Readers can explore the full collection of colour character illustrations on the author's personal Facebook page here:

https://www.facebook.com/profile.php?id=61581325000577

Contents

Chapter 1: Beginning at Green Mountain

The mountain mist lay thick and low, pressing down like a damp weight. The air was saturated, heavy enough to taste.

Beneath the carriage, the wheels ground through wet mud, carving deep grooves into the road—grooves so dark and gouged that for a moment it felt as if they were not cutting through earth at all, but through the tangled, chaotic remnants of her old dreams, crushing them into ruts she could never climb out of again.

Qin Nianyin lifted the edge of the curtain.

Cold wind, laden with moisture, slipped into her sleeve like a thin knife. The fog in the distance churned and rolled in pale layers, swallowing the road, swallowing the trees, swallowing everything that should have been clear. Then a long cry—sharp as an eagle's shriek—split the mist in a single stroke.

Hooves answered immediately after.

Rapid. Tight. Urgent—like war-drums striking on stone.

Her chest tightened.

This was not the sound of ordinary travellers hurrying along a road. It was too disciplined, too violent in its rhythm, the kind of sound that belonged to pursuit and ambush, not to merchants and pilgrims.

In the next instant, several dark silhouettes burst from the fog.

Blades flashed—white as snow, cold as lightning—cutting straight for the side of the carriage.

"Madam!" Mei's voice cracked.

She lunged forward and shoved Qin Nianyin back into the carriage compartment with all her strength. "Fall back—quickly!"

The carriage jolted violently. Wood groaned. Metal rang. The scent of incense ash—faint, powdery, familiar—was suddenly torn open by the stink of mud and rainwater, the two smells rushing into her nostrils at once as if the world itself had been struck and shaken.

Her fingers clenched the curtain fabric so hard the weave bit into her skin.

Before she could even glimpse the assailants' faces, the sharp clash of blades rang out at her ears—clean, vicious, unforgiving.

And then, in the middle of that chaos, a voice arrived.

Cold.

So cold it did not sound like it came from the road outside at all, but from a sealed place deep inside her—echoing across years like a sentence flung through time.

"Qin Nianyin… do you know what you are doing?"

That voice cut into her heart like a knife.

It was as if her entire life—her choices, her shame, her desperate bargains—were being seized by the throat and forced back into a memory she had tried to bury and lock away.

In that instant, the past flared open in her mind—clear, vivid, merciless.

* * * * *

Past Life — Jianyuan, Twelfth Year — East Wing of the Su Residence

Candlelight trembled.

The night was cool as water.

It was the one impulse she should never have had when she first entered the capital—reckless, humiliating, unforgivable.

But at that time, she had been terrified of being sent back to Jiangnan.

Terrified of becoming useless, discarded, erased.

So she had set down a woman's reserve, swallowed her dignity, and—when Su Zhang was drunk—gathered the last thread of courage she possessed and pushed open that door…

Qin Nianyin remembered those early days in the capital, how she lived in the Su Residence with constant caution, each breath measured, each step taken as if on thin ice. She also remembered how the affection she hid so carefully—so silently—had grown without sound, without permission, until it filled the spaces she could no longer control.

Her feelings for Su Zhang.

Her cousin—noble, cold, austere.

Like a solitary moon hanging above all others, untouched by warmth.

That night, the East Wing was so quiet that even the wind sounded distinct, so quiet that she could hear the brittle fracture of the small, humble wish inside her chest—as if it were breaking, piece by piece, with each step she took.

She came with a lantern.

Her fingertips clenched the handle; her palm was damp.

The hem of her skirt brushed over bluestone. The sound was so light it was almost nothing, as if moving softly could erase what she was doing—erase the impropriety, the shame, the fact that she was walking into a man's room at an hour she had no right to.

She pushed the door open.

The scent of wine drifted out—thick, sweet, oppressive.

Su Zhang leaned half against the couch, his collar slightly open, long hair disordered. His white robe was damp with spilled wine, clinging to the sharply defined lines of his body in a way that made her throat go dry.

He looked neither fully drunk nor fully sober.

But his gaze—clear as a cold pool—met hers and pierced straight through her.

He saw her.

He saw everything.

"Cousin." Her voice was low, like a candle flame trembling in wind, on the verge of going out.

She knew she was walking along a cliff's edge: one step forward was a bottomless abyss. One step back…

There was no back for her anymore.

She knew this embrace might bring her humiliation, not warmth.

But if she did not do it, she would have nothing at all.

This desperate, ugly gamble—this loss of face—was the only card she had left to play.

He lifted his eyes. A faint crease formed between his brows.

"At this hour," he asked, voice flat, restrained, "what are you doing here?"

She bit her lip and said nothing.

She only walked closer and placed the lantern on the small table. Lamplight spilled across her pale face; in her eyes, the desire she had suppressed for so long burned, not loud, but stubborn—mixed with a resolution that had already decided to ruin itself.

She lowered herself beside the couch and looked up at him.

"I only…" Her voice shook, and she hated herself for it. "I only wanted to see you."

Su Zhang's gaze darkened.

His voice left no space for bargaining.

"Leave."

Her fingertips trembled.

Yet she still reached out and tugged at his sleeve, the words coming out thin, unsteady.

"Cousin, I brought sobering soup. Would you… drink some?"

His brow tightened. With a flick of his sleeve, he pulled away.

"These trivial matters," he said coldly, "are for Xiuyan."

"Cousin…"

"Leave." Anger edged into his tone. "Do not make me repeat myself."

Before the sentence even fully settled, she braced herself on her knees and lunged forward—wrapping her arms around his waist.

For one breath, his body stiffened.

Something flashed in his eyes—so quick she could not name it. Surprise, perhaps.

Then coldness swept over it like frost, burying it at once.

"Qin Nianyin," he said, voice like forged iron, "do you know what you are doing?"

He shoved her away.

She fell to the floor, hair dishevelled, lips drained of colour.

"Don't drive me away," she whispered, shame and panic tangling together. "I only… I only…"

He looked down at her. His expression was indifferent, almost remote.

"Have all your lessons in feminine virtue and restraint," he asked, "been wasted on you?"

The words cut across her face like a blade.

She stared at him, stunned. Her cheeks burned as if slapped—hot, humiliating, exposed.

But inside, her heart froze.

Even the last trace of foolish longing—everything she had tried to protect—congealed into fragile ice.

In that moment, she finally understood.

He despised her.

"I'm sorry…" Her voice broke into a whisper, so faint it was nearly swallowed by the night. "I shouldn't have come…"

Su Zhang turned away.

His back was decisive, leaving no pause, no mercy, not even a glance.

She forced the tears back—forced them down until her throat hurt—and picked up the fallen lantern. Step by step, she walked out of the room.

The corridor wind was cold as knives.

Lantern-light swayed.

Only then did she realise the copper hook had loosened.

She removed the plain hairpin from her hair.

Carefully, she bent the tip into a fine hook; following the grain of the copper wire, she looped and clasped it, twisting and fastening until the hook held firm again.

She murmured, the words barely audible.

"Copper must follow its grain… but what of a human heart?"

She had followed his "grain" for so many years—careful, quiet, obedient—trying to please him, trying to fit herself into the shape he would tolerate.

And what had she gained?

Only contempt.

The lantern finally steadied.

She turned and vanished into the night.

The light bobbed in the frigid wind, unable to illuminate the flood of regret in her eyes—leaving only boundless silence behind.

* * * * *

Present Life — Qingshan Temple Gate

Outside the temple gate, the rain had just stopped.

Pine needles still dripped water into stone crevices—drop after drop, each sound crisp and cold, as if the mountain itself were speaking in a tone that allowed no warmth.

Qin Nianyin emerged from the side hall, holding an empty incense holder. When she stepped onto the stairs, mist curled around the stone steps like pale silk—and within that mist, a figure in an inky official cloak ascended from below.

Hair bound beneath a jade crown.

Brow sharp.

Nose straight.

Thin lips pressed into a single line.

A trace of snow-white inner robe showed beneath the outer cloak. His pace was neither fast nor slow, measured as if cut by a ruler—each step placed with the same calm precision she remembered too well.

As he drew nearer, that cold star in his eyes was stirred by the mountain wind—clear as winter well water.

She paused.

Her heart warmed first—warmth rising before reason could catch it, as if meeting him here, in this place of incense and vows, were an unexpected patch of sunlight breaking through fog.

"…Why have you come?" The words slipped out softly, almost without her permission.

Su Zhang stopped three paces away.

His gaze swept over the sandalwood ash on her sleeve. His tone remained even, controlled.

"You have been staying in the temple for three days. I have come to collect you."

He lowered his lashes, stepped aside, and placed a plain cloak on the stone railing.

"The night wind is heavy. Put this on first. The carriage is at the foot of the mountain." A pause—so slight, so precise. "If you have knelt too long during prayer these past days, your knees will swell."

Her fingers tightened around the incense holder without thinking.

A faint smile rose—small, involuntary.

He was usually rigid, strict to the point of being unapproachable. This kind of consideration was rare.

For one dangerous moment, she even thought—

Perhaps… perhaps in this life, some things truly were different.

Then he spoke again.

"Three consecutive days without the mistress of the inner residence returning—if that spreads," his voice remained calm, "it will be unseemly."

The warmth was scraped away as if the mountain wind had taken a blade to it.

So it was still this.

Still the Su family's face.

Still his reputation as a minister.

Her hand froze halfway toward the cloak. Sourness rose in her chest, and her voice tightened despite herself.

"So, I require others' approval," she asked, "even to visit Qingshan Temple?"

His brow moved—only the slightest fraction.

He maintained that familiar restraint.

"This is a matter of propriety."

A brief pause.

Then, lower:

"Your name is not only your own."

Propriety. Reputation.

The two words that had always sat most easily on his tongue.

She lowered her eyes, hiding the sharpness that threatened to break through.

"So the Minister fears gossip," she said flatly, "but not whether I am cold or warm."

For one heartbeat, his knuckles tightened inside his sleeve—as if something tried to rise and was pressed down again.

His voice turned heavier.

"I also brought the imperial physician. He is waiting below. Do not kneel any further. It will harm your health."

The small flicker of joy that had almost settled—almost—was ground into dust between "unseemly" and "propriety."

She turned her face away, her tone stubborn, as if arguing not only with him but with herself.

"I will not return today."

He looked at her.

His gaze passed over her lightly—like a shadow hiding something, or like a shadow that hid nothing at all.

"As you wish."

He turned. His robe brushed through the clean, rain-washed air. He took two steps—then stopped.

His profile was pale, cold. His voice was brief, clipped.

"If you change your mind before the Hour of Chen, I will have someone waiting outside the gate."

He did not look back.

Qin Nianyin returned to the hall.

She set the incense holder down and pressed her fingertip gently into the ash, leaving a clear impression.

A mark could remain.

But warmth could not.

Just like the tenderness he had shown her for a single breath—nothing more than duty and rules, something that would scatter the moment the wind rose again.

Chapter 2: An Unexpected Meeting

Three sticks of incense burned completely, their light smoke coiling upward in the air. Outside the temple hall, the evening drum sounded its first deep, muted beat. Pilgrims nearby turned their heads at the sound, and several older women pressed their voices low, exchanging quiet, compressed whispers. A wisp of incense smoke drifted askew, searing the back of Qin Nianyin's finger and leaving a fine, transient red mark.

Just as she was preparing to step back, a clear and cool female voice reached her from the dense shadows of the smoke: "Sister Nianyin, fate is indeed kind today; I never expected to encounter you here."

That long-unheard form of address felt like a dull blade, deliberately cutting open a chamber of memory accumulated over years of stillness.

A woman in a blue-green dress stood positioned before the altar—her facial features were familiar, and her expression was calm, yet she was separated from Qin Nianyin by countless years of elapsed time. It was Shen Lingyan.

The memory of their shared laughter and the joy of pinning flowers in their hair when they were both sixteen now felt like a life lived in another era. Since then, the cosmos had turned, and each had been irrevocably set upon her own destined path. The sudden sight of her old acquaintance caused a subtle tightening in Qin Nianyin's chest. She quickly curved her lips into a self-mocking smile: No wonder I saw him ascending the mountain earlier. It seems... he may not have made this difficult trip solely on my account.

The reason, most likely, is for Shen Lingyan.

Shen Lingyan offered a graceful smile and advanced slowly to perform a proper bow, her voice flowing with the clarity of mountain spring water: "We have not met for many years. I hope you have been in good health since then?"

Qin Nianyin returned the greeting with a respectful hand-salute, maintaining an entirely composed demeanour: "Sister Lingyan is safe and well."

Her knees, weary from the long prayer, were numb. She nearly lost her balance while rising and bowing, but she forced herself into rigid self-control, struggling not to let it show. She was saved from any sign of impropriety only when the attending maid quickly stepped forward to offer support, sparing her from a lapse in etiquette.

Shen Lingyan lowered her gaze slightly to the hand that was still trembling, her voice becoming gentle: "You are still determined to appear strong, as always."

Qin Nianyin lightly compressed her lips and smiled: "Sister speaks too kindly. At this stage in life, and at our age, there is no longer any need to discuss determination."

Shen Lingyan's expression shifted, and she sighed softly: "To meet here today was truly unanticipated. It suggests that the connection between us sisters has not been entirely severed by fate."

"It does," Qin Nianyin replied in a measured tone. "The affairs of the world are in constant flux; to be granted even this single meeting counts as a significant fortune."

Shen Lingyan's eyes were limpid, infused with a faint yet discernible trace of compassion: "I saw Minister Su's party from a distance, near the temple entrance, looking as if they were about to leave the premises. I suspected you might be with them, so I came inside along the path. Reflecting on the years we have each spent enduring our separate lives and drifting through the world, I felt a reunion was too precious to ignore, so I sought you out to offer my greetings. When one ages, it is easy to succumb to melancholy, alas..."

Qin Nianyin's expression did not change. She offered a slight inclination of her head and allowed her maid to assist her to a large, comfortable armchair. Her voice remained level: "Sister has taken too much trouble."

Shen Lingyan then sat down opposite her, her gaze subtly and quietly assessing Qin Nianyin from head to toe: "You persist in denying your stubbornness. Minister Su came in person, bringing the imperial physician to plead for your return, yet you still refuse to go home? Had he not been truly and deeply concerned and mindful of you, why would he undertake such a difficult journey up this mountain?"

Qin Nianyin lowered her eyes and offered a polite smile: "Sister has misunderstood the situation. Your younger sister simply appreciates the quiet atmosphere of the monastery and intends to stay here for a few extra days. My husband has heavy responsibilities at court; his occasional visit to burn incense is purely for the purpose of praying for safety."

"Ah, you truly are..." Shen Lingyan shook her head, sighing lightly, her voice carrying a gentle blend of fondness and resignation.

Qin Nianyin watched her calmly, the slight curve of her lips barely visible: "Sister has attained a lifetime of wealth, status, and high power. Why should you spend your breath sighing over me?"

Shen Lingyan paused, a moment of complicated feeling flashing in her eyes, and her voice lowered in pitch: "Because I possess that understanding. Because I truly understand."

"Understanding?" Qin Nianyin lifted her gaze, her tone still subdued. "Your sister is dim-witted. I respectfully request that Sister explain more clearly."

Shen Lingyan dropped her gaze behind her lashes. Her voice held both softness and a measure of tragedy: "Years ago, you risked everything you had, striving desperately for a sense of completion and fulfillment. Yet now, you have no parents-in-law to serve, no children to attend to below you; the entire Su Residence is silent and desolate..."

She paused, her smile becoming distinctly strained. "In what way is that state different from my General's Residence? The General has campaigned on the frontier for years, and I hear he already has a concubine by his side, who has even borne him his first legitimate son. I am left here alone in the capital, childless. In this enormous house, only I remain to keep watch. The splendour the world sees is, in the end, nothing more than a single, dim lantern."

Hearing this, Qin Nianyin felt a sharp tremor in her heart, and the temperature of her voice dropped slightly: "Sister, what is the true meaning behind these words?"

Shen Lingyan looked at her, her eyes calm and unwavering: "Do not be alarmed. I merely wished to say—for women like us, what we wish to redeem, we find no path to; what we long to love, we have no secure place to offer it. In the end, we are left only with a heavy account of past errors and the burden of emptiness. Do you not find this to be true?"

A light, clear ring from the wind chimes on the eaves broke through the prevailing silence.

Qin Nianyin's fingertips twitched, but her voice remained steady as she asked: "Sister has lived a life of great honour and glory. Setting aside the personal coldness around you, would you not consider that all your worldly desires have been met?"

Shen Lingyan was briefly stunned, then offered a quiet smile: "What difference exists between achievement and failure? It all amounts to nothing more than a momentary vision, a fleeting dream."

The wind passed the altar, stirring a single fine wisp of residual smoke. Shen Lingyan murmured softly: "...And a child was also wronged."

Qin Nianyin's heart leaped, and she instinctively clenched her fingers into fists. She looked up, her voice slightly muffled and hoarse: "To whom are you referring, Sister?"

Shen Lingyan's gaze was full of a vast, desolate weariness: "A child. Yes, there was one, early on. It is a pity... For women in our position, lacking a child nearby is sufficient reason for society to mock us for the rest of our lives."

Qin Nianyin stood motionless for several moments, the air in her chest heaving in uneven bursts. Ultimately, she managed only a quiet whisper: "Yes, I understand this point."

The sound was extremely soft, yet it felt like an inscription carved into stone, penetrating deep into her soul and marrow.

Qin Nianyin lowered her eyes, her lips curving into the faintest of smiles—it was not a denial, but a silent, private admission of self-censure. She pressed a fingertip into the incense ash; the acute pain forced out a short, cold breath of icy air.

A child. The loss was not Shen Lingyan's alone; she herself had also suffered such a profound deprivation...

Amidst the surge of disorderly thoughts, she heard Shen Lingyan continue softly: "My dear sister, Nianyin, is this not the very truth of our situation?"

Qin Nianyin avoided that pair of clear eyes, merely answering flatly: "Perhaps that is the case."

A short period of silence followed, broken only by the faint light of the eternal lamp. She suddenly raised her lashes, her smile now utterly cold: "The common world loves to debate right and wrong, yet those caught within the situation each have their own inescapable burdens. This existence is often profoundly difficult for women—Sister, do you agree?"

Shen Lingyan seemed momentarily startled.

Qin Nianyin's voice now held the sharp clarity of ice just beginning to crack: "I suffered two terrible floods when I was young, losing my family and home, forced into a wandering existence. I was fortunate to be taken in by my maternal aunt's family, the Sus, which saved my life and offered me a refuge. Nianyin is aware of all the vicious gossip circulating, but Nianyin does not fear the malicious rumours."

She looked directly at Shen Lingyan, every word articulated clearly: "The right and the wrong of everything I have chosen to do, I will accept and bear the consequences entirely myself. The position I hold now is that of a First-Rank Official Lady, personally granted by the Emperor—the Minister's wife."

The wind chimes on the hall eaves chimed softly once more. The two words, "Official Lady," landed heavily, like a physical weight, causing the atmosphere to settle and the air to grow heavy.

Shen Lingyan raised her lashes, her smile completely gone: "Those two words are heavy—so heavy that they make it difficult for one to breathe."

The two women stood opposite each other in complete, wordless silence.

After a long interval, Shen Lingyan sighed and turned, signaling her intent to leave: "In that case, I will not further interrupt the Minister's wife in her quiet meditation."

After taking two steps, she suddenly looked back, offering a simple, faint smile: "Take care."

With this, her maid and the attending women followed her, their forms slowly dissolving into the rising smoke.

Qin Nianyin felt a faint, inner scoff, yet found herself unable to weep. When she was on the brink of starvation back then, what principles could she possibly have afforded to uphold?

She lowered herself once more for a deep kowtow. A strand of pale smoke curled and clung to her fingertips. The breeze outside the main doors stirred a single lock of black hair on her shoulder.

It was as if someone from the hidden depths of the clouds was whispering a question—

If a next life were truly possible, would she still seek that sense of completion one more time?

She dared not answer. She merely lowered her gaze to the golden image of the Buddha. The golden statue remained an image of solemn compassion; only deep within her, something vital had quietly loosened its grip.

The evening drum sounded its second beat, indicating that the temple was about to close its doors. She suddenly understood clearly—if she did not now turn around and leave, the rest of this life would remain confined and trapped within the confines of this single door.

She pressed her palms together and, in her heart, spoke each word devoutly and respectfully—

Your disciple, Qin Nianyin, is deeply stained by sin, lost on her path, and has ruined a blessed opportunity. Due to a past covetousness for power and status, I forsook family ties and betrayed a good companion, leading to the estrangement of all people and a future of desolate solitude. Bowing before the Buddha now, I pray only to diminish all karmic debt, sever all attachments to this mortal sphere, and atone for this entire life. May those I have caused pain find lasting peace and comfort; may the affection I missed find its destined fulfillment. If a future life is granted, I do not ask to share old age with him, but only for an existence free of fault and regret, that I may cross this life in tranquillity. Amitabha. May the Buddha extend His mercy and guide me out of my darkness.

The clean incense had been wholly consumed, its light smoke spiralling upward towards the temple roof, seemingly establishing a silent link with the emptiness of the ether.

Her consciousness was nearing a state of total stillness; the only sound left was the gentle crackling of the ritual fire. Then, a soft, refined female voice suddenly spoke: "Benefactress, are you perhaps experiencing discomfort?"

Qin Nianyin opened her eyes to see a Buddhist nun standing beside the incense altar, dressed in simple robes, her expression benign and gentle, her hands pressed together in salutation.

"I thank you, Master, for your concern," she replied in a dry, low voice.

The nun smiled, retrieving a string of warm, polished sandalwood beads and placing them gently into her palm: "These are for meditation. They may assist in calming your heart."

The moment her fingers touched them, the warmth of the beads seemed to permeate her very being and seep into her heart. Her forehead suddenly felt a gentle warmth—as if an unseen, radiant light had descended from above.

A sound like a distant, profound chant seemed to enter her consciousness, arriving from the far reaches of the sky; it was deep and prolonged, yet possessed a strange intimacy, as though it were softly calling her name.

Her spirit was abruptly shaken. She instinctively lifted her gaze.

Through the rising mist of smoke, the massive golden Buddha seemed to incline its head slightly, its expression profoundly tranquil, looking directly down upon her.

She murmured softly: "Your disciple thanks the Master."

However, that nameless sense of agitation was now intensifying, rising in powerful, successive surges—like a forceful tide, entirely encompassing her entire being.

Chapter 3: The Su Family Precept

Qingshan Temple, wreathed in mountain mist, lay in profound silence. A biting chill permeated the air from the early spring. The cold, damp breeze beneath the eaves caused the candle flames to tremble subtly.

Qin Nianyin knelt before the incense altar, her hands cradling the three tall sticks of incense, shivering faintly from the pervasive cold. The rising tendrils of smoke drifted straight upward, seemingly conjuring a phantom image of the Buddha in the swirling mist, majestic and unattainable. A particle of ash quietly dropped, the red ember searing her hand, yet she appeared completely oblivious to the pain.

She lowered her eyelashes, fine beads of sweat breaking out on her forehead, allowing memories to flood her consciousness like a tide.

She recalled that in the first few years after their marriage, she had attempted to discuss the matter of an heir with him—not out of personal ambition, but from a genuine concern that the Su family line might be extinguished. That night, the candlelight flickered, and she spoke softly: "If this continues, with no son or daughter, how will we face the clan elders? Taking a concubine would be beneficial."

The teacup in his hand paused imperceptibly. The porcelain lid tapped gently against the rim of the cup, producing a sound that was crisp and cold. His brow twitched slightly, then immediately settled back into its level line.

"Has Madam perhaps forgotten the Su family's ancestral instructions?" His voice sounded outwardly steady, yet it was sharp and distinct, like a blade of cold steel.

She froze completely.

"The ancestors decreed that, in order to prevent disputes over succession from common-born children, offspring may be adopted from the clan, but concubines shall not be taken," Su Zhang's tone was calm, but every word was forged like iron, ringing with a chilling finality.

The candlelight reflected off the side of his face, illuminating a chiseled profile that was utterly devoid of warmth. In that precise instant, a barely perceptible flash of mockery crossed his eyes. She remembered it with perfect clarity—she could never discern whether that scorn was directed at her, or at the desolate failure of their nominal marriage.

After that evening, the vital energy in her heart seemed to have been entirely drained away.

They never shared a meal, there were no words exchanged, and though they shared a bed, they were strangers. When she turned over in the night, the pillow beside her was always graced by his rigidly straight back, separated from her by an inch of empty space that felt as cold and impassable as a solid wall.

She suddenly found the entirety of their marital relationship absurd—if a marriage was reduced to nothing more than a shared facade and maintaining outward appearances, what possible significance could it possess? The true irony lay in the fact that, years ago, in her fervent desire for prosperity, she had personally forced them both into this silent, deep well.

In the eyes of the world, her life was one of unparalleled prestige; yet in reality, the inner chambers of her home were steeped in isolation. The rain pattered against the bamboo shadows in the corridor while she sat alone at her desk copying scriptures; the garden burst into full bloom in spring, yet he never once glanced back at it. She saw these realities clearly, but she never revealed her sorrow or her joy.

This marriage had bought her a lifetime of profound honor. Perhaps, to her, this already represented 'fulfillment.' But whether this fulfillment was merely for public display or represented genuine contentment in her heart—that, she herself could not articulate.

She knelt prostrate before the jade steps, her heart clear and desolate—many things were nothing more than transient smoke passing before the eyes. What was gained and what was lost would ultimately return to dust.

Su Zhang had never owed her anything. In fact, it was she who owed him far too much.

In her previous life, she had used her "life-saving grace" as leverage to compel him to marry her. She claimed deep affection, but in truth, it was a presumptuous usurpation. His heart already belonged to another, and though she knew this, she forcefully intruded, purely to secure personal stability and honor. On their wedding day, his eyes were cold and heavy, yet she smiled brightly, receiving guests in the main hall. She forced herself to appear composed, though her heart trembled minutely within.

Su Zhang—a Tanhua scholar, elegantly composed and rigorously self-disciplined. Despite his clear unhappiness, he never once uttered a single word of complaint against her. In over twenty years of marriage, he never took a concubine, nor did he ever treat her harshly. She enjoyed every honour due to her rank, yet night after night, she fell asleep facing his back, only to wake in a chamber filled with cold silence.

Perhaps this lifelong emotional distance was this lifelong coldness was the most silent, yet most excruciating punishment he could inflict.

Twenty years as husband and wife amounted to nothing more than a legal bond—a marriage sought for power, a life lived for reputation, leverage used through kindness, and a written contract that trapped them both. She had once naively believed that by securing a high position, she could eventually win his heart. She failed to realize that this marriage, which was a cage for her, was equally a shackle for him.

The candlelight in the Buddha hall flickered, and the chanting flowed like water, yet her heart felt heavy and inert as stone.

She slowly closed her eyes, her fingertips touching the cool sandalwood of the altar. As her chest gently rose and fell, only a few words surfaced in her deepest thoughts—

" No more stolen love; no more a life wronged. "

The sound was as light as motes of dust, yet it carried an undeniable finality.

* * * * *

At one point in their past, she had just learned that she was carrying his child.

In the first few days, she clung to the news like a strand of warm light. She sat daily by the window waiting for his return, secretly imagining the surprised joy that might flash in his eyes when she finally told him.

That particular afternoon, he returned to the residence, a rare occurrence. She stood early in the corridor waiting for him, dressed in a plain, pale-green silk dress, her palm tightly gripping the sample for a tiny shoe she had newly embroidered.

The man who turned the corner of the corridor was still wearing his court robes. His expression concealed slight anger and deep fatigue, suggesting he had just been entangled in another dispute at court.

She had barely managed to call out, "Cousin," when he merely raised his eyes, fixing her with a gaze that was cold, like snow covering the ground in mid-winter.

"Is something the matter?" He did not slow his pace.

Her lips parted slightly, but before the words could leave her mouth, he had already turned and quickened his steps, leaving her with only one brief instruction: "We can discuss this when I return. I must enter the palace immediately."

In that moment, her hand was still tightly clasping the small shoes, but she was completely unable to utter a sound.

She convinced herself that another opportunity would arise.

However, once he left, he did not return for ten consecutive days. By the time he finally came back, she had already lost the child—that brief moment of surprise and excitement had existed only within her own heart.

She closed her eyes, surrendering to the profound grief. In the span of ten days, she went from overwhelming happiness to complete emptiness, all in one silent, private dream. And he had never known anything about it.

In an even earlier recess of her memory lay the water towns of Jiangnan.

That year, she was still too young to wear the hair-pin of maturity when a sudden, massive flood struck. Her father managed to push her onto the roof, but he himself never followed. Her mother, holding her infant brother wrapped in swaddling clothes, was transformed into a fleeting soul in the turbulent, muddy waters.

She spent an entire day and night curled up on the shaking, collapsing roof beam. When she was finally rescued, her fingers were deeply embedded in the wet wood, the congealed blood forming dark purple scabs.

After that trauma, she even forgot her own birth name, nothing remained of her identity but the lingering whisper of her childhood nickname, 'Nannan'.

Fortunately, her mother's cousin, Qin Shouyi, and his wife took pity on her and brought her into their home. They named her Qin Nianyin and raised her as their own daughter.

When she first entered the Qin Residence, she stood on the clean stone floor with her cracked, bare feet, awkward and unsure where to place her hands and feet. That period was brief but filled with warmth—her adopted brother taught her to read, her adopted sister showed her needlework, her adopted mother sewed clothes for her. They watched the lanterns during the Lantern Festival, saw the boat races on the Dragon Boat Festival, and offered prayers to the moon during the Mid-

Autumn Festival... She almost completely forgot she had once been an orphan.

Yet, in the twelfth year of the Jianyuan era, the great flood returned with devastating force. Her adopted father, a river commissioner, died on duty, and her adopted mother contracted an illness and passed away. Kneeling between the two coffins in the mourning hall, she suddenly realized that there was no one left in the world with whom she shared a blood connection.

"A-Yin..." Her adopted mother, in her last moments, pressed a sealed letter into her hand, her voice weak as the wind. "Go to the Capital... Find your aunt... She can protect you..."

Sixteen-year-old Qin Nianyin, clutching that letter, journeyed with her young maid Mei, enduring hardship until she finally stood before the gates of the Su Residence, gazing up at the golden plaque that declared it the "Minister's Residence."

Later, she manipulated the situation, using her claim of a life-saving grace to prompt Madam Qin to propose the marriage for her. On that occasion, Su Zhang was ambushed outside the capital. She happened to be passing on her way to burn incense at Qingshan Temple. She quickly ordered Mei to ride back to the capital for help, while she herself hid the injured Su Zhang among the scattered rocks, drawing out the critical, murderous moments.

She ultimately achieved her desire, becoming the young madam of the Su Residence, and later soaring to the prestigious station of a First-Rank Official Lady. However, Su Zhang remained consistently detached and cold, his words like sharp knives that daily chipped away at her vain illusions and self-respect.

She had genuinely wished to turn back, but she was too confined by the memory of her desperate, wandering childhood, sinking deeper and deeper into her schemes.

To gain favour among the capital's noble women, she exhausted every manoeuvre, even involving Shen Lingyan in her calculations and altering her destiny—a move that subsequently created deep resentment between the Su and Shen families, severing their long-standing friendship.

Su Zhang and she lived a life of pretence, Shen Lingyan was forced into a resentful marriage with the General Who Guards the Nation; and she herself, in the relentless struggle for power, lost her husband's heart and lost all genuine affection.

Chapter 4: Resolve to Part

The hour was swiftly approaching twilight, and the evening drum sounded its initial note. The deep, heavy resonance travelled from the distant peaks, gently permeating the quiet of Qingshan Temple. The setting sun cast a sharp, golden reflection upon the pagoda, the light filtering through breaks in the clouds to wash over the white stone steps, appearing like a thin layer of sacred illumination.

Qin Nianyin pushed herself up, finding support for her knees which trembled slightly from exhaustion. The residual heat of the incense ash still warmed her fingertips. She cast a final look back at the main hall; the massive golden Buddha statue stood solemn and compassionate, looking down upon the world of mortals, seemingly offering silent absolution even for the most concealed and shameful thoughts within her heart.

She stepped beyond the mountain gate. The fine spring rain had subsided, leaving the air damp and the mountain enveloped in swirling, moist mist. Mei rushed forward, holding a waxed paper parasol and gently securing her mistress's arm.

"Madam, please be cautious where you tread. The path is exceedingly slippery."

Qin Nianyin offered a genuine smile, her expression serene, yet her eyes held an untold complexity of apology and deep longing: "Mei..."

"Madam..." Mei started, her voice catching with hesitation, her eyes reflecting a distinct anxiety.

"What troubles you?" After so many years of companionship, Qin Nianyin immediately recognized the worrying look on Mei's face.

"Madam, why did you decide not to accompany the Minister back to the estate today?"

Qin Nianyin managed a small, quiet laugh. "I knew that was the very thing irritating you."

"Madam, if you continue this way, silently feuding with the Minister, when will this state of affairs ever conclude?"

Qin Nianyin leaned slightly upon Mei's outstretched arm. "There is no feud to speak of. Now that my aunt and uncle are gone, I simply lack the desire to return and face that cold, cavernous courtyard alone."

Mei tightly pressed her lips together, her eyes welling up with tears. "If only Madam had been able to bear a child..."

Qin Nianyin gently stroked her hand. Noting the fine lines etched around her maid's eyes, she whispered: "Even our Mei has reached this maturity of age."

"What foolishness is Madam talking about?" Mei quickly turned her face aside, but stealthily pulled back her hand to wipe away a tear.

Qin Nianyin's heart constricted sharply. Mei had been with her since childhood; her own youth had been quietly consumed, and she remained unmarried. Qin Nianyin was suddenly overwhelmed by the feeling that her debt to Mei was enormous.

"Starting from today, you must live your own life properly... You must not sacrifice yourself as you have done."

Mei was startled into silence. That current of melancholy combined with the unusual command sent a strong, unsettling premonition through her.

"Let us proceed. It is time we went home," Qin Nianyin commanded, her expression resolute.

Outside the temple gates, the deep echoes of the evening drum continued to roll across the mountain's vast, indistinct contours. Mei helped her into the coach, giving the driver instructions to commence the journey.

The heavy wheels ground through the moist, clinging mud, slowly beginning the descent. Qin Nianyin's fingers were tightly locked on her lap. With every yard they travelled, the unshakeable determination in her chest grew more intensely defined.

She was going to confront Su Zhang and propose a formal divorce. Immediately, without delay!

The thought, as if forcefully struck awake by the drum's beat, surfaced without any possibility of retreat.

"Make haste," she urged for the third time.

"My apologies, Madam, but this is the fastest speed the terrain will permit," the coachman respectfully called back.

Suddenly, a long, piercing sound, like the cry of a hunting falcon, sliced through the dense fog from the distance. The frantic drumming of horses' hooves rapidly approached, accompanied by the clatter of metal, carrying palpable menace through the forest.

Qin Nianyin's heart jolted with alarm. She was just about to lift the carriage curtain—

Several figures cloaked in black shot out of the mist like expertly aimed projectiles. The gleam of their blades was cold as snow, their malice instantly chilling.

"Madam! Withdraw immediately!" Mei violently thrust her mistress backward, placing her own body completely in the path of the danger.

The coachman whipped the horses in terror. The animals screamed, the carriage shuddered violently, and mud was flung up onto the curtained windows.

Peering through a narrow slit, Qin Nianyin could see four black-clad assailants advancing in measured, menacing steps. Their footwork was unnervingly precise, every move aimed at a swift kill. Eight accompanying guards were forced into the engagement, their swords striking metal in a shower of sparks.

"Insolent fools! Do you know who occupies this carriage?" one guard roared.

"Spare the useless talk, and prepare to die!"

The opponents instantly altered their formation. The leader raised a hand, and the other three pressed forward simultaneously, their attacks savage and without mercy—this was not a roadside banditry; these were trained assassins, committed to taking Su Zhang's life!

A chilling realization struck Qin Nianyin. The number of people wishing Su Zhang dead was truly vast—and she was merely an unwitting pawn drawn into the brutal game.

"Madam, I will hold them back; you must leave now!" Mei's voice trembled uncontrollably.

"Do not panic—we absolutely must not die here." Qin Nianyin clamped her jaw shut, desperately containing her terror. She had to survive and return—for the separation!

If her life were cut short at this spot, she would die still bearing his wife's name, her ancestral worship tied to the Su family. She could not accept that fate!

"Mei, the signal flare!"

"Oh, yes!" Mei quickly reached beneath the carriage seat and pulled out a small flare canister—a precaution Su Zhang had insisted upon against just such an incident.

Qin Nianyin swiftly yanked off her hairpin and used it to pry open the cap. The main fuse line was visibly damp from the rain; she twisted off the saturated section and quickly fashioned a shorter, dry fuse.

"Now, fire it!" she commanded in a low, sharp whisper.

The flare erupted in a blinding flash, tearing through the evening mist with a colossal blast that startled flocks of birds skyward.

The sound of horses' hooves surged closer in the distance; the reinforcements were arriving. The assassins in black immediately perceived their peril, their forms blurring as they melted back into the trees, disappearing as swiftly as shadows.

Qin Nianyin held Mei tightly, shaking from head to foot, her back soaked in cold perspiration.

"Madam, you—" Before Mei could utter a full sentence, a flash of cold light darted out from the mist again!

A solitary assassin surged from the wet ditch beside the carriage's rear, a short dagger sweeping past the carriage frame—the blade's shadow was swift as lightning.

"Madam, take care—!" Mei hurled herself forward with desperate speed. The blade instantly sliced across her chest. Blood erupted in a crimson spray, striking Qin Nianyin's face.

"Mei!" Qin Nianyin shrieked, the sound broken. She lunged forward to hold her, but her hands only met the warm, sticky substance of the copious blood.

Mei's eyes lost focus quickly, yet her lips continued to tremble. The last, faint trace of air forced its way from her throat: "Madam... Go... Quickly..."

Her fingers still clung desperately to Qin Nianyin's sleeve, as though fearing her mistress would fall alone into an abyss. In the following second, the strength in her grip completely failed. Bloody froth leaked from the corner of her mouth.

"Mei—!!!"

"No!" Qin Nianyin's cry was raw and desperate. But just as she reached out to pull Mei close, her own footing suddenly slipped; she lost balance completely!

The mist swirled violently. Her body swung precariously in the air, her fingers tenaciously hooked over the carriage's edge. The slick wooden carriage floor was smeared with blood, and her toes flailed uselessly in the void. Her vision was a maelstrom of white fog.

The wind howled past her ears, mixing with the horse's panicked screams and the shouts of the guards. Someone in the distance was calling her name, yet the sound was incomprehensible to her.

Only a terrifying blankness remained in her mind. Her knuckles were slowly giving way. The moisture of the fog was icy cold, feeling like countless needles piercing her skin.

In the final, split second before she fell, she saw the distant pagoda on the mountain peak glow with a tiny light, like someone igniting a lone lamp in the deep night.

She suddenly understood that fate itself might have completed its circle at this precise moment.

The resounding evening drum echoed, as if heaven and earth were reciting the final chant for her passage.

Her robes opened wide in the wind, like a pale flower unfolding on the brink of a sheer drop. In the flickering darkness, only a vanishing silhouette remained.

A flash of gold seemed to appear beneath the fog. A spiritual image of the great Buddha rose in her mind, solemn and compassionate. "If there is a next life..." Her lips formed the words, but the wind stole the sound.

A deep, sustained hum, like a tolling bell or a sacred chant, was carried on the wind, as if all things in creation were responding to her last desperate thought.

Her body abruptly plunged. The wind's speed tore at her eardrums. Her vision became a confused chaos of blood-red and white mist—in the last moment, she could only see Mei collapsed loosely in the mud, her blood flowing, staining her hairpin and the hem of her sleeve.

That final image was burned into her eyes like a searing flame.

Her anguished screams were swallowed by the valley, dissolving into an endless, bottomless echo.

The third, heavy beat of the evening drum sounded with a dull shock, like the final knell for her life.

The mountain wind ripped at her clothing; her ears filled only with the deafening roar of the wind and the violent hammering of her heart.

Deep within the thick fog, the golden Buddha stood firm on the mountain summit, its sacred features majestic, its gaze cast downwards, as if in boundless pity for all existence.

She opened her eyes wide, her chest heaving violently. The last, thin thread of her life's obsession was reduced to a single word—Regret.

A whisper seemed to graze her ear: "Karma is not yet resolved, the thread of connection is not yet concluded..."

The evening drum sounded again, as if counting the final measure of her days.

Her figure, like a maple leaf torn away by the gale, fell straight down into the immeasurable depths of the ravine.

Chapter 5: Return From the In-Between

Heaven and earth wavered, their outlines blurred and every colour seemed to drain from the world.

There was no wind in the air, yet a suffocating stillness pressed down on her, a silence so absolute it felt as though time itself had halted in this void.

Her hair and sleeves drifted in a slow, weightless motion, but not a single sound reached her ears.

Only her heartbeat remained—striking her chest with a hollow, solitary thud, echoing in the emptiness.

She attempted to call out, but no voice emerged. Even her breath was swallowed by the pale haze around her.

The mist seemed to have its own life, coiling upward with an eerie vitality, winding itself layers upon layers around her limbs.

It climbed from her ankles to her throat, enclosing and submerging her inch by inch.

She stared forward, dazed. A sudden emptiness opened within her chest.

If this was death, why did it still hurt?

The pain was not of the body but of the heart, as though someone had brushed a hand across the very core of her soul, leaving a lingering ache.

At that moment, a faint sound drifted from afar—low, distant, like the sound of a gust rising from the bottom of a deep, forgotten well.

She felt suspended between sky and abyss, caught between rising and falling in a state of weightlessness.

Every direction was blank and colourless, a vast expanse of cold, white emptiness.

She lifted a hand to test her surroundings.

Her fingertips touched nothing but thin, chilled emptiness and a biting, hollow void.

Am I dead?

The thought barely formed when a sound stirred by her ear.

The sound began as a gentle breeze brushing through early-spring willows, then swelled abruptly.

It echoed like waves crashing against a cliff—ancient, resonant, immeasurably distant.

A bell.

Its tone was deep and drawn out, as though struck a thousand years ago.

Each reverberation cut through the fog and sank into her spirit, knocking against her soul.

With every toll, the mist quivered and rippled slightly, and a faint path of pale, ghostly light began to take shape in the distance.

She stood still for a moment, uncomprehending.

Where was this place? What year was it? Whose body was she in now?

Yet the tolling of the bell persisted—a wavering pinprick of light like a flickering beacon, leading her forward, never allowing her to remain still.

She stumbled forward.

The haze stung her cheeks with its icy edge, and a tight pressure formed in her chest.

Each breath thinned and grew shallower little by little.

But something—someone—seemed to whisper at her ear, urging her to keep moving… forward.

She did not know how long she walked until her limbs grew heavy and even lifting her eyelids felt impossible.

Then, from within the sea of vapor, a glimmer appeared.

A temple rose into view—golden tiles and red eaves standing solemn and majestic.

A great bronze bell hung above the hall, its weight immense.

When it tolled again, the sound crashed through her like a peal of thunder, vibrating through her soul.

She halted. Her sleeves trembled lightly in the still air.

A trace of sandalwood drifted toward her—so familiar it pierced straight into her chest, making her heart skip with a sudden shock.

Something deep within her trembled sharply, as though struck with great force.

The bamboo shadows outside a study window, rustling in the wind;

The soft rustle of wind along a cold, lonely corridor;

The retreating back of a man turning away from her…

All the regrets and remorse she had buried so tightly broke open at once, flooding her without mercy like a collapsing dam.

The bell tolled again.

The fog dissolved.

Heaven and earth spun violently.

Darkness swept over her vision and her body dropped downward like a feather—

Sinking into warmth, into softness, into breath.

* * * * *

She opened her eyes abruptly, pulled back to consciousness by Mei's frightened cry.

Qin Nianyin's vision was still unfocused and chaotic.

Mei was already half-kneeling in front of her, eyes red with tears.

The leather water pouch trembled in her hands with the biting cold of early spring.

"Miss, please wake up."

Mei's voice was strained and urgent, cutting into the quiet air like a bell's ring that snapped through Nianyin's very mind and soul.

The surroundings were still except for the faint rustle of wind moving across the tender wheat shoots.

Green lined the narrow ridge, and in the distance, a shabby donkey cart waited nearby.

The driver slouched beneath a bamboo hat, half-asleep.

This was not a dream.

Pain pulled sharply through her body, especially along her skull, as though struck repeatedly by a heavy wooden mallet.

"Mei..." Her voice scraped out, nearly lost to a searing dryness.

"Miss, don't scare me like this." Mei's panic deepened.

Qin Nianyin suddenly lifted her gaze, startled by something far more tangible than pain.

"What... what did you call me?"

"Miss…" Mei answered, looking bewildered and full of concern.

"Miss, drink some water. You fainted just now. You frightened me to death."

She pushed the water pouch forward quickly.

Nianyin accepted it.

Her eyes fell on the faded blue jacket Mei wore, washed nearly to white.

Her hair was tied simply with a plain silver pin—it was exactly how she had looked when they first entered the capital.

Nianyin's fingers shook.

She reached for her wrist and felt the tight loop of old red thread her mother had tied before passing away, a protective talisman.

The sandalwood prayer beads given to her by the monk were gone, replaced once again by this thin, old thread.

Her heart tightened and sank heavily.

This mountain road was one she knew intimately—it was the same path she had taken into the capital in her previous life.

She had not yet entered the city. She had not met Su Zhang, nor the Crown Prince.

She had not yet stepped into the chain of events that led to that entire disastrous fate.

She had not yet forced a marriage. She had not yet begged for a child.

She had not yet lost everything in a cold and heartless game.

Relief swelled violently inside her, too large to contain.

Her vision blurred as tears fell onto her old skirt, darkening the dust.

The stains spread slowly, as though washing away the weight of her past sins and mistakes little by little.

She reached for Mei and pulled her into a tight, trembling embrace.

Her body shook. Joy, raw and overwhelming, rose until it nearly choked her.

A faint memory of blood flashing across her sight lingered, and cold sweat slipped down her spine.

Mei was alive. Still here. Still safe. Not yet lost to her.

The gratitude surged through her until it nearly unsteadied her breath.

"M…Miss, why are you crying again?" Mei asked in confusion, trying to support her.

"It's nothing."

Nianyin shook her head, laughing through her tears, her voice clear and firm.

She turned toward the north—the direction of the capital.

Through the drifting clouds, sunlight broke across the distant mountains.

The line of the peaks resembled the silhouette of a seated Buddha.

She closed her eyes. When she opened them, the uncertainty had cleared completely.

Her gaze was sharp, bright and inwardly renewed, as if something had been reforged from the ashes like a bird rising anew.

In this life, she would not allow the same tragedies to take shape.

She would no longer force herself upon Su Zhang.

She would not allow Gu Xiao to die again.

She would secure a good marriage for Mei.

These were no longer hopes; they were her vow and her destiny.

The wind rose along the mountain road, shifting the wildflowers at its edge.

They moved gently, almost as if offering quiet blessings for her return and a new beginning.

"Mei…" Nianyin said as she stood up, her voice as steady as a mountain, "we are going to the capital."

* * * * *

"Miss… Miss…"

Mei's anxious voice pressed against her ear. Qin Nianyin forced her eyes open once more.

Cold sweat covered her brow; her palms were chilled, as though whatever faint warmth she had regained had slipped away.

She must have drifted off without noticing.

Her lashes fluttered.

She looked at Mei with a dazed heaviness, her voice hoarse from repeated bouts of unconsciousness.

"Where are we now?"

"We are nearly at the outer official road of the capital."

Mei supported her carefully, worry tightening every word.

"You have been unconscious for quite some time. Does your head still hurt?"

Qin Nianyin gave a slow shake of her head. She lifted her gaze toward the road ahead.

In the distance, the high walls of the capital had begun to rise through the morning haze.

Outside the city gates, crowds gathered in restless waves.

Flags lined the battlements, snapping sharply in the wind, their colours bright against the sky.

The first signs of bustle and grandeur were already visible.

Inside that city lay everything she had missed in her previous life and everything she had sworn to protect in this one.

She smoothed back the few strands of hair that clung damply to her forehead.

A quiet resolve had settled across her features, steady and composed.

This time, she would face everyone with a clean heart and reclaim the life she once let slip through her grasp.

* * * * *

—— Capital City · At the Gate ——

By the time they approached the city gate, the sky had already dipped toward dusk.

From atop the high tower came a sudden, muffled thud of the evening drum—

The sound was heavy, carrying the cold that had seeped into the city walls over long years, vibrating through every brick and tile and shaking the air.

Qin Nianyin halted at once. Her chest tightened sharply.

That sound was identical to the drum she had heard before plunging off the cliff in her previous life.

The same low pulse that had seemed intent on counting down her final breath.

Her fingers curled instinctively against the collar of her cloak. She swallowed, the motion stiff and slow.

Only after a long moment did she draw in a deeper breath, forcing the surging memories back beneath the surface.

In this lifetime, no matter how deep the drum's echo, it would no longer be her death knell.

It was a warning.

It was a reminder.

The donkey cart swayed as it rolled past the city gate.

The streets inside were filled with people and carts, yet it was not overly crowded, likely because the sun was setting.

The day was nearing its end; the spring chill was biting, piercing through her padded jacket.

"It's so cold in the capital," Mei murmured, tightening her coat.

Qin Nianyin thought quietly that the cold of the capital was something she had long grown accustomed to—Only in another lifetime. She lifted the edge of the carriage curtain.

From a distance, she caught sight of the Su residence:

High walls capped with green tiles, a vermilion gate standing solemn beneath the dimming sky.

Two stone lions guarded the entrance, imposing and unmoving, exactly as she remembered.

* * * * *

Her gaze lowered, her knuckles tightening along the edge of her cloak.

That residence was the place she had, in her previous life, schemed her way into step by step with ambition and desperation.

Now, approaching it again, she was no longer that orphan girl filled with wild desires.

She entered the capital once more, but this time with clear eyes and a steady, calm heart.

Chapter 6: Returning to the Su Residence

At the second gate of the Su household, Mei carefully lifted the long-stored family letter and the admission token from her bundle, presenting them to the gate servant. The letter was the one Qin Nianyin's foster mother had entrusted to her before passing away; its envelope had grown soft at the corners, worn thin by the passage of years. The servant hurried inside to report their arrival.

After the report, the one who came out to receive them was Su Zhang's mother, Madam Qin, who personally led two elderly matrons as they arrived in a hurried pace.

The moment she saw Nianyin, she quickened her steps, her eyes warming with a gentle light and her smile softening into a welcoming glow. "It truly is our Nianyin who has arrived. This old woman thought her hearing had failed her for a moment."

She reached out with quiet tenderness and drew Nianyin into her arms. Her voice carried a soft, enveloping warmth, as if the little girl she once held upon her knee had never strayed far from her side.

"It has been years since you last came to the capital as a child. You have grown even more beautiful and graceful than I remembered."

Heat pricked faintly behind Nianyin's eyes. She bowed her head and murmured in a low, trembling voice, "Aunt."

Madam Qin gave her back a gentle, reassuring pat and replied with an affectionate chuckle. "I heard everything about the tragic events back home in Jiangnan. Since you are now stepping into the Su residence, there is no need to call me 'Aunt' anymore. I see it fit that you follow your cousin and Wan in calling me Mother."

Nianyin lowered her gaze, her voice hoarse and thick with emotion. "...Yes."

She had answered the words, yet a difficult, unspoken resistance stirred within her chest—in her previous life, she had indeed called this Marchioness 'Mother' for an entire lifetime, but she had done so as a daughter-in-law.

But those calls, tender and sincere as they once were, had eventually been met only with cold eyes, a desolate room, and total isolation.

Now that she had returned to this life, she no longer wished to face this woman with that same identity ever again.

Inside the gate, the bluestone path stretched beneath their feet, clean and vast. Two rows of crimson lanterns swayed gently with the spring breeze, releasing thin, coiling trails of fragrant smoke. From farther within the residence came the faint, elegant sound of a zither mingled with soft laughter, drifting through the air. The melody was gentle, yet it sent a subtle tremor through Nianyin's chest—the first time she had entered this household in her previous life, she had heard a tune just like this. Back then, she had stepped inside filled with bright longing; now, she felt only a thread of chilling coldness slide through her heart.

She lowered her head to salute and in doing so caught, from the corner of her eye, the sight of a newly planted camphor tree by the stone steps. The soil beneath it was still dark and damp, as though the years she thought were buried were quietly breathing and pulsing again below her feet.

* * * * *

"Do not stand at the doorway like fools. Come inside quickly to have some hot tea. It is late, and the air grows bitterly cold once evening settles." Madam Qin drew Nianyin toward the house with earnest warmth, while giving the servants several quiet instructions to prepare every necessity for her stay.

The central courtyard of the Su residence was broad, orderly, and impeccably clean. Spring had only just stirred; a few clusters of early plum blossoms had pushed out pale buds, their faint, cool fragrance trailing lightly through the air. Qin Nianyin walked step by step, feeling as though she were treading upon the very shadows of her past nightmares.

Inside the hall, the Marquis of Anguo, Su Ze, was already seated in a dignified manner, waiting.

His features were upright and square, his bearing steady and composed. When he saw her enter, he merely inclined his head a fraction. "Your journey to the capital must have been a long and tiring one."

"Thank you for your concern, Uncle," she replied. Her expression remained even, her gaze clear and steady, her manners neither lacking nor exceeding propriety.

Su Ze gave a small nod and did not pursue additional conversation. Yet from the corner of his eye, he studied her carefully—her expression was like the surface of a still, deep lake, devoid of joy or anger, as though he were observing a player at a chessboard.

The candle flames flickered lightly, casting a thin, soft warmth across the hall in shifting bands of gold.

Madam Qin kept hold of Nianyin's hand, assessing her for a moment before she smiled. "It has been several years since I last saw you, Nianyin. You have truly grown as graceful as jade. When you travelled north with my elder brother and sister-in-law, I worried the climate would not suit you. Yet now that I look at you, you seem even fairer and clearer than the young ladies raised here in the capital."

Nianyin lowered her eyes and listened quietly, allowing a light, faint smile to soften her lips.

Madam Qin continued, "Though you were adopted by my brother and sister-in-law, I have always treated you as one of my own children, with no difference. From today onward, you will stay here. Do not be a stranger."

"Nianyin has little fortune," she answered softly. "It is only by the grace and pity of Aunt and Uncle that I am able to find such peace today."

Madam Qin sighed, and a glimmer of tenderness and grief surfaced in her eyes. "You lost your parents early and followed my brother and sister-in-law as they travelled from place to place. Those years were truly not easy. Both of them were kind-hearted in life and in their final moments they entrusted you to me. How could I dare not do my utmost to care for you?"

Her tone was gentle, and a faint brightness gathered at the corner of her eyes, as though the tears from that farewell years ago had never dried.

Qin Nianyin lowered her gaze, her voice trembling slightly. "Aunt's kindness is heavy. Nianyin will forever remember it in her heart and never dare forget."

Madam Qin's smile paused for an instant. Her eyes shifted, as if casually, before she asked, "While you were in Jiangnan, did you ever correspond with Su Zhang?"

A small shock rippled through Nianyin's heart, yet her face remained as calm as ever. She slowly shook her head. "I did not."

"That is for the best." Madam Qin let out a quiet sigh, its intent difficult to discern. "His temperament has been cold and stubborn since he was a child. Now that his career is flourishing, I doubt he even remembers the matters of home. Should you cross paths with him, do not take his distance to heart."

Qin Nianyin lowered her lashes. "Aunt may be at ease. Nianyin has her own sense of proportion."

Her tone was obedient, but within her sleeves, her fingers curled ever so slightly. He had been her husband in her previous life—her burden, her karmic debt, which she had failed to repay even with an entire lifetime.

Midway through their conversation, Su Ze suddenly spoke, "Since you have returned, tell us your intention and plans for coming to the capital."

Madam Qin's brows drew together as though she meant to intervene, but Qin Nianyin had already risen with calm composure. She bowed and replied, "Uncle, during these years in Jiangnan, I studied calligraphy and embroidery. Now that I have reached adulthood, I wish to remain in the capital and establish a livelihood of my own to secure a place for myself. If the Su residence does not find it improper, I am willing to stay in the inner quarters temporarily until I find a place to dwell."

"What talk is this about starting a livelihood? A young girl has no need to show herself outside…"

Su Ze pressed down her unease. "Do not rush. Let her finish."

Madam Qin shot him a sharp glance before continuing, "Do not mind your uncle. From morning till night, all he speaks of is achievements and advancement. He has no end to his lectures. You are a young girl. Simply live here peacefully."

"Aunt, please be at ease. Nianyin understands."

Su Ze disregarded his wife's interruption and asked again, "Establishing your own livelihood? Have you made proper plans?"

Her gaze was as serene as still water. "In Suzhou, I learned embroidery, the making of floral hairpins and the blending of scents. I also possess a modest understanding of qin craftsmanship."

Her tone carried neither pride nor submission. Her eyes held the quiet certainty of someone who had walked out of disaster and returned alive.

Upon hearing this, Su Ze's brow lifted slightly—an almost imperceptible shift. He had assumed that his elder cousin's adopted daughter was coming solely to lean on the Su family's old ties. In his mind, he had intended only to settle her in the inner quarters and, at most, prepare a dowry before finding her a respectable marriage.

After all, was that not the usual fate for most women?

Yet she spoke of "establishing herself" and "earning a living," with not the slightest intention of clinging to anyone.

A trace of reassessment appeared in his eyes, mingled with surprise, and he looked upon her with a bit more weight.

But beneath that approval, a thin strand of cold reasoning slid past—this was not Jiangnan. Did she know the price a woman must pay to stand alone in this capital?

Su Ze studied her for a moment longer before finally nodding. "For a woman, the household is traditionally her domain. It is not fitting to show oneself too openly. Since you have come to the capital, remain in the inner quarters for now. Your aunt will see to the arrangements."

Madam Qin immediately added with a smile, "Yes, exactly. Do not speak nonsense. This is your home—there is no need to talk about staying 'temporarily.' As for managing a livelihood, a young woman should not expose herself to the world. If your parents look upon you from the heavens, they will surely hope for you to find a stable resting place. The capital is filled with hidden dangers. A girl finds it even harder to stand on her own. If you face difficulties, you must never keep them locked in your heart."

Qin Nianyin answered softly, "Yes, Aunt."

Her voice was faint, yet it brushed across her chest like a warm hand clearing away long-accumulated frost.

The candlelight fluttered across the hall, brightening and dimming, as though illuminating a deeper ripple within her.

She knew, beneath all this kindness, an old pattern of fate lay waiting.

And the man she was destined to confront—the one tied to her past and her debt—was somewhere in this capital, waiting in silence.

In this lifetime, she would still have to meet him.

She did not seek love.

She sought only to settle what she owed.

Chapter 7: First Encounter in This Life

Steady, unhurried footsteps approached from outside the door. His figure had not yet appeared, but the presence was already unmistakable.

That cadence—measured, composed, carrying a chill of restraint—was one she had once memorized down to her very bones in her previous life.

Qin Nianyin's fingers paused. Something in her chest tightened in response, as though an old string had been plucked without warning. That familiar calmness, that austere control, stirred her far more than she wished to admit. She already knew who had come. Only one person carried such a quiet, commanding breath.

Su Zhang—her refined, distant cousin, a man of rare talent and a temperament colder than frost.

He served as Chief Secretary of the Bureau of Appointments. Brilliant since childhood, reticent by nature, and sharp enough to be described as "near-demonic" in his wisdom.

Born into an erudite family, he had ranked as Tanhua in the imperial examinations. Emperor Xuanwen himself had bestowed the purple-gold belt upon him.

He had risen from the Hanlin Academy to the Ministry of Rites and now—remarkably young for such authority—held charge over the appointment and transfer of officials throughout the empire. It was a post at the heart of power, one that quietly shaped the destinies of countless men.

Yet he remained detached, principled, and unyielding. He neither formed factions nor sought patronage. Although he had a personal friendship with the Crown Prince, he never once crossed the line of propriety.

Those who spoke of him in court always used the same words: "Disciplined as jade, yet acting like iron." It was the Su family's ancestral virtue and also the very essence of his character.

Because of his formidable and often merciless political hand, he had accumulated countless adversaries. Even so, his official path had been smooth; at least, by the time she died in her previous life, he had already risen to Minister of Personnel.

Now, Su Zhang stepped inside wearing a dark indigo brocade robe. His posture was straight as a pine, his expression as remote as ever. The moment he entered, he bowed toward the elders of the household. "Father. Mother."

Madam Qin smiled and beckoned. "Come, meet your cousin."

Su Zhang's gaze brushed across Qin Nianyin, brief and unreadable. He inclined his head slightly. "The journey must have been tiring, Cousin."

The word "Cousin" landed lightly, yet a faint tremor stirred in her chest as though something fragile had been touched. Qin Nianyin faltered for half a heartbeat before smoothing over the reaction. Her lips curved gently while she reminded herself—

"This life is different. There is no need to lose your composure."

She steadied her breath, adjusted her sleeves, and allowed her expression to settle into something even and calm. By the time he approached, her face revealed nothing out of place.

The candle nearby flickered. His shadow fell across her skirts, cast through a thin layer of wavering light. The air seemed to tighten around her, as if his presence alone could press against her lungs.

It was an unspoken pressure, subtle yet unmistakable—an echo of those countless nights in her previous life when he worked beneath the lamplight, his figure solitary and immovable.

Her heart dipped, then loosened. This was good. If they could remain separate from the start—distant, unentangled—then repaying the debts left from another lifetime would be far easier.

Sensing her slight stiffness, Madam Qin gently held her hand and laughed softly. "Your cousin has always been quiet and rather cold. It isn't directed at you. He's simply older. Once you spend time together, you'll understand him. As long as I am here, you won't suffer the slightest grievance in this house."

Qin Nianyin lowered her eyes with a small smile. Her voice was gentle. "Nianyin knows that my cousin has always been quiet and restrained."

Her tone was light, but the end of her sentence trembled the faintest bit.

In the previous life, she had approached him again and again, only to meet a wall of coldness and the exhaustion in his eyes. In this life, he could remain as aloof as he pleased—she had no intention of repeating her old mistakes.

Su Zhang's expression did not shift. His tone remained even, composed. "The journey from Jiangnan to the capital is long and demanding. You should rest as much as you need. If your lodging proves inconvenient in any way, simply have someone inform the household."

"Thank you, Cousin." Qin Nianyin answered with respectful calm.

Their eyes met for only a fleeting second before both looked away. The brush of that moment stirred a strange ache beneath her ribs, a sensation sharp enough to feel like an old memory resurfacing without mercy.

Sensing the slight stiffness in the air, Madam Qin let out a warm laugh in a hurry. "Nianyin has just arrived and knows nothing of the capital. Zhang, you must look after her a little more. The two of you even studied together for a few days when you were children."

At those words, a vague image flickered in Su Zhang's mind—something small, soft, and dressed in pale pink, a blurred memory from too long ago.

Qin Nianyin, however, retained no such recollection. She only knew she had visited the capital once as a child, but she had been too young to keep anything clearly in mind.

Su Zhang's lips moved slightly, as if he might address the memory, yet he merely offered a restrained smile and let the thought pass. "I still have documents to review. I will withdraw for now. Father. Mother. Cousin—please excuse me."

He turned and left after speaking. His back remained straight as a pine, his steps steady, without the slightest hint of reluctance.

For a moment, the hall fell still.

Madam Qin exhaled softly and said in a gentle voice, "Your cousin has been this way since he was young. Even Wan complains that he is far too rigid. Do not let it trouble you. With time, you will grow comfortable around him."

Qin Nianyin returned a small smile. "Cousin is upright and disciplined. If anything felt improper, then the fault must lie in my own manners. I hope I have not caused Aunt or Uncle any amusement."

Her voice was mild, her tone smooth as still water. Yet her heart remained entirely unmoved.

In her previous life, she had loved precisely this icy, solitary part of him—loved it so much she had, in her drunken desperation, crossed every line to grasp at a marriage that should never have been forced. The result had been ruin for both of them.

In this life, she wanted nothing from him. Distance was a gift. She wished only for peace—no entanglement, no pleading, and certainly no misguided affection. "Let the well water not disturb the river water," she thought.

Madam Qin did not notice the shift beneath her calm exterior. Still smiling, she said, "You must be tired from the journey. Come, I will show you your courtyard. Would that be all right?"

"I trouble Aunt."

Qin Nianyin rose and followed her. But before stepping out, she could not resist glancing back over her shoulder.

Su Zhang's silhouette was long gone, swallowed entirely by the weaving shadows of the lantern light—like someone lost across lifetimes.

* * * * *

Not long after, light footsteps sounded from behind the screen— measured, graceful, touched by a chill that suggested disciplined restraint.

A young girl entered in a pale-blue bijia embroidered with bamboo patterns. She appeared fifteen or sixteen, her features delicate and finely shaped. Her complexion held a faint, cold fairness and her expression carried a trace of aloof pride far beyond her age.

She gave a proper curtsey. Her voice was clear, yet curiously distant. "Mother, Father. I heard our cousin has arrived, so I came to pay my respects."

When she had finished speaking, she lowered her gaze and offered Qin Nianyin a courteous bow—neither warm nor discourteous, held at a perfect, unapproachable distance.

Qin Nianyin's heart tightened. The faint coolness in Su Wan's eyes, the guarded stillness beneath them, felt like a thin layer of frost quietly separating the two of them.

In her previous life, she and Su Wan had been as close as sisters— sharing winter snows, keeping vigil together on long cold nights. Yet now, all that warmth seemed to have been scattered by a single sweep of the northern wind.

She pressed down the faint sting rising in her chest and returned the greeting with a gentle smile. "Hello, Sister Wan."

When the two finished their formalities, Madam Qin beamed. "Wan, I was just about to take your cousin to see her courtyard. What perfect timing. Nianyin is new to the capital and unfamiliar with everything. As the elder sister, you should look after her. When you have a free moment, host a small tea gathering and introduce her to the ladies of the city."

A flicker of impatience surfaced briefly in Su Wan's eyes, but she bowed her head. "Of course. I must welcome my younger cousin properly."

She looked up again. Her lips curved, yet the smile resembled the first thin crust of frost—elegant, cold, and fragile.

"Three days from now, at the hour of Wei, I will host a tea gathering in Ningfang Courtyard. Cousin, do attend on time."

Her tone was polite, but Qin Nianyin heard the subtle trace of testing and the quiet sense of granting favour from a position above.

Qin Nianyin's lashes lowered slightly. She curtsied and replied, "Thank you for your generosity, Sister Wan. I will certainly be there."

Her voice was soft and warm, but inside she was still and clear, like a pool of water untouched by wind. She understood well that Su Wan saw her now only as a rural relative with questionable upbringing.

But in this lifetime, she would neither compete nor cling. She intended only to restore—quietly, patiently—the reputation and affection she had destroyed with her own hands in the past.

Between the two young women, a subtle exchange had already begun behind the veneer of politeness.

Seeing this, Madam Qin grew delighted. "Sisters of the same family should be this close."

Qin Nianyin lowered her gaze with a faint smile. In her eyes, however, a restrained warmth flickered—an emotion kept carefully out of sight.

She refused to let fate repeat its cruel performance.

Even if their beginning was separated by a layer of frost, she was willing to wait for the day when the ice finally thawed.

Chapter 8: An Improper Gift

The following morning, gifts of congratulation began to arrive at the inner courtyard of the Su residence from various quarters.

Mei carried in a stack of exquisite wooden boxes, reciting their contents as she set them down one by one on the table. "This one is orchid powder, this is plum-blossom fragrance balm, and this is a purse embroidered with gold thread..."

Qin Nianyin opened each one in turn. The scents within ranged from delicate to rich, all customary tokens of goodwill exchanged among women—not exceedingly valuable, yet perfectly respectable and appropriate.

It was the final box that gave Mei pause when she placed it down; her voice softened noticeably. "This one... should be from the Young Master."

Qin Nianyin looked up. The box was slightly longer than the others, its brocade surface embroidered with a pattern of flowing clouds in fine silver thread.

She pushed open the lid. A white jade hairpin of mutton-fat purity glowed with a soft, warm radiance in the morning light. Its head was carved into the form of a budding plum blossom, the heart of which was inlaid with a single southern pearl. The pearl's lustre was subdued and quiet, like a dewdrop captured and held in stillness by time itself.

Mei could not suppress a soft gasp of admiration. "It's truly beautiful..."

Qin Nianyin lowered her eyes. Her fingertips brushed along the length of the jade pin, feeling its icy coolness seep into her very bones. A moment later, she closed the lid, her voice level and leaving no room for doubt or hesitation. "Return it."

The lessons of her past life had taught her: to accept was to invite an entanglement from which it would be difficult to emerge unscathed.

Mei was stunned. "Return it?"

"It is too valuable—it does not fit propriety," she murmured in a low, quiet voice. "Lest it give others cause for gossip."

Though she did not fully understand, Mei obeyed, returning the jade hairpin and conveying her Miss's sentiments.

* * * * *

Su Zhang's Study. The sunlight outside the window was just right, casting long shadows across the floor.

A servant reported in a respectful, hushed tone, "First Young Master, the Lady Cousin said… the gift is too heavy; she dares not accept it."

Su Zhang, who was in the midst of reviewing a legal dossier, paused his hand momentarily. His gaze shifted to the brocade box resting at the corner of his desk.

The white jade hairpin lay within, serene and unmoving. The southern pearl caught the slanting light, its beauty growing ever colder and more exquisite against the silk lining.

He reached out, his fingers lightly tracing the carved blossom at its head. The faintest of smiles touched his lips, as if he were merely acknowledging a trivial, everyday matter. "Understood. Put it away for now."

His voice was as temperate as ever, betraying not a sliver of emotion.

Only the smile failed to reach the depths of his eyes. It was like a thin layer of ice over a deep pool—no one could tell what currents moved beneath the frozen surface.

* * * * *

Afternoon - The Garden Walkway.

Su Zhang was on his way to the main house to pay his respects to his mother. As he turned the corner of the covered walkway, he saw a figure in plain, white silk approaching from the sunlit path opposite.

Qin Nianyin, who was also on her way out, paused slightly upon seeing him. She offered a shallow curtsey. "Cousin."

"Cousin." He stepped aside to let her pass, his voice mellifluous, yet his gaze seemed to linger on her for an uncalculated moment.

They were about to pass each other when Su Zhang, as if suddenly recalling something, turned and called out, "A moment."

Qin Nianyin stopped and turned back, her expression serene and untroubled.

"I heard you returned the hairpin." His tone was light, as if merely making casual conversation. "Did it not suit your taste? If that is the case, I can simply replace it with another welcoming gift."

Her eyes remained lowered, her voice even and detached. "The gift was too generous. One who has no merit does not receive such reward. I appreciate the sentiment behind your gesture, Cousin."

Su Zhang observed her expression, as if weighing her words. The faintest ripple of a smile stirred in the depths of his eyes, so slight it seemed it would scatter with the first breath of wind.

"In that case, I shall not insist." He nodded, turning slightly aside, his tone still gentle and measured.

Qin Nianyin bowed again, then turned and left.

Su Zhang remained where he stood, watching the plain, retreating figure grow gradually more distant. Only after a long moment did he himself turn and continue towards the main house. His fingers brushed against his sleeve—a seemingly absent gesture, yet one laden with deep contemplation.

* * * * *

On the afternoon of the third day, at the hour of Wei, the small gathering in Ningfang Courtyard had already been arranged with meticulous care. Spring warmth lingered in the air.

It was the fourth month, when the garden's flowers bloomed in steady succession. By the pavilion, the peonies were at their fullest—opulent petals unfurling in layered crimson and ivory, their fragrance drifting lightly on the breeze, lending an added delicacy to the tidy little tea pavilion.

Qin Nianyin wore a simple white gauze dress; the hem was embroidered with faint water-ripples in pale thread. At her temple she pinned only a single pearl blossom. The effect was clean and dignified, modest yet refined.

She had always understood the boundaries that came with her humble origins—she would not dare appear ostentatious, yet she did not wish to seem shabby or poor. This level of adornment struck precisely the right balance.

Mei leaned close and whispered, "Miss, we are almost at Ningfang Courtyard."

Qin Nianyin drew a soft breath, pressing down the faint unease tightening beneath her ribs. "Let's go," she replied quietly.

Several young ladies had already taken their seats inside the pavilion. Fragrant silks and jewelled hairpins lined the table—daughters of prominent families from the capital, each bearing the poise of status.

Su Wan occupied the main seat, dressed in lake-blue robes embroidered with slender silver vines. Her expression remained cool, her gaze carrying a distant nobility that kept others at a careful distance.

Qin Nianyin allowed her eyes to pass over the assembled girls. They were all familiar faces from her previous life.

Of course. Su Wan and Su Zhang shared the same mother. That reserved, unsmiling pride… seven parts of their temperaments matched without fail.

Seeing her arrive, Su Wan curved her lips in a small, practiced smile. "Cousin, you're here. Please sit."

"Thank you for the arrangement, Sister Wan." Qin Nianyin offered a courteous bow and took her seat, her movements calm and precise.

A girl beside Su Wan leaned close to whisper, her voice soft enough to pass as harmless. "So this is your cousin from the countryside? She looks a bit more presentable than I expected."

Another murmured beneath her breath, sharing idle gossip. "I heard she came because of the disaster back home. Staying in the Marquis of Anguo's residence… who knows how proper her background really is."

"So carefully dressed. Whether her elegance is genuine or merely borrowed remains to be seen. The capital is not a place where just anyone can sit at this tea table."

The words were gentle, yet each syllable carried a fine, barbed edge—a quiet probing meant to exclude her. Su Wan sipped her tea without replying. She neither agreed nor intervened, as if such remarks had nothing to do with her.

Qin Nianyin's expression did not alter in the least. She lifted the teapot and poured herself a cup, her posture serene and her face unruffled, as though none of the whispers had brushed against her ears.

Yet inwardly she noted: In my past life, I might have cared a little. But now—after all the honor and disgrace I've survived—such talk is scarcely worth a thought.

A warm, pleasant laugh drifted from the entrance. "Wan, why didn't you send word earlier? I nearly missed such an entertaining gathering."

The speaker was Shen Lingyan. She wore a moon-white gown embroidered with plum blossoms, her features refined, carrying a touch of heroism softened by gentle grace. Her manner was open and naturally affable.

For the first time that day, Su Wan's expression eased noticeably. "Lingyan, you arrived at the perfect moment. We're welcoming our cousin today. Join us and brighten the table."

Shen Lingyan seated herself beside Qin Nianyin, studied her for a breath and remarked with open surprise, "So this is Miss Qin? You have a calmer air than most young ladies in the capital."

"Greetings, Sister Shen." Qin Nianyin rose and offered a respectful bow, her smile soft at the corners of her lips. She remembered well that in her past life, Shen Lingyan had been one of the few sincere hearts who had extended even a little kindness to her.

Shen Lingyan paused suddenly, her brows lifting with amused curiosity. "Ah? How interesting. I haven't given you my name yet—how did you know I'm a Shen?"

A faint jolt ran through Qin Nianyin. Her fingertips curled inward before she steadied herself. She replied calmly, "On my way here, I thought I heard someone mention the 'Shen household.' When I saw Sister's extraordinary bearing and since you arrived slightly later, it was only natural to guess."

Shen Lingyan accepted the explanation with a light laugh and let the matter drop. "I see… that makes sense."

"And what about me? Can you guess my name as well?" A young girl in pale rose-pink spring attire leaned forward, smiling brightly.

Qin Nianyin recognized her instantly—Jiang Ying, second daughter of the Deputy Minister of Revenue. In her former life, Jiang Ying's affection for Su Zhang had turned bitter, and she had later fallen out with Su Wan.

Qin Nianyin returned an amused smile. "A figure as lovely as yours, Sister, seems less like a mortal miss and more like an immortal fairy who has just been struck down to earth by the Jade Emperor."

The remark drew soft laughter around the pavilion.

"Cousin is indeed quick-witted," Su Wan added politely.

Qin Nianyin inclined her head. "Thank you for the praise, Sister Wan."

With Shen Lingyan present, the atmosphere eased noticeably. The pointed remarks grew sparse. Qin Nianyin remained steady, answering with composed ease. She knew that in this life, her path would not mirror the previous one. She would not climb by clinging to others, but by her own ability and character.

Then, by chance, her gaze lifted. At the far end of the flower corridor stood a man in dark indigo court robes, a jade tablet held in his hand. His features were refined, his presence restrained. His eyes swept across the pavilion with a hint of cool detachment.

It was Su Zhang.

He appeared freshly returned from court, a servant standing quietly behind him. Through the thin spring light, he cast a single glance toward the small tea pavilion before turning away.

His expression was as severe as ever—the same face she had spent an entire lifetime growing accustomed to.

Qin Nianyin lowered her lashes. Her fingertip trembled for the smallest instant against the rim of her teacup before she steadied it again.

She took a slow sip of tea. The pale green brew tasted faintly bitter, yet she drank it with unbroken calm—as though she had seen nothing at all.

Chapter 9: The Tea Gathering at Ningfang

Within Ningfang Courtyard, the laughter of the various young ladies curled and lingered like delicate threads of silk. Some sat idly plucking at tea leaves as they chatted, while others leaned close to trade whispers in hushed, secretive tones.

The golden-glazed tea cups, painted with intricate blossoms, released a fragrant warmth that filled the air—yet even this heavy steam could not mask the cold, rising undercurrents of probing and calculation hidden within the noblewomen's words.

Su Wan wore a serene, proper smile on her face, her every movement measured, refined, and impeccably thoughtful. Her gaze swept slowly and deliberately across each face in the pavilion, yet it always withdrew in the final instant—as though held back by a layer of lucent, crystalline light.

It made her visible to others, yet kept her untouchable. That perfect reserve resembled a tightly shut door; no matter who you were, you were permitted only to stand beyond the threshold, never to cross into her world.

Qin Nianyin lowered her lashes, watching her silently. Something shifted faintly in the depths of her heart.

She recalled the Su Wan of her previous life. At that time, because of the connection between their mothers, they had once drawn closer for a brief period, but the warmth had faded quickly, and their paths had silently diverged.

Back then, Qin Nianyin had simply believed her cousin to be difficult to approach, a woman of high and solitary character. But now, looking again with eyes that had seen the end of life, she perceived another layer beneath that pride—

Su Wan guarded herself. She guarded herself against her, and she guarded herself against everyone else.

And that guardedness was not simply because Qin Nianyin came from humbler origins; it was more because she understood the plight of being a woman in this world.

The laughter in the courtyard was graceful and winding, accompanied by the low, steady melody of strings. T he shifting shadows of flowers brushed across the girls' faces, creating a bright and beautiful scene—yet beneath this radiance lay a thread of sharp, biting chill.

Fragrant mist rose and spiraled in the air, coiling almost invisibly around the tips of her hair. Even her breathing felt dyed with a sense of constraint.

When Nianyin lifted her eyes, she caught several pairs of smiling eyes studying her with cold scrutiny. In that instant, she truly understood: this so-called paradise of noble ladies in the capital was in fact a gilt cage. Behind every smile was a concealed blade.

In her past life, she did not know how many noblewomen had approached under the guise of friendship, when in truth, they only intended to use Su Wan as a bridge to reach Su Zhang—the accomplished, elegant, and brilliant young master of the Su family.

Even though he was cold and reticent, he remained the unreachable moonlight coveted by the hearts of countless high-born daughters in the capital.

As his legitimate sister, Su Wan had long grown weary of the honeyed words, the hidden schemes, and the heartless calculations that surrounded her.

To her, the Qin Nianyin of that previous life must have appeared no different from any other young woman harbouring ulterior motives— worse still, she was a cousin of faded origins who lived as a dependent under another family's roof.

Qin Nianyin's lips curved into a faint smile, though a touch of self-mockery and regret rippled beneath it. She admitted to herself: Su Wan had not misjudged her before. She had, indeed, possessed intentions toward Su Zhang. Ha.

Just as the thought settled, a clear, bright laugh sounded, and Shen Lingyan approached with a steady, graceful pace.

Born of a distinguished lineage in the capital, with her father and brothers holding high office, her bearing carried an innate ease and composure.

Unlike those noble ladies who competed with veiled barbs and honeyed but poisonous words, Shen Lingyan's features held a warm sincerity, her brightness like a clear spring revealing its depths at a glance.

Her gaze did not carry even a hint of condescension toward Qin Nianyin's origins. Instead, she noticed a certain quiet self-possession in those still eyes, and her heart stirred with a flicker of genuine appreciation.

"I heard Miss Qin newly arrived from Jiangnan," Shen Lingyan said with an easy smile, her tone sounding like casual talk yet holding a subtle probe. "How does that land of misted waters compare with our capital?"

Qin Nianyin inclined her head slightly. Her voice was as warm and gentle as spring water. "Jiangnan has many waterways, lakes, and harbors. In spring, the plum rains linger, fine droplets brushing the willow branches as the city fills with soft, hazy mist.

When autumn comes, the scent of osmanthus is everywhere. Near the Confucius Temple, boats glide along the river, and the strains of silk and bamboo music drift slowly across the water… It is quite different from the solemn and majestic grandeur of the capital. Small bridges and flowing currents, veiled by rain and mist—Jiangnan has its own charm entirely."

She had barely finished speaking when a noble lady in an apricot-yellow jacket let out a soft, mocking laugh. "It sounds refined enough, but with that much rain, I imagine the charm must grow tiresome and dull rather quickly."

Another noble girl, dressed in a verdant patterned silk skirt, ran her fingers along the pearls around her wrist and added lightly, "It's just a sentiment for smaller households to indulge in. For daily living, how could it ever compare with the bustle and brilliant prosperity of the capital?"

The words were delivered gently, yet the hint of high-flown condescension was unmistakable. Their gazes drifted over Qin Nianyin's simple attire and plain ornaments, as though they were measuring her value.

Qin Nianyin's expression remained composed, a faint, courteous smile touching her lips. "The capital is naturally the foot of the throne, its grandeur and atmosphere unmatched. Jiangnan's scenery is nothing more than an old memory; it hardly counts for anything."

Her tone was humble without being servile, neither forced nor weak, giving them no opening to find fault. Shen Lingyan turned to observe her.

In those calm, autumn-water eyes of Qin Nianyin, not a ripple stirred. Something unspoken flickered in Shen Lingyan's chest, a slight shift she could not entirely name.

Her smile deepened, and she settled in beside Qin Nianyin with a familiarity that required no invitation. "Jiangnan is known for its flourishing arts. Miss Qin, have you studied the qin, the brush, the board, or painting? I'm hosting a small gathering in a few days. If you have the leisure and interest, you should join us."

Such an unguarded and sincere invitation warmed Qin Nianyin's heart. Truly, she thought, had Su Zhang married Shen Lingyan in the past life, they would have been a match made in heaven.

In birth, talent, and bearing, they were equals; in temperament—one cool and the other warm, one still and the other active—they would have complemented each other flawlessly.

The more she considered it, the more she felt the sting of her own past folly. I really was hopeless back then, ruining something that should never have involved me.

She lowered her head in a graceful bow, her smile sincere. "Thank you for your kindness, Sister Shen. I only hope you won't mind my clumsiness. I know a little of painting and am slightly familiar with the qin."

Shen Lingyan blinked and joked, "What I fear most are those noble ladies who only speak in rules. I much prefer sisters who are as easygoing and interesting as you."

At this, Su Wan's hand paused over her teacup. She lowered her gaze and remained silent, her fingertip tracing the rim of the cup with slow, deliberate circles. A moment later, she looked up at Qin Nianyin. Something faint shifted in her eyes—this cousin was far more self-possessed than she had expected.

Perhaps… it would not hurt to observe her a little longer.

Tea fragrance curled through the air, and pear blossoms drifted lightly past the pavilion, creating tiny ripples on the surface of the white porcelain cups. Qin Nianyin brushed a thumb over the embroidered edge of her sleeve, her heart forming a quiet, firm resolve.

In this life, she would rearrange the board from the start—even if every step required her to walk along the edge of a blade.

* * * * *

Tea smoke drifted lazily in the air. Blossoms perfumed the breeze, and laughter wove through the pavilion like a thin thread of silk.

Qin Nianyin sat quietly, her gaze drawn—almost against her will—toward Su Wan resting her hand on the railing.

Her own fingertips brushed the embroidered edge of her handkerchief. That single familiar posture, that faint line between Su Wan's brows, tugged her thoughts sharply back to a dusk from her previous life, a dusk heavy as falling ash.

At that time, she had already become the mistress of the Su household. Yet her body was failing, every bone felt hollowed, and even warm broth had become difficult to swallow. No amount of incense could mask the thin, creeping scent of death clinging to the room.

The door had opened—not to Mei, but to Su Wan, long married and living far away. She stepped through the dim, silent corridor carrying a bowl of warm medicinal broth.

Her plain dress trailed behind her in a soft sweep. Her gaze was steady, tempered by years of wind and frost, but beneath it lay a quiet, settled kindness.

She sat by the bed and scooped a spoonful of the dark medicine, blowing on it gently. "Drink it," she said softly. "Listen to me. Don't be so quick to die. It isn't worth it."

Qin Nianyin had tried to open her eyes, tried to speak, but her throat was too dry. Su Wan set the bowl aside and tapped her chest lightly with cool fingertips. "Drink some," she murmured. "If you leave as well… then this Su household—no, this entire capital—will have no one left who truly speaks to me."

The words were mild, yet they carried the weight of years—steadfast affection buried beneath restraint. The bitterness of the medicine burned her throat, and the heat behind her eyes rose with it.

Only in that moment had she understood—Su Wan had never truly regarded her as an outsider. Even though they had drifted apart, when she had been most abandoned and alone, it was still those cool, unwavering hands that held her last sliver of breath.

When she returned to herself, the scene before her was once again the lively pavilion of Ningfang Courtyard. Qin Nianyin looked toward Su Wan across the distance and a faint, gentle smile curved her lips.

No matter how cold Su Wan seemed now, she could no longer mind—
because she remembered that bitter medicine and that pair of hands. The
past had dissolved. In this life, she sought only to live without shame.
She would never again fail any hand that once reached out to her.

Chapter 10: Spring's Palette in the Garden

After several rounds of tea had passed, Shen Lingyan let out a pleasant, light laugh and gently took Qin Nianyin's hand. "Sitting here for so long eventually grows dull and uninteresting. Let us go and take a stroll in the garden; the flowers there are currently blooming at their absolute peak."

Her tone was light and brisk, and within her eyes dwelt a genuine warmth and sincerity, which caused the rigid atmosphere of formal etiquette that had filled the room to soften by several degrees.

Qin Nianyin nodded in agreement and was just about to rise from her seat, when she heard Su Wan speak in her usual cool, indifferent, and level voice. "Since Mother instructed me to properly receive our cousin who has traveled from afar, I naturally must accompany you all for a stretch of the path."

Her tone was as clear and thin as water, and her expression remained entirely devoid of any ripples or waves. She smoothed the wide sleeves of her robe, rose ahead of the group, and led everyone forward into the garden.

The rear garden overflowed with lush greenery and a dense abundance of blossoms. Along the narrow, winding paths, the stones were mottled with patches of ancient green moss.

A gentle breeze, carrying the distinct scent of damp soil and fragrant flowers, brushed against their faces, causing the branches and leaves above to rustle with a soft, persistent sound.

A few finches had landed upon the railings; they flapped their wings, startling loose a cascade of fine, shattered flower petals that fell like rain.

A stone bridge arched gracefully over the water, where the willow shadows swayed back and forth with a lingering grace. Deeper within the garden, the crabapple trees had opened half of their heavy blooms— red and white blossoms intertwined and scattered in a chaotic beauty, resembling a display of silent fireworks frozen mid-air.

Shen Lingyan walked with high spirits and great interest. She pointed toward a particular peony bush and laughed heartily. "This peony has bloomed so beautifully! The flowers in my own courtyard haven't even formed their buds yet, yet here they are, opening first in the Su residence. It truly seems that your family's gardeners are exceptionally skilled in the craft of nurturing flowers."

Her movements were both refined and entirely natural, and that innate ease and aristocratic bearing of hers invited affection from everyone around her. Several of the other noble ladies chimed in with soft laughter to agree, their voices sounding clear and bright, like the clashing of fine jade and pearls.

Only Qin Nianyin walked quietly at the very back of the group, her expression flat and composed. From time to time, she lowered her head as her fingertips brushed lightly against the edge of a leaf. The lingering fragrance of the flowers coiled around her fingers, and that scent unexpectedly caused her heart to tremble faintly.

In her past life, she had also walked through this very garden side by side with Su Zhang. But back then, she was the formal Mistress of the household, and the garden—despite its abundance of flowers—felt so desolate and cold that it seemed as if no human warmth remained. Now, however, it was filled with the sounds of lively voices and cheerful laughter.

She forcibly suppressed these rising thoughts. When she lifted her gaze again, she caught Su Wan looking back over her shoulder. Their eyes met briefly in the open air—a moment of light so pale it was almost entirely transparent.

"Cousin, do you seem to dislike such noisy and lively gatherings?" Su Wan's voice remained faint and distant.

"People from Jiangnan are accustomed to remaining in quiet places," Qin Nianyin replied with a gentle smile, her voice sounding exceptionally mild and warm.

"The social climate of the Capital is different from that of the Southern lands. In time, you will naturally grow used to it." Su Wan inclined her head slightly, her demeanor remaining entirely calm and poised.

Shen Lingyan stepped in from the side to smooth over the atmosphere with a soft laugh. "The two of you standing together look exactly like figures stepped out of a masterpiece painting, making the rest of us seem like nothing more than common, secular guests."

Once she finished speaking, everyone rippled with laughter, and the atmosphere grew slightly warmer as the shadows of the flowers drifted across their sleeves.

Just at this moment, a tall and slender figure appeared, walking gracefully from behind the hanging-flower gate.

Su Zhang had already changed out of his formal court attire. He now wore a direct-seam robe of a pale indigo shade, tied at the waist with a simple, plain belt, and his dark hair was bound high. His temperament was as clear and lofty as white clouds in a mountain range, his steps unhurried and composed, carrying a relaxed ease that was utterly different from his severe and restrained demeanor in the imperial court.

The various noblewomen in the garden turned their heads at the sound of his approach, and the atmosphere suddenly stirred like spring water touched by a spreading ripple.

"It is Young Master Su," a low whisper rose among them, unable to hide a hint of irrepressible, pleasant surprise.

Shen Lingyan was the first to speak out. "Lord Su!" her voice was clear and crisp.

Su Zhang paused in his steps. He turned and inclined his head slightly in her direction. "Miss Shen." Then he offered a polite, cupped-hand bow to the rest of the group. "Ladies."

Shen Lingyan asked with a smile, "How is it that you have the leisure to come to the garden today?"

"My official duties are finished for the day. I am merely taking a moment of rest in the midst of this leisure," he replied in an even, steady tone.

The words were neutral, neither warm nor cold, yet as his gaze swept across the group, it paused—almost imperceptibly—on Qin Nianyin, who was standing in the far corner of the gathering.

She was dressed in a simple, plain robe, her eyelashes lowered, deliberately hiding herself outside of the surrounding excitement. Even the sound of her setting down her teacup was so soft it seemed she was afraid of disturbing anyone at all.

She seemed to wish only to be a wisp of a shadow that remained unnoticed by the world—yet, despite it all, his eyes fell directly upon her.

That faint, fleeting glance caused her heart to tremble. Noting his subtle, indistinct weight of attention, she deliberately refused to lift her head. Only after he had finally walked away did a ring of moisture remain along the rim of her teacup—though no one would ever know its true cause.

Su Zhang did not linger. His words were perfectly courteous yet remained distant and detached. "I ask that you ladies enjoy yourselves to the fullest. I still have important matters to attend to, so I shall take my leave first."

He bowed and withdrew, his figure disappearing gradually into the deep shadows of the flower-laden paths, leaving behind a ground littered with low-voiced sighs and lingering laments.

Several of the noble girls watched after his retreating figure with reluctant admiration, their eyes shimmering with a quiet, unspoken longing.

Only then did Su Wan speak in her cool, level voice. "My brother has always disliked noisy gatherings. The fact that he was willing to pause here in the garden for even a brief moment is already quite rare. I ask that you all do not take offense."

Shen Lingyan laughed. "Wan, you are joking. Lord Su is heavily relied upon by His Majesty and is burdened with ten thousand affairs every single day. How could anyone possibly find fault with him?"

One noble girl said teasingly, "The Su family is truly blessed by heaven—both the brother and the sister are such pristine and untouchable figures, like ice and snow."

Su Wan's expression remained entirely still, yet her gaze flickered— briefly and involuntarily—toward Qin Nianyin, who continued to sip her tea in total silence, as if the wave of emotion that had just passed through the garden had absolutely nothing to do with her.

"The spring scenery in the garden is at its best. There is no need to be constrained by rigid formalities and spoil the mood," Su Wan said as she lowered her eyes and plucked a stray petal from her knee, her tone remaining as calm as ever.

The others laughed softly.

"Lord Su is indeed as refined, noble, and self-possessed as the rumors say." "His bearing is so extraordinary; he actually seems more real and vivid than the immortals painted in scrolls." "It is a pity that he never speaks more than a few words to any woman..."

Their voices were filled to the brim with praise and adoration.

Only Qin Nianyin kept her eyelashes lowered. Her fingers slowly turned the teacup, her expression appearing faint and indifferent, yet she kept that single departing silhouette buried deep within the most hidden part of her heart.

She took a quiet sip of her tea and fell into step behind Shen Lingyan and Su Wan as they walked toward the deeper reaches of the garden. Her figure appeared slender yet firm in its resolve, as if she had soundlessly and completely bid farewell to the dreams of her past life.

* * * * *

The evening glow of the sunset reflected across the sky, and the shadows of the flowers in the garden grew long and slanted. The guests gradually began to disperse, until finally only Shen Lingyan and Qin Nianyin remained walking side by side.

"That Lord Su just now—he truly is your cousin?" Shen Lingyan asked with a teasing lilt in her voice, her tone carrying a hint of mischief.

Qin Nianyin's fingertips tightened for a brief second, but she immediately masked the reaction and offered a gentle smile. "He is the son of my Aunt. I have heard that he has been exceptionally intelligent since his childhood."

"Intelligent?" Shen Lingyan lifted a brow, a half-smile playing on her lips. "He certainly has a great reputation for talent, but from the sound of it, the two of you don't seem particularly close or familiar?"

Qin Nianyin nodded her head lightly and said, "We met only once when we were very young. Naturally, we are not familiar with one another."

At those words, Shen Lingyan laughed outright. "Then you naturally must not know this: in my view, your cousin seems more like someone who is excessively humble yet entirely devoid of emotion—a man like that is the absolute hardest to read."

After she finished speaking, Shen Lingyan set her teacup aside and glanced around the surroundings, as though she were searching for someone in particular, and asked in a seemingly careless manner. "By the way, I heard a rumor… are you an adopted daughter?"

The sudden bluntness of the question caused Qin Nianyin to freeze for a heartbeat. However, she quickly regained her composure and nodded with a quiet, steady smile. "Yes. My adoptive parents were my Cousin's uncle and aunt."

If it had been her previous life, without the scars and the harsh lessons of everything she had endured, she likely would not have been able to handle such a direct question from Shen Lingyan. She would have been both ashamed and frightened.

"Ooh…" Shen Lingyan murmured, appearing as if she didn't truly care about the answer, her eyes even refusing to linger on Qin Nianyin. "That is indeed quite pitiful…"

Qin Nianyin did not answer. She merely looked toward a nearby pool of spring water. The surface of the water reflected the light of the setting sun, and the waves sparkled like scattered, broken pieces of gold.

"Miss Shen, all things in this world follow their own cause and consequence. When Jiangnan suffered the great flood, I was fortunate to be taken in by my adoptive parents. To me, that was a true blessing."

"Yes, yes… a blessing," Shen Lingyan echoed absently, her eyes still scanning the surroundings in all directions.

"Is Miss Shen looking for someone?"

Only then did Shen Lingyan withdraw her gaze. She smiled and brushed the question off. "It is nothing. I was simply taking a casual look around."

The two of them continued walking side by side beneath the deep shadows of the long willow branches. A breeze stirred, carrying with it a light fragrance of blossoms.

From afar, at the curve of the veranda where it met the path, the sound of a man's low, muffled cough drifted through the quiet air.

Su Zhang stood beneath the eaves. He seemed to be listening to the conversation between the two women, yet he also appeared entirely detached, as if the words carried no weight. The slanted light of the evening cut across his brow, hiding the indistinct emotion in the depths of his eyes within the deepening dusk.

He watched the two figures as they walked side by side. For a brief instant, his expression shifted slightly. Between his fingers, he snapped the stem of a newly fallen flower blossom.

The coolness of the broken stem touched his fingertips. The petals slipped through his hand and scattered at his feet. A passing breeze brushed against his sleeve, and it seemed as though something within him had fractured in total silence.

Dusk settled more deeply. Qin Nianyin remained unaware of the gaze lingering behind her. She only sensed that the hour had grown late and turned to Shen Lingyan with a quiet smile. "Sister, it is time we headed back."

Shen Lingyan paused for a moment. Looking at Qin Nianyin's serene and indifferent profile, an indistinct and reflective emotion suddenly stirred within her.

—Some people return to the world reborn, yet they are no longer the same as the person they once were.

And fate, perhaps, began to shift and turn again at that very moment.

The moon began to rise, veiling the garden in a thin layer of evening mist. When Qin Nianyin glanced back at the flower-lined path, the sound of a temple bell drifted through the haze—sounding distant and near all at once, as if it were echoing from a dream of her previous life.

Her fingertips trembled slightly. A tide of emotion stirred faintly in her chest—the past has not yet gone far; its consequences have not yet scattered. This road ahead may still be filled with thorns—but she would, in the end, walk it one step at a time.

The wind skimmed the corners of the eaves. The lanterns flickered. She lowered her gaze and whispered a voice meant only for herself:

"If Heaven grants me one more chance… in this life, I would sooner betray the heavens themselves than betray my own heart."

Chapter 11: Gu the Howling Wind

Suddenly, a burst of frank and unrestrained laughter came rushing in from afar, like a bolt of spring thunder that violently cleaved through the garden's heavy hush.

"Zijun! Hurry and come look at what your lord has brought! Freshly brewed Mantangchun! I had to thicken my face and pester that old devil at the winery for half a month before I finally managed to trick this single jar out of his hands!"

A tall, broad-shouldered figure strode out from between the narrow flower shadows of the passageway, a wine jar in hand, following the stone path straight to the pavilion.

The newcomer wore an ink-dark brocade robe, cinched with a jade belt, his brows as sharp as swords and his eyes as bright as stars, heroic spirit spilling from his very posture.

Laughter blazed at the corners of his eyes and mouth—wild, arrogant, and unrestrained—yet in the lift of his hand and the turn of his shoulder, there was a keen edge of sharpness that no one could afford to underestimate.

It was Gu Xiao—the Marquis of Zhongwu.

The Gu clan had served as a military house for generations; both his father and elder brothers had died on the battlefield. He himself had been raised within the palace under the Empress's care, and though born with a title high enough to live in ease for a lifetime, he still refused to sit quietly and enjoy his soft privilege. On campaign, he was ruthless and decisive in his killing; yet in private, he forever wore that careless, roguish air—tongue unbridled, laughter nonstop, as though the world were nothing but a place for his amusement.

People in the capital often joked that this Marquis Gu kept all his temper and pride openly on his brows and in his smile, yet hid his sharpest blade beneath his drunken laughter.

He halted beneath the pavilion steps and, through the railing, cupped his hands in a bold salute, grinning brazenly. "What sort of auspicious day is this? The Su residence is actually this… flower-bright and bustling?"

The pavilion curtain dipped half an inch, and the chatter at the table stalled at once.

Shen Lingyan lifted a sleeve to cover her mouth, laughing lightly. " Marquis Gu, you truly are still as mouth-uncovered as ever. Three sentences from you, and you leave people with nowhere to hide."

Su Wan's brows tightened, displeasure entering her voice. " Marquis Gu, this is a ladies' gathering within the inner residence. I trust you will keep proper restraint."

Gu Xiao did not care in the slightest. His long legs carried him forward in one stride, and he was already seated on the long bench. He poured himself tea as if it were his own house, smacked his lips after one taste, and did not forget to offer his critique. "The tea's not bad. It's just that it doesn't feel as satisfying as wine."

When the words fell, his gaze shifted—then landed squarely on Qin Nianyin.

Those eyes that had been laughing with teasing mischief instantly gained a sharper focus and a clear interest. It looked like a casual sweep, yet he examined her from head to toe with startling thoroughness—how her fingertips rested lightly on her knees, the faint movements hidden beneath her sleeves, even the calm, neither-servile-nor-proud curve of her lips. All of it was taken in.

"This young lady," he said, his voice half-playful and half-genuine, "looks unfamiliar. How is it that I've never seen you before?"

His tone could pass as a joke, yet his gaze was as keen as a knife, as though he meant to peel away layer after layer of secrets from her eyes.

Qin Nianyin lifted her gaze unhurriedly, meeting that slightly insolent scrutiny head-on. A clear, faint smile touched her lips. "This one is Qin Nianyin. I came from Jiangnan to the capital, and for now, I am lodging temporarily at the Marquis of Anguo's residence."

The smile at his mouth deepened, as if he had tasted something rare and exquisite. He murmured her name, savoring the sound. "Qin Nianyin… a good name."

Throughout the tea gathering, Qin Nianyin had sat quietly, her brows and eyes mild and her words few—yet there was not the least trace of shyness, nor the least hint of timidity.

That was the strange part.

Gu Xiao turned his teacup slowly between his fingers while watching her from the corner of his eye. He had seen plenty of Su-family tea gatherings; the noble daughters who attended were either delicate and soft-spoken, or stiff with affectation. A few teasing remarks from him would make them blush or drop their heads no matter what.

But this Qin Nianyin—neither a titled daughter of a great house, nor anything more than a guest living under another family's roof—sat as steadily as if she belonged at the center of the table.

Something stirred in his chest. He angled his body slightly toward her. "First time in the capital, seeing so many high-born ladies and distinguished guests—are you truly not the slightest bit afraid?"

Qin Nianyin smiled lightly, her voice gentle yet not weak. "Afraid? Not to that extent. My aunt treats me as her own child, and my cousin and elder sister are both kind and broad-hearted. Since no one in the Su residence regards me as an outsider, why should I be afraid?"

Gu Xiao's brow lifted, and the laughter in his smile gained a thin thread of mockery. The Su siblings? Kind and broad-hearted? If anyone in the capital heard her sincerity, they would laugh until their teeth fell out.

As if catching the flicker in his expression, Qin Nianyin added in a calm tone, "Besides, this one is not visiting the capital for the first time. When I was young, I once came with my parents to pay a visit at the marquisate."

Gu Xiao stared at her for several breaths. Then he gave a low chuckle, his voice deep and the meaning unclear. "Wonderful."

Qin Nianyin lifted her eyes to him, her expression unruffled and her voice silent.

Gu Xiao did not continue the exchange. He only rocked the teacup lightly in his hand, his gaze turning thoughtful, as if weighing something.

At the side, Su Wan cut in coldly. "My brother did stop here for a moment earlier, but he has already left ahead of you. If the Little Marquis wishes to find him, you may go to the study."

Gu Xiao bared his teeth in a lazy grin. "Of course I'll go find him. But there's no rush. It's lively here—this young master wants to sit a little longer."

Shen Lingyan laughed behind her red sleeve, a soft burst of sound. Qin Nianyin only gave a faint, polite smile, lowered her eyes, and sipped her tea—as if all his teasing talk were nothing but wind passing her ears.

But in her heart, a thin chill rose.

Gu Xiao—indeed—was unchanged from her previous life: charming and flamboyant, laughing lightly, and careless of restraint, living with that devil-may-care arrogance. Only she did not know whether, in this life as in the last, he would still… die for the country on distant sands, his blood staining the yellow desert.

And she—could only call him once in a dream: "Come back."

* * * * *

After Gu Xiao left amid laughter and jokes, Qin Nianyin lowered her gaze. Her fingertips brushed unconsciously along the rim of her teacup, but inside her chest, old dreams rose one after another—burning hot, and yet ice-cold.

In her previous life, she had not had much direct contact with Gu Xiao. She only knew him as Su Zhang's closest companion, and as the young hero of the court whose star was rising by the day. Later, he was ordered to lead an expedition to the borderlands, commanding troops against the enemy with an inspiring and lofty bearing. Victories arrived in rapid succession, shaking the capital with high morale. The common people spoke of him everywhere, praising him openly: "The Gu family are loyal martyrs. The young general is a man of promise."

But good times do not last.

The border situation changed suddenly. During a campaign to suppress bandits, Gu Xiao was ambushed. It was said that his most trusted deputy, Liang Dong, had colluded with the enemy and betrayed him—leaking military intelligence and exposing their route and formation—until the entire force collapsed in ruin.

In that battle, Gu Xiao fought until the very last moment. He died on the battlefield. No body was recovered, and not a single bone returned. Only a corner of his blood-soaked battle clothing was found amid the chaos and brought back to the capital.

When the news reached the palace, the Empress wept and collapsed in the Golden Throne Hall, nearly wishing to follow him into death. The Gu household, a family of loyal heroes, had all perished on the battlefield; their line was extinguished.

The Gu family had been the Crown Prince's most solid support. With Gu Xiao's death, it was as if one of the Crown Prince's wings had been snapped off alive. The winds in court shifted overnight. Factional strife intensified. The Crown Prince came perilously close to being deposed—

had he not kept a steady head in crisis and engineered a reversal, the position of heir would already have fallen into another's hands.

And she, at that time, was already the mistress of the Su household, a first-rank titled lady—status high, power great—yet she was unable to change any of it. She could only watch, helpless, as a young hero's blood stained the desert sands, not even knowing where his soul had gone.

And she hated the self she had been then—her eyes and heart had been filled only with seeking power. She had devoted herself to pleasing Madam Su, to securing Su Zhang's favour, and to tightening her own position. But toward Gu Xiao—toward a man so loyal and brave—she had never offered even a single sincere act of concern.

Now, seeing that old acquaintance again… he was still as before—arrogant, unrestrained, laughter bright across his face, and his youthful spirit blazing as he strode past her.

Yet in her heart, a sudden stab of pain rose, sharp and merciless—as though she saw him stepping across the white bones of the road ahead, running, step by step, toward a death already written. Now she carried twenty years of memory from her previous life, and she was seeing this fierce flame again.

She felt like an elder who knew the ending, watching him ride in bright clothes and bold laughter toward a destined abyss. The pity born from the distance of years mingled with a crushing helplessness, flooding her chest.

"…If I can change things earlier," she whispered, eyes lowered, her voice so soft it was nearly unheard, "can I protect him… even for a stretch of the road?"

The words were quiet, but they fell into her heart like a resolute anchor of decision. Shen Lingyan, hearing only indistinctly, turned in confusion. "Sister Nianyin, are you perhaps unwell?"

Qin Nianyin returned to herself. She smiled faintly and shook her head. "It's nothing. The tea has simply gone cold."

She pushed aside the old cup and poured herself a fresh one. Steam curled upward in thin threads, but her gaze grew clearer and clearer.

She knew she could not remain doing nothing again—even if the road ahead was steep with obstacles, and even if her ability was limited, she still had to exhaust every means she could to help him rewrite the calamity written into his fate.

The lamplight in Su Zhang's study was sharp and clean. On the desk, a pot of tea released a faint, coiling steam of warm white mist, and the fragrance of sandalwood rose slowly in steady, mesmerizing curls.

Gu Xiao pushed open the door with the ease and familiarity of one long accustomed to the place. A wine pot was in his hand, and his face had already split into an unrestrained grin.

"I swear, Su Zijun, your study is even gloomier and more deserted than your family's main hall. Outside, it is all songbirds and silk sleeves, lively chatter and joyful laughter—a bustling garden of spring. But here? This room feels more like a cold ancestral shrine."

Su Zhang did not even lift his head. His voice was level, without warmth or irritation. "If you continue to spout such nonsense while clutching that wine, you can find the door back out yourself."

"Ooh, giving me a cold face before I've even had a single drink? Who has provoked you now?" Gu Xiao laughed as he dropped onto a seat, uncorking the wine pot with a practiced, casual flick of his fingers.

"This is freshly brewed Mantangchun. If it is not to your taste, then I shall enjoy the entire jar by myself."

Su Zhang finally sent him a brief, sideways glance. He set down his brush with deliberate calm and accepted the cup of wine. "If you could manage to speak a few less words, I might be persuaded to share a drink with you."

"That won't do. Wine without conversation—how is that any different from being a mute?" Gu Xiao took a small, appreciative sip, a spark of mischief glinting in the depths of his eyes.

"Your household was incredibly lively today. A whole line of young ladies sitting there as neatly as a prized peony garden. A rugged, coarse man like me nearly didn't dare to enter the gates."

Su Zhang's tone remained as flat as a still lake. "Yet you barged in anyway."

"Hey, that was me being polite." Gu Xiao suddenly lowered his voice conspiratorially. "By the way… your cousin who just arrived—Qin Nianyin?"

Su Zhang's brow drew down a fraction, a heavy shadow settling there. "What of her?"

"Nothing much." Gu Xiao's grin turned sly and knowing. "I just found her rather pleasant to the eye. A girl of humble yet delicate grace from a humble house, yet she doesn't put on airs. She has that gentle, nurturing grace that only the Jiangnan lands can produce. Truly soft on the eyes and pleasing to the soul."

Su Zhang did not offer a reply. He merely raised his cup and drank the wine in silence.

Gu Xiao's smile deepened, becoming pure mischief. "If not for your own sister's gaze being so cold it could freeze a man's blood within his bones, I might have seriously considered choosing a wife from your household. Forming ties through marriage—how convenient that would be. And this little cousin of yours… I truly find her interesting. Do you want to help your brother here and match us up?"

His words had hardly faded when Su Zhang set his wine cup down upon the table with a heavy, dull, and decisive knock. His voice grew several degrees colder, cutting through the air like a blade.

"If you insist on continuing with this ridiculous drivel, then there is no longer any need to share this wine."

Gu Xiao was momentarily taken aback. "Why the sudden temper?"

"She bears the surname Qin, but for now, she is considered a daughter of the Su family." Su Zhang's tone was restrained yet edged with an unmistakable and sharp warning. "You would do well to restrain that unbridled and irresponsible nature of yours. Like Wan, she is not someone you should ever treat with your usual, thoughtless frivolity."

"It's not the same," Gu Xiao muttered, puckering his lips in a small show of defiance. "I wasn't being indecent; I only mentioned her in a casual, passing manner—"

"Enough." Su Zhang's interruption was sharp and piercingly cold, his eyes looking as if they were suddenly covered by a thin, impenetrable layer of ice. "Regardless of whether it is a jest or your true heart—stay far away from her."

Gu Xiao raised a brow. After a long moment of silence, the laughter in his smile faded away by slow degrees as he studied the other man's profile.

Su Zhang did not elaborate or explain further. He turned back toward his desk, picked up his brush again, and his back remained as silent and immovable as a great rock.

Gu Xiao watched him for a long moment, then took a sullen, quiet sip of wine, muttering under his breath. "Truly… a difficult, stubborn slab of ice."

* * * * *

Days later, beneath a clear and brilliant sky, the inner courtyard of the Su residence was unusually quiet. Sunlight slanted across the space, falling over the bluestone corridor in neat patterns, broken into precise squares of light and shadow by the intricate lattice windows beneath the eaves.

The wind chimes hung from the eaves rang with a crisp, light sound, intertwining with the distant, melodic calls of birds. It sounded very much like the soft murmur of a small stream trickling from the hidden depths of time.

Qin Nianyin had just paid her morning respects at the main hall. Her aunt had rewarded her right then and there with a magnificent length of satin. The fabric was as soft and smooth as flowing water; she carried it with both arms, and her view was mostly obscured by the bulk of the gleaming material.

As she rounded a corner of the corridor, a sudden gust of wind swept through the courtyard. It lifted several loose strands of hair across her eyes, blurring her vision. She raised a hand to brush them back, yet her footsteps never slowed or hesitated.

And then—"Thud!"

She collided squarely and heavily with a figure as solid and as immovable as a mountain of stone. The length of satin in her arms nearly slipped to the dusty floor. Her chest jolted with the impact of the collision.

She looked up to meet a pair of strikingly clear and cold eyes. They were like the surface of a frost-covered lake—devoid of anger, yet instinctively making one withdraw every possible explanation.

Her lips parted slightly. She had intended to offer an apology or an explanation for her clumsiness. But looking into the depths of those eyes, the words suddenly felt redundant and unnecessary.

A faint, weary sigh brushed through her heart. She simply lowered her head and said in a low voice, "I was impolite."

Her voice was not high, yet it carried an unmistakable sense of propriety and a clear, defined distance.

She tightened her hold on the satin and walked past him with measured grace. Her sleeve brushed lightly against his broad shoulder, carrying with it a faint, lingering trace of sandalwood incense. Her pace was neither hurried nor slow, as if nothing of importance had happened at all.

Behind her, the man stood still for a moment, his figure paused in the light. Something flickered faintly in his eyes, but he only lowered his gaze a fraction and continued on his way.

Just then, another figure approached from the side corridor—Su Wan, her face showing a plain and unmistakable displeasure. "Was that the Lady Cousin just now?"

Su Zhang gave a slight, nearly imperceptible nod.

"In my view, she has likely set her heart on you, Brother. She has surely moved her intentions toward you." Su Wan let out a cold, sharp sneer.

Su Zhang's expression did not change in the slightest. He merely cast her a cool glance, his tone as sharp and as cold as a metal blade. "A young lady who has not yet left her family's inner chambers should be mindful of her propriety and the weight of her speech. Guard your tongue, lest you be laughed at by those outside."

Despite her brother's scolding words, Su Wan showed no sign of embarrassment or shame. She merely lifted her chin and continued to walk side by side with him with effortless familiarity. "Brother is also going to pay respects to mother? Then let us walk together."

Not far away, Qin Nianyin had already moved several yards down the corridor. Yet the offhand, teasing remark Gu Xiao had made that day seemed to echo persistently in her ears.

The corners of her lips lifted in the slightest, most invisible curve, and she thought to herself—In this life, I will never, ever repeat those disastrous past mistakes.

Sunlight poured down at the far end of the corridor, stretching her silhouette thin and long against the stone. Along with that silent, resolute oath, her shadow gradually dissolved and vanished into the depths of the light.

The night was deep and the dew was heavy; the moonlight was as pale and clear as liquid silver.

Su Zhang set down his brush and sat in deep, silent thought for a long, aching moment. He walked over to the small side table and poured himself a cup of the Mantangchun wine that Gu Xiao had brought.

Before the wine even touched his parched lips, his heart was already as tangled and messy as a ball of wet hemp. His brows knit together, and a layer of indescribable, heavy exhaustion settled in the depths of his eyes.

Without realizing it, he leaned his weight against the desk—and sleep claimed him almost at once.

Dreams seeped into the lake of his mind quietly, like a wisp of spring wind. It was gentle in its touch, yet resolute and inescapable in its intent.

In the haze of the dream, he saw a man seated alone in a still, secluded courtyard. The ground was paved with old, weathered bluestone, and apricot blossoms drifted down from above in silent, white flurries.

A warm lantern glowed unsteadily against the darkness of the night, its flame flickering like a heartbeat. The figure felt familiar—hauntingly, painfully so—yet he could not see the face clearly through the shifting mist.

Someone was laughing softly, draping an outer robe over his cold shoulders. Their fingertips brushed lightly against his skin with a sense of intimacy and natural tenderness. The voice was as mild and as pleasant as a lingering fragrance: "It is cold outside. You must not allow yourself to catch a chill."

He tried to lift his gaze to see the speaker's face clearly, to finally know who she was. But the voice only circled his ears, clear yet ungraspable, while the features remained obscured by the stubborn fog of the dream.

The scene shifted abruptly.

He lay upon a sickbed, weak and fevered, his breath coming in shallow, ragged bursts. That same figure stayed faithfully by his side, feeding him medicine spoon by painful spoon.

The voice now carried a sharp hint of anger born of a deep, agonizing heartache: "Su Zhang, it has come to this—just how long do you intend to torment the both of us!"

"Do you really hate me that deeply…?"

"Please… I beg of you, stop torturing yourself… and stop torturing me…"

Every word and every sentence felt like fine needles and silk threads sewing together his fractured, broken soul. Although his limbs felt weak and heavy as lead, because of that person's presence, he felt a warmth and a peace he had never known in his waking life.

He heard himself let out a low, quiet, and bitter laugh. But then, in the dream, he reached out and struck the medicine bowl to the floor. The sound of the porcelain shattering sharply cleaved the still night in two, and a sudden, agonizing pain flared in the center of his chest.

He realized with a shock—the sick man in the dream was himself.

But before he could look closer at the person beside him, the figure and the courtyard were swallowed by a thick, encroaching fog. The voice drifted farther and farther away, yet it was still calling out to him—"Zhang… Zhang…"

The cry was like a sob, threaded with grief, striking directly into the softest and most vulnerable part of his heart.

Su Zhang jolted awake in his chair. His forehead was drenched in cold sweat and his back was soaked through his underrobe.

He gripped the embroidered quilt tightly, his heart drumming against his ribs like a hammer. For a long moment, he could not distinguish the remnants of the dream from the reality of the quiet, candlelit room around him.

The candle flame flickered wildly in a draft, its shadow clinging tremulously to the wall. He raised a hand to press against his temple, his brows locked in a deep, painful frown as he whispered into the silence— "…Absurd."

It was only a dream. How could a mere dream leave his heart pounding with such terrifying force? And who—who in this world could make him so willing to entrust his entire life, so willing to face the storm and fire together?

He was always calm and self-disciplined, a man who never believed in the omens of dreams. Yet the lingering sorrow and that strange, aching familiarity from the dream clung to him like ivy. It was tight, tenacious, and utterly impossible to sever.

The person in the dream... he did not remember them. And yet, it felt as though he had never truly, in all his years, forgotten them at all.

Outside, a faint breeze passed through the night air. Pear blossoms loosened from their branches and drifted past the window, pale as the remnants of a dream.

Su Zhang lowered his eyes, his lashes casting long shadows, and said in a soft, barely audible murmur— "Truly… I have gone mad."

Chapter 13: If One Could Find a Kindred Heart

Sunlight slanted through the lattice windows of the main hall, warm yet subdued, and a muted ripple of raised voices—the sound of a lingering disagreement—filtered through the half-closed screens.

Qin Nianyin paused just as she was about to step over the threshold, instinctively withdrawing the foot she had started to move.

Inside, Madam Qin sat on the main seat, her expression gentle in countenance, yet her voice was unyielding and determined in tone. "...Nonsense! Since ancient times, there is a reason for families of equal standing to match, but Zhang is no longer young; it is time his marriage be settled. There are many young ladies of fine reputation and character in the capital, and I see no reason to bind ourselves strictly to noble houses and powerful clans. As his mother, I only seek a woman who is warm-hearted and virtuous, someone who can understand and tolerate Zhang's temperament. That is the only way for a marriage to endure."

She knew her son's nature better than anyone; he had possessed an incredibly deep will since childhood, and she feared he would not easily marry a daughter of a great family just to satisfy his father's desires.

Marquis Su Ze lifted his tea, his brow knit in a faint frown. "That is nothing but a woman's sentiment. Zhang now follows the Crown Prince, and his future is limitless. If he were to gain the support of a powerful house through marriage, it would be like adding wings to a tiger. Besides, the Second Lady of the Shen family is a childhood friend; her temperament and appearance are both perfectly suited to him."

Madam Qin sighed and shook her head. "The Second Lady Shen may be radiant, gracious, and possessed of a noble lineage and a fine mind, but she may not necessarily be able to endure Zhang's solitary pride and coldness."

"A gentleman's temperament is like bamboo or pine; character can naturally be shaped and tempered after marriage," Su Ze countered with a light tsk.

Madam Qin cast her husband a sidelong glance. "You know his cold nature; on the surface it doesn't show, but in his bones, he is extremely self-disciplined and cannot abide even a single trace of false affection. When you were in office, do you remember? Which of those noble daughters didn't first respect your rank before they ever looked at who you were as a man?"

Su Ze snorted. "My rank was not low in those days; what fault was there in that? Zhang is a man; he will naturally know how to distinguish the true from the feigned."

The argument had reached an impasse when a soft voice came from outside: "Uncle, Aunt, Nianyin has come to pay her respects."

Madam Qin's eyes brightened instantly. "Come in, child."

Qin Nianyin stepped inside, dressed in a simple and elegant blue gown, a white-jade pear-blossom pin adorning her temple. Her brows and eyes carried a gentle, luminous, and clear composure.

Madam Qin smiled as she entered. "You've come at just the right time. Your uncle and I were just discussing your cousin's marriage. Tell us— in a marriage, is it more important to value lineage or temperament?"

Qin Nianyin stilled, her lashes lowering quickly to hide the jolt of surprise in her eyes. Beneath her wide sleeves, her fingers curled by a fraction as a wave of emotion rose in her heart.

His marriage?

Having lived through a previous life, she understood too well: if Su Zhang married into a powerful house, it would undoubtedly aid his political career. Yet most of those noble ladies admired nothing but his fame and the protection of his wings; few would truly respect his true nature—that of a man who guarded his integrity in principled poverty.

In the previous life, he had spent his days in cold solitude. Aside from a few young servants and elderly maids, no one was ever allowed to draw near him.

In court, he preferred to be a "Lone Minister," loyal only to the imperial power. Because of this, he had incurred the enmity of countless people, eventually leading to the tragedy where she was driven off a cliff and Mei was stabbed.

She thought to herself: How could a man like him ever entrust his life to hollow fame? Yet every person has their moments of winter and isolation; if he could have one person to " A companion to share his quiet hours," to warm his wine and hold his books, it would be worth far more than all the empty etiquette of a grand estate.

Qin Nianyin lowered her lashes and offered a faint, gentle smile. "Aunt, you tease me. Such a matter is far beyond anything Nianyin dares to speak on."

Madam Qin gave her embroidered fan a light shake and laughed. "Ah, it is I who have grown foolish, asking such a thing of a young lady who has not yet stepped beyond her inner chambers."

But Su Ze spoke up. "No harm done. Since your aunt has raised the question, go ahead and speak your mind. It's nothing more than idle household talk."

Qin Nianyin hesitated for a moment, then inclined her head. "In that case, Nianyin will obey."

In her previous life, he had married her—a woman with neither pedigree nor talent—and they had lived as a couple in name only, a hollow union that left them both lonely for a lifetime. In this life, she only wished for him to find a true companion who could aid him, comfort him, and cherish him, so that he would no longer spend his years in such cold silence.

After a moment of deep thought, she spoke softly. "My cousin is a paragon among men, a man of peerless grace. He is naturally the choice of many young ladies in the capital. If one speaks of lineage, it would certainly serve as wings to lift him further…"

In her mind, the image of that slender, solitary figure flickered—his back to her as he walked through long corridors, courtyards, and across stone bridges.

Her voice grew quieter. "But marriage, in the end, is made of the long years of rice and salt. If he can find one person who knows his true heart, respects his integrity, and understands the hardships of his long winters and summers… that would be the rarest and most fitting companion."

The hall fell into a brief silence. A flicker of appreciation and relief shone in Madam Qin's eyes, while Su Ze said no more, simply lowering his head to sip his tea.

"Very well," Madam Qin said with a smile, swaying her fan. "In a few days, it will be the Festival of the Flower Goddess, and the capital will be very lively. Let Zhang accompany you and Wan. It will save you the trouble of the journey, and he can keep you safe."

She beckoned Qin Nianyin closer and whispered into her ear with a playful laugh, "This time at the festival, take a proper look for me—see which young ladies have kind tempers and which possess extraordinary talent. And you, child, must keep your own eyes open as well."

"Aunt… I would rather not go," Nianyin replied quietly. Her lashes trembled, yet she did not say the words: that she had already vowed never to become anyone's wife in this lifetime.

"That won't do. You've been in the capital for several days and haven't stepped outside properly. Go out and enjoy the bustle, otherwise, you'll grow stifled staying indoors." Madam Qin took her hand and gave it two soft, comforting pats.

Qin Nianyin could only press her lips together and remain silent, unwilling to argue. She thought to herself: Very well, let it be.

Madam Qin assumed she was simply being shy and chuckled. "The words of a matchmaker may be sweet, but nothing compares to what one sees with their own eyes. Enough, let us speak of it no more."

* * * * *

The lamplight wavered faintly, and the study around Su Zhang was so still that the only sound was the soft, rhythmic glide of his brush.

The scent of ink lingered in the air, but then, almost without conscious intent, the tip of his brush traced an outline on the paper—a small, delicate figure.

It was a little girl in a pink blouse and skirt, her two short braids tilting unevenly over her shoulders as she chased after a butterfly.

His brush halted abruptly.

He stared at that touch of pink on the paper, and his chest felt as if it had been struck by a soft blow. Somewhere deep within his memory, a door that had been closed for a very long time began to ease open in the silence.

It was an afternoon drenched in sunlight, a courtyard where butterflies fluttered in swarms. He had been only seven, squatting on the stone steps to carve a bamboo sword. Suddenly, a small, round shadow burst out from the flower shrubs. A flash of pink silk cut across the sunlit courtyard before colliding heavily into his chest.

The impact knocked him backward, and the bamboo scrap clattered to the ground. The little girl stared at him in startled silence for a heartbeat—and then burst into a loud, shrill cry.

The crying was both sharp and strangely soft, a sound so piercing it seemed to make the entire courtyard tremble.

He was momentarily at a loss, and could only crouch down awkwardly and whisper to comfort her, "Don't cry. I don't blame you."

To his surprise, she only sobbed harder. She threw herself into his arms, her tiny hands clutching tightly at his robe, her tears and nose running freely onto his sleeves.

From not far away came the anxious, hurried call of a woman: "Yinyin! Where is Yinyin?"

It was his aunt's voice.

He lifted his head and saw her hurrying over with a worried expression. He carefully tried to push the small pink shadow in his arms toward her, but the little girl refused to let go, her grip surprisingly strong.

"No—Yinyin wants Big Brother!" she wailed between hiccups. Her face was flushed red, yet her words were unmistakably clear.

He froze for a moment, and finally could not resist asking in a low voice, "What is your name?"

"Yinyin," she replied through her sobs, her tears sparkling like jewels in the sunlight. "I'm called Yinyin."

That was the very first time he had ever heard that name.

The remnants of the memory unravelled slowly, and the study returned to its tranquil stillness.

Su Zhang set the brush aside and stared at the pink-robed silhouette on the paper for a long time without speaking. The candle flame trembled, as though a breeze had slipped through a narrow seam in the window, lifting the pages on his desk.

He reached out to press the paper down, but his fingertips trembled almost imperceptibly.

"Yinyin…"

He called the name in his heart. His voice was extremely low, as though speaking to the past, or perhaps to himself.

Outside, the night was deep. The wind brushed through the bamboo shadows in the courtyard, and for a moment, it seemed as if the distant sound of a child's laughter rose in the air, only to be quickly carried away by the wind, leaving behind nothing but the empty room and the faint, lingering fragrance of ink.

Chapter 14: Whispers Beneath the Garden Pavilion

Spring reached the capital at last, yet it did not arrive bright.

After the first thaw, rain returned in thin, persistent sheets. Mist clung to the city day after day, layering the streets in pale veils until even noon carried a muted, dimmed light. And within the imperial court, the wind was sharper still.

The Crown Prince, Li Duan, had grown into a man of age and reputation. He was praised for virtue and ability alike, yet the matter of a Crown Princess remained unresolved—suspended, undecided—casting a heavy shadow over every faction that watched the Eastern Palace.

The Second Prince, Li Xuan, had long since ceased to hide his ambition. Backed by the strength of his maternal clan, he drew ministers to his side with quiet patience, gathered influence over military appointments, and, behind a façade of propriety, allowed an undeniable power to congeal around him.

The Third Prince, Li Su, was younger and outwardly low-profile, his steps cautious and his words measured—but even behind him, faint movements stirred, as though another current was beginning to gather under the surface.

The predator stalks its prey, blind to the danger behind. So it was in every court session: silk sleeves, polished phrases, and beneath each exchange, the glint of steel.

Songxue Court lay behind Su Zhang's study, a small courtyard secluded and elegant. Spring rain had only just ceased. Pear blossoms, heavy with water, drooped from the branches like softened silk; the ground was carpeted with damp white petals, their fragrance cool and clean—so tranquil it should have eased the heart.

Yet at the stone table, Su Zhang sat in a moon-white robe with a jade belt at his waist. His features were refined and calm, his gaze steady as ink-washed painting… and still, a tautness lingered at the edge of his composure, betraying how little the court's storms had truly left him untouched.

He poured a cup of warm tea for the man opposite and slid it across the table. His voice was even, but not light.

"What brings you here with time to drink tea today?"

Gu Xiao lounged against the low table as if he had come to idle beneath blossoms rather than step into a nest of politics. His brows lifted, his tone languid, answering a question with another.

"Where is your little cousin?"

Su Zhang's brow tightened. "Why bring her up?"

"To chat with her, naturally."

"Enough." Su Zhang cut him off before the jest could be dressed as innocence. "Stop talking nonsense. There is no possibility between you and her."

The refusal landed cleanly, colder than the rain-washed air. And beneath it, there was something else—a flicker of irritation sharpened by a lingering unrest he himself did not welcome: the echo of dream images he had not yet fully shaken.

Gu Xiao's long fingers flicked a stray lock of hair from his brow, the gesture lazy, almost flamboyant. "That is not for you to decide. Who can say? I am, after all, handsome as carved jade and charming beyond reason—"

"That is enough." Su Zhang's tone cleaved through his boasting without hesitation. "Speak of something useful."

Gu Xiao's mouth curved, amusement lingering. But at the shift in Su Zhang's voice, he finally let a fraction of sobriety seep back in. Su Zhang did not waste the opening.

"During today's court session, the Second Prince's faction raised the matter of northern unrest again. They urged reinforcement—loudly— calling for the Tiger Guards to be moved. You knew of it?"

"And if I did? And if I didn't?" Gu Xiao replied as though commenting on the weather. "I hold no real office. Only a hollow courtesy title collecting dust."

"Be serious." Su Zhang's brows drew together.

Gu Xiao let out a short, humourless breath—half a laugh, half a scoff. "You are only telling me this now? What part of me has ever been serious?"

Even so, his expression shifted. The easy roguishness withdrew by degrees, and a sharper edge showed through. He glanced toward Su Zhang's face—so composed and yet so clearly weighted—and gave a quiet sigh, his tone taking on faint mockery.

"Fine. It is nothing more than an excuse. Northern tribes raid the border every year. That is hardly news. Why would it warrant a spectacle—why force the matter to the point of mobilizing the Tiger Guards?"

Su Zhang nodded faintly, his eyes dark as deep water. "Unfortunately, it seems even a few elder ministers have been won over. Their speeches today were earnest—too earnest—full of 'preventing danger before it arises' and 'safeguarding the realm.' One would think failing to raise troops amounts to dereliction."

He paused. A thin breath—cold amusement—passed through his voice.

"The Second Prince's true aim is likely not the Tiger Guards at all," Su Zhang said, his tone lowering. "It is the Imperial Guards."

Gu Xiao's fingers tapped the table once—steady, deliberate. The last of his earlier levity faded from his brow, leaving behind the clear sharpness of someone born under a military banner.

"The Imperial Guards exist solely to defend the capital," Su Zhang continued. "If Li Xuan gains influence over them, the door will be open—and military power will slip from rightful hands. The position of Crown Prince may then…"

His voice trailed off, but the unspoken ending hung in the air like a blade.

"I know what this means," Gu Xiao murmured at last. "But this game is not one Li Duan can win easily."

Su Zhang fixed his gaze on him, severe now, the calm sharpened into something like command.

"Have you ever considered," he said quietly, "that the Empress has hinted more than once for you to take a post within the Imperial Guards? The seat of commander—if it fell into your hands—would not only protect you. It would shield Li Duan. It would shield the Empress. It would secure your own future."

Gu Xiao shook his head. His eyes gleamed with the untempered, dangerous clarity of youth—a pride that refused to be softened.

"If I enter the Imperial Guards, I bind myself with chains. Today the Crown Prince is kind to me. By blood, he is practically my kin." His voice was not loud, yet each syllable struck like iron hammered on stone. "But when the winds change? In court, loyalty and affection are as cheap as dust."

A faint gust stirred through the courtyard. Pear petals shifted on the wet stone like pale, silent ash.

"The Tiger Guards," Gu Xiao said, the decision firm in his throat, "are where I intend to go."

At the mention of the Tiger Guards, something in the air seemed to tighten.

Once, that name had made the frontier tremble.

They were the army of the Gu family—the Iron-Blooded Tiger Legion. From the days of the old Gu General, the family had defended the northern borders for thirty years without retreat. Within the ranks, the Gu name was not merely respected; it was obeyed as the spine of the army itself.

Gu Xiao's elder brother, Gu Changyuan, had inherited their father's command. Despite his youth, he led tens of thousands into battle, cutting down enemy lines with a ferocity that turned victory into legend. Wherever his banner flew, enemy courage froze.

But glory is fickle. Power shifts faster than smoke.

In the brutal northern campaign that followed, the old Gu General and his eldest son both fell. The Tiger Guards were ripped apart, their losses so severe that even triumph tasted like blood. And at the very moment the front line bled, the court seized its chance: scholars submitted memorials, officials spoke of "proper order" and "central control," and the imperial decree arrived swiftly.

The Tiger Guards' command was stripped away.

Their remaining structure was taken over by the Secretariat for Military Affairs, then folded under the Imperial Guards.

Thirty years of Gu authority vanished overnight.

In the city, commoners lamented. Among veterans, tears fell as they cried, "The general may be gone, but the tiger's spirit remains!"

Yet even spirit fades.

With the old general and Gu Changyuan buried beneath border sands, the last trace of the Tiger Guards' dominance slowly dissolved into dust—until all that remained was a name, a memory, and a bitterness that never quite cooled.

Su Zhang's gaze tightened, as if that history had pressed against his ribs.

"You know well Li Duan is no longer who he once was," he said. "He has grown steadier. More wary of the dangers beneath the surface. You and I studied beside him for years. Now—when he needs people the most—he has no one he can rely on. If we refuse to move, if we stand by while shifting shadows twist through the court… how long can he endure?"

Gu Xiao held his teacup between his fingers. For a long moment, he did not speak.

Pear blossoms lay across the ground, wet and pale. Their fragrance was cool—refreshing, and yet stifled beneath the weight of spring rain, as though beauty itself had been muted into restraint.

At last, Gu Xiao said, low and reluctant, "I will think on it."

Su Zhang exhaled slowly. He brushed away a pear petal that had drifted onto the table, his tone easing by a fraction.

"Then think carefully. Just not for too long."

Gu Xiao let out a brief laugh—neither agreement nor refusal. He turned the teacup in his hand, his voice returning to that lazy ease mixed with youthful arrogance.

"The Imperial Guards are fine. But with no official post to my name, what merit do I have to justify walking straight into their ranks? Even the Empress cannot elevate me without cause."

Su Zhang studied him for several breaths, then spoke again, quiet and weighty.

"Right now, the winds rise and fall by the hour. Even the smallest post must be chosen with care."

He paused—as if adding the next words were incidental, yet the weight was unmistakable.

"And there is another matter. Have you noticed? The Second Prince's people are not only pressing the northern border issue. In the Ministry of Revenue, they have been clinging to the southern flood-control funds— demanding a complete reassessment of allocations, delaying repairs."

Gu Xiao's brows drew together. "Spring floods in the south will arrive soon. If the defences are not restored in time, disaster will strike."

"They know that," Su Zhang said, a cold smile curving at his lips. "Jiangnan has always been Li Duan's foundation. If calamity erupts during flood season, responsibility will fall on the Ministry of Revenue and the local governors. The Crown Prince will shoulder blame whether he deserves it or not."

Gu Xiao's grip tightened around the porcelain. His knuckles paled.

A muted unease rippled beneath his calm.

Su Zhang continued, his voice low, almost severe.

"We are already inside this struggle. Whatever concerns the Crown Prince is ours as well. We are his faction, his people. We cannot continue acting like boys who believe passion alone can set things right."

A breeze drifted through the courtyard. Pear petals fell in slow, steady waves, weightless and white, like snow that refused to melt.

Gu Xiao lowered his gaze. He did not agree, nor did he refute. He only let out a faint, almost careless laugh.

"I know my limits."

The words carried a trace of mirth, but the meaning was unmistakable: he would not be pressed further.

Su Zhang watched him quietly. In the depth of his eyes, concern flickered—too subtle to name, impossible to conceal.

The two men fell silent.

The courtyard was deep and still, spring muted into restraint. Only the steady fall of pear blossoms broke the hush, as if bearing silent witness to the first stirrings of a storm not yet born.

They exchanged a brief smile—understanding shared, worry unspoken.

And not far away, behind a cornered side gate, Qin Nianyin stood perfectly still, watching the scene unfold without a sound.

Her fingers clenched around the handkerchief in her hand. Her knuckles whitened.

In her previous life, she had watched Gu Xiao accept the northern appointment. She had watched him ride out with pride—and then fall into an ambush, betrayed by his own deputy. His body was never recovered.

The Gu clan—loyal for generations—was then falsely accused of colluding with the enemy.

The entire family was executed.

The capital ran with blood.

And the Gu clan had been the Empress's only remaining support. Gu Xiao's death had been half a death sentence for the Empress—and for Li Duan.

From that moment on, the Crown Prince lost half his strength.

The court descended into chaos.

Nothing could be reversed.

Qin Nianyin lowered her gaze.

A chill spread through her chest, sharp and bitter, mingled with a sorrow that tasted like old iron.

This time… she would change it.

For him. For her family. For the realm. No matter the cost.

The wind rose in the courtyard.

Pear blossoms scattered like drifting snow, as though the heavens themselves were murmuring a quiet lament.

Gu Chang Xiao
顧長嘯

Chapter 15: As Far Apart as the Poles

In the imperial study, daylight slanted through the gilded lattice windows and fell across two memorials laid open on the desk.

Red seals, black ink ——one on the left, one on the right ——quietly opposed one another.

One was from the Ministry of Revenue, titled Memorial on the Allocation of Military Funds for the Northern Frontier.

The other was from the Ministry of Works, titled Reexamination Report on Jiangnan's Flood-Control Repairs.

Emperor Xuanwen reclined against the carved dragon throne. His brows were drawn tight and his fingers slowly rubbed along the edge of the memorial as though he meant to wear away the gold-lacquered dragon motif.

The hall was so silent that even a falling pin would have sounded like thunder. Only the soft rustle of paper and the slow rhythm of his breathing filled the air.

"Beiyang..." he said under his breath, eyes shifting to the second document.

"...Jiangnan."

North and South ——two arteries of the realm.

One concerned the fortification of the empire's borders; the other, thousands of miles of riverbanks.

A eunuch presented tea with extreme care. Seeing the emperor's dark expression, he scarcely dared breathe. In the corner, a bronze clepsydra dripped steadily, each drop seeming to grind time itself thinner.

Emperor Xuanwen lifted the cup but did not drink.

On the surface of the tea, two memories surfaced ——layered, distinct.

The first was from ten years ago: the Jiangnan floods.

Waves like rampaging beasts had devoured fields and towns. Wooden houses overturned. Cries of terror echoed across the waters. White bones floated among the mud-laden currents.

He had still been the Crown Prince then and had gone personally to the disaster zone. He remembered the eyes of a child struggling in the murky water ——eyes emptied of hope.

That look had carved itself into him like a blade, one he could not forget even after a decade.

The second memory came from five years prior: the northern frontier.

Snow and wind sharp as knives; battle banners cracking in the air.

Armoured soldiers charged through blood-stained drifts, spears thrusting into enemy lines.

The wind carried both the screams of the dying and the heat of fresh blood.

He understood well that the border's lifeline was paid for with men's lives.

The tea cooled. He slowly set the cup aside and looked once more at the memorials on his desk.

If the northern frontier did not receive its funds, the soldiers would lack food, armour and winter gear. The border would be a hollow wall —— ready to collapse.

If Jiangnan's floodworks were not repaired, the spring floods would burst through the embankments and hundreds of thousands would drown in mud and ruin.

His fingers tapped the desk ——a quiet, metallic rhythm.

"Both are matters of life and death," he murmured, "yet both demand silver..."

The treasury was nearly empty. Salt-tax revenues had only just begun entering the accounts; the Inner Court's funds could not be moved lightly.

His father's admonition echoed in his ears ——

Do not neglect relief work, nor military defence.

Gilded light flickered across the pillars, harsh as knives.

This realm was one he had secured with his own hands, yet every inch of land seemed to demand blood from him.

More troubling still was the revenue shortfall this year.

In the spring, rain had soaked Jiangnan for months. Floodwaters lingered long after the plum season. Seedlings drowned.

In the north, early frost struck, ruining millet and wheat.

Hedong suffered drought; Guanzhong faced plague.

Several provinces failed to deliver salt taxes on time; transport officials reported dozens of boats overturned, with tens of thousands of taels lost.

Tax shipments were delayed again and again.

Outside, an announcement rang out.

A eunuch entered and bowed deeply.

"Your Majesty, Minister Wen Cong of the Ministry of Revenue and Vice Minister Shen Ting of the Ministry of Works request an audience."

Emperor Xuanwen's voice was flat.

"Summon them."

The two officials hastened inside and knelt side by side.

Wen Cong, nearly sixty and sweating heavily, raised his voice:

"Your Majesty! The memorial from the northern garrison is an urgent plea. The front line has grain for only half a month. Armor and winter coats have not been replenished for long. Should the delay continue, the army's morale will crumble!"

Shen Ting stepped forward at once, memorial clasped in both hands.

"Your Majesty, the re-examination of Jiangnan's embankments lists forty-five sections requiring reinforcement. The spring floods are imminent. One misstep and last year's disaster will return tenfold. Homes and granaries have yet to recover. Should the river burst its banks again, no fewer than a million people will be displaced."

Wen Cong interjected urgently.

"If the northern defences fail, enemy cavalry will sweep south. Jiangnan would not be safe either!"

Shen Ting refused to yield.

"Once floodwaters rise, counties fall into chaos. Long before military stipends arrive, troops will need to be diverted for riot control. That is disorder preceding defence."

Their voices sharpened.

Shen Ting pressed on, louder than before.

"Does Your Majesty still recall the breach at Runzhou during the late emperor's reign? A hundred li of devastation ——public outcry, prefectural offices burned, granaries plundered. Three battalions of the northern garrison were summoned to assist the disaster relief, leaving the border empty and nearly overrun!"

Wen Cong's face turned pale, yet he argued back.

"And the outcome? Jiangnan spent two full years rebuilding its embankments ——at a cost of three million taels. If we repeat that now, how is the treasury to endure? It is not that I disregard the people, but if the army loses morale, the nation will not survive!"

Shen Ting let out a cold, humourless laugh.

"Morale can be raised. The people's trust, once broken, cannot. Should unrest erupt in Jiangnan, there will be no taxes to collect and no men to conscript."

Wen Cong bowed again, anger flaring.

"Your Majesty, the treasury is already exhausted. Last year, the Ministry of Works spent three hundred thousand taels repairing five prefectures of embankments ——payments still unpaid. If we open the coffers again, what shall we rely on next?"

The commercial taxes reported by the Ministry of Revenue had also plummeted.

Markets were desolate. Money houses had collapsed one after another, triggering a chain of bankruptcies.

Salt merchants north of the river jointly petitioned for reduced taxes.

Last month, Wen Cong had begged permission to draw from the Inner Court's funds to fill the deficit, but the Director of the Inner Court refused, citing "heavy palace expenditures."

Emperor Xuanwen still felt a cold anger coil beneath his ribs.

Palace expenditures.

A polite phrase for extravagant renovations and endless robes for the consorts.

While the people froze and starved, how could the palace blaze with lamps and silk without becoming a jest to the world?

He rose slowly and looked toward the muted daylight beyond the half-open window.

His voice was steady, final and edged with frost.

"Send word to the Inner Court: From this day forward, all expenses for palace music, ceremonial attire and garden renovations are to be suspended. Expenditures from the Wardrobe Bureau and Inner Treasury shall be reduced by half."

The eunuchs pressed low to the floor, breath held, cold sweat sliding down their temples.

"Further," Emperor Xuanwen continued,

"the monthly stipends of the Empress and Noble Consort shall be reduced by thirty percent. Should there be objections, the Secretariat is to record them in full. I want all under Heaven to know that the court will share hardship with the people ——beginning at the top."

When he finished speaking, he lowered his gaze to the two memorials on the desk.

A faint, weary desolation passed through his eyes.

"If Heaven offers no aid," he murmured, "then I must save us myself."

Shouts rose again ——arguments blurring into noise.

The pressure in the hall thickened.

"Enough."

His single command cracked through the air.

Both officials dropped to the floor without daring to speak another word.

Another eunuch hurried inside.

"Your Majesty, an urgent dispatch from Lin Wang, Governor of the Northern Garrison!"

Emperor Xuanwen's eyes hardened.

"Bring it forward."

The military courier scroll was presented and unrolled. The imperial scribe read aloud:

"Cold winds have struck early. Frost has not yet lifted. There are three hundred and seventy-six cases of frostbite among the troops. Grain stores will last fifteen days; salted meat only seven. We request immediate allocation of armour and provisions and ask that local officials be permitted to advance half of the salt-tax revenue to alleviate our desperate need."

The hall fell silent ——heavy, metallic and absolute.

Only the thin trembling of the paper seemed to move.

Shen Ting lowered his voice.

"Your Majesty, the Northern Garrison… it has barely recovered from last year's campaign. To request silver again so soon ——there may be exaggeration within the ranks."

Wen Cong immediately countered, his tone sharp with offense.

"Mind your words, Lord Shen. General Lin is famed for integrity. Who in the court is unaware of the hardships suffered in the Northern Garrison?"

Emperor Xuanwen's cold gaze swept across the two men.

Silence crashed over the hall like a falling stone.

He rose from the throne and walked toward the grand map of the empire.

The northern border sprawled in deep ink-black mountains; Jiangnan stretched in blue veins of river and lake.

His fingertips hovered between the two regions, pausing for a long, steady breath before moving again ——as though weighing countless lives against the fate of a nation.

"In the late emperor's time," he said quietly, "the South River was sacrificed to defend the northern frontier. The borders were held, but corpses lined the riverbanks."

He exhaled, the sound almost like a sigh.

"I will not repeat that choice."

A faint laugh escaped him ——soft, almost pleasant, yet entirely devoid of warmth.

"What a burden you place upon me."

He returned to his seat.

The jade brush touched each memorial in turn, lifting, lowering, then lifting again ——each movement deliberate, each hesitation heavy with consequence.

At last, he closed his eyes and drew a slow breath.

"Summon the Crown Prince and the Second Prince to the hall."

The command was spoken neither loudly nor quickly, yet a thin current of frost ran beneath every word.

A sharp "Yes, Your Majesty!" echoed from outside.

The eunuchs hurried away to relay the order, followed by another decree: the officials of the Ministry of Revenue and the Ministry of Works were to withdraw only half a step, not leave the vicinity and return the moment they were called.

The sky darkened without warning.

A mass of shadowed clouds pressed in from the northwest, spring thunder murmuring within their depths.

Before the thunder itself arrived, wind swept into the hall, lifting the corners of the memorials and rustling them with a brittle, unsettling sound ——as though even Heaven held its breath for the decision to come.

The air grew heavier, its weight sinking into stone and bone alike.

These two petitions were no simple dispute between north and south, nor between soldiers and households.

They were the collision of livelihood and destiny ——of the people's survival and the empire's future.

Chapter 16: The Floriate Assembly

Spring had barely unfurled its first true warmth when the capital welcomed its most anticipated annual celebration ——the Festival of the Flower Goddess.

On the opening day, blossoms reached their peak and crowds surged like a rising tide.

That morning, the sky was pale and clear. A gentle breeze drifted through the budding willows and across the branches heavy with spring blooms. Fragrance spilled through every street and alley.

At the lakeside of Hundred-Flowers Islet, brilliantly coloured pavilions stood in rows, spring banners fluttered overhead and both common townsfolk and noble young ladies arrived in their finest attire, their laughter shimmering beneath the morning sun.

According to tradition, eight young girls between the ages of ten and twelve were selected each year ——half from within the palace precincts, half from the capital's noble households.

Dressed in identical celestial robes, crowned with flower circlets and carrying baskets of fresh petals, the eight girls would step from the Flower Goddess Altar and walk the Imperial Avenue, scattering blossoms all the way to Hundred-Flowers Islet.

It was meant to symbolize the descent of spring blessings upon all under heaven, a ritual known as "Hundred Flowers Descending Blessings, Ten Thousand People Receiving Spring."

These eight children were selected from noble clans, subjected to rigorous assessment of their lineage, learning, talent, and appearance.

For the wealthy houses of the capital, having a daughter chosen was a supreme mark of prestige; it served as a lucky omen, a source of family honor, and a way to secure a sterling reputation before the girl reached marriageable age, providing significant leverage for future alliances.

Drums echoed along the street; petals drifted like falling clouds and children darted through the flower rain with shrieks of delight.

Young scholars craned their necks above the crowd, searching for the elegant figures of the city's maidens.

Amid the noise and the cascade of blossoms, a small group drew particular attention ——not for extravagance, but for the quiet grace and distinguished bearing each carried.

To encourage young men and women to discreetly observe one another, the festival grounds were arranged along the riverbank: men on one side, women on the other, separated by no more than several paces of water.

A single small bridge stretched across to connect the two banks; it preserved the propriety expected between the sexes, appearing as if separated by a thousand mountains and rivers, while allowing them to speak across the water as if they were barely an arm's length apart.

Spring warmth lingered lightly in the air. The river rippled in silver threads and willows trailed their new-grown green.

Su Wan had invited Shen Lingyan to accompany her to the festival. Su Zhang, at Madam Qin's instruction, escorted a few younger sisters.

Qin Nianyin wore a pale-apricot gown patterned with faint woven blossoms. A moon-white sash embroidered with gold circled her waist and her hair was adorned with only a single jade flower-pin ——neither extravagant nor overly simple, maintaining perfect decorum.

Standing beside Su Wan and Shen Lingyan, whose noble birth was reflected in their richly adorned attire, Qin Nianyin appeared like a quiet spring orchid beneath a soft drizzle: understated, serene and naturally refined.

She stood beneath a peach tree at the water's edge, speaking quietly with a few young ladies.

A breeze swept through; petals loosened and drifted down like rosy clouds, brushing her shoulders before scattering across the ground—and also falling into Su Zhang's field of vision.

Polite greetings passed among the group. Throughout the exchanges, Su Wan maintained a poised smile, yet her words were sparse and her expression faintly cool.

Anyone attentive enough could sense the polite distance and alienation that lay beneath her smile.

Su Zhang, dressed in plain robes, stood quietly at the head of the old stone bridge on the men's side. He spoke not a single word.

But when he lifted his gaze across the water, it met hers.

His eyes did not cross forests nor rivers, yet it felt as though countless unsaid thoughts had already been carried across to her.

He saw her smile faintly at something another lady said, saw her lower her head to pluck a fallen blossom from her sleeve ——an action that looked accidental, yet perhaps not entirely so.

His expression shifted by the smallest measure; his fingers tightened slightly around the edge of his sleeve, yet he did not step forward.

Preparations for the festival had begun days earlier, and the marketplace had long been adorned with lanterns and streamers.

Every major shop ——embroidery houses, incense stores, jade ateliers ——launched new hairpins, sachets and painted fans to capitalize on the season.

The crowd flowed like weaving silk. The lakeside teahouses and wine pavilions had long been booked by scholars and gentry, their balconies hung with tasselled lanterns that swayed as though drifting on waterlight.

Music floated above the river. Children chased tiny festival boats shaped like lotus petals, their laughter intermingling with the melodies of silk and bamboo.

Girls compared flower hairpins while young men exchanged improvised verses across the water.

Spring itself seemed to gather, ready to spill from the edges of the scene like an overflowing scroll.

At the bridgehead, Su Zhang's gaze skimmed across the drifting petals and the indistinct ripple of movement on the opposite bank.

A single peach blossom fell into the river, its reflection trembling as it faded downstream ——his own expression seemed touched by the same faint hue.

Across the way, Qin Nianyin adjusted the pin in her hair.

A petal brushed her fingertip and sent a small, involuntary tremor through her hand.

She felt a distant gaze settle upon her ——steady, unwavering, almost too direct to meet, burning her until there was nowhere to hide.

Sensing the flicker of distraction, Shen Lingyan lifted her fan to hide a smile. "Sister, on such a day, if you feel the slightest spark of inspiration, why not offer a verse?"

Qin Nianyin paused. A soft smile curved her lips.

"Sister jokes. My thoughts are elsewhere today; my heart is not on such things."

* * * * *

The procession of the flower maidens had just passed.

Petals swirled through the air, ribbons fluttered and the soft strains of flutes and zithers drifted above the lively crowd as people composed poetry and drank for pleasure.

Young women moved like blossoms themselves, their fragrance and trailing sleeves forming ripples of colour.

The city's young gentlemen walked with easy confidence, their manner graceful beneath the canopy of spring.

Inside one of the riverside pavilions, several noble ladies reclined behind gauzy curtains.

Their layered gowns flowed like clouds and their laughter rose and fell in light, shimmering waves.

Outside, the sunlight flashed through the pearl-beaded curtains, scattering flecks of gold across embroidered sleeves and brocade shoes.

Steam curled from fine porcelain teacups and as it rose, the conversation drifted ——inevitably ——toward the newest young ladies who had recently arrived in the capital.

A girl in a gown of deep stone-blue lowered her gaze with a languid smile. She idly twirled a plum-blossom hairpin between her fingers as she spoke, her tone carrying three parts pride and seven parts dismissal.

"I heard," she drawled, "that for this year's poetry gathering, even that Qin girl ——whatever distant place she crawled out from ——had the audacity to attend and join the fun. Someone even delivered an invitation on her behalf."

A pretty girl in a pale-yellow vest giggled behind her sleeve.

"Her? I heard she's merely a dependent living off old family ties, a person of leisure. And now such a person dares to sit among us and discuss poetry?"

Another young lady with long, narrow eyes added with a soft, cutting tone,

"The Qin family had some reputation in the past, perhaps. But their days of grace are long gone. And her mother was born of humble stock. The only reason she can stand in the capital at all is due to that sliver of connection to the Su family's collateral branch."

Their voices were neither loud nor soft, but each word landed with a cold gleam.

Some girls hid their amusement behind fans; others exchanged glances, their expressions rippling like sunlight on water ——curiosity mixed with thinly veiled ridicule and mockery.

A slightly older young woman spoke in a gentler tone, yet her gentleness was threaded with needles.

"Enough. A poetry gathering values talent, not pedigree. If Miss Qin truly possesses any ability, no one will dare look down on her."

The words seemed mild, but the faint curve of her eyes carried unmistakable mockery ——an anticipatory delight, as though she were waiting to witness a staged embarrassment.

Someone murmured in agreement, "True enough… though let us hope she doesn't lose her elegance and make people laugh at this fine gathering."

A clear cascade of laughter followed.

The pearl ornaments dangling from the pavilion roof trembled gently, tapping against one another like raindrops striking glazed tiles in early spring ——pleasant in sound, yet edged with chill.

Across the river, young scholars were stepping forward one after another to compose verses.

The theme for the gathering was "Spring Arrives as Fate Allows." Wine had already circulated several rounds and poetic enthusiasm surged.

Half-dazed with drink, someone called out loudly, "Lord Su ——the illustrious jinshi ranked third, famed throughout the capital! If today's gathering ends without a poem from Lord Su himself, would that not disappoint the Flower Goddess on her sacred day?"

Others joined in with laughter and eager shouts.

"Lord Su's verses flow as naturally as breath. Even an impromptu poem from him surpasses the prepared works of most present. Let us borrow some of the explore-flower-ranking scholar's brilliance today!"

In an instant, every gaze turned toward Su Zhang.

He lifted his eyes, calm and unhurried, the corner of his mouth curving with quiet composure.

Rising, he offered a courteous bow. "If everyone insists, then I shall offer a humble verse."

He walked to the flower platform. Behind him, the shadows of blossoms stretched across the ground and the breeze brushed against his sleeves, causing the jade pendant at his waist to strike with a soft, clear sound.

His voice, cool and steady, carried across the water like a stream flowing over smooth stone as he recited a seven-character quatrain of his own making:

In winter's chill air, the jade hare lights the rivers;

In spring's soft breath, bright kites sweep across the heaven.

If the mortal world were to seek where beauty lingers ——

It lingers where passing years keep faith with the green mountains.

冬寒玉兔照三川，

春暖彩鳶飛九天。

人間若問何處好，

青山有約共流年。

The moment the final line left Su Zhang's lips, the gathering went utterly still. Not a whisper, not even the soft rustle of silk.

Then, like a tide retreating and rushing back again, quiet murmurs of astonishment spread through the pavilion and along both banks.

Su Zhang stood at the centre of the crowd, his composure unruffled, his expression calm as unshaken water.

He seemed almost unaware of the eyes fixed upon him ——yet it was impossible for those eyes to look elsewhere.

The wind brushed past him; the blossoms behind him swayed and even that faint movement seemed to echo the measured cadence of his verse.

Across the river, Qin Nianyin held a porcelain cup between her fingers. Her grip wavered.

The fragrance of warm tea drifted upward, yet her pulse beat faintly against the cup's rim.

She had read this poem countless times in her previous life; she had copied it, recited it, collected it in her heart until every character felt like an old friend.

But none of those years of remembrance could match the impact of hearing it spoken here, spoken now, spoken by him, in a voice as steady as mountain springs spilling into a deep lake, as quiet as a night breeze slipping through hanging curtains, carrying a cool clarity and deep intent that pressed gently, almost painfully, against her chest.

Around them, conversation resumed, light and teasing.

A young gentleman approached Su Zhang with an easy smile and murmured just loudly enough for others to hear, "Lord Su, such a poem surely carries a hidden sentiment. Might it be meant for someone in particular?"

The remark drew soft laughter.

Qin Nianyin lifted her gaze before she could stop herself. Her eyes collided with Su Zhang's.

His were dark as inkstone pools, still yet impossibly deep, carrying something unspoken beneath their surface as if a hundred thoughts flickered there, containing ten thousand words.

Then, with a quiet, practiced ease, he looked away, leaving behind only the faintest tremor in her breath.

Chapter 17: The Princess's Admiration

By his side, Second Princess Li Jing kept her gaze fixed on Su Zhang, unable to hide the admiration shimmering in her eyes. She had dressed with deliberate care today ——scarlet cross-collar robes, narrow sleeves, every fold immaculate.

Her brows were bright, her manner poised and cultivated. Yet none of it earned even a single lingering glance from Su Zhang.

Once the poetry recitation concluded, the host had wine brought forth and the guests drank in leisurely rounds. Seizing the moment, Li Jing filled a cup herself and carried it to Su Zhang with a bright smile.

"Since the tanhua possesses such boundless inspiration," she said, her tone half teasing and half challenging, "why not compose another verse for us? I shall reward you with three cups."

The words held a delicate lilt, coquettish and faintly provocative.

Conversation around the pavilion fell still. Everyone knew that once a princess spoke thus, refusal was no longer an easy option; she had opened her golden mouth, and a decline would be seen as a slight.

Qin Nianyin lowered her gaze, a quiet worry stirring in her chest on Su Zhang's behalf.

Su Zhang, however, remained composed. He accepted the cup with a slight bow. "Your Highness is too generous. This humble servant's talent is meagre. To be so favoured already leaves me uneasy."

The line was courteous without being ingratiating, respectful yet offering no room for presumption.

Hearing him decline again, Li Jing's smile finally stiffened; her voice cooled by a shade. "Is the tanhua truly as cold-hearted and cold-faced as the rumours claim? If I did not understand propriety, I would not personally pour the wine, nor lower myself by leaving my seat."

Su Zhang's expression did not shift. His voice was even, almost tranquil. "Your Highness's favour humbles me. Yet I was raised in a life of sparse means and long study. I know little of such refined delights and I would never dare misunderstand the gracious intentions of a noble lady."

What sounded like modesty was, line by line, an unerring return of her own phrase ——"gracious intentions" ——pressed neatly back into her hands. Clear-cut. Controlled. Leaving her with no further ground to take.

Li Jing gave a short, brittle laugh. Her fingertip tapped lightly against the jade cup. "Now that you are the tanhua, should you receive my regard, many would beg for such fortune."

"I have studied the classics," Su Zhang replied, bowing again with calm restraint. "One must know one's place and know when to advance or withdraw."

"And if I truly force the matter," she asked softly, "what then?"

The pavilion fell utterly silent.

A subtle tension rippled through the air.

Several ladies lifted their eyes in veiled curiosity; a few young officials shifted uneasily. Some were waiting for a spectacle. Others were holding their breath for Su Zhang.

He paused only briefly, not in hesitation but in thought. "If Your Highness insists," he said steadily, "I would not dare disobey. Yet if my inadequacy should tarnish Your Highness's name, that would be a grave offense. The mere thought chills me; I would not dare act recklessly."

On the surface, it was obedience.

In truth, he had used the threat of "tarnishing her name" to push back with impeccable formality, sealing off every path she might try to take.

Around them, no one spoke. Several lowered their heads, feigning deafness. Even the incense on the table seemed to falter, its smoke wavering as if the air itself had paused.

Li Jing swept her sleeve sharply as she rose, her skirt brushing across the flower-strewn floor, trailing a faint trace of fragrance. Her steps were quick, edged with wounded pride, yet she fought to maintain the appearance of grace.

At the threshold of the pavilion, she forced one last composed remark: "Since the tanhua possesses such lofty integrity, I shall not press you further."

The pavilion fell into a profound, breath-held quiet.

The guests kept their eyes lowered, each absorbed in private thoughts. What had happened moments earlier resembled a stone dropped into a still pond ——its surface remained placid, yet beneath that calm an undertow had begun to swirl.

Everyone understood that Su Zhang had just given the Second Princess a firm but impeccably courteous rebuff. The quiet boldness in his refusal, the steadiness with which he held his ground, was far more startling than his title as the tanhua.

Several young noble ladies who had previously entertained thoughts of him silently withdrew those hopes. If even a princess was turned away without a foothold, how could any of them expect to enter his regard?

Only Wen Wan, seated beneath the patch of willow shade, felt her fingers grow pale around her sleeve. She pressed her flicker of unwillingness and caution deep into her chest, burying it where no one could see.

Across the pavilion, a few guests exchanged subtle glances. Someone hid a smile behind a cup of tea. Another lady covered her lips with her sleeve, whispering lightly to the friend beside her. Their laughter remained muted, but their meaning was clear.

From her seat near the edge, Wen Wan—the daughter of the Minister of Revenue—lifted her gaze with quiet deliberation. Something new flickered beneath her composure: a blend of restraint and hesitation.

Su Zhang had dared reject a daughter of the imperial blood before so many eyes. That level of detachment and resolve was not something to be taken lightly.

At the corner of the pavilion, Qin Nianyin sat silent, her fingers slowly tightening within her sleeves. Her breath wavered, breaking its steady rhythm.

She knew well that Li Jing's bold gesture toward Su Zhang had been a declaration of interest and she also understood the princess's temperament: proud, impulsive, accustomed to forcing what she could not obtain.

In her past life, she had once witnessed this very scene.

Back then, he had been as cold as winter frost and she had stood on the margins ——unable to speak, unable to intervene.

Now, as destiny looped back on itself, she sat neither too close nor too far from him. Yet her heart felt like a leaf in wind, floating without anchor.

Abruptly, Su Zhang inclined his head. He set down his cup and glanced in her direction in a way that seemed almost unintentional.

That single look ——light as a stray feather ——lifted her from her turmoil as though drawing her out of water.

Then, in a low murmur soft enough to pass for a private thought yet clear enough for those nearby to hear, he recited:

"White dew gathers upon the jade steps through the long night. The long night invades the silken stockings.

The jewelled curtains fall and through their crystal glow she gazes at the autumn moon."

He raised his cup and drank. The wine slid down his throat with no visible shift in expression, his face as composed as before.

The original poem by Li Bai portrayed a secluded beauty, spending a solitary night watching the moon beyond crystal curtains. Now, offered here, its meaning had shifted ——turning into a veiled rebuke aimed at one who mistook her own illusions for affection.

Someone who recognized the reference gave a faint, stifled sound and dropped their gaze to hide a smile.

Qin Nianyin's pulse tightened. She knew this poem from her previous life. Delivered now—so precise, so cutting—it was a blade wrapped in silk.

She lifted her eyes. Su Zhang looked utterly calm, as if he had plucked the verse without thought, without weight.

From a distance, the verse reached Li Jing's ears mid-stride. Her face turned red and white in succession, but there was nothing she could say. She bit down on her anger and walked away quickly.

And yet the look in her eyes made one thing unmistakable: she was now all the more determined to obtain him.

At the main seat, the host of the gathering forced a laugh and raised his cup high.

"Master Su's poetic talent is truly renowned! If any of our guests still feel inspired, why not take up a new theme—'Spring slips away too easily, youth cannot be reclaimed'—and each compose a verse?"

Those with sense quickly voiced their agreement, easing the tension and brightening the atmosphere once more.

Outside the pavilion, the spring light remained soft and clear. A breeze skimmed across the lake, scattering a field of ripples like shattered glass.

Qin Nianyin gazed across the lake and let a faint smile rise at the corner of her lips. She understood now—this life was no echo of the previous one.

Those hidden malice and sidelong glances no longer had the power to touch her. She would not bow beneath them again.

Under the swaying petals, a jade table held freshly brewed yellow wine and delicate honeyed fruits. Young nobles gathered around it, discussing verse and critiquing each other's writings, their animated conversation filling the pavilion with an easy warmth.

Qin Nianyin remained seated in a quiet corner. Her pale gown softened her features, lending her an almost painted grace.

A young scholar—nervous yet earnest—approached and presented a folded sheet of poetry with both hands.

She took the page and read it carefully. Her brows lifted by a fraction and her voice held genuine praise as she returned the page.

"The rhyme settles naturally and the shift between lines carries strength. It is a fine poem. Thank you for allowing me to read it."

Her tone was gentle, without the slightest hint of empty courtesy.

Colour rushed instantly to the scholar's ears. His eyes brightened with a mixture of joy and disbelief.

"G-Girl Qin… if you… if you like it… I ——my name is Xie Zongyang… I…"

The words tangled in his throat, each syllable tumbling out in fragments. His cheeks had flushed nearly scarlet.

From a short distance away, Su Zhang leaned against one of the stone steps. His long, cool gaze narrowed by an imperceptible degree and his fingers tightened inside his sleeve.

He watched Qin Nianyin smile at the trembling scholar—watched the way her nod carried a soft, almost luminous gentleness—and a thin, piercing ache ran beneath his ribs.

That smile, offered to someone else, rippled like spring water.

And he found it deeply, sharply displeasing.

His mind flickered to the dream from the previous night ——

A blurred figure had draped a robe over his shoulders, offered him medicine, murmured with a tender reproach that softened into warmth.

The fragments felt so real they threatened to pull him under, as though they belonged not to a dream but to a memory.

That inexplicable sense of recognition, that unshakable familiarity —— he nearly knew, with unsettling certainty, that the woman in his dream had been Qin Nianyin.

What he could not understand was this: Why had he awakened sitting still for several breaths, with a hollow sensation pressing at his chest? Why had the thought of losing something unnamed left him so profoundly restless?

He loathed that loss of control.

Su Zhang lowered his gaze, burying the strange remnants of that dream deep in his heart.

Yet when he looked toward Qin Nianyin again, his eyes darkened further, their depth impossible to discern.

"…Do you like it?"

The ache beneath his sternum spread, silent and insistent, like a hidden current rising from the depths of a well.

Even he could not say whether it was because her smile had nothing to do with him, or because her slight hesitation unsettled him in ways he could not name.

Chapter 18: The Northern Frontier and the Southern Floods

Within the imperial study, the air felt dense with restraint. Everyone standing along the sides had unconsciously quieted their breathing.

Beyond the tall doors, two figures stepped inside at nearly the same moment. Their robes brushed across the golden floor tiles, producing a faint whisper of fabric.

Imperial guards lined both sides of the hall, their bronze halberds reflecting the firelight ——cold gleams sharp enough to cut. Dusk gathered at the windows. The last trace of gold spilled through the lattice, casting a long bar of light that stretched all the way to the dragon desk.

The doors opened fully, and the two men entered together, kneeling in unison.

"Your sons greet Father. May Emperor Xuanwen enjoy peace and health."

Emperor Xuanwen sat with his back to the fading light, silver beginning to thread through his temples. His gaze was hard as iron. Gold-threaded dragons on his robe shifted subtly with each measured breath.

He lifted a hand and indicated the two memorials on the desk. His voice was low, firm and allowed no dispute.

"Dispense with formalities. Speak plainly. These two memorials —— one from the northern frontier, one from the southern provinces —— each holds weight. State your positions."

The Crown Prince, Li Duan, stepped forward first.

"Father, spring floods approach. If the river defences in Jiangnan are not reinforced immediately, a breach would bring devastation across a hundred li ——lost lives, ruined fields and heavy tax deficits. Your son requests that fund be temporarily drawn from the inner treasury to meet the urgent need. Once the river defences are secured, the army's supplies can be replenished within half a month, ensuring the northern front does not suffer delay."

He bowed again, voice steady yet resonant, like water striking stone ——quiet, but carrying force. His gaze was steady and determined as he stood with his head lowered.

The Third Prince Li Xuan responded next, his tone courteous and mild.

"In your son's view, the border is far more pressing. Each day the military lacks supplies, the frontier walls weaken. Flood prevention must also follow its natural timing; if we rush the work, we risk clogging the waterways and causing an even greater collapse. It would be wiser to supply the north in full and allow Jiangnan to conduct smaller repairs for now. Major reconstruction can wait until summer or autumn, once the water level falls."

As he spoke, he raised his head just slightly. His voice remained smooth, but a faint glimmer of sharpness hid in his eyes ——a gleam that flickered like a blade wrapped in silk. That faint smile of his was like a sharp edge hidden in a roll of silk.

Silence descended. The slow drip of the water clock became painfully distinct and nearly a full incense stick passed before someone dared to speak.

Minister Wen Cong of the Ministry of Revenue stepped out from the line. His sleeves brushed the floor as he bowed. His voice was cautious, almost to the point of trembling.

"Your Majesty… when I reviewed last year's river-defence accounts, several allocations from the autumn disbursement were not properly verified. The Ministry suspects some funds have yet to be accounted for, their direction unknown… I fear that if we disburse again now, we may merely throw more silver into a void of waste."

Emperor Xuanwen's gaze darkened. "Unaccounted for?"

The two words struck the hall like a hammer. Every official held their breath.

A vice minister dropped to his knees, sweat rolling down his forehead. "Your Majesty, your servant dares not draw conclusions. I beg for an imperial edict to allow the Censorate and the Ministry of Works to re-investigate before more funds are released."

Li Duan lifted his eyes at that, his voice turning colder. "At a moment when lives in Jiangnan hang by a thread, will we delay repairs over a single suspicion? And when disaster strikes again, who shall bear the responsibility?"

His tone remained calm, yet the fingers hidden in his sleeves curled inward, tightening slightly.

Li Xuan chuckled softly. "Elder Brother's words are severe. Investigating is a matter of prudence, not obstruction. If corruption truly exists, we must first cleanse the officials and rectify the administration, otherwise any subsequent effort will be wasted."

The smile on his lips appeared gentle, like a breeze passing through bamboo, but it carried a hidden chill.

Li Duan's gaze shifted ever so slightly before he spoke again, his tone steady yet carrying unmistakable resolve.

"Jiangnan is not merely another region, Father. It is the empire's granary and the artery of all river transport. When floods erupt in Jiangnan, the entire realm trembles. It is not just one corner of the land; it affects the very pulse of the nation. If repairs are delayed because of a single suspicion, then by the time the northern front is reinforced, the grain boats would already have been halted, the transport routes severed. And when the border soldiers stand with empty stores… with what, then, shall they guard the frontier?"

His voice lowered, gaining weight.

Li Xuan let out a soft laugh, his tone gentle, almost courteous.

"Elder Brother seems to forget that the northern frontier is no less vital. Should the border fall, Jiangnan will naturally have no more fear of floods, because ——"

He paused, letting the silence stretch. Something sharp flickered at the bottom of his eyes, amusement mixed with provocation and a sneer.

" ——because the enemy would already be marching straight into the heartland."

Li Duan's expression did not change, but his breath released in a thin, controlled stream.

"So Second Brother means," he said quietly, "that the lives of Jiangnan's people weigh less than the lives of the frontier troops?"

In that instant when he lifted his eyes, the force of his stare was like a burning torch.

Li Xuan remained bowed. "Your son merely believes that with limited imperial funds, the state must first secure its borders and only then repair riverbanks. Moreover, Jiangnan's water disasters are not new. Silver was allocated ten years ago and again three years ago. Why, then, must it be repaired yet again?"

The air froze. No one dared breathe.

The candles flickered under an invisible draft, casting jagged shadows across the dragon desk.

Emperor Xuanwen tapped his fingers against the desk ——three slow, heavy taps. Each one landed like distant thunder.

"So you suggest ——that someone has swallowed the silver?"

The Emperor's voice was low, but each syllable struck like an axe cleaving through stone.

Li Xuan lowered his gaze further, yet his stance held firm. "Your son dares not accuse without proof. But if corruption indeed exists within the Ministry or the local offices, then allocating funds before the truth is uncovered would only create another man-made disaster."

Li Duan's brows tightened sharply. His eyes rose like unsheathed steel. "And what evidence does Second Brother possess for this suspicion?"

Li Xuan's tone remained calm, almost serene. "If we investigate, we shall know."

His words fell into the hall like a pebble dropped into a frozen lake —— no ripple, only silence. A hush swept through the chamber. Wind slipped through the door crack, stirring the bamboo screens and producing a faint, brittle sound.

Emperor Xuanwen's gaze slowly moved between his two sons. Memories surfaced —— the black waves of Jiangnan's flood swallowing homes and children's cries; the blood-soaked battlefield of the northern frontier where soldiers froze where they fell. The empire's north and south ——one civil, one martial ——held together by lives and sacrifice.

After a long, weighted silence, he exhaled a long sigh.

"Very well. Jiangnan's riverworks will remain with the Ministry of Revenue for re-verification. The northern frontier shall receive immediate disbursement. But regarding the Jiangnan matter, Li Duan, Li Xuan ——you will investigate it together."

His voice was not loud, yet it fell like a verdict.

Both Li Duan and Li Xuan answered in unison. As they lowered their heads, the light flickered, catching the chill in each pair of eyes.

Li Duan's heart surged beneath his composed surface. He understood at once that this so-called "joint investigation" was, in truth, a test of imperial sons ——another silent measure of the Emperor's judgment.

Li Xuan, however, allowed himself the faintest inward curl of amusement. *Heaven aligns with me. How convenient; it spares me the effort of persuasion.*

Emperor Xuanwen continued.

"The northern military provisions ——are to be disbursed immediately. As for Jiangnan's riverworks ——draw three parts from the Inner Treasury at once to answer the present urgency. The remainder shall be withheld until further review. The Censorate, together with the Ministry of Works and the Ministry of Revenue, will descend upon Jiangnan within three days to verify the ledgers. A full report is due within twenty days. The Crown Prince shall oversee the matter. The Second Prince shall supervise its progress. Should either of you delay or deceive, I will not pardon it."

The two princes bowed deeply and struck their foreheads to the ground.

Their voices ——"Your son obeys" ——echoed against the gold-laid bricks, reverberating until even the bronze incense tripod gave a faint tremor.

Emperor Xuanwen stood silent for a long moment before he finally spoke again.

"As for the imperial envoy to be sent to Jiangnan… the man must be sharp-eyed and steady-tongued, one whose words and intentions align. I shall consider it further."

When he finished speaking, he rose. The dying light of dusk split his silhouette into two uneven halves. He appeared to be pondering, yet also seemed like a solitary figure speaking softly to his own shadow.

From the bronze incense burner, the smoke rose in a thin, unwavering column. The curling haze gathered above the dragon desk, forming a pale ring. It resembled an invisible chain ——binding the riverbanks of Jiangnan to the frozen fields of the northern frontier and binding as well the Emperor's own weary deliberations.

Outside the Hall of Governance, the sky deepened to indigo. Thunder murmured far beyond the eaves and the wind gathered strength, stirring the clouds as though echoing the silent confrontation within.

From this moment on, a struggle intertwining the fate of north and south ——the empire's lifeblood, its clans and its power ——quietly stepped onto the stage.

* * * * *

The palace gates had barely closed when a low wind swept across the stone steps, carrying with it a muted sense of foreboding.

Li Duan and Li Xuan walked side by side as they left the Imperial Study. Attendants made room for them from a distance, not daring to approach. Their shadows trailed across the steps ——one long, one slightly shorter ——stretching toward the deepening dusk.

Li Duan was the first to speak, his tone quiet and level. "Second Brother, your words in the Imperial Study were admirably sharp. Father seemed rather pleased."

Li Xuan lowered his hands and offered a respectful bow. His expression was humble, even deferential. "I dare not claim credit. The northern frontier is in urgent straits. Your younger brother could not withhold what must be said."

Li Duan let out a soft laugh, stripped of warmth. "'What must be said'? You sound as though your remarks had been prepared long beforehand. Even the discrepancy in the Ministry of Revenue's ledgers ——you pointed it out as though by chance."

Li Xuan's voice remained serene. "Your brother merely glanced through some older ledgers last night. I noticed a few inconsistencies and mentioned them. If it troubled you, I shall draw up a detailed account in the coming days."

Li Duan slowed his steps and turned to look at him. His words dropped to a low rumble.

"The debate over northern supplies concerns the entire realm. Yet with one remark about 'waste,' you made Jiangnan's repairs falter yet again. Do you know how many people still live under the shadow of that broken embankment?"

"You are right, Elder Brother." Li Xuan's tone grew calmer, almost gentle, "but your younger brother also knows that the frontier soldiers go into battle wearing tattered furs. If the delay stretches another ten days, they may not live long enough to return. Civilians can rebuild. If the army breaks, the border itself is lost."

A cold glint passed through Li Duan's gaze. "So, in Father's presence, you wished to imply that I lack foresight?"

"I would not dare." Li Xuan smiled faintly, the corners of his lips soft yet unreadable. "I only thought ——if there is even a hint of corruption in the accounts and Father does not investigate, what would the world think of the two sons of the Emperor?"

Li Duan fell silent for a moment before stepping down the next stair. His voice, when it came, was icy.

"Very well. Investigate, then. If there is corruption, I will see it punished myself. But if nothing is found ——Second Brother, you will remember this day clearly, and you will pay this debt."

Li Xuan lowered his gaze, his smile deepening like a ripple spreading through still water. "Elder Brother may rest assured. Your younger brother has always had an excellent memory."

Chapter 19: The Burdens We Carry

The annual Flower Goddess Festival was always held along the banks of the Zhaoyang River, where the water glimmered like liquid jade and drifted past in languid currents.

Thousands of blossoms competed for brilliance on both shores and whenever a breeze swept through, petals scattered like drifting willow flakes, filling the air in a flurry of soft colour.

Music poured from silk strings without end, mingling with the laughter of scholars and maidens; the scene rivalled the very flowers that bloomed, each striving for its moment of radiance.

Qin Nianyin sat alone in one quiet corner, her plain robes lighter than falling snow. Subtle orchid embroidery traced the edge of her sleeves and the shadow cast across her lap rendered her as still as autumn water ——silent, unmoving, as though she did not quite belong to this bustling world.

Before her rested a cup of pale tea. Two stray crabapple petals floated on its surface, tinting its clarity with a faint coolness.

A breeze off the river brushed past her hair, carrying the lightest trace of fragrance ——something akin to orchid, perhaps a hint of osmanthus ——so delicate it nearly vanished the moment one sought it.

From the distance came the sound of children chasing flower boats, their laughter threading through the instruments' lingering tones.

Just as the gathering reached a peak of laughter and conversation, a sharp cry split the air.

"Is that girl in plain robes the orphan taken in by the Qin family?"

The voice was clear and cutting, like a cold needle striking against jade.

The speaker was Zheng Mingzhu, the legitimate daughter of Marquis Tongbo.

She had taken several cups of sweet osmanthus wine and though her cheeks were faintly flushed, her anger surged like a sudden blaze. She rose abruptly; the gold beads of her hair ornament swung with the movement, flashing harshly beneath the sun.

The banquet fell silent at once.

All eyes turned toward the corner ——toward Qin Nianyin.

The word orphan struck the gathering like a stone tossed into still water, sending ripples of surprise and murmured speculation across the seats.

Some sons of noble houses lifted their brows with thinly veiled amusement; others whispered behind their sleeves. A few young scholars from humble families stiffened at the slur, uncertain whether to speak or remain silent.

Gu Xiao had been lounging casually against a vermilion railing, folding fan swaying lazily between his fingers. But at those words, the fan snapped shut with a crisp crack.

He drew breath to speak ——only to have Shen Lingyan step quickly into his path. Her lips curved with an elegant smile, eyes bright with sharp intuition.

"Sister Zheng seems a little drunk," Shen Lingyan remarked lightly. "Allow me to accompany you to clear your head."

She reached forward as though to guide her away.

"Wait."

The single word unfurled across the air like the ripple of a pebble dropped into clear water.

Qin Nianyin rose without haste. Her hem brushed across the stone steps, sending three crabapple petals drifting to the ground. Her features remained composed, her tone soft yet unwavering, carrying easily through the entire pavilion ——outweighing even the wind moving through the flowers.

"Since Miss Zheng has asked, I shall answer."

There was no anger in her voice. Instead, it held the temperate softness of early spring ——gentle, yet undeniably steady.

She walked from the shadowed corridor into the open, standing among the sea of blossoms. Behind her, red walls and green tiles framed her quiet figure, while crabapple petals fell like scattered light.

A hush settled.

Someone murmured, "She dares respond?"

Another leaned forward, curiosity ignited.

Qin Nianyin's expression remained placid. Her gaze swept lightly across the crowd as she spoke.

"Today is the Flower Goddess Festival. It should have been an occasion for enjoying spring and exchanging verse. But since my background troubles some people, I do not wish for idle rumours to linger. A person's birth may differ in station or circumstance, yet it should not be wielded to shame them."

Having lived one full lifetime before this, she now looked upon the brightly dressed youths and spirited maidens before her as one might regard younger generations ——mischievous, spirited, yet transient in their concerns.

She had not intended to respond at all. But she was now residing in the Su household; her aunt, Madam Qin, treated her with genuine affection. She would not allow careless gossip to bring even a shadow of trouble upon the Su family.

This life is no longer the same as the last. I will not let old wounds reopen ——not for myself and not for those who shelter me.

She finished speaking with a slight nod, her voice clear and ringing like jade chips falling into a bronze vessel.

"If everyone is truly curious, then allow me to explain.

My late father, Qin Shouyi, once served as the seventh-rank magistrate of Yonghe County.

He was upright and honest, donating half of his salary each year to provide medicine for the poor.

In the third year of Yonghe, when the floods struck, he personally led the yamen runners into danger and saved more than a hundred refugees — —yet in the end, he contracted the plague and passed away."

She drew a piece of green jade pendant from her waist and lifted it for all to see.

"This jade was bestowed by the late emperor to commend my father's service in the disaster relief.

I wear it today not to flaunt anything, but simply as a keepsake of my departed parents."

A breeze swept across her sleeves, making the jade tremble slightly and glow with a gentle sheen.

The moment her words landed, the entire hall fell silent.

Shen Lingyan's expression shifted. She set down her wine cup and said coolly,

"So, Miss Qin is the daughter of a meritorious official. Madam Qin has spoken sincerely. Mingzhu, you should apologize."

Zheng Mingzhu's lips tightened. Her flushed face turned pale.

"I… I only repeated what others said…"

A few moments later, several poor-scholar guests rose quietly and bowed.

"Magistrate Qin was a righteous man. We hold him in great respect."

A number of older scholars also nodded, murmuring praise.

"This young lady is truly well-taught."

Qin Nianyin continued gently,

"My father lived and died for the people. I have no regrets on his behalf.

Though I was orphaned young, I was fortunate to be raised with care and to be sheltered now by my aunt's family.

Thus, I only ask that everyone refrain from addressing me as 'orphan girl' again."

Her tone was warm and proper ——neither servile nor overbearing —— yet it left no room for anyone to argue.

"Yes, yes… after all, she's protected by the Su family. Who would dare lose face like that…"

The murmurs spread and Zheng Mingzhu grew flustered. At last she bowed with a burning face.

"Miss Qin, I spoke out of turn. Please forgive me."

Qin Nianyin returned the bow with a faint smile.

"You are forthright by nature. I took no offense."

In that instant, the tense atmosphere finally melted away ——like ice thawing into spring water.

Standing by the pillar, Gu Xiao unconsciously rubbed the rib of his folding fan with his fingertip.

His gaze slid toward Su Zhang.

Su Zhang, usually so calm, was strangely unsettled today.

He held a cup of Biluochun tea, yet had not taken a sip.

The porcelain trembled faintly in his grasp.

Suddenly ——

Crack.

The cup split open.

Tea dripped through his fingers, blooming a dark stain across the peacock-blue brocade of his robe.

"Interesting."

Gu Xiao leaned in, his voice a quiet whisper by Su Zhang's ear.

"Why would Zijun lose his composure to this degree?"

Su Zhang said nothing.

His gaze stayed riveted upon Qin Nianyin ——

In that single moment, every blossom in the garden seemed to dim.

She alone stood bright as a blade catching dawn light.

Without warning, the dream from the previous night rose before him ——

Under wavering candlelight, a woman had bent over his wounded hand, gently wrapping the bandages.

Tied around her wrist had been a thin red cord.

 and today, Qin Nianyin wore that same red cord.

Qin Nianyin lifted her gaze.

By coincidence or fate, her eyes met his across the courtyard.

She caught sight of the tea stain spreading on his sleeve, the tension in his clenched fist.

A flash of comprehension crossed her expression ——quick, delicate ——

before she allowed her features to settle once more into composed serenity.

Despite the turbulence rippling through him, Qin Nianyin raised her head again, her expression placid.

Her voice emerged soft but unwavering, like still water stirred by a passing breeze ——

gentle in tone, yet each word struck with crystalline clarity.

As her final words landed, the wind brushed past her sleeves.

Petals of crabapple blossoms drifted down, catching in her dark hair; each petal trembled faintly in the air, as though adding to her an aura untouched by dust.

A hush fell over the gathering.

Somewhere distant, the silk- and-bamboo ensemble had fallen silent without anyone noticing.

Only the shifting shadows of blossoms stirred.

At that moment, Xie Zongyang stepped forward.

He clasped his hands in salute.

"Miss Qin's words remind me of what my late father often said ——

That loyalty and righteousness bear no relation to one's birth.

Only the heart stands clear before the sun and moon."

Qin Nianyin turned to him, her expression unchanged, offering a slight, courteous smile.

"Master Xie."

She lowered the jade pendant and bowed with unhurried grace.

"I thank everyone for witnessing this matter today. In a sense, it has brushed the dust from my father's memory. Let the matter end here. May it not be brought up again."

Crabapple petals rose with the wind once more, scattering across her clothing, clinging to the faint curve of her sleeves and hair.

——The red glow in his dream… was no different from what he beheld now.

He lowered his eyes.

The blood on his palm had dried long ago, leaving only a stark red slash across the skin.

His thoughts gradually tightened, settling into something cold and quiet beneath the sighing of the wind.

He murmured under his breath, barely audible even to himself:

"That woman in the dream…who… was she…"

Chapter 20: In the Eye of the Storm

The breeze swept past the flowering crabapple, carrying its fading scent farther and farther away.

The tea cup in Su Zhang's hand had long been set down; even so, the joints of his fingers tightened faintly beneath his sleeve. Every word she had spoken earlier felt as though it had carved straight through the dusted layers of memory sealed within his chest ——

the woman in his dreams,

the red cord beneath lamplight,

and that unwavering voice that refused to bow.

All of it surged upward, refusing to be suppressed.

The jade pendant caught between his fingertips made the slightest sound against his palm. He did not feel the sting. What he felt instead was the strange tearing at his composure, a sudden wrench of emotion he could not steady.

Blood seeped between his fingers, tracing its way into his palm, yet he did not glance at it. His gaze remained locked upon Qin Nianyin ——

She was neither angry nor seeking forgiveness.

She simply stood there, calm and unmoving, cold yet resolute, like an orchid braving the wind.

Gu Xiao noticed the scene and tilted his head, lowering his voice with a hint of amusement.

"Zi Jun, your cousin is quite something ——neither servile nor arrogant… there is a particular dignity to her. I should go speak with her ——"

Su Zhang pressed a hand against him.

"Do not go."

"Su Zhang!" the imperial physician exclaimed, startled. The sight of blood in Su Zhang's palm prompted him to step forward, but Su Zhang lifted a hand to stop him.

His expression remained severe and when he finally spoke, his voice rasped out from low in his throat.

"Sharp-tongued."

The words came out quietly, almost dragged through grit.

Then he rose and walked toward Qin Nianyin.

"Zi Jun, where are you going?"

"I will return shortly."

* * * * *

It was unclear when Su Zhang had left the gathering, but now he stood three steps behind her. His expression remained composed, yet his gaze carried a weight sharp enough to halt the words on Xie Zongyang's lips mid-sentence.

He then shifted his attention to Qin Nianyin. His eyes lingered briefly on the red cord tied around her wrist before he spoke, his tone low enough that only those standing closest could hear.

"Quite a tongue you have."

The four words carried no clear praise, nor any clear reproach.

Without waiting for her reply, he turned toward the surrounding guests and addressed them evenly:

"The spring light is at its best. Do not let quarrels dull the afternoon. The magnolias in the garden have just come into bloom ——perhaps everyone might enjoy a walk."

Only after saying this did he look toward Qin Nianyin once more. His tone remained the same steady calm as always, but there was no mistaking the note of quiet command beneath it.

"Come with me."

The sound of voices faded as they walked deeper beneath the drooping willows.

Layer by layer, the breeze scattered the noise of music and conversation across the flower isles, until only the soft slap of river water against stone remained.

Su Zhang stood beneath the shade, hands clasped behind his back. The sleeve at his wrist still carried traces of tea that had not fully dried. When he looked at Qin Nianyin, his gaze was cool and when he spoke, his voice pressed low, as though meant only for her.

"What happened just now ——you did not need to speak."

Qin Nianyin met his eyes quietly, her gaze as calm as water. She neither nodded nor offered any justification.

Su Zhang continued,

"The place was wrong. The person was wrong. With so many eyes on the flower gathering, every word you say becomes another thing for people to talk about."

Qin Nianyin lifted her lashes and gave a soft, almost weightless smile.

"So that is how it is. Then today… was it I who broke decorum?"

"I did not say you broke anything," Su Zhang replied. His tone eased, though the edge beneath it did not disappear. "But I do not care for that sharp tongue of yours. This matter did not require you to speak at all. You still have… people behind you."

The unspoken Su family hung plainly between them.

Her gaze cooled, though her voice remained composed.

"I only spoke of my foster father's truth."

She had not intended to argue further, yet she found herself increasingly weary of how he wielded the word "propriety" as though it were a tether.

"Truth also depends on the setting," he said after a brief pause, his words growing more blunt. "Had you remained silent, Mingyan would have smoothed the matter over. The Su family would have shielded you. Why place yourself at the very edge of the storm?"

Qin Nianyin lowered her eyes and brushed a bit of dust from her sleeve, her voice soft enough to nearly dissolve against the wind.

"But if the wind keeps blowing toward the Su family's name, that… unsettles me."

He faltered for a heartbeat, thrown off by her use of the word unsettles. His brow tightened.

"I brought you out today. Naturally, I will protect you. Those words you spoke ——charitably interpreted, they were dignity. Less charitably, they were a blade. The world does not always praise the latter."

Qin Nianyin held still for a moment, pushing down the slow, rising heat of irritation.

Last lifetime, he used 'propriety' on me again and again. And now, in this life, he still will not let it go?

She raised her gaze. Her eyes were cool, almost faint.

"Whether I care or not… what does that matter to anyone else?"

The question made the thin anger in his eyes finally surface.

"It matters because it concerns you. If someone bears a grudge against you ——if a single careless word implicates the Su family ——who will clean up after you?"

She studied him, then allowed a small, almost imperceptible smile to lift the corner of her mouth.

"So tell me, cousin ——what troubles you more? Me? Or the Su family?"

He stiffened. When he spoke again, his voice had chilled.

"Both. But if you were not of the Su household, why would I bother saying any of this?"

She lowered her eyes without answering.

Inside, however, calm ripples spread one after another ——quiet, resigned, unhurried.

He was the same in the last life ——guiding her with 'rules,' holding up a shelter above her, yet tying an unseen rope around her ankles. She did not blame him; she was simply tired.

Seeing her silence, Su Zhang assumed she had conceded. His voice softened, as though explaining something rather than admonishing.

"I am not reproaching you. Only reminding you ——today's outcome favoured you, yes, but it also means the Marquis of Tongbo's household has now made note of you."

"I never intended to befriend them," she replied, lifting her eyes again. Her tone remained gentle. "Still, since cousin dislikes me speaking too much, I shall speak less in the future."

Her obedience ——so swift, so unresisting ——struck him harder than any retort.

For a long moment, he said nothing. Then, finally, he murmured,

"Not less. Just… wiser."

Qin Nianyin nodded.

"All right. I will learn."

A breeze came from the river, carrying a faint scent of crabapple blossoms. She shifted her stance slightly, as if preparing to leave.

"It's getting late. Aunt should be returning to the manor. If cousin has nothing else to instruct ——"

He suddenly cut in, his tone sharp.

"What were you trying to do, chatting and laughing with Xie Zongyang?"

She paused and turned back to him. Her expression was still calm.

"He spoke a fair word for me. I thanked him. That was all."

"That was all?"

He let out a short laugh without any warmth.

"To anyone watching, it looks like the Su family's young lady getting friendly with a new rising noble at the flower festival."

Her brow moved slightly ——just a small reaction.

In her last life, he reacted the same way whenever she spoke more than a few sentences to someone. He reminded her of rules, reputation and consequences.

She could tolerate it then.

She could tolerate it now.

So, she answered softly.

"Understood. I will be more mindful."

He stared at her and the uneasy feeling in his chest only grew, as though her composure was pushing him further away instead of calming him.

Then he asked abruptly,

"The red cord on your wrist ——where did it come from?"

Qin Nianyin lowered her gaze and lifted her hand slightly. She wrapped the red cord once around her wrist bone.

"My foster mother tied it before she passed. For protection. And to remember her."

She turned, intending to leave and end the conversation.

But his voice came again, colder than before:

"If you really want to avoid causing trouble for the Su family, stop confronting people in public."

She stopped walking.

After a brief hesitation, she answered without turning back:

"It won't happen again."

Will this ever end?

* * * * *

Qin Nianyin looked at him and spoke at an even pace, her tone steady and unhurried.

"I will not compete with anyone. If Miss Zheng had not first called me an 'orphan,' I would not have said more than a few words. If cousin wishes to rebuke me, then let it be for caring too much about my father ——not for speaking two heavy sentences."

His expression darkened.

"That… is not what I meant."

"I know it isn't."

Her brows and eyes softened, the sharp edges folding away.

"You worry for me. You fear that if I take one wrong step, everything will collapse. I understand."

She paused, her voice dropping lower.

"It's just that, in my last life, I listened obediently for far too long. In the end… it didn't bring me anything."

He did not catch it clearly. Instinctively, he asked,

"What?"

Last life?

The words brushed past him before he could grasp them.

She lowered her gaze, as though folding every emotion back into herself.

"Nothing."

"Make it clear."

He had clearly heard something, but her voice had been too soft to distinguish. He refused to let it pass.

Only after she steadied her breathing did she speak again, barely above a whisper.

131

"Cousin, I will remember the rules you've mentioned. You may rest assured."

Her calm, almost detached acceptance left him without a response. His fingers curled involuntarily, knuckles tightening beneath his sleeve. After a long moment, as though he had finally made up his mind, his tone hardened.

"If you truly want peace for the Su family, then listen to one thing —— here in the capital, speak less, meet fewer people and show fewer edges. Restraint is protection."

Qin Nianyin looked at him, silent.

Then she turned and walked away, step by step, her skirt brushing through the shadowed branches. Her voice drifted back toward him —— flat, without temperature:

"Rest assured. I will do as you say."

The words in his throat dissolved into nothing. After a long stretch of stillness, all that remained was a faint exhale ——barely a sound —— and a tide of unspoken regret.

A breeze rose from the river, scattering petals and distant voices.

He stood where she left him, watching her figure slip into the shifting light and shadow and a cold, unmistakably clear thought surfaced in his mind ——

——The Marquis of Tongbo's Zheng household has failed to teach their daughter properly. Though today's events were masked as a flower gathering, they have in truth damaged propriety and disrupted order. If a warning is not delivered early, trouble will follow.

The jade pendant hidden in his sleeve warmed under the pressure of his grip, while his palm remained cold.

After a moment, he pushed his emotions down, straightened his robe and stepped back toward the crowd.

Music rose again by the riverbank. His expression had already returned to the familiar chill ——like a sheathed blade, quiet, yet capable of cutting through anything.

Chapter 21: Speak Not of Love

Princess Li Jing stormed away, sleeves snapping in the wind. Before long, Princess Li Rong arrived under the curtain of willow branches, moving slowly with the support of her maid. She glimpsed her younger sister's indignant face and let the corner of her lips lift in a quiet, almost idle smile.

"Again?" she murmured. "Turned away once more?"

Li Jing stamped her foot, anger flushing her eyes red. She bit out through clenched teeth, "Su Zhang is utterly blind to his own fortune!"

She spun around, only to find Li Rong stepping out from the pavilion ahead.

Draped in pale blue court robes, her waist bound by a soft belt threaded with gold, Li Rong's bearing held a serene luxury. Yet her brows and eyes were cool, distant and untouched by sentiment.

She looked Li Jing up and down with a faint, unreadable smile. "So, you failed again?" She had long been aware of her sister's infatuation with the newly crowned imperial scholar.

Li Jing's nose stung. She turned her face away, forcing her voice to remain steady. "Who cares for him? Su Zhang must be blind. I lay a path straight to the clouds at his feet and he refuses it. He will regret it one day!"

Li Rong flicked open her silk fan and approached at an unhurried pace. Her tone seemed casual, almost gentle, yet every word struck cleanly. "You know he is the Emperor's chosen tanhua and that His Majesty already decreed he is to assist the Crown Prince."

Li Jing froze for a breath, still stubborn even as confusion crept into her voice. "And so what? I like him. If I marry him, wouldn't that be better?"

"Like him?" Li Rong gave a soft laugh. A flicker of pity surfaced briefly in her eyes. "You truly are a child still. Far too innocent."

"Why would you say that…?" Li Jing's grievance spilled to the surface at once.

Li Rong extended a slender finger and tapped her lightly on the forehead. "Silly girl. If you truly married him, you would be driving him straight into a dead end."

"How could that be?" Li Jing's face drained of colour. Her voice shot up in disbelief.

Li Rong adopted the patient tone of one offering earnest counsel, yet her words grew sharper with every syllable. "If he were to take a princess as wife, what future would remain for him? The entire Su clan would be placed on the chopping block. Even he himself might not live to see the next year."

Her voice softened, yet the clarity in it only cut deeper. "Is there a single political storm in court that has not claimed lives? He now stands in the Emperor's favour. His fame is rising. If you reach toward him at this moment, it is the same as driving a blade into his back. Jing, you do not understand. Those seemingly gentle scholars… with a single stroke of the brush, they can bury a household. If Su Zhang is wise, the one he must avoid is not you. It is the throne standing behind you."

She paused, her gaze dimming with something older, something wearier. "Speak not of affection. Even one private word may be used as evidence against him. You smile and his heart must tremble. You speak one sentence, and he must sever every path of retreat."

Li Jing swayed, her face white as moon-ash. Her voice caught, thin and trembling. "It… cannot be so serious."

Li Rong folded her fan shut. Her tone dropped low. "We were born into the imperial family. Marriage has never been something we choose. The Empress and your mother, Concubine Chen, arranged your future long ago. In three years' time, your betrothal to the heir of Nanping Commandery will be settled. Su Zhang? Banish all thought of him."

Li Jing's lips trembled. She choked out, "And what about you, Elder Sister? Are you willing to be married to that…"

"The grand Consort Prince?" Li Rong arched a brow, letting out a soft breeze of amusement. "Zhao Ziqi is obedient. He endures what he should, and he knows what ought not be asked. That alone makes him rare."

She let her smile deepen by a breath, her voice dropping to that thin edge between courtesy and quiet mockery. "As for everything else… I find myself sufficiently satisfied."

Then, with deliberate lightness, she added, voice nearly a whisper, "His health is excellent and his skills are… commendable. What grievance would I possibly have?"

Li Jing's face turned scarlet in an instant, reddening all the way to the tips of her ears, like a shrimp plunged into boiling water.

Li Rong leaned in toward her sister's ear, voice dropping to a whisper that carried the softest curve, yet not a grain of warmth. "If you truly wish for freedom… you may as well follow my example and keep a few favourites of your own. He knows. He dares not speak. The days still pass."

She lifted a hand and smoothed a loose strand of Li Jing's hair, tucking it gently behind her ear. The gesture was tender, but her tone was cold enough to frost steel. "Jing, remember this. To live unrestrained, you rely on power, not on devotion."

Li Jing stared at her in mute astonishment. Her eyes held shock, confusion and the raw fear of someone tasting the world's bitterness for the first time.

Not far from the sisters, behind the long colonnade, a tall figure stood motionless.

Zhao Ziqi, the grand Consort Prince, kept his hands folded within his sleeves so tightly that his knuckles blanched beneath the fabric. He listened without a sound. Each word, each light remark, sank into him like needles driven into bone.

His gaze held no rage, no ripple ——only a lifeless stillness.

At last, he stepped back, letting the shadows of the willow branches swallow him whole, as though he had never been there at all.

A breeze stirred. Leaves wavered. A lone peach blossom drifted down onto his shoulder. He did not lift a hand to brush it away.

Spring was bright and generous, yet his heart only sank deeper into its own frozen dark.

* * * * *

That night, Zhao Ziqi returned alone to the Princess's residence.

The palace grounds lay quiet. Servants withdrew far from sight, none daring to approach. He shed his outer robe, dampened by night dew and walked slowly into his study.

Petitions lay untouched on the desk. The candle burned low, the last inch of the wick trembling. The flame stretched long shadows across the floor.

He stood still for a long time before finally lifting a hand to touch a white porcelain lotus lamp. She had once chosen it for him herself, saying it would steady the mind and sharpen clarity.

Now, his fingertips met only cold porcelain.

The lamps she had picked, the jade she had fastened at his waist, the words she once spoke ——grow old together ——all of it felt like some distant, cruel jest.

He lowered himself into his seat, his eyes hollow, his mind replaying the whisper that would not leave him: keep a few favourites…

He bowed his head and closed his fingers around the cracked jade pendant in his palm, as if clutching a piece of rotted memory that no longer held shape.

After a long silence, he let out a faint laugh, so soft it barely stirred the air. "Enough… enough…"

The candle gave its final shiver and died. The study was swallowed in darkness. Outside, sparse stars drifted like scattered silver dust, faintly illuminating the solitary outline of his figure.

That night, he understood with absolute clarity: whatever bond they once called marriage had crossed a point from which it would never return.

* * * * *

The next morning, in the flower hall.

Li Rong sat before her dressing table while a maid arranged her hair. She wore a long gown of silver-red brocade threaded with gold. Her face bore no powder, only a thin layer of fragrant cream that left her skin smooth as polished jade. Her expression remained cool and unyielding.

In the bronze mirror, her striking beauty reflected back at her, yet there was no softness in it, only a faint trace of distance. Her fingertips brushed the dangling bead on an ornate hairpin, moving slowly, as though waiting for a question whose answer she already knew.

"Your Highness," the maid said softly, "the grand Consort Prince waits outside. He says he has something to report."

Li Rong lifted a brow. "Did he say what matter?"

The maid hesitated, bowing her head without speaking further.

A slight curve touched Li Rong's lips, something resembling a smile but devoid of any warmth. She reached for a gilt hairpin shaped like a blooming flower and slid it into place with a languid motion, her eyes holding a glint that was neither amusement nor irritation ——merely a cool dismissal.

"Tell him to go to the side hall," she said. "My toilette is not yet complete. I have no leisure to listen to his trifles."

With that, she picked up a storybook from the table and let it fall open in her lap. The pages drooped downward, untouched. She did not turn them. She merely lowered her gaze, as if the thin sheet of paper itself were enough to keep unwelcome people firmly outside her world.

* * * * *

In the side hall, Zhao Ziqi sat in silence for a long time.

In the end, the summons never came.

He rose, brushed his sleeves into order and stood for a moment before leaving. As he stepped toward the threshold, he turned back and looked at the tall vermilion doors. His gaze was steady, cool and faint.

From behind the doors came the soft murmur of a woman speaking with her maid, their laughter drifting lightly. It was distant, yet clear enough that it might as well have been meant for him alone.

His lips tightened. At last, he turned and walked away.

The high doors remained shut.

Behind them, Li Rong stood in the shadowed interior, her fingers grazing the dangling fringe of her gilt hairpin. Her eyes held no ripple.

She did not follow him. She did not order anyone to keep him back. She simply instructed the maid to refill the tea ——her voice even, untouched ——as though the man who had just stood outside had never been there at all.

She had long understood that sincerity only turned into vulnerability. Better to withdraw her hand than reach forward. Better to let affection bury itself so deep that even she would not touch it.

The world moved like a chessboard. She preferred to stand upon the high terrace and observe the game, not be drawn into its knots.

Marrying Zhao Ziqi had been a political bond from the start. Once, she had allowed herself a foolish hope, believing they might grow old side by side. But with time she learned: wherever true feeling existed, chains would follow.

Better to remain free of love and live by power alone.

137

Chapter 22: Aiding Xu Wencai

The poetry gathering was at its height, the pavilion brimming with laughter and bright chatter.

Yet Qin Nianyin excused herself from Shen Lingyan halfway through and quietly slipped away.

Mei held up a small white silk parasol, following close behind. She could not help muttering in a low voice, "Miss, leaving so early today… Young Lady Su will surely blame us."

Qin Nianyin only smiled lightly, neither agreeing nor denying it.

The two walked until they reached a secluded lane. Before they could pass, a burst of noisy shouting rose from the front.

At the entrance of an inn, an argument seemed to be unfolding. The inn attendant was loudly berating a young man dressed like a scholar.

"Hurry up and go! No silver and you still want to stay at an inn? Get moving—don't block the business!"

Mei clicked her tongue at the sight. "Miss, look. That attendant is far too fierce."

Qin Nianyin glanced over as well. The two were still quarrelling.

"Brother," the scholar pleaded, voice strained yet restrained, "have mercy. I'll find work in the next two days—I will pay. Where can I possibly go right now?"

"Get lost!" the attendant barked. "No silver and you still dare lodge here?"

At that instant, a memory flashed through Qin Nianyin's mind—sharp and swift, as if the past life had struck the present with a single cold spark.

In her previous life, around this time, there had indeed been a scholar who was driven out of an inn for lack of money. After that, he missed the spring examinations. In the end, he threw himself into a lake and died. The matter had been discussed in the capital for a long time.

What made it the talk of the city was not merely that he failed, but the reason he failed: that fallen scholar had been plotted against by a companion. He was forced to drink a wine laced with purgatives, missed the following day's examination, saw his name absent from the list, and—heart broken beyond repair—ended his life in the water.

That man had been Xu Wencai.

Now that fate had looped back and she had returned, Qin Nianyin did not wish to see him tread that same path again. If her rebirth could shift anything at all, then she hoped this young scholar's destiny would quietly turn today—right here, without anyone even realizing.

"Out! Out, out, out!" the inn attendant roared, hands on his hips. A rag was gripped in his hand as he drove away a thinly dressed youth. "No copper on you and you still dare to loiter? This place isn't a charity den!"

The young man looked about seventeen or eighteen. His features were clear and handsome, but his clothes were washed so often they had gone pale. Near his feet lay several scattered pages from old books.

He bent down, stubbornly picking up the fallen volumes. His brows held a hard, unyielding set. He did not argue back. He did not explain. He only pressed his lips together, letting the insults wash over him as he gathered what belonged to him.

Mei spat softly in disgust and complained under her breath, "People in the city are far too snobbish. The moment they see someone poor, they kick them while they're down."

Qin Nianyin slowed to a stop. She lowered her eyes and thought for a brief moment, then said, "Mei. Give him the silver we brought."

Mei froze, then hurriedly tugged at Qin Nianyin's sleeve corner, whispering anxiously, "Miss… he… we don't even know what sort of background he has. Is it really appropriate to do this?"

Qin Nianyin's voice remained gentle. "Just treat it as doing someone a small kindness. Mei."

Mei pouted, looking completely unwilling, but she still fished out a small embroidered purse. She weighed it in her palm, her face pained as though she were cutting off her own flesh, and muttered, "This is the private savings we scraped together with such effort… Miss has to write this down for me! Put it on the account! You must owe me one clear entry!"

Qin Nianyin's eyes curved in faint amusement. "Of course I'll remember."

Mei snorted, then strode forward quickly.

She shoved the purse straight into Xu Wencai's hand and clucked her tongue loudly. "Scholar-brother, today you're lucky. You ran into our young lady, who's soft-hearted. Otherwise, these streets are cold and empty—who would still have spare silver to give to anyone?"

Xu Wencai went still. Both hands clenched around the purse. His throat moved—he seemed to want to speak, yet could not. His lips parted, then closed again, words stuck somewhere deeper than his chest.

The inn attendant's eyes spun the moment he saw silver appear. His face changed instantly; a smile bloomed so fast it looked practiced.

"Ah—misunderstanding, misunderstanding!" he exclaimed, voice suddenly syrupy. "Young brother, please come inside! Just now it was this lowly one who had no eyes! No eyes at all!"

Mei rolled her eyes and planted her hands on her hips. "Just now, who was it shouting this isn't a charity den? Now you're smiling brighter than flowers—what happened?"

The attendant laughed awkwardly, bowing repeatedly. "Yes, yes, yes— young lady, be magnanimous! This humble shop treated you poorly, deserves to be punished, it does!" As he spoke, he even raised a hand and lightly slapped his own cheek twice, putting on a show.

Mei found it ridiculous and couldn't help huffing. She turned and walked away.

Only then did Xu Wencai come back to himself. He hurried after them, clasped his hands, and bowed deeply. His voice shook faintly.

"This humble one is Xu Wencai. Thank you, young lady—and thank you, this young maiden—for your helping grace. If one day I have the chance, I will surely repay it."

Qin Nianyin gave a light smile, calm and detached. "No need to thank me."

Xu Wencai stared at her, dazed, as if he understood yet did not. He nodded slowly, uncertain where to place his gratitude.

A spring breeze swept through the lane. The faint scent of apricot blossoms drifted up, soft and clean.

That small encounter at the alley's end—no one in the capital knew it— had already quietly altered the trajectories of more than one life.

Mei turned her head back and shot Qin Nianyin a subtle look, whispering, "Miss saved this little scholar… but don't let him latch onto us."

Qin Nianyin laughed and gently shook her head. She reached out and rubbed Mei's forehead lightly. "You said it wrong. It wasn't I who saved this little scholar. That silver was Young Lady Mei's private savings."

Mei's eyes widened in shock. "Miss, how can you play tricks like this? You said you'd write it down on the account! Heavens—Miss isn't going to pay me back, is she?!"

Xu Wencai accepted the purse, yet he did not hurry back into the inn. Instead, he stood where he was, watching Qin Nianyin's retreating back. His eyes reddened slightly. He drew a deep breath, hugged his books close, and chased after her again.

He stopped in front of her, stood firm, and bowed with hands clasped. His voice trembled more than before.

"Young lady—please wait."

Qin Nianyin turned her head to look back.

Mei pouted at her side and muttered, "He really is latching on."

Xu Wencai stood in the spring wind, lean and clear-boned, his youth sharp with stubborn pride. He drew out a battered book from his arms and offered it with both hands.

"This humble one is Xu Wencai. My family has been a scholarly line for generations, but I was born at the wrong time. When I was young, our household fell into ruin; my parents died. I could only go to distant relatives and live under another's roof, at their mercy."

His voice grew lower, rougher.

"This year, I came to the capital for the examinations. I spent everything—just for one chance to change my fate. But last night… the place I lodged… someone set me up. Something was mixed into the wine."

He swallowed hard, as if forcing the words through his throat.

"My belly cramped like it was being torn apart. I missed the sitting. If the young lady had not helped me today… Xu—Xu…" His voice broke; he forced it back together. "…Xu fears he might not even have been able to keep my life."

As he spoke, his voice sank further and further, thick with an ache he could not swallow. The book in his hands trembled slightly.

Qin Nianyin looked at the worn copy of the Book of Songs commentary. The pages were yellowed; the edges were frayed; yet it had been wiped so clean it looked like someone had tried to polish dignity back into it.

Something stirred in her heart. She asked softly, "Have your relatives ever looked for you?"

Xu Wencai forced a bitter smile. "Relatives?" He gave a short, hollow laugh. "They would rather I live or die on my own. They drove me out when I was still young. This time coming to the capital—every step was scraped together with blood. I only wanted one chance."

Mei, hearing this, could not help the pity in her eyes. She lightly nudged the hem of Qin Nianyin's skirt and whispered, "Miss… he really is pitiful."

Qin Nianyin's expression softened a fraction. "Do you have somewhere to go now?"

Xu Wencai bowed deeply. "If the young lady does not disdain me, Xu is willing to serve under your household as a clerk. I will give my all— exhaust myself for you, even unto death."

Mei waved her hands quickly, laughing as though to defuse it. "Oh dear, our young lady is a noble person. We don't take in wandering scholars as retainers."

Xu Wencai's face stiffened. He lowered his head and said nothing.

Qin Nianyin saw his silence and felt a small softness rise in her chest. "Stay at the inn for now. Rest and recover. Let me think—see where you can be placed."

Even as she spoke, Qin Nianyin felt troubled. She herself was living under someone else's roof—how could she truly settle another living person?

Xu Wencai's whole body shook. Then he suddenly knelt and kowtowed three times, his forehead striking the ground with heavy thuds.

"Xu… in this life and all lives to come—willing to serve the young lady with my life!"

Mei startled badly and hurried forward to pull him up. "Oh, oh—get up, get up! Our young lady isn't the kind who takes someone's indenture contract!"

Xu Wencai's eyes were red, but his voice was firm. "The young lady saved me from the pit. Xu will carve this into my bones. Even death will bring no regret."

Qin Nianyin couldn't help laughing. She pointed to Mei beside her. "Young master, you thanked the wrong person. This young lady is called Mei. She is the one who saved you. That pouch of silver in your hand—it is her personal savings."

"Miss!" Mei's face turned bright red.

And it wasn't only Mei—Xu Wencai's face also flushed. He bowed again, even more solemnly. "This unworthy scholar thanks Young Lady Mei for saving him. I will surely repay today's grace—knotting grass, holding the ring—never forgetting it."

Mei looked at his earnest, scholarly manner and could only sigh. She waved a hand repeatedly. "Forget it, forget it."

In her heart, she could only think: fine. With him this sincere, just treat it as losing money to ward off disaster.

Chapter 23: First Thoughts on Crafting a Hairpin

At the mouth of the alley, the spring breeze lifted, and apricot blossoms drifted down—petals settling across a shoulder like scattered silk.

Qin Nianyin looked quietly at the youth before her. In that still gaze lay a faint sting of memory: in her previous life, he had been utterly alone—brimming with talent, yet destined to end up buried in the rivers and roads of the world, his name swallowed by cold water and distant dust. The thought made something sour tighten briefly in her chest.

In this life, she hoped that what she had done today—this small rescue, this handful of silver—might be enough to break that thin line of ill fate that clung to Xu Wencai.

She reached out, helped him up properly, and said softly, "Xu Wencai, I will only ask you one thing—do you dare to begin again from the very start?"

Xu Wencai lifted his eyes. In the clear black-and-white of his gaze, sparks flared—small at first, then suddenly bright. His reply came like a blade striking stone.

"I dare!"

Mei stood to the side with her hands on her hips, muttering under her breath, "This brat… he does have a bit of backbone."

Qin Nianyin covered her lips and let out a low laugh, then murmured, "Good. That's enough."

She turned her head and glanced toward the end of the alley. Dusk had already spilled its rosy light across the long street, as if hinting that another, entirely new path of fate was quietly unfurling from this moment onward.

And everything that happened here—every word, every movement—fell into two pairs of eyes hidden in the shadows.

"I say, Zijun," Gu Xiao clicked his tongue in admiration, voice low and amused, "your little cousin really is full of surprises at every turn."

Su Zhang's gaze remained heavy as he watched the mistress and maid depart. He did not answer.

* * * * *

After they left the alley, Qin Nianyin drew her thin gauze closer about her shoulders. She lifted her chin slightly, looking toward the sun as it sank deeper into the dimming sky.

Mei sneaked a glance at her young mistress, careful and tentative, and said softly, "Miss… saving Young Master Xu was a good deed, yes—but we still have to find a way to keep ourselves fed."

Sigh. They really had become penniless now.

Qin Nianyin smiled faintly, but her eyes held a darker weight. "I know. If we only rely on the Su household to support us, then it will be no different from the last life."

Mei blinked, confused. "Last… what?"

Qin Nianyin's mouth halted at once. Only then did she realize she had spoken too quickly. She immediately corrected herself, smoothing it over as if it were nothing.

"Nothing. I meant… what happened before. Earlier matters."

"Oh." Mei did not dwell on it. She simply went right back to fretting.

Qin Nianyin, however, remembered the day she had entered the residence—standing before the Marquis, making her vow in a clear voice: she would establish herself, live by her own hands, and not burden her kin.

Now that those words had been spoken, how could she break them so easily?

Mei scratched her cheek and frowned, muttering, "But the two of us don't even have a single decent piece of jewellery. And we want to do business? In the capital, even a small shop costs a thousand gold to start. Us… are we supposed to do it with nothing but our mouths?"

Qin Nianyin was just about to answer when a bright, sweet voice floated from the street corner—lively and crisp.

"Come and see! Have a look! Freshly made velvet blossoms! Wear one on your hair—bring fortune and blessings!"

The two turned toward the sound.

A small stall stood there, bright brocade spread neatly across its surface, covered in velvet-flower hairpins. Soft pink, pale yellow, lake green, silver white—each one trembled and swayed, dazzlingly eye-catching. Several young ladies crowded around, holding the blossoms up, picking and comparing, laughing as they teased one another without end.

Qin Nianyin's heart stirred.

She crouched down and examined the velvet flowers carefully. At a glance, the workmanship was rough—the silver threads messy, the colours a touch vulgar. Yet, despite that, a single velvet-flower hairpin could sell for thirty coins.

Thirty.

Her brows lifted slightly. A faint, almost invisible smile curved her lips.

Mei edged closer and whispered, "Miss… you're not thinking of making this, are you?"

"Why not?" Qin Nianyin laughed softly, her eyes quiet and clear. "Velvet flowers take time and effort, but the cost is low. We can start with ordinary hair ornaments first. Buy scraps of cloth, silver thread—add a bit of thought, sketch a few patterns… I think we can make new styles."

Mei stared. "B-but there are endless styles in the world. How can you learn them all?"

Qin Nianyin only smiled, and in her gaze there was an unusual steadiness—calm, unhurried, as though she already knew the shape of what was to come.

Scenes from her previous life flickered before her eyes. She had grown up surrounded by such things; she knew well that within three years, what would become most fashionable in the capital would not be these coarse velvet blossoms at all, but delicate, intricate, layered floral embroidery hairpieces—fine and clever, stacked petal upon petal, nothing like the crudeness of the present.

"The most valuable thing in this world," she said slowly, "is not quick hands."

"It's new thinking."

"Scraps, silver thread, floral hairpins—make them so refined that noble ladies fight to wear them. Then we'll have our first bucket of silver."

Mei listened until she was completely stunned, then clapped her hands in delight. "Miss, that's brilliant! But buying cloth, buying silver thread… that still costs money."

She patted her own chest, then drooped at once. "But… we just used up every bit of loose silver to save someone."

Qin Nianyin sighed lightly, helplessness threading through her voice. "Yes. Skill without capital—what can it do?"

Mistress and maid exchanged a bitter smile. Mei tugged at her sleeve, muffled and gloomy.

"Then… should we pawn my hairpin?"

Qin Nianyin paused and looked at her.

Mei pursed her lips, but her eyes flashed with a small, bright light. "I'm only a maid. It's useless for me to wear a hairpin anyway. Better to do something real—something that earns silver! I want to make money properly!"

Warmth rose quietly in Qin Nianyin's chest. She reached out and gently held Mei's hand.

"No," she said softly. "That hairpin… was the one I gave you for your coming-of-age."

Mei turned her head away at once, grumbling as if embarrassed. "W-who said I was wronged… I just… I just want to get rich with you, that's all!"

They looked at one another and smiled.

The evening breeze swept through the streets and alleys, scattering the last chill of dusk—and at the same time, opening a different road before them.

They walked back laughing and talking, shoulder to shoulder.

At the turn of a long street corner, Mei suddenly slapped her forehead hard.

"Miss! We don't have a single coin left—what do we do? Making velvet flowers still needs materials. We have to buy them first!"

Qin Nianyin's expression did not change. Her gaze swept lightly toward a pawnshop by the roadside.

"It's fine," she said evenly. "I have a way."

She drew out a small jade pendant from within her clothing. It was smooth and warm as cream, yet time had worn it dull until it no longer shone. It was the keepsake her foster mother had left her on her deathbed—carrying the weight of old affection and a past tenderness she could not name aloud.

Mei jolted and immediately grabbed her sleeve.

"Miss, no! Absolutely not! This is what Madam left you—how can you pawn it?"

Qin Nianyin's smile thinned, becoming faint. "Only temporarily. Once we have silver, we'll redeem it."

With that, she stepped inside.

The old shopkeeper examined her for a long time. Suspicion came first, but when he recognized that the pendant—though old—was fine mutton-fat jade, his manner immediately turned more respectful.

"Miss," he said, "this jade has good quality. Two hundred coins—will that do?"

"Fine," Qin Nianyin answered briskly.

She took the silver note, turned, and walked out.

Mei was still uneasy, her face full of worry. "Miss… can we really turn ourselves around with just this little money?"

Qin Nianyin smiled slightly. "Don't look down on a small sum. If the method is right, it's enough to open the road."

She brought Mei straight to a cloth shop and then a thread shop.

When she chose materials, she was painstakingly careful: the finest cocoon-white silk, the brightest lake-blue thread, several packets of scrap satin, and thin copper pieces.

Mei watched roll after roll go into their bamboo basket and couldn't help muttering, "The way our Miss spends money… you're calmer than someone spending money to buy back her life."

Qin Nianyin turned her head with a smile. "If it's worth spending, then it isn't waste."

By the time they returned to the small courtyard, night had fallen fully.

Qin Nianyin spread her work across the table. Under the lamplight, her fingers moved with nimble precision—threading the needle, drawing it through, again and again.

She used thin copper as the base, then covered it with silk thread, layering it in overlapping folds. The stitches were tight and dense, each one fine and exact. Before long, the shape of a begonia blossom appeared—its centre bright with silver as its veins, its petals soft pink like clouded sunset.

Mei's eyes widened to their fullest.

"Heavens… Miss, your hands are like immortal craftsmanship!"

Qin Nianyin only smiled. Under the lamp, her fingertips trembled faintly—not from weakness, but from something deeper.

She knew it.

With each stitch, she was not only sewing a flower.

She was sewing her new life.

"Tomorrow," she said calmly, "we go to the Baihua Isle riverside. We won't set up a stall yet—first we test the price."

Mei blinked. "Miss is going yourself?"

"Yes," Qin Nianyin replied simply. "If I can't see the market clearly, how can I do business?"

She placed the begonia gently beneath the lamp. The flame swayed; the flower's light looked almost like fire.

Mei lowered her voice. "Miss… you really mean to start from here?"

Qin Nianyin lifted her eyes. In them was softness, but also an unshakable resolve.

"If fate is to be changed," she said quietly, "then I have to do it with my own hands."

The night wind brushed past. The lamp flame trembled slightly.

That newly embroidered begonia—small, bright, and new—glowed quietly in the darkness, like a hope lit and held steady.

Chapter 24: On Duty in the Study

Dawn's first light had just begun to break. The sky was washed in a faint, pale whiteness. A thin mist enveloped the streets, and from afar, the cries of early vendors were already drifting through the air.

Qin Nianyin, accompanied by Mei, walked slowly along the slightly damp bluestone slabs.

The marketplace was already alive with noise — voices rising and falling, people brushing past one another. The scents of tea broth, fried cakes, and the medicinal tang from the dye workshops mingled together, forming a dense, bustling atmosphere that pressed in from all sides.

Mei, still drowsy, rubbed her eyes and complained in a low voice,

"Miss, it's barely light… and we're already heading out. This really is going to wear a person down…"

Qin Nianyin's hair was tousled by the morning breeze, yet her expression remained clear and untroubled. Her voice was gentle, calm, without a trace of impatience.

"Without enduring hardship, how can one establish oneself? If one wishes to be self-reliant, one must begin from the smallest details."

As they walked, she observed everything with care. She first stopped by stalls selling velvet flowers and beaded ornaments, quietly asking after prices. Then she moved on to ready-made clothing shops, memorising the cuts, the colours, the way fabrics were displayed, all of it stored away in silence.

Reaching a corner, she noticed a small stall laid out with scraps of fabric and coils of silver thread. The materials were not luxurious, but they were even-textured and durable, clearly chosen for practicality rather than appearance. She reached into her purse, counted out silver, and selected several colours without hesitation.

Mei saw at once how light the purse had become. She could not help drawing in a quiet breath.

"Miss… our capital isn't much to begin with. How can we afford to spend like this?"

Qin Nianyin smiled faintly, as if the concern were expected.

"For a small business, what matters is refinement. These alone are enough to make dozens of hair ornaments."

They worked until dusk. By the time the sky darkened, their feet were sore and their legs ached, yet because their hearts now had something to hold onto, the fatigue felt lighter than it should have. When they returned to the residence, night had fully fallen, lantern light and drifting mist intertwining into a hazy, indistinct glow.

Back in her room, Qin Nianyin carefully put the fabrics away. Together with Mei, she rolled up her sleeves and began to try her hand at making something.

Her hands moved swiftly. Needle and thread passed cleanly between her fingers, stitch after stitch tight and precise. Petals layered one over another, silver thread carefully placed to form the flower's core.

Before long, the outline of a floral hairpin emerged — supple in posture, quietly elegant, carrying a freshness that set it apart.

Mei's eyes lit up at once.

"Miss, your craftsmanship is amazing! If this were sold, people would definitely fight over it."

Qin Nianyin lowered her gaze with a small smile. Yet within her chest, something steadied itself, firm and unyielding.

In this life, she would rely on herself — step by step — and live with clarity.

A soft cough suddenly sounded from the corridor.

Both of them looked up at the same time. Su Zhang stood in the shadows, hands clasped behind his back, his posture upright, his gaze calm and unreadable.

"Nianyin."

His voice was cool, carrying a quiet authority that did not invite refusal.

At the sound, Qin Nianyin's heart tightened. Startled, she hurriedly gathered the items on the table and wrapped them together.

"Cousin?"

In her surprise, she did not even notice that he had not called her "cousin" as before, but had spoken her given name directly.

Her thoughts raced at once.

Why had he come to her small courtyard?

What business could he possibly have here?

Su Zhang's gaze fell upon the fabric clenched tightly in her hand. His brow furrowed slightly, but he said nothing.

"Cousin…?" she tried again, her voice low.

He drew his expression back into composure and spoke evenly,

"Since you say you have leisure, starting tomorrow, at the Mao hour, come to my study."

She froze.

"The study… for what purpose?"

"Grinding ink. Sorting documents. Recording matters."

His tone was steady, leaving no room for debate.

"Others are not fit for this duty. The one I want is you."

The words fell one after another, heavy as stones. Qin Nianyin's chest trembled slightly; she did not manage to respond in time.

His gaze was intense, yet tightly restrained, as if something were being held firmly in check.

"I ask you to come because I trust you — and because I do not wish for you to be entangled with people and matters you should not approach."

Qin Nianyin lowered her eyes and asked quietly,

"What do you mean by that?"

He did not answer.

He simply looked at her.

That gaze advanced like a tightening lock, step by step, leaving her nowhere to retreat.

She steadied herself and forced calm into her voice.

"Cousin already has study boys and assistants. I cannot take on such a role."

In this lifetime, she did not wish to draw near him — not even half a step.

"The study boys are clumsy," he replied indifferently. "Their copying is unreliable."

"I am not skilled in official documents or the classics either."

Her brows knit together as she continued to refuse him, her tone still cool.

His eyes sharpened. His voice remained light, yet allowed no withdrawal.

"Reading and copying are trivial matters. Qin Nianyin — must you continue to refuse again and again?"

Her breath caught.

"Since you know this places me in difficulty, why insist so forcefully?"

In the depths of her heart, a cold thought surfaced:

In her previous life, this man had always been indifferent. Why, in this life, did he insist on pressing others so hard?

His expression did not change.

"If you are unwilling to help, that is also acceptable. But you live in the Su residence, eat from the Su residence, receive its monthly stipends — and yet claim to have nothing to do. Is this not your place of shelter?"

The words cut coldly into bone.

Qin Nianyin fell silent. She wished to argue, yet found nothing she could refute.

Su Zhang's gaze remained calm, yet it felt as though it had already locked onto her thoughts.

"If you consider me your cousin, then I will take it seriously."

"Take what seriously?" she blurted out before she could stop herself.

His voice dropped.

"Take seriously that you intend to spend your entire life confined within the Su residence — safe, complacent, accomplishing nothing?"

The sentence pierced straight through the years of her previous life.

Her heart jolted; her gaze dimmed at once.

After a long pause, his tone eased slightly.

"If you truly wish to stand on your own, you must first learn to restrain your sharpness. Working by lamplight at night — if others were to see it, how would you explain yourself?"

His gaze swept over the cloth clenched in her hand, then over Mei's alarmed expression. With that, he turned and walked away.

Qin Nianyin's ears burned red, anger and frustration tangling together in her chest.

He reached the doorway without slowing. His voice drifted back, light and cool.

"Tomorrow, at the Mao hour. Do not be late."

His departing figure was solitary and cold, yet beneath it lay an insistence that could not be hidden.

She stood there, staring after him.

A spark of defiance flared sharply in her chest.

"If I must go — then I will make him see that I am not someone to be handled so easily."

Mei startled.

"Miss… what do you mean?"

"Let us see who yields first."

Her voice was low, cold, resolute.

Since she could not refuse him, then she would make him be the one to ask her to stop helping.

Was that not simple?

All she needed was to create a few minor mishaps in the study he so treasured.

In her previous life, she had once accidentally spilled a small cup of water on his desk. For that alone, she had been barred from the study for an entire year, forbidden from approaching that so-called "important" place ever again.

The lamplight flickered.

Qin Nianyin's eyes settled into quiet resolve, as though she were making a vow in the stillness of the night.

Not far away, in the shadows, Su Zhang's lips lifted by the faintest degree — almost imperceptible.

If she wished to contend, then he had patience to spare.

* * * * *

That same day, the study lay in utter silence. The lattice window was half open, morning light slanting inward.

Qin Nianyin bent over the desk, transcribing. Her expression was focused, yet her thoughts were unsettled; the tip of her brush trembled from time to time.

"There is an error in that character."

Su Zhang spoke without approaching. From across the desk, his finger indicated the margin. His tone was steady, absolute.

Her chest tightened. She hurried to correct it, yet in her fluster the brush slipped again, and a droplet of ink splashed onto the page. She looked up and met his gaze.

There was no anger. No warmth.

Only a stillness that fixed her in place, leaving her nowhere to hide.

"Focus."

His voice was light, yet struck like a bell against stone, sending her nerves into further disarray.

She forced herself to steady her breathing, gathered her scattered thoughts, and resumed writing.

Moments later —

"The stroke order is incorrect."

His voice was not loud, yet each word landed like a hammer beside her ear.

Her fingers tightened. She did not look up.

"I will correct it."

He remained where he stood, hands clasped behind his back, gaze lowered.

"If you truly wish to stand on your own, you must first learn restraint. If your heart is unsettled, how can you stand firm?"

A tremor passed through her chest.

The coldness of the previous life — the pressure of this one — felt no different.

Light and shadow mottled the desk. His silhouette stretched long across her hands, like an invisible shackle.

At last, she lifted her eyes, a cold edge glinting within them.

"Why must you press so relentlessly, Cousin?"

He met her gaze for a long moment. His voice dropped low.

"Relentless? Is that how you see it? Very well."

The words cut like a blade.

Past and present collided — two parallel lines crossing at last, steel striking steel.

Her expression flickered. She turned away, choosing silence. The brush descended again, each stroke edged with stubborn resolve.

Su Zhang stood quietly for a time, his gaze fathomless. Then he turned.

As he left, he spoke one final line, low and restrained:

"Nianyin — do not err again."

Her heart jolted. The ink beneath her brush trembled.

That voice, heavy and restrained like chains, bound her in place — and reminded her without sound:

There was no retreat left on this path.

Chapter 25: Nianyin's Dilemma

"You..." Qin Nianyin retreated an inch, her back pressing against the chair—no room left to withdraw. Her throat was dry, her voice thin as a gossamer thread. "Cousin, please... stand farther away."

Su Zhang looked down at her, his eyes cool and detached, yet his voice was pressed exceedingly low. "Farther? Is this close? I certainly don't perceive it as such."

Each word was indifferent as cold iron, heavy enough to steal her breath.

Her thoughts churned wildly, but they were abruptly severed by his next question—

"You wish to pair me with Shen Lingyan?"

A violent tremor ran through her. Her eyes snapped up to meet his, only to find a gaze of unfathomable depth. Within it lay an almost amused, almost mocking light—yet beneath that sheen, a honed blade waited.

She was struck dumb, a sudden chill blooming in her heart. She had not even acted yet; she had barely begun to move. And still, he had already seen through her.

"A cousin's good intentions." He withdrew his gaze, his tone turning light, almost absent, as he pivoted to the window with his hands clasped behind his back. His figure was solitary and austere, as though his earlier proximity had been nothing but an illusion.

Yet how could she treat it as nothing? Her knuckles were white, her breath in disarray, her chest tight as if it had been squeezed.

Her fingers were clenched so tightly that the joints ached, nails biting into her palm. She forced her shoulders to remain still, forced her gaze not to waver, yet the heat beneath her skin betrayed her—rising too fast, too sharp, as if her body had reacted before her mind could command it otherwise. Every breath felt shallow, drawn too quickly, as though the space around her had quietly narrowed.

He had already turned away.

That was the most unbearable part.

The distance he created was deliberate, precise—neither retreat nor apology. Standing by the window, his posture composed and upright, he looked exactly as he always did: restrained, proper, untouched. As if the closeness moments ago had never occurred. As if she had not been the one forced back against the chair, left with nowhere to retreat.

The room itself seemed to conspire in that contrast. The faint rustle of silk, the low scrape of paper as he shifted, the steady rhythm of his breathing—calm, unbroken—all of it sharpened her awareness of her own disarray. The faster her pulse raced, the more unbearable his composure became.

If he acknowledged nothing, then she was left alone with everything.

And he—he acted as if nothing had happened. He idly lifted a scroll and flipped it open, the casual rustle of paper sharpening the contrast between her heat and his composure, leaving her even more at a loss.

The teacup on the desk was slightly askew; water splashed onto her sleeve. She jerked her hand back, but heard him speak in that same even tone. "Scalded?"

The words were flat, devoid of tenderness. Yet he had already bent down, drawing a handkerchief to blot away the moisture.

His movements were steady and deliberate—neither distant nor intimate, controlled to the point of cruelty. His fingertips brushed along the side of her wrist, their warmth impossible to ignore, like a shackle clicking shut.

Qin Nianyin's heart gave a sudden, violent jolt. Her entire body stiffened, her breath nearly losing its rhythm.

"Su Zhang!" She finally snatched the handkerchief back, her voice rising slightly in urgency, her face burning as if on fire. "You... this is going too far!"

He straightened slowly, his expression unchanged, his voice cool and unruffled. "Too far? Wiping water for you is merely a trivial gesture."

The chill in his tone, paradoxically, flustered her more.

Her chest heaved as she fought for composure, yet a thread of cold defiance curled at the corner of her lips. "Cousin has always been known for upright restraint. Yet today, you press me at every turn. If we are truly speaking of service... Nianyin is not some delicate flower. I might just be able to return the favour."

With that, she pressed the handkerchief back into his palm, her gaze clear and bright, carrying a subtle challenge.

Su Zhang lowered his eyes, staring at it. A long moment passed before the barest hint of a smile touched his thin lips.

Her heart tightened. She meant to pull away, but he seized her wrist in one swift motion. The grip wasn't brutal—yet it offered no chance of escape.

"If that is the case—" His voice was deep and cold, nearly oppressive. "Then begin by finishing transcribing this volume."

Having spoken, he guided—or rather, compelled—her back to the desk. His presence loomed close, his breath silent, yet it trapped her utterly.

The candle flame flickered. The scroll lay unopened. But between them, the tension stretched like a fully drawn bowstring, taut to the point of snapping.

* * * * *

Qin Nianyin lowered her head to refill his tea, her eyes shifting faintly. "Uncle and Aunt have long been concerned about your marriage prospects, cousin," she said, her voice gentle and measured. "Your literary reputation has never waned. If you truly have intent, why not convey your heart through poetry? Words infused with feeling naturally move others."

Su Zhang's brush paused mid-stroke. After a moment, he replied evenly, "If there truly were a worthy woman, why would I need to rely on words to please her?"

A faint, knowing smile touched Qin Nianyin's lips. "As you wish. I only heard Miss Shen is particularly fond of handwriting that reflects the person. If she were to see your hand... she would likely find it hard not to be moved."

Her words were not heavy, yet they pierced like fine needles, slipping in without a sound.

Su Zhang finally lifted his gaze, his eyes deep as a still well. "You make a fair point. However—" He paused, his voice lowering, pressing down with weight. "What of you, Nianyin?"

She started slightly, then quickly regained her composure. "I dislike such ostentatious brushwork the most."

"Oh?" He let out a soft laugh, unhurried, yet carrying an undeniable pressure. "You didn't answer me earlier. Do you truly intend to matchmake me with Shen Lingyan?"

A tremor passed through Qin Nianyin's heart, but she calmly smoothed her sleeve and picked up a brush. "Miss Shen is of noble birth; her conduct is refined and upright. She is indeed a rare and excellent match."

Su Zhang suddenly leaned in, his shadow falling across her desk, his voice nearly brushing her ear. "Yet I feel—perhaps you are the superior one."

The words were uttered very softly, but they fell into the lake of her heart like a heavy stone, the ripples lingering long after.

Her fingertip twitched, ink splattering. Heat instantly flooded her cheeks. She knew full well this was provocation, a deliberate test—yet her emotions still surged beyond her control.

Suddenly, hurried footsteps approached from the corridor. Before she could even think, Su Zhang caught her wrist, his fingers settling precisely at her pulse. His voice was a low command: "Hush."

In the next instant, with a swift turn, he drew her behind the standing screen.

In the shadow of carved wood, the cramped space meant for one now held two. Their breaths mingled; sleeves brushed, with no room to retreat.

"You... what are you doing?" she whispered, her voice tight.

A sliver of light filtered through a gap, falling diagonally across his stern profile. So close, she had the distinct illusion of being locked into this narrow world by him alone.

"Quiet," he murmured, his voice hoarse, his breath brushing her ear like night wind through willow leaves—soft, yet carrying an unyielding weight.

Qin Nianyin stood holding her breath, her heart drumming like thunder. She knew this was improper, yet there was nowhere to withdraw. That sense of being coerced wrapped around her like invisible chains, binding her fast.

* * * * *

The footsteps halted just outside the door. A voice called softly, "First Young Master, are you inside?"

It was the steward.

Su Zhang listened for a moment but made no sound. Behind the screen, Qin Nianyin—already unnerved—found the atmosphere turning stranger still.

A doubt rose unbidden: the scroll on the desk—where had it gone?

She shifted a fraction, but before she could steady herself, her knee brushed his. The protest died in her throat as his arms suddenly barred her shoulders, pressing her back against the carved screen.

Su Zhang braced his hands on either side of her, trapping her within that narrow space. Qin Nianyin trembled and looked up, meeting a pair of eyes that held a faint, knowing smile.

"What are you moving for?" His voice was extremely low, his breath close to her ear, tightening every nerve. "With such noise, do you truly want to be discovered?"

"You... move aside," she whispered urgently, furious at the cramped quarters that left her no room to retreat.

Her heart grew more frantic. There had been no impropriety between them—none—and yet this posture, this hiding, made it look like something else entirely.

He acted as if he hadn't heard her reproach. His gaze darkened, and he murmured, slow and deliberate, "Don't move."

Qin Nianyin fell silent, her face burning. And just then, the steward outside asked again, hesitant, "First Young Master? If it's inconvenient, shall I return later?"

"Inconvenient." The corner of Su Zhang's mouth lifted slightly. His voice was gentle, yet he leaned closer still, his whisper almost grazing her ear. "Isn't that right, Cousin?"

The softness was worse than harshness. Heat flushed from her neck to her fingertips, her thoughts dissolving into chaos.

She seethed inwardly: If you meant to answer, why not answer plainly? Why whisper into my ear like this?

After a moment, the footsteps outside receded. The study returned to silence.

Yet behind the screen, neither of them moved a fraction.

One breath, two—time stretched, seemingly frozen.

Finally, Qin Nianyin gritted her teeth and whispered, "Su Zhang, if you do not step back now, I will call someone."

"Go ahead." His tone remained mild, yet the challenge beneath it was unmistakable. "Only then, it may be hard to explain whether you stepped into my arms yourself... or I left you with nowhere to retreat."

Qin Nianyin trembled with anger but was left speechless, able only to spit out in a low voice, "You... are truly detestable."

He let out a soft laugh. His already handsome features took on an even more beguiling edge in the dimness.

In the quiet room, it was as if the world had shrunk to the sound of their breathing, tangled together in too narrow a space.

She leaned against the screen, cheeks burning, heart pounding like a frantic drum. His proximity was so overwhelming that for a moment she almost felt she had stumbled into a dream.

Su Zhang gazed at her for a long time, then finally sighed—softly. A trace of gentleness flashed through his eyes, brief as melting spring snow.

He withdrew his hands and took a step back. The movement was light, careful—yet it felt as though an invisible chain around her had been lifted.

"Enough," he said, calm as ever. "He has gone. You may come out."

She stood dazed for a long moment before raising her sleeve to cover the heat in her face and stepping out sideways. She had taken only two steps when she heard him add, still even, "Had the screen not been so confining, I might not have been quite so... discourteous."

His words hovered between apology and excuse, tinged with teasing—a complete departure from his usual solemn restraint.

Qin Nianyin turned her head and met his gaze, warm as polished jade, faint ripples shifting within. For a heartbeat, her thoughts slipped out of order.

Biting her lip to hide her discomposure, she said coldly, "Lord Su is truly admirable in self-restraint—worthy of your reputation as one of the capital's famed talents."

"Self-restraint?" He raised an eyebrow, a smile playing at his lips. "That depends on whether Nianyin is willing to give me the chance to be restrained."

Half sincere, half jesting—soft and seamless—yet every word hooked straight into the heart.

Unable to refute him, her frustration only deepened, her emotions in turmoil.

In her past life, they had mostly met in cold opposition. In this life, she had somehow ended up having to spar with such a rogue.

She said no more, flicked her sleeve and made to leave. She had taken only two steps when he called again, mild as if remembering something trivial. "The books?"

She stopped, frowning slightly. "What books?"

"The scrolls you were airing earlier." His voice remained gentle, yet held a note of mischief. "It's already dark. Aren't you going to put them away? Or... did seeing me speak with Miss Shen make you forget your task?"

She stood where she was, her back to him, her voice very low. "There is no need for Lord Su to concern himself. I will remember."

With that, she walked away quickly, the hem of her skirt brushing over the threshold like a breeze skimming water.

Inside the study, Su Zhang watched her retreating figure. His fingertips tapped lightly against the desk, a smile faint in his brows, his gaze deep and far-reaching

Chapter 26: A Craft of Hopeful Blossoms

Qin Nianyin had spent consecutive days recently "on duty" in Su Zhang's study, without a single day's break.

Remembering the various unusual ocurrences in the study yesterday, a restless anxiety churned uncontrollably in her heart. She felt her very breath growing stifled and tight, instinctively dreading setting foot in that room again.

It was not fear alone, but a sense of being quietly cornered—of having her composure tested again and again without warning. Even now, the memory of his proximity, deliberate and unhurried, lingered like a pressure she could not easily shake.

Those ambiguous, provoking methods... She admitted she was no match for them. In terms of boldness and strategic pursuit, he was a completely different man from the cold, detached figure of her past life, leaving her increasingly disconcerted.

In her former life, his indifference had been distant and predictable; now, this calculated intimacy left her with no clear ground to stand on. She could neither advance nor retreat without exposing herself.

While her thoughts wandered chaotically, her fingertips never stilled. Her plain hands flew deftly, velvet flowers and silver thread intertwining in her palms. In a moment, an exquisite velvet hairpin took shape.

Mei, squatting nearby, watched wide-eyed and couldn't help whispering, "Miss, this hairpin is truly beautiful, but will it really sell? I've asked around... there are at least ten or so shops in the capital making floral hairpins."

Without looking up, Qin Nianyin offered a faint smile. "What they sell is craftsmanship. What I sell is thoughtful design. The style is uniquely new, the workmanship meticulous and the price is fair. Someone will recognize its worth."

Though her words were soft, they carried a firm certainty. In her previous life, elevated by Su Zhang's favour, what kind of jewellery or rare trinket had she not seen? Her discerning eye would not be wrong.

Back then, silver and gold had come to her without effort, placed in her hands by others. Now, every piece she crafted was weighed not by status, but by whether it could truly sustain her.

As the noon hour approached, Qin Nianyin carefully wrapped the finished hairpin, tucked it into a small bundle and stood to go out.

Su Zhang was away today attending to business. She finally had a moment's respite and didn't have to go "on duty" in his study. Eagerly, she pulled Mei along toward the bustling East Market.

Mei followed, full of doubts yet not daring to dissuade her. The two walked through nearly every lane of the East Market, inquiring about shopfront conditions. Though their legs grew sore and numb, they also found it novel and enjoyable.

"Miss, it seems this business might be hard to manage," Mei muttered quietly, a note of discouragement in her voice.

Everything in the capital was expensive and shop rents were particularly staggering.

Yet Qin Nianyin's expression remained composed. Her voice, though not loud, was steady and assured. "Do not fear. What we are selling is skill. Let us visit a few more shops. We will surely meet someone who recognizes true value."

She knew well that confidence alone would not open doors—but hesitation would close them all the same.

* * * * *

At last, she paused before a small shop. From her sleeve, she took out several hairpins and placed them lightly on the counter.

The shopkeeper was a slick, sharp-eyed man ——quick to see through everything. Though the ornaments in her hand were not luxurious, their designs were fresh and unusual.

Still, he pretended to be lofty.

"These designs… passable, I suppose. But the workmanship is rather rough."

Of course, Qin Nianyin knew her current conditions were limited. Her pieces were far from exquisite ——the polishing, the tools, the equipment ——everything she lacked showed clearly. She could not yet produce truly refined work.

Each flaw was a reminder of her position now: without backing, without resources, relying solely on her own hands.

The shopkeeper added,

"Things from little households like yours… may not sell at all."

Qin Nianyin's expression remained calm. Her voice stayed gentle and poised.

"This is fine velvet-flower silver thread. No other shop in the capital carries such designs. It may not be as valuable as gold or jade, but the colours are versatile, the shapes novel and the cost affordable. You may try placing them in your long counter. I believe many girls with smaller budgets will be quite fond of them."

She paused for a moment, then lifted her chin with a pleasant, steady smile.

"Just set them out on your counter for three days. I guarantee it ——by the third day, not a single one will still be there."

The shopkeeper blinked, clearly not expecting that level of confidence.

and why shouldn't she be confident?

These styles would become wildly popular in the capital within a year ——she remembered it vividly from her past life. What everyone else saw as odd or unfashionable, she knew was simply ahead of its time.

That certainty gave her the boldness to speak like this.

Still, a small sigh pressed against her chest.

To earn a single coin, she had to smile, bow her head, talk nicely and even recommend herself.

Across two lifetimes, this was the very first time she had lowered her pride to this degree.

In her previous life, she had never once needed to bargain, to persuade, to endure dismissal with courtesy. Now, every word she spoke carried the weight of survival.

So, this is what it truly means… to build one's own livelihood.

No wonder so many people fail halfway.

The shopkeeper snorted, folding his arms with a half-mocking look.

"You do talk pretty well. Fine ——twenty wens. That's what I'm willing to pay."

Little Mei instantly bristled.

"Twenty? You're practically stealing them! At that price, we might as well hand them to you for free!"

But Qin Nianyin kept her composure. She gathered the hairpins back into her sleeve with a soft, unhurried movement, the picture of courtesy.

"Very well. If we cannot agree on a fair price, I shall try my luck at other shops. Someone out there will certainly recognize their worth."

She turned as if to leave.

The shopkeeper's expression changed immediately ——panic flickered across his face. He hurried around the counter and blocked her way.

"Alright, alright ——thirty wens! That's the highest I can go!"

He tried to sound firm, but the edge of desperation slipped through.

After several rounds of bargaining, the deal closed at fifty wen each.

In the end, the shopkeeper selected three pieces ——discounted to a total of one hundred and thirty wen.

It was not a great profit, but it was her first successful sale.

Both women felt a quiet swell of satisfaction.

It was a small beginning, yet it marked a line she had crossed on her own strength alone.

They were just about to return by another route when, stepping out of the shop, a sudden commotion burst behind them.

"Make way ——!"

A horse neighed wildly.

People scattered in panic.

Little Mei grabbed her with all her strength, yet they were still pushed apart by the chaotic crowd.

"Miss ——watch out!"

Qin Nianyin's eyes fell on the few unsold hairpins dropped to the ground ——her hard-earned work scattered in the dust.

Her heart clenched painfully.

"My hairpins ——!"

She bent instinctively to pick them up, but before her fingers reached ——

A heavy deer-leather boot came down.

A sharp crack.

The silver thread flattened instantly beneath the heel.

Her brow twitched. A cold, cutting anger surged up.

"You ——"

Her words had not finished when she looked up and saw a man in refined clothing, handsome features and the bearing of a noble family's young master. Her hand stilled, but her voice remained steady: "Compensate me." Staring at the broken hairpin in her hand, she felt a sharp pain in her chest and her anger rose. She did not care who he was; princes and nobles were nothing new to her, not after her previous life.

The man raised a brow, surprised that this young woman did not back down and a faint smile curved his lips. "And why should I?"

"You stepped on my hairpin," she said, her voice not loud but each word clear. "This kind of workmanship and design is hard to find in the capital."

The man laughed lightly. "It is neither gold nor jade ——just a few little flowers. And you dare say it is rare in the capital?"

Qin Nianyin's gaze cooled as she said, "To you, they're little flowers. In my hands, they're hard-earned coin." These hairpins were made in styles she knew would soon be all the fashion among the capital's noble ladies, and that certainty kept her tone calm and confident.

Her composure drew the attention of those nearby, and many paused to watch.

The man's gaze swept over the remaining intact velvet-flower, silver-thread hairpins in her hand, and interest flickered in his eyes. "May I ask, young lady—how many more pieces of this 'hard-earned coin' do you have?"

Qin Nianyin did not avoid his eyes and replied evenly, "If you truly wish to buy, I naturally will offer them. But buying and selling has its price ——whether noble or common, it depends solely on whether you can recognize their worth."

He narrowed his eyes slightly. "Are you implying that I can't recognize quality?"

"No," Qin Nianyin replied calmly. "A gentleman dressed like you must be well-born and knowledgeable. But men do not always understand what pleases a woman's eye. A hairpin cannot be judged by how expensive its materials are. A simple design often carries more spirit."

He let out a soft laugh. "Your tongue is sharper than the pin itself."

She lifted her gaze to meet his, her expression steady and composed. "There's no need for extra talk. I only want compensation."

Had this been her previous life, she would never have cared about such a trivial amount. Yet now she was haggling with a stranger in the middle of the street over a few coins.

The realization washed over her with a quiet heaviness ——this road to standing on her own feet would not be smooth; it would be filled with thorns.

The young man raised an eyebrow, then crouched to pick up the crushed hairpin. He turned it between his fingers.

Under the sunlight, the silver threads gleamed faintly. With a careless twist, a hidden needle pricked his skin, drawing a small bead of blood.

He paused, the teasing fading from his face and murmured, "It is finer work than I assumed. Not something an ordinary hand could make."

Qin Nianyin remained indifferent. "If you understand its worth, then you should also know how much it deserves."

A soft murmur rippled through the surrounding crowd. Her composure, her refusal to bow or yield, drew respectful glances.

The man's lips curved again, though this time his amusement was tinged with something else. "A very sharp young lady indeed."

With that, he reached for the silver pouch at his waist. A flick of his fingers sent several small silver pieces into her palm ——far more than the price of a single hairpin.

"This silver," he said, mounting his horse, "buys your pin… and an apology."

He swept his sleeve and with a light tug of the reins, the horse sprang forward. Dust stirred behind him as he disappeared into the street.

Mei stared after the fading figure, wide-eyed. "G-girl… that one must be some nobleman's son, right?"

Qin Nianyin lowered her eyes. In her palm, the scattered silver glinted coldly in the fading light. Her voice was quiet. "Whoever he is, the money is real."

She tucked the broken hairpin away. When she finally lifted her head, her expression had steadied ——calm, clear and resolute.

"In this world," she murmured, "debts must be repaid. Today, at least he paid cleanly."

With that, she turned and continued down the street. The twilight gradually swallowed her silhouette, yet her steps carried a firmness that had not been there before.

Chapter 27: I Will Remember You

"Your humble servant, Su Zhang, greets Your Highness, the Third Prince."

A faint flicker crossed the young man's eyes—sharp, unreadable—as though the title both amused and irritated him.

Su Zhang was about to speak again when a calm yet unmistakably authoritative voice sounded from behind him. Warm on the surface, final in its weight, it left no room for dispute, no space to feign ignorance, no path to retreat.

It was not loud, yet it cut cleanly through the noise of the street and laid the man's identity bare, as if the air itself had been split open by a single sentence.

Only moments earlier, Su Zhang had been at Linfeng Pavilion, conferring with several officials. He had not expected that, on his way back, he would come upon a disturbance in the street—and that Qin Nianyin would be standing at its centre, her back too straight, her posture too unyielding for a place where power could crush a person without leaving a trace.

Qin Nianyin stiffened.

She looked again at the young man before her. His features were handsome, his smile open and effortless, exactly as she remembered from her previous life: the same brows, the same bright arrogance curving his mouth, only sharpened now by youth.

The Third Prince, Li Suo.

A cold shock slid down her spine. How had she not recognized him? How could she, of all people, have been blind to a face that had once sat so high above the world?

Her earlier impulsiveness struck back like a slap. Regret came too late and too sharply. She had stepped forward without thinking, demanded compensation in the middle of the street, spoken as though the man before her were merely another privileged passerby.

And yet today, he wore no princely regalia. Dressed like a wealthy noble son out for leisure, he looked far younger than the Li Suo of her memory. The man she had known was a cold-eyed, middle-aged emperor, every glance a blade, every smile a warning. This youth, loose in posture and bright in laughter, scarcely resembled that distant shadow at all.

Li Suo glanced back.

Su Zhang had already stepped forward. His sleeves were neat, his posture straight, his expression respectful—yet beneath it all lay an unshakable, mountain-cold steadiness. His manners were impeccable, his tone measured, but the air around him seemed to cool by a degree. It was the kind of calm that did not bend, the kind that made others hesitate before taking another step.

"So, it is Lord Su." The Third Prince lifted a brow, a hint of a smile touching his lips, as though he had discovered a more interesting piece on the board.

Su Zhang inclined his head slightly. His voice was deep and steady, carrying a weight that did not ask permission to be felt.

"This young lady is Qin Nianyin, a distant cousin of mine. She has only just arrived in the capital and is naturally outspoken. If she has offended Your Highness, I ask for your pardon."

Qin Nianyin immediately lowered her gaze. She adjusted her expression with practiced ease and stepped into a graceful curtsey, the sort of movement learned not for elegance, but for survival beneath other people's eyes.

"This humble girl, Qin Nianyin, offended Your Highness in her ignorance. I beg your forgiveness."

Li Suo observed them with faint amusement, then turned his head, as though mercy were something he dispensed for sport.

"You are there. Bring me a gold ingot."

A guard stepped forward at once and drew a solid piece of gold from within his robe. Li Suo tossed it toward her with careless ease, as if its value meant nothing at all, as if he were flicking a coin to a performer for an amusing display.

"Here. A reward for you."

The weight nearly made her fingers tremble.

Still, she accepted it calmly and bowed again, forcing her posture into neatness even as her chest tightened with mingled heat and cold.

"Many thanks, Your Highness, for compensating my loss."

She was genuinely pleased. A gold ingot was no small thing—enough to buy breathing room, enough to dull the sharpest edge of today's humiliation.

And yet, beneath that brief flicker of delight ran a thin thread of bitterness.

In her previous life, she had lived surrounded by wealth and privilege, never once stirred by a few taels of silver. Gold and jade had come to her without effort, placed into her hands as naturally as water finds its course.

Now, because a few hairpins had been crushed, this ingot made her heart leap—quick, helpless—as if poverty had trained gratitude into her bones.

This kind of poverty… even she found it laughable.

This kind of smallness… was real enough to sting.

Li Suo blinked, then burst into hearty laughter, the corners of his eyes sharpening with mischief. The sound was bright, but it carried the edge of someone long accustomed to watching others bend.

"So, the hairpins were ruined, and that is this prince's fault. Very well. Another day, I will come buy several more of your little 'living silvers.' Tell me—will you still sell them to me then?"

"If Your Highness does not mind the humble craft of a country girl, I would be honoured," Qin Nianyin replied, lowering herself again. Her tone held neither fear nor flattery, only a composed confidence that refused to kneel in spirit even while her body bowed.

Those hairpins, even at their finest, were not worth a single gold ingot.

If the Third Prince insisted on being taken advantage of—if he wished to play the generous fool before the street—she would hardly refuse.

A fool with power was still power, and power was not something she could afford to offend.

Li Suo cast Su Zhang a sideways glance, his lips lifting slowly.

"Lord Su has taught his cousin well. Straightforward. Bold. Your little miss certainly opened my eyes today."

His gaze returned to Qin Nianyin, his smile deepening with interest.

Her features were refined, her temperament gentle but far from weak. She met him evenly, without shrinking, as though she had learned long ago that lowering one's eyes did not guarantee safety.

Rare. Very rare.

He threw back his head and laughed aloud, letting the sound carry down the street and turn the marketplace into a stage. Then, with a smooth motion, he swung onto his horse.

Just as he gathered the reins to leave, he turned back once more, this time looking directly at Su Zhang.

"Truly a coincidence," the young prince said lightly. "Who would have thought this prince would encounter such an amusing scene in the marketplace today?"

Playful. Deliberately teasing—the kind of teasing that tested boundaries without ever staining the speaker's hands.

Su Zhang's expression did not shift. His reply was steady and cool, polite enough to be flawless, cold enough to be unmistakable.

"Your Highness flatters. Coincidences such as these are hardly unheard of in this world."

Li Suo's gaze lingered on Qin Nianyin a heartbeat longer. His smile deepened, the interest no longer subtle, like a hunter who had noticed an unexpected spark in a quiet animal.

"Girl," he said lazily, "I will remember you after today."

In all his years, this was the first time anyone had dared demand compensation from him face to face—not with trembling lips, not with tearful pleading, but with a steady spine and clear eyes.

With that, he lifted his whip. The horse surged forward, and he rode off in a sweep of wind and dust.

Only a drifting farewell echoed behind him, light as silk, sharp as a hook.

"Mountains high, rivers long. Until we meet again."

A moment later, a cold, low voice sounded behind Qin Nianyin, threaded with a rare trace of displeasure, as though control had slipped for the briefest instant.

"Do you know who that was?"

"Earlier, I did not," she answered honestly. "Now I do."

Su Zhang stared at her, the calm in his eyes tightening into something harder.

"Do you know what would have happened if you truly angered the Third Prince?"

"I do." She nodded.

She was no longer the honoured wife of a high minister. She was no longer seated safely within a household, shielded by a name and a title. Now she was merely a dependent, a guest beneath the Marquis' roof—low in status, with no influence, no leverage.

If anything went wrong, a single sentence from someone with power could decide guilt or innocence. Proof would not be required. Only someone willing to point.

Su Zhang watched her in silence for a long moment.

Finally, he asked, his voice low, "Are you frightened now?"

Qin Nianyin's expression did not change. She said nothing—neither admitting fear nor granting him the satisfaction of denial.

He continued, his questions clipped and controlled, as if forcing himself to remain rational.

"This business you are running—was it planned by you alone?"

"At present, only Little Mei and I are involved," she replied calmly. "No one else knows. If it grows in the future, I will rent a shop, register it properly with the yamen, pay the required taxes, and follow all regulations."

Her tone was even, almost formal, as though she had already mapped the road ahead step by step, as though order itself could keep misfortune at bay.

Su Zhang's gaze darkened; a fleeting shadow crossed his eyes.

"Then why did you not tell me sooner?"

Qin Nianyin lowered her gaze. Her smile was soft, courteous enough to sound harmless, yet edged sharply beneath.

"Cousin, you are occupied with matters of state. Such trifles as women's accessories should not fall within the scope of your concerns."

Gentle words. Blade-sharp meaning.

It sounded like deference, but it was distance.

It sounded like consideration, but it was refusal.

Su Zhang fell silent for several breaths. Something unnameable stirred in his chest—half irritation, half disbelief—as though he were looking at someone who no longer fit the shape he had assigned her.

When he spoke again, his voice was low.

"You know now that he is the Emperor's third son, Li Suo, titled Prince of Qinping. And still, you dared block a prince's path in public and demand silver from him. Do you truly not consider the consequences?"

Qin Nianyin turned to face him. Her expression was calm, her voice unhurried, as though she were stating an obvious truth.

"Not knowing, I committed no offense. Before today, how would I recognize a prince dressed as a noble youth at leisure?" She lowered her eyes, steady and unruffled. "I only asked for the silver owed for the hairpin he damaged. Nothing more."

In this lifetime, she had no reason to cross paths with princes at all.

She had seen Li Suo before—only in her previous life, when he had already become the cold, sharp-eyed emperor whose every gesture carried unquestioned authority.

The young man she encountered today was nothing like that distant figure. His smile was open, his gaze bright with youthful arrogance, his presence that of a privileged noble enjoying the streets of the capital.

The gold he had tossed her was his own extravagance, given as casually as one might flick away a leaf. She had not begged for it. She had not asked for more than what she was owed. If he wished to scatter gold for amusement, that was his choice. She had only demanded justice for her labour.

Su Zhang's gaze swept over her. His voice carried a cool edge, colder now for having been shaken.

"Are you truly this naïve, or are you deliberately acting without restraint?"

"I already said I did not recognize him," Qin Nianyin replied. Her tone remained calm, yet the chaos of moments earlier had left her eyes faintly red—not with tears, but with restrained fury, with the sting of being judged.

"To me, he was nothing more than a passerby who stepped on my hairpin. And if earning one's livelihood counts as acting without restraint, then the whole of the capital should be punished."

Her voice stayed even, but the displeasure beneath it was unmistakable.

Su Zhang let out a quiet, derisive snort. "Sharp-tongued." The slight curl of his lips betrayed the easing of his earlier tension, though the look in his eyes remained hard, as if the aftertaste of fear still lingered.

Thinking back on the disturbance, even he could admit a flicker of unease. It had not been the Third Prince alone that unsettled him, but the thought of what might have happened had a single word gone wrong. It seemed that whenever matters involved her, the composure he prided himself on grew unreliable, as though one loose thread threatened to unravel the whole.

Qin Nianyin felt her temper burn. Why should he be the one to chide her? Did he intend to supervise every breath she took, dictate what she could or could not do, simply because she lived under his roof?

Su Zhang's voice deepened, cold and rigid, the restraint in it sounding almost like anger with nowhere acceptable to land.

"If I had not happened to pass by, how would you have handled the situation? You live beneath the Su family's roof now. Every word and action reflects upon this household. These street-corner entanglements—intentional or not—trample the Su family's reputation."

So that was what troubled him.

In his eyes, she had never placed the Su family—or him—within her calculations. Perhaps that was the true irritation: not merely that she had risked trouble, but that she had done so without turning to him first, as though he were not part of the equation at all.

Qin Nianyin gave a soft, humourless laugh, turned away, and refused to argue further.

Su Zhang watched her walk off, his fingertips tightening at his side. A quiet storm gathered behind his composed expression, for even now—after he had arrived in time—the image of her standing alone before a prince in the street refused to leave his mind.

Chapter 28: The Solace of a Quiet Heart

When she turned away without expression and prepared to leave, Su Zhang felt another surge of anger rise sharply in his chest, sudden and fierce, as though the mere sight of her retreating back were an affront he could not simply ignore.

"Stop."

His voice cut cleanly through the air, low and cold.

She halted.

Qin Nianyin turned back slowly. A muted chill rested in her gaze as she lifted her chin with deliberate calm before speaking. "Does Master Su still have further instructions for me?"

For an instant, he met the steady coolness of her eyes. Something unbalanced stirred beneath his ribs, and the anger he had been ready to unleash weakened by a subtle degree.

He had intended to ask whether she lacked silver, whether she needed support—an offer he would never have voiced to anyone else—but she did not grant him the chance to begin.

"The dignity of the Su household may indeed be as precious as gold," she said, her tone quiet, yet sharpened by restrained resolve, "but these hands earn their silver through honest work. I have done nothing disgraceful. If other steps on my hairpin, am I expected to apologize instead of seeking compensation?"

Her voice did not rise, yet each word landed with steady clarity.

"If the Su Prefecture fears that someone as coarse as I might stain its reputation, then perhaps I should leave sooner rather than later, so as not to provoke your displeasure."

As she finished, her lashes lowered slightly. The calmness in her expression was so composed it bordered on ice.

"Even if I live under the Su roof, I am not someone who allows herself to be stepped upon."

He had not anticipated that his stern tone would provoke such a direct, cutting reply. Watching her avert her gaze—refusing even to acknowledge him further—he felt most of his anger ebb away before he realized it had begun to fade.

After a moment of silence to steady himself, Su Zhang looked down at her once more. His voice, though softened, left no room for argument.

"First, tell me how you came to be here today. You should have been in my study."

Before leaving, he had assigned her several tasks, issuing precise instructions he expected to be followed. She was certainly not meant to be wandering the streets.

"And how did you happen to pass by?" she countered, her tone calm, yet unwilling to yield.

She frowned slightly. In her previous life, they had lived beneath the same roof for twenty years. How had she never discovered this side of him?

The side that questioned everything. That demanded explanations for every step she took and insisted on knowing her every movement.

In just a few days, the two of them had exchanged more words than they had in two decades.

Su Zhang's eyes narrowed faintly. His tone remained cool, but this time he offered an explanation—something he rarely did.

"I was in the teahouse across the street, discussing matters with several officials of the Ministry of Rites. I saw a familiar figure pass by the window. It appeared to be Li Suo, so I came to confirm."

He did not add that it had been her silhouette he noticed first, not the prince's.

The explanation caught her off guard. She had expected reproach or interrogation, not this calm, precise account. For a moment, she found herself at a loss for words.

She had spoken only out of irritation—yet he answered in earnest.

He was nothing like the Su Zhang she remembered from twenty years of marriage.

"I was merely making a few hairpins," Qin Nianyin said at last. "I wanted to see whether they might sell."

Su Zhang frowned slightly. A complicated shadow crossed his expression before he let out a brief, cold laugh.

"Since you have leisure for such crafts, direct your efforts to my study. The scrolls require cataloguing—attend to them volume by volume. Any need for silver is to be brought to me. I will not have you wandering beyond the gates."

"…"

Was he attempting to hire her with money?

"What is it? Are you unwilling?"

She was, indeed, unwilling—

but she did not know how to say it.

The memories of her previous life rose unbidden. Su Zhang was not a man who altered his decisions lightly. Once he chose a course, no argument could sway him.

"Master Su jests," she replied, keeping her tone even. "The scrolls have been nearly sorted over the past three days. The remaining work may be taken over by Xiuyan."

"And how would you know they are nearly sorted?" His voice cooled, carrying a quiet reprimand. "Three days, and you believe yourself already entitled to a sense of accomplishment?"

Qin Nianyin pressed her lips together. She wished to disengage, but he continued pressing—question after question—leaving her no room to breathe, let alone retreat.

She lived beneath another's roof. Her food, clothing, and lodging were all provided by the Su household. What were three days of work compared to the cost of her daily upkeep?

"Very well," she said softly. Her tone remained gentle, yet her words were firm. "If it is a task assigned to me, I will see it done."

At least this way, she would not feel as though she were simply eating and living in the marquis's residence without offering anything in return.

Su Zhang raised a brow. An unreadable trace of amusement flickered across his expression, though he said nothing. The faint curve of his lips was neither mockery nor warmth—it hovered somewhere in between.

If she was willing to remain by his side, then so be it.

That alone eased something in him he refused to name.

She added quietly, "A debt is a debt. I will repay them one by one."

Her words bore two meanings—settling accounts from both her past life and the present—and she spoke them without hesitation.

When she finished, she turned and walked away with Mei at her side. Her steps were steady, her bearing composed, her departing figure untouched by fear or disorder, as though she had long anticipated today's confrontation and had prepared herself for it.

Su Zhang remained where he stood.

His palm closed around a small fragment of silver from the broken hairpin that had fallen earlier.

It lay cold against his skin—cold enough to bite—and he stood motionless for a long while, his expression unreadable.

* * * * *

Su Zhang stood alone by the window of his study.

The deepening dusk filtered through the lattice, scattering uneven shadows across his pale, moon-white robe. Outside, the pear blossoms in the courtyard were in full bloom—clusters of pure white crowding noisily along every branch, an eruption of spring that clashed sharply with the cold stillness surrounding him.

He had never cared for such noisy vitality.

His fingers drifted absently to the inside of his sleeve, brushing against the chilled fragment hidden there—

the broken piece of silver hairpin she had dropped at the street corner.

Its edges were sharp, nearly enough to cut his fingertip. That faint sting anchored him, paradoxically, amid the turmoil he had yet to tame.

"The Su family's dignity… I am not someone to be stepped upon."

Her voice—cool, with a barely perceptible tremor—echoed in his ears as though she still stood before him. He could picture her with unsettling clarity: the slight lift of her chin, the tight line of her lips, those eyes— always striving for calm, yet far too transparent for their own good.

Why had he been angry?

Lowering his gaze, he examined the storm within himself—a storm he had neither anticipated nor welcomed.

It was not because she had contradicted him. He was not so petty.

Nor was it solely because she had provoked Li Suo; the lingering fear remained, yet he believed he could shield those beneath his roof.

So, where had that inexplicable surge of anger come from?

Yes—

it had struck him when she turned away from him, her back straight, her departure resolute, as though he—and the entire Su household—held no claim over her at all.

As though she could sever herself from all of it with one effortless motion.

How could she?

How dare she… appear so ready to walk away?

"Even if I live under the Su roof, I am not someone to be stepped upon."

She had drawn a line—between herself and the Su family.

In her eyes, the name he represented had become something capable of trampling her.

That thought lodged in his chest like a thorn, and a cold, unfamiliar ache spread with it—an emotion he neither wished to name nor knew how to banish.

The realization slid beneath his skin like a cold needle, piercing straight through the composure he relied upon so instinctively.

The Qin Nianyin he remembered had not been like this.

When she first entered the residence a month ago, she had been cautious, soft-spoken—a girl from Jiangnan with lowered eyes and drawn-in shoulders, carrying the timid deference of one living beneath another's eaves.

But somewhere along the way, that obedient shell had fallen away.

What remained was a woman with edges—clear, sharp, impossible to ignore. Her gaze had grown luminous, even cutting, as though it could skewer through any pretense.

The change was too swift. Too abrupt.

As if she had become an entirely different person.

He remembered the moment he had trapped her behind the screen.

In that narrow space, her breath had been startlingly close—warm, uneven, brushing the shell of his ear.

He had felt the tension seize her spine, the way she went rigid like a startled sparrow, ready to bolt at the first opening. And in that instant, there had been no romantic indulgence in his mind, no fanciful speculation.

Instead, it was something far cruder—almost primitive—an urge to confirm that she was there, within reach, unable to flee.

When had he become so… undignified?

When had he begun relying on such near-shameless tactics to keep a woman from slipping beyond his grasp?

"Any need for silver is to be brought to me."

The words had escaped him before thought could intervene. Even he had been momentarily stunned. Since when did Su Zhang offer money—proactively, no less—to maintain a connection?

He had always scorned those who bound others with gold or silk, idle nobles who used wealth to decorate their own emptiness.

Yet in that moment, he had found no better method.

It was as though only by doing so could he strike a crack in the hardened shell she was building around herself.

Only by doing so could he make her ask for something—depend on something—so she would not slip away.

Slip away from the Su household…or slip away from him?

The thought rose like ghost-fire, flickering hot and unsteady, unsettling every breath he took.

He opened his palm.

The fragment of her hairpin lay there, catching the last traces of dusk. It was far from flawless, slightly rough, uneven in craftsmanship.

Yet there was an unmistakable earnestness in its making.

This was her symbol of self-reliance—the wings she was attempting to forge for herself.

He ought to crush it.

He ought to grind that foolish notion beneath his heel and end the absurd impulse before it took deeper root.

But the cold touch of the silver shard pressed against his skin, merging strangely with the fevered heat roiling beneath his ribs.

Ice and ember, burning in the same breath.

He shut his eyes.

Two opposing forces collided violently within his chest.

Reason urged distance—order, restraint, the calm he had always maintained.

But something deeper, more instinctive, more possessive roared in defiance, demanding that he seize this unpredictable force and hold it fast.

To control it.

To keep it close.

To prevent her from ever turning her back and walking away again.

To make her copy texts, grind ink, confine her within the study—

all gestures that appeared to be discipline, that appeared to uphold the dignity of the Su household.

But beneath that veneer… was there something far less righteous at work?

Something he himself refused to name?

Was it simply that he wanted her close?

Nothing more.

Nothing less.

"Nianyin…"

Her name slipped soundlessly from his lips, a faint movement of breath and tongue, yet weighted with a tenderness and conflict he scarcely recognized in himself.

Outside the window, the final trace of daylight was swallowed whole by the descending night.

The study remained unlit, the curtains drawn low. His tall silhouette stood motionless in the darkness. In his palm, a thin fragment of the broken hairpin caught the fading light, its dull gleam reflected in his eyes—restless, contained, and unwilling to settle.

He understood, however unwillingly, that something fundamental had shifted.

Not today. Not merely during the quarrel in the street—but long before.

Perhaps from the moment she stepped into the capital.

Or perhaps from the instant she shed that fragile layer of timidity and stood before him with a clarity and steadiness he had never anticipated.

From that moment onward, the world had begun to tilt, and he—proud of his constancy, certain of his discipline—had been utterly unprepared for the chaos rising within him.

For the quiet disorder tightening its grip.

For this slow, inexorable upheaval that felt less like inconvenience and more like war being waged beneath his ribs.

He remained where he was, swallowed by the darkness. In his palm, the fragment of her hairpin glimmered faintly, the only light left in the room.

Chapter 29: Like My Own Daughter

Leaving the suffocating pressure Su Zhang had cast over her, Qin Nianyin moved swiftly through the covered corridor with Mei following close behind.

Her sole desire was to return to the sanctuary of her small courtyard, to firmly bolt the door, and to painstakingly reassemble the frayed remnants of her composure.

The strained calm she had rigorously imposed on herself during their confrontation was already beginning to dissolve.

What rushed in to fill the vacancy was a deep, pervasive exhaustion that settled right into her bones.

In her previous life, twenty years as his consort—twenty years marked by cold wars, silent tables, and polite salutations that were nothing more than crystallized frost—had long ago rendered her insensible to pain.

But in this unexpected second existence, in only a handful of days, his persistent pressure, his probing gaze, and that vague, unsettling entanglement pressing between them were, somehow, more profoundly depleting than the two decades she had once stoically endured.

Every step felt precariously like treading on wafer-thin ice.

She was forced to constantly defend herself from his meticulous scrutiny, to meticulously conceal every hint of anomaly, and simultaneously to parry that sudden, forceful authority he occasionally deployed—a latent strength that disquieted her far more acutely than his former indifference ever had the capacity to do.

Her thoughts were hopelessly entangled, her heart in profound disarray, when a gentle, welcoming voice arrested her steps.

"Nianyin."

She lifted her head sharply.

Standing at the entrance of the floral pavilion was her aunt, Madam Qin (Qin Huiniang), radiating warmth and serene composure. Two maidservants stood near her, holding precious bolts of richly embroidered satin. Madam Qin's smile conveyed nothing but pure, unadulterated affection.

"Aunt," Qin Nianyin greeted, forcing the wave of internal distress back into a rigid silence as she executed a low, graceful curtsy.

"Come here, child," Madam Qin beckoned, taking her hand with a gesture of genuine, heartfelt connection. "I have just received a shipment of exquisite new Hangzhou silks—the colours are vibrant, and the material is yielding to the touch. I immediately thought to have fresh spring attire tailored for all you young women. Come and inspect them. Tell me which hues appeal to you most."

Before she could articulate a refusal, Madam Qin had already drawn her into the pavilion's warm embrace.

Inside, the air was saturated with a soft fragrance, creating an atmosphere that felt intimate and domestically secure, utterly alien to the icy detachment she had just fled.

Madam Qin guided her towards the comfortable, cushioned couch and began deliberately spreading the luxurious fabric across her lap, smoothing each bolt with a careful, attentive hand. The fine silk brushed lightly against Qin Nianyin's skin, feeling light and restoratively warm, offering a sense of unexpected solace.

"Observe this piece—the blue-green shade enhances your fair complexion. And this apricot yellow; it is such a cheerful, animated colour. Our Nianyin, of course, is flattered by anything she chooses."

Her voice was profoundly tender, her gaze brimming with an open, maternal affection that lacked all reservation.

"Aunt..."

Qin Nianyin felt a sharp constriction in her throat, signalling the imminent threat of tears.

Such unreserved warmth—such open, uncomplicated familial kindness—was precisely what she had craved throughout her entire past life in the Su household, yet had never once been granted.

Now, in this renewed existence, the warmth was tangible, close enough for her to fully absorb. It instantly thawed a part of her spirit that Su Zhang's coldness had ruthlessly frozen rigid mere moments ago.

It felt, for a fleeting instant, as though she were a small, desperately navigating vessel that had finally sighted a quiet, sheltered harbour—a place secure enough to allow her weary soul a moment of profound rest.

A place that dangerously tempted her to discard every layer of caution.

"Silly child, why are you so intent on maintaining such formality?" Madam Qin chuckled softly, the sound melodious and light.

Noticing the distinct shadow of fatigue etched between her brows, she gently repositioned Qin Nianyin and placed her hands firmly upon her shoulders, beginning to massage the tense muscles with the careful, measured pressure only a deeply solicitous elder possessed.

Qin Nianyin closed her eyes, nearly collapsing into the unexpected comfort of the warmth.

Mei, ever perceptive to her mistress's subtle distress, advanced with a cup of hot tea and began to gently pound her legs with practiced, steady hands, further alleviating the acute physical tension that had been tightly coiled inside her.

Madam Qin let out a soft, protracted sigh, her tone heavy with rich emotion.

"If your mother were still living and could witness how beautifully you have matured... she would be immensely proud. I sincerely regard you as my own cherished daughter, child. I only hope that you will be content to remain closely settled here with me. We women could at least provide comfort and companionship to one another."

Her carefully chosen words flowed into Qin Nianyin's troubled heart like a restorative stream of heat, meticulously smoothing over the raw, frayed edges of her sorrow.

Nianyin inclined her head slightly. "I, too, hold Aunt as my true mother."

Hearing this solemn affirmation, Madam Qin's smile deepened noticeably, and her fingers resumed their gentle kneading, their pressure now even lighter and more deliberately soothing than before.

The room settled into a period of tranquil intimacy, the only sound the faint, delicate shhh of silk sliding gently against silk.

But the soothing calm was not destined to endure.

In what appeared to be an innocent shift in conversation, Madam Qin spoke again, her voice dropping into an even softer, more confidential register.

"Speaking of which... Nianyin, what are your personal thoughts regarding your cousin Zhang?"

A sharp, audible clatter instantly followed.

The delicate jade pendant tassel she had been lightly handling slipped completely from her fingers and fell sharply onto the polished, resonant tile floor.

She froze instantly—every muscle in her body became taut—like an individual suddenly plunged into an unforeseen bath of ice water.

Then she jolted upright as if violently struck, spinning around so quickly that her hair momentarily lifted with the motion. Her complexion utterly drained of all colour.

Her voice emerged strained and constricted, edged with a raw panic she could not entirely suppress.

"Aunt must never, ever allow such a thought to take root!"

Her reaction was intensely visceral, so abruptly disproportionate, that Madam Qin and the attending servants stared at her in profound astonishment.

A moment earlier, she had been wrapped safely in delicate maternal affection.

Now, she looked terrifyingly like a cornered young animal, her composure instantly shattered, her eyes wide with a mixture of fear and absolute revulsion—as if her aunt's kind, suggestive inquiry had been a vial of deadly poison deliberately placed into her hands.

Recognizing the devastating loss of control, Qin Nianyin forced herself to draw a slow, deliberate breath.

She lowered her gaze, desperately fighting the frantic, painful hammering of her heart. When she finally spoke again, her voice was low, but its manufactured steadiness was unnaturally rigid, every word selected with painstaking caution.

"Cousin Zhang possesses the formidable bearing of a dragon and a phoenix. His future trajectory is exceedingly bright, and he will, without question, one day be allied with a princess or the daughter of a preeminent noble family. I, who was born to such humble circumstances, consider merely being welcomed into this household by Aunt to be an overwhelming blessing. I would never dare to harbour even the slightest, most inappropriate thought. In this life, my sole objective is to firmly establish my independence and repay Aunt's immense kindness in whatever small measure I can. Nothing more, I assure you."

She spoke rapidly—too rapidly—as if pausing for even a moment would grant fate the opportunity to seize her by the ankle and violently drag her back into the very abyss she had only just escaped.

Each word was deliberately extracted from a chamber of ice, coming out hard, absolute, and devoid of warmth.

She was not merely issuing a response to her aunt.

She was delivering a stringent warning to her own treacherous heart.

A vow, cold and final: she must never, under any circumstances, repeat the mistakes of the past.

That union had not been a marriage in any true sense.

It had been a meticulously gilded tomb—a desolate prison where all her emotion, her innate warmth, and every vestige of hope had slowly, painfully desiccated into dust until nothing remained but profound chill and emptiness.

Su Zhang.

Just the single, isolating thought of that name—Su Zhang—being coupled with the word marriage was enough to send a devastating tide of familiar coldness crashing through her chest.

Cold, desolate nights from her entire previous life.

A rigid, perpetually averted back, straight and utterly unyielding.

A marriage of outward courtesy, hollow and deserted as an abandoned shrine.

An unending emotional wasteland concealed beneath the meticulous veneer of public respectability.

The memories surged forth with overwhelming force, thick, suffocating, and for a terrifying moment, Qin Nianyin found herself utterly unable to draw a steady breath.

The kind smile on Madam Qin's face was utterly frozen in place.

She studied the sudden defensiveness that had sprung up around her posture, and the guarded tension in her eyes.

After a long, strained silence, Madam Qin finally exhaled, the sound a thin, drawn-out sigh of palpable regret.

"It was inexcusably thoughtless of me to suggest it..." she murmured apologetically.

She reached out and gently gathered Nianyin's now-icy hands between her warm palms, patting them softly, as though attempting to physically warm away the terror she had accidentally elicited.

"I only thought... if such an enduring bond could be forged, then we would truly become one indissoluble family. You could reside in this household openly, securely, for the remainder of your days. But it seems... your aunt does not possess that particular fortune."

One family.

The powerful phrase struck her like a sharp needle-prick.

She yearned intensely for family.

She desperately longed for a sense of true belonging.

But if the necessary price of that profound warmth was the surrender of her essential freedom, her sanity, her very sense of self, then the cost was infinitely too great to bear.

She could already see the tragic trajectory with chilling clarity.

If she agreed, she would knowingly step onto another path meticulously paved for her, a route gilded and beautiful in its exterior, yet utterly devoid of genuine warmth—a destiny almost identical to the agonizing one she had endured in her previous life.

She lowered her head, deliberately avoiding Madam Qin's gentle, disappointed gaze. Her voice was soft, yet possessed an unshakeable, quiet certainty.

"It is I who lacks the necessary fortune to accept such immense kindness. The Su household has demonstrated extraordinary generosity towards me, and I will remember it for the rest of my life. But... this particular arrangement must never, under any circumstances, proceed."

The air in the pavilion turned unnervingly still.

The warmth that had so recently filled the room dissipated entirely, leaving behind only a quiet, heavy stillness, like dust settling over a securely sealed, forgotten chamber.

Madam Qin's sigh lingered palpably between them, faint but impossible to overlook.

Qin Nianyin rose to her feet, her movements deeply respectful but imbued with final, absolute resolve.

"If Aunt has no further specific instructions, Nianyin will respectfully take her leave."

Madam Qin watched her intently for a long, searching moment, her lips parting as though she were struggling to utter a final plea.

But in the end, she simply lifted a weary hand, the gesture soft and profoundly defeated.

"Go, child. Rest well."

Qin Nianyin fled the flower hall almost in a rush.

She did not permit herself to slow her pace until she had traversed a considerable distance down the long, covered corridor.

Only when the cold spring wind sharply brushed against her cheeks did the frantic, violent pounding in her chest begin to subside, each ragged breath slowly returning to a semblance of steady rhythm.

Yet the deep fear cloaked in maternal warmth—the sheer terror that had surged beneath Madam Qin's gentle affection—did not dissipate. Instead, it sank deep into the core of her spirit, heavy and immovable as a submerged stone.

She understood with chilling clarity that once certain decisive words were uttered, once a possibility was consciously given life, nothing could ever fully revert to its original, neutral state.

Inside her sleeve, her fingers continued to tremble faintly.

Madam Qin's tenderness was sweetness meticulously laced with subtle poison.

Su Zhang's very existence was a looming descent into a trap she remained acutely aware of—and yet found she could not entirely evade.

Could she truly find lasting security within the confines of this Su household?

The pressing question jabbed painfully against her ribs like a concealed dagger.

If she truly sought freedom—absolute, uncompromised independence— if she wished never again to be shackled by another person's expectations or the remnants of a previous lifetime, then her meticulously planned path to self-sufficiency had to accelerate dramatically.

Much, much faster than she had originally calculated.

She exhaled slowly, attempting to dissipate the intense pressure that continued to build relentlessly in her chest.

Back in the flower hall, Madam Qin watched her departing silhouette with a sigh that carried both immense helplessness and genuine maternal concern. She murmured softly to the elderly attendant standing beside her:

"What a truly excellent child she is. And she and Zhang... they seem well-suited enough. How could she have reacted with such profound vehemence? Is it possible that Zhang has somehow deeply offended her, without our knowledge?"

The experienced attendant dared not hazard a reply.

Madam Qin only shook her head once more, troubled and utterly unable to reconcile the profound, defensive distance she had just witnessed in the young girl's eyes.

Chapter 30: The Iron Tree Blooms

The Study: A Fateful Counsel

The lamplight flickered gently in the study, and a heavy atmosphere settled over the pervasive silence.

Upon Su Zhang's return to the residence, a servant immediately reported that Gu Xiao had been waiting for him in the study for a considerable time.

The moment he stepped into the room, he observed Gu Xiao seated casually, pouring himself tea, his posture relaxed.

Gu Xiao's tone was light, yet he came straight to the point: "Guess what I stumbled upon? I went to see the Empress this morning and overheard a few pieces of idle gossip."

"Indeed," Su Zhang acknowledged with a slight nod, offering no further questions.

Gu Xiao hooked a long, slender finger and pointed directly at him. "You are not going to ask what it was?"

Su Zhang settled into his chair, picked up a volume of writings from his desk, and leisurely began to turn the pages, adopting an unhurried, attentive posture.

His manner clearly communicated: Speak if you wish, or be swift about your departure if you do not.

Gu Xiao immediately conceded the battle. In terms of composed composure and reserved temperament, he readily admitted he could not match the gravity of this Tanhua scholar.

He then proceeded to relay the entirety of the rumour he had heard that day. "It is said that the Second Princess has petitioned the Emperor repeatedly in recent days, seeking an imperial decree for marriage—to you."

Su Zhang's fingertip paused. He gently set the scroll aside, his gaze revealing neither surprise nor pleasure: "What was the Emperor's final decision?"

Gu Xiao shook his head. "He has not yet given his consent, but in my estimation, he will likely not be able to delay granting the marriage between you and the Second Princess for much longer."

Su Zhang remained silent, his fingers tapping soundlessly on the desktop as he sank into deep contemplation.

This intelligence was neither entirely unexpected nor completely foreseen.

Seeing his friend's silence, Gu Xiao curved his lips into a smile, which held a degree of self-satisfaction: "This information was privately released by the Empress herself. She intimated that the Emperor has always regarded the Second Princess's marriage as critically important, and if the Crown Prince's succession encounters instability, it is highly likely that he will use you as a strategic counter-piece."

He finished speaking with an expression that clearly demanded praise.

Su Zhang merely offered a calm, unconcerned reply: "My thanks for your trouble."

"Ha, you truly lack appreciation! And here I am, having rushed straight from the palace to deliver this news." He was utterly vexed by Su Zhang's perpetually unflappable, composed demeanour.

The two of them, along with others, had served as the Crown Prince's study companions since childhood. Boys were naturally prone to mischief, yet Su Zhang had consistently maintained this air of a senior scholar, which was thoroughly disheartening to his peers.

Su Zhang glanced sideways at him, a faint, wry smile touching his lips: "Are you so eager to relay this information today because you fear I will become the Imperial Son-in-Law and steal your thunder before the Crown Prince?"

Gu Xiao was momentarily stunned, then scoffed: "Don't be absurd. If you truly marry the Second Princess, I fear your prestige will not even begin to rise before your destiny is entirely manipulated by the Imperial Family. I am here to save your life, my friend."

Su Zhang allowed himself a rare, soft laugh, his refined appearance enhanced by a touch of cultured elegance.

This unexpected display of amusement caused Gu Xiao to marvel: "What extraordinary good fortune has occurred before my arrival today, that it has managed to crack this millennium of ice surrounding you?"

Su Zhang gave his friend a warning look. "Do not speak nonsense."

"Seriously, observing your refined, handsome appearance, never mind the Second Princess, if I had been born a woman, I would probably fight fiercely for you myself."

"If you continue with this foolish talk, I shall have you removed," Su Zhang retorted, his smile fading, quickly resuming his solemn air.

"Very well, I shall cease my jests. My true purpose in coming today is because..." He paused, his tone becoming serious. "Zi Jun, you must think this through clearly. A marriage to a Princess is not a matter of private affection; it is a critical piece on the Imperial chessboard. If you make a misstep, you will not be the one placing the move; you will be the piece being moved."

At this, Su Zhang could not help but cast a glance of profound disdain at his friend.

Did he truly believe he needed this advice?

Su Zhang lowered his eyes, remaining silent for a moment. After a pause, he spoke in a measured tone: "If the situation is indeed as you describe, but I am entirely unwilling to be positioned in that move, how can I withdraw from the game?"

Gu Xiao regarded him intently for a long period, then shook his head and offered a complex smile: "If you truly hold a strong aversion to this course, you will likely need another person—one for whom you would risk Imperial displeasure rather than obey the decree."

Perhaps that is the result the opposing faction truly desires.

If Su Zhang incurred the Emperor's disfavour over this matter, the Crown Prince's party would naturally lose a significant source of support.

A weighty silence descended upon the study following this stark pronouncement. The lamplight reflected a momentary flicker of profound emotion in Su Zhang's eyes. His gaze deepened, and he finally responded in a low voice: "If the situation truly escalates to that point... I can only destroy this entire chessboard with my own hands."

Gu Xiao offered a characteristic, playful smirk: "You remain admirably calm. That is easily said. But do you possess a concrete strategy yet?"

Su Zhang gave him a brief look, his tone unhurried but distinctly unwilling to elaborate further. "The water will flow where the channel is prepared. A solution will naturally present itself."

Gu Xiao frowned, then subtly shifted the subject, the laughter completely vanishing from his face as he spoke: "The General Who Guards the Nation departed for the Northern Frontier yesterday."

As he spoke, his voice changed, and a rare, intense fire ignited in his eyes: "I hear that last time on the Northern Frontier, the situation was extremely perilous. He swept through the enemy lines single-handedly—that is truly... exhilarating!"

Su Zhang's lips curved faintly. He offered no reply, merely listening quietly.

Gu Xiao suddenly clenched his fist, his gaze becoming clouded with disappointment: "I, too, wished to join the campaign this time, to personally earn distinction... Unfortunately, the Empress prevented me. She claimed that I am the last remaining member of the Gu family and cannot be put at risk."

With that, he let out a cold laugh, abruptly shaking his half-sleeve vigorously, as if attempting to shake off his mounting frustration: "Protecting me like this, they have only succeeded in protecting me into uselessness."

Su Zhang watched him for a long moment, his tone entirely placid: "The glorious achievements of your father and brothers are remembered by all. Your aunt, the Empress, merely wishes to preserve your life."

Gu Xiao laughed coldly: "But if life is preserved without purpose, how does that differ from a caged beast? Tell me, Zi Jun, you must not become confined like me, trapped in a golden cage, only able to sit and await the will of fate."

His primary reason for rushing straight from the palace was this very concern: he did not want Su Zhang to be shackled by a Princess, finding himself unable to advance in court and unable to realize his lifelong ambition.

His eyes grew sharp and heavy. He shifted his meaning, injecting a note of clear warning: "The political situation is unstable. If you truly marry the Princess without gaining tangible power to solidify your position, even your esteemed Shen family will inevitably be dragged into the political mire."

Su Zhang was silent for a brief interval, a thread of coldness suddenly tracing the line of his lips: "I thank you for today's disclosure."

He paused, then his voice dropped to a low murmur, a flicker of an emotion difficult to decipher surfacing in his eyes: "Furthermore, if I already have a person I care for, and I truly marry the Princess, should I then be expected to surrender my beloved to another?"

"What? A beloved?" Gu Xiao was momentarily stunned, then turned to look at him with a knowing, half-amused expression: "Did I hear that correctly? There is someone that even you, Minister Su, cannot put aside?"

Su Zhang's brow furrowed slightly. In a rare moment of candour, he replied in a subdued voice: "There is such a person."

"What noble family does this young lady belong to?" Gu Xiao was thoroughly astonished, his friend's frankness igniting an immense curiosity.

Had the thousand-year-old iron tree finally flowered?

After a pause, Su Zhang looked out the window where the lamplight flickered, his gaze profound: "We are still in the preliminary stages. Until the final moment, it is best not to disclose certain matters."

Gu Xiao could scarcely believe what he was hearing. Was there truly a beauty in the capital that Minister Su could not immediately win over?

"Who in the world is this miraculous person?" His curiosity was reaching a fever pitch.

"The walls have ears. I will tell you the details when the time is right."

Gu Xiao understood the implied caution and wisely refrained from asking further questions.

It was entirely possible that spies from the palace frequented the residence. If the identity of the woman were revealed, certain factions might take adverse action against her.

Gu Xiao let out an impressed "Tsk," then remarked: "I never realized you were capable of such deep affection."

So fiercely secretive, like a protective parent.

His voice was laced with teasing, yet a flash of genuine respect appeared in his eyes: "It is true, if this person exists, you must protect her even more carefully, ensuring she does not become a casualty in the court's power games."

Su Zhang quietly gripped his teacup, offering a slight nod: "That is certainly my intention."

Chapter 31: Embodying the Imperial Will

The following morning, within the East Warming Pavilion of the Taiji Hall, coils of rich amber-coloured smoke drifted slowly from a gilded beast-shaped incense burner. The heavy, lingering scent of dragon-musk permeated the air, lending the chamber a solemn, almost oppressive stillness.

Emperor Xuanwen reclined against a brocaded couch, his eyes half-shut as he listened to the memorial being recited aloud.

Before him stood Wen Cong, Minister of Revenue, his posture appropriately deferential and his head bowed. A senior eunuch waited at the side, utterly silent and motionless, like a statue carved of pale jade.

"...Your Majesty," Wen Cong began, his voice steady despite the beads of perspiration that had begun to gather visibly at his temples, "His Highness the Crown Prince and His Highness the Second Prince have jointly concluded their preliminary review of the case concerning the missing funds allocated for the Jiangnan river embankment works. A comprehensive picture is now beginning to take shape."

A faint sound escaped Emperor Xuanwen in slow acknowledgment, yet his expression revealed absolutely nothing of his thoughts. "Continue."

"Yes, Your Majesty."

Wen Cong swallowed hard, struggling to maintain his composure.

"According to the cross-examination of the Ministry of Works' documents and the ledger records maintained by our Ministry of Revenue, thirty thousand taels were allocated last year for the project. Of that substantial sum, approximately five thousand taels remain entirely unaccounted for. The accounts were prepared with extraordinary deceit; without painstakingly comparing multiple documents, the discrepancy would have been nearly impossible to detect."

The Emperor's eyes snapped fully open. A shard of cold, penetrating light flickered there, sharp enough to cause Wen Cong's heart to give a violent jolt.

After a long, measured breath, that sharp glint receded.

"How coincidental," the Emperor murmured, his voice returning to its characteristic, serene calm. "Speak further on this matter."

Wen Cong bowed even lower in deference.

"Of the missing total, three thousand taels passed directly through the hands of the former river inspector, Liu Mingyuan. That man, however, died suddenly of illness last month. The remaining two thousand, evidence strongly suggests, may lead to an Assistant Administrator serving under the Zhejiang Provincial Administration Office. The proof remains incomplete at this stage. His Highness the Crown Prince advises delaying any overt move, so as not to prematurely alert the involved parties."

"Died of sudden illness?"

The Emperor's tone remained remarkably mild, yet the chilling undercurrent of his words seemed to drop the temperature of the entire chamber.

He said nothing further regarding that specific demise. Instead, his voice shifted, becoming almost conversational.

"The spring floods in Jiangnan will commence shortly. The old embankments remain desperately fragile, and the new funds have yet to be officially released. The Crown Prince demands the immediate allocation of money, while the Second Prince demands a thorough investigation. Both stood before Us yesterday, arguing until their faces were flushed crimson and their voices were utterly hoarse."

He tapped a single finger on the edge of the couch. "Wen, you oversee the Empire's entire purse. What is the counsel you would offer Us?"

The question was deceptively simple in its formulation, yet Wen Cong felt a suffocating tightness immediately seize his chest.

He answered slowly, with the utmost caution and precise articulation.

"Your Majesty, I believe the integrity of the embankments must be stabilized as an immediate priority. The safety of the common people cannot, under any circumstances, be jeopardized. Yet, if the corrupt officials responsible remain unpunished, even newly allocated funds may vanish like mud sinking irrevocably into the river. Therefore, the essential repair work and the covert investigation should proceed simultaneously, without delay."

He hesitated perceptibly. "There is… one critical matter to consider further."

"Speak."

"A singularly trustworthy official must be dispatched immediately to Jiangnan. This individual must possess the capability to meticulously oversee the repair efforts, ensuring all funds are used for the populace, while concurrently continuing the covert investigation into the shortfall. This person must possess a deep understanding of administrative affairs, must not fear challenging the entrenched power of regional officials, and, crucially, must remain politically neutral aligned with neither the Crown Prince's nor the Second Prince's factions." The words were spoken with extreme care, yet the meaning was unequivocally clear—the Minister must be an independent operator.

The chamber fell into an utter, profound stillness. Only the delicate smoke of the incense continued to sway in the silence.

The Emperor tapped the couch again, the rhythm deep, unhurried, and regular, like the muffled beat of a distant drum. Wen Cong silently counted the beats, knowing full well this deliberate cadence meant His Majesty was meticulously weighing the grave matter.

After a long, protracted pause, the Emperor asked,

"And whom does Wen, in his wisdom, have in mind for this perilous assignment?"

Wen Cong had thoroughly anticipated this specific query. He still feigned a brief moment of intense deliberation before offering his reply.

"There is one candidate whom I would humbly put forward, though his experience in major administrative matters is admittedly shallow."

"Name him."

"The newly appointed Langzhong of the Ministry of Personnel's Selection Office—Su Zhang."

The rhythmic tapping ceased immediately, cutting the silence.

Wen Cong rushed to elaborate further.

"Though Langzhong Su Zhang is young, he ranked as a Tanhua in the Imperial Examination. His scholarly aptitude is exceptionally sharp, and his personal conduct is rigorously upright. He is widely regarded as a man of impeccable, jade-like integrity.

The Su family has historically maintained a stance of complete neutrality, entirely uninvolved in factional disputes. Sending him would, therefore, invite the fewest suspicions from any contending side.

Furthermore, the Ministry of Personnel naturally maintains supervisory ties with all provincial administrations. For him to inspect the river works as a Langzhong is perfectly aligned with his official duties and entirely above board."

He paused deliberately, then added the weightiest sentence of his argument:

"And—this is critically important—Langzhong Su Zhang holds personal acquaintance with both the Crown Prince and the Second Prince. Not favouritism, but simple acquaintance. His appointment, more effectively than anyone else's, would clearly manifest Your Majesty's true, impartial intent."

The moment those carefully chosen words fell, the atmosphere within the hall shifted almost imperceptibly.

Between the Crown Prince and the Second Prince, power already hung in a precarious, dangerous balance; what Emperor Xuanwen required now was a solitary minister—one who was neither partisan nor unduly beholden to anyone.

The Emperor remained profoundly silent for a long period. His gaze passed idly through the beaded curtain, drifting toward the distant, obscured reaches of the palace grounds, as though he were looking beyond the high walls at that calm, clear-featured young official.

On the day of the palace examination, the strokes of Su Zhang's brush had thundered with the spirit of wind and storm, his talent unmistakable and formidable.

Assigning him to the Bureau of Selections had been intended as a period of refinement. Sending him to Jiangnan now would either temper his character into resilient steel or ruthlessly break him upon the political field.

"Su Zhang…" The Emperor repeated the name under his breath, his tone impossible to read. "It seems this man has encountered quite a few… 'fortuitous happenings' lately?"

Wen Cong's heart gave a faint, nervous jolt. He could not discern whether His Majesty referred to the recent chance encounter with the Third Prince in the marketplace, or to the persistent rumours that the Second Princess intended to propose marriage. He could only respond with cautious ambiguity.

"Langzhong Su Zhang is exceptionally diligent and upholds justice, Your Majesty. He has never once overstepped his station. As for idle gossip circulating in the city… it is hardly reliable evidence."

Emperor Xuanwen offered no verbal response. He merely closed his eyes, his voice sinking into a low, measured murmur.

"We shall observe the situation for a few more days."

The curling smoke of the dragon-musk incense rolled upward like slow, invisible tides, gradually enveloping the entire warm pavilion in a cloud of oppressive fragrance.

* * * * *

Two full quarters of an hour had elapsed, yet Qin Nianyin remained perfectly motionless, her gaze fixed intently on the heavy brick of gold lying squarely on the table before her. She had not uttered a single word.

The ingot sat solid and square, its brilliant yellow glow catching the lamplight, gleaming with a clarity that seemed capable of reflecting the deepest avarice hidden within a person's heart.

Her arms were folded tightly before her chest. Her brows were furrowed ever so slightly, and her lips were pressed into a tense, unyielding line. She looked as though she stood paralyzed at the fork of an impossibly difficult choice.

Mei propped her cheeks in both hands and leaned in closer, her eyes round with open astonishment.

"Miss, heavens above—I have never seen a single piece of gold this immense in my entire life!"

She reached out with exaggerated care, only to violently jerk her hand back the instant her fingertips brushed against the cold metal, as though the ingot had literally scalded her skin.

"If—if we took this down to the shops to exchange for silver, we could probably afford to open three entire stores! Three!"

Qin Nianyin did not reply immediately. She let out a quiet, subdued breath, her voice low and edged with calm weariness.

"It is gold, yes. But it is not enough to purchase three stores. And in this world, no gold is ever given without a heavy price exacted in return."

Her tone was gentle, yet it carried a profound weight forged from an entire past life—one irrefutable truth she had learned at enormous cost: nothing of value was truly free. Every perceived boon ultimately demanded a dear sacrifice.

Mei blinked slowly, then muttered in a small voice, "But… it is still gold…"

Seeing Mei's wide-eyed, absolute innocence, Qin Nianyin could only sigh inwardly. It was no fault of the girl. Had she herself did not live an entire lifetime in the very heights of power, she too might have believed this single ingot of gold represented sudden, boundless fortune.

She remained silent for another long moment. Her gaze lowered to the ingot once more, her eyes gradually darkening with thought. Thoughts twisted and circled relentlessly, threading through past memories and future cautions, until she finally seemed to settle upon an absolute decision.

At last, she reached out and briefly brushed her palm over the gold's surface. The metal felt faintly warm beneath her skin, and a strange heat rose abruptly within her chest—a complex mixture of firm resolve and something far more fragile, harder to accurately name.

In her previous life, such a modest amount of money would not have swayed her at all. She would have dismissed it without a second glance.

But now—now the circumstances were entirely different.

Now, this ingot represented the very first capital she possessed since she had stepped into her second life. Something wholly, unequivocally her own.

"Mei!" she suddenly straightened her posture, her expression tightening with profound clarity. "We really must think this through. Should we not start by looking immediately for a place to rent?"

Mei nodded so vigorously her head bobbed, eager and breathless with barely contained excitement. Yet before Mei could utter another word, Qin Nianyin's resolve suddenly fractured. Her shoulders slumped; her brows tightened painfully as she let out a soft, defeated sigh.

"Come. I... I will go and beg him."

The mistress and servant had barely followed the covered corridor through several turns before they reached the exterior of Su Zhang's study. A warm, yellow light glowed through the lattice window, and the very moment Qin Nianyin saw it, the determination she had so painstakingly mustered shattered once again.

"Miss?" Mei blinked in confusion when her mistress suddenly came to an abrupt halt.

Inside, the lamplight still burned steady. Su Zhang sat absorbed at his desk, deep in his work, the light pooling around him like a quiet, reflective river. It washed over the calm, straight line of his brows, rendering his expression as composed and distantly handsome as ever.

That particular sight struck Qin Nianyin with unexpected, painful force—

Just like in the last life… in the moment when she had been at her absolute lowest, he had sat beneath this very same kind of lamplight yet had not once lifted his eyes to look at her.

Her feet rooted themselves to the ground as if they were physically nailed there. Her chest tightened sharply, an intense, breathless pressure blooming beneath her ribs. One single word from him might open a potential path for Xu Wencai—it might even save his entire future.

But she understood all too well the devastating implications of such a formal pledge.

It was not merely a simple favour owed; she would be intentionally placing her dignity and pride directly into his hands, allowing him to turn it over, inspect its worth, and weigh it as he pleased.

Mei looked timidly toward the half-open door, her voice barely above a whisper.

"Miss… will you still go in?"

Qin Nianyin offered no answer. She held the small pouch of gold tightly, her fingers pressing so hard that the edges of the ingot bit painfully into her palm. Firelight flickered through the corridor, in its trembling, fragile glow, a faint, stinging ache rose from somewhere deep inside her heart. She drew a slow, deliberate breath and finally forced her gaze away from the brightly lit doorway.

"…Mei, return to your room first. Allow me to consider this properly for a little while."

"Yes, Miss."

Chapter 32: Becoming Entangled

The night wind carried a faint chill, setting the corridor lamps trembling, their flames wavering as shadows swayed like drifting thoughts. Qin Nianyin stood before the study door, her sleeves lifted lightly by the passing breeze. The hour for tea had long since passed, yet she had not taken a single step inside.

She had already rehearsed her words countless times in her mind—how she should respond if he met her with cold sarcasm or sharp questioning; how she ought to begin if he greeted her with silence. Yet in the end, no amount of preparation could overcome the hesitation and quiet dread that bound her in place now.

The lamplight dimmed slightly. Su Zhang remained seated beneath it, his brow faintly drawn, his expression unchanged from the past.

Suddenly, she felt it—every plea she had ever made of him, every moment of concern, every offer of assistance, each one like a fine thread pulling her backward, drawing her step by step toward those years she could no longer bear to face.

She refused to be dragged back.

Xu Wencai was not hers to bear. If she begged for him today, for whom would she beg tomorrow? Pitiful people were never few.

If she could not release this fragile impulse toward kindness, she would eventually be bound hand and foot by sentiment, worn down by obligation and unable to move forward.

The thought steadied her. She exhaled softly and turned to leave.

The gold remained clenched in her palm. Her fingers were white at the joints, yet she felt no pain.

She walked forward until she stood before the carved vermilion door.

A thin streak of candlelight seeped through the gap and the stillness inside pressed against her like a tightening net, drawing her breath taut by inches.

Her fingers lifted ——only an inch from the door.

In that suspended moment, even her breath halted. She almost knocked.

Almost.

But just before her fingertip fell, an inexplicable hesitation rose from the depths of her chest ——as if a gentle hand pressed down upon hers from behind. Her heart sank sharply; her fingers trembled and at last she drew her hand back.

She lowered her arm and turned away. Her sleeves brushed the shadows before the door without a sound.

She departed lightly, quietly, without disturbing anything. The lamplight in the study remained steady. Everything appeared unchanged, as though no one had ever stood outside.

Only at the far end of the corridor, within a stretch of dim shadow, did a tall, lean figure stand watching her retreating silhouette in silence, his gaze deep and unreadable.

Su Zhang withdrew his eyes and returned to his desk. His brush had never ceased moving—yet at the very next stroke, it faltered.

He had known she was outside the entire time. She had lingered for so long… and still left without saying a single word.

Lowering his gaze, he slowly ran his fingertips along the brush shaft. He did not realize his grip had tightened until a fine crack split across the bamboo.

The faint rustle of her sleeves brushing against the stone floor seemed to linger beside his ear, each soft sound stretching the night longer and darker.

It had been nothing more than her back turning away, yet it cut more sharply than any spoken refusal.

The wavering flame cast a slanted shadow across the documents on his table—like a cold blade slicing into the centre of his chest, inch by inch.

The curve of his lips thinned, cooling into something faint and restrained.

"In the end, you left after all," he said softly. "Afraid of being bound to me?"

That night, the study glowed with a quiet, wan light. The window paper had yellowed slightly with age. Su Zhang remained bent over the desk, the strokes of his brush smooth and swift, yet a heavy weight settled between his brows.

"What exactly are you hiding from me?" he murmured, his voice low and hoarse. The smile at his lips was shallow and cold mockery, perhaps, but also… disappointment.

He summoned his attendant, Yefeng, in a tone that was not loud, yet carried a firm, undeniable steadiness.

"Tomorrow, go make discreet inquiries with the maid serving the young cousin. Find out whether she has faced any trouble recently."

"…Yes."

Yefeng blinked, momentarily taken aback. Though he did not understand the reason behind the command, he still answered with proper respect.

"Remember ——do not arouse suspicion."

"Yes, young master."

Yefeng bowed and withdrew. As he stepped back into the corridor, he could not help letting a quiet thought slip across his mind: Since when has the young master begun paying such close attention to that cousin, who has always been distant and polite to a fault?

He, after all, had never bothered with his own legitimate sister beyond basic courtesy. Never a single unnecessary word, never a hint of sentiment.

By the hour of Wei (1-3pm) the next day, the sky was clear, the sunlight warm and steady.

In the rear courtyard of the Su household, the apricot blossoms had only recently fallen. Pale petals lay scattered in soft layers across the stone path. A passing breeze stirred them lightly, carrying a faint sweetness through the air.

Yefeng walked in through the small side gate, humming a carefree tune, a paper-wrapped parcel of sugar cakes swinging lazily from his hand. Just as expected, he ran into Mei—who was carefully carrying a basket filled with rose-petal water.

"Oh my, Miss Mei ——what a perfect coincidence."

He quickly stepped aside to clear the path, the corners of his eyes curving with a warm, easy smile.

"Look at me ——another half-step and I would have dropped all this sugar cake."

Mei steadied her basket. Seeing it was him, she smiled cheerfully and gave him a polite curtsey.

"Brother Ye. Working so hard, even in this heat?"

Yefeng lifted the paper parcel slightly.

"The kitchen just made a fresh batch of osmanthus sugar cakes. I'm taking some to the stewards as a treat ——and brought two pieces for myself while I was at it."

As he spoke, his gaze casually swept over the basket in her hands. The pale red petals caught his eye. He leaned in slightly and inhaled.

"Ah ——sun-dried rose petals? What are you making with these, Miss Mei?"

"For my lady's hand and face wash," Mei answered brightly. She seemed in unusually good spirits. "She can't stay under the sun and the petals soften the skin."

Yefeng blinked and spoke in an idle, conversational tone.

"So particular? Why not buy Jade Skin Cream outright? All the highborn young ladies in the capital use that."

Mei paused. A faint sigh escaped her as she lowered her voice.

"That Jade Skin Cream costs a great deal. Too much silver for us. Besides… this method was taught by the former Madam…"

Her voice trailed off. Her lips moved, as though she meant to add something, but halfway through she seemed to realize the impropriety of her own words. Her eyes lowered at once. She swallowed the rest.

Yefeng caught the shift instantly. His expression did not change as he asked,

"The former Madam… was she very fond of your lady?"

Mei had intended to brush the question aside. But the moment the topic was touched, something warm and painful stirred in her chest, stirring up memories that had long settled into silence. She could not hold it back.

"Fond? Of course she was." Her voice softened into something fragile. "Though my lady was adopted, Madam raised her as if she were her own flesh and blood. Every day, she chose her meals herself, selected her fabrics, and whenever she had a spare moment, she taught her to read and to write… Even this method of preparing flower water came from Madam. In those days, who in the household did not praise how carefully and delicately my lady was raised?"

Her voice dimmed as she went on.

"But after the flood… everyone who cherished her was gone. Nothing like now ——this residence feels so cold, so empty…"

Yefeng let out a faint, sympathetic sigh.

"Ah… then the young cousin is truly a pitiful one."

"Compared to others, my lady and I were already fortunate. During last year's flood… the streets were filled with cries, corpses piled like hills… many entire families didn't survive."

"Oh? That tragic?"

Yefeng widened his eyes with deliberate exaggeration, playing the part naturally.

Before Mei could continue, she abruptly stopped. A flicker of alarm crossed her face; she lowered her head in a hurry, as if trying to push her own words back into her throat.

"I ——I spoke nonsense. Brother, don't take it to heart."

Yefeng lowered his gaze slightly, studying her expression. His voice remained gentle, warm as ever.

"What nonsense? Your lady is kind hearted and carries herself with dignity. Someone ought to cherish her."

Mei's cheeks flushed a soft red. She mumbled a vague reply and dipped her head.

"I should go back. My lady still needs me."

Yefeng smiled, watching her figure recede along the garden path. Once she disappeared around the bend, his expression shifted—the light fading, shadow settling in its place. He replayed every word she had heard, committing each detail carefully to memory.

The sky darkened by degrees. One by one, the lamps in the study were lit, their glow flickering softly against the papered windows.

Quiet as a shadow, Yefeng slipped back into Su Zhang's study and bowed deeply.

"Reporting to Young Master: it is just as we suspected. Xu Wencai is a failed scholar. The young cousin encountered him by chance along the roadside, saw that he was destitute, and took pity on him. But… she never came to seek your assistance."

Su Zhang's brush paused for barely a breath—the faintest hesitation— yet even that fleeting break revealed something beneath the surface. A glint passed through his eyes before he replied in an even, unreadable tone.

"I see."

After a long silence, he murmured,

"Anything more?"

Yefeng rubbed the back of his neck, hesitating before speaking.

"Mei said that in the Qin household, the late Madam treated the young cousin exceedingly well. Though she was not her birth daughter, Madam raised her as one—perhaps even more tenderly than most would their own. Not like here, in the Su residence, where she is… ah… rather restrained."

"Is that so?" Su Zhang's voice was low and calm, impossible to read.

Restrained?

The single word flickered through Yefeng's mind, but he did not dare pursue it. The atmosphere in the room felt subtly altered—quiet, cool, yet faintly weighted. He immediately lowered his head, standing as still as stone.

The lamp flame swayed gently. Ink continued flowing across the memorial drafts beneath Su Zhang's hand, each stroke smooth and disciplined.

Only the slight furrow between his brows betrayed that his thoughts had already drifted far away ——carried off by something he could not ignore, something that continued to tug at him despite himself.

Chapter 33: A Small Favour

Evening had just begun to settle when Qin Nianyin received word that Su Zhang wished to see her.

The message was delivered with a level of formality she had not anticipated and as she made her way along the covered corridor toward the study, a quiet unease tightened in her chest.

The air carried a faint coolness, and each footstep seemed to echo louder than usual against the stone tiles, as though urging her toward something unknown.

Inside the study, the lamps had already been lit. Their warm glow stretched across shelves stacked with scrolls and documents, yet the light did little to soften the atmosphere.

Su Zhang sat behind the long desk, his posture straight, his head slightly bent as he wrote. His brush moved with steady, assured ease ——each stroke fluid, decisive, a rhythm too calm to read.

The lamplight outlined the sharp line of his cheek, casting a cold silhouette across the room.

Qin Nianyin stood at the threshold for a beat too long before speaking.

"Cousin?" Her voice barely disrupted the silence.

The sun had nearly dipped below the horizon and only a short time ago Yefeng had come personally to summon her.

She had followed without question, though her heart had tightened with every passing moment.

What does he intend this time? Another rebuke? Another reminder of the distance between us?

Su Zhang did not respond immediately. Instead, the brush in his hand paused mid-stroke. The faintest tremor of stillness settled over the room before he finally raised his gaze.

"I heard," he said, his tone as cool as the light glancing off the inkstone, "that you rescued a scholar on the road a few days ago."

The words struck her sharply ——too sharply.

"Ah?"

Her composure slipped for an instant, a flicker of unease revealing itself before she forced her features back under control. "How… how did you hear of such a trivial matter, Cousin?"

A subtle curve formed at the corner of his mouth, though it held no mirth ——more a shadow of thought than a smile.

"Acts of kindness have their way of being noticed."

"It wasn't anything worth mentioning," she said quickly. "I simply saw someone in distress. He was penniless, had missed the examination, had been turned out of the inn and he was ill… so I asked a physician to tend to him. That was all."

Su Zhang set the brush down with deliberate precision.

"Oh? I was told you also sent Mei with the silver you carried ——and had clothes and meals prepared for him. That is not what I would call a small gesture."

Her fingers curled inward, clutching the fabric of her sleeves. Her breath faltered, though she forced a strained smile.

"That man… he was pitiful. It was nothing more than a chance encounter. I simply felt unable to look away."

His gaze sharpened ——quiet but incisive ——before he repeated her words, softer and more dangerous than before.

"Unable to look away?"

Her lashes trembled. She turned her eyes aside, voice thinning.

"It was just a small favour…"

"A small favour?"

He leaned back slightly, the faintest shadow settling into his features.

"You nearly emptied your entire purse for a stranger. Does that still qualify as small?"

The reprimand was not loud, not harsh, yet it landed like cold water sinking into her bones. Her throat tightened and the words forming on her tongue scattered helplessly.

"What is his name?" he asked.

The question sliced through the room with unsettling clarity. Her heart thudded painfully, each beat echoing against her ribs. Her grip tightened until her knuckles whitened.

"…Xu Wencai," she whispered at last.

The name, once spoken so often in her past life with indifference, emerged now with an unfamiliar weight. In that former life, even as husband and wife, they had remained distant. He had always been restrained, courteous, measured. Certainly, never like the man before her now: never pressing, never revealing ripples beneath the surface.

She found herself momentarily unsteady beneath the force of it.

"Xu Wencai," Su Zhang repeated softly, tasting each syllable, as though committing it to memory or marking it.

Silence fell once more. The lamplight

flickered, stretching their shadows long across the floor. The weight of the unspoken settled between them like a thin, invisible veil ——one he had no intention of lifting and one she was afraid to touch.

Qin Nianyin held her breath, her chest rising and falling in small, uneven tremors, as if bracing herself for the reprimand she believed would fall at any moment. Yet Su Zhang merely looked at her, calm to the point of indifference and said,

"Do you understand the situation you are in?"

The quiet severity of the words stunned her. Before she could stop herself, her eyes lifted to his.

"The silver you have," he continued, tone mild but every syllable landing with the weight of iron, "And the future you rely upon, neither is secure. If you truly intend to live with clarity, then stop exhausting yourself for people who have nothing to do with you."

Her lips parted with a faint tremor. A protest gathered in her throat, yet the moment she tried to speak, something inside tightened painfully, forcing the sound back down. Her chest felt uncomfortably constricted.

Su Zhang did not give her the chance to argue.

"As for Xu Wencai, I will make arrangements. But remember ——do not take such matters into your own hands again."

She stared at him in silence, emotions tangled ——surprise, frustration, confusion and something she dared not name. None of it found its way to her tongue.

"I said I will handle it."

He lowered his gaze again, picking up his brush, the stroke sharp and cold against the paper.

"In the future, whatever you encounter ——pass it through me first."

The dismissal was clear. Qin Nianyin pressed her trembling fingers into her sleeves, bowed her head and withdrew. She kept her steps steady, though her heart felt anything but.

Inside the study, the lamplight did not flicker. It held steady, casting a sharp glow over Su Zhang's desk. His fingers tapped against the wood once, twice ——measured, controlled ——before he spoke.

"Yefeng."

The attendant stepped inside at once, lowering his head. "Young master."

"Investigate Xu Wencai. His origins, background, teacher, current circumstances. I want results quickly."

"Yes."

Yefeng hesitated, his eyes flickering upward as though he wished to say more. But the moment he saw the young master's expression ——calm, distant, utterly untouched by emotion ——his voice stilled.

"Understood."

Neither master nor servant noticed the presence lingering in the shadows of the far corridor.

Leaning against the red-painted railing, Su Wan watched from a distance as Qin Nianyin stepped out of the study. Her gaze was cool, unreadable, following the graceful silhouette until it joined Mei.

The two walked together through the slanted shade of blooming branches, exchanging a few soft words and quiet laughter.

Su Wan's lips lifted in a faint, icy curve.

There it was. Sisterly affection? Mutual kindness? Nothing but a mask. Running to the study every few days ——was that not merely an excuse? All under the guise of "familial closeness," yet clearly meant to cling to a man who had never liked letting anyone near him since childhood.

* * * * *

The small courtyard was enclosed by sparse bamboo, their slender shadows swaying over a pool dark as ink. A light pavilion stood at the centre; its four sides draped with thin gauze.

When the breeze brushed through, the lamplight behind the veil wavered and stretched into a golden apricot-shaped glow.

Li Jing sat on the eastern side, a porcelain tea cup held delicately between her fingers. Her fingertips traced the rim in absent circles and the faint shade at her eyes seemed paler than the night itself.

Footsteps approached ——soft, unhurried.

The gauze lifted slightly, revealing Li Suo entering with his hands clasped behind his back. The night wind still clung to his robes, bringing with it a faint, cooling edge. A lazy, effortless smile played across his brows.

"You're a little slow tonight, Third Brother."

Li Jing raised her eyes at him, her tone half playful, half reproachful.

Li Suo took the seat opposite her. He pointed casually at the tea cup in front of him.

"Go on then. What did you call me here for?"

Li Jing did not circle around the matter. She leaned forward, lowering her voice.

"I want a way to win Su Zhang."

Outside the pavilion, bamboo leaves rustled against one another, a whisper like fine rain sliding across stone. Li Suo glanced at her once ——and unexpectedly let out a laugh.

"Give up."

Li Jing puffed her cheeks slightly.

"That's exactly what the Eldest Princess said. The two of you sound as though you rehearsed your lines together."

"No need for rehearsal."

Li Suo lifted the lid of his cup and tapped it lightly against the edge.

"That man is a blade Father intends to keep. A sharp one, at least for now. A blade is meant to cut down enemies, not be stuck into a princess's embroidered shoes. You want him as your consort, or tucked into some comfortable idle post? Father will never agree."

"Consort or not, I don't care."

Li Jing tilted her head, eyes bright with firm intent.

"What I want to know is whether I can win his heart."

Li Suo gave a helpless chuckle.

"His heart? That's far harder than securing his rank."

He lifted his gaze fully to hers, voice settling into a calm, almost clinical tone.

"Su Zhang weighs everything on a scale. And the weight on that scale… is not you."

Li Jing fell silent. After a moment, she began tapping a folded fan against the faint water marks on the table, the motion small but restless.

"He looks at everyone so coldly," she murmured. "If I step forward, he steps back half an inch. If I withdraw, he acts as though nothing ever happened."

"That," Li Suo said, setting down the cup lid, "is precisely why your Third Brother has a bit of practical advice for you."

He tapped the wooden table twice with his fingertips, the sound crisp, like knocking sense directly into her thoughts.

"Eat what there is to eat. Drink what there is to drink. Whatever is within reach, enjoy it. Don't gamble your life and don't gamble your heart. Maintain your distance and you'll keep your title and your seat secure."

"What does that even mean, 'enjoy what you can'?"

Li Jing glared at him, her voice rising in indignation.
"You say it so easily!"

"There are plenty of beautiful things in this world."

Li Suo arched a brow, his smile hovering somewhere between amusement and indifference.

"Silks, fine horses, flower banquets, talented scholars. If you can hold it in your hand, then hold it. If you cannot, one glance is more than enough."

"I refuse."

Li Jing pressed her lips together, stubbornness rising like a spark catching on dry wood.

"What I want is that when he turns his head, his eyes find only me. What I want is one lifetime, one person and no one else."

Li Suo regarded her in silence. A breath of wind slipped through the gauze curtain, lifting a stray wisp of hair at her temple. His smile faded, and when he spoke again, his tone had dropped a shade deeper.

"If you truly mean to give your heart," he asked quietly, "have you asked yourself whether you can withstand the fall when your hand slips?"

Li Jing's fingers tightened around the folded fan in her palm.

"You are a princess."

Li Suo's voice was slow, steady, almost weighty.

"Your footing does not depend on any man's favour. Admiration may be a poem, but it cannot become your lifeblood. If you want to test your luck with him, fine. But start from afar. A line of verse. Three brief meetings. Do not cross propriety. Do not offer private gifts. If he looks back, then you take one measured step forward."

His methodical, detached reasoning left Li Jing blinking at him.

"And if he does not look back?"

Li Suo let out a soft laugh, the corner of his mouth lifting in a hint of mockery.

"If he does not, you close your fan. Treat it as a well-performed play, nothing more."

Li Jing spoke barely above a whisper.

"Why must it be so complicated?"

His smile returned, gentler, rippling outward like concentric rings on a spring night's lake.

"Because those two words, restraint and measure, are the dignity of a princess."

Li Jing studied him for a moment, then her brows curved as she suddenly smiled.

"Then tell me this. Will he look back?"

Li Suo lifted his tea cup, tasting it with deliberate leisure, as though the answer could wait.

"You'll only know if you try."

"How am I supposed to try?"

He set the cup down, the soft click echoing beneath the pavilion roof.

"Less eagerness. More poise. Don't rush. Don't chase."

Li Jing glared at him, but the glare quickly dissolved into reluctant laughter, laughter carrying a faint, helpless ache.

"Then you've said a whole lot of nothing, haven't you?"

Li Suo rose and swept a hand lightly across the hanging gauze.

Moonlight spilled in, pale and cool, drawing silver edges along the bamboo shadows outside.

"I'll give you two more lines," he said.

"Don't put yourself into someone else's heart too easily, and don't let anyone press you into the dirt."

Li Jing nodded slowly. Then, as though a thought had quietly resurfaced, she asked:

"And if he still refuses to look at me?"

Li Suo huffed a soft laugh.

"Then look at someone else."

She let out a small, helpless sound, half a laugh, half an exhale, as though he had finally punctured the last stubborn breath sitting in her chest.

Beyond the gauze curtain, bamboo shadows slanted across the stones; beads of night dew gathered at the tips of the leaves like tiny lanterns, trembling once before dropping into the dark pool below.

When they parted, Li Suo lifted a corner of the curtain for her. He turned slightly, the moon at his back, and said:

"Remember,
better to find someone who carries you in his hands
than for you to spend your life carrying him."

Li Jing murmured an acknowledgment, the sound soft as a thread. Her gaze dipped, grew shadowed, then brightened, steadying itself.

She folded her fan with great care, so lightly it was as though she were pressing away that restless heat at her heart and sealing it shut.

"All right," she said. "I'll keep my footing first… and watch slowly."

Li Suo nodded and stepped out of the pavilion.

A breeze moved the gauze behind him, the fluttering fabric drawing a quiet curtain over a lesson given without raising a single voice.

Chapter 34: Petty Obstacles

Qin Nianyin and Mei were carrying a small, embroidered pouch as they walked along the stone path toward the front courtyard. A faint trace of bamboo lingered in the wind, lending the early evening an uncommon ease, light, unhurried, almost peaceful.

But before they reached the corner, a shadow fell sharply across their way.

A slim figure stepped out, barring the path.

"What are you holding in your hand?"

Su Wan stood with her arms folded, posture rigid, her expression cut from frost. Her voice carried no warmth at all, only scrutiny and a thin strand of disdain beneath it.

Mei halted on instinct, shoulders tightening. She shifted as if wanting to skirt around, but Qin Nianyin raised a steadying hand, stopping her.

Nianyin herself remained composed. Her gaze stayed even, her smile courteous as she offered a calm greeting.

"Cousin Su Wan."

Su Wan gave a cold, sharp exhale ——barely a sound, but its edge was unmistakable.

"I advise you," she said, her tone brittle, "to stop wandering into the study whenever you have nothing else to do. My brother has matters to attend to. He does not have the time to indulge idle visitors."

Nianyin stiffened for half a breath. She had not intended to argue.

Yet in that instant, a long-buried image flickered across her mind ——an echo from her former life, a memory of Su Wan's marriage collapsing, her reputation dragged through the mud.

Her eyes rested briefly on Su Wan's face. The familiar pride was still there, sharp and upright, yet something beneath it felt fragile, as though the shell had been polished too thin. Nianyin understood with sudden clarity that this was the very moment when fate had once begun to tilt, quietly and without warning.

She remembered, with too much clarity, that it had been around this time in her past life when Su Wan had gone to Gui Bao Pavilion to choose jewellery.

She had spent enormous sums without hesitation, drawing the envy of the noble girls in the capital.

That display of wealth had also drawn the attention of Lu Chengqian.

He excelled at studying weaknesses.

One glance at her proud bearing and extravagant manner and he had already begun to scheme.

Gui Bao Pavilion stood along a riverside, its carved beams and painted walls reflecting in the water. Arching bridges and slow-moving currents made it a gathering place for the refined and idle ——elegant, serene, deceptively picturesque.

The wind shifted. Shadows of bamboo shook across the ground, thin and wavering.

When Nianyin spoke, her tone was light ——barely heavier than falling dust ——yet something in it seemed to settle into place, like a game piece dropped onto a board.

And another memory slipped in ——

She recalled lying ill for years in that forgotten lifetime, breath faint, life fading thread by thread.

It had been Su Wan who knelt by her sickbed, holding a bowl of medicine with both hands, feeding it to her spoon by spoon.

How strange, she realized, that the very arrogance and coldness that had once suffocated her now looked almost pitiable, even endearing. What she saw now was not cruelty, but blindness: the unguarded confidence of someone who had never learned how vicious the world could be.

Su Wan had been born into a high household. Like her brother Su Zhang, she possessed both talent and beauty.

As the Su family's only daughter, cherished by both the Old Madam and Su Madam, she had been raised like a pearl, too bright to be slighted.

Naturally, she looked down on the young noblemen and aristocratic ladies who circled Su Zhang endlessly.

Yet she had given her heart quietly and earnestly to a young scholar of humble birth, Lu Chengqian, known for his refined demeanour and clever speech.

What she did not know was that Lu Chengqian's elegance was nothing more than a veil.

He was cunning, calculating.

Soon after their marriage, he shed his mask. He reclaimed his original surname and revealed a darker temper, spiteful, narrow, and selfish.

Before the marriage, at a poetry gathering, he had exchanged verses with Su Wan, their harmony drawing admiration from all the young ladies present. Su Wan had convinced herself she had found a rare confidant.

Ignoring the difference in status, she had begged her parents for the match. She believed, naively, that though he came from a concubine line, he was diligent and would one day be her equal.

But Lu Chengqian had studied her well. He knew her pride and knew that she saw sincerity where there was only pretence. He played the part of the aloof gentleman, earning her trust and her heart. And once the marriage was sealed, he discarded the act.

He suppressed her brilliance, resented her reputation, and sneered at her lineage. Worse still, he whispered poison into the world, spreading rumours that she bullied her husband and that she lacked virtue.

What truly shattered Su Wan's heart was what happened in the second year of her marriage.

Lu Chengqian placed high in the imperial examinations, earning the rank of jinshi, and was promoted swiftly to an Assistant Minister in the Ministry of Revenue.

Almost immediately afterward, he took in a concubine, the daughter of a wealthy merchant family.

To the outside world, he announced coldly: "Though the Su lady is noble by birth, she lacks virtue. She is unfit to preside over the household."

From that moment on, Lu Chengqian enjoyed everything he had coveted: rank, wealth, a beautiful concubine with money behind her.

Fame and fortune came to him hand in hand.

And Su Wan, who had once been his stepping stone upward, became the very stepping stone he trampled without hesitation.

She continued to bear the nominal title of principal wife. She still dressed finely and still appeared proper in public. But the truth was plain: authority had slipped through her fingers. The entire household listened to the concubine.

Rumour had it that the concubine was Lu Chengqian's childhood sweetheart, someone close to him since they were young.

In Qin Nianyin's previous life, this was also the period when Su Zhang, newly rising in his career and burdened with secret assignments from the Crown Prince, was constantly away investigating major cases.

He barely slept and rarely returned home. The running of the Su household fell largely to his mother and to Su Wan.

Su Zhang had never liked meddling in inner-courtyard affairs. He believed his sister was clever, dignified, and proud in the right measure, fully capable of choosing a suitable husband for herself.

He never looked beneath Lu Chengqian's polished facade to see the greed and ambition hidden underneath.

By the time he returned to the capital and finally sensed that something was amiss, it was already too late. Su Wan had been married off into that modest household, already trapped and already reduced to nothing more than a tool for another man's ambitions.

Outwardly, Lu Chengqian treated her with indifference and distance. Yet within the court, he relied heavily on the Su family's reputation to climb quickly. In secret, he even aligned himself with political enemies for the sake of power.

And Su Zhang, seeking to protect his sister, unknowingly smoothed Lu Chengqian's path further, enabling the very ambition that would one day destroy her. At that time, Nianyin herself had still been the wife of a high minister.

She possessed a measure of influence among the noblewomen and had, in discreet ways, supported Su Wan, letting her at least maintain the outward dignity of a principal wife. Su Wan could still step out in fine attire and proper ceremony.

But within the inner residence, she had already lost everything.

Su Zhang had not been blind to this; he had thought of intervening.

But one quiet sentence from his mother stopped him:

"She chose him of her own will."

And so he had fallen silent.

All he could do was watch ——watch his once brilliant, proud sister lose the light in her eyes, little by little, until they finally went dark.

Eventually, she severed all ties with him.

Stopped writing.

Stopped visiting.

Stopped hoping.

In the end, because she remained childless, the concubine's son pushed her aside entirely. When she finally gathered the courage to ask for a separation, Lu Chengqian trapped her instead ——accusing her of adultery with an outsider.

Her reputation crumbled instantly.

She was locked away in a remote courtyard, alive in name only.

Nianyin remembered that day clearly ——Su Wan coming to her sickbed, feeding her a bowl of medicine. She wore silk and brocade, but her complexion was ashen, her spirit held together by the faintest thread.

Thinking of this, Qin Nianyin's eyes shifted. Her earlier softness withdrew, replaced by a composed seriousness. She understood then that some words, once spoken, could not change fate ——but silence, too, was a choice, and one she could no longer make.

She looked directly at Su Wan and spoke evenly:

"Cousin Su Wan… I will be honest with you. Though I have little skill, I once learned a small technique for reading faces when I was young."

She deliberately slowed her speech, watching Su Wan's expression with careful precision. Then she let a faint crease form between her brows, followed by a quiet sigh ——a sigh touched with worry and regret, as though witnessing something that pained her deeply.

"In my opinion… it would be best if you refrain from going out these next two days. Some spirits are troublesome. The safest place for you is within the residence."

Su Wan froze, a flicker of uncertainty passing through her eyes before cold amusement replaced it.

"Are you cursing me?"

"How could I?" Qin Nianyin's tone remained gentle, unhurried. Her gaze did not waver.

"I'm merely offering a kind reminder. Especially where there is water… it is better to avoid than to approach."

When her words fell, Qin Nianyin did not add another sentence.

She simply looked at Su Wan, quietly and steadily.

It was precisely this lack of insistence, this refusal to explain or justify, that pressed down on the air like an invisible weight.

The wind brushed over the treetops; petals quivered faintly on the stone path.

A chill, subtle yet unmistakable, seemed to rise from somewhere, though no one could have said which heart it came from.

Su Wan's expression shifted. A flicker of uncertainty flashed through her eyes before she forced a brittle smile onto her lips.

"So, you truly believe you can read faces? Pretending to divine ill omens, aren't you afraid the capital will laugh at you?"

"I wouldn't dare invite mockery," Qin Nianyin replied. Her tone remained mild, but a veil of quiet mystery settled over it.

"It's only that, when I glanced at you just now, I noticed your brow dimmed, your complexion slightly off. And your eyes… there is a faint bluish cast to them. It looks rather like…"

She paused, letting the stillness grow between them.

"…a misfortune tied to water."

Her voice was not loud, calm and almost conversational, yet every word landed with distinct clarity.

There was nothing dramatic in her delivery, only a truth spoken as though she were observing the weather.

But beneath that composure lay a quiet resolve.

This, she thought, is the least I owe her from the last life.

She had already repaid a fragment of what Su Wan once gave her, a warning, small yet sincere.

For these coming days, she truly must not leave the residence.

Chapter 35: The Misfortune of Old Man

The Su Residence

Su Wan's expression shifted violently; the colour first drained away, then returned in a hot, blotchy flush of anger and indignation.

Her lips tightened into a thin line, but her voice still clung stubbornly to its brittle edge.

"Utter nonsense! Do not use such ridiculous tricks to try and frighten me."

At her side, the maid Zixin unconsciously took a protective half-step closer, as if attempting to shield her mistress from something invisible but present. Her voice dipped low, thin with unease.

"Miss... this servant feels a little unsettled by this talk."

Qin Nianyin lifted her hands in a small, helpless gesture, her brows softened with feigned innocence.

"Whether you choose to believe it or not, Cousin, that is entirely your prerogative. I merely offered a passing warning. And if one day... by some unfortunate chance—"

She deliberately did not finish the sentence, letting the unspoken prediction hang heavy in the air.

Mei was already shaking with violently suppressed laughter, her cheeks flushed bright red. Her head was bent as she bit down hard on her lip, her shoulders trembling uncontrollably.

Su Wan's face alternated rapidly between an ashen pallor and livid fury. At last, she snapped her sleeve away sharply.

"Ridiculous! As if I would ever believe your absurdities."

She spun abruptly on her heel to walk away—

But the hem of her skirt caught sharply on the raised corner of a nearby stone slab.

Her body pitched forward in a sudden, alarming lurch.

A faint, high-pitched chime rang out from the small bell sewn into her sleeve, crisp and startled, like a frightened sparrow unexpectedly taking wing.

Zixin reacted instantly, catching Su Wan securely by the arm, though her own hand trembled faintly from the shock.

Qin Nianyin watched the fleeting moment with eyes that deepened perceptibly by a shade. Her voice was soft, almost indistinct beneath the sound of the wind:

"As I said... her fortune is unsettled."

Mei leaned close to Nianyin, whispering with immense effort to contain her broad grin.

"Miss, just now you looked exactly like an immortal scolding mortals. I didn't even dare draw a full breath."

Nianyin only curved her lips slightly. Her eyes remained calm, reflective—like the surface of still, deep water.

"A warning is all I offered. Whether she chooses to heed it... is entirely her own decision."

Wind pushed through the branches overhead, scattering shifting shadows across her gaze.

Since the past had returned, since time had looped and offered her another chance—

Anything she could possibly change, she would not wilfully ignore.

Even if all she could offer was half a sentence, or a fleeting, meaningful glance, she would still fulfil whatever small duty she now owed to those in her orbit.

* * * * *

The Su Residence: A Cautious Kindness

That afternoon, the sun hung warm and heavy above the quiet courtyard.

Qin Nianyin held a small bamboo parasol, waiting just beyond the corner gate for Mei.

Today, their plan was to slip out of the residence again—quietly and discreetly—to continue their search for a suitable storefront location.

But the moment they stepped past the corner of the auxiliary building, they paused abruptly.

A rickety wooden cart leaned crookedly against the path.

Two of the Su manor's kitchen hands were helping an elderly vegetable vendor unload his baskets. The old man's back was sharply bent like a drawn bow, but his face was alight with pure, unadulterated joy.

Snatches of lively, congratulatory conversation floated through the warm, sunny air.

"Congratulations, old Zhou! Heard your boy's finally getting married soon?"

"Aye, aye—after all these years of saving, we finally pulled through. At long last, my lad will have himself a good wife!"

His deeply lined face glowed with a happiness that was far too bright for his worn, patched clothes.

Qin Nianyin stopped instantly in her tracks.

A memory—a vivid, painful fragment from her previous life—surged up like a swiftly breaking tide.

It had been only three or five days before this very wedding was set to occur.

The vegetable seller's future daughter-in-law… was viciously sold off by her own greedy stepmother to Chunhua House, the local brothel, under the claim that the family was desperately in need of money.

And the dowry old Zhou had painfully offered was simply deemed "too little."

The old vendor's tragic story unwound completely in her mind—how his son, upon learning the devastating truth, had flown into a blind, desperate rage and violently barged into Chunhua House in the dead of night, only to be beaten so savagely that the bones in his leg snapped like dry branches.

A red wedding had tragically turned white overnight; the shock and grief had crushed the old man's spirit entirely. Not long after, illness claimed him, and he never again came to deliver vegetables—leaving the Su residence short on fresh produce for weeks.

The memory flickered sharp and cold across Qin Nianyin's gaze, a glint of ice that passed as swiftly as it came.

She closed her oil-paper umbrella and stepped forward with a gentle smile, stooping slightly to lift one of the wicker baskets herself. The vegetables were still damp with morning dew; she carefully brushed aside a stray leaf before helping the old man secure the rest of his load onto his cart.

"Congratulations, Uncle Zhou," she said lightly, her tone warm but carefully measured. "Your young master must be blessed indeed. May the wedding proceed smoothly and may the couple grow old together in happiness."

The old vendor bowed again and again, visibly flustered by her unexpected courtesy, gratitude written plainly across his weathered face.

Nianyin dusted a smear of soil from her fingertips, her smile curving with a casual, unassuming grace. "Only… with the happy day drawing so close, the bride's family must be terribly busy. Uncle Zhou, do keep an exceptionally careful eye on things. When joy is at hand, that is precisely when one must be most prudent. A single lapse in vigilance can entirely spoil a celebration."

The old man blinked, looking genuinely puzzled. "What… what exactly do you mean by that, Miss?"

"Oh, nothing much at all." Her voice softened further, turning almost conspiratorial as she leaned in slightly closer. "This is the capital, after all. Naturally, none of the nasty things that sometimes happen in small, remote villages would ever occur here."

Her lashes lowered, casting a shadow over the faint, pointed meaning in her eyes.

"But where I lived before," she continued in a low whisper, "I heard more than a few sorrowful tales… of certain unscrupulous parents who, dissatisfied with the initial bride price, hatched other cruel schemes just before the wedding day. Quite shameful, wouldn't you say?"

The words were carefully veiled, yet sharp enough to cut directly through any lingering illusions.

The old vendor froze completely, the colour draining rapidly from his cheeks as the horrifying realization of her implied warning dawned. He bowed deeply once more, promising that he would remember her caution well and attend to the matter immediately.

Only after he shuffled quickly out of earshot did Mei—who had arrived halfway through the exchange and listened with mounting disbelief—finally let out a poorly stifled snort of laughter.

She pressed a hand to her mouth, her shoulders shaking with mirth. "Miss, your foresight is absolutely uncanny! Truly uncanny! If you ask this servant, you should set up a fortune-telling stall yourself immediately. With skills like yours, it would be a crime not to earn some silver!"

Qin Nianyin shot her a mock glare of exasperation. "What utter nonsense."

But Mei merely sidled closer, her eyes bright with mischief. "Really! You would make a fortune. And think of all the good karma you would accrue! Imagine it—outside our shop, a grand wooden sign: All wishes granted, all misfortunes dispelled—"

Nianyin could not help the small, genuine laugh that escaped her. Exasperated yet clearly fond, she tapped the girl lightly on the forehead. "You have certainly changed your tune, haven't you? Not so afraid of me sounding mystical anymore? Fortune-telling is hardly so simple. Sometimes, knowing too much is ultimately more of a burdensome weight than a blessing."

Her words drifted softly in the morning air—half jest, half profound truth, and entirely reflective of the heavy weight she alone carried.

* * * * *

The noise of the streets faded rapidly as they walked farther from the gate, the heat and bustle of the city seeming to remain firmly shut out beyond the courtyard walls.

Qin Nianyin pushed the door open and stepped inside their small room. The lamplight flickered; in its warm golden glow, she opened her palm. The gold piece resting there shone brilliantly, casting a brighter gleam across her eyes.

Mei leaned in, muttering under her breath, "Miss, does silver in the capital grow wings? That shop we just visited—a single hairpin costs three taels!"

Nianyin's lips curved faintly, though her expression stayed calm and reflective as still water. "Capital prices adhere to the logic of the capital."

In her past life, she had been the powerful mistress of the Minister's household, tossing out rewards of a hundred taels without even lifting an eyelid. Now she had to meticulously weigh the value of every single tael with careful thought.

The sharp contrast followed her everywhere like an ever-present shadow—yet it only served to make her all the more clear-headed and determined.

* * * * *

230

The next morning at the hour of Chen (between 7 and 9 a.m.), the weather was slightly cool and crisp.

Qin Nianyin rose early, washed, dressed neatly, and left quickly with Mei, carrying a small cloth bundle. Inside were several hairpins and ornaments she had hurried to finish the night before.

The materials were not inherently expensive, but the stitches were delicate, and the designs were fresh and innovative styles rarely, if ever, seen on the common market.

These designs were less a result of "clever tricks" than the direct result of her years of cultivated taste and astute social observation as a high official's wife in her past life, allowing her to stay ahead of current trends and accurately grasp the subtle preferences of noblewomen.

She planned to walk around today—first, to thoroughly learn the current market prices, and second, to try her luck at selling. If there happened to be a suitable storefront, she could begin preparing the necessary arrangements early.

But just as they reached the front entrance of Changchun Inn, a sudden sound came from directly above—

"Tap."

Something hit her lightly at the side of her forehead.

She looked down and found, lying on the stone path… a single peanut.

Mei nearly jumped in anger, scanning the windows furiously. "Who is so ill-mannered!"

Qin Nianyin lifted her gaze. On the second floor, beside the street-facing window, the shutters were half open. Someone lounged lazily against the frame, rolling peanuts idly between his fingers, his expression one of bored leisure, framed by a half smile.

It was the Third Prince of Great Zhou—Li Suo.

Her expression did not change; only her brows tightened faintly in irritation. She continued forward. Just as she was about to step over the inn's threshold, she was stopped abruptly by the guards stationed at the staircase.

"Miss, the upper floor is reserved for honoured guests—"

Before he could finish, Li Suo's voice drifted down from above, unhurried and casually dismissive:

"Let her ascend."

The guard paused uncertainly, then stepped aside.

Qin Nianyin nodded slightly and ascended the stairs, maintaining an unhurried, measured posture. With each graceful movement of her hem, her calm expression settled further, the faint frown already vanished.

When she reached the table, she did not immediately sit. She stood quietly by the side, her hands lowered respectfully, her voice even and steady:

"Your Highness invited me upstairs—does Your Highness have specific instructions for me?"

Li Suo leaned further into the window's shadow, amusement lingering at his lips.

"Your brows were furrowed so pitifully. I was afraid you'd cause yourself injury from sheer vexation, so I thought you might sit, drink a cup of my tea, and calm your nerves."

He gestured vaguely toward the empty seat opposite him.

Qin Nianyin offered no outward reaction, but after a moment of careful consideration, she sat across from him, her back rigidly straight.

Li Suo poured two cups of tea for himself, then casually asked,

"Early in the morning, sneaking around like a common thief, looking everywhere—what exactly are you plotting?"

She instinctively glanced down at the small cloth bundle resting on her lap. She paused slightly, her expression serene and composed.

"Just walking around, looking at available storefronts," she said gently, neither adopting a humble nor a haughty tone.

Storefronts?

Li Suo gave a short, cynical half-smile, looking at her with genuine, amused interest.

"You? You want to open a shop?"

"Mm."

"That's simple enough. Why not simply ask your dear cousin? Wouldn't he readily provide you with one?"

She acted as though she hadn't heard the question, offering no response whatsoever.

Li Suo chuckled lightly.

"Otherwise… beg me, and I will personally give you one?"

Only then did Nianyin visibly react, as if remembering her duties.

"If there is no further matter, Nianyin will respectfully take her leave. Your Highness, please enjoy your meal."

"Ah—wait, don't go yet."

Chapter 36: The First Silver Earned

Qin Nianyin steadied the turbulent currents of her mind, meticulously ensuring that she did not betray even a flicker of disarray or panic.

After all, having spent an entire previous lifetime amidst the exalted heights of luxury and holding a station of profound eminence, such mundane, street-level affairs as the opening of a shop had never once manifested within the fabric of her existence; in those former years, there had always been efficient stewards and managers to handle every triviality of commerce.

"Does Your Highness have further instructions for me?"

"Speak then—what is the reason for your pursuit of a storefront?"

Upon hearing this inquiry, Qin Nianyin allowed a faint, subtle smile to curve her lips, choosing not to offer much in the way of elaborate defense or justification: "One cannot simply consume the food and dwell within the halls of another for nothing; it is only right that I should perform some tasks that lie within the modest scope of my own capabilities."

Li Suo arched a single brow, his eyes shifting with a brief, languid and predatory turn, his tone carrying an unmistakable air of insolent nonchalance: "Could it be that Su Zhang can no longer afford the cost of your maintenance, that he has forced you to emerge into the world to beg for a meager livelihood?"

As the final syllable of his speech fell, he paused with deliberate intent, waiting with keen eyes to observe the slightest ripple of her reaction.

Qin Nianyin's countenance remained as unruffled as a still pond; she merely returned the porcelain teacup in her hand with agonizing slowness to the small table, her expression projecting an aura of serene and unshakable tranquility.

"Your Highness jests with me; the manner in which the Su Residence has hosted me has never been anything less than kind and generous." Her voice remained faint and airy, yet every word was imbued with a deep, resonant and steady composure.

With this single, measured sentence, she neither over-explained her circumstances nor compromised her own self-possession; amidst her flawless and meticulous etiquette, she also effectively and cleanly blocked any further intrusion into the topic of conversation.

The glint of interest within Li Suo's eyes grew visibly deeper; he was just about to part his lips to tease her further with his sharp wit when a sudden burst of dainty, silver-bell laughter drifted in from outside the doorway— "Third Brother, what a truly remarkable coincidence to encounter you this day!"

A group of noble young ladies, adorned in attire as vibrant and variegated as a garden of blossoming flowers, filed into the chamber in a single, graceful line. The one who walked at their lead was none other than Shen Lingyan—the cherished daughter of the Grand Tutor Su.

The several young mistresses, one after another, paid their formal respects and performed their elegant salutations to Li Suo.

Shen Lingyan had been a companion to the imperial princes since their shared childhood, and she was well-accustomed to addressing them by their familial rankings, as ordinary folk might, when they were away from the rigid confines of the court.

The several female guests, suddenly finding themselves in the presence of the Emperor's third son, also felt their hearts bloom with a flurry of joy and proceeded to take their seats one after another in a rustle of silk.

They were not like Su Wan, who possessed the privilege to frequently enter the palace precincts; in their daily lives, they did not easily find the opportunity to behold the countenance of an imperial prince.

Moreover, the Third Prince was born with a scholarly and refined temperament, appearing as handsome and elegant as a piece of flawless jade; he was widely considered the most fair-featured and striking among the three princes of the realm.

Shen Lingyan's keen eyes caught sight of Qin Nianyin sitting in the quiet corner almost instantly; she was briefly seized by a startle, but immediately shielded her lips with her hand, masking a smile as she spoke with an air of practiced affection: "Oh, is this not the Su Residence's Cousin Nianyin?"

Qin Nianyin had no choice but to rise and offer her own formal salutations, all the while secretly lamenting the bitterness of her misfortune in the silent depths of her heart.

Shen Lingyan laughed and exchanged playful jests with the other noble ladies, making herself entirely at home as she took a seat without any hint of ceremony. Someone's gaze happened to flicker across the small, wrapped bundle cradled in Qin Nianyin's arms, and they inquired with curiosity: "What fine treasures is the Cousin carrying with her today?"

Mei was just about to move and shield the bundle from their collective view, but Shen Lingyan, possessing an incredibly sharp and discerning eye, deftly drew the parcel toward herself and unrolled it to inspect the contents—

Lying there in profound silence were several floral hairpins and intricate head-ornaments; their workmanship was nothing short of exquisite, and their patterns were strikingly novel, bearing absolutely no resemblance to the monotonous and indistinguishable wares typically found in the city's ordinary shops.

Shen Lingyan's eyes brightened with a sudden luster, and she exclaimed in a voice of genuine, pleasant surprise: "These styles are truly clever, ingenious, and fresh!"

The several noble ladies crowding beside her also leaned closer, clicking their tongues in a chorus of wonder and admiration.

"Indeed, this particular design of butterflies fluttering amidst a cascade of flowers has never once been glimpsed on the market before!"

"This plum blossom pin, crafted with such artistry that it appears as if it is just at the precipice of blooming, is made with such lifelike and vivid detail!"

"This one here is surely the most marvelous of all; it is as delicate and intricate as a true, living winding vine—"

Shen Lingyan was the first to extend her hand, selecting a green-beaded floral ornament; her eyes shone with delight as she laughed and remarked: "This workmanship is so remarkably intricate! To think that green beads of such diminutive size are not disordered in the slightest degree; your handiwork is truly exceptional. Did you craft this with your own hands?"

Qin Nianyin offered a slight, modest bow and replied with a contained and graceful smile: "In reply to the young lady, this was indeed fashioned by my own hand; though the base materials are coarse and humble, they prevail through the sheer novelty and freshness of the style. If the lady does not find them beneath her disdain, then please, I beg you to take them."

These patterns were the very designs that would become overwhelmingly popular and fashionable in the years to come; she possessed an immense and unshakable confidence in these few hairpins.

While idly toying with the floral pin, Shen Lingyan blinked her eyes with a mischievous glint: "That simply will not do; if I am to take them,

I must provide silver in return, for I, Shen Lingyan, am not the sort of person to acquire another's efforts for nothing."

A charming and spirited young lady sitting beside her giggled and chimed in: "Sister Yun'er, this gesture of ours is called 'offering patronage and support'; how could it be considered taking advantage for nothing?"

Having uttered this, she also selected a piece for herself—a pink blossom entwined upon a delicate branch, simple in form yet vibrantly spirited and vivid; unable to part with the treasure, she pinned it into her hair at the temple and peered into the polished bronze mirror, her smile becoming even sweeter and more satisfied: "Does it truly look well upon me?"

"It looks well, indeed it looks marvelous! If paired with a gown of pale pink, you would be the very first little flower-spirit of the spring season to attract a swarm of bees and butterflies!" Another lady teased playfully, drawing a chorus of lighthearted laughter from the entire assembled company.

Mei watched the scene from the side with her nerves stretched as taut as a bowstring, yet Qin Nianyin remained perfectly calm, self-assured, and possessed; with a smile, she took a small square of red velvet cloth from the bundle and spread it flat upon the table, arranging the remaining floral pins into a neat and orderly row.

Shen Lingyan inquired with a high degree of interest: "How did it ever occur to you to create such things to sell for the sake of earning money?"

Qin Nianyin answered in a soft, melodic, and humble voice: "The circumstances of my family are straitened and meager, and I merely wish to earn some small coins to provide for the sustenance of my household."

Hearing her speak in such a humble and plain manner, the noble ladies could not help but feel a few involuntary sparks of sympathy and pity for her, failing entirely to notice the Third Prince, Li Suo, who sat at the side and could not resist letting out a short, scoffing, and derisive laugh.

He most certainly did not believe for a single heartbeat that a dignified and wealthy Su Residence could not afford the cost of maintaining a single cousin of the house.

"To possess such exceptional skill and such a resolute ambition is quite commendable, indeed."

Shen Lingyan smiled and fished a solid tael of broken silver from the folds of her robes, placing it firmly upon the table: "I shall take all of these that remain; you must remember to craft more, and bring them for me to inspect in the days to come!"

The other several young ladies also pulled out pieces of broken silver one after another from their pouches, insisting with great earnestness on purchasing one or two pins before they eventually departed.

Qin Nianyin offered her thanks repeatedly with graceful bows, and Mei also busied herself with the task of tidying up the table, her heart secretly blooming and opening with a jubilant joy.

By the time everyone had finished selecting their desired hairpins and departed the upper floor in a cluster surrounding Shen Lingyan, Qin Nianyin looked down at the heavy, cold weight of the broken silver in her hand, feeling only a surge of profound warmth rising in her heart.

This was the silver she had earned in this life, truly and unequivocally through the labor and toil of her own two hands!

* * * * *

Li Suo took the entirety of this scene into his sight, the corners of his thin lips curving into a faint, elusive, and indiscernible arc of amusement.

"What an interesting and peculiar little girl."

His voice was low, husky, and slow in its delivery, as if spoken with a casual ease, yet also as if he were meticulously savoring the discovery of a fresh and novel plaything. His fingertip lightly and rhythmically tapped the rim of his porcelain teacup; every single strike seemed to be measuring and calculating her ultimate worth. The glint of interest buried within the dark depths of his eyes was as profound as a hidden undercurrent, making it utterly impossible for any observer to discern whether it was genuine admiration or something of a far more complex nature.

In the mere blink of an eye, Qin Nianyin's several handcrafted floral pins were sold out completely, yielding a substantial and unexpected sum of silver.

Mei was so overwhelmed with delight that she nearly embraced her mistress and spun in jubilant circles on the spot.

Qin Nianyin meticulously maintained her humble, smiling, and deferential demeanor, yet her heart was as jubilant as a flower in the peak of its bloom—she had never once imagined that she, too, could rely on the strength of her own hands to earn the silver necessary for her very survival.

She quietly and firmly tightened her grip on that ingot of broken silver, hiding it within the deep shadows of her sleeve, and hiding it even deeper within the recesses of her heart.

This one instance of fortunate and providential success must absolutely never be the last.

Chapter 37: A Hint of Interest

As the laughter and light chatter of the noble ladies faded into the distance, a profound quietude finally reclaimed the upper floor of the establishment.

The bustling clamour from the streets below grew muffled and remote, leaving only the sound of the wind as it lightly brushed against the corners of the window curtains.

The flickering shadows cast by the remaining candles danced softly upon the walls, confining the space within an atmosphere of still, heavy oppression.

Having unexpectedly secured this initial pittance of income, Qin Nianyin instinctively directed her gaze toward the Third Prince, Li Suo, who sat in silent poise, elegantly sipping his tea.

He was a figure of unhurried grace and effortless composure, his countenance strikingly handsome—marking him unequivocally as a nobleman of the highest caliber.

"Your High—" she began, an impulse to offer her gratitude surfacing for a fleeting second, only to be immediately suppressed and swallowed in the following instant.

This paltry sum of silver was surely less significant than a single strand of hair in the eyes of the Third Prince.

She was no longer the exalted wife of a Minister; given her current station, what necessity was there to utter such redundant words? Furthermore, she harboured absolutely no desire to initiate any further entanglements with those belonging to the Imperial Family.

Qin Nianyin withdrew the final, fading trace of her smile. She lifted the now-empty cloth bundle, executed a low, graceful curtsy toward Li Suo, and spoke with measured, steady composure: "Your Highness, if there are no other matters to attend to, this humble woman shall take her leave."

Unexpectedly, Li Suo leaned languidly against the back of his chair, his fingertips beginning to tap lightly against the surface of the table.

The rhythm was slow and distinctly audible, each strike seemingly protracted with deliberate intent, causing the very air to solidify for a suspended moment.

His voice carried a tone of underlying laziness, yet it failed to mask that undeniable sense of potent, non-negotiable authority: "Wait."

Her steps paused for a fraction of a heartbeat. She turned, her posture remaining perfectly dignified and respectful, as she responded quietly: "Does Your Highness have further instructions?"

Li Suo did not offer an immediate reply. Instead, he half-closed his eyes, his gaze moving across her figure with the slow, deliberate manner of a predatory cat, scrutinizing her at his leisure and without the slightest urgency.

He held his jade fan closed, using it only to tap lightly against his open palm—a casual motion that nonetheless conveyed a clear, calculated appraisal of her worth.

His eyes, framed by the interplay of shadow and light, held an ambiguous quality; the candlelight reflected fragmented glints within them, which seemed to glide over her person like the flicking tongue of a serpent.

She had encountered such intrusive and discerning gazes countless times within the Imperial court of her past life—monarchs, high officials, and powerful aristocrats all shared the habit of surveying the world with an air of amused, entitled contemplation.

Her chest tightened painfully, yet she meticulously maintained her mask of calm, forcing herself to draw a subtle, stabilizing breath to remain anchored. Li Suo's lips curved slowly into a smile, revealing an unspoken, private amusement; clearly, her carefully guarded restraint only intrigued him further.

He remained silent for a considerable duration, and she likewise kept her lips tightly closed, unwilling to be the first to speak.

The only sounds that remained were the faint, distant noise of the marketplace filtering up from outside and the gentle sighs of the wind. Finally, he spoke.

"Your name... is Qin Nianyin?"

She lowered her gaze and affirmed: "Replying to Your Highness, it is." Her tone was neither hurried nor slow, yet beneath the concealment of her sleeves, her palms were instinctively clenching into tight fists.

She vaguely recalled that in her previous life, this Third Prince was renowned for being the most difficult to predict, a man whose actions rarely adhered to conventional lines.

Every time his speech momentarily lapsed, her heart instinctively tightened, only to slowly relax when his expression returned to its usual half-smile.

She recognized this exact form of psychological testing—she knew she must appear neither timid nor lose the necessary humility of one in a lower position. She had to navigate a balance as fragile as thin ice between these two extremes.

"The cousin of Su Zhang and Su Wan..."

He seemed to be tasting the words, his lips curving with an arc of vague significance. "You possess considerable nerve. For a mere child, you are quite adept at the art of business."

Hearing this, Qin Nianyin could not help but inwardly purse her lips... *A mere child?*

Your Highness has no inkling that, in spirit and mind, this young woman is fully twenty years your senior...

His gaze shifted slightly, falling upon the faint bulge of the purse tucked within her robes, his tone becoming subtly teasing and mischievous: "Well now, since you have secured a profit, are you not planning to share a portion of it with me?"

Qin Nianyin offered no verbal response. Instead, she instinctively clutched the bundle containing the silver even tighter. The action was swift yet controlled, a gesture that clearly conveyed her refusal.

Li Suo gave a light, cynical chuckle: "Those noble ladies—had they not been acutely aware of my presence here, would they ever have possessed the patience to sit down and select your wares?"

Having finished his piece, he waited in silence to see how she would calculate her response.

Qin Nianyin paused for a moment before raising her eyes to meet his. A shallow, almost imperceptible smile touched her lips, like a faint ripple upon the surface of clear water; her look was neither fearful nor overly bold. Her words were spoken with careful deference, yet they lacked any hint of servility.

"I am indebted to Your Highness's exalted status for drawing such attention. I am deeply aware that my humble craft only received the favour of the young mistresses due to Your Highness's formidable reputation. However, I believe this small sum of silver is less than a single hair's breadth of Your Highness's vast fortune, and I would not presume to offer it. To diminish Your Highness's grand standing with such a trifling and meagre amount would truly be a transgression on my part."

She harbored no further illusions of clinging to power in this life. She wished only that every stitch and every piece of needlework she produced would be honest and worthy of her own heart and effort.

Li Suo's eyebrow lifted slightly, the glint of interest in his eyes deepening even further.

"Oh? Then what was it you were about to say just moments ago, before you stopped yourself?"

"...It was nothing of significance."

Her voice remained mild and even. She offered a slight inclination of her head, performing a second salute: "If Your Highness has no further need of me, this humble woman shall not impose upon your time."

She turned and departed, her back remaining composed and entirely dignified. Mei silently rushed to follow in her wake. Li Suo did not pursue the matter further.

Only after her silhouette had vanished entirely did he turn his head and instruct his personal guard: "Investigate this cousin of the Su Residence; find out exactly what her origins are."

The guard acknowledged the command and quietly retreated. Li Suo picked up the final peanut and flicked it with his finger—a light *clink* echoed as it landed precisely in his teacup, causing tiny ripples to spread across the surface of the tea. He chuckled softly, speaking half to himself, as if making an internal promise: "A person such as that... how could she merely be an ordinary young girl?"

* * * * *

Downstairs.

Qin Nianyin maintained an unhurried, measured pace, yet she did not break her rhythm for a single inch, as if she were using this steady tempo to soothe her own slightly disordered heartbeats. The small cloth bundle in her hand was already noticeably damp, a consequence of her having gripped it tightly for far too long.

Mei could not help but whisper in a low voice: "Miss, the Third Prince was terrifying... just now he kept staring at you, and I felt as though I could barely draw breath."

Qin Nianyin replied calmly: "Do not be alarmed."

243

Though her voice was light, her expression was as cool and clear as water. She knew well that the attention of the powerful was never a true blessing.

Having stood at the pinnacle of power in her past life, she had witnessed too many true intentions and concealed dangers lurking beneath polite smiles. In this life, she desired only to rely on herself to walk a clean and independent path.

Yet, destiny seemed to have already laid its snare, relentlessly drawing her back into a familiar and dangerous vortex. S

he lowered her gaze, looking at those few pieces of fragmented silver in her hand, securing them tightly and hiding them within her sleeve. Then she spoke softly: "Let us go. This road, we have only just begun to travel."

—This time, she vowed she would not allow herself to fall back into the mire.

* * * * *

Leaving the inn, Qin Nianyin and Mei turned into a quiet, secluded side alley.

Mei looked around meticulously, ensuring no one was following them. Only then did she retrieve the small cloth pouch from her bosom, carefully pouring the accumulated fragmented silver into her palm.

The afternoon sun slanted down, catching the silver and making it glint faintly. A gentle breeze blew in from the alley entrance, carrying the warmth of the afternoon and the lingering scent of tea from the shops; a few stray willow catkins brushed against her sleeve before she casually flicked them away.

Though such days were lean and meagre, they possessed a long-awaited sense of ease. Qin Nianyin listened to the quiet clink of the coins, the long-standing tension in her heart finally loosening slightly—as if she could at last see a faint, tangible outline of a future she could depend upon.

Mei began counting, her voice low but barely concealing her excitement: "One ingot, two ingots... Miss, we truly made a profit this time!"

She looked up at Qin Nianyin, her eyes curving like bright new moons in a smile. Qin Nianyin could not help but be infected by her joy, her brow softening slightly. She looked down at the handful of fragmented silver, her voice gentle and thin: "We did not earn a great sum, and we are still far from the capital needed to buy a storefront... but it is enough to purchase a few more chairs."

Though her tone was airy, her fingertips tightened slightly—it was a sensation of careful yet firm security. Just as she spoke, a low, light laugh suddenly sounded above them.

"Well now, are we dividing the silver?"

They both looked up abruptly to see a figure leaning against the wall. The sunlight caught his features, revealing a handsome, uninhibited countenance. Dressed in a simple blue-green robe, he stood with his arms crossed, watching the scene with an air of amused spectatorship.

It was none other than—Gu Xiao.

Chapter 38: An Admission of Guilt

Gu Xiao wore a dark-ink brocade robe with subtle woven patterns. His long arms were crossed loosely over his chest and a hint of playfulness lingered on his thin lips as he cast a languid smile at the mistress and her maid. His posture was carefree ——almost recklessly elegant.

"Counting silver with such joy? Then let me join the fun. Whoever sees it gets a share ——don't you think that's fair?"

As he spoke, he extended an open hand, grinning as though he truly expected payment.

Qin Nianyin gathered the silver in her palm, slow and steady, her eyes giving nothing away.

"Master Gu has quite the refined taste," she replied calmly.

Her tone was composed ——neither shy nor irritated ——and that unexpected steadiness made Gu Xiao pause, surprised.

Qin Nianyin offered him a faint, polite smile and turned as if to leave.

"Master Gu, please help yourself. I imagine you have more pressing matters. We won't keep you."

But behind her came his unhurried footsteps and his sleeves flicked as he followed along, voice ringing with theatrical ease:

"Well now, since I've discovered your little secret of dividing silver, shouldn't you at least buy me a cup of tea to keep me quiet?"

Qin Nianyin halted just a fraction, casting him a sidelong glance.

"Master Gu has run out of tea at home?"

Truly peculiar ——first the Third Prince, then this Gu Xiao. Men with coffers overflowing, yet both so distracted by the mere weight of a few pieces of silver in her pouch.

Gu Xiao only laughed, utterly unabashed.

"Oh, it's there and plenty of it. But tea someone else pays for ——now that's the fragrant kind."

He lifted a shoulder in nonchalance.

"You wouldn't understand. Free tea is the priciest and the best."

Qin Nianyin said nothing more. She had no intention of engaging with him. She gave a small curtsey and prepared to depart.

Seeing this, Gu Xiao didn't grow annoyed. He simply trailed after them, speaking as though strolling through a spring garden:

"No matter. I was heading to find your noble cousin anyway. I'll walk you two there ——nice and convenient."

"No need to trouble yourself, Master Gu."

"Just humour me. So many turns in these streets ——drop a coin and you'll never see it again."

"Master Gu, if you keep saying so much, everyone will soon know I have silver on me."

"I'm only afraid you'll grow bored. Thought I'd chat with you along the way…"

"Thank you kindly, Master Gu, but Nianyin has no wish to chatter…"

"Hey, don't be ungrateful now. This young master ——"

The sun sank lower, stretching the alley into a long ribbon of gold and shadow.

The three walked, he in front, the other two behind, shadows drawn thin across the stone path.

A soft breeze stirred, lifting the hem of Qin Nianyin's robes. The silver in her pouch clinked faintly, a tiny, scattered sound.

She lowered her gaze to the small cloth bag, and an almost invisible smile touched her eyes.

She found it faintly ironic — first the Third Prince, now Gu Xiao.

Men whose coffers overflowed, whose names alone could command entire streets to bow aside, yet both had lingered over the sound of a few scattered pieces of silver in her pouch.

But it was not the silver that mattered.

The soft clink of silver in her pouch was a quiet sound, yet it felt more substantial than all the jewels she had possessed in her previous life. In that former existence, pearls and jade had adorned her, but every step she took had been guided by another's will. From this moment onward, she knew with quiet certainty: her life would no longer find shelter beneath anyone else's wings.

When Qin Nianyin received the summons to the study, a faint sense of foreboding had already settled within her. Inside, the subtle fragrance of sinking incense drifted in languid curls.

Su Zhang sat at the centre of the room, his long fingers tapping lightly against the desk as he reviewed a memorial. The atmosphere was cold, so still it seemed to stifle the very air.

Qin Nianyin kept her head lowered, fingertips gripping tightly at the corner of her sleeve.

She could hear the wind brushing through the bamboo shadows outside, soft, rhythmic, like each stroke was striking against her chest.

The sound was light, almost imperceptible, yet it brought back every memory of the moments before he used to grow stern in her previous life, those silences, that stillness. Before every storm, he had been just like this: wordless, quiet… a quietness more frightening than anger.

Su Zhang let out a quiet "Mm."

A single syllable ——light but weighted with authority.

The study door closed with a muted creak, cutting off all sounds from outside.

Incense burned steadily, its thin trail of smoke spreading like cool mist over a still pool. In the centre of the room, Su Zhang stood with his hands clasped behind him ——black robes, obsidian waist sash, a tall and austere figure.

In that instant, Qin Nianyin felt her steps grow heavy, as though she were walking into a solemn court of judgment.

She had expected rebuke, but not this weight —

not the suffocating gravity of authority pressing down without a single word raised in anger.

In her previous life, Su Zhang had been cold, distant, restrained to the point of inhuman calm. Even when the court stormed and blood was shed beyond palace walls, he had remained unmoved, his silence sharper than any blade.

Yet now, standing before her, every line of his posture spoke of vigilance — not personal displeasure, but something heavier, more dangerous.

Politics.

* * * * *

She held her breath as she approached, a fine sheen of sweat gathering at her temples.

"Where were you just now?"

His voice wasn't loud, yet it struck straight at the heart with its chill.

She pressed her lips together without answering, standing there in a daze, wanting to explain yet feeling it would be pointless.

Since when… did her every movement need to be reported to him?

Su Zhang slowly turned. His gaze was deep and severe, pressing down on her inch by inch, as though he had already seen through all her movements today.

His voice dropped from low to frigid, each word falling heavy like a stone into water.

"Entering an inn without reporting. Speaking and laughing with the Third Prince. Staying away from the study for half a day."

Each line landed like a hammer.

Only then did she begin to understand.

His accusations were not truly about her wandering the streets, nor about a handful of idle words exchanged over tea. They were born of fear — not fear for himself, but fear that with her fate now bound to the Su household, she was still moving blindly through the capital's shifting currents.

The Su family had already placed its banner beneath the Crown Prince.

And the Third Prince — every smile he offered, every step he took closer, carried calculation beneath its surface.

If she mis stepped, if she stood even briefly on the wrong side of power, she would not fall alone.

The air grew tighter, squeezing the breath from her chest.

Qin Nianyin's heart jolted. She instinctively lowered her head, fingers clutching tightly at the edge of her sleeve.

Across two lifetimes, she had only ever been treated with courtesy —— when had she ever been listed and scolded like this?

And worst of all, the person doing it was him, the man who, in her previous life, had been cold as winter frost and almost never reproached with more words than necessary.

His gaze swept down, cool and unyielding, mistaking her silence for defiance. His tone sank further.

"Acting in this manner ——do you or do you not know your fault?"

Acting?

Know her fault?

Faced with his relentless accusations, Qin Nianyin's throat tightened. She refused to answer, yet her fingers curled so hard inside her sleeve that half-moon dents were about to form.

"Why do you not speak?"

His voice lowered further, the chill so sharp it was hard to endure —— not agitated, but unbearably cutting.

"Do you think this place is what? A street market's farce? A children's schoolyard?"

In the wavering candlelight, his expression was shadowed and severe, the restraint in his tone only making the edge sharper.

Qin Nianyin kept her lips pressed tight, her chest rising and falling too quickly.

She had merely gone out to look for a shop, to sell a few hairpins ——

how had it escalated into a crime worthy of Heaven's wrath?

She looked down, silent, while something inside her coil tighter and tighter.

The scent of sandalwood grew suffocating. The light on his profile carved his features into something even colder.

This man ——this was not the Su Zhang she had known, but a true regent minister: one who allowed no challenge, no carelessness.

In her last life, he had been a man of ice, unmoved even by court tempests ——yet now, before her, his emotions leaked through every word, every breath, refusing to let go.

"Nianyin."

He spoke her name in a voice so low it was colder, heavier.

The suddenness of it shocked her heart into a jump.

That voice was too close ——so close it felt like it brushed the shell of her ear.

She instinctively stepped back half a pace, only to be forced into stillness again by his presence.

"The Su family now stands under the Crown Prince's banner. And the Third Prince ——what kind of man is he? Every smile, every step he takes toward you may well be calculation.

Do you truly believe the hearts of the world are as simple as you see them?"

He stepped closer.

His gaze was a sharpened blade, pressing down coldly.

Her palms were slick with sweat. A wave of helpless bewilderment rose in her chest.

This Su Zhang ——felt almost like a stranger.

So that was the truth of it.

All the sharpness in his tone, the iron restraint in his words — none of it was truly about her. She could hear it now, beneath every cold accusation he cast her way. It was fear.

Fear that now her fate was bound to the Su household, yet she still moved through the capital without sensing the undercurrents beneath its calm surface. Fear that a single careless step, a moment of misplaced trust, might place her on the wrong side of power — and that when the tide turned, she would be swept away with no strength to resist.

The Su family had already pledged itself beneath the Crown Prince's banner. And the Third Prince — every smile he offered, every step he took closer — carried calculation beneath its ease.

If she mis stepped, she would not fall alone.

All that severity, all that relentless pressing — it was the weight he bore as a regent minister, the vigilance demanded by his position, pressing outward in the only way he knew how.

Her chest trembled. Something lodged in her throat.

A long moment passed before she forced out a faint whisper:

"…It may have been a misunderstanding."

Her voice nearly broke.

"We met by chance. He merely… tossed me a few peanuts."

Su Zhang's brows tightened; his eyes grew even colder.

"Precisely because you are this simple-hearted… you are the easiest to worry for."

His tone was low and tightly restrained, yet every word struck like a chisel on stone.

"If you remain this careless ——how is the Su residence supposed to protect you?"

Chapter 39: Virtue and Restraint, Once More

The candle flame quivered with a slight, erratic tremor, the room sinking into a stillness so profound that one could hear the faint, dry rustle of parchment.

Su Zhang remained locked in a long, weighted silence, his countenance gradually frost-hardened as he struggled to suppress the surging tides of irritation within his chest. At last, he lifted his heavy gaze and spoke, his voice dropping into a low, resonant register that brooked no contradiction.

With a leaden expression, he stood with one hand clasped rigidly behind his back while the other tapped rhythmically upon the mahogany desk—a slow, deliberate cadence that exhaled an undeniable aura of oppressive authority.

"Nianyin," he began, his voice measuring out the words with cold precision, "Are you aware that for a woman, the foremost virtue resides in the capacity for restraint?"

Qin Nianyin started, her shoulders stiffening as she instinctively lifted her eyes to meet his. She encountered a gaze as piercing as a torch's flame, pressing down upon her with such force that her chest constricted, a spark of sharp displeasure igniting in her own heart.

Virtue... restraint. Again.

She had clung to those very anchors from her previous life all the way into this one; had it not been enough?

Maintaining his severe, unyielding visage, Su Zhang continued, "Though your years are few, you are no longer a mere child.

To engage in clamorous socializing with men outside, to exchange private words and laughter in full view of the world... if such whispers spread, how shall the populace judge you? How, in the days to come, shall you find a footing to stand upon in this world?"

As the final syllable of his speech fell, he became aware—in a sudden, jarring instant—of the imbalance that had crept into his own tone. It was no longer a simple, righteous admonition; rather, it felt like a restless, frantic agitation that had been forcibly stifled, a turbulence he himself had not yet found the leisure to trace to its source.

She stood before him with her head bowed low, her spine pulled taut and her fingertips clenching within her sleeves until the knuckles turned a stark, bone-white.

That posture of silent, unyielding endurance—which ought to have granted him a measure of relief—instead only served to make the air in his chest feel more stifled and wretched. He realized, with an abrupt clarity, that his words were no longer steered solely by the rudder of reason.

Yet the decree had been uttered; the authority of his station had been asserted. To retract his words now would only betray a heart of uncertainty.

Thus, he chose to press onward, veiling that nameless, fleeting loss of control under the guise of cool composure, continuing his lecture in the name of a distant, rational restraint.

Each word struck her heart like the cold clang of hammered iron.

Qin Nianyin bit her lower lip, the skin paling beneath the pressure.

Having been lectured and rebuked for so long, even her well-practiced patience finally reached its breaking point. Her nose began to prickle with a rising sourness, and she could no longer suppress the surge of her own indignation.

"Lord Su," she began, her voice trembling slightly with suppressed ire, "Your Lordship is surely being over-corrective to the point of unreason. I merely walked the marketplace this day in the company of my maid; I have committed not the slightest act that could be deemed a loss of virtue..."

"Whether or not virtue has been lost is not for you to decide," Su Zhang interjected coldly, his brows knitting into a deep, severe furrow. His countenance exhibited a gravity more profound than she had ever witnessed. "It is determined by how the eyes of the world perceive you."

Qin Nianyin could only swallow the remainder of her words, relapsing into a stifled silence.

The fire in his heart showed no sign of receding; instead, it seemed to gather momentum. "Nianyin, remember this well: for a woman to guard her virtue, she must guard not only her person, but also her heart, her conduct, and her reputation. Each must be held with equal vigilance."

By the time he finished, Qin Nianyin had utterly surrendered to the futility of argument. She lowered her head, feeling only a suffocating gloom and a leaden weight pressing upon her heart.

Su Zhang's voice finally softened by a marginal degree, and he drew a deep, labored breath. "Innocence is a fragile thing, easily shattered; a reputation, once tarnished, is nearly impossible to salvage. If you act wilfully out of a moment's impulse, you will find that when regret finally arrives, it arrives far too late."

Observing her despondent expression, he did not allow his tone to yield; instead, it grew several degrees colder.

"Even with Gu Xiao, you must not be familiar to the point of recklessness. You must maintain the proper defences and boundaries that exist between man and woman."

His voice grew heavier still, his eyes flashing like unsheathed blades. "Eh...?" Qin Nianyin was momentarily stunned, her mind clouding with even greater bewilderment.

Why, in all the world, was Gu Xiao being dragged into this now?

Su Zhang's gaze remained riveted upon her, his tone deep and laden with a terrifying solemnity. "Who is Gu Xiao? He is my closest, most trusted friend, but he is also a scion of a noble and ancient household serving the court. If the world sees you together, they will indulge in all manner of wild speculation. As a cousin residing within the Su Residence, people will inevitably question your motives for approaching him. Do you truly believe you can withstand the relentless gossip of the multitude?"

Qin Nianyin snapped her head up, staring at him in sheer disbelief.

What was he implying?

The way he rebuked her—never repeating a single word, each phrase polished and spotless—truly marked him as a scholar of the classics!

Ah, so that was the heart of it. At its root, he believed her station was too lowly, that she was unworthy of being associated with a man like Gu Xiao!

She pressed her lips into a tight line. She wanted to defend herself, but beneath the suffocating, magisterial pressure of Su Zhang's presence, she chose once again to remain silent.

What was there to explain?

That she held no romantic intent toward Gu Xiao? Or that she, having lived two lifetimes, merely spoke a few extra words to him in hopes of helping him evade the calamities of his previous life? No matter how she phrased it, the words would ring hollow. Better to say nothing at all.

"Since you are a member of the Su household, your every word and gesture must be governed by an extraordinary prudence. The criticism of others is a minor matter, but if the reputation of this residence is implicated—if you provide the malicious with a pretext to exploit—can you truly bear such a responsibility?"

There was an unconscious, frantic urgency in his voice. His gaze lingered for a moment on her slightly trembling eyelashes, and a nameless, suffocating anger welled up once more in his chest.

"In summary, Nianyin, remember this." He moderated his tone slightly, yet its severity remained absolute. "In your interactions with men—no matter who they may be—you must maintain an appropriate distance and observe the proper limits of decorum. Do not... do not make me worry for you any further."

Qin Nianyin lowered her head, her heart a cauldron of grievance and stifled resentment, yet beneath it all, an inexplicable, subtle emotion began to quietly ferment.

Very well. She admitted it. Her current station was indeed humble. She ought to keep her distance from these esteemed noblemen, lest people believe she harbored ambitions of social climbing!

She had been at fault this day. Having occupied a position of high authority for so long in her previous life, she had forgotten the precise movements of advance and retreat required when one's standing is low.

A mere cousin dwelling under another's roof, constantly associating with such luminaries—it was only natural that people would whisper.

* * * * *

Having uttered those words, Su Zhang was suddenly seized by a wave of profound powerlessness. He lowered his gaze to conceal his shifting emotions, a bitter, silent smile curling within his heart.

He had intended to offer counsel in the name of an elder brother, yet he found himself utterly unable to suppress the inexplicable, gloomy turbulence simmering in his soul.

The more he spoke, the more disordered his thoughts became.

He knew with absolute certainty that she should not be entangled in the webs of power; he knew he ought to remain a cold, detached observer. Yet, the moment the sight of her—bowed head, bitten lip—imprinted itself upon his eyes, his chest felt as though it were being gripped by an invisible hand, tightening until it ached.

The candle flame flickered, the light and shadow dancing across the curve of her cheek. In that moment, the hidden thread of tenderness in his heart was amplified beyond his control.

Qin Nianyin kept her head lowered, her shoulders trembling with a faint, rhythmic vibration, her fingertips digging into the fabric of her skirt. A mountain of grievance and stifled frustration had accumulated in her chest, yet she found no vessel into which she could pour it.

Su Zhang watched her in a heavy silence, his gaze appearing cold and detached, yet his own chest was tightening.

A sudden, wild impulse rose within him—to reach out and smooth a stray lock of her hair, or to steady the trembling of her shoulder. His fingertips twitched with the ghost of a movement, but he halted midway.

He lowered his lashes, forcibly crushing that impulse, the knuckles of his hand clasped behind his back turning a stark white from the strain.

A moment later, he said only in a frigid tone, "Remember, Nianyin. Never again let me worry for you in this manner."

With those words, he turned his back to the candlelight, allowing the gathering shadows to swallow his features.

Qin Nianyin felt the sting of grievance deepen. A burning warmth gathered in the corners of her eyes, but she stubbornly refused to let a single tear fall.

Meanwhile, as Su Zhang stared at the unfinished scrolls upon his desk, the tenderness in his heart transformed into a deeper, more oppressive anger—one so heavy it disrupted the very cadence of his breath.

It was only Gu Xiao. It was only the Third Prince. He knew well that neither was a man of frivolous character, yet why—why did he find it so utterly unbearable to see her in close proximity to them?

He did not understand what was happening to him. Why was he, a man always so celebrated for his cool self-possession, losing his equilibrium because of her?

This strange, alien sentiment was like a burgeoning fire, igniting quietly in the deepest recesses of his being.

He glanced down at her trembling shoulders, and his heart clenched again, only for him to harden it once more.

Why?

Her transgression was merely a few extra words shared with the Third Prince; he knew his fury was unwarranted, yet the mere image of their shared laughter caused a sharp pain in his chest, as if he had been pricked by invisible thorns.

He could not control the urge to rebuke her, to bind her, to insist that she follow only the path that he himself had deemed acceptable.

This mentality... even he found it jarring and discordant.

He furrowed his brow, averting his gaze so that she might not see the flicker of his own wretched disarray. The room fell into an utter, tomb-like silence, so quiet that even the sighing of the wind through the bamboo grove outside was clearly audible.

Qin Nianyin remained with her head bowed, speaking not a word for a long duration. Seeing her despondent state, a trace of weariness flickered across Su Zhang's brow.

He lowered his voice, saying, "Enough. These words were not intended to instill a heart of fear. I merely wished you to understand that behind you, there stands not only yourself, but the entirety of the Shen household."

As long as you dwell under the Su roof, your name is bound to both houses—what befalls you will not stop at your own doorstep.

He paused, a momentary silence falling before he spoke again with a slow deliberation. "...Regarding the matter of Xu Wencai, I have already made the necessary arrangements for you. He may enter Songhe Academy on the morrow."

Qin Nianyin was momentarily frozen, her eyes instantly igniting with light. The accumulated grievance and the unshed tears in her eyes now shimmered together in a soft mist. "That... that is truly wonderful." Her voice trembled slightly, yet it carried a profound note of relief. Her rebirth had, at last, altered the destiny of another.

Su Zhang looked at her, and a slow, faint curve finally touched the corners of his lips. "Since you harbor such concern for his future, I have acted to fulfill your wish."

Qin Nianyin nodded with a fierce vigor, the tears swirling in her eyes as she struggled with all her might to contain them.

"You may withdraw now," his tone turned heavy once more. "Return and reflect meticulously upon your actions."

Reflect?

With her eyes rimmed in red, Qin Nianyin performed a formal curtsey and turned to depart, her steps hurried and frantic, as if staying a heartbeat longer would cause her composure to crumble into a deluge.

The night breeze brushed against her cheeks. Her shoulders and back continued to tremble slightly, her lips pressed into a tight, stubborn line, her heart churning with a sour, acrid bitterness.

In her previous life, he had been as cold as ice. In this life, he bound her at every turn.

She whispered a low, bitter laugh to herself. "It is truly... more than one can bear."

Step by step, she walked farther into the night, the moisture in her eyes growing more pronounced. In her former life, he had bestowed upon her glory and wealth. In this life, he bestowed upon her shackles.

She lowered her eyes, pressing her emotions deep into the recesses of her heart, yet her chest felt leaden and suffocating.

Once her silhouette had vanished into the darkness, the study finally settled into a complete, absolute stillness.

Su Zhang stood motionless, his hands clasped behind him. Only after a long duration did he finally exhale a deep, weary sigh.

The moonlight spilled in, the shadows of the bamboo swaying. He lifted his head to gaze out, his brow marked by an increasing vexation.

The official documents upon his desk remained unturned. His fingertips tapped lightly against the wood, and he let out a low, soft laugh—a sound that was dark and laden with a biting self-mockery.

He was unwilling to ponder it deeply, yet found himself utterly unable to stop the thoughts from rising.

The incense smoke curled upward in its languid dance. His gaze gradually darkened, his voice dropping to a murmur that was nearly inaudible.

"...Could it be that I have truly... fallen under a spell?"

He, a man always so steady and self-controlled, had finally—on this very night—given birth to a rare and terrifying tremor of uncertainty and disquiet.

Qin Nianyin returned to her chambers. Mei hurried forward to help her remove her cloak, her face clouded with concern upon seeing her mistress's pallid complexion and the lingering tension around her eyes.

"Miss, just now… was the reprimand severe?" she whispered, unable to fully conceal her indignation. "He is too unfeeling. With just a few words, he makes one feel utterly ashamed and small."

Qin Nianyin remained silent, merely casting a faint, weary glance in her direction.

Mei bit her lip, muttering under her breath, "Miss… the rules in this residence are so strict and cold, not at all like the warmth and ease of our time in Jiangnan…"

"Enough," Qin Nianyin's voice was very soft, laced with a weariness that seemed to seep into the quiet room. "That is past. None of it can be returned to."

Mei, still unwilling to relent, pressed, "But Miss did nothing wrong…"

Qin Nianyin's fingers stilled momentarily. "Right or wrong is not for me to decide," she replied, her tone even lighter, as if the words themselves held no weight she could claim.

In her current humble position as a dependent, what right did she have to speak? Any further explanation would merely sound like a feeble excuse.

Having said this, she moved to remove her hairpins, her movements exceedingly slow and deliberate, as if trying to use these mundane, rhythmic sounds to suppress the stifling anger and helplessness coiled in her chest.

She knew, of course, that Su Zhang's words were not entirely without reason. Yet, precisely because of this, her heart felt even more troubled, tangled in a knot of resentment and reluctant understanding.

What had he said? Nothing more than to make her recognize her station and status, observe womanly virtues, preserve propriety and cease her delusions of climbing the social ladder ——each sentence a blade, each striking true and leaving a familiar, cold ache.

After her muttered complaints, seeing her mistress's despondent expression, Mei's heart softened. She added gently, "Perhaps the Young Master is also concerned for you… and spoke hastily out of worry."

A lump caught in Qin Nianyin's throat. After a long moment, she let out a soft sigh, the sound barely disturbing the stillness. Lowering her head, she twisted a corner of her garment, her expression returning to a calmness that felt like a thin veneer, yet tinged with a trace of bitterness.

She was angry with him, but even more so with herself.

How could she have been so foolish? For the sake of a few pleasant words, she dared show a cold face to a prince? For a handful of peanuts, she went to argue with someone as if she still had the standing to do so?

Who was she? Who was she in this life?

No matter her memories of a past life, no matter her ability to earn silver or understand the times, now she was merely a 'cousin' living under someone else's roof in the Su residence — a guest whose welcome was contingent upon her silence and compliance.

They could crush her with a single finger , and the world would not blink.

She gently bit her lower lip. After a long silence, she finally said in a low voice, "Enough. I acted rashly today. I deserved the reprimand. I cannot speak of grievance." The words tasted like ash.

Before her words fully faded, a young servant entered, presenting a card.

Mei took it, her face lighting up with a smile as she handed it to Qin Nianyin. "Lady Lingyan is hosting a chrysanthemum viewing tomorrow. She has invited Lady Wan and specifically mentioned your name, inviting you to attend as well."

Qin Nianyin's fingers paused slightly. She accepted the card and examined it for a moment, the fine paper cool against her skin.

"Since the invitation is so gracious, I naturally must attend," she said, her voice clear and mellifluous, a practiced social grace softening her expression with the faintest trace of warmth.

As she spoke the final phrase, she seemed to smile casually, her fingertips lightly twisting the corner of the card, yet the pressure subtly tightened, belying the ease of her manner.

She lowered her gaze to the card, her eyes appearing gentle, yet concealing a degree of imperceptible indifference and aloofness , like a still pond that reflected light but gave no depth.

* * * * *

The next day, the light rain had just ceased, leaving the world washed in a clean, damp gloss.

A thin, pearlescent mist lingered among the trees and pavilions. The chrysanthemums in the rear garden of the Su estate were in full, glorious bloom, great clusters of fiery gold, snowy white, and deep wine-red, like radiant brocade spread across the earth. The young ladies moved among the flowers, their light laughter and the soft rustle of silk drifting like fragrant smoke.

Shen Lingyan was already waiting under the flower-covered corridor. Seeing Qin Nianyin arrive, she approached with a radiant smile. "Younger Sister Nianyin, come quickly! We were just about to start comparing our appreciation of the flowers. Had you been a step later, you would have lost."

Su Wan also nodded with a smile, yet her courtesy was distant, her demeanour not revealing any particular closeness , a polite mask perfectly in place.

Qin Nianyin responded with a slight smile, answering gently, "Sister Lingyan, Sister Wan, your refined interest is high. Nianyin naturally will accompany you. However,… I am not very knowledgeable about appreciating chrysanthemums. I fear I may invite laughter." Her humility was a well-worn shield.

Shen Lingyan pulled her to a spot beneath a particularly splendid canopy of blooms. Just as they were about to sit, a sudden, delighted exclamation was heard: "Ah, Lady Chen! The flower in your hair is truly beautiful and unusual! Where did you get it?"

All eyes turned as one towards a pretty young woman with delicate features who wore a hairpin flower tucked diagonally into her chignon. It was not made of gold, jade, or gems, but crafted from silk ribbons and beaded strings into the shape of a clinging vine with tiny blossoms, —— unique, elegant and quite charming.

The woman smiled shyly, a faint blush touching her cheeks. "It was made by Lady Qin."

She then proceeded to narrate the amusing incident of their chance meeting at the teahouse days before, her tale animated and engaging, where Qin Nianyin had given each of them a handcrafted hairpin flower.

Before the light chatter could subside, its pleasant hum still hanging in the air, another young woman pursed her lips into a smile, her tone now meaningful and laced with subtle provocation. "Speaking of which, it wasn't only Lady Chen present that day… His Highness, the Third Prince, was also there."

As these words fell, a palpable ripple passed through the gathering. The assembled young ladies turned their gazes uniformly towards Qin Nianyin, their eyes glittering with a sharp, volatile mix of astonishment, speculation and envy. The atmosphere instantly grew still and charged.

"The Third Prince? Younger Sister Nianyin actually took tea with His Highness the Third Prince?" The question was a dart, thinly veiled as curiosity.

Qin Nianyin's heart jolted violently, abruptly recalling the warning in Su Zhang's study ——she absolutely must not become associated with the Third Prince in any way! Panic, cold and swift, tightened her throat.

"Nothing of the sort!" Her voice rose abruptly, betraying her alarm before she could steady it. "His Highness is a person of such stature! That day, it was merely a few words of jest. How would Nianyin dare to presume to converse with him!"

"Aiya, Younger Sister Nianyin is so modest," said another, her smile not reaching her eyes. "With Lady Wan and Lord Su as your connections and now the favour of His Highness the Third Prince, who wouldn't look at you differently?"

"…" Unwilling to be drawn further in, Qin Nianyin had no choice but to force herself into a stiff, strained silence.

A young lady of the Liu family, her eyes shifting with feigned innocence, feigned a sigh. "The Third Prince has always held himself aloof, a moon beyond reach. To gain a glance from him is something many would dream of but never obtain."

Another added, her tone a perfect blend of jest and pointed earnestness, "Who's to say… this little hairpin flower might one day become a token of love from a royal consort!"

A wave of tittering laughter , edged and knowing, passed through the group, the probing and scrutinizing gazes intensifying, weighing her like a commodity.

Qin Nianyin's heart tightened, but she forcibly maintained her composure, slightly lowering her eyes to veil their distress, her tone gentle and temperate. "What nonsense. It was merely a coincidence." She poured every ounce of calm into the words.

She struggled to suppress her emotions, inwardly chiding herself for her earlier loss of control.

Not far away, a young woman of the Zhao family let out a soft, disdainful humph, her fingertips viciously crushing a chrysanthemum blossom to pieces.

This subtle but violent action did not escape Qin Nianyin's notice. She couldn't help but laugh inwardly, a cold thread of amusement, though her face remained composed and gentle.

"Nianyin is well aware her skills are insignificant. These little trinkets I make are merely for my own amusement. If they do not please, you are all free to simply disregard them as if they were never there."

Her tone was light, yet her words skilfully navigated attack and defence, leaving no room for reproach and gracefully dismissing their barbs.

The expressions of several young ladies shifted slightly, but they found no grounds for rebuttal.

Suddenly, the Zhao young woman spoke coldly, her voice clear and cutting, "Those with any discernment naturally understand the cleverness of this hairpin. Those who only know how to pile up gold and jade probably haven't learned how to write the words 'elegance' and 'refinement'."

She was usually sparing with words, but this time her protection was unmistakable, her tone leaving no room for courtesy.

The Wang young lady's expression stiffened. Forcing a smile, she changed the subject, causing the atmosphere to cool momentarily into awkwardness.

Su Wan's tone grew even colder as she said with a derisive laugh, "Everyone wearing the same gold and jade is, conversely, rather vulgar. It's far inferior to my cousin, who can create her own distinctive style. Unlike some, who only rely on their family background, utterly devoid of refined taste."

She did not name names, but everyone understood whom she was protecting and whom she was mocking , the lines drawn plainly in the air.

The Zhao young woman's face turned pale with anger. She let out a cold humph and turned her head away.

Shen Lingyan hurried to smooth things over, her voice a practiced melody of harmony. "Today is a gathering to appreciate flowers. Let's not allow idle chatter to spoil our mood. I have long admired Younger Sister Nianyin's cleverness and was actually hoping to request another hairpin to gift to an elder."

The lively Liu young lady also laughed, "Well said! I'd like one too, to match my new gauze dress. It would look absolutely lovely."

Shen Lingyan added with a smile, "Younger Sister Nianyin, if it's not too much trouble, I would also like to purchase a few to give as gifts. They would be quite suitable."

Qin Nianyin responded with a warm smile, the perfect picture of gracious humility, "If Sister Lingyan does not find them beneath contempt, Nianyin would naturally offer them. How could I dare speak of payment?"

Her tone was soft and graceful, her manner poised and generous, making her seem exceptionally dignified by contrast.

The scent of chrysanthemums, moist and heavy, hung in the rain-freshened air. A petal, dislodged by the fine rain, settled quietly beside Qin Nianyin's embroidered shoe, a tiny, perfect spot of fallen gold.

The undercurrents of that moment seemed to be gently smoothed away with it, leaving on the surface only the picture of a pleasant garden party.

Chapter 41: A Particular Gift

After the conclusion of the Chrysanthemum Banquet, the carriage rocked with a rhythmic, languid sway on its journey back to the Su residence.

Within the confined sanctuary of the carriage, the lamplight flickered with an uneasy cadence, casting long, wavering shadows that intensified an atmosphere already heavy with a stifling, silent oppression.

Qin Nianyin sat ensconced within the carriage, her peripheral vision catching the stark, crystalline coldness of Su Wan's countenance.

Su Wan's eyes emitted a frost-like chill, a gaze that deliberately kept the world at a daunting distance. Qin Nianyin sighed inwardly—the brother and sister were truly forged from the same unyielding mold; even this peculiar brand of frigidity was shared in every chilling detail.

Remaining utterly composed, Qin Nianyin retrieved a small, dark-lacquered wood food box with a grace that seemed effortless. Her voice, when it emerged, was soft and melodic, yet possessed a scrupulous sense of measure: "Sister Wan, the toil of the journey is wearying. Perhaps you would care to first moisten your throat with a little something?"

Su Wan's gaze remained immovable, fixed upon the tapestry of street scenes unfolding beyond the window, as if she were entirely deaf to the offer.

Qin Nianyin's expression remained as unruffled as a still pond, her tone as casual as if she were merely drifting through idle conversation: "These are peach shortcakes gathered from the banquet; they remain crisp and fragrant. Would you care to sample a piece?"

There was no response, only the monotonous grind of the wheels.

"There is also the hibiscus cake; it is sweet without being cloying, and the color is quite pleasing to the eye." Her tone remained light and even, as if she were calmly narrating a matter of the utmost insignificance.

Finally, Su Wan emitted an almost imperceptible huff of breath—a sound between a scoff and a sigh.

She turned her head at last, her tone flat yet betraying a thin, taut thread of suppressed irritation: "You... when you were fashioning those head-ornaments, why did you not first offer a single branch to me? To let the outsiders seize the priority—it makes it seem as though I am somehow inferior to them."

Qin Nianyin was momentarily startled, but she grasped the truth in an instant. Though the words were couched in casual complaint, they vibrated with a genuine, wounded pride—it was not the ornament she craved, but the recognition. At the banquet, the noble ladies had crowded around Qin Nianyin with effusive praise, leaving Su Wan to stand in the shadows of neglect.

A subtle, knowing smile touched Qin Nianyin's lips. "Those ornaments were, after all, mere wares intended for the marketplace. Had those ladies not truly harbored a genuine affection for the craft, they would not have been so eager to part with their silver."

The sound of the carriage wheels provided a persistent, low-level drone.

Qin Nianyin paused, her tone softening even further, as if she were treading carefully to avoid bruising the other's delicate pride: "My hands are coarse and unskilled; I must spend several more days in careful study and refinement before I can produce a piece that is truly satisfying. If you, Sister, were willing to adorn yourself with my work, it would be my profound honor."

She paused again, her gaze reflecting a sincere and open warmth. "If it meets your approval, Sister Wan, I shall naturally prepare a piece for you. However, that specific ornament must be crafted with a slower, more meticulous hand—I shall take my time to fashion one of exceptional quality, one that is truly worthy of your bearing and innate grace."

She curved her eyes into the shape of crescent moons, adding with a delicate balance of gravity and jest: "Naturally, it would be a token of my heart's true regard."

The corner of Su Wan's mouth quivered, threatening to arc upward. Though she was loath to admit defeat, a faint, unmistakable warmth began to ripple and spread through the dark depths of her eyes.

Seeing this, Qin Nianyin ceased her persuasion. She understood that a person of Su Wan's temperament held no stock in empty flattery or fawning subservience; she trusted only the weight of genuine intent.

Rather than wielding a glib and silver tongue, it was better to let the truth flow like deep, silent waters, allowing the other to perceive the sincerity for herself.

Upon their return to the residence, Qin Nianyin instructed Mei to carefully stow the handcrafted ornaments within a fine wooden box. The beadwork was intricate, the labor complex, and tucked within was a short, elegant note:

"I have newly arrived at this residence and have been favoured by Sister Wan's care. This small token of my heart is offered with the utmost respect, though it is far from adequate to express my true sentiments."

Though Su Wan remained sparse with her words upon receiving the gift, she spent a long duration within her chambers, trying the ornament on before the polished bronze mirror. In the wavering dance of the lamplight, the corners of her lips curved into a faint, almost invisible arc of satisfaction.

Meanwhile, in a distant corner of the courtyard, a servant of the Su household watched this exchange from afar.

His expression was neutral, yet he turned and vanished into the shadows—as if he were a messenger preparing to relay every observed detail to someone who was never meant to know.

* * * * *

The following morning, a thin, silver mist had yet to disperse, clinging to the eaves like a lingering dream. Though the season was turning toward the heat of summer, the dawn still carried a biting chill that seeped into one's bones.

Qin Nianyin arrived at the study at her customary hour, before the mark of Mao. Just as she approached the threshold, the heavy, muffled sound of a low cough echoed from within—a sound that was suppressed and weighted, like the distant rumble of thunder pressing against the chest.

Her steps faltered. Peering through the narrow, partially open crack of the door, she beheld Su Zhang.

He was dressed in a simple, moon-white robe, leaning wearily behind his desk. His complexion was a stark, bloodless white, and his lips were so pale they appeared nearly translucent.

A scroll lay half-turned in his hand, his brow was locked in a tight furrow, and his shoulders trembled with the violence of each stifled cough.

Her initial, visceral impulse was to rush inside and offer her concern, but the moment she took a single step, she halted abruptly. She lowered her lashes, forcibly swallowing the words that had risen to her throat, tasting the ash of her own hesitation.

Xiuyan's voice drifted from within, laden with a palpable anxiety: "Young Master, the Imperial Physician was most explicit. No matter the bitterness of the concoction, you must consume the medicine on schedule. Your cough has grown increasingly severe; if you continue this delay, I fear the damage to your lungs and spirit will be irreversible."

Su Zhang's voice remained flat and level: "It is but a minor cough; there is no need for such excessive alarm. The medicine is too arid—I find I cannot stomach it."

"But these past few nights, you have slept so poorly that your strength is waning. When the fits take you, you can scarcely find the breath to—"

"I know my own limits," he interrupted. His voice was steady, yet it was layered with an undeniable weariness that brooked no further argument.

Just as Xiuyan prepared to renew his plea, he turned the corner of the corridor and spotted Qin Nianyin standing by the door. She held a tea tray in her hands, her expression veiled beneath the shadow of her lowered lashes, making her thoughts impossible to decipher.

His eyes ignited with a desperate hope. Lowering his voice, he whispered: "Young Lady Cousin, you have arrived at the most fortuitous moment... The Young Master has become increasingly dismissive of all counsel, refusing his medicine at every turn. If you were to speak, he might—just might—be willing to listen."

Qin Nianyin remained silent for a long, heavy heartbeat before she offered a slight, measured nod: "I shall try."

When she stepped into the study, her footsteps were as light as fallen leaves. The bitter aroma of the medicine mingled with the scent of ink and aged paper, hanging in the still, oppressive air.

Su Zhang lifted his gaze. His eyes fell first upon the tea tray in her hands, then moved slowly to her face, his expression a mask of unruffled calm.

Qin Nianyin placed the teacup upon the red sandalwood tray beside his desk, her tone entirely mild: "The temperature of the tea is precisely correct. The medicine is also here. If Your Lordship has no other pressing matters, it would be best to consume them both at once." Her voice was level and unhurried, devoid of any superfluous pleasantries or deliberate coldness—as if she were merely a servant fulfilling a mundane duty.

The corner of Su Zhang's mouth twitched with a ghost of a movement. In the end, he said nothing. He merely lowered his gaze, staring at the dark liquid in the bowl as if seeking some hidden truth within the shadows of his own fingers.

As she turned to depart, his voice suddenly emerged, deep and resonant: "If this gesture is born only from the request of another, there is no need to force yourself."

Qin Nianyin's steps did not falter for a single inch. Her tone remained equally even, equally detached: "I am merely delivering tea. It does not constitute a forcing of myself."

The silence that followed descended upon the room like a layer of frost—soundless, cold, and absolute.

After a long, agonizing moment, he reached out, grasped the bowl, and drained the bitter medicine in a single, unhesitating draught.

As her silhouette receded into the distance, the faint, flickering emotion he had hidden so deeply within his eyes was once again repressed, returning to a state of hollow calmness. Yet, the porcelain bowl in his hand still vibrated with the residual warmth from where her fingers had gripped it moments before.

* * * * *

As Qin Nianyin withdrew from the threshold of the study, her heart was a churning cauldron of turbulent emotions. The image of him—bloodless and pale, yet still forcing his spine into that unyielding, straight line—haunted her. She found that she could not bring herself to utter even the simplest word of concern.

She could not say it; she dared not say it.

Her heart hammered against her ribs with such violence it felt as if it might shatter the bone. She could only cloak herself in a shroud of feigned indifference, acting the part of a distant relative who shared no bond of blood or spirit with him.

In her previous life, he had always been plagued by these coughing fits during the changing of the seasons, yet his hatred for medicine was legendary.

Back then, she had knelt by his sickbed, tearfully begging him to take his cure, keeping a solitary vigil by his lamp through the long reaches of the night. She had even held his hand, her voice trembling as she whispered, "Does it hurt? Does it hurt terribly?"

Even then, he had offered her no more than a few cold, clipped words in return, maintaining his impenetrable wall of aloofness.

She could not help but let out a silent, self-mocking laugh. Now, with a new life before her, it was he who was ill and she who held the power to take the initiative—yet she found herself unable to even ask, "Are you feeling better?"

By the time she reached the courtyard, the sky had turned a leaden, oppressive gray, a low ceiling that seemed to press the very breath from the world. A sharp, cool wind wormed its way through the folds of her gown. It was clear that rain was imminent.

Suddenly, her steps came to a dead halt. Standing there, watching the frantic swaying of the bamboo shadows, her mind became a tangled, inextricable mess.

The image of his shoulders trembling with each cough replayed incessantly in her mind, as did that brief, flickering flash of expectation in his eyes when he had looked up at her.

She had seen it. She had captured that silent, desperate hope in his gaze.

But she did not want to respond, nor did she dare to. Even though he had strove to conceal his vulnerability, she had seen his waiting and his weariness with a devastating clarity.

"What am I doing..." she murmured to herself, her heart filled with a sharp, internal chiding. "What in heaven's name am I doing?"

Her fingers unconsciously twisted and worried the fabric of her sleeves. Finally, she pivoted on her heel with a sudden, sharp motion, her steps quickening as if she were fleeing from her own suffocating hesitation, heading straight for the sanctuary of the kitchen.

Chapter 42: Sweet Pear Soup

When the stove fire roared to life, Qin Nianyin suddenly felt a scorching heat in the center of her palms; only then did she realize with a jolt that she had actually proceeded with this endeavor.

Her fingertips trembled with a rhythmic vibration as she sliced the pears; the blade strayed and veered several times as she pared the skin, and when it came time to add the red dates, she found herself adding two more than intended.

She was far from adept in the culinary arts. In her previous life, there had always been an army of maids and servants to organize every morsel of her sustenance; rarely indeed had there been an occasion for her to personally kindle the fire for soup or porridge.

Yet, a bowl of Rock Sugar and Snow Pear was one of the few offerings of hers that he had been willing to accept in that former existence.

He harboured a deep-seated aversion to medicine; it had been so in the last life, just as it was now. He had habitually and coldly rejected her overtures and gestures of kindness, yet that specific pear soup was the rare exception when he seldom turned her away.

Spoon by agonizing spoon, she simmered the pear until it was rendered soft and yielding, adding a few goji berries to draw out a subtle fragrance, all for the sake of soothing that stubborn cough of a man who refused to dutifully consume his medicine.

Every single drop of that decoction seemed to scorch her very heart.

Qin Nianyin lowered her gaze to the shimmering, reflective surface of the soup within the earthenware pot, and she could not help but let out a low, cold laugh—a sound of biting self-mockery. "Qin Nianyin," she murmured, "you are truly without a shred of resolve. He would not deign to spare you a second glance in the last life, and yet, having arrived in this one, you still find yourself unable to let go?"

But, in the end, she truly could not let go.

She meticulously ladled the essence into a ceramic bowl, fitted the lid securely, and then—with a lingering caution—wrapped it again and again in a protective cloth napkin before finally summoning Mei.

"Deliver this invitation to the Shen estate. Say that I am inviting Sister Lingyan to come tomorrow to inspect the newly crafted velvet-flower hairpins... Also..." Her voice faltered into a brief, suspended silence as she bit her lip, then she added, "Just mention, as if by accident, that...that Cousin is feeling somewhat indisposed."

Mei was momentarily taken aback, her gaze fixing upon her mistress's eyes, which were rimmed with a faint, telltale redness. Just as she was about to voice a question, she was cut short by a sharp gesture.

"Do not say that I specifically instructed you to speak of it. Under no circumstances must you say that."

She turned her back, her voice becoming as light as a passing breeze, swallowed up inch by inch by the encroaching night. Only she herself knew that in this incarnation, she no longer wished to forcefully impose her affections upon him with that same aggressive insistence of the past.

She merely wanted to perform this small act for him in the shadows of silence. She hoped, with a desperate fervour, that he would remain unaware.

Even if the person who arrived to tend to him was not her, and even if he might feel a flicker of disappointment.

She would much rather be misunderstood as being cold and indifferent than to ever again approach him with such reckless haste. In this life, she had to proceed with a more profound caution. Yet, no matter how meticulously she guarded herself, this wellspring of affection still managed to irrepressibly overflow the boundaries she had set.

* * * * *

Qin Nianyin gently pressed the lid onto the porcelain bowl of Rock Sugar and Snow Pear soup.

Hot steam escaped in languid curls from the narrow gap, carrying with it the delicate, honeyed aroma of red dates and goji berries.

She handed the tray to Mei, her voice suppressed into the faintest of whispers: "Take this to Xiuyan. Tell him it is a throat-soothing soup newly simmered in the kitchen, and ask him to deliver it to the Young Master. Remember—at all costs, you must not reveal that it was I who prepared it."

Mei stood frozen for a heartbeat, her mouth parting as if to protest, but in the end, she merely bowed her head in compliance. "Understood, Miss."

Not long afterward, Xiuyan entered the study as was his custom. Seeing Su Zhang with his brow tightly furrowed, the corners of his eyes flushed with a feverish red, and his voice sounding painfully hoarse, the attendant quickly brought forth the bowl of pear soup: "Young Master, this is a fresh batch of snow pear soup from the kitchen. They say it is an essence to moisten the lungs and quiet the cough. They requested that I bring it for you to sample."

Su Zhang's head was thrumming with a violent ache, and he did not spare the matter a second thought, merely dismissing it with a wave of his hand. "Set it down."

After a moment, he reached out and lifted the lid of the vessel. A mist of hot steam billowed upward, and the fragrance permeated the air.

He ladled a spoonful into his mouth; it was warm without being scalding, a gentle and sweet moisture.

The snow pear dissolved almost instantly upon his tongue, and the lingering aftertaste of red dates and goji berries permeated his throat, actually managing to suppress the violence of his cough by a degree.

He was momentarily dazed, his tongue appearing to be suddenly snagged by a hook of memory—this flavor was unmistakably familiar.

Yet, for a fleeting instant, he could not recall exactly when or in what place he had ever savored such a taste before.

"Xiuyan."

"Yes, Young Master. I await your instructions." Xiuyan hastily abandoned the mundane tasks he was tending to and bowed with a respectful deference.

"This sweet soup... is it the first time the kitchen has delivered it?" Or had they sent it before, and he had simply been too preoccupied to notice?

"Uh..." Xiuyan was seized by a startle, stammering as his mind spun frantically to find an escape, for the Young Lady Cousin had forbidden him from speaking the truth. "Yes... ha-ha, it should be the first time. I believe it is a folk remedy for coughs from the hometown of the cook, Old Li."

"I see." Su Zhang remained deeply puzzled by the hauntingly familiar taste.

What flickered through his mind like a lightning bolt was the clink of a teacup being set upon a table, the serene expression of a woman with her eyes cast down, and those slender, delicate fingers—adorned with a touch of scarlet lacquer—as she held the bowl.

But he remained outwardly unruffled, merely finishing the entire bowl of soup in a heavy silence.

The wisp of doubt and the stirring of an unknown heartbeat, like ripples across the surface of a pond, slowly fanned out, only to subside once more into a hollow calm, as if nothing of consequence had ever occurred.

* * * * *

The night grew deeper, and the sound of the wind brushing against the corners of the curtains brought a sharp chill.

Mei returned in a frantic haste, and the moment she stepped over the threshold, she lowered her head to report: "Miss, the Shen estate has sent word... Miss Lingyan accompanied the Madam to the suburban villa early this morning and has not yet returned. I waited for a long duration, but ultimately, the person did not appear."

Upon hearing this, Qin Nianyin's hand faltered for a fraction of a second. A shadow of light flickered within the depths of her eyes, but she merely forced a faint, distant smile. "So be it. There will be other opportunities in the long days ahead."

Her voice was exceedingly light, so airy it seemed as if it would vanish the moment the wind caught it. Falling amidst the wavering lamplight, it was impossible to discern whether the tone was one of consolation or of bitter self-mockery.

She walked to the window, her fingertips pushing open half of the carved wooden lattice.

The night wind, heavy with moisture, surged inside, instantly extinguishing the residual warmth of the lamp.

Qin Nianyin stood there, fixed in place for a long time, quietly gazing toward the direction of the faintly lit study in the distance. Her gaze was deep and devoid of ripples, and for a long, protracted duration, she uttered not a single word.

Chapter 43: Refusing a Royal Marriage

The sun grew increasingly fierce, its golden light slanting in from the white jade steps outside the hall.

In the Imperial Study, Emperor Xuanwen reclined slightly in his grand master's chair, rotating a smooth, warm jade bead between his fingers. Deep within his gaze lay an amusement that resembled a smile yet wasn't quiet.

The three princes and Su Zhang stood in rows to his left and right, each countenance inscrutable, quietly awaiting the imperial command.

"Zijun," Emperor Xuanwen's tone was mild, yet held a note of probing, "you are no longer young in years. Is there someone who has captured your heart?"

Su Zhang stepped forward slightly with a bow, his expression reverent. "Matters of marriage and children naturally follow the commands of one's parents. In reply to Your Majesty, this humble official has no specific desires."

Emperor Xuanwen gave a light laugh. "Do not try to deceive Us with such high-sounding excuses. If you do not give your nod, could your parents possibly overcome your stubborn nature?"

"This matter is still under discussion by my esteemed elders at home."

"In that case ——" Emperor Xuanwen's lips curved faintly, his voice mild yet carrying an authority that allowed no refusal.

"Today, We shall decide for you. The palace holds many talented women and remarkable beauties.

If you truly have no wish to choose for yourself… then We may well bestow one upon you ——

say, Lady Jing. What of her?"

"Your Majesty!"

Su Zhang dropped to his knees at once, robes sweeping the floor as he bowed deeply. His voice was firm yet reverent.

"This unworthy minister is dull of wit and meagre in ability. I dare not presume to ascend to a station that stands shoulder to shoulder with the Imperial House."

As these words fell, the air in the hall solidified instantly.

Crown Prince Li Duan lowered his eyelashes, his expression unchanged, as if he had long anticipated this.

Second Prince Li Xuan's brow arched slightly. He covered his lips with a light laugh; his meaning tinged with scorn.

Third Prince Li Suo leaned against a pillar, his sword-like brows slightly raised, a mix of mockery and amusement deepening in his eyes.

Emperor Xuanwen's brow furrowed slightly, his voice sinking. "Minister Su, you would refuse a marriage personally selected by Us?"

Su Zhang bowed again, his tone neither haughty nor servile. "This humble official knows his own foundations are humble and weak. I fear bringing disgrace upon Your Majesty's grace. The Second Princess is heavenly in grace and beauty, a noble scion of the golden bough. Should she be wed to one such as I, any slight hardship incurred would leave me unable to sleep or eat in peace. I truly dare not arrogantly accept such an honour."

As he lifted his gaze, his eyes were clear and bright. Each word was earnest and thorough, simultaneously self-deprecating and demonstrating loyalty, leaving no opening for criticism.

Li Duan pressed his lips into a slight smile, his steady demeanour hinting at a trace of approval.

A cold light flashed in Li Xuan's eyes, though a faint smile still played on his lips. His tone held a note of sarcastic amusement. "Minister Su's loyalty is so profound that he would discard a royal marriage as if it were worthless. Truly, a pillar of the state."

Li Suo, fanning himself lightly, chuckled low. "Zijun, I've heard Jing holds considerable affection for you. Now that you've publicly refused the marriage, I'm afraid her heart will be broken."

Su Zhang lowered his eyelashes slightly; his voice was like a blade cleaving water.

"The Princess Ninghua is, of course, bright as the moon, far beyond the reach of ordinary men. But this humble official's ambition lies in the court halls. I wish to devote my entire life's strength to supporting the realm. To take a royal consort would mean…"

He paused, breath tightening, before continuing softly: "…resigning my post to avoid suspicion ——and that would waste Your Majesty's painstaking cultivation of my abilities.

The welfare of the people is paramount; personal matters are light.

I only wish to remain worthy of Your Majesty's grace ——

and would have no regrets even in death."

"It seems Minister Su's eyes are as lofty as the heavens, looking down even upon Our daughter."

"This humble official dares not. The Princess is a child of gold and jade, a natural phoenix. It is this humble official who is unworthy."

Emperor Xuanwen pondered for a moment, thoughtful. "Very well. Consorts in this dynasty cannot hold key positions in the capital. If Minister Su were to wed the Princess, it would be difficult to break this ancestral rule and We have no wish to set such a precedent."

"This official thanks Your Majesty." Su Zhang bowed low once more in reverence.

The Emperor lightly tapped the armrest with his fingertips, after a moment of contemplation, before slowly speaking.

"Since that is the case, We shall not keep you entangled in matters of the heart... The annual taxes from Jiangnan have been unclear lately, the canal transport funds are in deficit and the Ministry of Revenue has repeatedly memorialized without resolution. We intend to send you south to investigate, granting you the authority of a Special Imperial Censor in addition to your post as Director of the Bureau of Appointments in the Ministry of Personnel. Are you willing to undertake this trial?"

The hall instantly became as silent as a cicada in cold weather; even the sound of the wind seemed to freeze.

Jiangnan presented a facade of prosperity and flourishing commerce, but beneath the surface, influential clans were deeply entrenched and their interests intricately interwoven. To investigate corruption there was tantamount to plucking sustenance directly from a tiger's jaws.

Li Duan's fingertips twitched slightly within his sleeves, as if giving silent assent. Li Xuan turned his head slightly, a cold glint flashing in his eyes as he chuckled softly.

Li Suo leaned halfway against a hall pillar, the corner of his mouth hooked in an arc of ambiguous interest.

Anyone could see that by refusing the marriage to the Second Princess, Su Zhang had already provoked the Emperor's displeasure.

Now, the Emperor sending Su Zhang on this mission to investigate the Jiangnan taxes was ostensibly a mark of significant trust and delegation of authority, but in reality, it was a manoeuvre to compel him to handle a perilous situation, serving as a tacit reprimand for his defiance.

If he handled this matter well, he would naturally gain the Emperor's favour directly. If he handled it poorly, ending up in prison with clanking chains was a distinct possibility.

Su Zhang stepped forward and made a bow, his voice deep as a bell. "This official is willing to accept the command to go south, vowing to investigate the malpractices thoroughly, restore clarity to Jiangnan and not disgrace the mission."

Emperor Xuanwen tossed a jade ruyi sceptre. It landed on the dragon desk with a clear, crisp sound. His words were sonorous: "Good! We shall await your return after achieving merit and then discuss marriage again!"

Li Suo raised an eyebrow. His tone was mild yet concealed a sharp edge. "Investigating malpractices is no minor matter, Minister Su. You must be prudent. If there is any misstep… what is lost may not be merely an official."

His words were like a stone cast into water, sending ripples of undercurrents.

Su Zhang's expression remained unmoved. He slowly inclined his head, his voice steady. "This official, bearing Your Majesty's profound grace, will naturally perform his duties with caution and not betray the trust placed in him."

Emperor Xuanwen finally nodded, his tone sinking. "Since that is the case, you have half a year. Return to Us a clear and honest Jiangnan."

For a moment, the hall was utterly silent, save for the incense smoke coiling upwards from the gilded bronze censer, quietly locking this clash of sharp tensions into the path leading south.

"This official receives the decree."

Su Zhang, his figure tall, bowed deeply once more. His robes spread like ink upon the steps before the throne. Though he uttered not a word, his presence was as weighty as a mountain pressing down.

* * * * *

The court session concluded. Outside the hall doors, the golden roof tiles reflected the sunlight; the long steps stretched out like flowing water.

Just as Su Zhang stepped out of the hall, he saw Crown Prince Li Duan approaching.

The sunlight reflected in his eyes, condensed into a profound depth.

He said in a low voice, "The matter of refusing the marriage was handled flawlessly. Even this hot-potato mission of the southern inspection has fallen into your hands ——Zijun, quite the capability."

Su Zhang bowed in salute, his tone neither warm nor cold. "Your Highness praises me. Zhang dares not entertain any distractions."

Li Duan's gaze shifted, seemingly glancing unintentionally towards the not-too-distant Li Xuan. The smile on his lips did not fade, but his eyes held a probing depth and unspoken meaning.

Li Xuan approached at a leisurely pace, a smile still gracing his lips, though his voice carried a slight chill. "The waters of Jiangnan run deep. You must be cautious."

As his words fell, he flicked his sleeve and passed calmly by Su Zhang's shoulder.

Below the steps, the wind stirred abruptly, as if pulling invisible strings ——moments later, a trusted follower received a command from the shadows of a corner and swiftly departed.

And by the colonnade pillars, Third Prince Li Suo leaned against the railing, lightly fanning himself. His gaze was calm yet brimming with keen interest, as if observing prey about to enter the snare.

On the distant imperial way, officials filed out in a steady stream. Brocade robes billowed, and the sound of black boots upon the steps was a rhythmic tide, yet not a single man dared to look back.

In the hearts of all was a single, unspoken understanding: this journey to Jiangnan was not merely an investigation into corruption; it was a test of the blade's own temper.

The gaze of the Crown Prince's faction, the scrutiny of the Second Prince's, and the watchful eyes of the Third Prince's—all would converge upon that one scroll of a memorial, upon the single man who would write it.

Su Zhang's mind was a pool of perfect stillness, yet the pressure of those converging undercurrents was a tangible weight against his skin. He recalled the Emperor's final decree in the hall—Half a year is the limit

The words cold and heavy as forged iron, settling upon his shoulders like the burden of a mountain.

He walked on, hands clasped behind his back, his strides as measured and unyielding as an iron ruler, the hem of his robes snapping in the wind.

 Before his mind's eye, the landscape of Jiangnan took vivid shape: the intricate malpractices of the Grand Canal, the labyrinthine deficits in the annual taxes, the old, powerful families with roots sunk deep into the fertile soil, and beneath the glittering surface of its lakes and rivers, the waiting blades, unseen but keenly felt.

He knew this journey was walking on knife blades, yet also an opportunity to establish his authority.

Suddenly, a dreamlike shadow flitted through the depths of his mind: a woman turning her head with a soft smile, her gaze like gentle water.

His expression tightened slightly, immediately brushing away that thread of agitation. His steps, instead, grew even more resolute.

The skies of the Great Zhou dynasty appeared calm and tranquil, yet undercurrents had long been churning.

On this journey, he must ——calculate every single step.

Chapter 44: No Need for Concern

When the stove fire roared to life, Qin Nianyin suddenly felt a scorching heat in the centre of her palms; only then did she realize with a jolt that she had actually proceeded with this endeavour.

Her fingertips trembled with a rhythmic vibration as she sliced the pears; the blade strayed and veered several times as she pared the skin, and when it came time to add the red dates, she found herself adding two more than intended.

She was far from adept in the culinary arts. In her previous life, there had always been an army of maids and servants to organize every morsel of her sustenance; rarely indeed had there been an occasion for her to personally kindle the fire for soup or porridge.

Yet, a bowl of Rock Sugar and Snow Pear was one of the few offerings of hers that he had been willing to accept in that former existence.

He harboured a deep-seated aversion to medicine; it had been so in the last life, just as it was now. He had habitually and coldly rejected her overtures and gestures of kindness, yet that specific pear soup was the rare exception when he seldom turned her away.

Spoon by agonizing spoon, she simmered the pear until it was rendered soft and yielding, adding a few goji berries to draw out a subtle fragrance, all for the sake of soothing that stubborn cough of a man who refused to dutifully consume his medicine.

Every single drop of that decoction seemed to scorch her very heart.

Qin Nianyin lowered her gaze to the shimmering, reflective surface of the soup within the earthenware pot, and she could not help but let out a low, cold laugh—a sound of biting self-mockery. "Qin Nianyin," she murmured, "you are truly without a shred of resolve. He would not deign to spare you a second glance in the last life, and yet, having arrived in this one, you still find yourself unable to let go?"

But, in the end, she truly could not let go.

She meticulously ladled the essence into a ceramic bowl, fitted the lid securely, and then—with a lingering caution—wrapped it again and again in a protective cloth napkin before finally summoning Mei.

"Deliver this invitation to the Shen estate. Say that I am inviting Sister Lingyan to come tomorrow to inspect the newly crafted velvet-flower hairpins... Also..." Her voice faltered into a brief, suspended silence as she bit her lip, then she added, "Just mention, as if by accident, that... that Cousin is feeling somewhat indisposed."

Mei was momentarily taken aback, her gaze fixing upon her mistress's eyes, which were rimmed with a faint, telltale redness. Just as she was about to voice a question, she was cut short by a sharp gesture.

"Do not say that I specifically instructed you to speak of it. Under no circumstances must you say that."

She turned her back, her voice becoming as light as a passing breeze, swallowed up inch by inch by the encroaching night. Only she herself knew that in this incarnation, she no longer wished to forcefully impose her affections upon him with that same aggressive insistence of the past.

She merely wanted to perform this small act for him in the shadows of silence. She hoped, with a desperate fervour, that he would remain unaware.

Even if the person who arrived to tend to him was not her, and even if he might feel a flicker of disappointment.

She would much rather be misunderstood as being cold and indifferent than to ever again approach him with such reckless haste. In this life, she had to proceed with a more profound caution. Yet, no matter how meticulously she guarded herself, this wellspring of affection still managed to irrepressibly overflow the boundaries she had set.

* * * * *

Qin Nianyin gently pressed the lid onto the porcelain bowl of Rock Sugar and Snow Pear soup.

Hot steam escaped in languid curls from the narrow gap, carrying with it the delicate, honeyed aroma of red dates and goji berries.

She handed the tray to Mei, her voice suppressed into the faintest of whispers: "Take this to Xiuyan. Tell him it is a throat-soothing soup newly simmered in the kitchen, and ask him to deliver it to the Young Master. Remember—at all costs, you must not reveal that it was I who prepared it."

Mei stood frozen for a heartbeat, her mouth parting as if to protest, but in the end, she merely bowed her head in compliance. "Understood, Miss."

Not long afterward, Xiuyan entered the study as was his custom. Seeing Su Zhang with his brow tightly furrowed, the corners of his eyes flushed with a feverish red, and his voice sounding painfully hoarse, the attendant quickly brought forth the bowl of pear soup: "Young Master, this is a fresh batch of snow pear soup from the kitchen. They say it is an essence to moisten the lungs and quiet the cough. They requested that I bring it for you to sample."

Su Zhang's head was thrumming with a violent ache, and he did not spare the matter a second thought, merely dismissing it with a wave of his hand. "Set it down."

After a moment, he reached out and lifted the lid of the vessel. A mist of hot steam billowed upward, and the fragrance permeated the air.

He ladled a spoonful into his mouth; it was warm without being scalding, a gentle and sweet moisture.

The snow pear dissolved almost instantly upon his tongue, and the lingering aftertaste of red dates and goji berries permeated his throat, actually managing to suppress the violence of his cough by a degree.

He was momentarily dazed, his tongue appearing to be suddenly snagged by a hook of memory—this flavour was unmistakably familiar.

Yet, for a fleeting instant, he could not recall exactly when or in what place he had ever savoured such a taste before.

"Xiuyan."

"Yes, Young Master. I await your instructions." Xiuyan hastily abandoned the mundane tasks he was tending to and bowed with a respectful deference.

"This sweet soup... is it the first time the kitchen has delivered it?" Or had they sent it before, and he had simply been too preoccupied to notice?

"Uh..." Xiuyan was seized by a startle, stammering as his mind spun frantically to find an escape, for the Young Lady Cousin had forbidden him from speaking the truth. "Yes... ha-ha, it should be the first time. I believe it is a folk remedy for coughs from the hometown of the cook, Old Li."

"I see." Su Zhang remained deeply puzzled by the hauntingly familiar taste.

What flickered through his mind like a lightning bolt was the clink of a teacup being set upon a table, the serene expression of a woman with her eyes cast down, and those slender, delicate fingers—adorned with a touch of scarlet lacquer—as she held the bowl.

But he remained outwardly unruffled, merely finishing the entire bowl of soup in a heavy silence.

The wisp of doubt and the stirring of an unknown heartbeat, like ripples across the surface of a pond, slowly fanned out, only to subside once more into a hollow calm, as if nothing of consequence had ever occurred.

* * * * *

The night grew deeper, and the sound of the wind brushing against the corners of the curtains brought a sharp chill.

Mei returned in a frantic haste, and the moment she stepped over the threshold, she lowered her head to report: "Miss, the Shen estate has sent word... Miss Lingyan accompanied the Madam to the suburban villa early this morning and has not yet returned. I waited for a long duration, but ultimately, the person did not appear."

Upon hearing this, Qin Nianyin's hand faltered for a fraction of a second. A shadow of light flickered within the depths of her eyes, but she merely forced a faint, distant smile. "So be it. There will be other opportunities in the long days ahead."

Her voice was exceedingly light, so airy it seemed as if it would vanish the moment the wind caught it. Falling amidst the wavering lamplight, it was impossible to discern whether the tone was one of consolation or of bitter self-mockery.

She walked to the window, her fingertips pushing open half of the carved wooden lattice.

The night wind, heavy with moisture, surged inside, instantly extinguishing the residual warmth of the lamp.

Qin Nianyin stood there, fixed in place for a long time, quietly gazing toward the direction of the faintly lit study in the distance. Her gaze was deep and devoid of ripples, and for a long, protracted duration, she uttered not a single word.

Chapter 45: No Fondness for Sweets

Su Zhang's steps were heavy as he returned to his study. The hem of his robes swept carelessly against the desk corner, stirring a fine veil of dust into the slanting afternoon light.

His features were arranged in their customary calm, yet the fingertips of one hand moved unconsciously, tracing the faint, persistent tremor he had concealed within his sleeve — the physical ghost of an unsettled heart.

Those chestnut cakes Qin Nianyin's maid, Mei, had delivered to his father's quarters… he had dismissed it as insignificant earlier. Now, in the quiet solitude of his room, the thought returned with nagging insistence, coiling tighter around his mind.

"Xiuyan." His voice was a clear, cool note in the stillness.

Xiuyan appeared promptly from the side chamber, bowing. "Your instruction, Young Master?"

"The chestnut cakes?" Su Zhang asked, his face a perfect mask of indifference, yet the question carried an undertone so faint it verged on self-doubt.

Xiuyan blinked, confusion plain on his face. "Chestnut cakes, Young Master? This servant… does not understand."

Su Zhang was silent for a moment, replaying Mei's words: 'She sent some to every courtyard…'

"It's nothing," he said finally, the ghost of a self-mocking smile touching his lips. He truly wondered what spell had come over him.

Xiuyan scratched his head. "If the Young Master wishes for chestnut cakes, this servant can go to the kitchens at once to have some prepared." It was peculiar. Since when did his master, usually so austere, concern himself with such trifling treats?

A change, subtle as a shadow passing over stone, crossed Su Zhang's expression.

"Let it be." He raised his eyes, their usual clarity now clouded, heavy as if dusted with a morning frost.

—So, it was. In the entire Su residence, he was the one who had been overlooked.

A spark of irritation, hot and sharp, ignited in his chest, quickly fanned into a smoldering discontent. It rose within him, a slow, bitter tide.

Xiuyan scratched his head again, bewildered by this uncharacteristic vexation. "This servant will just go and check with the kitchens, to be sure…"

"It is unnecessary." Su Zhang cut him off, lifting a hand to press against his temple. His voice remained measured, a stark contrast to the turbulence it veiled.

Xiuyan swallowed his words. The air around his master today felt dangerously charged—like the thick ice over a deep winter river, bearing immense, silent pressure from the dark currents below, poised to shatter with a catastrophic roar at the slightest provocation.

Su Zhang turned away and walked alone to the window. He gazed out at the courtyard where the pear blossoms had all fallen, a carpet of faded white against the dark earth.

In his eyes, emotions long suppressed churned and roiled, reaching a fever pitch of intensity with nowhere to escape.

* * * * *

Dawn light, pale and tentative, gilded the world. A thin, almost translucent layer of pear blossoms lay scattered like discarded silk across the courtyard stones.

Qin Nianyin walked the gravel path, the package of chestnut cakes warm against her chest. Mei trotted beside her, whispering, "After all that delivering to the other courtyards, this little bit is all we have left for ourselves. It won't be enough, I'm sure of it."

"You! Is your mind a bottomless pit meant only for food?" Qin Nianyin chided, though her eyes held affection.

"Young Lady, you tease me too much." Mei pouted, then smiled. "But Young Lady, have you heard the news? Young Master Cousin has received a great commission from the Emperor! He's to go south to investigate some important matter. Our Young Master Cousin is truly exceptional."

Qin Nianyin's smile vanished. Her expression cooled, the playful light in her eyes snuffed out in an instant, replaced by a sombre, familiar unease.

She remembered. In her past life, Su Zhang had undertaken this very journey to Jiangnan.

And she remembered with chilling clarity—the courier roads had been treacherous with mud that year.

The official boat was moored for the night on a dark, still stretch of river. Someone had seized that opportunity.

Sabotage.

A stealthy, night-time assassination attempt. He had almost been lost then, tumbling into the inky, cold water, his body never to be found.

If not for his preternatural vigilance and a staggering twist of fortune, his bones would have long since settled in the silty bed of some Jiangnan waterway.

The memory constricted her heart like a cold hand, but she mastered it, forcing the feeling down.

This life is different; she reminded herself sternly. She knew the shape of fate now. A carefully worded warning would be enough. She must not overreach, must not entangle herself in his world as she had before, inviting only his eventual weariness and disdain.

Mei looked up at the softening sky, a dreamy, tender light blooming in her gaze. "Young Lady, do you remember… back when we were small, living there? The street vendors with their sticky-sweet, candied lotus root, the sound of laughter from the kite-flyers by the lakeside pavilion… Oh, to see it all again would be…"

As she spoke, a smile surfaced on her face—a bright, unguarded expression from a simpler time, her voice thick with nostalgia and yearning. "If we could go to Jiangnan together… it would be like stepping back into those days. Wouldn't that be wonderful?"

Listening, a sharp, poignant ache stabbed through Qin Nianyin's heart. Her fingers tightened minutely on the fabric of her sleeve.

Jiangnan. The land where she and Mei had spent their childhood. But Jiangnan was also the land that had taken everything from her in a raging, muddy deluge. Her feelings for it were a tangled, inseparable knot of profound love and equally profound resentment.

* * * * *

Lost in this bittersweet reverie, she looked up and saw him.

Su Zhang was approaching from the far end of the covered walkway. His form was tall and straight, his dark robes billowing slightly with his stride, his entire presence as poised and immutable as an ancient pine.

Qin Nianyin, her mind elsewhere, did not register his proximity until it was nearly too late. She started, taking a half-step sideways with a soft, startled gasp. "Ah—!"

"Awareness is a virtue, even on familiar paths." His tone was neutral, offering neither warmth nor censure. His glance fell, and by chance, it landed on the cloth-wrapped package she held close.

Not a single line of his face altered, yet deep within, it felt as if a taut, silent string had been plucked, sending a single, pure vibration through him.

The sullen, heavy cloud that had settled in his study dissipated in that instant, vanishing as if it had never been. Unknowingly, unconsciously, the strict line of his mouth softened, the very corner lifting in the faintest suggestion of a curve.

—So, she had been bringing it to him. Herself.

Qin Nianyin gathered her scattered wits, recognized him, and quickly dipped into a curtsey. "Cousin. Forgive my clumsiness. I was not watching my step."

Su Zhang did not acknowledge the apology. His voice remained mild, almost casual. "Give it to me." He extended his hand, palm upturned, to receive the package.

For a heartbeat, Qin Nianyin simply stared. Then her fingers clenched instinctively around the parcel, and her body moved of its own volition—a subtle but unmistakable retreat of half a step.

That slight movement, neither grand nor dramatic, landed in Su Zhang's perception with the weight of a stone dropped into still water.

The air between them grew thick, suspended.

His outstretched hand hung in the empty space between them. His expression did not flicker, yet beneath the composed surface, his heart constricted violently, as if pierced by a needle of ice.

—So, the cakes were not meant for him.

It was he who had misinterpreted. He who had, in his silent anticipation, woven significance from ordinary courtesy.

Qin Nianyin, too, felt the abruptness of her reaction. Her eyes darted away momentarily. "These… these are rather crushed," she murmured, her voice barely louder than a sigh. "They are not presentable. I will… I will make a fresh batch tomorrow. For you."

Her words were light, meant to dismiss, but they could not entirely conceal the thread of flustered awkwardness that ran through them.

Su Zhang lowered his gaze to her face. His eyes were deep, unreadable pools. He offered no reply. After a silence that stretched too long, he simply turned away. "Unnecessary," he stated, the word cool and final.

He took a step, then paused, as if an afterthought had struck him. He did not look back. "I have never had a particular taste for sweet things."

The words were delivered lightly, carelessly, like a dry leaf skittering across stone. They held no discernible emotion, and yet their very detachment made them sting all the more sharply.

Xiuyan, who had been hovering at a respectful distance, hurried to follow. His master's posture was rigidly correct, his pace even, yet Xiuyan could sense a tumultuous undercurrent swirling beneath the calm exterior. He scratched his head in frank bewilderment.

But… hadn't the Young Master just this morning asked specifically about those very chestnut cakes? How could he now dismiss them with such indifference?

The shift was too abrupt, too complete.

He stole a glance. Su Zhang's back was a straight, unyielding line, his gaze fixed on some distant point ahead. His dark robes swept the ground with a sound like frost scraping stone. Not a trace remained of the faint, unguarded softness that had momentarily touched his features.

Xiuyan sighed inwardly.

Truly, the most fathomless mystery in this world was the heart and mind of his Young Master.

* * * * *

The study was enveloped in a silence as deep and still as undisturbed water. The only sound was the occasional, crystalline shiver of the wind chime hanging from the eaves.

Afternoon sunlight, thick and golden, slanted through the intricately carved window lattice, painting a shifting chessboard of light and shadow upon the polished surface of the desk.

Pear blossoms lay scattered like forgotten jade across the floor; the branches outside stood nearly bare.

A passing breeze stirred, and the last few clinging petals detached, twirling silently through the air before coming to rest, one by one, beside the dark pool of the inkstone.

Su Zhang stood before his desk, motionless as a statue carved from cold jade. His fingertips rested on an unread memorial, but the characters swam before his eyes, formless and meaningless. His consciousness was held hostage elsewhere.

What filled his mind, replaying with relentless clarity, was not affairs of state or imperial edicts, but the fleeting, tangible memory of her fingertips brushing against his as she offered—then withdrew—the simple cloth package.

Suddenly, with a swift, uncontrolled motion, he swept his jade-handled brush aside. It struck the hard corner of the desk with a sharp, jarring crack.

A splash of ink flew, landing not as ordered characters, but as a chaotic, spreading stain—a dark bloom of disorder that could not be undone.

Beyond the window, the shadows of branches danced in the wind. He watched them, but felt only a suffocating tightness in his chest.

Her every gesture, her slightest hesitation… they pulled at strings within him he had not known were so taut.

That instinctive retreat of hers was no mere movement; it was a needle, fine and sharp, finding its mark deep in a place he rarely acknowledged.

He closed his eyes. The bones of his hands stood white and prominent where they were clenched within the folds of his sleeves. His breath was held, painfully shallow. That he could be so unravelled… by a parcel of cakes, by a glance, by half a step backward…

After a long, heavy interval, he turned his back on the room, standing alone in the fading light.

The flame of the single candle guttered, casting wavering, restless patterns across the stark contrast of inkblot and pale petal. He did not speak.

He merely stood, allowing the suppressed, formless turmoil within him to churn and seethe—a heavy, silent tempest with no shore upon which to break.

Chapter 46: A Matter of the Heart

Outside the estate gates, a fine, silk-like rain fell. Water droplets gathered at the eaves and dripped steadily onto the blue-grey stone paving below, splashing up tiny, ever-widening ripples.

Just as Su Zhang reached the front entrance of the residence, his gaze was caught by an ornate carriage with a golden canopy, unmistakably of imperial make, halted at the mouth of the lane. Its curtains of sheer, light gauze were partially drawn, and it was surrounded by a solemn retinue of palace eunuchs—its presence was both grand and imposing, a silent disruption of the rainy afternoon.

The lead eunuch hurried forward to intercept him, his voice sharp and clear as he announced, "Lord Su, the Second Princess, Li Jing, requests your presence for a word."

The current Emperor had no Empress-born daughters, only three princes and these two princesses. The world knew the Second Princess, Li Jing, held the title Ninghua, while the Eldest Princess, Li Rong, was titled Ningyuan.

Su Zhang's brow furrowed, a subtle, almost invisible crease. His gaze, however, remained as calm and unrippled as a deep lake. He merely gave a slight nod of assent and followed the eunuch around to the front of the imperial carriage.

The carriage curtain was half-rolled up. Inside, the Second Princess Li Jing reclined against silk cushions. She was clad in a cloak of pristine white fox fur over a brilliant crimson gown woven with gold thread. Her features were classically, coldly beautiful, her bearing inherently noble and distant. Yet, the faint redness and slight swelling around her eyes betrayed a vulnerability that was utterly at odds with her regal demeanour.

"Su Zhang." She called his name softly, her voice hoarse, as if from unshed tears or a sleepless night.

Su Zhang halted three paces away—a precise, respectful distance. He clasped his hands formally and bowed deeply from the waist. "Your subject pays his respects to the Second Princess."

The Second Princess Li Jing stared directly at him, not blinking. She bit the corner of her lower lip, a small, fraught gesture. Her voice was pressed very low, meant for his ears alone. "This Princess asks you…

were you aware of His Imperial Majesty's intention to bestow this marriage?"

Su Zhang kept his gaze lowered, his profile a study in composed detachment. "Your subject was aware," he replied, his voice even.

"Then why…" Her breath hitched slightly. "Why did you defy the decree?" The tremor she had been holding back finally seeped into her words.

Within the carriage, the scent of expensive sandalwood incense hung gently in the air, yet the atmosphere felt stifling, almost suffocating.

Su Zhang's expression showed no fluctuation. It was as if carved from jade. "Your subject is dull and incompetent," he stated, the self-deprecation rote and hollow. "I dare not ruin Your Highness's entire life. Moreover, I bear the weighty responsibility for flood control in Jiangnan and dare not entertain distracting thoughts."

His words were a skilful argument, perfectly courteous on the surface, yet the refusal beneath was delivered flawlessly, a wall without a single chink or weakness.

The Second Princess Li Jing's fingers clutched convulsively at a corner of her fox fur cloak, the fine hairs crumpling in her grip, her knuckles turning white against the dark lining. Her voice now held a panic that bordered on pleading. "Do you know… if this marriage does not proceed, His Imperial Majesty will most likely—"

She cut herself off abruptly, biting the tip of her tongue so hard she tasted copper. The tears that had threatened now pooled, shimmering, but she would not let them fall in front of him.

Su Zhang remained silent, his head still slightly bowed, a statue of respectful obduracy.

The Second Princess Li Jing drew a deep, shuddering breath, forcing the corners of her lips upward into a terrible, brittle smile. "This Princess has heard… the royal family of the Barbarian Frontier has a new Khan. He urgently seeks a marriage alliance with the Great Zhou imperial house to stabilize his kingdom's fortune." She paused, the words like stones in her throat. "If I do not marry you… I will be sent far away. To the Barbarian Frontier. To keep company with savages."

As she spoke the final words, her voice finally broke, shaking uncontrollably.

Inside the carriage, the lamplight flickered in the damp breeze, casting wavering shadows across her face—a face that was now as pale as fine rice paper. Her eyes, those famously proud eyes, were filled with a tumultuous sea of emotion: grievous 委屈, crumbling pride, and a profound, helpless sorrow.

Su Zhang closed his eyes for a brief moment—a fleeting concession to the weight of her words. When he opened them, he still bowed in formal salute. "Your subject is incapable. But I believe that should such an event occur, the capable ministers and tiger-generals of our court would not stand idly by. They would not allow Your Highness to suffer such a disgrace."

But he still showed not the slightest intention of relenting. The subtext was colder than the rain: her fate was not his to change.

The Second Princess Li Jing looked at him, the tears welling in her eyes finally overflowing, tracing silent paths down her cheeks. Finally, with a sudden, furious motion, she swept the carriage curtain fully aside and stepped down from the carriage, her composure in tatters. She pointed a trembling finger at him, her voice a low, wounded demand. "Su Zhang! Am I… am I so utterly unworthy in your eyes?"

In the wind and rain, her magnificent robes—the crimson and gold, the white fur—flapped and snapped loudly around her, as if she stood alone and defiant against the entire, immutable will of Heaven.

Su Zhang merely bowed his head lower, his posture ramrod straight yet unmoving as solid, ancient ice. He offered no comfort, no concession.

The Second Princess Li Jing stared fixedly at him, anger and grief intertwining in her gaze like venomous vines. Her voice trembled, barely audible over the rain. "This Princess asks you… where do I lack? By what right… by what right do you refuse me!"

Once the words were out, she herself seemed startled by their raw desperation, but the floodgates were open now, and the tears rolled forth, impossible to stop, mingling with the fine rain on her face.

Su Zhang inclined his head slightly further, his demeanour the very picture of respectful yet absolute aloofness. "Your Highness is a child of gold and jade, a noble scion of the highest order. Your subject is of lowly status and shallow virtue. I truly dare not aspire so high." The words were polished, perfect, and utterly final.

"Hypocrite!" the Second Princess Li Jing hissed through gritted teeth, her body shaking with a fury born of humiliation and heartbreak. "If this

Princess wishes to marry you, it is her own choice! Do you think… do you think this Princess cares one whit for the gossiping words of others?"

Su Zhang's hand tightened almost imperceptibly within the wide sleeve of his official robe, but his face remained an impassive mask. "Your subject's mind is decided," he repeated, each word measured and cool. "I beg Your Highness… not to force one who is unwilling."

The Second Princess Li Jing was furious beyond measure, her pride in ribbons. Finally casting aside all remaining regard for her status and dignity, she surged forward a step, her hand darting out to grab the sleeve of his robe, as if by physically holding him she could anchor his will, make him stay.

"Su Zhang—!"

Yet he, anticipating this, shifted his stance with a fluid, subtle motion. With a light, almost dismissive flick of his wrist, the silk of his sleeve slipped through her desperate fingers, evading her touch completely.

This subtle, yet devastatingly resolute, action stabbed into the Second Princess Li Jing's heart more painfully than any outright rejection.

She froze on the spot, her arm still outstretched, her eyes wide with a disbelief that quickly curdled into a deeper, more intimate humiliation.

Seeing the attendants and eunuchs surrounding them quickly lower their eyes, studying the wet stones at their feet, pretending blindness, her chest heaved violently. Gritting her teeth until they ached, she spat the words with bitter, wounded hatred, "Do you truly… not care in the slightest for this Princess's… face?" The last word was a whisper, laden with the weight of her entire royal identity.

Su Zhang finally lifted his gaze to look at her directly.

His eyes were deep and cold as a mountain tarn in winter, his voice as sharp and chilling as a blade being drawn across new snow. "Your subject's duty is solely to uphold the propriety between ruler and subject. I dare not… overstep recklessly."

He emphasized the last two words, drawing an uncrossable line in the space between them.

The Second Princess Li Jing stared fixedly at him, her breathing ragged. Her voice dropped to a low, hoarse, and urgent whisper. "If you said this Princess was unworthy, so be it. Let us leave it at that. But the Princess asks you one thing—just one thing—"

She took another half-step forward, ignoring the rain soaking the hem of her splendid robes. The rims of her eyes were a furious, heartbroken red. There was almost a hint of entreaty in her stance now, a princess reduced to pleading. "Su Zhang… is there already someone you admire in your heart?"

Li Jing thought to herself that the Su and Shen families had been close for many years. Shen Lingyan had grown up with the Su siblings since childhood, like green plums and a bamboo horse. It was entirely possible… no, it was likely… that Su Zhang's beloved was Shen Lingyan.

Su Zhang was taken aback by the directness of the question. His initial, trained instinct was to deny it immediately, to offer another polite deflection.

But in that lightning-fast, unguarded instant, a stubborn, clear, and quietly beautiful figure suddenly flashed, unbidden, through the careful architecture of his mind—Qin Nianyin.

Her subconscious half-step back when holding the chestnut cakes, the protective instinct in that small retreat. Her slightly furrowed brow, bathed in lamplight, as she secretly worked on hair ornaments away from prying eyes.

Her drowsy, utterly unguarded appearance when she had dozed off in his study, her head nodding gently…

Fragmented, seemingly insignificant images surged into his heart, a silent, powerful tide.

Su Zhang's knuckles tightened slightly where they were hidden in his sleeves. Even he himself felt a strange, unfamiliar stagnation in his chest, a tightness that was somewhat inexplicable, somewhat alarming.

The Second Princess Li Jing stared, unblinking, waiting. Her voice was low, hoarse, scraping with urgency. "If you claim this Princess is unworthy, so be it. But tell me… who, exactly, is the one in your heart?"

The sound of the rain around them seemed to grow heavier, as if the heavens themselves were leaning in to listen. Water droplets fell from the eaves in a steady, accusing rhythm, drip… drip… drip… as if urging him, pressing him to give an answer.

She took that final, vulnerable step closer, the scent of her imperial incense mingling with the petrichor. "Su Zhang… answer me?"

As these words fell into the damp air, the surrounding attendants, as if controlled by a single string, automatically held their breaths and retreated to a discreet distance, melting into the grey curtain of rain.

Only the two of them remained, standing in stark opposition in the fine, misting drizzle.

Su Zhang was silent for a long, suspended moment. The internal struggle was invisible, a war fought behind his calm eyes. Finally, with a slowness that felt like fate itself unfolding, he gave a single, slight nod.

"Yes." One word. Dry, succinct, and utterly irrevocable, it escaped his thin, usually disciplined lips.

Once spoken, even Su Zhang himself was momentarily stunned. A faint, unprecedented ripple of chaos disturbed the perfect stillness of his mind. Had he… had he actually admitted it?

The Second Princess Li Jing stared blankly, as if the single syllable had physically struck her. Her face abruptly lost all remaining color, turning a ghastly white against the dark frame of her fur hood. Almost subconsciously, her lips formed the name she had already decided upon: "Is it… Shen Lingyan?"

Her heart trembled faintly, a sickly mix of dread and a desperate hope for a comprehensible reason—if it was Shen Lingyan, she could still understand. She could still, perhaps, grudgingly accept.

After all, Shen Lingyan was a noble lady from a prominent family, their statuses were comparable, and she had long been woven into the fabric of the Su family's life.

Yet Su Zhang shook his head, a firm, definitive motion. His voice, when it came, was low but carried an unshakable firmness. "It is not."

"Then…" The Second Princess Li Jing's voice was a strangled thread. She gritted her teeth, the question forced out through a wall of pain. "Which family's daughter is it?"

Su Zhang looked up at her, meeting her devastated gaze fully. His own eyes were as deep and still as untouched ink. Each word he spoke was deliberate, clear, and distinct, leaving no room for ambiguity or false hope. "She is merely an ordinary maiden from a modest family. Not of noble birth, nor from a powerful clan. Just a true ordinary lady."

The Second Princess Li Jing looked as if she had been struck a physical blow on the head. She stared at him dumbly, her mind refusing to process the words.

Her lips moved soundlessly for a moment before a lost, broken whisper emerged. "Not Shen Lingyan… and not a noble lady? You… you would refuse this Princess… for such a woman?"

Su Zhang did not speak further. He offered no explanation, no justification. His gaze remained steady and calm, without a trace of evasion or apology. His silence was more eloquent than any argument.

The Second Princess Li Jing could scarcely believe it. Shock and fury warred on her pale, rain-dampened face, twisting her beautiful features.

Her voice quivered, not with sadness now, but with a kind of incandescent, bewildered rage. "What does she possibly have? What virtue, what talent, what power… that makes you… makes you disregard your future, defy an imperial decree, and still… still choose to protect her?"

Su Zhang took a slow breath, the cool, wet air filling his lungs.

When he spoke again, his voice was low yet carried a profound, unshakeable certainty. It was as if he were making a vow to himself as much as delivering a final, absolute severance to her. "Qing zhi suo qi, hao wu li you. Where affection arises, there is no reason, no 'why.' It simply… is. If you demand an answer… it is simply that, in the space of a single thought, in the quiet of my heart… it is already, entirely, her."

As these words were spoken into the misty air, the sound of the rain around them seemed to hush, as if holding its breath.

Even the lamplight within the nearby carriage appeared to flicker and dim for an instant, as if acknowledging the gravity of the confession.

The Second Princess Li Jing stood rooted to the spot, her body rigid, every line of her form screaming tension.

It was as if all strength, all hope, all the fiery pride that had sustained her, had been violently drained away, leaving only a hollow shell.

She looked at this man standing before her, cold and remote as a peak dusted with eternal snow.

The emotion that now flooded her eyes was no longer merely the sting of rejected love or wounded pride. It had crystallized into something darker, more potent: a raging, helpless tide of hatred—for him, for the unknown woman, for the cruel, indifferent turn of her fate—and a crushing, all-encompassing powerlessness.

Chapter 47: Seeking Entry into the Imperial Guard

The Second Princess, Li Jing, fixed her gaze upon his eyes for a long, agonizing duration, until at last, she lowered her lashes in a defeat of profound disappointment, allowing a bitter laugh to escape her lips.

—She believed him; or rather, she dared not do otherwise.

Su Zhang remained rooted to the spot, his gaze heavy and sunless, his palms suffused with a bone-deep cold. He himself had not yet perceived that the name he had never uttered had already begun to quietly take root within the deepest recesses of his heart.

With only a few terse sentences, he had shattered the final, fragile illusion harbored within her chest.

Princess Li Jing tilted her head back, struggling with all her might to force back the encroaching tears. She gritted her teeth in a show of stubborn defiance, forcing a brittle smile: "Very well, Su Zhang. Remember this—this was the path you chose for yourself!"

Having spat out these words, she pivoted sharply and climbed into her imperial carriage. The heavy curtains fell at once, shielding a countenance that could no longer restrain its surging emotions.

And Su Zhang remained there, standing motionless amidst the fine, drifting rain. His features betrayed neither joy nor sorrow; he merely arched his hands in a formal bow of salutation, then stepped aside, intending to depart.

In the midst of this cold stalemate, the rhythmic thunder of hoofbeats echoed from the end of the alley.

Gu Xiao arrived on horseback, draped in a silver-gray cloak that exhaled an aura of frigid authority. Having witnessed the scene from a distance, he allowed a mocking smile to curve his lips. He spurred his horse until he reached them, dismounting with a fluid motion and clasping his hands in a theatrical display of surprise: "Oh? What a fortuitous encounter. Xiao pays his humble respects to Her Highness, the Second Princess."

Finding that the newcomer was an acquaintance, Li Jing was seized by a renewed surge of shame and indignation. Wishing for nothing more than to vanish on the spot, she barked an order for the carriage to return to the palace.

Gu Xiao watched the retreating imperial carriage with a cold sneer: "That temperament of Princess Li Jing is truly... quite something."

Su Zhang offered a slight, acknowledging nod and began to walk.

Gu Xiao hastily caught up, his voice dropping to a low, guarded murmur: "Wait. In the corner of the left alley—someone is watching us."

Su Zhang's pace did not falter by a single heartbeat. He merely slanted his posture slightly, moving out of the direct line of sight. The two of them moved in perfect unison through the narrow lane, their boot soles kicking up fine, scattered sprays of water from the bluestone path.

Gu Xiao spoke with a half-smile that didn't reach his eyes: "Lord Su is certainly basked in glory today. Not only has he secured the devoted favour of the Second Princess, but even the flies in the shadows have begun to follow his scent."

As they reached a turn, Gu Xiao came to an abrupt halt, his gaze sharpening: "Shall I act as bait for you and hook that tail out into the light?"

Su Zhang tilted his head slightly, his eyes reflecting a profound, glacial chill: "No need for haste. Leave them. They may yet serve a far greater purpose."

The two men exchanged a glance, a silent and mutual understanding passing between them, and their smiles vanished simultaneously. The rain wove a fine tapestry around them, and the wind grew increasingly taut. On the bluestone road, only the silhouettes of the two men remained, walking shoulder to shoulder until they were swallowed by the mist and the distance.

* * * * *

The following afternoon, within the "Pearl Pavilion"—a jewellery establishment where gemstones and jade were displayed in exquisite disarray—the air was thick with a heavy, sweet fragrance.

Qin Nianyin had just handed over a newly crafted floral hairpin to the shopkeeper for appraisal when a burst of boisterous, unrestrained laughter erupted from the doorway: "Aiya! Is this not the little cousin of the Su family?"

Turning her head, she beheld Gu Xiao. He was adorned in a luxurious brocade robe, stepping into the shop with a swaggering, arrogant gait. One hand rested lazily against a jade display shelf as his gaze swept a slow, measuring circle between her and the shopkeeper.

"What are you selecting? Which piece do you fancy? I shall buy it." His tone was one of effortless entitlement. With a grand sweep of his arm, he declared loudly: "This Young Master is in an excellent mood today. If the lady fancies any item, have the shop wrap it at once and deliver it to the Su Residence."

Qin Nianyin merely cast a sidelong glance at him before turning back with an air of indifference. She meticulously counted the silver ingots she had just earned, securing them within her purse, and spoke to Mei: "Let us depart."

Before her words had fully faded, Gu Xiao blocked their path, wearing a rakish, indolent grin: "What is this? Do you look down upon a gift from this Young Master?"

Mei was on the verge of speaking, but Qin Nianyin silenced her with a single, sharp look.

Qin Nianyin lifted her gaze to meet his, her voice not loud, yet every word was etched with a crystalline clarity: "This silver you intend for gifts—did Master Gu earn it through his own labour?"

Gu Xiao froze, the grin on his face faltering for a heartbeat.

"This..." He pursed his lips, his voice turning stubborn: "The wealth of the Gu Household belongs to this Young Master by right. Sooner or later, it is mine to spend. What difference does it make?"

Upon hearing this, Qin Nianyin's expression turned cold. Her voice remained low, yet it sliced through his heart like a honed blade, inch by agonizing inch: "The prosperity and glory the Gu House enjoys today— was it not forged by your father and brother at the cost of their very lives? You have never set foot upon a battlefield for a single day; you have not a single military merit to your name. And yet, here you are, squandering gold like water, using the glory they bought with their blood to purchase the hollow favour of others?"

Gu Xiao stood stunned, his composure crumbling as his face flushed a violent red before turning a stark, ashen white.

"If you truly wish to gift me something," she said, her tone calm yet anchored in an unassailable logic, "then wait until the day you use silver earned by your own hand to speak with me."

With that, she flicked her sleeve and departed with Mei, turning her back upon him without a second glance.

Gu Xiao stared at her retreating silhouette, so incensed that he stamped his foot in frustration, shouting toward her back: "Fine! For the sake of that one sentence of yours, do not think this Young Master cannot earn his own silver!"

Everyone within the Pearl Pavilion stood aghast. The shopkeeper murmured in a low, trembling voice: "Master Gu... truly has a resolute spirit."

Gu Xiao let out a cold snort, turned, and strode away with great, sweeping steps, his cloak billowing behind him like a storm cloud.

* * * * *

Within the Imperial Garden, the hues of autumn were deepening. Beside the pond, the fallen leaves of the phoenix trees lay in mottled patterns, and every passing breeze sent ripples dancing across the water's surface.

The Empress leaned against a jade balustrade, idly feeding the fish, when an attendant's voice broke the silence: "The Young Marquis of Zhongwu requests an audience."

"At this hour?" She felt a touch of surprise, yet she maintained a smile: "Bid him enter."

Moments later, Gu Xiao burst into the garden with a frantic energy. Without even unfastening his cloak, he declared in a resonant voice: "Aunt, your nephew wishes to join the Imperial Guard. Might I trouble my Aunt to make the necessary arrangements?"

The Empress was so startled she nearly scattered the fish feed into the water. She cast a suspicious glance at him: "What did you say?"

"I wish to enter the Imperial Guard." His tone was resolute, his chin lifted high, his gaze burning with a fierce, sudden light.

The Empress set down her teacup and could not suppress a laugh: "Do you have a fever? In the past, how many times did I offer to arrange a post for you in the Imperial Guard, only for you to refuse with a single word? You said you would either join the Tiger Guards or live as a wealthy idler, accompanying your old mother in a life of leisure."

Gu Xiao gave a dry cough, averting his face in embarrassment as he muttered: "...That was before."

She narrowed her eyes, staring at him with a knowing, half-smile: "Oh? Only a few months have passed—how did your nature shift so violently? Tell me, who was it that provoked you so?"

Gu Xiao's skin burned under her scrutiny. He bit his lip for a long while before finally grumbling in a low voice: "...I was merely... looked down upon by a young girl."

The Empress erupted into a sudden laugh, yet she did not continue her teasing. Her gaze turned sombre, falling upon the ceremonial blade strapped to his back.

The youth, who had remained silent for so long, suddenly straightened his spine, his tone becoming quiet and unwavering: "Your nephew knows that my father and elder brother both perished upon the battlefield; their loyal souls are not far. If I continue to wither away in this state of decadence, I fear I shall have no face to meet them when I pass into the next life."

The moment these words left his mouth, a heavy silence descended upon the chamber.

Gu Xiao lowered his head, as if suppressing a violent tremor of emotion. He had thought of going to the border; he had seen the broken banners and the bleached bones of the day his brother fell in his dreams many times. Yet every time he mentioned it, the Empress would only say coldly: "The Gu family cannot afford to have no one return ever again."

She was afraid; he knew this.

So he had said nothing. He played the fool, he laughed, he caused trouble—he lived his life like a weed that could never bloom, allowing the world to mock him as a profligate and a wastrel, all for the sake of not adding to her burden of worry.

But this time, he had been truly provoked to the core.

Not for any other reason, but for that girl's cold accusation—*Are you not ashamed to squander the military glory of your father and brother?*

He had no answer for her. But he felt that he must, at last, do something.

The Empress let out a long sigh, remaining silent for a long duration before she finally nodded: "The post in the Imperial Guard is to protect the capital; you will not go to war, nor will you be deployed to distant lands. If you wish only to stand upon your own feet rather than throw your life away... then I shall mention this matter to the Emperor."

A faint light ignited in Gu Xiao's eyes, and he responded in a low voice: "Yes. I thank my Aunt."

She looked at that face, which had finally taken on an air of earnest resolve, her heart a cauldron of conflicting emotions. Finally, she asked: "Who is she? That girl."

He immediately waved his hand, the tips of his ears turning a secret, vivid red. "Just... just a young girl, that is all."

Watching him struggle to maintain his pride despite his reddened ears, the Empress laughed once more, nodding: "Then you must put forth your best effort. Our Xiao must not be looked down upon by the ladies."

She chuckled, watching his retreating silhouette, shaking her head as she whispered: "For the sake of a girl's single word, a youth finds his ambition... not bad at all."

After Gu Xiao departed, a profound stillness reclaimed the inner hall.

Chapter 48: Merely Adding Inconvenience

Outside the window, the wind rose, stirring the gauze curtains; lamplight flickered, its glow wavering faintly against the walls as the night deepened.

The Empress reclined on her couch, idly rotating the teacup in her hand several times, the porcelain rim clicking softly beneath her fingers.

Though a smile graced her lips, her gaze remained fixed on the hall doors that had just been shut, lingering there for a long while, as if weighing something unseen.

"Looked down upon by a young girl?" she murmured under her breath. Her eyes held not a trace of mockery, but instead revealed a glint of amusement and curiosity, the kind born of long experience rather than idle gossip.

For so many years, she knew that child best—his tough talk but soft heart, his seemingly frivolous exterior that masked a core deeply concerned with others' opinions, always more sensitive than he allowed others to see.

He never spoke of defeat lightly, yet he was willing to change his nature and actively seek employment for a young girl, even bending his pride to do so… This was truly unprecedented.

The Empress chuckled softly, set down her teacup, and instructed the maid standing nearby, her tone light yet deliberate: "Send a reliable person to investigate. See if Xiao has had any dealings recently with any young lady from a noble family. She should be no more than seventeen or eighteen, not of high birth, her features likely quite comely, and her temperament… probably one that doesn't hold him in much regard."

The maid was taken aback and couldn't help asking, cautiously, "Your Majesty, this is…?"

The Empress smiled faintly. "It's merely a sudden curiosity. I wish to know what kind of remarkable girl could make that stubborn boy change his ways so thoroughly."

She inclined her head slightly and added, almost as an afterthought, "There's no hurry. Investigate slowly, no need to alert outsiders. Let us see which family has produced such an interesting maiden."

Having spoken, her eyes smiling, she picked up her teacup again, and a smile suffused her lips, lingering longer than before.

* * * * *

Within the Su residence study, it was quiet as ever. A light breeze from outside rustled the window gauze; before the desk, documents were piled high like mountains, their edges casting layered shadows beneath the lamplight.

Qin Nianyin entered from outside, the sleeves of her robe still carrying a few strands of fragrance from the flower market, light and fleeting. Seeing Su Zhang leaning over his desk writing swiftly, she bowed in greeting.

"Cousin, are there documents to organize today?"

Su Zhang did not speak, but merely lifted a hand to point at the stacks of notes and official letters beside the desk. "Those volumes on the right are recently copied entries on southern administrative affairs. They are somewhat disordered and still require you to sort them out."

His tone was mild and temperate, as if asking for her help with a trivial, insignificant matter, yet his posture remained rigid, betraying a habitual restraint.

Qin Nianyin assented softly, rolled up her sleeves, and sat down beside the desk. Her plain hands turned pages, categorized, and straightened edges with practiced familiarity, each movement precise and unhurried.

The look in her brows and eyes held a faint resemblance to the woman from Su Zhang's dreams, subtle enough to be unsettling.

A document on the desk slipped from its pile accidentally. She reached out to pick it up. The neatly folded official missive was tucked back between her fingers, and she handed it to him without comment.

"Nianyin." His voice was low and hoarse, as if weighed before speaking, yet his gaze remained fixed on her lowered lashes.

His tone seemed offhand, but each word appeared to have been measured for a long time. "His Majesty has ordered me south to investigate a case… The road to Jiangnan is long, travel is arduous. If you are willing, perhaps… accompany me."

Qin Nianyin, originally focused on the documents in her hand, paused minutely at his words, her fingertips trembling imperceptibly before stilling again.

She looked up at him, dumbfounded.

Accompany him?

These two words were like a small stone dropped into the centre of a lake, stirring up disturbing ripples circle after circle, spreading far beyond what she could immediately suppress.

Her heart jumped. Emotions that had lain dormant for a long time seemed abruptly awakened, brushing dangerously close to the surface.

But she quickly suppressed that fleeting moment of hesitation. Lowering her eyes with a light laugh, she spoke gently, her tone carefully smoothed. "Cousin, this journey is official business. Nianyin, being a woman, would only add inconvenience if I accompanied you."

Her tone was as pliant as the spring breeze brushing willow branches, yet it carried a distinct boundary and a lucid sense of distance, leaving no room for misinterpretation.

She remembered this journey from her previous life. She had expended great effort and careful arrangement to finally accompany him to Jiangnan. It was on that very journey that the party was ambushed.

She had taken an arrow meant for him, nearly losing her life, which later allowed her to use the life-saving grace to pressure him into marrying her. But in this life, she was unwilling to become entangled with him again.

In this life, she refused to use her own blood to purchase a loveless shackle.

Regarding the assassination attempt during the Jiangnan journey, a subtle reminder from her would be sufficient. Given his intelligence, he would certainly be able to protect himself.

Su Zhang was slightly taken aback, the pause lasting no more than a breath, yet enough for his fingers to still against the desk.

He had thought she would hesitate, would shyly lower her head, or softly ask him, "Is it truly permissible?" Then, under his insistence, finally nod in fulfillment of her wish.

He had never made such a request of anyone before; this time, he had broken precedent by speaking it aloud.

The result was that she did not hesitate for even a moment, lightly and dismissively pushing it away, her composure unbroken.

A sudden, indescribable irritation welled up in his heart. His chest felt as if pressed down by a lump of lead, heavy and suffocating.

"Inconvenience?" he repeated in a low, cold laugh.

A storm gathered in his eyes as he set the document in his hand down heavily upon the desk.

His voice was pressed low, yet cold enough to pierce the bone. "Do you know how many dangers lie along the road to Jiangnan? Do you imagine I ask you to accompany me for my own convenience?"

Qin Nianyin was startled by his sudden outburst of emotion. She looked up at him and saw faint anger emerging between his handsome brows. Even he, usually so composed, seemed somewhat out of control now, the restraint in his gaze visibly strained.

She bit her lip, still maintaining a soft yet resolute tone. "Cousin, you have shown me the utmost care and concern, and Nianyin is deeply grateful. However, this journey is fraught with peril. It is best to prioritize official duties. I am merely a woman; my accompaniment would only add unnecessary inconvenience. Therefore, remaining in the capital is the more prudent and thorough course."

Her words were appropriate, impeccable, like a soft yet solid wall, yielding in sound but unmovable in intent.

The light in Su Zhang's eyes dimmed slightly.

It wasn't that she didn't trust him, nor that she was rejecting his protection.

It was simply that she had chosen to stand on the side of "propriety"— choosing to yield, choosing to remain aloof and untouched, beyond the reach of his concern.

His palms tightened slightly within his sleeves, his knuckles turning white.

Clearly her words were gentle, a smile still lingered on her lips, yet it was more sobering than having ice water thrown in his face.

He wanted to say: "It's not just to protect you. I want you by my side." But the words, reaching his lips, were ultimately swallowed back.

He, usually taciturn and cautious in speech, now found himself tongue-tied and flustered before her, his emotions in turmoil.

"Very well. Since that is the case, as you wish."

His voice was low and hoarse. He finally conceded a step, turned and left. His retreating figure was tall and slender, solitary and cold as a blade's edge under the lamplight.

Qin Nianyin watched his retreating back disappear. Her fingertips gripped the edge of the table tightly. Her lips trembled slightly, but she did not follow him.

Her palm still retained the lingering warmth from his brief touch moments before. Though it was merely a fleeting contact, it felt as if it had seared her heart.

She murmured softly, "Su Zhang… you must return safe and sound."

* * * * *

Su Zhang walked to his desk and gently placed a hand upon the pile of unread documents, remaining silent for a time.

The files and cases before him still stood piled like mountains, yet they failed to spark the slightest interest in him now.

His gaze was profound, but his expression began to grow rigid.

His fingers unconsciously traced the lines of text on page after page, while his mind circled back to the scene moments before—the expression on Qin Nianyin's face when she refused to accompany him, cool and resolute, as if it had become a thorn in his heart that he was unwilling to uncover.

Suddenly, he swept a hand out, casting the jade writing brush aside. It struck the desk with a clear, sharp sound.

The brush lay askew on the table, a thin film of moisture already glistening over the black ink.

"Truly laughable," Su Zhang murmured under his breath, his tone carrying a note of self-mockery.

He gazed out the window at the pear blossoms still drifting down, but his heart could no longer find a moment's peace.

Qin Nianyin's casual actions and gestures had already stirred the emotions pent up within him.

He understood the root of it all was not those chestnut cakes, but her alternating coldness and warmth, always keeping him guessing, uncertain. He had never felt so perturbed before.

He felt, inescapably, that he had become entangled—her gaze, her movements, every small, seemingly inadvertent gesture was like a fatal talisman branding his heart.

Su Zhang let out a bitter laugh, as if he had finally recognized one thing: what he was experiencing, enduring, and suppressing were nothing more than his own unwillingness to face the fact—the ineffable attraction she brought, drawing him deeper into a whirlpool from which he could not extricate himself.

He stood up, turned his back to the desk, closed his eyes for a moment and drew a deep breath, attempting to force that surge of anger back down.

In this moment, he suddenly felt he ought to do something.

Not for her, or for himself. Merely for that familiar yet utterly foreign emotion within his heart, to give himself an outlet.

Chapter 49: A Thorn on the Journey

The night had deepened. The lamp wick flickered faintly. Beyond the curtains, no wind stirred; a profound silence enveloped everything.

Qin Nianyin sat before the low table by her bed, a light gown draped over her shoulders. She clutched a piece of pure white notepaper, unable to put brush to it for a long while.

She had thought that after calmly uttering the words "merely adding inconvenience," she could suppress that inner fluctuation, could confine this transient emotion to the soundless lake of her heart. Yet when night fell and silence reigned, those unspoken words instead grew increasingly clamorous, like drums, like thunder.

She closed her eyes. The image that surfaced in her mind was his retreating figure from moments before —— his shoulders and back held ramrod straight, yet with an indescribable loneliness.

The Su Zhang of now was in his prime, his demeanour cultured, refined, and upright, his words modest and courteous. Both court and commoners praised the Su young master as possessing both virtue and talent.

His features were handsome and clear, his eyes like autumn water under moonlight. In speech, he possessed both a scholar's quiet restraint and the noble ease of a scion from a prestigious family.

 Simply standing in a blue robe at the front steps was enough to attract the admiration of young ladies from various houses, fitting perfectly the saying —— a jewel of a man on the road, a peerless young master in the world.

Pity she was no longer that ignorant young girl who would lose her composure over a handsome face and the allure of high status and glory.

Her mistakes in her previous life had been too grave; she had long since learned not to lose herself beneath his distinguished appearance.

This journey south to investigate the salt case had also occurred in her previous life.

This road was fraught with perils, with various factions watching like tigers eyeing their prey. Certain parties in the capital had long been restless.

She understood clearly in her heart that those people would absolutely not wait until he set foot in Jiangnan to strike —— the truly fatal blow often came midway.

In her previous life, it had never been the destination that claimed lives, but the stretch of road where vigilance dulled and escorts grew careless. The capital's invisible hands were patient and ruthless; they preferred shadows to spectacle, silence to chaos.

* * * * *

Moonlight spilled quietly outside the window, filtering through the bamboo blind to cast dappled patterns on the floor, leaving the room half in light, half in shadow, much like her own disordered thoughts.

Qin Nianyin sat alone under the lamplight, a blank letter held between her fingertips. A slight dampness from her palm lingered, the corner of the paper slightly crumpled from her grip.

From her experiences in her previous life, she already knew that this journey to Jiangnan would involve an ambush —— those forces hidden within the capital would ultimately be unable to restrain themselves, attempting to ensure Su Zhang "never reached Jiangnan and never returned."

If she stood by and did nothing, perhaps she could sever this tangled predestined relationship completely.

So long as she remained silent, so long as she chose distance, fate might finally loosen its grip. No more debts of blood, no more ties forged through sacrifice and coercion.

But the look in his eyes that day when he said "accompany me" still lingered in her heart, refusing to fade.

 It had not been insistence, nor command, but a quiet expectation that unsettled her far more than force ever could. That brief, restrained moment had betrayed a reliance he himself might not yet have recognized.

That year, on his first journey to Jiangnan, he was ambushed on the road, and an arrow pierced his knee —— an injury not fatal, but one that never fully healed.

After returning to the capital, he continued attending morning court as usual, walking normally. Others noticed nothing amiss. It was only after their marriage that she learned that on overcast or rainy days, his gait slowed slightly and he would sometimes lean on an armrest for a brief moment.

It was said that after being wounded in that encounter, he walked dozens of li alone to the courier station without raising any alarm. When the imperial physician examined him, he merely said mildly, "An old injury. Do not trouble yourself."

It was years later, while managing household affairs, that she happened to glimpse a reference in an old file and realized the assassination attempt that year was no minor incident.

Buried among routine memorials and expenditure logs, the report was brief, almost deliberately understated — precisely the sort of omission that concealed danger rather than dispelled it.

Now, facing the same situation again, she could not stand idly by. Yet if her words were too revealing, it could easily attract scrutiny, even bring disaster upon herself.

Su Zhang was inherently deep-minded and keenly perceptive. If he detected the slightest trace, he would surely follow the clues, ultimately leading to her.

She lowered her head. Initially intending to write, she paused her thoughts in an instant. Ink hovered at the tip of the brush, trembling faintly, as though mirroring the conflict in her chest.

After pondering for a long moment, she shifted the brush to her left hand, lifted it, and wrote six characters.

She had deliberately written only six characters, leaving behind no signature, no salutation, and not a single trace that could point back to her.

Six characters — no more, no less — enough to warn, insufficient to accuse.

The handwriting appeared somewhat unfamiliar and slanted, yet remained clear and controlled.

She gazed at that line of characters for a long time, her fingertips slowly pressing against the still-damp ink, her expression calm.

After a considerable while, she folded the letter properly and sealed it within a plain envelope.

The lamplight flickered. She leaned over the desk, her temple lightly touching the letter, her eyes serene and softly tender.

If he was willing to believe it, she would have no regrets, having done her small part.

But now —— how was this letter to be delivered into his hands without leaving a trace?

She gently rubbed the envelope in her palm. The sound of Mei's footsteps outside the courtyard seemed to reach her ears. Qin Nianyin lifted her gaze, her eyes glimmering faintly where the lamplight and moonlight met. This matter could not be entrusted to another.

She calculated secretly in her heart: Should she quietly entrust it to Xiuyan? Or should she personally place it among the documents on his desk at night?

Whichever method, it must leave no trace. Otherwise, if he questioned it, she would certainly be unable to conceal it.

She pressed the letter gently against her chest, closed her eyes, her breathing even, as if she had finally reached a certain resolution.

* * * * *

In the quiet of the afternoon study, the only sound was the occasional breeze beyond the curtains, lightly rustling a few pages of documents.

Su Zhang was bent over his desk reviewing papers, a trace of weariness between his brows, when he heard footsteps approaching the door.

Yefeng entered, holding a plain white letter in his hands. Clasping his hands in salute, he said, "Young Master, this was just delivered."

Su Zhang looked up, scanned the letter —— plain paper without pattern, sealed very simply. He took it, turned it over, raised an eyebrow slightly, and said in a tone neither cold nor warm, "There is no name written on it. For whom is it intended?"

Yefeng scratched his head, slightly puzzled. "The servant boy said a child of seven or eight delivered it. Dressed cleanly, holding this letter, said it was for 'the Eldest Young Master Su.' Didn't give a name, didn't leave a message."

Seeing his master's sombre silence, a sign of latent displeasure, he felt very uneasy. After a pause, he added, "The child ran off after handing over the letter. The servant went after him but couldn't catch him. If you are concerned, Young Master, I will have someone investigate immediately."

Su Zhang did not speak. His fingertip rubbed the letter. The paper was somewhat thin, feeling slightly rough to the touch. He leaned forward slightly and opened the envelope.

The handwriting before his eyes came into view —— only six characters.

江南行中有刺 - A thorn awaits the Southern journey

In an instant, his pupils darkened slightly, his knuckles tightening imperceptibly. The warning was blunt, stripped of flourish or explanation, yet it struck with unsettling precision — too precise to be idle mischief, too restrained to be provocation.

Su Zhang's fingertip lightly touched the plain white paper —— thin and coarse, the colour yellowish, with faint rough edges visible in the fibres. This was the cheapest variety sold in common bookshops, often used by schoolchildren for practice or for leaflets and notices sold on the streets.

It did not seem like a careless act, but rather a deliberate one. Whoever had written this understood restraint — and understood him.

His brow furrowed slightly. He examined the front and back of the letter, confirming only these six characters.

No opening. No signature.

The handwriting was uneven and slanted, as if written with the left hand, yet not deliberately disguised. It seemed more like a natural concealment by someone unwilling to leave traces.

He looked at it quietly for a while, then folded the letter and tucked it into his sleeve, his eyes growing increasingly sombre. He could not help but become suspicious. Who was kindly warning him? Or was it intentionally creating mystery? More troubling still was the possibility that this person knew exactly how he thought — and exactly how little was required to place him on guard.

"A thorn awaits the Southern journey?" His tone was neither cold nor warm. He made no sound, but closed the letter and instructed in a low voice, "There is no need to investigate."

Yefeng was taken aback. "Young Master?"

Su Zhang had already set the letter aside, his expression normal, his tone calm. "The journey to Jiangnan approaches. Rumours easily cause disorder. There is no need to mobilize forces."

Yefeng still seemed somewhat hesitant, but in the end, he tactfully withdrew.

When the room had returned to silence, Su Zhang picked up the letter again, gazing at those six characters for a long time ——

The handwriting appeared extremely slanted, as if deliberately concealing the original script.

He betrayed no emotion but lowered his eyelashes almost imperceptibly.

Dangers on the road to Jiangnan?

He closed the letter. The expression in his eyes had quietly changed, no longer as calm and clear as before.

Chapter 50: The Imperial Guard Uniform

Spring sunlight was clear and unwavering; the sky shone at its fullest.

Light sifted through the drooping willows of the Su Manor, mingling with blossoms that cast drifting shadows upon the flagstone path, forming layered halos upon the stone in a quiet, luminous shimmer. In that bright stillness, even the air seemed washed clean—soft, warm, and deceptively harmless.

Suddenly, from beyond the manor gate burst a rapid volley of hoofbeats ——crisp, sharp, striking stone in an urgent rhythm.

The sound came hard and fast from the street corner, as if the rider had not slowed once, not even to announce himself.

Yefeng had just lifted his hands to close the gate when he glanced up and saw a figure leap from horseback in one fluid motion, landing with clean precision, his robe flaring behind him like unfolded crane wings caught in the wind.

The descent was too neat to be mere bravado; it was the kind of practiced decisiveness that belonged to someone newly placed under strict military drill.

The youth stood tall, his posture straight as a spear shaft. He wore a newly issued uniform of the Imperial Guards ——deep crimson armour trimmed in dark lacquer, tailored closely to his build, emphasizing the raw vitality of someone still half a boy, half a blade.

The cut of the armour hugged him just right, making his youth look even more insolent, even more unrestrained.

Silver clasps on the armour gleamed under the sun; at his hip hung a regulation longsword whose narrow arc of exposed steel flashed with a cold, restrained glint. His spirit was bright, his expression fierce and unbound.

Beneath that fierce brightness, there was also something sharper—an edge of ambition that did not bother to hide itself.

It was Gu Xiao ——newly admitted to the elite Shen Ce Battalion of the royal Imperial Guard.

He strode forward in long, confident steps, each movement swift yet with a trace of wind, his boots knocking crisply against the stone path, rhythmic and decisive.

His pace was light, almost careless, yet every footfall landed with a clear, deliberate beat, as if he meant the entire manor to hear him.

Yefeng had barely lifted a hand to salute when Gu Xiao's palm landed firmly on his shoulder. The boyish arrogance on his face was undisguised, a grin stretched wide with mischief and pride—half rogue, half conqueror, as if the world owed him applause.

"Well now, Brother Ye, still recognize this young master?"

He lifted his chin, gave his new armour a showy shake ——silver clasps chiming. The metal fittings rang out cleanly, bright and insistent, like a small victory being announced to whoever dared to look away.

"How is it? Does this outfit suit your eyes?"

Yefeng's mouth twitched. He looked Gu Xiao over from head to toe before forcing a polite bow, the instinctive caution of a servant rising faster than any compliment.

"Master Gu has always been striking. This… is the uniform of the Imperial Guard, is it not? Has Master Gu entered the Shen Ce Battalion?"

"Of course!" Gu Xiao snapped his sleeve with theatrical flourish, the metal fittings clinking lightly.

"My archery is unmatched, my courage unparalleled ——naturally they recruited me. Well? Impressed?"

His tone was playful, yet a shard of sharp ambition flickered beneath it, quick as a blade's reflection—gone the moment one tried to pin it down.

Before Yefeng could answer, Gu Xiao lifted his brows.

"Where's your young master?"

"My apologies, my lord… he is not at home at the moment."

"Not home? Even better. I'll go in and wait."

Before the sentence finished, Gu Xiao had already nudged Yefeng aside with a single effortless sweep of his arm ——light in appearance, yet impossible to resist.

It was not a shove that looked violent, but it carried the casual authority of someone who had never been denied. His step shifted and in the next moment he walked straight into the Su Manor.

Yefeng reacted too slowly; he reached out belatedly to block him, but Gu Xiao was already several paces ahead. The distance between them widened as if the manor itself had decided whom it would obey.

"Master Gu! The young master did not instruct us to receive guests today ——if you enter like this, I… I do not know how long you might have to wait!"

"No matter!" Gu Xiao called over his shoulder, half a laugh in his voice.

His hands folded behind his back, he strode boldly through the moon gate like the rightful owner of the estate returning to inspect his grounds.

The posture was so natural it was almost infuriating—too familiar, too unbothered by propriety.

The garden was in full bloom, crabapple blossoms freshly opened, pear flowers beaded with dew.

He paused before a side chamber to study the flowers; the next moment he drifted toward a corner of the covered walkway to kick at loose stones; then he lifted a curtain to peek inside a guest room with complete lack of restraint. (pear flowers like they had been washed in dew; the garden looked as though spring itself had just arrived and refused to leave.)

"This room isn't it… nor that one…"

He appeared to be looking for something ——or someone ——or perhaps he was simply wandering without purpose.

But the longer Yefeng watched, the more alarmed he became. Gu Xiao's gaze was too active, too quick; it did not look like idle roaming so much as a man mapping a place he intended to claim.

Guests did not enter manors this way. And this particular guest feared neither heaven nor earth. Wearing an Imperial Guard uniform only amplified his already domineering aura. The uniform did not just decorate him; it legitimized him, turning his arrogance into something others had to swallow.

Helpless, Yefeng trailed behind him cautiously, hardly daring to breathe too loudly. Anxiety churned in his chest ——What exactly is this Gu family young master trying to do? If the young master returned to find this chaos, how was Yefeng to explain that the Su Manor had been treated like a playground?

Gu Xiao's gaze swept the courtyard in a single swift arc.

His steps shifted as though he were searching for a trace, or confirming whether someone had been present.

He turned where the shadows lay thickest, lingered where footprints might pass, glanced once toward the inner path that led deeper into the residence—as if he expected the person he wanted to appear at any moment.

Unable to endure the tension, Yefeng finally asked in a hushed voice, "Master Gu… whom are you searching for?"

Gu Xiao turned, amusement in his gaze sharpened by directness. His expression carried that same half-mocking, half-cutting frankness that always made people feel as though they were being toyed with.

"Where is your young miss ——the cousin?"

"Ah…" Yefeng stiffened, neither retreating nor approaching, unable to answer yet unable to remain silent. His throat went dry, and for a moment he wished the willows would drop their leaves to cover him.

But Gu Xiao did not wait for his reply.

He stepped out into the central garden, made his way to a small stone pavilion and sat down on a stone stool with the ease of a man entirely unconcerned with propriety.

His posture was relaxed yet commanding, as though the entire manor belonged to him. He sat as if he had been invited—no, as if the invitation was unnecessary.

He lifted his face toward the sky. Sunlight fell across his eyes, leaving pale gleams like frost upon steel. He gave a soft laugh, murmuring almost to himself,

"Not a bad view."

Then he propped one leg forward, spine straight, hands loosely folded behind him. The pose looked casual, but the message was clear: he would not move until he got what he wanted.

"Very well. I'll sit here. Have your young miss come for a chat."

Cold sweat instantly gathered at Yefeng's temples. His mind produced only one silent cry ——

Do you think this is your own home?

He swallowed, bowing low.

"I ——I will go inform the young master."

But both men knew he would not dare truly summon the young miss. His only choice was to hurry off to find his own master first. Even running felt dangerous, as though the wrong step would turn this into an offence the manor could not afford.

* * * * *

Afternoon sunlight drifted across the courtyard, the branches stirring in the breeze, scattering shadows onto the quiet ground.

The manor looked tranquil from afar, yet the air inside carried a tautness that did not match the gentleness of spring.

When Su Zhang returned from the outer courtyard and stepped through the moon gate, Yefeng approached hurriedly, ledger in hand, yet clearly uneasy. His steps were too quick, his breath slightly off—signs that something had already gone wrong.

Su Zhang cast him a calm glance. "What is it?"

Yefeng swallowed. "…Master Gu arrived wearing a completely new Imperial Guard uniform. He is… currently seated in the back-garden pavilion, saying he wishes to wait for you." He hesitated, as if the rest of the truth tasted bitter.

Su Zhang halted. His expression did not shift; he merely responded with a neutral hum. The pause was so light it almost seemed like nothing— yet it was enough to make Yefeng's spine go straighter.

"What did he say?"

Yefeng's gaze flickered. After a moment of hesitation, he whispered, "He first claimed he came to see you. Later… it seemed… he wished to see the young miss." The last words came softer, as if he feared even the blossoms might hear.

The corridor fell still.

"Did you send for her?"

Yefeng shook his head immediately.

"No, young master. I came to report to you first. No one in the manor dared to stop him, so he remains sitting in the pavilion." He did not add the rest aloud—how Gu Xiao had wandered through rooms like a lord inspecting property, how he had spoken of "chatting" with a young lady as though it were his right.

Su Zhang was quiet for a breath. Then, with the faintest pause of his step, he said ——his tone unchanged, steady and even —— "I understand."

The words were light, yet enough to silence Yefeng entirely. He bowed his head and retreated to one side.

Su Zhang lifted his gaze toward the eastern wing. Branches cast shifting shadows; blossoms swayed in the wind.

Though his expression did not change, the folding fan in his hand slowly closed, its frame pressing firmly against his palm and remaining still. The fan's edge bit into his skin just slightly, a pressure that betrayed what his face refused to show.

* * * * *

When Su Zhang arrived at the back garden, his expression held the same unshaken calm. If there was displeasure, it sat too deep to be seen.

Gu Xiao lounged against the pavilion railing in his deep-red armour, silver clasps catching sunlight so brightly it almost stung the eye.

Seeing Su Zhang approach, Gu Xiao lifted a hand in an easy wave. His smile was unabashed ——bold, careless, impossible to fend off, like a bright blade flashed too close to the eyes.

A soft breeze stirred the flower shadows in the pavilion. Gu Xiao turned slightly, speaking as though making idle conversation, as though he had not just forced his way into the manor without a single announcement.

"You're just in time. This is the new Shen Ce Battalion uniform. What do you think?"

The silver clasp gave a faint flash ——youthful pride radiating from every line of him.

Su Zhang gave it a brief glance, his tone clear and cool.

"It fits."

Gu Xiao snorted a laugh, sprawling back onto the stone seat, his long legs stretching out.

"Fine, don't flatter me. Either way, I've been sitting here an entire hour ——consider it helping you guard your courtyard."

Su Zhang replied mildly,

"No need to guard anything. Next time you have leisure, take a fast horse outside the city ——more exhilarating."

"Sure, exhilarating," Gu Xiao waved dismissively. "But dull."

He paused. His gaze slid sideways, as if he were listening for footsteps that never came, as if he were annoyed by the absence of the person he had wanted to see.

"Your young miss happens not to be here, so I waited for you. Wanted to ask something."

Su Zhang turned his head slightly.

"You were looking for her ——for what reason?"

Gu Xiao flicked a loose strand of hair back over his shoulder, speaking in a lazy tone, as if the question itself were beneath serious answer.

"To let her see this uniform, of course. A man should have someone comment when he changes into armour."

If there was hidden meaning beneath those words, Su Zhang did not acknowledge it. He answered simply,

"Very well. In a few days, I intend to bring her with me to Jiangnan."

The ease on Gu Xiao's face vanished instantly.

As though shoved without warning, he jerked upright and sprang to his feet.

The words he meant to shout She cannot go, surged hotly to his throat. His jaw tightened so hard it looked as if he might crack a tooth through sheer restraint.

But at the final moment, he forced them down.

Realizing how abrupt his reaction had been, he swallowed hard. His expression tightened, then smoothed out again. He sank back into his seat, drumming his fingers twice against his knee as if nothing had occurred.

The motion looked careless, but it was the kind of tapping a man did when something inside him refused to stay quiet.

Su Zhang observed the entire sequence ——the flare, the restraint, the suppression.

His lips curved faintly.

"What is it?"

Gu Xiao lifted his eyelids, expression half teasing, half veiled.

"Nothing."

"Xiao," Su Zhang said suddenly, his tone so direct that even the flowers beyond the pavilion seemed to fall silent, "To be frank, did you come today because you've developed feelings for her?"

Gu Xiao froze. The sunlight on his armour seemed to harden; even the air around him turned sharper.

A heartbeat later, he barked out a laugh ——clear, bright and impressively unruffled.

"Feelings? Hardly. I merely…"

Su Zhang lowered his gaze slightly.

"Yes, or no?"

Gu Xiao held his eyes for several breaths before allowing a slow, easy smile to surface. The smile was smooth, practiced—too smooth, as if placed there to cover something that would otherwise show.

"Talking about feelings is far too sentimental… nothing of the sort."

"No?" Su Zhang nodded, expression unchanging.

"Very well. I will take your word for it."

Chapter 51: Genuine Delight

The moment Qin Nianyin stepped into the rear garden under Su Wan's guidance, the sky was just right. The daylight lay at its gentlest.

Warm spring sunlight filtered through the layered osmanthus leaves outside the pavilion, breaking into scattered flecks of gold that drifted across the stone floor like fragments of an unhurried dream.

Upon the stone table inside the pavilion, two porcelain tea cups rested side by side.

Both were still faintly warm; pale steam curled upward in soft threads, carrying with it the clean, green fragrance of freshly brewed leaves.

Qin Nianyin's steps paused ever so slightly — she gave a faint start. Had someone been here just moments ago?

The quiet warmth left in the air had not yet scattered.

"Sit."

Su Zhang's voice held no weight of emotion. It sounded like a casual instruction, yet allowed no refusal, lodging itself beneath her ribs with an unmistakable firmness. His tone was placid, as if offhandedly giving an order, yet brooked no doubt.

As she approached the table, her gaze flicked instinctively toward the two cups — one on the left, one on the right — still aligned in a way that suggested a conversation cut short. She couldn't help but glance at the two teacups, a quiet puzzlement rising within her: If there had been a guest here just now, and the guest had already left, then why summon her?

Su Zhang did not hurry.

He reached for the clay teapot with the slow precision of a man entirely in control of the moment, his movements so leisurely they bordered on provocation. He tilted it to refill both cups.

The stream of pale tea fell clean and unbroken, releasing another faint breath of fragrance that drifted between them like an invisible veil.

Only after the scent had settled did he speak, voice calm and unhurried. "Gu Xiao was here a moment ago," he said lightly. "He waited an hour for you."

Qin Nianyin froze in place.

Her eyes swept instinctively across the pavilion pillars, then toward the garden path beyond the flowers — searching, though she already knew she would find no one. Her steps paused slightly; her gaze swept subconsciously over the pavilion pillars and the foliage — but where was there any sign of a person?

"Then… where is he now?"

"He just left."

The answer came lightly, without ripple, as if the matter held no particular significance. Su Zhang's tone was breezy and detached.

Qin Nianyin gave a quiet "oh," neither surprised nor relieved, and did not press further.

But the doubt deepened.

If the guest had already gone, then what purpose did calling her here serve? Her heart grew even more perplexed.

She bowed slightly.

"In that case, I shall —"

"Wait."

Only the single word — soft, level, almost lazily spoken. Yet it caught her like a hook, halting her mid-step. His two faint words were like a lightly cast hook, reeling her in and holding her fast.

"Sit."

With no room to refuse, she returned to the stone bench, a faint crease gathering between her brows. She had no choice but to return to the stone stool, a slight frown knitting her brow.

Su Zhang slid one of the tea cups toward her. "This year's newly arrived spring tea," he murmured in a low voice. "Taste it."

The request sounded simple.

Yet the quiet weight in his tone made her lift the cup despite her confusion. Qin Nianyin was somewhat baffled, but seeing he seemed to have something to say, she lowered her gaze and lifted the teacup.

The tea glowed with a clear green sheen, delicate as the first leaf of the season. She took a sip — light, astringent, with the faint sting of freshness unique to new tea.

Silence unfurled between them.

Only tea fragrance lingered, drifting between breath and sunlight, settling into the small pauses of the afternoon. For a moment, the pavilion fell quiet, leaving only the scent of tea and the shadows of flowers.

Su Zhang watched her set the cup down.

He seemed to be waiting — letting the silence ripen into a shape that suited him, as if waiting for the right moment.

"Today," he finally said, his voice neither rushed nor slow, "Gu Xiao came mainly to let you see his new Imperial Guard uniform."

Qin Nianyin blinked once, genuinely taken aback. A faint glimmer rose in her eyes, soft and bright, a genuine flicker of light. "He has truly entered the Imperial Guard?"

"Mm."

Su Zhang gave a quiet acknowledgment, but his gaze remained pinned to her face, intent on catching every flicker across her features. His eyes were locked on her face, as if carefully capturing each subtle change. "You're pleased?"

"Of course."

The words escaped her without thought. Her lips even curved with a faint, unguarded smile.

and then the smile dimmed — subtly, like a candle touched by a passing breeze. Yet in the next instant, that smile was gently submerged by a sour ache rising from the depths of her heart —

He lived this time.

Last lifetime, Gu Xiao had ridden to the northern frontier, never to return. In her previous life, he had gone to the border, died on the battlefield, and not even his remains had returned to the capital.

His bones vanished beneath wind-scoured sands; there had been no remains to bury, no closure for the living. Perhaps… this life, entering the Imperial Guard meant staying in the capital. Perhaps he could avoid that doomed death in the northern frontier.

If joining the Imperial Guard meant remaining in the capital, if it meant he would not be dispatched to the border again, then perhaps — just perhaps — he might finally slip free of that grim fate laid out before him.

Her joy was not for his status. Her happiness was not for Gu Xiao's prospects.

It was for his life. It was... for his safety.

She lowered her gaze to the tea, letting the steam veil the faint ache that surfaced in her chest. She lowered her lashes, hiding this tremor within the scent of tea.

Su Zhang watched the changes in her expression. His fingers brushed the rim of his own cup, slow and steady. After a long moment, he asked quietly in a light tone: "Happy... for him?"

Qin Nianyin looked up, startled, instinctively meeting his gaze. His gaze held no sharpness, yet it seemed to reach straight through her lashes, searching beneath the calm she wore.

That gaze was calm as water, yet seemed able to see through her eyes into the thoughts in her heart. Her lips parted slightly; she thought to deny it, yet felt it unnecessary, so she followed the scent of tea and whispered softly, "Yes. He... finally has a place of his own."

A subtle light flickered and then narrowed in Su Zhang's eyes, a hint of a smile that wasn't a smile. "Is that all? Simply because he has a place?"

She did not answer. Her fingertips circled the teacup gently, tracing the smooth curve in deliberate avoidance, as if evading.

Su Zhang drew back his gaze. His voice returned to its tranquil, almost distant calm, back to that breezy detachment. "Mm, so long as your heart is at ease then."

Tea fragrance drifted lightly through the pavilion. The shadows of osmanthus branches swayed in silence outside. The length of the stillness between them stretched and stretched, until Qin Nianyin felt the faint unease settle along her spine.

The prolonged silence made her somewhat uncomfortable. Just as she was planning to take her leave, he finally spoke again — calmly, almost idly, yet each syllable cut with quiet precision.

Su Zhang's gaze remained on Qin Nianyin, his tone unhurried: "Gu Xiao has never been a sentimental man. If he chose to wait here an entire hour merely to see you... he likely bears intentions toward you. Do you have any thoughts about that?"

"...Thoughts?"

"If he were to pursue you —"

"Impossible!"

The words burst from her before reason could intervene, sharp and immediate enough to tremble against the spring air. Qin Nianyin almost immediately raised her voice.

Su Zhang did not flinch. He merely angled his gaze toward her, unhurried, observing the startled tension in her shoulders, the shock widening her eyes. Su Zhang watched the startled expression that abruptly flashed across her face without changing his expression, his tone unchanged.

His own voice remained perfectly level. "And why," he asked softly, "is it impossible?"

Qin Nianyin's reply came without a breath of hesitation, decisive and unequivocal. "Because I, Qin Nianyin, have no such intention toward Young Master Gu. None whatsoever. Nianyin has absolutely no thoughts regarding Young Master Gu."

Her voice was steady; her expression clear and sincere. No hidden fluttering, no uncertain pause. Her tone was blunt, her expression genuine, not feigned. No attempt to disguise or soften the truth.

Su Zhang studied her for a long, measured moment. The tight, muted heaviness that had been lodged beneath his ribs — born from the brief fear that Gu Xiao's mind might collide with his own — began to loosen, thread by thread.

That dull, stifling feeling in his heart, born from the momentary fear that his brother's thoughts might clash with his own, slowly eased somewhat.

The pressure eased. His posture relaxed by an imperceptible degree.

He placed his cup back upon the stone table. The shadow within his eyes thinned, its chill receding. His tone also became somewhat more at ease. "In that case," he said quietly, "finish your tea before you go."

Qin Nianyin blinked, caught off guard by the abrupt shift, but she murmured a soft assent. She picked up the tea and took a sip. The temperature was just right, yet a slight bitterness spread on the tip of her tongue.

The pavilion fell silent once more. Su Zhang kept his gaze lowered, his tone notably lighter when he finally asked, as if casually: "Then… what do you think of Gu Xiao?"

Qin Nianyin faltered for a heartbeat. Why is this not over yet? She set the tea cup down with deliberate calm, her posture straight, and said solemnly: "What kind of person Young Master Gu is, cousin surely knows better than I do."

Su Zhang lifted his eyes, his tone neither salty nor bland. "From a man's perspective, he is not lacking. His appearance is striking. His family background is noble. Among the young ladies of the capital, many would gladly look his way." He paused. "And you?"

Qin Nianyin's expression did not shift. "Cousin need not say more. I've already said, Nianyin has absolutely no thoughts of aspiring to Young Master Gu."

Su Zhang seemed as though he wished to press once more — but ultimately all that escaped him was a quiet hum, the faintest acknowledgment, before he looked away.

Sensing the moment had loosened, Qin Nianyin rose and bowed politely. "If Cousin has no further instructions, I shall return first."

He did not stop her.

She stepped out of the pavilion, her figure soon swallowed by the drifting patterns of osmanthus shadows. Su Zhang watched her back just disappear into the depths of the osmanthus shadows when brisk footsteps approached from outside the courtyard.

Gu Xiao. He strode in with the careless vigour unique to him. The dark red Imperial Guard uniform gleamed sharply beneath the sun, every metal clasp catching light like scattered fragments of a blade.

He looked entirely self-assured, radiant with energy, as if he had just returned triumphant from a fast ride through open fields.

"Zhang!" Gu Xiao lifted a hand and greeted him with a grin that rippled through the pavilion. "I was halfway home and thought — better say a word to your cousin's lady first. Next time I come, I intend to give proper notice. Can't have her missing me again."

Su Zhang's expression remained unchanged. "She is gone."

Gu Xiao paused mid-step. A hint of disappointment flickered, then vanished beneath an easy shrug. "Ah, that's a shame." He settled himself against the stone railing as though the pavilion belonged to him.

The breeze shifted; the tea on the table had already cooled to a wan, pale color. Outside the pavilion, the sound of the wind gradually grew heavier; the tea on the stone table had already turned cold.

Su Zhang stared down at his untouched cup. For a moment, his fingers tightened around the porcelain. Then the cup touched the stone table with a soft, decisive click — a sound quiet enough not to echo, yet sharp enough to sever the thin veil of peace lingering in the air.

He stared at the light reflected in the cup, then suddenly paused. The porcelain cup was placed back on the table with a soft tap — the sound wasn't loud, but it coldly severed the surrounding stillness.

"Gu Xiao." He suddenly called Gu Xiao with a serious expression, lifting his eyes, their colour deep. Seeing his solemn expression, Gu Xiao's heart suddenly skipped a beat. "What is it? What's with that look? Quite frightening."

"Qin Nianyin came earlier," Su Zhang said, his tone not loud but carrying an undeniable finality. "I asked on your behalf. She has no interest in you."

Gu Xiao blinked. Then he laughed — bright, careless, utterly unbothered. "What? I never said she had to. I merely thought your cousin's lady is interesting, nothing more."

Su Zhang's gaze fixed on him without wavering. His lips pressed into a thin, controlled line. After a breath, he spoke again, voice low. "Gu Xiao. Do not forget what you just said." His voice was low, like an iron hammer held in the throat for a long time finally falling.

The breeze outside stirred the osmanthus leaves, rustling in uneasy waves as if echoing the strain in his tone. The osmanthus shadows outside the pavilion rustled in the wind, as if covering up that momentary, almost out-of-control coldness for him.

Gu Xiao froze for the briefest instant. Then he threw his head back and laughed again — louder, freer, as though to scatter the tension with sound. But Su Zhang no longer engaged. He lifted his cup and drained the cold tea in a single swallow.

The bitterness slid into his chest, sharp and piercing and the chill settled deep — locking itself in the quiet chambers of his heart. The clear bitterness entered his mouth; the suppression in his chest had already turned to ice, deeply locked within his heart.

Chapter 52: A Son of His Blood

Night pressed heavily over the palace grounds, thick and unbroken, the entire imperial city submerged in a darkness as deep as ink.

Only the vermilion palace lanterns trembled faintly in the wind, their warm glow sliding across the cinnabar steps and stretching into a long, narrow shadow that wavered like a silent omen.

The faint scent of sandalwood drifted through the air, rising and dispersing in slow, curling strands.

From the far distance came the muffled strike of a bronze gong announcing the hour, the sound lingering for a breath before being swallowed whole by the wind threading through the long palace corridors.

Second Prince Li Xuan stood beneath the sweeping eaves of the hall, hands clasped behind his back.

Silver-white lantern light fell slantwise across his shoulders, catching on the folds of his robe while the night wind stirred the hem with a subtle, deliberate movement.

His expression held a languid calm, the kind born of one who had already predicted the shape and outcome of the conversation long before it arrived.

From the stone steps below, a man in a blue-patterned court robe approached at a hurried pace.

The sound of his boots striking the stone rang sharply in the quiet night, clear and crisp in the night's stillness.

"Assistant Minister Du," Li Xuan remarked without turning fully, casting only the briefest glance toward the man.

Du Mao bent into a deep bow, his back nearly folding in half. "Your Highness."

Li Xuan cast him a displeased look, a glance of clear annoyance. "What urgent matter requires you to seek me out at such an hour?"

"Th-there is… a matter… truly urgent…" Du Mao bowed even lower, hands clasped in salute, his voice trembling despite his attempts at restraint.

Li Xuan tilted his head slightly, examining him with a sidelong, derisive glance. "Look at you, so agitated you're quivering. Speak. What grave matter brings you here?"

The man swallowed, throat bobbing. He lowered his voice to a near-whisper, his brow tightly furrowed. "Your Highness… the matter in Jiangnan… I fear it will be investigated."

Li Xuan betrayed no surprise. He merely lifted his chin a fraction, signalling him to continue.

Du Mao wet his lips. His Adam's apple bobbed before he finally managed to say: "During last year's floods, the embankment section under Jiangning Prefecture's charge… it was, after all, rushed. If anyone were to examine the accounts in detail, they wouldn't match up. In the end, it's likely to… to implicate this humble official."

His voice shook harder now. Sweat seeped into the hair at his temples, catching the dim lantern glow. He paused. Cold sweat had already seeped from his forehead into his sideburns. Lowering his voice further, he added: "Your Highness knows as well, the figures for materials and labour at that time… we did indeed make some… adjustments."

Li Xuan looked at him sideways, a trace of a smile that was not quite a smile at the corner of his mouth. "What's this? Are you afraid?"

Upon hearing this, Du Mao immediately became even more obsequious, bowing again with clasped hands. "Y-your Highness, this humble official is naturally afraid!"

Li Xuan snorted lightly, his face showing clear disdain. "With the little courage you possess, what great undertaking could you possibly shoulder?"

"'This servant simply fears… in case of the unexpected…'" Du Mao's voice shook as he struggled to swallow. "'That flood last year claimed over a hundred lives, left thousands homeless… what if His Majesty were to find out we had a hand in it…'"

Before he finished, Li Xuan's lips curved again ——this time with a faint, icy amusement. "And if he learns it? I am his son by blood. Will he kill me for it?"

Having spoken, he waved a dismissive hand, as if he had already lost all interest in Du Mao's cowardice.

The wind shifted beneath the eaves, lifting the edges of his robe. Under the eaves, the night breeze brushed past. He suddenly turned, his gaze settling on the pitch-black sky beyond the palace walls. His voice was gentle, almost offhand: "Since you fear it, then perhaps… we should harness that very momentum."

Du Mao blinked, stunned. He was dumbfounded. "Harness… the momentum?"

"The Crown Prince enjoys preaching 'governance and relief,' does he not?" Li Xuan's tone remained soft, but the edges had sharpened. "Send this matter to his desk. Once His Majesty asks, the Crown Prince will have to answer. If he knew and failed to report it, he is unvirtuous. If he knew and shielded the culprits, he is derelict."

He paused, letting each word settle like blades. Li Xuan's tone was unhurried, yet each word was as sharp as a blade. "Two paths. Both are dead ends."

Du Mao's eyes widened, shock flooding his face. He stared, eyes wide. "Your Highness means…?"

"'Look at you. Useless as a bear in a trap. You've been eating rice for nothing.'" Li Xuan looked at him with open disdain. He lifted his gaze. The lantern light reflected in his eyes, revealing a hint of fierce, untamed ambition. "'This is the perfect chance to cause him some trouble. If my Crown Prince brother can't even handle this trifling matter, what right does he have to sit on that throne?'"

"Your Highness… you… you mean to implicate the Crown Prince?" Du Mao's voice cracked into a squeak of terror. His knees nearly buckled. Du Mao's voice rose in shocked disbelief, his body trembling even more violently. Frame the Crown Prince? How could a minor official from Jiangnan dare to do such a thing?

But Li Xuan seemed to find nothing amiss with the idea; on the contrary, he was brimming with confidence. The lantern light flashed in his eyes like the glint of a blade's edge. "If this matter comes to light and His Majesty demands answers, he will either be guilty of withholding information or of favouritism and shielding the guilty — either way, he'll have a bitter cup to drink."

"But… but…" Before Du Mao could finish speaking, Li Xuan's eyebrows shot up sharply, his expression turning fierce. "What? You've already taken the silver, and now at this critical juncture you want to back out?"

"Your servant ——your servant would never ——!"

Li Xuan snorted coldly. His voice cut cold. "Don't forget, we're on the same boat now. If I fall, you needn't think you'll survive either."

The words fell like thunder.

Du Mao felt as if struck by lightning. In an instant, understanding dawned, and the heavy stone in his heart was surprisingly lightened by a flicker of perverse relief. His fear twisted into a grotesque form of reverence. "Your Highness's plan is… it is brilliant ——truly a masterstroke!"

Li Xuan said no more, merely raising a hand to dismiss him. Du Mao hastily bowed with clasped hands and retreated into the dark shadows of the corridor. The sound of his boots faded into the distance, as if swallowed whole by the night.

Under the eaves, the night wind slipped past, causing the palace lanterns to sway slightly. The gold-and-red light and shadow played across Li Xuan's profile, blurring warm and cold into an indistinct mix.

He turned and stepped into the hall, his figure soon consumed by the drifting light within, leaving behind only that whispered "masterstroke" echoing colder than before.

* * * * *

At that same moment, the Eastern Palace remained brightly lit despite the deepening night. Crown Prince Li Duan stood before his high desk, where scrolls, bamboo slips and memorials piled one atop another like a small mountain.

The wavering candlelight threw long shadows across his brow. The flickering candle flame cast its faint light on the deep furrow between his brows, making that shadow appear even more profound.

"Your Highness," his adviser murmured, presenting a sealed report, "this is a confidential dispatch from the Jiangnan inspection office. It confirms discrepancies in last year's embankment accounts."

Crown Prince Li Duan took it. His fingertip hesitated over the seal for a moment before slowly breaking it. His eyes scanned the page, stopping at a column of figures. The discrepancy wasn't merely missing silver—it was the blood and lives crushed beneath those numbers.

His gaze swept the contents ——then stopped abruptly. The discrepancy was not merely missing silver. It was the lives buried beneath those figures.

"Not only accounts," he said softly. His voice was low but carried a weight like deep water. "There were deaths."

He closed the scroll, but did not issue orders immediately. Instead, he turned to look out into the deep night beyond the window, his gaze seeming to pass through the palace walls and travel thousands of li into the distance. His gaze passed beyond the palace walls, stretching over darkness as though reaching toward the distant rivers and embankments of Jiangnan.

If the waters surged again this year, not only would the people along the river suffer, but the court would be forced to divert troops southward, which in turn would leave the northern frontier dangerously exposed.

And the northern frontier, that was the one place where he could afford absolutely no weakness. —and that was the critical pass where he could not afford the slightest mistake. One misstep, and both the northern frontier and the southern waters would likely be lost. The adviser stood with hands at his sides, not daring to urge him.

Crown Prince Li Duan pulled back his thoughts, his tone as calm and even as usual: "Re-examine the old records meticulously. Do not make a sound. Whoever approved, whoever supervised, whoever meddled midway—quietly note it down according to the clues. Do not let outsiders become aware."

"Yes, Your Highness." The adviser bowed and withdrew.

The study grew quiet again, leaving only the faint sound of paper rustling slightly in the candlelight. Crown Prince Li Duan lowered his gaze to look at an unrolled river defence map on the desk. The lamplight reflected on the lines depicting water ripples, creating an illusion of surging tides beneath the surface.

He tapped a finger gently on the mark representing Jiangnan, lingering in thought. After a long silence, he uttered in a low voice: "Pacify the waters first, then secure the borders." This was his unwavering conviction.

Outside the window, the night surged like a tide, layer upon layer pushing deep into the palace grounds, enveloping the entire Eastern Palace in an atmosphere of quiet yet restless unease.

Yet the night was not over. A wind crept in from under the eaves, scattering the final memorial on the desk. Li Duan reached out to press it flat, his fingertip touching the line of writing where the ink was not yet dry: "The Jiangnan embankments required labour exceeding ten thousand. The people's resentment boils over."

He stared at it for a long while. An old teaching surfaced in his heart: 'A ruler governing the state should guard against close confidants, not enemies.' But within these deep palace walls, between confidant and enemy, who could truly distinguish clearly?

The candle flame flared and dimmed, casting overlapping, swaying silhouettes on the wall, like countless pairs of watching eyes. He finally composed his expression, took up a brush, dipped it in ink, and secretly wrote three characters in a corner: Su Zhang. That was the man he trusted. Then he gently blew the ink dry and resealed the dossier once more.

Chapter 53: A Stroll Through the Night Market

Crown Prince Li Duan closed the dossier with deliberate care, sliding the rolled river-defence map to the side of the desk before lifting his hand in a quiet gesture toward the attendant. "Prepare the palanquin. We are going to Xining Palace."

The route that led to Xining Palace cut through the inner administration courts of the imperial city. Even at this hour, the corridors glowed with steady lantern-light.

The Imperial Guards on duty stood in two ordered rows, armour plates catching and reflecting the red glow of palace lamps, each faint gleam betraying the hard edge of cold metal beneath their ceremonial discipline.

As the Crown Prince approached a turn in the covered walkway, he caught sight of a figure standing straight-backed beside the shadow wall ——a young man in newly issued dark-scarlet armour, hand resting lightly on the hilt of his blade.

Even from a distance, the sharp burnish of the golden clasps on his uniform marked him as a fresh inductee of the Shen Ce Battalion.

It was Gu Xiao.

He turned at the sound of approaching footsteps and the crisp movement of his salute echoed faintly beneath the high beams. "Your Highness."

Li Duan paused, studying him for a heartbeat. His expression did not soften, but something faint ——something nearly warm ——passed through his gaze. "Gu Xiao. So, it truly ended this way. You held out longer than most, but in the end even you could not escape Her Majesty's hand."

Gu Xiao allowed himself a brief smile, restrained and measured, though the bright edge of ambition in his eyes remained entirely undimmed. "Your Highness overstates it," he said evenly. "Since I could not enter the Huben Army nor take service at the frontier, remaining in the capital and doing real work is preferable to holding an idle title and letting it grow moss."

Li Duan inclined his head slightly. His gaze lingered for a moment on the newly affixed insignia resting on the young man's shoulder, as though weighing not the metal itself, but what it signified. "It is well that you think so," he replied. "A man with resolve will find a place to build merit no matter where he stands. What matters is not the ground beneath his feet, but the direction of his will."

"Your Highness speaks true," Gu Xiao answered. The faint arch of his mouth carried a trace of self-mockery, yet the youthful hunger for achievement beneath it was unmistakable. "Of course," he added lightly, "the splendour of the capital can hardly compare to the hardship of the frontier."

A fleeting, nearly imperceptible smile brushed across Li Duan's lips.

He heard the hidden meaning clearly, yet chose not to expose it. "Your ambitions point both south and north," he said calmly, "but for now, observe more and learn more. There is no need to force your pace. Some roads are not crossed by haste."

"Yes, Your Highness." Gu Xiao bowed, fists clasped with respectful firmness.

Li Duan nodded once more. His voice dropped slightly, lower than the flickering lantern-light around them, carrying a weight that brushed the air between them like a passing chill. "Do not brood over it. Entering palace service is no small matter," he said. "Especially now that Su Zhang will soon depart for Jiangnan. There are… few people left around me whom I can trust."

The final words were spoken softly, almost conversationally, yet cold enough to settle like frost in the space between them.

Gu Xiao's steps stilled and one brow lifted, half amused and half startled. "So, His Highness places me among the 'trustworthy'?"

Li Duan returned the look with calm, steady eyes. "You are straightforward. You work for the matter itself, not for fame or flattery. That is precisely what this palace lacks."

He let his attention drift briefly toward the far end of the corridor, where flames from a brazier cast long, shifting shadows across the ranks of armour. "Do not think serving within the palace is easier than riding into battle. Blades may not fall at the city walls, but they glint just as sharply within sleeves and smiles."

Gu Xiao's expression steadied, losing its earlier lightness. "Understood."

The Crown Prince continued, "With Su Zhang traveling to Jiangnan, there will be those who seize upon last year's floods to stir up trouble again. The reconstruction of the dikes demands a vast treasury. The northern garrisons also have an insatiable appetite for funds. When state coffers are strained, schemers multiply."

Gu Xiao's voice lowered, the youthful vigour in his tone reining itself into a tightly wound focus.

"Yes, Your Highness. Your concerns are well-founded." Gu Xiao's voice lowered, the vigor of youth drawing inward into a taut line of focus. "If Your Highness requires anything, one order is enough."

Li Duan looked at him and a soft, barely visible smile flickered again ——gone before it could fully form. "My cousin has grown."

Gu Xiao's lips twitched but he did not reply. Instead, he bowed more solidly, shoulders firm beneath the new armour.

"Be at ease. Serve your post well. Matters of court ——leave them to me."

"Yes, Your Highness."

"Go on," Li Duan said, motioning him back to the line of guards. "Observe more. Think more. Speak less. Merit does not depend on where a man stands and even less on how loudly he shouts."

Gu Xiao stepped back and bowed deeply, his "Thank you for the instruction, Cousin. I will remember it," spoken with deliberate familial respect.

The Crown Prince lifted a hand in brief acknowledgment before continuing down the lantern-lit passage.

Behind him, the interlocking glimmer of blades and armour rang in the quiet air with a faint, distinct metallic sigh ——one that followed him like a warning.

* * * * *

Dusk had thickened into early night by the time Qin Nianyin and Mei stepped out of the tailoring house. Stray threads still clung to the hem of Qin Nianyin's sleeve and the warm glow of newly lit lanterns cast gentle halos across the stone street.

They had barely turned the corner when Qin Nianyin spotted a figure standing beneath the corridor pillars ahead.

The man wore a gleaming set of dark-scarlet palace guard armour —— new enough that the polished shoulder plates caught and scattered the lantern-light like a thin sheen of water.

The muted patterns along his bracers shimmered subtly and the sword at his waist rested with the easy authority of someone unused to standing idle. Even his eyebrows carried a young soldier's quiet pride.

She paused, realizing at once why he was positioned so precisely where the street opened into light.

He was waiting for her.

Mei tugged lightly at her sleeve. "Miss… look ——it's Young Master Gu."

"Qin Nianyin."

Gu Xiao stepped forward with a bright, unabashed grin. There was an unmistakable spark in his eyes ——as though the armour itself had lent him three extra inches of height. "Well? What do you think?"

Her gaze swept over him briefly. "It fits well. Looks good."

"Not just good ——impressive, isn't it?" he added, lifting a hand to tap lightly on the metal of his shoulder guard. The ring of metal-on-metal chimed crisply. "Not everyone gets to wear the armour of the Imperial Guards."

Her lips curved slightly. "Congratulations, General Gu. You've achieved what you hoped for."

Her tone held no mockery, only calm and sincere happiness for him.

That unguarded honesty struck Gu Xiao squarely in the chest. Something skipped, sharp and unexpected, disrupting the easy rhythm he had rehearsed. All the lines he had planned, the half-jokes and lightly boastful remarks meant to sound effortless, tangled at once and lodged awkwardly in his throat.

He lifted a hand and rubbed the back of his neck, a habitual gesture whenever he found himself at a loss. Heat crept faintly to his ears, betraying him even as he forced his expression into something relaxed and casual.

"Well…" he began, then paused, searching for the right opening. "In a few days, the capital will be holding its monthly night market." His gaze flicked away for a heartbeat before returning. "So, I thought… maybe… would you like to go?"

She hesitated, her breath catching for the briefest moment as she prepared to decline, the refusal already forming at the edge of her lips.

Sensing it, he hurried on, words spilling faster than intended, tripping slightly over his own urgency. "It's nothing formal," he added quickly. "I just wanted to thank you. If you hadn't said what you did that day, I'd probably still be wasting time at the estate." His voice lowered a fraction, more earnest now. "I would never have had the chance to join the Guards."

Qin Nianyin blinked. "I said something?"

"You don't remember?" He laughed sheepishly. "At Pearl House —— you asked me whether the silver I spent was 'earned by myself,' and said I was living off family wealth."

She couldn't help letting out a soft laugh. "It was just an offhand remark."

"But I took it seriously." His voice dropped, quieter, tinged with a restrained earnestness that felt oddly vulnerable coming from him. "A man should have something of his own to stand on… otherwise, how could he be worthy of…"

He suddenly stopped, realizing he had gone too far.

Qin Nianyin turned slightly, and the lantern-light softened the edge of her profile. She had meant to tease him, but the seriousness in his expression made her ask gently, "Worthy of what?"

Gu Xiao froze. The question hit too squarely; words tangled. After a long moment, he muttered, "Nothing."

She laughed quietly. "Look at you ——already a palace guard, yet still speaking like this."

His ears turned red again. He quickly changed the subject. "So… the night market. Are you going?"

Qin Nianyin looked at him ——looked at that earnest expectation he tried so hard to disguise and after a brief silence, she nodded. "All right."

The capital's mid-month night market—how many years had it been since she last saw it? Not since her previous life, after she had married Su Zhang. A sudden, fleeting desire rose within her: to see that worldly bustle one more time.

She had not walked the bustling mid-month night market in years, not since marrying Su Zhang in her previous life.

For one fleeting moment, she found herself wanting to see it again, to feel the pulse of a world she had long abandoned.

"Really?" His eyes lit instantly.

"Really."

Gu Xiao broke into a grin so wide even the lanterns seemed to flare brighter against the polished sheen of his armour. "Then it's settled. I'll come for you at the start of Shen hour."

"Hm." She nodded gently, accepting the promise.

She turned toward home, her steps composed and graceful beneath the lantern-glow. Gu Xiao remained where he was, watching her retreat into the warm haze of light. Only after she had vanished from sight did he realize his smile remained.

It was not the triumphant grin of someone who had shown off his new armour.

It was the startled, quietly blooming smile of someone who was beginning to fall.

Chapter 54: A Monument for Her Father

Night had settled deeply over the Su Manor, draping its courtyards in a hush that made the flickering lamps appear even brighter against the darkness. A thin wind swept down the eaves, carrying with it a few dry leaves that skittered across the stone floor.

Beneath the roof's shadow, the copper lantern swayed almost imperceptibly, its warm glow stretching and shrinking the silhouettes cast upon the ground, long then short, steady then wavering.

Mei walked ahead with careful steps, glancing back at Qin Nianyin as she whispered, "Miss, the young master said he has something to discuss with you. He asks that you go to the study."

Qin Nianyin's steps slowed. It was already late and for him to summon her at such an hour inevitably stirred a ripple of unease in her heart. Yet her hesitation lasted only a breath; she did not turn away.

The door to the study was half-open, a muted sliver of light spilling onto the veranda. Inside, the candlelight was warm and steady.

Su Zhang stood with his back to her; a scroll of aged records unfurled in his hands. Only when he heard her footsteps did he place the scroll down and turn toward her.

"Sit." His voice was calm in a way that did not allow refusal.

Qin Nianyin settled before the low table. Her gaze flicked over the scroll he had just been reading and she caught a few characters amid the dense text—"Former Jiangnan Prefect, Qin Shouyi." Her breath hitched. Her father's name. Her fingers curled against her sleeve without her noticing.

Su Zhang did not speak immediately. He simply lifted a cup, tasting the tea with a slow, measured movement, as though the time it took for the steam to rise was a part of the conversation itself. Not until he set the cup down again did, he say, "Do you still remember much of your uncle's work during the Jiangnan flood that year?"

Qin Nianyin jolted faintly. Her eyes lowered. "Of course I remember. During that flood… my father gave his life to protect the people and so—"

Her voice cut off of its own accord. The tremor hiding under her breath was too raw to let out.

"Yes," Su Zhang said softly. "For that flood, he exchanged his life for thousands of households' safety."

His tone was unadorned, but the words landed heavily—as though a silent weight had dropped into the stillness between them.

"Yet even so," he continued, "because of the prevailing political tides, not even a stone statue was left behind."

Qin Nianyin tightened her grip on her sleeve, the nails hidden inside the fabric pressing deeply into her palm. After a long moment she asked quietly, "What… do you mean by this?"

Su Zhang lowered his gaze and pushed a sealed memorial toward her. "The court has resolved to rebuild the Jialing dike. Alongside this, they intend to erect statues for those who contributed to flood relief in past years. Your father, though he did not personally oversee the works, played a key role in allocation of resources and in submitting memorials that guided the operation. For this, he received imperial commendation."

His tone deepened by a shade. "This inspection trip is not only to observe the rebuilding—it is meant to honour past merit and reinforce the benevolence of the throne."

What he did not say, but what lay plainly between the lines, was that this entire arrangement had been steered by him—manoeuvring between ministers, smoothing resistance, weaving the strands of court politics until the outcome seemed natural. It honoured the past, soothed the people, pleased the emperor… and left her with no room to refuse.

The candlelight flickered across her eyes, revealing disbelief, then rising urgency—quickly restrained behind lowered lashes. "Is this… truly settled?"

Her fingertips trembled slightly as she touched the surface of the memorial. The strokes of ink seemed to pulse with the weight of history—her father's history, the Qin family's pride, the story too long buried in dust.

Watching her expression shift, Su Zhang's voice remained steady, yet there was a distinct undertone of direction—of persuasion that felt deliberate. "When the statue is erected, for you to be present is not merely a comfort to the departed. It will allow the world to remember the old merits of the Qin family. It is good for you… good for your adoptive father and for my uncle."

Qin Nianyin lowered her gaze. For a moment she struggled for air as if something invisible had settled across her chest. "But I…"

She wanted to say she did not wish to go—did not want to follow any arrangement that kept her bound to him, to his household, to the long shadow he cast across her life. But father's merit—those words locked her firmly in place.

Su Zhang saw the conflict and gave the final push with quiet precision. "This trip will also re-examine the flaws in the flood response that year. Your father bore no fault, but I would not have others speculate or slander his name. With you there, no one will dare." The flame wavered once, illuminating his eyes—calm, resolute, unyielding.

Qin Nianyin lowered her gaze again and in that moment understood he had left her no path but this one. For her father, for the Qin family, she had no grounds for refusal.

A breath passed. A second. At last, she spoke, though her voice was barely above a whisper. "I… understand."

Su Zhang exhaled silently—a release so subtle it was almost imperceptible. The curve of his lips lifted by a fraction, faint enough to disappear if one blinked.

He resumed his usual composure, returning to the desk and picking up a brush as though the matter were settled. "In that case, begin your preparations tomorrow. The journey south is long; you need not bring much—only what is necessary."

Then he looked up at her, gaze steady. "At the government office in Jiangnan, the statue of Qin Da-ren will stand. His name will not vanish into obscurity." The light across the table trembled, the shadows shifting. Her heart tightened with each word, as though a hand were closing slowly around it.

Then, unbidden, another thought chased through her mind—the memory of danger, the knowledge of the assassination he would soon face. A sudden wave of determination rose in her, startling even herself.

Su Zhang's fingers traced the rim of his teacup in an idle motion that belied the intent behind his words. "If you remain in the capital, you will miss this opportunity."

Her fingers curled where they hid inside her sleeve. She swallowed, throat tight, unable to form an objection. She did not want more entanglement with him. But for her father's name—She could not refuse.

The room fell quiet. The faint sound of tea settling in the pot drifted through the stillness, each drop soft yet painfully clear.

When she finally lifted her eyes, his gaze met hers. For a heartbeat her chest tightened so sharply she almost drew back. She had thought of many excuses—many ways to distance herself from him. Yet none of them could be spoken now.

After a long silence, she drew in a slow breath and said with newfound steadiness, "Then… I will accompany you to Jiangnan."

Su Zhang's lips curved at the corners—not in triumph, but in the faint, inevitable satisfaction of someone receiving a result long expected. "Good. Prepare well. Your affairs—I will see to them."

A moment later he added, almost offhandedly, "As for Xu Wencai, I have already arranged a place for him at a local academy. He will have food and lodging and he may resume his studies while awaiting the next provincial examinations." The words were light, almost casual. Yet each syllable struck like a pin hammered firmly into place, securing another thread she had not expected him to touch.

Outside, a gust of wind swept across the courtyard, shaking the lantern flame and rattling the window paper. It was as though the night itself had whispered a warning—the road to Jiangnan would not be peaceful.

As Qin Nianyin rose to take her leave, Su Zhang's voice stopped her. "Wait."

She halted and turned.

His expression remained calm, but his tone had softened into something quieter, deeper than before. "Jiangnan is far… and not a place free of danger. That you will accompany this journey as the daughter of the Qin family… pleases me."

She blinked, unable to decipher the flicker behind his words. Pleases him? Why?

Yet before she could ask, he lifted his gaze—dark eyes catching hers with a heat that startled her. "It is nothing. Go prepare." The words landed like a gentle weight, half comfort, half command—both impossible to ignore.

Qin Nianyin lowered her head. Her fingers trembled faintly within her sleeve. After a long moment she replied softly, "I… understand."

Su Zhang returned to his desk, lifting the river map and smoothing its edges with a practiced hand. "Along the way, if we pass any of the reconstruction sites, you may see them for yourself." His tone seemed light, but the implication beneath it was unmistakable: Now that she had stepped into his plan, she would not step out easily.

Qin Nianyin felt her heart sink, little by little. This trip, wrapped in the name of commemoration, was no simple journey—it was a move in a deeper game.

A sudden gust battered the window again, stirring the lantern flame into trembling arcs of light. She steadied her breath, bowed and said, "If there is nothing else, I will begin my preparations."

"Go." Su Zhang's gesture was calm, yet his gaze lingered on her as she turned away.

Only after she disappeared beyond the door did he close the river map with a quiet thud. His fingers tapped the table twice, a hint of satisfaction threading through his low murmur. "With her along… all the better."

Outside, Qin Nianyin stepped into the cold night breeze and instinctively pulled her cloak tighter. Half the moon was swallowed by drifting clouds, its fractured glow scattering across the ground like broken silver.

Mei hurried up to her. "Miss, did the young master ask you to—?"

Qin Nianyin answered faintly, "He wants me to go to Jiangnan."

Mei blinked, then beamed. "But that's wonderful! To erect a statue for the old master—that is a great honour!"

Qin Nianyin smiled—softly, faintly—yet none of the warmth reached her eyes.

The wind swept through the long corridor again, carrying a faint scent of medicine and cold stone. And somewhere deep in her heart, a quiet, uneasy premonition began to form: This journey… would not only be for her father. It would bring with it a storm she could not escape.

Chapter 55: Buying a Little White Cat

The last streaks of sunset had not yet faded from the horizon, yet the night market was already overflowing with people, the crowd moving like a slow-rolling tide under the dimming sky.

The lingering glow of dusk clung to the rooftops like embers that refused to cool, while the growing bustle below filled the street with restless warmth.

Shops on either side had thrown their doors wide open, their lamps blazing gold as colourful banners snapped sharply in the rising night wind.

The air pulsed with overlapping voices ——sugar painters calling out their designs, lantern sellers shaking their wares and hawkers raising their cries in bright, rhythmic waves.

Gu Xiao had been waiting at the gate of the Su residence long before the hour and the instant he saw her step out from the side entrance; he moved toward her with unhidden eagerness.

His grin carried the buoyancy of the lively crowd behind him as he said, "Perfect timing ——the night market is just getting lively."

"Have you been waiting long?" she asked, unable to ignore the nervous impatience in the way he had straightened the moment she appeared as if he had been waiting for her far more eagerly than he meant to show.

Her voice contained a thread of quiet curiosity, for something in his expression shone too brightly to be dismissed.

"Not long at all, just a quarter hour," he replied with a light, easy smile. It was, of course, far from the truth ——he had already waited nearly an entire hour, pacing and glancing toward the gate every few breaths as though afraid she might pass unnoticed.

Qin Nianyin took in the sight of him dressed not in armour but in a dark brocade robe, his martial sharpness softened by civilian clothing. Without the rigid lines of metal and leather, he seemed unexpectedly handsome ——effortlessly so ——with a freer, more unrestrained air that lent him a boyish charm.

"Shall we look at the lanterns ahead first?" he asked, lifting a hand to gesture toward the glow at the end of the street. The lights seemed to ignite a reflection in his eyes, making them gleam like strings of lanterns swaying in the evening wind.

The lantern stalls stretched in a bright ribbon along the riverside, each paper creation glowing from within.

Fish-shaped lanterns swam in midair on thin sticks, revolving horse lanterns cast circles of light across the ground and palace lanterns in crimson and gold swayed like blossoms in a warm breeze.

Children darted among them with unrestrained laughter, their shadows skipping across the stone pavement.

Gu Xiao bought a lotus-shaped lantern from one of the vendors and placed it gently into her hands. "There's a custom here," he said, his tone almost conspiratorial. "Set the lantern afloat on the river and it brings good fortune and good luck."

She lowered her gaze to the delicate petals of coloured paper and murmured with a faint, amused curve of her lips, "Isn't that something done on Qixi?"

He laughed openly. "Merchants take every chance to make a little more silver. Paint it as a blessing and every month becomes a festival."

The night market swelled around them, crowds pressing in from every side, voices overlapping without pause, filled with warmth from the countless oil lamps overhead. Their light pooled across the street, turning the crowds into an ever-shifting tapestry of shadows and colour.

As they passed a sugar vendor's stall, Gu Xiao reached out and snapped off a strand of glossy candy. Held up to the lantern light, the sugar caught a glimmer like spun gold.

"Try this," he said, bringing it toward her lips.

Qin Nianyin turned her head away with a furrowed brow, leaving him to let out a soft, self-deprecating laugh before taking a bite himself. The candy broke crisply. "Sweet," he said lightly, "And good for chasing off tiredness."

"Are the palace guards always this busy?" she asked, letting the noise of the crowd settle between them like a buffer.

"Busy enough," he replied. He pointed toward a pair of armoured soldiers patrolling in the distance. "Look ——those two are from my unit. We drill from dawn to dusk and even at night we rotate between patrol and garrison duty. I didn't know until I joined that guarding a city takes more strength than fighting a battle. On the battlefield you use a single surge of energy. In the palace, you stay sharp every hour of every day ——one stray sound in the wind and you're already reaching for your blade."

She listened quietly, a faint glimmer tugging at her eyes. "That's good," she said softly. "Having something to do is always better than having nothing." as if the thought itself resonated with her more than she let on.

"Of course," he answered with a slight lift of his chin. "Serving with a blade under the emperor's roof, protecting the people of the capital, earning decent pay ——certainly better than lazing around at home."

He paused, then added thoughtfully, "A few days ago during my shift, a caravan from Jiangnan passed through. They were transporting bolts of Suzhou silk. The sheen was nothing like what we see here in the capital."

Her lashes lowered. "Jiangnan has always been finer."

Gu Xiao tilted his head to look at her. "You're from Jiangnan, aren't you?"

"Yes," she replied, her tone serene yet distant. After a moment of hesitation, she added, "In a few days, I'll be returning to Jiangnan with my cousin."

At that, the water he had cupped from the river slipped through his fingers in a sudden cascade as though the thought had knocked the strength from his hand.

He straightened at once, his brows drawing tight as he reached out and gripped her shoulder with unexpected urgency.

"What's wrong?" she asked, puzzled by the sudden solemnity in his eyes.

He shed the usual ease from his expression and said, with a gravity he seldom used, "Can you… not go?"

She blinked, startled. "Why not?"

For a heartbeat, he had no answer. Indeed ——what right did he have to ask such a thing? By what standing, and with what right, could he ask her to stay?

Recovering her composure, she replied gently, "My cousin said the court intends to honor the officials who once managed the flood relief. They wish to raise a stone statue in memory of my foster father. As his daughter, I must return."

Gu Xiao rubbed at the back of his neck, his frown deepening. Concern darkened his voice, though he spoke stiffly, almost defensively. "But… Su Zhang is cunning. You shouldn't let him trick you."

"Trick me?" She looked at him, bewildered. "What do you mean?"

He faltered, words tangling uselessly on his tongue, until at last he muttered, "I just mean ——you mustn't… fall for him."

She stared at him, stunned, before her brows drew sharply together. "What nonsense. I have no interest in my cousin Su Zhang. And besides, this has nothing to do with you."

His ears flushed red, but he pressed on anyway. "But I like you. I hope you'll consider me."

She froze, breath caught in her throat.

Had she heard correctly?

He hurried on, as if afraid hesitation would steal his courage. "My family may be a military one, but I'm the only one left. No mother-in-law, no concubines, no petty household quarrels. If you married me, you'd never need to endure any of that, any of the petty, grinding troubles that wear a person down day after day. And I'm good with horses and the bow ——I can protect you."

A quiet, incredulous laugh escaped her ——not mocking, but touched with a bewildered sincerity. "Don't forget, you still have your imperial aunt. The Empress will choose your marriage for you."

"And you?" he countered instantly, eyes fixed on her. "Who will choose your marriage?"

She pressed her lips together. In her heart, the answer had long been clear ——she intended never to marry again in this lifetime a resolve she kept to herself, never meant to be spoken aloud.

But aloud she said only, "If fate brings someone suitable, then it will. There's no need to rush."

A breeze stirred across the river, sending ripples of lantern light trembling across the water. Gu Xiao watched the gentle line of her profile and something within him tightened with quiet, unmistakable longing.

"All right," she said suddenly, her voice brisk, her gaze turning away as if to dispel the tension gathering between them. "Shall we keep walking? If not, we may as well go back."

"Of course we'll keep walking," he said quickly. He swallowed his protest, for he would take whatever time she was willing to give him.

The night market grew louder as they moved on. They passed stalls of candied hawthorn, steamed buns, embroidered purses and Gu Xiao kept trying to find new topics to fill the silence. Then a delicate sound threaded through the din ——a soft, wavering mewls.

He glanced toward the noise.

A vendor approached them, With a bamboo basket. Inside, curled together like tufts of snow, were three tiny white kittens, each with clear blue eyes. The man's smile brimmed with practiced enthusiasm.

"Sir, miss ——care to buy one? True Persian breed, white as fresh jade! A joy to keep in any household. And the two of you look so well-matched holding such a little creature would make the picture even more harmonious."

Gu Xiao blinked, then let out an involuntary laugh. His eyes glimmered with a hint of mischief as he leaned in to tickle one of the kittens beneath its chin. "They are rather cute."

The vendor grew even bolder. "A handsome young gentleman and a lovely lady ——why not take home a fortune-bringing kitten together?"

Colour rose faintly to Qin Nianyin's cheeks. She opened her mouth to decline, but Gu Xiao had already pulled out a piece of silver and placed it decisively in the vendor's hand.

"This one," he said, scooping up the kitten.

"Why did you suddenly buy a cat?" she asked.

"Because they're adorable," he said simply. "I'm giving it to you."

"I don't want it," she rejected at once, stepping back as though to avoid the snow-white bundle.

"It's from my own silver," he said quickly, with a stubbornness almost childlike. "Not from my family's purse. Didn't you say a man should earn his own keep? This is something I bought with my own effort."

She shook her head. "I won't keep such a delicate pet. It would be it would only suffer for being kept by someone like me. If you truly like it, then keep it yourself."

He stared at her, at the kitten purring trustingly in his arms and then, with visible reluctance, placed it back into the basket. "Fine. Forget I said anything."

Sensing the tension, the vendor bowed himself away into the sea of lanterns and voices. The kittens' soft cries faded into the crowd.

Gu Xiao clasped his hands behind him, walking a few paces in thoughtful silence. She, however, simply turned toward the river again, serene and unbothered, as though she had deliberately set the moment aside.

Neither of them noticed the tall figure standing some distance away— watching in deliberate silence, careful not to be seen, wordless, as their silhouettes drifted farther down the lantern-lit street.

The next morning carried with it the lingering coolness that follows a night of steady rain; the air in the courtyard felt freshly washed, the stone slabs still holding traces of dampness.

Qin Nianyin had just finished her morning grooming, her hair pinned neatly and her sleeves still smelling faintly of warm water. She was about to sit down and begin her breakfast when Mei came hurrying in from outside, both arms wrapped around a perfectly square bamboo basket.

Her steps were brisk and her face was bright with an excitement she made absolutely no effort to hide.

"Miss," she announced, unable to keep the smile out of her voice, "Young Master Gu sent this over."

A small tightening formed between Nianyin's brows. A faint, unmistakable premonition rose from the depth of her chest ——quiet, certain and not at all pleasant.

She set her silver spoon aside and shifted her gaze toward the bamboo basket.

The lid was tied carefully with thin cords and a cloth draped securely over the top. From within came the lightest rustle, the soft, whispering sound of something alive shifting against wicker.

"Shall we open it?" Mei asked at once, already reaching eagerly toward the cloth.

Nianyin pressed her lips together in a thin, resigned line.

 and just as she expected ——when the cloth was lifted, a burst of snow-white fur gleamed in the morning light, dazzling as frost under the sun. It was the very same Persian kitten from the night market, with its pale coat and crystal-blue eyes.

Mei gasped, her eyes lighting up as though she had found a piece of hidden treasure. "Oh heavens ——what a beautiful little creature!"

She crouched down beside the basket, leaning close. Inside, the kitten blinked up at her with an innocent, unguarded expression. Its tail flicked lightly and it let out a soft, velvety mewl that seemed designed to invite affection.

Nianyin walked over and lowered herself into a half-crouch by the basket. She extended a finger through the bamboo slats and lightly stroked the kitten's chin.

At once, the tiny creature tilted its head, its pink tongue darting out to lick her fingertip before nudging its head insistently against the door of the basket. Its downy fur brushed her skin, soft enough to tingle against her palm.

A faint smile touched the corner of her lips ——so faint it almost wasn't there ——but her eyes remained cool and clear. So this was exactly what she had expected.

Her refusal the night before had clearly meant nothing to him. Instead of stepping back, he had simply chosen a more clever, more irresistible method to force the gift into her hands.

She withdrew her hand and said lightly, "Mei, return the cat."

"Return it?" Mei's eyes widened, a clear expression of reluctance filling them.

"Yes. Return it."

Mei stayed crouched in the corridor, still teasing the ball of snow-white fur with a sprig of grass. The tuft of grass hovered mid-air as she hesitated. "Miss… but what if Young Master Gu won't take it back?"

Nianyin glanced at the kitten's bright blue eyes and let out a small, curved smile ——one that held a different meaning entirely. A memory flickered across her mind from her past life: Su Wan feared cats.

Not merely disliked them ——she avoided them as though they were poison. Even the sound of a meow was enough to drain her face of colour.

"You don't need to send it back yourself," Nianyin said gently. "Bring the cat with you. We're going to Ningfang Court."

* * * * *

In the afternoon, sunlight filtered through the carved lattice windows of Ningfang Court, scattering pale golden patterns across the polished floor and the cushioned seat before the divan.

Su Wan reclined against the beauty couch, her posture composed and elegant, slender sleeves trailing beside her as she examined the newly arrived Song brocade samples. The tranquil scene seemed untouched by anything outside its delicate order.

Qin Nianyin entered with Mei at her side, a bamboo basket hanging from her hand. Inside the basket, the kitten lay curled in a quiet white ball, scarcely moving.

Qin Nianyin deliberately walked closer ——close enough for the basket to fall naturally into Su Wan's line of sight ——yet her expression remained perfectly serene, as though she noticed nothing at all.

"Wan-jie," she greeted softly.

Su Wan lifted her gaze, responding with a faint, distant hum. She was just lowering her eyes back to the brocade samples when a gentle "mrr ——" drifted from within the bamboo slats.

The ball of snowy fur shifted, catching a spill of sunlight; its coat shone like sifted frost and its blue eyes glimmered with crystalline clarity.

Su Wan's expression changed at once. Instinctively ——almost violently ——she recoiled, drawing back against the cushions. The brocade sample in her hand slipped free and fell to the floor with a sharp, brittle snap. Her brows tightened as though seized by pain. "W-what… what is that thing?"

Qin Nianyin made a small show of looking down only then, as if noticing for the first time. "This? It's the Persian cat Young Master Gu sent over last night. Why? Wan-jie does not like it?"

A flash of unmistakable panic crossed Su Wan's eyes. She waved both hands in hurried refusal. "Take it away ——quickly. I have never liked such creatures. They scratch and tear clothing and I cannot bear them near me. Take it away at once!" She turned sharply to Mei, her normally measured tone quivering with urgency. "Hurry and send the little thing off. Su Manor does not allow cats ——you did not know?"

So, she still fears them.

Qin Nianyin swallowed the rising laugh, smoothing her expression into wide-eyed innocence. Su Wan's terror of cats was something she had known in her past life all too well. "Is that so? As your cousin, I had never heard of such a rule."

She released a small, helpless sigh, then addressed Mei with gentle deliberateness. "Very well. Take the cat back to Young Master Gu. Tell him Su Manor forbids keeping pets like this."

"Yes, Miss," Mei replied at once, face stern with dutiful gravity.

When they stepped out of Ningfang Court, the kitten inside the basket had nestled back into a doze, its tail swaying in tiny, rhythmic motions.

Qin Nianyin carried the basket by its handle and a faint, nearly invisible smile brushed the depths of her eyes.

Su Wan.

* * * * *

By evening, dusk had begun to settle over the Gu residence. Shadows lengthened across the courtyard and the fading light pooled like ink along the flagstones. Gu Xiao was practicing archery in the open yard, his posture steady, bowstring drawn to its fullest.

The arrow shot forth with a clean crack, slicing through the air and striking the centre of the target. Only one arrow remained in his grip when hurried footsteps came rushing from the corridor.

His young attendant entered at a brisk pace, slightly winded, a bamboo basket dangling from his hand. Inside, the snow-white Persian cat lay curled in a soft cloud of fur, its long coat drifting like mist, the tips of its ears trembling faintly with each movement.

"Master Gu," the attendant reported, catching his breath, "this was sent over by the Su Manor. They also specifically said ——Su Manor cannot keep cats, because Second Miss Su is afraid of them."

Gu Xiao lifted an eyebrow, slowly lowering his bow before turning fully toward the basket.

"Specifically said?" he echoed, his voice low, the corners of his lips lifting into a faint, unreadable curve that was not quite a smile.

The message was spoken for his ears alone; that much was obvious. They wanted him to understand that the refusal did not come from her own will. Yet… afraid of cats?

The image of her smiling under last night's warm lantern glow flickered across his thoughts and an unexpected heaviness tugged at his chest. So, this lovely creature ——in all its softness ——could not remain by her side.

He extended a hand, letting his fingertips glide along the bamboo slats as he brushed the kitten's fur through the gaps.

The Persian cat lifted its head, gazing at him with gem-bright blue eyes, clear and innocent like moonlight resting on a lake. Gu Xiao's smile deepened, though a thread of regret lingered beneath it.

"A pity…" he murmured quietly. Then another thought unfurled in the depths of his mind ——If not a cat, then something else. She must accept at least one token from me.

He handed the basket back to the attendant. "Keep it well," he instructed, his tone allowing no argument. "And do not send it back again."

When he turned toward the house, the last streak of gold in the sky had softened into a warm afterglow.

His footsteps were unhurried, steady, yet the faint lift at his lips never faded ——he was already considering what he ought to send next, something she would have no way to refuse, no matter how gently she tried to push it aside.

* * * * *

Night had deepened; autumn insects chirred softly in the shadows and the silhouettes of osmanthus trees swayed in scattered patterns across the courtyard.

Qin Nianyin had just set down her teacup and was about to extinguish the candle for the night when a sharp tap struck the wooden lattice of her window ——light and crisp, like a pebble flicked by a deft hand.

Her brows drew together. Two more identical taps followed, crisp and deliberate. Suspicion rose within her. She stood and walked toward the window.

When she pushed open half of the shutter, a gust of cool night wind brushed across her face. Moonlight lay pale upon the courtyard ——and beneath the courtyard wall stood a familiar figure.

A low "shh ——" escaped his lips. Gu Xiao pressed a finger to them, his features carved cleanly beneath the moonlight, dark brows and eyes forming a distinctly handsome silhouette.

In his arms rested a bamboo basket and inside, the snowy Persian cat lay curled into a perfect ball, its sapphire eyes unblinking as they stared up at her.

Qin Nianyin paused, her gaze falling briefly to the cat before her tone hardened. "Gu Xiao, what is the meaning of this?"

"Xiaobai missed you," he replied, far too righteously for someone trespassing into another household in the dead of night.

"Xiaobai?" She raised a doubtful brow.

"Yes. That's his name."

She fell silent. The sheer simplicity of the name ——so blunt it required not a shred of thought ——left her momentarily speechless. The entire matter struck her as absurd.

"It is late. You barged into the Su residence ——and into my small courtyard besides. What exactly do you intend to do?" Her voice turned cold.

Gu Xiao lifted a hand to the back of his neck, scratching lightly with faint embarrassment. At last, he lowered his voice. "That day… the night market. I asked you something, but you didn't answer. So, I thought ——I'd ask again."

"What question?"

"I… like you. Could you… give me a chance?"

Moonlight washed a thin layer of silver over the line of his cheek. His voice was earnest ——far too earnest ——but it earned only her glacial refusal.

"Impossible. Take your cat and leave."

"Why?" he demanded, anxious.

"There is no why. Go back." The moment the words left her lips, she shut the window with a firm bang.

Silence hovered outside for a moment before his low voice rose again. "I won't leave. I know you're still listening, so I'll speak… Perhaps you think I'm unreliable, but I'm serious about you. You're Zijun's cousin ——I would never treat you lightly."

As he spoke, she could faintly hear the rustle of him adjusting the kitten in the basket, his tone dipping between quiet murmurs and lighter notes.

His monologue drifted on and on beneath the night sky, until his voice was carried farther away and the courtyard sank into stillness once more.

Behind the shuttered window, Qin Nianyin pressed her back against the wooden frame, her fingertips digging into her palm so sharply they left crescents in her skin.

She did not understand how things had reached this point. In her previous life, she and Gu Xiao had barely exchanged a handful of words.

The silence outside stretched a few more breaths before his voice returned ——softer, yet resolute. "Miss Qin, I swear to the heavens —— everything I said is true. I will never fail you."

He paused, then hurriedly continued, as though afraid she might shut him out completely. "Since I was young, I've wanted to follow my father and brother into battle ——to defend the borders of our country. My mother died early. I was the only one left in the household. So… I cherish the people around me."

"Maybe you think I'm careless, even frivolous, but my martial skills are excellent. If you were willing to marry me, I would strive hard in my career. I'd give you a home that is steady and safe."

His voice, carried through the cool night air, bore an earnestness tinged with the unpolished sincerity of youth. "You're the first girl who ever spoke to me like that ——not like others who only look at my family background and nothing else. I won't force you. Just… think about it for a few days before giving me your answer. All right?"

He spoke as though confiding his heart to the night itself, unreserved and persistent. Only when footsteps from the night patrol approached did he at last fall silent, his presence retreating down the walkway until the yard was quiet again.

Behind the window, Qin Nianyin remained still, her nails cutting deep into her palm. She could not fathom how matters had spun so wildly astray. In their previous life, she and Gu Xiao had been little more than distant acquaintances.

She wanted to tell him to stop wasting his attention ——but she knew he would not listen. Perhaps the only solution was for her and Su Zhang to leave the capital sooner.

Given time and distance, his feelings would fade. After all, judging by his temperament, he was not someone possessed of long patience.

* * * * *

The night was heavy and silent, yet the candle in the study had not been extinguished.

A faint rustle sounded from outside ——almost imperceptible —— before a shadow melted out from the darkness. The hidden guard appeared without a whisper, dropped to one knee and reported in a subdued voice, "Someone has entered the Su residence."

Su Zhang lifted his gaze. His expression did not shift in the slightest, his voice calm and cool. "Who is it?"

The guard bowed his head even lower. "Our investigation shows it is Young Master Gu."

For a heartbeat, the room quieted entirely. The candle flame swayed, casting thin ripples of light across the scholar's desk. Su Zhang's fingertips paused briefly atop the paper before him. After a short silence, he spoke with the same faint, unhurried tone: "For what purpose?"

The hidden guard replied, "Master Gu was With a white Persian cat in his arms. He went directly to the young lady's courtyard. They spoke through the window lattice. At first the young lady opened the window but later seemed displeased and closed it. Young Master Gu continued speaking alone outside for quite some time before departing. Fearing they might be alerted, our men did not dare approach too closely, so the exact words cannot be confirmed."

Su Zhang listened quietly until the end. His eyes revealed not the slightest disturbance ——no anger, no surprise, no emotion at all.

Yet the brush in his hand had been gripped so tightly that the slender bamboo shaft bent under the pressure, curving as though it might snap at any moment.

Chapter 57: First Glimpse of Kingfisher Feathers

Dusk fell quickly that evening; the sky sank into shadow as a thin veil of twilight pooled over the courtyard. The first candle had only just been lit inside the room when the courtyard gate was tapped twice in a soft, measured rhythm.

Mei went to answer and soon poked her head back in, lowering her voice as though sharing a secret. "Miss, Young Master Su is here." Qin Nianyin had been bending over the table, gathering the garments she had left out earlier, when the gate creaked open from the outside.

She froze, barely having time to turn before Su Zhang's tall, composed figure stepped into the small courtyard. In the dimming light, his silhouette carried a faint halo from the lantern glow behind him; his expression was as calm as ever, his footsteps measured, steady, wholly unhurried.

Behind him, Xiuyan followed closely, lifting a carved wooden cage with both hands, the utmost care in his movements.

Curled inside the cage was something small and snow-white. The tiny creature rested quietly, its fur soft as newborn frost; under the lantern light its pair of round, dark eyes gleamed even more brightly, full of crystal clarity, fixed curiously upon her.

"What is this ——" Qin Nianyin could not help speaking, her tone threaded with confusion, a faint sense of foreboding rising in her chest.

Su Zhang came closer, set the wooden cage lightly upon her table and spoke with a tone so mild it sounded almost casual, as though merely commenting in passing.

"I happened to pass through the marketplace today. This little creature looked rather pleasing, so I thought you might like it and brought it back for you."

For her?

At that, Qin Nianyin was rendered momentarily speechless. First Gu Xiao and now Su Zhang ——were the two of them competing to send her small animals? What exactly were they thinking?

Besides, the esteemed and perpetually busy Su Zhang "happened" to stroll through the marketplace today? and furthermore, had the leisure to buy a sable?

She lowered her gaze to inspect it. The little snow-white sable twitched its ears lightly inside the cage, its tail resting lazily against its side, its demeanour impeccably gentle.

When she reached out, touching the wooden slats to test its reaction, the little creature merely blinked its large, glossy eyes and stayed entirely unafraid, as though it trusted her by instinct alone.

Xiuyan, who had been standing aside, stiffened for a moment when he heard Su Zhang's explanation. Young Master had ordered him —— ordered him ——to procure a pure white sable of the finest appearance within three days, no matter the price.

And now, with a single breath, it had become something he "happened" to encounter by the roadside?

Qin Nianyin did not miss the faint stiffness in Xiuyan's posture, nor the care with which the cage had been handled. She understood at once— this was no chance encounter, but a choice deliberately rendered weightless. He had wrapped effort in the language of coincidence, as though naming it otherwise would bind her too tightly.

The young master, speaking so lightly, had no idea that he and Yefeng had nearly run their legs off through half the city to find this one creature with its rare snow-white fur and decent breeding.

Qin Nianyin lifted her eyes toward Su Zhang, the corners of her lips curving in a small, helpless smile. "It is indeed adorable. But this sort of thing… perhaps send it to Sister Wan instead. She would surely like it."

"No." Su Zhang shook his head, his expression tranquil but With an unmistakable edge of finality. "She has feared such animals since childhood."

"Then give it to Miss Shen Lingyan," Qin Nianyin offered without thinking.

The moment the words left her mouth, his brow tightened ever so slightly. "Why should it be given to her?"

Qin Nianyin faltered. Naturally because she is your sweetheart and you should be the one currying her favour… Yet when the thought reached her lips, she altered it into something more neutral.

"Sister Wan has helped me greatly these past days. I ought to return her kindness. This little creature is rare and charming. So I thought I might… offer it on her behalf."

"If that is the case, I shall prepare a proper gift for her myself." Su Zhang cut her off, his tone steady, unhurried. "What is it? You do not like this sable?"

Qin Nianyin found herself unable to answer. After a moment of silence, she finally said, "It is not a matter of liking or not. It is simply that ——"

Apparently fearing her refusal, Su Zhang spoke again at once, leaving her no time to finish. "Even if you do not like it, keep it for me for a few days."

She had originally intended to return the sable, yet when she saw his expression ——unmoved, unreadable ——she knew too well what would come if she refused outright.

She could already imagine the quiet reproach that would follow—spoken not in anger, but in reason. That she lived under another's roof yet would not even trouble herself to keep a small creature for a few days. That she drew boundaries too sharply, as though every kindness were a debt she feared to owe. He would not say it outright, but the meaning would settle all the same. And so, she chose delay over refusal, knowing time itself could soften what words could not.

He would claim she was living under another's roof yet unwilling to lend even the smallest assistance. After a moment of quiet, she reached out and accepted the cage.

Her fingertips brushed the warm wooden frame and the small creature inside shifted, curling deeper into a corner as though seeking comfort.

She spoke softly. "Then… I shall keep it for now."

Su Zhang responded with a single, low hum. His gaze lingered briefly on the cage in her arms before passing over her face in the same calm, unreadable way.

Only then did he turn to leave. As the candlelight flickered, his figure receded into the night, merging so smoothly into the darkness that it felt as though he had never stepped into the courtyard at all.

The room was left to her and Mei alone. Mei leaned in to look at the sable, her eyes shining. "Miss, this little thing is truly spirited!" Qin Nianyin pressed her lips together, saying nothing.

Yet she could not escape the feeling that this small cage, soft though it seemed, had suddenly added another layer of entanglement she could neither name nor untangle.

* * * * *

The following morning, as the first hint of dawn paled the edge of the sky, the streets of the capital were already waking. Vendors pushed their small carts along the roads, calling out their wares; steam rose from bamboo baskets, carrying with it the warm, comforting fragrance of freshly made breakfast.

Qin Nianyin stepped out with a square brocade box of pale lotus hue cradled in her arms.

Inside the box lay the velvet-flower hairpins she had rushed to finish the night before ——one in a vivid crabapple red, bright as the first blush of spring; one in a faint, mist-soft pink, delicate as drifting smoke; and one fashioned of silver-threaded plum blossoms, its bead-set stamens gleaming with cold purity.

The small shop she frequented to deliver these pieces sat just around the corner on the main street, its sign shaded by a newly embroidered crimson awning. The shopkeeper was bent over an account book with an assistant when she stepped inside.

Recognizing her, he hurried forward, his smile warm. "Miss Qin, your timing is perfect. As it happens, the entire batch you delivered a few days ago has already sold out. There are still several distinguished customers waiting for new pieces."

As he spoke, he accepted the brocade box and opened it; delight flashed immediately across his eyes. "Exquisite work as always."

Qin Nianyin murmured a few quiet instructions, ready to take her leave when something at the edge of her vision caught the light ——an unexpected hint of vivid green, like clear water reflecting the feathers of a passing bird. She turned her head.

Beneath a glass display dome at the corner of the counter rested a kingfisher hairpin.

The bird's head dipped in a graceful arc, its long tail raised just so; its feathers were layered in shades of turquoise and deep blue and at the very tips, threads of gold shimmered faintly, as though the creature might lift from its stand and take flight the very next moment.

She bent toward it without thinking, her voice unconsciously softening. "This hairpin… is beautiful."

The shop owner's lips curved into something between amusement and admiration. "You have a sharp eye, Miss. This is a piece made with dian cui ——kingfisher feathers set into gold filigree. A full set of headpieces made in this craft would cost no less than a hundred taels."

(Dian Cui-Kingfisher feathers set into gold filigree)

"Dian cui…" Qin Nianyin tasted the word inwardly. Through the thin pane of glass, her fingertip nearly felt the cool gleam radiating from the feathers, a sharpness that seemed to sink straight into her heart.

Seeing her interest, the shopkeeper leaned closer and lowered his voice. "This was made by a rather eccentric master craftsman ——little-known, difficult to approach.

He only makes one complete set of ornaments each year, never takes apprentices and no amount of silver will persuade him otherwise. This set came to my shop only after calling in several layers of favours."

A glimmer flickered briefly in Qin Nianyin's eyes. One set a year… If I could learn such a craft, the standard of my workshop would rise far above the ordinary. And more importantly ——no one would be able to copy it so easily.

What truly caught her breath was not the beauty alone, but the barrier it represented. One maker. One complete set each year. No apprentices, no repetition, no dilution. If such a craft passed through her hands, it would not merely elevate her workshop—it would place her beyond imitation. In a world that devoured skill through copying, rarity was its own kind of armour.

Feigning casual curiosity, she asked, "Where does this master live?"

"Oh? Does Miss Qin wish to buy a piece?"

"No. I wish to learn."

The shopkeeper immediately shook his head. "That will not do. The master has been explicit ——he takes no apprentices. One set a year is enough for him to drink wine and eat well. I heard someone once tried to beg him for instruction, knelt outside his door for three days and three nights and still failed."

"Even so… I should at least try."

The shopkeeper hesitated, then relented. "Well, since you're determined, I suppose it does no harm to attempt it. Who knows ——perhaps fate will favour you. The master lives west of the city, near Willow Lane. Go south past two small streets, close to the old docks." Just then a regular customer entered the shop and he hurried away with a genial greeting, leaving the matter at that.

Qin Nianyin lowered her gaze as though the conversation were finished, yet in her heart the address was already carved with absolute clarity. Her fingers brushed lightly over the velvet flowers at her sleeve and a quiet, resolute thought settled in her chest like a stone dropping into still water ——

This craft… she would see it with her own eyes. And if fate allowed, she would learn it with her own hands.

Chapter 58: The Peanut and the Prince

After leaving the jewellery shop, Qin Nianyin had already begun planning to seek out the kingfisher feather artisan according to the shopkeeper's directions while the sky was still early.

West Willow Lane was not exactly close, so she intended to take her time winding her way along the main street, taking the opportunity to observe the shops along the route and note potential business opportunities.

The sun climbed higher. Shops lined both sides of the street, a continuous stream of people filled the thoroughfare. Banners fluttered; the cries of street vendors and porters, the creaking of carriage wheels and the sound of storytelling from teahouses interwove, converging into the bustling daily life of the capital.

As she walked, Qin Nianyin paid attention to the business methods of the shops along the route.

From the display of fabrics in the silk and satin stores to the tactics used by rouge and powder shops to attract female customers, she observed everything carefully, silently committing it to memory, hoping her own small business could eventually find a viable path.

She did not merely look — she compared. The silk shops favoured brilliance and excess, layers of colour meant to dazzle at first glance, while the finer pieces were kept deliberately high and out of reach.

Rouge sellers relied on noise and novelty, calling out exaggerated promises, yet the truly steady customers were drawn not by voices, but by familiarity. Qin Nianyin noted all of it. What sold quickly was not always what endured; what appeared refined was often mass-produced beneath a different name.

In Jiangnan, craft survived through patience. In the capital, profit thrived on spectacle. The two were not enemies, she realized — but they could not be treated the same. If she were to stand firm here, she could not rely on the quiet confidence that had once sustained her work elsewhere. She would need distinction that could not be mimicked easily, something that invited admiration without inviting imitation.

As she walked, she began quietly rearranging her plans. Not larger scale — but sharper edges. Not louder appeal — but clearer ownership. The capital rewarded those who understood its rhythm, not those who fought it outright.

The moment she turned into the busier street, Qin Nianyin felt it — that subtle shift in air that preceded trouble rather than danger. Not the kind that raised one's pulse, but the kind that demanded composure. She slowed her steps almost imperceptibly, lifting her gaze to take in the second floors of the surrounding buildings. Taverns, private rooms, carved railings — places where idle eyes lingered above the street, unseen yet watching.

In the capital, accidents were rarely accidents. Attention, once drawn, rarely remained harmless. She reminded herself to keep her posture steady, her pace unhurried. A woman alone, moving with purpose, invited curiosity; one who appeared unbothered discouraged pursuit.

She had nearly cleared the intersection when the sound came — light, deliberate, unmistakably intentional.

Just as she turned onto a busy street, low laughter came from the carved railing of a tavern's second floor ahead. Amid the cacophony of voices, something suddenly cut through the air ——"Ding" ——striking her squarely on the temple.

She swayed slightly, instinctively raising a hand to touch the spot. Her fingertip encountered not blood, but half a peanut.

Qin Nianyin looked up. A man leaning against the tavern's second-floor railing was smiling at her ——a smile tinged with laziness and playful insolence, his eyes clearly sparkling with teasing light.

The Third Prince, Li Suo, dressed in a moon-white martial attire, his long hair tied up with a jade crown. He held another peanut between his fingers, slowly twirling it.

Seeing her look up, he slightly lifted his chin, pointed a long finger at her, then crooked it, signalling her to come upstairs.

This series of actions was as composed as summoning a teased kitten.

Qin Nianyin stood silent for a moment, sighing inwardly ——she had intended to find the kingfisher feather master, but had the misfortune to run into this idle Third Highness.

She looked up and met his gaze, reading a mix of amusement and an air of non-refusal in those smiling, yet not quite smiling, eyes.

Indeed, who let him be a prince?

She had no choice but to temporarily set aside her original plan. Lifting her skirts, she approached, pushed open the tavern door and ascended the wooden stairs.

As the wooden steps creaked faintly, the scent of wine and the sound of stringed music from upstairs grew nearer. The Third Prince Li Suo's figure by the carved railing also became clearer ——like a smiling face hiding an unknown card, quietly awaiting her arrival.

The moment Qin Nianyin stepped onto the second floor, she saw the Third Prince reclining by the window, his teacup slightly tilted, a playful smile gracing his lips.

"Last time I saw you, you were looking around like a wary little sparrow," he drawled. "Today, you walk with your head down the whole way. What are you thinking about? A young girl like you, with such heavy thoughts?"

Before his words faded, she did not respond. Instead, she walked past him to the table, picked up the pot and poured a cup of tea, her movements deft and natural. The fragrance of tea rose from the porcelain cup. She lifted her head and took a drink, sighing softly, "So thirsty."

Her demeanour was as composed as if she were in her own small courtyard, not restraining herself in the slightest.

Li Suo was momentarily taken aback, then laughed dismissively ——the noble daughters he had met, regardless of their inner thoughts, always maintained proper decorum, afraid of being too casual or lacking in propriety. This one before him, however, seemed utterly unconcerned with others' opinions.

Qin Nianyin, receiving his scrutinizing look, also laughed inwardly —— he probably thought she was naturally uninhibited. Little did he know she was a transmigrator; how could she be intimidated by his noble aura?

Li Suo slowly swirled his teacup, his tone shifting. "I heard your cousin will soon depart for Jiangnan?"

"..." Qin Nianyin frowned slightly, disliking the overly familiar way Li Suo referred to Su Zhang.

Li Suo glanced at her amusedly, his eyes full of interest. "What? Your cousin Su Zhang is a paragon among men. Don't you have any thoughts about him?"

Qin Nianyin suddenly became serious and stood up to leave. "If Your Highness continues with such jokes, Nianyin will take her leave."

"Aiya, aiya, sit, sit. I was just joking with you."

Qin Nianyin sat back down as instructed, her expression displeased. "Your Highness, this common girl knows her status is lowly. Not only towards Cousin Su Zhang, but towards any young master from a prominent family, this common girl absolutely holds no other thoughts. Your Highness can rest assured."

Hearing this, Li Suo was somewhat surprised, his regard for her rising a notch. He smiled. "Then drink your tea. Let's not talk of these things."

"Yes, thank you, Your Highness." She replied mildly, not wishing to answer too deeply.

He looked up at her, a hint of smugness in his expression. "There's another matter you should bear in mind ——the court's commendation this time for those who rendered service in flood control, the swift erection of your foster father's statue… it wasn't entirely Su Zhang's doing. This Prince also contributed significantly."

Seeing his expression that seemed to say, 'praise me now,' Qin Nianyin was slightly taken aback.

Li Suo lightly tapped the teacup lid with his fingertip. His tone seemed casual yet carried a note of laughter and deliberate credit-seeking. "That foster father is yours, not Su Zhang's. This Prince's efforts naturally mean it's a favour you owe. This Prince doesn't want that Su Zhang to take all the credit."

Watching his seemingly nonchalant yet actually quite calculating manner, she couldn't help but let out a soft laugh. "In that case, then Nianyin, on behalf of her foster father… thanks Your Highness. Once the statue is completed, Nianyin will certainly inform her foster father before it. I will tell him Your Highness contributed significantly to this endeavour and must ask him to bestow his blessings upon you."

"Sharp-tongued." Li Suo's gaze paused, then he slowly raised an eyebrow. "So you mean to say, you are also accompanying Su Zhang on his Jiangnan journey?"

"Yes."

"Interesting." Li Suo tossed a peanut into his mouth, his roguish, dissolute charm not diminishing his noble air.

She pressed her lips together and did not answer, only lowering her head to slowly sip her tea, allowing his gaze to scrutinize her face in detail.

Seeing her indifferent expression, Li Suo, conversely, felt a stir of interest. The teacup in his fingers turned halfway. He smiled and said, "Jiangnan is a fine place. The landscape is soft and graceful; the people are clever and spirited. Su Zhang is going on official business. And you? To enjoy the scenery and amusements?"

Qin Nianyin looked up, her brow arching very slightly. "Your Highness is mistaken. This journey is not for pleasure, but solely to honour my ancestor."

Li Suo uttered an "Oh," the mockery in his tone diminishing abruptly, seeming genuinely somewhat surprised.

"You are different from those young ladies who only care for romance and moonlight. So valuing sentiment and duty ——no wonder Su Zhang is willing to take you along."

"Your Highness praises me too highly." She picked up her teacup, her voice unhurried. "Sentiment and duty are merely common human principles. Nothing particularly rare about them."

Li Suo stared at her profile. The lamplight trembled in the shadows of her lashes, a faint glow settling at the corner of her lips, like a strand of coldness masked by the tea fragrance. He suddenly leaned closer, his voice low and slow. "If this Prince also wants you to owe a favour, what then?"

Qin Nianyin was forced back half a step by his sudden proximity, but her gaze remained steady. "Your Highness is a noble Prince. Nianyin cannot presume to bear it."

Li Suo's smile deepened. "Your words are clever. This Prince has never seen anyone refuse a favour so outright."

"If Your Highness truly wishes to accumulate virtue, please bestow that favour upon the common people of the world, not upon me." Her tone was calm, yet held an undeniable chill.

For a moment, the atmosphere grew slightly tense.

Li Suo stared at her, then suddenly laughed dismissively, shaking his head with a sigh. "Look at you, clearly young in years, yet you speak like a stern old matron. Truly amusing."

A stern old matron?

Hearing this, Qin Nianyin's heart paused. Heh, little did he know, her mental age was indeed that of an old woman.

"Your Highness flatters me." She stood and bowed, the hem of her robe swaying slightly with the movement. "The hour is late. This common girl has important matters to attend to and will not further disrupt Your Highness's tea enjoyment."

"Go on." Li Suo waved a hand lazily, still leaning by the window, watching her descend the stairs.

Qin Nianyin's retreating figure gradually faded into the lamplight. The sound of stringed music continued within the tavern. Li Suo lightly tapped the tabletop with his fingertip.

After a long moment, he murmured to himself, "This person is indeed interesting. A pity, her status is somewhat too low."

He looked up towards the twilight at the street corner, the corner of his mouth hooking upwards. That smile held both interest and a degree of calculation.

The wind rose on the street. When Qin Nianyin stepped out of the tavern, the last of the sunset glow had already scattered. She sighed inwardly, lifting her gaze to look into the distance ——

As she stepped back onto the street, the echoes of the tavern did not follow her — yet the weight of the encounter did. Princes collected debts lightly, she thought, as though favour itself were a game. They offered assistance not to relieve burdens, but to mark possession.

What unsettled her was not his words, nor his interest, but how easily power mistook proximity for entitlement. She had declined politely, cleanly, yet even that refusal would now be noted, remembered, measured.

And so, her resolve sharpened. If she were to move within this city, she would do so on terms that belonged unmistakably to her. Not as someone granted passage by others, but as someone whose value could not be casually claimed.

Only then did she lift her eyes toward the west.

Willow Lane lay to the west. The sky was gradually darkening, yet she remained determined to seek out that artisan. Because she knew that only by mastering her own craft could she truly stand firm in this city filled with power and frivolous laughter.

Chapter 59: An Ambush Encountered

Before dawn, beyond the courier road outside the capital, the carriages and horses were already prepared.

The sky had not yet fully brightened. A pale wash of grey lay over the streets, neither night nor morning, as if the city itself were holding its breath.

Qin Nianyin wore plain, light-coloured garments. There was no ornament upon her save for a single velvet flower hairpin tucked into her hair. Her features were composed and cool as she sorted her travel belongings with Mei, folding each item with deliberate care, as though order alone might still the unease beneath her calm.

Suddenly, a sharp rhythm of hoofbeats broke through the stillness from the corner of the street.

Mei looked up in surprise. Before she could speak, the sound had already drawn near. A rider reined in hard. Gu Xiao swung down from his horse in one clean motion, a bamboo cage held firmly in his arms. Within it, a mass of snowy-white fur was curled tight, motionless save for the faint rise and fall of breath.

"Nianyin."

He strode towards her, his voice bright, his eyes catching the faint light like the first edge of sunrise. There was an openness to his expression, unguarded and earnest, as though the world before him were simple and straightforward.

"Little White," he said, lifting the cage slightly. "I'll keep her for you for now. The journey to Jiangnan will be long, boats and carriages the whole way. It won't be convenient to bring her along."

Qin Nianyin paused.

Her gaze fell to the bamboo cage. For a moment, she said nothing. Then her brows drew together, just slightly.

"No need," she replied. "I don't want it."

Gu Xiao froze.

The words seemed not to land at first. Then his expression darkened, a faint shadow passing across his features.

"Don't want it?"

The corner of his mouth lifted into a restrained, displeased curve. His tone, however, still carried the stubbornness of youth, pressed flat but not extinguished.

"Since you accepted Su Zhang's little white ferret, why can't you accept my little white cat?" he said. "You're clearly favouring one over the other. That's not fair."

The moment the words left his mouth, Qin Nianyin felt her chest tighten.

She looked up at him in shock.

How did he know?

For a heartbeat, her thoughts scattered. Then she forced them back into order. Her face cooled at once, her gaze settling into stillness, like water sealed beneath a thin layer of ice.

"That ferret was only under my care temporarily," she said evenly. "There is no further involvement. Young Master Gu need not think too much."

Gu Xiao's throat moved.

It looked as though he wished to argue, as though there were words pressing hard behind his teeth. Yet her detached expression cut those words short before they could form. The distance in her eyes left him nowhere to step.

After a moment, he drew in a slow breath, as if forcibly pressing down the frustration tightening in his chest. He hugged the bamboo cage closer to himself, his fingers tightening around its edge.

"You…" he said, then stopped. When he spoke again, there was undisguised annoyance in his voice. "You always speak so decisively."

Qin Nianyin lowered her lashes.

She did not look at him again.

Outwardly, her composure did not waver. Inwardly, she let out a quiet sigh.

The matter of learning jewellery craft would have to wait until she returned from Jiangnan. There was no space left now for such plans, not when this journey already carried the weight of unseen danger.

This road ahead would not be smooth.

Waves and storms awaited her, far more treacherous than she had first imagined.

Hoofbeats began to rise around them as the convoy prepared to depart. Orders were called in low voices. Harnesses were checked once more. The stillness of dawn fractured into motion.

Gu Xiao remained where he stood.

He watched as Qin Nianyin turned away, her figure gradually receding into the line of carriages. Inside the bamboo cage, the white fur shifted slightly, a small movement that seemed almost questioning.

Yet no movement, no call, could bring her steps back.

* * * *

The sky was just beginning to pale.

A thin veil of morning mist drifted across the streets as the convoy moved forward in single file. Hoofbeats and the rumble of carriage wheels overlapped and echoed, weaving together into a restrained, low rhythm, like the opening notes of a sombre overture.

Inside the carriage, Qin Nianyin sat beside Mei.

The curtain swayed faintly with the movement of the wheels. From beyond it came Su Zhang's occasional instructions, spoken in a low voice, firm and measured, carrying the decisiveness of long-honed discipline. Yet beneath that steadiness lay a faint restraint, an urgency held tightly in check.

Since setting out, he had lifted the curtain more than once.

Each time, his gaze lingered for a fraction too long, as though words pressed against his lips only to be swallowed back again.

Qin Nianyin remained silent throughout.

She leaned lightly against the carriage wall, her posture composed, one hand closed around a handkerchief in her lap. Outwardly, she appeared calm. Inwardly, her thoughts were drawn taut, stretched tight as a bowstring pulled to its limit.

She gave him no opening.

Mei noticed it nonetheless. After watching her mistress for a time, she leaned closer and whispered, "Young Lady… what is it? You seem unsettled. Your spirit hasn't been at ease since we set off."

Qin Nianyin's gaze slid past the window lattice.

She did not answer.

Instead, she calculated in silence.

When will they strike?

The note had already been delivered. No name. No seal. Just a few stark lines, written plainly enough to leave no room for ambiguity.

He should have received it by now.

If Su Zhang believed it, if he had taken precautions, then perhaps this journey might yet pass without disaster. But if he had dismissed it—

Then she would have no choice but to watch this road herself, from beginning to end.

Outside the carriage, Su Zhang finally spoke again.

"Nianyin."

The curtain trembled slightly as his voice carried through the morning air, lowered by the wind, edged with restraint.

Qin Nianyin did not lift her eyes.

She pressed her lips together, then spoke quietly, "Mei. Lower the curtain."

Mei hesitated for half a breath, then obeyed.

The curtain fell.

Su Zhang's voice was cut off at once. Only the sense of his presence remained, close and unyielding, following alongside the carriage like a shadow that refused to disperse.

Qin Nianyin withdrew her gaze and placed a hand against her chest.

The note had been written clearly.

There is danger on the Jiangnan journey.

Nothing more. Nothing less.

She could only hope he had believed it.

The wheels rolled over the bluestone road, their steady rhythm striking her heart like a warning bell, one beat after another, refusing to fade.

* * * * *

Su Zhang rode at the head of the convoy.

His posture remained straight in the saddle, his pace unhurried, his control over the horse precise. To any onlooker, there was nothing amiss.

Yet his thoughts were far from steady.

Again and again, his mind returned to that note.

The handwriting had been clean, sharp, without flourish. The words were cold, direct, stripped of ornament, as though written by someone who neither sought favour nor feared consequence.

It read like guidance.

It also read like a trap.

Su Zhang had always been cautious. Without knowing the sender's identity or intent, he could not determine which it was.

To trust it might mean stepping straight into a snare laid with care.

To doubt it might mean missing the only chance to avert disaster.

For a brief moment, his thoughts turned to another anonymous message he had received days earlier. That one, too, had arrived without warning, the ink barely dry, yet it had pointed unerringly toward truths he had not yet confirmed.

Too accurate.

Too timely.

A faint crease formed between his brows.

Who was this person?

How did they know his movements so precisely?

Was this warning offered out of goodwill, or was it bait, meant to guide him where someone wished him to go?

Su Zhang's eyes darkened.

At last, he pressed the questions down, sealing them beneath the discipline he had honed over years. Doubt would not serve him now. Indecision even less.

Only one conclusion remained, cold and unavoidable.

If this person dares to warn me from the shadows, he thought, then sooner or later, they will reveal themselves.

The convoy continued forward, unaware that the road ahead had already been marked.

* * * * *

The sky gradually darkened.

Clouds gathered low and heavy above the official road leading into Jiangnan, pressing down upon the land with a sense of quiet oppression. The road itself was broad and well-kept, flanked by dense woodland that closed in on either side as the convoy advanced.

Without warning, the rhythm of hoofbeats dulled.

The sound did not vanish. It was simply swallowed, muffled by the trees, as though the forest itself had drawn closer, leaning in to listen.

Inside the carriage, Qin Nianyin's heart tightened.

Almost at the same moment, Su Zhang's gaze sharpened. His posture shifted subtly in the saddle, fingers tightening around the reins. He did not look back, yet his attention was fully alert.

The air had changed.

Then the shadows moved.

From among the trees, black figures surged forth in a sudden wave. Dozens of men in dark clothing burst onto the road, blades flashing, arrows already nocked.

"Ambush!" one of the guards shouted.

The escort reacted at once.

With a sharp crack, concealed mechanisms along the sides of the carriage sprang open. Reinforced wooden panels snapped outward, locking into place and forming a temporary barricade around the carriage. Steel met steel as the guards engaged the attackers at close range, the clash ringing sharp and violent through the forest.

Shouts erupted. Metal struck metal. The sound of battle tore through the stillness like a blade.

Inside the carriage, Mei's face drained of colour.

She clutched Qin Nianyin's hand tightly, her fingers cold and trembling. Qin Nianyin herself felt every nerve in her body drawn taut, her ears filled with the harsh, relentless ring of weapons colliding.

Then a familiar voice cut through the chaos.

"Who are you?" Su Zhang demanded, his tone cold and forceful. "Who sent you?"

From the opposing side came a low, mocking laugh.

"If the King of Hell has marked you for death at the third watch," the voice sneered, "who dares keep you alive until the fifth? This arrow will take your life."

The words had barely fallen when the air split.

A sharp whistle tore through the space, followed by another, and another. Arrows flew in rapid succession, their speed and force like rolling thunder.

Qin Nianyin did not think.

She moved.

In one swift motion, she shoved aside the protective panel and surged forward, throwing herself out of the carriage. There was no calculation, no hesitation. Only instinct, raw and unfiltered, driving her body toward Su Zhang.

The next instant, pain exploded.

A flying arrow tore through the air and drove straight into the back of her right shoulder.

"Nianyin!"

Su Zhang felt his heart jolt violently, as though the blood had been torn from his veins in a single breath.

Crimson spread at once across her clothing, dark and vivid. He did not pause. Without hesitation, he raised the whistle at his waist and blew hard.

The sound was piercing and long.

It cut cleanly through the noise of battle.

Almost immediately, another force erupted from deeper within the forest. Armed figures poured out, engaging the attackers from the flank. The balance of the fight shifted in an instant.

Su Zhang did not look back.

He bent down, scooped Qin Nianyin into his arms, and turned sharply toward the carriage. His movements were swift and decisive, yet his grip betrayed him. His hands were shaking.

Mei cried out and rushed forward, but Su Zhang's gaze swept over her, sharp as a blade.

"Down," he said coldly.

Mei froze where she stood, every muscle locked, unable to take another step.

The curtain fell.

Bloodshed, shouting, and the clash of steel were shut out at once.

Inside the carriage, the space felt impossibly narrow.

Su Zhang laid Qin Nianyin down with care, but the moment his hands reached her back, they trembled violently. He tore at the fabric of her clothing, urgency overriding restraint.

"No!"

Qin Nianyin struggled weakly, pressing her hand against the torn cloth. Her eyes were filled with pain and shame, her voice unsteady. "You cannot…"

"What cannot be done?" Su Zhang snapped, his control shattering. His eyes burned red as he leaned closer. "You are bleeding like this. Am I to stand by and watch you die?"

The fabric gave way.

The arrow was buried deep in her flesh, the wound dark with blood. Su Zhang tore a strip from his own sleeve, his fingers shaking as he pressed it firmly against the wound to slow the bleeding.

"Why?" His voice was hoarse, almost a shout. "Why did you take the arrow for me?"

Qin Nianyin's face was ashen, her breathing shallow. Her lips trembled as she forced the words out. "I… I do not know… I only… acted on instinct…"

This was a mistake, she thought faintly. If I could turn back time by even a moment, I would hide properly. I would not do this again.

Her vision blurred.

Pain surged, overwhelming what little strength remained. Her body slackened, consciousness slipping away.

Su Zhang stared at her, frozen.

His hand was still pressed to her wound, blood seeping between his fingers. His chest felt as though it had been split open by a blade, the pain so sharp he could barely draw breath.

Outside, hoofbeats thundered and blades continued to clash, yet it all felt distant, muffled, as though separated by layers upon layers of water.

In his eyes, there was only her.

Her face, pale and unmoving, became the only world he could see.

* * * * *

The carriage lurched forward as the horses were urged on.

Inside the narrow space, the smell of blood spread quickly, thick and metallic, pressing into every breath. The floor trembled beneath them, each jolt sending a sharp ripple of pain through Qin Nianyin's body.

The arrow remained embedded deep in the back of her right shoulder.

Blood seeped steadily from the wound, soaking through the cloth that Su Zhang had pressed there moments earlier. Her face had lost all colour, her lips pale to the point of translucence, her breathing shallow and uneven.

Outside the carriage, hurried footsteps approached.

A physician had been summoned, but the moment he learned that a young lady lay wounded inside, he stopped short. He did not dare enter. Instead, he spoke through the carriage wall, his voice low but urgent.

"The arrowhead is lodged deep," he said. "You must stop the bleeding first. Only then can you break the shaft. The medicine is here. Follow my instructions exactly."

A small bundle was passed in through the opening.

Mei's eyes were already red with tears. Her hands shook as she reached out. "Let me do it," she said in a trembling voice. "I have served Young Lady the longest. I can do this. I can."

Before Su Zhang could respond, she pushed her way into the carriage.

Then she saw the wound.

The sight struck her like a blow. Mei clamped a hand over her mouth and nose, her shoulders jerking as tears burst free. Her voice broke completely. "Young Lady… how could the Young Lady be hurt like this…"

Su Zhang's face darkened.

He did not raise his voice. He did not need to.

His gaze alone was enough to freeze her in place.

Without a word, he reached out and pushed her firmly back toward the door. His voice was low, cold, and absolute. "Out."

Mei staggered back, her sobbing cut off mid-breath. She did not dare argue. The door fell shut again, leaving only the two of them inside.

The space felt smaller still.

Su Zhang lowered his eyes to Qin Nianyin.

She lay nearly unconscious, her lashes damp with sweat, her body trembling faintly. His fingers hovered for a moment before touching her again. They were shaking.

The blood beneath his palm was hot, yet he felt cold to the bone.

"Do not pull the arrow yet," the physician's voice came again from outside. "Stop the bleeding first."

Su Zhang pressed his lips into a thin line.

He tore another strip from his sleeve without hesitation. His movements were not gentle, nor were they practiced, but they were precise. He pressed down hard at the edge of the wound, forcing the medicinal powder into the torn flesh.

Blood mixed with powder and ran over his palm.

Qin Nianyin shuddered violently, a low sound tearing from her throat despite her unconsciousness.

Su Zhang's breath caught.

Cold sweat slid down from his temples, soaking into his hair. He had stood on battlefields before, had seen men torn apart by blades and arrows alike. Yet never had he felt such panic claw at his chest.

Nothing was within his control.

She is mine, a voice roared relentlessly in his mind.

Only mine.

If anything happens to her, there will be no retreat left for me.

"Break the shaft now," the physician urged, his tone sharpening. "If you delay, she will bleed out."

Su Zhang drew in a harsh breath.

He steadied his hands by force, gripping the exposed arrow shaft firmly with both palms. His eyes darkened, a red tinge creeping into their depths.

Then he snapped it.

The sound was dull and abrupt.

Qin Nianyin cried out once, a sharp, broken sound that seemed to tear straight through him. Her body convulsed, then went limp once more, consciousness slipping away again.

For a moment, Su Zhang felt as though something inside his chest had collapsed entirely.

His fingers loosened around the broken shaft. He nearly dropped it.

He leaned forward suddenly, pressing his forehead against her cold cheek. His breath came ragged, his voice hoarse and barely held together.

"Qin Nianyin," he murmured, each word scraped raw from his throat. "You are not allowed to die."

Blood and medicine mingled in the air, heavy and suffocating.

The carriage continued to jolt onward through the night, the sounds of pursuit and retreat fading gradually into distance. Yet within this narrow space, Su Zhang finally understood what this single arrow had done.

It had not only torn through her flesh.

It had ripped open what he had buried deepest in his heart.

He loved her.

He wanted her.

And in this lifetime, no matter the cost, he would not let go.

* * * * *

Night pressed down heavily upon the camp.

Inside the tent, lamplight burned low, casting unsteady shadows across the canvas walls. Li Xuan sat alone, his posture still, his expression unreadable, fingers resting lightly on the rim of a porcelain teacup that had long since gone cold.

The tent flap stirred.

A trusted subordinate entered swiftly, lowered his head, and knelt on one knee. His voice was kept deliberately low. "Your Highness. The matter in Jiangnan… has failed."

The teacup struck the table with a sharp crack.

Li Xuan's eyes flew open. In a single motion he rose to his feet, the lamplight catching the hard edge of his gaze. "How did it fail?"

The subordinate's forehead glistened with sweat. He did not dare lift his head. "According to what we have gathered, Su Zhang had already made preparations. The carriage concealed mechanisms. The escort activated them at the critical moment. There was also another group providing covert protection. The men in black suffered heavy losses. None managed to escape."

"Prepared…" Li Xuan repeated softly.

His fingers tightened around the folding fan in his hand. A sharp snapping sound rang out as one of the ribs cracked cleanly under the pressure.

His eyes narrowed inch by inch.

"Whose people were they?" His voice was calm, but beneath it lay a chilling edge. "Li Duan's? Gu Xiao's? Or…" He paused, the corner of his mouth lifting slightly. "Or death soldiers he has cultivated in secret?"

The subordinate hesitated, then answered carefully. "This subordinate has not yet confirmed it. But to protect him with such discretion and precision, the backing must be considerable."

Li Xuan let out a short, humourless laugh.

"So," he said slowly, "Su Zhang is not as simple as he appears."

He turned and began to pace the length of the tent, each step measured, heavy. His voice grew darker with every word. "I once thought he was nothing more than a pedant clinging to a spotless reputation. Clean hands. Clean name. A man easy to deal with."

He stopped abruptly.

"But now," he continued, "he moves with hidden guards, concealed mechanisms, and forces that even my people cannot trace."

His grip tightened again around the broken fan. Was it Li Duan? he wondered. Or Gu Xiao, acting on impulse as he always does? Or has Su Zhang been hiding fangs all along?

"If Li Duan sent men to protect him," Li Xuan said aloud, "then the Eastern Palace has already bound Su Zhang to its side. And if it was Gu Xiao…" His lips curled faintly. "That man never lifts a finger without expecting something in return."

He raised his head, eyes glinting coldly in the lamplight. "No matter which it is, this cannot be allowed to continue."

The subordinate lowered his head further, not daring to breathe too loudly.

"This Jiangnan journey," Li Xuan said in a low, deliberate tone, "must remain under my control. There can be no further mistakes."

He stopped pacing.

"Su Zhang," he said quietly, each syllable weighed and sharpened, "must not be allowed to live long enough to steal my momentum."

The lamplight flickered.

Shadows leapt across his face, carving his features into something harsh and unforgiving. In his eyes, killing intent stirred openly now, no longer concealed.

Outside the tent, the night wind passed silently through the dark.

And somewhere far away, on the road to Jiangnan, blood had already been spilled.

Chapter 60: So That's How It Is

The capital, the Eastern Palace.

Candlelight trembled across the desk, throwing shifting shadows over stacked memorials and the neat edge of the inkstone. Crown Prince Li Duan held a wolf-hair brush between his fingers, the tip still wet with ink, as he reviewed the day's petitions line by line. His posture was composed, his expression unreadable, until swift footsteps sounded beyond the screen.

A palace eunuch entered at a near-run, stopped, and bowed low. His voice dropped to a careful hush. "Your Highness, a message has arrived from Jiangnan."

Li Duan's brush halted mid-stroke. A single bead of ink gathered at the tip, threatening to fall. He lifted his eyes. "Speak."

"The assassination attempt… failed." The eunuch's throat tightened; even the words seemed dangerous to carry. "Minister Su appeared to have made preparations in advance. He sustained only light injuries. However,… the young lady travelling with him… took an arrow meant for Minister Su. She is currently receiving treatment."

Li Duan straightened abruptly, the sleeve of his robe brushing the edge of the desk. The candle flame jumped as if startled by his movement. His gaze darkened at once. "What?"

The eunuch pressed his forehead lower, not daring to meet that look. His voice trembled, but he forced himself to continue. "The black-clad assailants were completely routed. They seemed to be intercepted by a covert force in the woods. This servant does not dare to speculate as to their origin."

For a brief moment, the room was so silent it seemed the air itself had been pinned in place. Li Duan's fingers loosened. He set the brush down slowly, with the restraint of someone placing away a blade. His fingertips pressed against the desk as he spoke, each word weighed before it left him.

"What were the other casualties?"

"The report states that only two among the retinue suffered fatal injuries. Minister Su is largely unharmed. But that young lady is gravely wounded. The arrow entered through the shoulder, nearly piercing through."

Li Duan's gaze lowered, as if he were reading an invisible line of text on the lacquered surface. He remained still for a long while, his expression cold and stern as iron. When he finally spoke again, his voice was very low, but it carried a decision that could not be disputed.

"Since there are those who seek his life, the Jiangnan journey must not fail."

He lifted his eyes slightly. In the candlelight, his pupils looked like dark embers held under ash. His words were slow, steady, and heavy with consequence.

"Jiangnan's waterways form a dense network. The people's livelihoods are bound to sericulture and the silk tax. In recent years the weather has been unseasonable; floods and droughts come without pattern, and the margin by which common households survive has grown thin. If corruption and embezzlement further disturb what little stability remains, then tens of thousands of homes will suffer. Minister Su's journey is not merely to investigate bribery. More than that, it is to steady the region and pacify the people. If harm comes to him on the road, it will not only mean I lose a capable assistant. It will mean the people lose a thread of hope to hold onto."

His voice pressed even lower, deliberate to the point of severity. "Dispatch another group of shadow guards. Have them follow at a distance and provide covert protection. Ensure Su Zhang reaches Jiangnan safely. No matter what unforeseen events arise along the route, there must not be the slightest error."

"Yes, Your Highness." The eunuch received the order as if receiving a sentence carved in stone, then withdrew with measured steps, careful not to make a single unnecessary sound.

Li Duan remained alone under the candlelight. He did not return to the memorials at once. His fingertips tapped the desk lightly, once, twice, the quiet rhythm betraying nothing yet suggesting everything. A thin, indescribable chill rose beneath his ribs.

If there truly is someone reaching out from the shadows along this journey, then someone is deliberately opposing my Eastern Palace.

* * * * *

Within the palace hall, candlelight blazed bright enough to gild the carved beams overhead. The memorial on the imperial desk had been unrolled only halfway when a eunuch hurried in, dropped to his knees, and presented a sealed report with both hands.

Emperor Xuanwen scanned it briefly. The change in his expression was immediate and violent, as if a storm had crossed his face in a single breath. He slammed the document onto the desk so hard the bronze censers in the hall shivered and released a dull, humming vibration.

"Such audacity!" His voice cracked through the stillness like a lash. "To dare lay hands on Minister Su right under Our very eyes!"

The officials below the dais fell into hushed silence. No one moved. Even the rustle of robes seemed to vanish. The air grew oppressive, thick enough to feel like it might congeal.

Emperor Xuanwen's chest heaved. He roared again, each word biting. "Investigate this for Us. Conduct a thorough investigation. We want to know precisely who stands behind this. If someone truly dares to stir up trouble in Jiangnan, let them not blame Us for showing no mercy!"

The ministers answered in unison, voices layered and taut. "Yes, Your Majesty."

The Emperor's face remained thunder-dark. His gaze swept across the hall, sharp, measuring, and then finally settled on one figure standing below. His voice paused, the fury cooling by a fraction into something harder and more controlled.

"Li Suo."

"Your son is here." Li Suo stepped forward with a casual smile, as if the weight in the room were no more than a passing cloud. His demeanour carried a hint of languor, the sort that had long since become both his shield and his reputation.

"This matter, we entrust to you." Emperor Xuanwen's tone was stern, yet within it a thread of expectation glimmered, faint but unmistakable. "You have the most leisure time. Do not idle about all day, filling the capital with gossip about your frivolity."

Li Suo did not flinch. The corners of his lips curved, half-roguish, half-playful. "Imperial Father, set your heart at ease. Your son will naturally devote himself to this task. Besides, a leisurely prince such as I also needs to find some amusement. Investigating culprits is arduous work. One might as well consider the selection of a proper consort along the way. When your son takes a wife, she must naturally be one who pleases his heart, a delight to behold day after day."

"You." The Emperor was both angered and, despite himself, faintly amused. He raised a hand and scolded, "Perpetually unreliable. We cannot be bothered with you."

Li Suo only bowed, respectful in form, unrepentant in spirit. His grin did not fade.

Emperor Xuanwen rose and flicked his sleeve in dismissal, but his retreating back seemed heavy, as if the burden of the throne pressed visibly against his shoulders. The rage in his heart dissipated somewhat, leaving behind a thread of weariness that no anger could burn away.

He understood the undercurrents at court. The rivalry between the Crown Prince and the Second Prince, Li Xuan, grew more intense by the day, sharp enough to draw blood even when no blade was bared. If he allowed the Third Prince to become entangled in the struggle for position and power, then conflict among his three sons would be inevitable, and one would surely be harmed.

Li Suo's frivolous, unserious manner gave him headaches. Yet it also afforded him a measure of secret relief. At least this son could still preserve some ease and freedom, a life not yet swallowed by the dragon court's hunger for victory. At least, for now, there was one who might be spared the path that ended in fraternal strife and blood within the palace walls.

* * * * *

The room was profoundly still. The candle flame flickered, casting mottled shadows along the walls.

Su Zhang sat alone before his desk. His robe was smeared with blood and dust, the stains dark and uneven; between his fingers, traces of blood still clung with a tacky sheen, not yet fully dry. Scene after scene replayed in his mind with cruel clarity: Qin Nianyin pushing herself forward without hesitation, throwing her body between him and the oncoming arrow.

In that instant, his heart had felt as if brutally cleaved open.

Xiuyan approached with careful steps, as if afraid even his breathing might offend. He advised in a low voice, "Master, you should wash and change your clothes first. If you remain like this, the chill from the injury may enter your body, and you risk catching a chill..."

Su Zhang lowered his head, staring at the blood on his palm. His voice, when it came, was hoarse to the point of rasping. "Why..."

Xiuyan froze, uncertain whether he had heard correctly. "Master?"

Su Zhang lifted his gaze. His eyes were as deep and unfathomable as a cold pool, the surface calm, the depths terrifying. His tone softened into something mild, almost gentle, yet it carried an unmistakable command.

"You may withdraw. Your service is not required here. I will attend to myself shortly."

Xiuyan opened his mouth as if to protest, then closed it again. He did not dare to press further. He bowed and withdrew quietly.

Only Su Zhang remained, the candle flame standing solitary beside him. He lowered his eyes again, watching the dark red lodged between his fingers. In his chest, however, something churned that he had never known in such force: agitation, fear, and a kind of helplessness that made his throat tighten.

What if she had truly died?

He did not dare to follow the thought any farther.

* * * * *

An indeterminate length of time passed. The figure on the bed stirred slightly.

Qin Nianyin's lashes fluttered as she slowly opened her eyes. The air was thick with the scent of medicine, layered with a faint metallic tang that clung to the back of the throat. Instinctively, she reached a hand back. Her fingertips touched the thick bandage on her shoulder, the tight binding, the ache that pulsed even beneath the numbness.

Startled, she caught her breath and abruptly clutched the bedcovers tighter around herself, as if she could conceal the wound through sheer will.

"Awake?"

The low voice came from beside her.

She turned her head. Su Zhang sat at her bedside, turned slightly away from the candlelight. The flicker left the planes of his face in shadow, sharpening his features into something cold and restrained, as if he had carved himself out of discipline alone.

"The wound was treated by me." His voice was hoarse, roughened by strain. "The medicine was also applied by me."

He paused, the silence stretching taut, and then continued, stubborn insistence pressing through the restraint like a blade against its sheath.

"Set your heart at ease. After today's events, I will assume responsibility."

Qin Nianyin went still.

A surge of memory rose too fast to stop. In her previous life, she had used a life-saving grace to force him into marriage. She had stood with her back against the cliff of her own desperation, believing she had no other way. In this life, it was again a life-saving grace, and now it was he who spoke of taking responsibility, as if duty and honour were chains he placed on himself without question.

Her heartbeat pounded once, hard, and then she forced it down. Her tone remained mild, controlled. "That is unnecessary. At a critical moment between life and death, it was merely instinct. There is no need to stand on such ceremony."

"No." His gaze settled on her face, heavy and unwavering. There was a resoluteness in it that she had never seen before, not even when he had been cornered. "This matter affects your reputation. I must assume responsibility."

She offered a faint smile, the curve small, but threaded with stubbornness. "If one does not marry, then naturally there is no effect. This minor matter is of no consequence."

The atmosphere in the room solidified at once.

Su Zhang lowered his eyes. His knuckles whitened, not from pain but from the force with which he restrained himself. In his heart, the understanding was brutally clear.

No matter how she refuses, this time I will not let go.

* * * * *

Su Wan walked along a bluestone path, her fingers tightening around the handkerchief tucked into her sleeve. The late light lay across the garden in quiet bands, soft enough to feel deceptive.

Her original intention had been simple: to go to the riverside and admire the lotus blossoms. Yet Qin Nianyin's words from not long ago kept returning, uninvited, repeating like a warning that would not fade.

"Sister, if you can avoid the waterside, it would be best to do so."

The tone had been mild, almost casual. But beneath it was a conviction that had tightened Su Wan's heart in a way she could not explain.

Her steps faltered. She looked ahead. A waterside pavilion stood not far off. The water shimmered; the faint fragrance of lotus blossoms drifted on the breeze. It should have been peaceful. Instead, a quiet unease crept up her spine, as if the beauty itself were bait.

Su Wan deliberated, and then finally spoke to her attendant maid in a low voice. "Never mind. We will not go. Turn back."

The maid startled, thinking she had misheard. "Young Lady, did you not say you wished to see the new lotuses…"

"It is unnecessary." Su Wan's voice was firm. She turned, preparing to return.

At that moment, a tall, slender figure approached from the opposite direction.

The man wore a blue scholar's robe. His steps were unhurried; his features were clear and bright, the sort of handsomeness that seemed crafted for gentleness, like a graceful tree swaying in wind. He appeared not to have noticed them. As he passed, there came a crisp ding from his waist.

A jade pendant slipped free and fell to the ground.

Su Wan moved by instinct. She bent slightly, hand reaching down. Her fingers were nearly upon it when she paused.

Qin Nianyin's warning surfaced again. Avoid the waterside. Avoid what is entangled with the waterside. A thread of caution flashed through Su Wan's mind, cold and quick. In the end, she withdrew her hand and said mildly to her maid, "Go. Remind him."

The maid called out in a clear voice, "Young Master, wait. You have dropped something."

The man halted as though only then realising. He turned back. Seeing the jade pendant lying quietly on the stone, a flicker of apology crossed his eyes. He returned at once, bent down himself to retrieve it, and then bowed towards Su Wan.

"My thanks for the young lady's reminder. My apologies for the discourtesy. I am Lu Chengqian."

His voice was warm and clear. His manner was measured, carrying the cultivated air of someone who had lived among books and propriety.

Su Wan inclined her head slightly but did not speak further. She had always understood social boundaries. Yet another thought rose, unwanted but persistent.

Qin Nianyin had told her to avoid the waterside. Did the man before her also have some connection to that entangled fate?

Her heart tightened. Unwilling to become further involved, she prepared to leave with her maid.

Unexpectedly, Lu Chengqian took a step forward, his tone earnest. "Might I ask the young lady's esteemed name?"

A faint frown touched Su Wan's brow. Her usual gentleness cooled, a trace of impatience surfacing despite her effort to keep it hidden. She rarely showed aloofness in front of others, but being pressed so directly for her name stirred a defensive distance.

"My apologies." Her voice was cool. She turned to leave.

The air grew stiff, as if the garden itself had held its breath.

Then a laughing voice cut in from the side, frivolous on the surface, with a sharp edge concealed beneath the amusement.

"Aiya. Who might this esteemed scholar be? A proper literate man, yet he chases after a young lady to ask her name. What sort of propriety is this?"

Su Wan froze and looked up.

Gu Xiao approached with his hands clasped behind his back. The evening light touched his brow and eyes. A lazy smile still sat on his lips, as if he had wandered in merely to pass the time. Yet his eyes were cold and keen, like a honed blade that caught light only when it chose to.

Lu Chengqian's face darkened instantly. He forced a bow of greeting. "So it is Young Master Gu."

The newly appointed high official of the Imperial Guard, the Empress's own nephew. His reputation had spread through the capital like wildfire; who did not know of him? Recognised or not, Lu Chengqian had no choice but to acknowledge him.

"Since that is the case," Gu Xiao said, his smile unchanged, his tone meaningful, "should you not be on your way?"

The words were calm. The firmness beneath them was not.

He shifted his body with an ease that looked casual, and yet in that single movement he placed himself between Su Wan and the scholar. His stance did not threaten, but it blocked all of Lu Chengqian's possible paths forward, leaving no space for persistence.

A flash of unwillingness crossed Lu Chengqian's eyes. In the end, he could not linger. He bowed again and withdrew.

Su Wan lowered her lashes. Her fingertips tightened around the edge of her handkerchief, then slowly loosened as relief crept in. The breath she had not realised she was holding finally escaped.

Indeed, as Qin Nianyin had said, she should not have gone near the water.

* * * * *

Gu Xiao watched Lu Chengqian's retreating figure until it faded into the distance. The coldness in his brow and eyes dissipated little by little. When he turned back, his expression returned to his usual open cheer, as if the sharpness from a moment ago had never existed.

"Young Lady Su," he said, and there was a rare touch of seriousness in his voice. "In future, when you go out, it would be prudent to bring more attendants. The capital looks peaceful on the surface, but in the shadows there are many with ill intentions."

Su Wan nodded slightly. The lingering unease still showed in her face, faint but present. "Just now… thank you, General Gu, for resolving the situation."

"It was nothing." Gu Xiao lifted an eyebrow, brisk as always. Then his tone shifted, matter-of-fact, as if what he said required no explanation. "Besides, you are Su Zhang's own sister. Naturally, I should look out for you a bit more."

Something stirred in Su Wan's chest. She lowered her eyes and asked softly, "If that is the case… what about Lady Qin? Does she also count as a 'younger sister' in your estimation?"

Gu Xiao paused. For a heartbeat he looked genuinely taken aback, and then he could not help but laugh. Under the moonlight, his handsome features lit with that spreading smile, bright enough to be almost dazzling.

"That is not the same." His voice dropped, low and firm, the certainty in it unmistakable. "My heart is inclined towards her."

As soon as the words left him, a flash of vexation crossed his eyes, lingering like a splinter he could not pull out. His tone cooled abruptly, jealousy barely restrained.

"It is just that Su Zhang has taken her to Jiangnan."

He articulated the name "Su Zhang" with particular emphasis, as if the syllables themselves tasted bitter.

Su Wan listened, her heart sinking slightly. She turned her face away to hide the complexity in her eyes. In her hand, the handkerchief tightened again, the fabric creasing under her grip.

So that is how it is.

Chapter 61: My Care

The courier station stood nestled beside a murmuring stream. A damp chill, born of the recent rainfall, seeped through the window seams, carrying with it the fresh, earthy scent of wet foliage.

Within the inner chamber, the lamplight burned low, its feeble glow struggling against the oppressive air. The closing aroma of medicinal herbs lay heavy, barely masking the underlying metallic tang of blood.

Each breath she drew was saturated with the inescapable, bitter astringency of the decoction.

Consciousness returned to Qin Nianyin with agonizing slowness. Her awareness drifted, buoyed and submerged in a turbid, watery darkness. When her eyes finally fluttered open, the light outside the window had deepened from a pallid dawn grey to the profound indigo of approaching dusk.

The slightest movement sent a searing pain, like a lick of flame, shooting through her shoulder and back. She drew a sharp, involuntary breath and only then did she hear the exceedingly soft query from behind the painted screen: "You are awake?"

Su Zhang parted the curtain and emerged. He still wore the same blue robe, unchanged from before, its front marred by faded, washed-out bloodstains.

Dark shadows of fatigue lingered under his eyes, yet his composure remained unshaken. It was only at the precise moment he witnessed the tremor in her lashes that his formidable self-restraint seemed to tighten imperceptibly.

Recognizing the figure before her, Qin Nianyin could not suppress a frown. "Why is it you?" she asked, her voice a dry rasp. "Where is Mei?"

"Do not move just yet," he instructed, bypassing her question. He leaned forward, retrieving the bowl of medicine warming on the bronze brazier. He brought it to her lips, the steam curling faintly between them. His voice was hushed, almost a whisper. "It is bitter. You must endure it."

She turned her face away slightly. "I will manage myself," she insisted, her voice hoarse and faint.

He did not argue. He merely placed the bowl securely within the reach of her fingertips but did not withdraw his presence entirely ——the pad of his finger rested lightly on her wrist, as if gauging the strength she could muster.

Qin Nianyin lowered her gaze and, after a moment's hesitation, accepted the bowl.

Pressing her lips together, she swallowed the concoction mouthful by painful mouthful. The bitterness was a sharp blade on her tongue, yet its very intensity served to push back the wave of dizziness threatening to overwhelm her.

"The medicine is finished," she announced, setting the empty bowl down, her voice still unsteady.

The unspoken message hung clearly in the air between them: You may leave now.

He took the bowl from her, his demeanour suggesting he had not registered her implicit dismissal.

She fell silent, offering no further comment. A moment later, as if a thought had suddenly occurred to her, she asked again, softly, "Where is Mei?"

"Keeping watch in the outer chamber," he replied, his gaze steady upon her. "I will see to changing your dressing now."

Her fingertips tightened their grip on the bedding. "That is not necessary. Summon Mei to attend to it."

He was silent for a beat, a visible effort of restraint. After a brief pause, he stated, "I have been the one changing your dressings these past several days."

A longer silence ensued from her. "It is truly improper to trouble you so, Cousin."

"Nianyin, the words I spoke that day stand. I must naturally assume responsibility ——"

"Say no more ——" A cough cut her off. The sudden motion tugged viciously at her wound, wrenching a sharp hiss of pain from between her clenched teeth. "Let this matter be laid to rest. Do not speak of it again."

Su Zhang's gaze remained fixed upon her, profound and unreadable. The flickering candlelight cast shifting patterns of light and shadow across the sharp planes of his face. Finally, he posed the question in a low voice, "You... are unwilling?"

"Yes!" The reply left her lips without a moment's hesitation.

The swiftness and finality of her answer struck him with unexpected force, causing his heart to stutter in his chest. Driven by instinct, he pressed further, "Why?"

"Cousin is, by nature, a paragon among men, a gentleman of peerless jade-like quality. Nianyin harbors no intention of aspiring to such heights…" Another cough racked her frame, stealing her breath.

Seeing her agitation escalate, Su Zhang moved swiftly forward, his hand rising to pat her back and ease her breathing. But she shifted away from his touch with unmistakable deliberateness, leaving his raised hand suspended in the air, a mere three inches from her.

"Do not agitate yourself," he urged, a thread of concern weaving through his steady tone. "You will risk reopening the wound. You must understand, while you are a cousin of the Su family, we share no blood tie. Moreover, my family holds no particular regard for ——"

Qin Nianyin turned her head away fully, presenting her back to him in a gesture of clear and final refusal. "No more. I am weary. Cousin, you should also take your rest. Let Mei attend to me."

Confronted with her unwavering resolve, Su Zhang had no choice but to temporarily swallow the words poised on his tongue. Within the voluminous sleeves of his robe, his long fingers clenched into fists, the knuckles standing out white against the strain.

* * * * *

The following morning, a thin mist still clung to the world, reluctant to disperse. Mei entered With a basin of hot water, her eyes rimmed with red, her footsteps so light they seemed to tread upon cotton.

As she carefully loosened the bandages, the dark, bruised stain of blood seeping through the gauze on Qin Nianyin's shoulder was revealed. Mei's hands began to tremble. "Young Lady…"

"Mei."

Tears welled in Mei's eyes, her nose sniffling. "Young Lady lost so much blood… this servant was terrified."

"Do not fear." It was Su Zhang's voice. He had come to stand behind them, methodically laying out the medicinal powders and fresh gauze. "Proceed as the physician instructed."

Qin Nianyin frowned. Why was he still here?

He did not overstep the bounds of propriety, only offering support by holding her forearm when she needed to turn. His palm was warm and steady. T

he application of the powder sent a sharp sting deep into the wound, forcing beads of cold sweat to her skin. Qin Nianyin bit down on her lower lip until a faint trace of blood bloomed there.

Mei, flustered, fumbled with the bandage, tying it into a stubborn knot she couldn't undo. Su Zhang reached over, his knuckles deftly working the knot loose and securing the dressing with practiced efficiency. His tone remained perfectly even. "Next time, proceed more slowly."

Mei assented repeatedly. Once the maid had withdrawn, the room settled back into silence. Qin Nianyin leaned against the pillows, consciously regulating her breath, one slow cycle after another. From outside the window came the sound of birdsong, fragmented and distant.

"Yesterday…" he began suddenly, his voice as light and dry as a fallen leaf, "I made myself clear. Upon our return to the capital, I will inform my parents and dispatch a matchmaker to formally propose marriage."

Qin Nianyin looked at him but did not speak. A long moment passed before a faint; shallow smile touched her lips.

She lowered her eyelids. "Cousin, when I took that arrow, it was not to demand anything in return. It was merely ——" She paused, as if searching for the right words, " ——merely an instinctive act."

He observed her for a while, an expression hovering between a smile and something else on his face. His voice dropped very low. "I know."

Instinctively, she had protected him with her life.

He refused to believe she held no affection for him whatsoever!

She lifted her gaze and met his eyes squarely. Her heart clenched inexplicably. His gaze held something she couldn't name ——it was not the familiar aloofness of the past, nor was it coldness. It was a determination that advanced upon her with the relentless force of a rising tide.

"Rest now," he said, carefully smoothing the quilt over her. "We will change the dressing again this afternoon."

The words "Let Mei do it" formed on her tongue, but in the end, she swallowed them unspoken.

She understood clearly in her heart that once he had settled on a course of action, she possessed no power to alter it.

"Sleep a while longer," he stated mildly. "Once you have recovered your strength, we will continue our journey."

His words, like a hidden needle, pricked delicately at her heart. She averted her eyes, fixing her gaze silently upon the patterns of light and shadow playing across the papered window.

* * * * *

On the second day, her fever subsided somewhat, only to return with the fall of night.

Hovering in the liminal space between wakefulness and sleep, dreams and reality overlapped like shifting tides: the relentless rain of her past life, the piercing arrow of this present one, the faint tremor of wind chimes under eaves and the sound of someone's breath, disconcertingly close to her ear.

Her lashes grew damp, a fine layer of cold sweat coating her brow. Suddenly, a warmth covered her forehead ——a palm With a mingled scent of medicinal herbs and faint tea. With exceptional patience, he repeatedly wiped the moisture from her skin.

"Drink some water." He helped her sit up, supporting her to lean against his shoulder. She rested there for a moment before realizing her weight was almost entirely supported by him and made a flustered attempt to sit upright. A sharp pain shot through her shoulder and back, disrupting her breath into ragged gasps. Su Zhang's voice was low. "Do not move."

His tone was never raised, yet it carried an undeniable, compelling force. Qin Nianyin ceased her struggles, allowing herself to remain in that fleeting haven of stability for a few precious breaths.

She could hear the deep, steady rhythm of his heartbeat from within his chest, like a drumbeat, pulling her back from the brink of confusion, one measured thud at a time.

"Su Zhang." She suddenly called him by his full name.

Hearing her address him so directly, his chest constricted violently. A strange, nameless agitation rushed from the core of his being out to his limbs, the final, swallowed syllable escaping as a soft exhalation from his throat.

"Mm."

"Do not speak again of 'assuming responsibility'." Her eyes remained closed, her tone feather-light, yet each word was enunciated with perfect clarity. "I owe you nothing. And I have no wish to use this as a pretext to become a pawn in anyone's game."

He was silent for a long time, so long she thought he would not answer. Finally, his reply came, uttered so softly it was almost inaudible. "Very well. I will not utter those two words again." He paused, the silence itself weighted with meaning. "But I will act upon them."

Her lashes lowered gently. She did not speak again.

Chapter 62: I Will Walk on My Own

On the afternoon of the third day, the rain finally stopped and the clouds broke apart. Pale light filtered through the eaves, and the relay station, which had felt sealed in dampness for days, seemed to breathe again.

A palace attendant arrived with a sealed missive from the Crown Prince. Xiuyan waited in the outer corridor, head lowered, hands folded, not making a sound. Only when Su Zhang called did he step forward.

Su Zhang read the communiqué from beginning to end without changing expression. When he finished, he slid the command slip into his sleeve and spoke in a calm, clipped voice, as if issuing orders on a battlefield rather than in a lodging house.

"Divide our personnel into two groups again. Prepare both overt and covert forces. Double the patrols inside and outside the relay station. Keep two physicians in attendance at all times."

Xiuyan acknowledged at once. "Understood." He withdrew without hesitation, already turning the orders over in his mind and measuring what needed to be rearranged.

Su Zhang turned back into the inner chamber.

Qin Nianyin was already half upright. She was attempting to bind her hair on her own. The movement was painfully slow, her fingers threading through dark strands and hairpins as though she were wrestling with the pain itself. Each time her arms lifted, the strain tugged at her shoulder and back, and her breath tightened faintly.

Su Zhang stepped closer. "Let me."

She startled, instinctively wanting to refuse, yet the moment she tried to raise her hand again the pull of the wound stopped her. After a brief pause, she murmured, very softly, "The hairpin. Shift it slightly to the left."

He adjusted his gesture according to her direction. The velvet-flower pin settled askew in her black hair, one bright point of colour, like a touch of spring caught on morning frost. When his hands withdrew, he took half a step back, and only then realised his own heartbeat had not remained steady.

"Thank you," she said, so quietly it was almost swallowed by the hush of the room.

He answered with a noncommittal sound, his tone even. "From here, if we travel another two li by evening, we will reach the next relay station. If you can endure it, we depart tomorrow."

"I can." She did not hesitate. The reply came too quickly, too cleanly, as if she refused herself the option of wavering.

By early morning, the procession rolled out of the relay station. Wind from the river docks carried the scent of damp grass and wet earth. The stone steps beneath the mountain gate were slick with residual moisture. Su Zhang signalled Xiuyan to proceed ahead, while he himself walked at Qin Nianyin's side.

They did not speak. Yet their footsteps fell into a quiet, matching rhythm, as though they had agreed without words to place each step on the same stone.

When they entered a secluded side courtyard, the morning temple bells sounded in the distance. Each resonant peal travelled across the air and lingered, long and slow, as if the sound itself had weight.

Beneath the covered corridor stood an empty long couch. Wind swept through the walkway and made the lamp flames tilt and flicker, as though even the fire could not keep its balance. Qin Nianyin paused there for a moment, then suddenly said, "Mei, fetch my cloak."

Su Zhang studied her. "Are you cold?"

She shook her head. "To cover my shoulders."

"It's unnecessary for now. Use mine." Without further comment, he unfastened his own cloak and draped it over her shoulders, arranging it with steady hands.

The cloth carried the scent of wind and medicine. The moment it settled, a memory rose without warning. Years ago, on a night she did not speak of, her father had once draped a robe over her in much the same way. The warmth of that old gesture, long gone, returned as an ache that had no name and nowhere to go. Her chest tightened, faintly, as if something inside had been nudged awake.

"If this journey proceeds smoothly," she said after a moment, voice controlled, "there will be a great many people present on the day the statue is erected."

"There will," Su Zhang replied. "You must stand at the forefront."

She lowered her gaze and let out a small, almost unreadable smile, neither affirming nor denying.

Just before dawn on the fourth day, Qin Nianyin was roused by the faint sound of fabric brushing against itself. The lamp still burned. In its light, she saw Su Zhang at the desk, grinding ink, his back a silent silhouette against the steady glow.

At the sound of her stirring, he turned at once. "Did I disturb you?"

"No." Her gaze rested on him without moving away.

He set the brush down, crossed the room, and sat on a small stool beside her bed. His posture remained composed, but his attention was fixed with an intensity that did not soften.

"The wound," he asked quietly. "Does it still hurt?"

"It's much better." She shifted slightly. "Only a little itch remains."

"Do not scratch." His hand caught hers as it moved towards the bandage. His fingers were firm, not gentle, but not harsh either. "It will inflame."

She withdrew her hand quickly from his grasp, as if the contact itself startled her more than the admonition. Her eyes darted aside, avoiding the heat of his gaze, avoiding whatever it was in him that felt too close.

He did not explain further. She did not press. Between them there existed a subtle understanding. They did not dissect every nuance, but when the road demanded it, they could place their feet on the same path without being told.

Su Zhang rose and brought warm water for her to rinse her mouth. She took it, then spoke abruptly, as if the thought had been lodged in her throat for some time.

"Some time ago, the Third Prince intercepted me at a tavern. He said the matter of the stone statue carried some of his credit as well, and he pressed me to remember his kindness."

Su Zhang's eyes paused for the slightest instant. Then he gave a faint, controlled smile, as if nothing in the world could truly surprise him. "Indeed. He contributed some effort."

She watched him, and a subtle curve touched her own lips. "Then I truly owe him a debt."

"Regarding this matter, do not trouble yourself." His voice remained level. "I will address it."

He adjusted the lamp, lowering the flame. "Return to your rest."

She closed her eyes. Night hung from the beams like a heavy drape, pressing into every corner, leaving no space for the mind to wander without touching something sharp.

In the darkness, her voice came soft and clear. "Su Zhang."

He answered at once. "Hm?"

"On this journey, I will walk on my own," she said. "No matter where it leads."

He was silent for one measured breath, then replied, "Understood."

After a pause, he added, the words low, almost restrained to the point of pain. "And I will be at your side."

He did not say protect. He did not say take responsibility. Only at your side. It felt like an unspoken boundary drawn between her autonomy and his resolve, a line neither of them named, yet both of them recognised.

The lamp finally guttered out.

Beyond the window, the river murmured, a hushed, distant conversation that never ended. Lulled by that sound, she sank into deep sleep, into a dream without arrows and without rain, filled only with slanting sunlight and velvet flowers.

Over the next two days, the procession altered its route.

Her injury improved day by day. At first she could sit up unaided. Then she could take a few steps while supporting herself against the window ledge.

Finally, she managed to stand by the stone couch for the length of a burning incense stick without swaying. Each small recovery loosened the tension in Mei's face; colour returned to her expression, and her eyes no longer looked permanently on the verge of tears.

Su Zhang did not relax his vigilance for a single moment.

By day, he attended to documents, route arrangements, and travel logistics, reading reports and issuing instructions with the same steady precision. By night, he still personally inspected her wound. The amount of medicine he applied was never too little and never too much. His hands remained impeccably steady. His words remained few.

Sometimes he sat in silence beneath the window, lamplight flickering, the tip of his brush moving softly across a scroll. The room would be quiet except for the scratch of ink and the faint shift of flame.

Qin Nianyin, half awake at times, would glimpse his profile cut out by the firelight. His presence felt near enough that she could almost reach for it, and yet immeasurably distant, as if some invisible space remained between them that neither dared to step across.

In those moments, she suddenly could not tell whether the ache pulsing in her chest came from the old wound at her shoulder and back, or from a heart remembering a former life.

On the third night, he came as usual to change her dressing.

Mei carried in water and then withdrew, tactful enough to retreat to the outer corridor without being told. The room was left with only the two of them, the air heavy with medicine and quiet.

The instant the medicinal powder touched her skin, she could not suppress a slight tremble. Su Zhang's fingertips tightened, as if his own breath had caught along with hers.

After a long moment, she said abruptly, as if testing the sound of the words. "Had you not come, they would have managed competently."

"I know," he replied evenly, without looking away from the bandage. "But I needed to see for myself."

"See what?" she asked.

He did not answer.

Silence spread like invisible ripples across the wooden floor, widening, pressing outward, leaving nowhere to hide from what was not being said. A considerable time passed before he finally murmured, voice low.

"To see you safe."

She turned her face away at once, refusing to let him witness the fleeting warmth that sparked in her eyes. And strangely, the pain in her shoulder and back did not feel quite as sharp.

Another day dawned, clear and bright.

The moisture of Jiangnan drew nearer at last. The wind carried the scent of rice fields, and the astringent sweetness of mulberry leaves. A report arrived from the forward relay station. Thirty li ahead lay the boundary of Jiangning.

Su Zhang stood at the river dock with his sleeves gathered, watching a line of white sails billow taut in the wind. The water looked calm, but the currents beneath were never simple. Everything in Jiangnan was like that.

Xiuyan came to receive instructions regarding their route. After a few quiet words, Su Zhang turned and re-entered the building.

Qin Nianyin could now bind her hair herself.

Before the bronze mirror, she pinned the velvet-flower hairpin in place, paused, then removed it and replaced it with a more subdued blossom, plainer in colour, quieter in presence. When she saw him, she rose and offered a slight bow.

"I am ready to proceed."

"Slowly." His voice was controlled, but his attention went straight to the injury. "Mind your wound."

His hand moved instinctively to support her elbow. The moment his fingers touched her sleeve, he released her again, as if catching himself. She gave no sign that she noticed. She only offered a faint smile, calm enough to make the gesture seem like nothing at all.

"Jiangning is near," she said. "I want to see the embankment first."

"The embankment first," he affirmed with a slight nod. "Then the stone."

Their eyes met, and neither looked away.

It was as if what each of them held in their hearts, her resolve and his obsession, had been distilled into these two simple statements. Plain words, ordinary words, yet carrying a weight neither of them named.

Wind swept across the threshold and lifted the hem of her robe. Qin Nianyin tightened her grip on her handkerchief and turned.

Su Zhang followed, half a step behind.

As the door closed, the medicinal scent within had not yet fully dissipated, but it was already being replaced by the river breeze, cool and damp, carrying the promise of a different world ahead.

That wind seemed to have a voice, as if saying that from this moment on it would be difficult to tell where one ended and the other began.

The road ahead still held uncertainties. But their hearts were settled.

She walked through the doorway step by step. He followed beside her in the same measured rhythm, neither overstepping nor falling behind.

Chapter 63: Exorbitant Taxes and Miscellaneous Levies

In the early autumn of Jiangnan, the river embankment was squared off with fresh earth. Grass had not yet found time to sprout. Both banks were festooned with red silks.

The air vibrated with the clamour of gongs and drums. Beneath makeshift canopies, vendors sold steaming osmanthus-sweetened lotus root, stuffed buns and bean curd pudding.

The crowd surged like a tide towards the curtained area at the levy's head. They all strained to catch a glimpse of the Honourable Virtuous Official's countenance.

Qin Nianyin stood at the crowd's rear margin. Mei stood a step behind her. Wind puffed from the water's surface, with a damp, raw odour.

She gathered her cloak closer, drawing a deep breath. This familiar scent from her childhood stung at her eyes, threatening tears.

"Miss," Mei murmured, her own voice thick with emotion, "to be back… it truly is good."

A child nearby cradled a small cloth tiger in both hands. He craned his neck to ask his mother, "Mother, are we to kowtow to Lord Qin today?"

The woman's face glistened with perspiration, yet her eyes shone with delight. "We must. Lord Qin saved our homes and our fields all those years ago." She glanced back at Qin Nianyin and added, smiling, "You have also come to give thanks, miss?"

Qin Nianyin offered a faint smile. "I have come merely to see."

When the curtain dropped, a collective inhalation swept the common folk. The stone statue towered over ten feet tall. It was clad in official robes, a jade belt cinched at its waist. Its features were dignified, bearing an eighty or ninety percent resemblance to Qin Shouyi.

Gilded inscriptions filled the base in orderly lines: 'The new embankment stands completed, ensuring the peace and security of the myriad families. Advocates and overseers ——' followed by the names: Cao Ji, Seal-Keeper of Jiangnan Prefecture; Tongpan Liu Xiao; several village chiefs.

At the place of the signature, one name was carved excessively large and deep. It seemed almost to strain, wanting to leap from the stone itself.

A wave of acclamation erupted at once. "Honourable Virtuous Official!" "We kowtow to Lord Qin!" Some wept. Some laughed. Others pressed forward homemade glutinous rice cakes.

Someone cried out, "Lord Qin was incorruptible! He would not want our ritual offerings!"

Another voice echoed, "Lord Qin was a true Virtuous Official!"

Qin Nianyin did not step forward. Her gaze lowered, settling intently upon the seams of the foundation. Her expression darkened immediately.

——The stone was coarse, with chips and gaps. Chisel marks appeared fresh. Even the inlaid gold powder was not yet fully dry. She turned. She moved slowly with the flowing crowd, walking around to the statue's rear. There, she crouched. With her fingertip, she lightly brushed a corner. Her finger came away dusted with gold powder and grime.

"What is the meaning of this?"

Mei, after one look, also observed, "Miss, the workmanship of this statue seems rather crude."

"A rushed endeavour," she uttered under her breath.

Su Zhang was jostled by the populace to the statue's front. His lapels were tugged by one pair of rough hands after another. He raised his hands, steadying people, urging them not to kneel. Beside him, Cao Ji beamed, his eyes nearly vanishing into his face.

He cupped his hands and announced loudly, "This was the spontaneous wish of the elders! This official merely presided, claiming no merit. The virtue of Lord Qin's flood control in his time deserves the incense and reverence of all people!"

"Who spoke of wanting incense?" Qin Nianyin's voice was not loud, yet it sliced clearly through the gongs and drums. She positioned herself before the inscriptions. She raised a hand, tracing the deeply carved signature. She turned her face slightly, a very faint smile touching her lips. "It is, nonetheless, carved with considerable force."

Cao Ji, caught by her glance, stiffened slightly. "This young lady…?"

"The people's donated silver carved your names with such neatness." She retreated half a step. Her gaze swept over the several donation boxes nearby. The scale beams and pans beside them gleamed with grease.

The counterweights were darkened from handling. A thin man before a donation box was quietly exhorting, "Even a single coin adds up,

accumulating small into great, to erect a virtuous statue for Lord Qin —
—"

Qin Nianyin approached. She reached out, lifted a counterweight and
hefted it in her hand. Suddenly, she smiled. "Quite heavy."

The thin man hastened to say, "The young lady has a keen eye! This
weight is full measure ——"

Qin Nianyin placed the counterweight back. Her fingers brushed over
the notches on the scale beam. "The markings seem shifted somewhat
forward." She lifted her eyes to Su Zhang. Her gaze was quiet and cold.
"Short measures and light weights, accumulating small into great… it
rather aligns with your slogan, does it not?"

A wave of murmuring passed through the crowd. Cao Ji's countenance
altered. He stepped forward, cupped his hands with a strained laugh.
"The young lady must misunderstand. These are all voluntary actions by
the elders. How would we dare any private gain?"

Qin Nianyin disengaged from further dispute with him. She lifted her
skirt slightly. She walked a slow circuit around the statue's base. She
stopped at another section of the inscription ——where, in fine script, a
list of "contributing merchants" was densely carved. It even included
items like river-crossing fees, scale taxes and boat taxes. She tapped it
with her finger. "These… are newly established collection items, beyond
the embankment work itself?"

Cao Ji gave a dry laugh. "Merely temporary necessities ——"

"Temporary necessities?" Qin Nianyin looked back towards the crowd.
"That woman there, may I ask how many times your household has paid
the river-crossing fee this year?"

The woman who had been holding her child earlier answered timidly,
"Three times… Each time they said it was needed for the embankment
repairs."

"Your embankment is repaired now." Qin Nianyin looked at her, her
smile exceedingly gentle. "Will they still collect it?"

The woman stared blankly. Her lips trembled slightly. "They… they said
the accounts are not yet settled."

At this moment, Su Zhang, who had been standing silently aside, finally
spoke. His voice was not raised, yet it subdued the scene. "You dare to
enrich yourselves under the guise of the court's decree? Such audacity."

"Su ——Su, Your Excellency... This is all... the intention from 'above.' This lowly official merely..." Cao Ji trembled from head to toe, almost unable to stand upright.

Su Zhang cast a cold glance upon him. His voice was like iron. "Do not speak nonsense. Henceforth, not a single coin unrelated to the embankment works is to be collected. Seal-Keeper Cao Ji, submit all account ledgers to the prefectural office in their entirety. Within three days, I require sight of every entry, every stroke."

Cao Ji's sleeves shook. His expression shifted rapidly. Finally, he assented with a strained smile. "Yes."

The crowd's noise dispersed slowly. The setting sun cast its light obliquely upon the water. Its rays stretched the statue's silhouette into a long shadow. Qin Nianyin stood within the shade. For a long time, she did not speak.

Su Zhang approached her. His voice was low. "...Regarding the statue today, you were subjected to impropriety."

"You are not at fault." Her tone was mild. Her fingertips toyed with the wooden bead at her sleeve. Her gaze alighted upon his chest, then moved away. "The fault lies with these corrupt officials. Is rectifying such matters not precisely why Your Excellency Su is here?"

"It is." He followed her words. A trace of a smile and a touch of gravity resided in his eyes. "We cannot allow these contemptible individuals to besmirch the unsullied reputation Lord Qin maintained throughout his lifetime."

Qin Nianyin lifted her head to look at him. She was silent a moment. "My adoptive parents showed me kindness as weighty as a mountain. What I myself cannot accomplish, Your Excellency Su achieves for me now. I thank you here, in their stead."

He gazed at her, his expression subtly stirred. The wind lifted the wisps of hair at her temples, pressing them against her ear. Su Zhang averted his eyes. "Must you persistently address me as 'Your Excellency Su'? Do not forget, Lord Qin was also my maternal uncle."

She looked at him. A thread of wariness lay within her gaze.

Su Zhang released a soft sigh. "When you first entered the Su residence, you called me 'cousin' several times. Why has it grown more distant since?"

She pressed her lips together. Struck by the faint, almost elusive note of regret in his words, a fine, sharp ache bloomed in her chest. Ill at ease, she turned her face away. Her line of sight returned to the tall, yet undeniably crude, statue.

The benevolent visage of her adoptive father superimposed upon the cold stone image before her. Grievances from a former life and gratitude in this one tangled intricately, like knotted hemp in her heart.

Uncertain how to respond to this complicated, inexpressible sentiment, she could only suppress the tumult, settling it into a semblance of placid indifference. "Given the context of our official duties now, addressing you as 'Your Excellency Su'… feels more comfortable."

He stood beside her. He did not speak further. He simply watched quietly with her. The statue's shadow, drawn long by the setting sun, fell between their own shadows. It resembled a boundary, both separating and connecting them.

Chapter 64: Sealing the Accounts and the Granary

The prefectural office under the night sky resembled a dark crate. Two lanterns flanking the main hall flickered in the wind, their flames wavering, casting dancing shadows on the walls. The courtyard was so quiet one could only hear the chirping of autumn insects.

As Su Zhang traversed the covered corridor, Xiuyan followed behind, arms laden with scrolls upon scrolls of ledgers. Qin Nianyin walked beside him, holding a lantern.

After Xiuyan deposited the ledgers on the desk, Su Zhang opened the first one. The scent of ink carried a hint of dampness, mixed with fine grit ——clearly copied in haste and hastily hidden away.

Seal-Keeper Cao Ji, summoned to stand below the dais, had dishevelled robes and hat, yet sweat beaded on his temples. He looked at the thick stack of account books on the desk, a strained smile plastered on his face. "Your Excellency Su, these are merely informal circulating records, hardly reliable ——"

"Let this official examine them carefully before deciding," Su Zhang said, not looking at him. He simply raised a hand, opened the ledger and his fingers skimmed rapidly over the numbers.

They paused at one entry: 'River-Crossing Fee,' collected three times in ten days, the amounts increasing each time. The 'Scale Tax' notches were shifted forward half a point ——this half-point equated to ten taels of silver. "Are you using the lives of commoners crossing the river to fulfill your duties to the court?"

"Your Excellency Su!" Cao Ji's voice rose sharply.

Su Zhang ignored him. He unfurled another scroll. "This is the donation ledger. The front pages list commoners' names. The latter pages are… the roster of merchants. How strange.

Why are the merchant names identical to those on the 'Embankment Materials Supply' page in another account book? 'Supply' comes first, 'Donations' follow ——did you first receive donations from the merchants, then use those donations to buy materials from those same merchants?"

You could have heard a pin drop in the hall.

"A truly clever scheme. Procuring embankment materials requires no silver at all. In fact, this way, all the funds allocated by the court end up in your pockets."

Su Zhang tapped a knuckle lightly on the edge of the desk, his voice low and even. "Seal-Keeper Cao Ji, how do you explain these accounts?"

Cao Ji swallowed, the smile on his face widening. "Common folk affairs have always been handled thus. Your Excellency Su governs waterworks. Why be so particular about these minor details of money and grain? Moreover, the erection of the statue was an imperial decree. It genuinely unites the people's hearts, sharing the court's concerns ———"

"The people's hearts are not your playthings. You exploit Lord Qin's unblemished name to collect donations..." Su Zhang interrupted him, his tone calm. "Erecting the stone statue was indeed the court's decree, for which public funds were already allocated for Lord Qin's memorial ———not for you to collect private sums from the people."

Cao Ji's smile finally cracked. A cold glint flashed in his eyes. "Your Excellency Su, you come from the capital. Can you truly be unaware of whose pockets this silver ultimately fills?!"

Su Zhang's gaze rested on him for a moment. "Then you tell me. Whose pockets does it fill?"

"This..." Cao Ji's eyes darted around, his face alternating between pale and flushed, unsure whether he should divulge the truth.

Su Zhang gave a cold laugh. "Magistrate Cao, at this moment, you should be considering three things.

First, who authorized these newly established collection items?

Second, whose idea was it to have the donation ledger and the supply ledger overlap?

Third, from which budget item were the funds for the statue diverted?"

Cao Ji opened his mouth, but the words caught in his throat. The lantern light suddenly dipped lower in the wind. Qin Nianyin turned her face slightly, her gaze sweeping past the hall's entrance ———there were scattered footsteps, as if someone was loitering in the courtyard.

"And one more thing." Su Zhang picked up the final ledger, glanced through it and suddenly smiled. "This page is interesting. This column records three dan of lime, two dan of white sand. Yet what I saw at the embankment today was fresh, unpacked earth and crumbling stone seams. Where did the lime and white sand go?"

Cao Ji's head jerked up. Beads of sweat slid down his forehead, falling into his collar. He trembled, forcing a laugh. "Your Excellency has a keen eye… This… this is merely negligence by this lowly official ——"

Su Zhang closed the ledger. He placed his palm flat on the paper surface, the wooden bead on his finger pressing a shallow impression. "Magistrate Cao, if you still remember those elderly folk kneeling and kowtowing on the embankment today, cease using this official jargon as a shield."

"Your Excellency, this lowly one was only following orders!" Cao Ji's face was red, his tone vehement.

Su Zhang's voice was icy. "The lady you saw on the embankment that day is the daughter of Qin Shouyi, named Qin Nianyin. Magistrate Cao, you exploit the court's decree and Lord Qin's posthumous reputation for personal gain. And Lord Qin was my own maternal uncle. Tell me, does that grant me the right to ask a few questions here?"

Su Zhang suddenly stood up, his robes brushing past the corner of the desk. "Guards!"

Two yamen runners entered. His voice was steady. "Seal the accounts. Seal the granary. Seal-Keeper Cao Ji is to be temporarily detained, pending further investigation when the imperial envoy arrives from the capital."

The lantern light in the hall flickered, the atmosphere pressed down to the point of suffocation.

Cao Ji was now drenched in sweat, pinned firmly beneath the dais by two yamen runners, his knees nearly crushed against the floor. His lips were pale, his voice trembled uncontrollably. "This lowly one… this lowly one was only following orders!"

Su Zhang's voice was icy. "Whose orders?"

His knuckle rapped sharply on the desk, the sound falling like a hammer blow. "Speak!"

"This… this…" Cao Ji's throat seemed knotted, his eyes darting wildly, veins bulging at his temples as if wrestling with an internal war.

"If you do not confess in full detail, this official will immediately order the arrest of your entire family ——"

Upon hearing this, his face turned deathly pale. His body went limp, as if the last supporting bone had been broken. His voice suddenly rose sharply, edged with a nearly hysterical sob. "It was ——it was the Crown Prince!"

The words echoed abruptly through the hall, striking straight against the roof beams.

The yamen runners started uniformly. Xiuyan drew a sharp breath. The lantern in Qin Nianyin's hand swayed, its flame shuddering as if on the verge of extinction.

Having shouted it, Cao Ji himself seemed stunned. His lips quivered uncontrollably, as if he had just realized he had uttered the unspeakable. His body went completely slack, his forehead knocking hard against the floorboards as he trembled repeatedly. "This lowly one… this lowly one deserves death, this lowly one deserves death…"

Su Zhang's eyes darkened abruptly. He let out a cold laugh. "Preposterous slander! Guards ——drag him away!"

As the two runners stepped forward, the furtive footsteps outside the hall suddenly grew louder. A small crowd had gathered at the courtyard gate, holding lanterns, hesitating to enter.

Someone whispered, "I heard they're investigating the accounts now." Another voice added, "Finally, a Virtuous Official has come!"

Qin Nianyin turned her head and saw the woman who had been holding her child standing at the front, her lantern shade made of homemade paper, a few smudges of dirt in the corners.

She recalled the woman's words from the daytime ——"We must kowtow" ——and a pang of sorrow struck her heart, which she forcibly suppressed, directing her gaze instead to Su Zhang's profile.

He was also looking at her.

It lasted only a moment, like the moment a gust of wind suddenly steadies a flickering flame. In his eyes, she saw a concealed light —— self-reproach, a protective instinct and an unspoken, aching tenderness.

She lifted her eyes to meet his and offered a faint smile. "I am not standing in front of you, either."

His hand rose instinctively, gently touching her right shoulder where the arrow had struck. His voice was hoarse. "Here… does it still pain you?"

She immediately evaded his touch. His hand could only fall back to his side, helplessly.

"Just a slight ache, that's all. Your Excellency Su need not concern yourself."

Su Zhang stiffened slightly, then nodded. "Regarding the matters to come, I will send official dispatches." He paused, lowering his voice. "You need not always place yourself in front of me…"

"I haven't…"

As these words fell, a vast emptiness seemed to open between them, leaving no words to bridge it. From outside the hall, someone shouted, "Your Excellency Su is a Virtuous Official!"

Another voice cried out, "Your Excellency Su is a good official!"

The yamen runners acknowledged the order and departed. The lantern light flickered again, illuminating the lines of her profile ——fine yet hard, like a blade freshly honed.

Su Zhang stood in place, watching her figure until it disappeared into the shadows of the corridor. Only after a long moment did he finally withdraw his gaze.

A sudden chill seized him, as if the river wind had found its way beneath his robes, blowing straight against his heart.

Chapter 65: Crisis on the Frontier

In the Capital

Within the court, the political winds blew fiercely. Urgent dispatches from the northern borders arrived one after another in the main hall. Beacon fires once again rose from the frontier towns, each character in the reports sharp as a blade.

Gu Xiao stood amidst the ranks of officials, watching the memorials being passed to the imperial desk. A dull ache throbbed in his chest.

——His father and elder brothers had all fallen in battle, purchasing decades of peace for the frontier with their blood and bones.

and he? He was kept in the capital, clad in brocade robes, bearing a military officer's rank, yet trapped day after day within vermilion walls. He watched civil officials debate military provisions, unable to set foot himself upon that wind-swept, sandy land.

As the debate raged endlessly around him, his hand clenched into a tight fist inside his sleeve. His blood surged, hot and restless, almost breaking through his skin.

A sudden, stark understanding dawned on him: if he remained confined to the capital for the rest of his life, allowing his aunt to arrange everything for him ——be it his career or his marriage ——he would ultimately become a caged beast, a existence worse than death.

——This is not what living should be.

A voice roared repeatedly in his breast: "If I cannot go to the front and fight the enemy, I have no face to confront the spirits of my father and brothers in the afterlife."

In that moment, the scales in his heart finally tipped.

He made his decision: No matter how his aunt, the Empress, might try to obstruct him, this time, he would seize back control of his own path.

* * * * *

The weather in the palace had turned cool. Leaves from the parasol trees fell one by one onto the blue-brick paths, crunching crisply underfoot.

Gu Xiao walked through the long, covered corridors. The main hall was brightly lit. The Empress was reviewing reports with her palace maids. Seeing him enter, her gaze softened. "Xiao, you've come. Good. Your aunt was just about to speak with you."

"Yes, indeed. Xiao also has words for Aunt."

"Your aunt has sent people to inquire about the one who holds your affection…" She paused, her eyes holding a mix of pity and resolve. "Her background is too humble. It would be a slight to you, unworthy of the Gu family."

A tightness gripped Gu Xiao's chest, but a stubborn light ignited in his eyes. "Worthy or not is for me to decide. It is her that I desire."

"Ah-Xiao ——" The Empress frowned. "This is not to your detriment, but for your own good. If you marry her, your future prospects ——"

"Future prospects?" He let out a sudden, cold laugh, his voice trembling with suppressed emotion. "Aunt, in this life, I have already followed your wishes, remaining in the capital, turning away from the battlefield. And now, can I not even marry the woman I love? Is this what you call 'future prospects'?"

He bowed in formal salute, but when he straightened, the usual levity was absent from his face. He simply looked directly at the Empress.

Noting his unusual expression, her smile faded. "What is it? You seem burdened with heavy thoughts lately."

"Aunt, the reason for my visit today is indeed to report a matter of great importance." Gu Xiao shed his customary playful demeanour, his expression uncharacteristically solemn.

The Empress's heart gave a sudden lurch. "Xiao, what is it? Why this countenance?"

"Aunt, as the Empress, you must already be aware that the border crisis is critical." Gu Xiao's voice was low, but it could not suppress the turmoil beneath. "I have requested to be sent to the front."

The memorial in the Empress's hand trembled. A sharp glint flashed in her eyes before she softened her tone. "Do not speak nonsense! The Gu family has only you, its sole male heir left. How can you take such a risk?"

A heavy weight settled in the Empress's chest. She sought to explain further: "Ah-Xiao, you must understand, all of this is for you, for the continuation of the Gu family line ——"

"This is not for my good!" Gu Xiao suddenly interrupted her, his voice rising, his eyes flashing crimson for an instant. "Aunt, do you know, there are times when Xiao truly feels life holds little meaning. If I could achieve glory on the battlefield like my father and brothers, even death in combat would be preferable to being trapped here in the capital, subjected to these endless calculations day and night!"

The Empress's face paled drastically. She rose abruptly, her sleeve quivering in the lamplight. "You will not speak of this again! The Gu family has only you! You absolutely cannot go to the battlefield!"

Silence filled the hall, so profound one could hear a pin drop.

Gu Xiao breathed heavily, then suddenly lowered his gaze, his voice growing calmer, yet colder. "If you truly insist, I remain here, then do not hinder me from pursuing her. She has never promised me anything. She has never even looked directly at me. But she is the only thought that makes me feel life is worth living."

A sharp pain stabbed through the Empress's heart. Her breath quickened; for a long moment, she could not speak. The lantern flame flickered, stretching the shadows of her shock and anger long and deep across her face.

Gu Xiao finally lifted his head. His eyes were like steel tempered in fire, each word enunciated with perfect clarity. "Aunt, you may protect my person, but you cannot protect my heart. My resolve is firm."

* * * * *

In the Palace

The autumn ambiance deepened within the palace grounds. Winds whispered through the groves of red maple trees, their shadows rustling as leaves fell.

The hall was brightly lit. The Empress sat in the seat of honor, yet her expression was colder than the lamplight.

Gu Xiao bowed in salute. When he raised his head, his eyes and brows were sharp as blades. "Aunt, the Tiger Guard Army at the frontier has been defeated. The enemy forces are now pressing close beyond the passes. Although I am the last of the Gu line, to shrink back in the capital now would be the true disgrace to our family's name!"

The Empress's face changed. She rose abruptly. "Xiao! Do you not understand this journey holds life and death in the balance? Your father and brothers all died on the battlefield. Your aunt has exhausted her efforts to protect you until this day, hoping precisely for the continuation of the Gu bloodline!"

Gu Xiao's fists clenched tightly, but his voice remained low, steady and unshaken: "Precisely because of this, I cannot act the coward. If the descendants of the Gu family only know how to cling to safety, who will remember the blood and bones of my father and brothers? Aunt, you wish to protect the Gu family's reputation. Here and now, the proper course is to let me stand upon the battlefield!"

The Empress felt a violent tremor in her chest. Her fingers clutched tightly at her sleeves.

He took another step forward, his voice firm as iron. "I ask Aunt to set her heart at ease. I will not recklessly discard my life. If I return, the frontier stabilized, His Majesty will undoubtedly place even greater reliance upon you. Your position within the palace will be unshakable."

Silence filled the hall. The lantern flame flickered, stretching the shadows of the Empress's internal struggle long across her face.

She gazed at him, finally releasing a low, shuddering breath. "Your resolve is fixed?"

Gu Xiao nodded firmly. "It is."

The Empress was wordless for a long moment, the rims of her eyes reddening. She slowly reached out a hand, as if to stop him, but ultimately let it fall. "So be it… Go. But promise your aunt ——you will return safely."

A flicker of emotion passed through Gu Xiao's eyes. He bent slightly at the waist, his tone resolute. "I will return safely."

In that moment, the lamplight cast his silhouette straight and tall. The Empress stared blankly, suddenly feeling she could no longer control this young man ——he was no longer just the orphaned son of the Gu family, but one truly about to set foot on the sands of war, to strive for that glory forged in blood and fire.

* * * * *

The Eastern Palace

Late night in the Eastern Palace. Lamps burned quietly.

The Crown Prince closed the last secret missive, a faint smile touching his lips.

The letter stated clearly: The Second Prince had ordered Cao Ji, the Jiangnan Seal-Keeper, to add the words "Crown Prince" to the official records, wishing to use this to implicate him in injustice before the court.

"Just as I thought," he said softly. "Second Brother has outsmarted himself this time."

His advisor, Du Mao, could not help but whisper, "Your Highness, since we know it is the Second Prince's scheme, why not report it first to prevent losing advantage at court?"

The Crown Prince shook his head, his expression mild and unhurried. "In recent years, my brothers and I have exhausted methods planting spies in each other's ranks. Our Father Emperor abhors fraternal strife above all. If I were to expose it first, I would inevitably be seen as overly forward and on the contrary, Father would begin to suspect me of having a petty or narrow mind."

He paused, his gaze lowering to the candle flame, his voice growing even quieter. "Tomorrow, we need only wait quietly for the truth to reveal itself. Second Brother's step-by-step scheming suits my purposes perfectly. When that forged entry appears in the court and Minister Su examines it closely, Father Emperor will perceive everything with discerning clarity."

Du Mao remained uneasy. "Your Highness does not fear long nights invite many dreams?" (i.e., complications may arise)

The Crown Prince smiled slightly, his demeanour composed. "Our spies report that Second Brother has no further moves to make. Tomorrow, he will deliver himself into Father Emperor's grasp with his own hands."

The candle flame jumped, illuminating his gentle expression, making it appear all the more poised.

It seemed all of this was merely a process of waiting quietly for the flower to bloom.

Chapter 66: A Sincere Thank You

The Jiangnan night was deep, the river swollen, its surface reflecting the moonlight like a peacefully unfurled silver screen.

Su Zhang and Qin Nianyin walked side-by-side along the embankment. The wind carried the faint, sweet scent of rice ears. The common folk on either side had gradually dispersed, leaving only the night watchman tapping his wooden clapper in the distance.

Su Zhang spoke abruptly, breaking the quiet. "The people's praise for Lord Qin this day was genuinely heartfelt. I believe that once this statue is erected, it will further proclaim my uncle's achievements, ensuring his fragrance endures for a hundred generations."

Qin Nianyin's fingertips lightly traced the blue bricks of the levy. Her voice was very soft. "The people's sincerity is real. It is just that I…" She paused, seeming to weigh her words.

Somehow, perhaps it was the overwhelming beauty of the moonlight, or perhaps the vindication of her family's name ——suddenly, a feeling of utter exhaustion washed over her.

Su Zhang turned his head to look at her. Under the moonlight, her features were pale and serene yet held a profound weariness.

"Just that what?" he asked.

She lowered her gaze with a faint smile, tinged with bitterness. "Cousin, you may not know… In my childhood, after the first great flood, I became a refugee. I never knew my birth parents. I was fortunate to be adopted by my foster parents and found shelter. Though our family was not illustrious, I was cherished. They treasured me as one would a pearl or jade; my elder brother protected me. At that time, I truly believed my whole life would be like that."

Her voice gradually softened. "But then another great flood came and once again, my family was destroyed, my loved ones lost. It was only after that I understood… sincerity, protection… they can turn to ashes in a single night. Your Excellency Su has probably never known the taste of true hunger."

A tightness gripped Su Zhang's chest. Each of her words felt like a stone dropping into the cavity of his ribs.

He had studied legal codes since youth, later entered officialdom, achieved success while young ——his path had been smooth, sheltered.

How could he comprehend the flavour of "having one's entire world obliterated overnight"?

He had always believed that reading countless case files, adjudicating numerous injustices, amounted to "understanding the people's hardships." But looking at her profile now, he suddenly understood —— the blood and tears in written words and the blood and tears lived firsthand, existed in two entirely separate realms.

In that moment, he even felt a sense of shame. Had she not unburdened herself today, had he not witnessed what he had these past few days, he, Su Zhang, might never have truly grasped the suffering of the world.

His gaze remained fixed on her face. The gentle breeze stirred, tousling a few strands of her hair against her cheek, but it could not hide the trace of aching sorrow in her eyes.

He said, his voice low, "The suffering of the people is the responsibility of the court."

Qin Nianyin did not deny it, only offered a light smile. "That is why, when I saw the statue today, my heart was also in turmoil. It wasn't because of the names on the statue, but because of the people… Their willingness to dig into their own pockets to build it… that sentiment, I cannot help but be moved by."

She halted her steps, looking toward the tall statue at the levy's head. In the night wind, its contours stood out with a stark, almost glacial clarity, the moonlight dragging its shadow long across the ground.

"They truly remember." Her voice held a tremor for the first time. "So, what my parents did… it was not in vain."

Su Zhang reached out a hand, but stopped mid-air. He wanted to tuck that stray lock behind her ear, but ultimately restrained himself, saying only, "The contributions made by Lord Qin and his wife… there will always be those in this world who remember."

Qin Nianyin turned to look at him. The coldness in her eyes was somewhat less than usual, like ice beginning to thaw, revealing a hint of soft water beneath.

"Your Excellency Su," she said softly, a smile touching the corners of her lips. "For today's matters… thank you."

This "thank you" was different from the cool politeness of days past. It held a genuine gratitude within it.

Su Zhang's heart shook violently. In that moment, he even felt that all the people's cheers, all the accolades and praise for his achievements, could not compare to this single sentence from her.

"It is this official's duty. You… need not thank me."

But Qin Nianyin shook her head with a soft laugh, whispering, "You… do not understand."

She was not only thanking him of today, but also the whim of her past life ——who had ensured she wanted for neither food nor clothing in both lifetimes, who had freed her from the fear of her family being destroyed and loved ones lost.

Even though him of that past life had not loved her, the care and honour he had bestowed upon her then and the enduring fame secured for her foster father in this life, were tangible debts of kindness.

* * * * *

The night over the Jiangnan prefectural office was profound and heavy. Wind howled through the corridors, causing the two lanterns flanking the main hall to flicker violently, their shadows dancing erratically on the walls.

The atmosphere within the hall was austere and suffocatingly still. Only the occasional pop and crackle of the candle flames intertwined with the soft rustle of turning pages.

Su Zhang sat upright behind the official desk, his robes settled heavily around him, his expression severe and cold. Xiuyan stood by head bowed attentively, arms cradling thick ledgers. Qin Nianyin sat quietly to the side; the lamplight falling across her features rendered them pale and detached.

Cao Ji knelt before the desk, his attire dishevelled, his topknot askew. Cold sweat beaded on his forehead, trickling down his temples, yet he dared not lift his head.

He heard the methodical turning of pages, each rustle like a hammer blow against his heart.

Suddenly, Su Zhang's finger halted on one page. His brows slowly drew together.

He lifted his gaze, his voice low and cold, yet it cut through the night air like a blade's edge. "...Here. This is incorrect."

Xiuyan hurriedly leaned closer. The page specified ——'Fifty thousand taels of silver, designated exclusively for His Highness the Crown

Prince's disaster relief.' Yet the accounts preceding and following it failed to connect seamlessly. The silver's whereabouts were unaccounted for.

"Young Master, for the Crown Prince's disaster relief… didn't the court allocate separate funds?" Xiuyan ventured cautiously.

Su Zhang responded with a cold laugh. He slammed the ledger shut on the desk.

His gaze, sharp as a knife, fell upon Cao Ji kneeling below. "Disaster relief funds require a directive from the Ministry of Revenue and disbursement from the inner treasury. This page lacks the Ministry's seal. The handwriting differs from the previous page. The ink shade is not even consistent ——it's still fresh. Magistrate Cao, do you present such a crudely fabricated record to frame the Crown Prince?"

"This…" Cao Ji's face turned ashen. His lips and teeth chattered. Cold sweat streamed down his brow.

Su Zhang suddenly rose to his feet, his robes swirling. His voice was as cold and sharp as the snap of frozen iron. "The Crown Prince, embezzling? Preposterous! This is clearly a last-minute addition. Cao Ji, if you truly dare to falsely accuse the Eastern Palace, that constitutes the crime of deceiving the Emperor! Punishable by the extermination of your entire clan!"

He enunciated the final four words slowly, each one striking like thunder.

Cao Ji shuddered violently. His legs nearly gave way; his body trembled uncontrollably.

Qin Nianyin, watching from the side, felt her own heart constrict. In the flickering light, she saw the icy gleam in Su Zhang's eyes ——a gaze that seemed capable of tearing a person apart.

"I… I…" Cao Ji's throat worked, his voice dry and hoarse. "This lowly one… was only following orders…"

Su Zhang took a step closer, his palm striking the ledger heavily. His voice was low yet razor-sharp. "Whose orders?!"

Deathly silence filled the hall, broken only by the sputtering of the lamp wicks.

Su Zhang tapped a knuckle lightly on the desk. His voice was frigid. "Cao Ji, this official asks you: earlier, before everyone, you implicated the Crown Prince. Now, you turn and accuse the Second Prince. Your words are full of contradictions. Is there a single shred of truth in your mouth?"

Cao Ji's face altered dramatically. His lips trembled; his eyes darted about shiftily, as if a fatal weakness had been exposed. Yet he still stubbornly persisted. "This lowly one… is wronged! I was only following orders…"

"Whose orders?" Su Zhang's gaze was piercing. His voice dropped even lower. "The Crown Prince? Or the Second Prince? Or… is it someone else entirely?"

He suddenly slapped the ledger hard, its pages fluttering. "Here, fifty thousand taels, marked 'Crown Prince disaster relief,' yet the accounts are broken before and after, the silver untraceable. You think such a clumsy forgery can escape this official's notice?"

Qin Nianyin's cold voice added from the side, "You believe that merely scribbling the words 'Crown Prince' allows you to shirk responsibility? The mouths of the people will not permit you to distort the truth!"

Su Zhang's eyes darkened further. His voice fell like an iron hammer. "This official gives you one final chance. If you continue to prevaricate and conceal, tomorrow your entire family will be thrown into the dungeons. Your clan will be exterminated, leaving you no chance of ever recovering!"

"I… I…" Cao Ji trembled from head to toe. His eyes rolled wildly. His lips quivered incessantly, yet no sound would emerge.

Su Zhang's gaze remained fixed on him, sharp as a honed blade, chilling him to the core.

Finally, as if the last supporting bone in his body had snapped, Cao Ji collapsed utterly. His forehead struck the blue brick floor with a heavy thud. His voice was ragged, broken:

"It was ——it was the Second Prince!"

The cry was almost heart-rending, shocking the yamen runners in the hall into visible dismay.

Xiuyan drew a sharp breath. The lantern in Qin Nianyin's hand wavered slightly, its flame guttering as if on the verge of extinction.

Su Zhang, however, remained unmoved, his expression unaltered.

He merely issued a cold command: "Guards, take him into custody. Seal the accounts. Seal the granary. All documents are to be meticulously catalogued within three days and submitted to the capital."

"Acknowledged!" The runners responded, dragging Cao Ji away.

The lantern light in the hall illuminated Su Zhang's profile, stern and unyielding as iron.

He lowered his gaze, looking at the ledgers on the desk, yet a shadow stirred in his heart.

The Second Prince... while he harboured ambitions for the throne, could such intricate planning and cunning truly be his alone?

His eyes grew darker. He murmured under his breath, "This scheme... may not belong solely to the Second Prince."

Qin Nianyin lifted her eyes to look at him, her heart suddenly tightening. This man, standing squarely in the storm's eye, remained so calm and decisive, single-handedly protecting the Crown Prince's integrity.

She whispered softly, "If my father's spirit in heaven knows of this, he would surely be at peace."

Su Zhang started at her words, turning to look at her. A misty light shimmered in her eyes, though she struggled to suppress it, allowing only a faint smile to touch the corners of her lips.

"Your Excellency Su... thank you."

Su Zhang's chest constricted violently. In that moment, he felt that even the people's cheers, the accolades of fame and achievement, could not compare to this single, sincere "thank you" from her.

——Heavy as a mountain, yet it ignited a flame within his heart that refused to be extinguished.

Chapter 67: Framed

The main hall of the capital was sombre, the beat of the drums heavy. Officials stood in rows on both sides, the air frozen solid. Only the candle flames wavered in the draft.

At the hall's entrance, Su Zhang strode in, holding a thick stack of case files in his arms.

"Your subject, Su Zhang, pays his respects to His Majesty."

The Emperor lifted his gaze, his expression unreadable. "The Jiangnan case. Is there a result?"

"Reporting to Your Majesty." Su Zhang bowed, then placed the files heavily upon the imperial desk. His voice was clear and resonant. "Over three years of water management in Jiangnan, funds allocated totalled three hundred thousand taels.

 Less than one-third was actually used.

The remaining two hundred thousand and more flowed entirely into the hands of over a dozen officials and local powerful families. Your subject has thoroughly investigated the accounts and testimonies one by one. This case implicates a wide circle. It is not the private corruption of one man, but the rot of an entire region!"

A wave of astonishment swept through the hall.

The Second Prince smiled faintly, his eyes sweeping over the Crown Prince. Just wait until the Crown Prince's name is revealed, he thought inwardly, see how he defends himself then.

The Emperor's face was overcast, but he remained silent, his gaze fixed on the files.

Su Zhang opened the second volume, his voice rising again. "Furthermore, within the accounts, there is an entry stating 'Fifty thousand taels of silver, designated exclusively for the Crown Prince's disaster relief.' This entry is fabricated. These funds never reached Jiangnan at all."

Upon these words, an uproar filled the hall. The Second Prince could not suppress the upward curve of his lips, his eyes nearly smiling.

The Crown Prince's face turned pale. He seemed on the verge of speaking, but stopped himself.

Just as the atmosphere in the hall congealed, Su Zhang suddenly paused. His voice deepened. "However ——"

The entire assembly held its breath.

" ——upon detailed examination of the files, your subject discovered that the handwriting for the words 'Crown Prince' differs from the preceding text. The ink is also fresher, clearly added later. Cross-referencing with testimonies reveals that Cao Ji, the Jiangnan Seal-Keeper, acting on a secret decree from the Second Prince, intended to frame the Crown Prince!"

"What!" Exclamations of shock erupted throughout the hall.

The Second Prince's face changed drastically. He immediately shouted, "Preposterous! You, a mere Director of Appointments from the Ministry of Personnel, dare to make such vicious and unfounded accusations!"

Su Zhang responded with a cold laugh. He flung another scroll heavily onto the floor of the hall. Several account books spilled open, the handwriting distinct. "Here is Cao Ji's written confession in his own hand, corroborated by the testimony of over a dozen officials. Second Prince ——the evidence is irrefutable. Do you still deny it?"

The Second Prince's face alternated between livid and pale. He whirled around. "Father Emperor, your son has been framed!"

The Emperor slammed his hand on the desk. The sound shook the hall, causing all officials to bow their heads in unison. "Silence!"

The hall fell utterly quiet, save for the crackling of the candles.

The Emperor's gaze, sharp as a knife, fell coldly upon the Second Prince. "You, a Prince of the Blood, do not contemplate assisting your brother. Instead, you engage in fabrication and false accusation, seeking to place the Crown Prince in an unjust position! Guards!"

"Here!" The guards responded in unison.

"Take the Second Prince to the Imperial Clan Court! Await their investigation and clarification before deciding his punishment!"

The Second Prince, Li Xuan, his face deathly pale, was forcibly restrained by the guards. He still cried out hoarsely, "Father Emperor! Your son is innocent! Innocent! This matter… it was not done by your son…" His voice faded into the distance, finally suppressed beyond the palace gates.

The hall returned to silence.

That momentary hesitation was quickly swallowed by the silent, flickering lamplight.

The officials in the hall collectively held their breath. None dared to lift their heads.

The Emperor drew a deep breath and turned his gaze to the Crown Prince, his tone slightly softer than before. "Crown Prince, in this Jiangnan case, you were originally wronged. Fortunately, Minister Su has clarified the truth. Do you understand the stakes involved here?"

The Crown Prince, Li Duan, prostrated himself in a kowtow, his voice trembling. "Your son understands! I thank Father Emperor for his discerning judgment! I thank Minister Su for his rescue!"

The Emperor looked again at Su Zhang. A trace of approval finally flashed in his eyes. "Minister Su, a scholar, can distinguish loyalty from treachery, safeguarding the stability of the state. You are truly a pillar of the court. Your merit in this case shall be recorded in the Veritable Records."

Su Zhang lowered his head in a deep bow, his sleeves sweeping over the cold imperial steps. Yet in his heart, he understood perfectly ——the uproar filling the hall at this moment was merely the beginning of the prologue.

* * * * *

Autumn

A crisp autumn breeze swept through the Su residence courtyard as the lanterns were about to be lit.

The sound of hoofbeats came from beyond the gate. Just as Qin Nianyin was about to enter the estate, she looked up and saw Gu Xiao approaching, With a small wooden cage. Inside, a snow-white kitten poked out its head, mewing plaintively with innocent eyes.

"Xiao Bai?" Qin Nianyin was taken aback.

Gu Xiao set the cage down, his eyes unable to conceal his reluctance. "I am departing for the frontier. Xiao Bai has a mischievous nature and with no one to care for him… I can only trouble you to look after him temporarily."

Qin Nianyin gazed at him quietly for a moment, then bent down to take the cage. Xiao Bai stretched, leaped out through the cage door and with practiced ease, jumped into her arms, purring and rubbing against her palm.

No one to care for him?

Could the entire Marquis' estate truly find no one to care for a single cat?

The courtyard fell silent for a beat. Gu Xiao's throat tightened. He said in a low voice, "When I return, you can give him back to me… alright?"

Qin Nianyin lowered her head to play with Xiao Bai. She had intended to refuse once more, but the thought of his imminent departure for the borderlands made her hold back the words of refusal.

"Then, I will care for him for now. You… must return safely."

She bowed her head, her thoughts churning. She felt she had forgotten something, but no matter how hard she tried, she couldn't recall it.

Gu Xiao stared at her, his lips moving several times before he finally asked, "Then… will you wait for me?"

Qin Nianyin started, then shook her head, her voice leaving no room for doubt. "I will not. Even if you asked me one hundred times, my answer would remain the same. Everyone has their own path. General Gu has chosen to go to the frontier. On behalf of the common people, I thank you and the Tiger Guard Army for your sacrifice. But in matters of the heart, I will not wait."

It felt like a heavy blow to Gu Xiao's chest, yet he only offered a low laugh, tinged with bitterness. "I won't listen. You don't have to agree, but I promise I will return as quickly as I can."

He paused, his eyes suddenly turning sharp. "During this time, could you please… not consider anyone else. Especially ——Su Zhang."

Qin Nianyin was stunned. She lifted her eyes to look at him, a trace of bewilderment surfacing in her gaze. "Why… does everyone assume I have feelings for him?"

"Promise me?"

Qin Nianyin nodded. "I promise you."

She would not consider Gu Xiao, nor would she consider Su Zhang. Indeed… she would not consider anyone!

The wind rustled through the treetops, With away her unanswered question. Gu Xiao did not reply. He simply turned, his spine ramrod straight and walked away.

Qin Nianyin looked down. Xiao Bai purred in her arms, softly nuzzling her palm. Yet she felt a profound heaviness in her heart, unclear whether it was for Gu Xiao, or for those specific words ——"especially Su Zhang."

* * * * *

In the Capital, Spring Bright Tavern

In the capital, within a private room on the second floor of the Spring Bright Tavern overlooking the street.

Outside the window, lanterns stretched like a river of stars, the bustle of the market streets unceasing. Inside, however, only two men were present. The wine vessel stood clear and cool, a half-burnt candle guttered on the table.

Gu Xiao drained his cup in one go and set it down heavily. "The Jiangnan mission, which you spearheaded, has finally concluded successfully. This memorial reached the capital, greatly pleasing the Sacred Emperor. You ought to be pleased with yourself."

Su Zhang smiled slightly, raising his cup in return. "You are the one truly poised for great achievements. This journey to the frontier, if you return victorious, will secure military glory for generations to come. I, Su, offer you a toast in advance."

Their cups met with a clear, resonant clink.

After a moment of silence, Gu Xiao suddenly turned his head, his gaze intense. "Zijun, before I depart, I have one thing to say."

"Speak."

"We are brothers, after all. I ask only one thing of you ——before I return, do not make your move first." Gu Xiao's tone was grave, as if suppressing a fire within his heart. "I intend to win her heart myself."

"Her?" Su Zhang let out a cold laugh. "To whom do you refer?"

Gu Xiao snorted softly. "You are an intelligent man. You must have seen it long ago. Don't play the fool. I, Gu, admire your little cousin."

Su Zhang's eyebrow arched. He slowly set down his wine cup, his voice cold and direct. "I beg your pardon, but that is a request I cannot grant. Regarding her, I am also determined to succeed."

The atmosphere instantly tightened. The candle flame jumped in the draft.

Anger rose in Gu Xiao's eyes, the veins on the back of his hands standing out, as if he might throw a punch the next moment. But his fist, clenched halfway, suddenly loosened.

He laughed coldly. "Forget it. Even if you have such intentions, when has your little cousin ever looked at you directly?"

Su Zhang's expression darkened and he immediately retorted, "Oh? Did she tell you that she returns your affections?"

At these words, Gu Xiao was struck speechless.

The two men stared at each other for a long moment, then simultaneously let out a derisive snort.

Gu Xiao shook his head. "Heh. It seems neither of us has the upper hand. Well, that sets my mind at ease."

Su Zhang raised an eyebrow, draining his cup in one swallow. "You don't have the upper hand. It's impossible for her to be moved by you."

"Hah, likewise," Gu Xiao sneered.

They drank again together. The aroma of wine rose between them, the atmosphere shifting from the brink of conflict to a tart, unspoken understanding.

Finally, Gu Xiao raised his cup, his voice low but firm. "A final cup, a final word ——take care of yourself."

Su Zhang met his gaze and finally raised his own cup, draining it completely.

The candle flame flickered. Between the two men lay both rivalry and a deep-seated camaraderie. The night wind howled outside the window, carry that single "take care" into the endless streets, as if etching their brotherhood into the clear, potent liquor of this shared drink.

Chapter 68: An Apprenticeship Sought

After returning to the capital, Qin Nianyin found no peace within her heart. The Jiangnan campaign had concluded, the purge of corruption was complete, and the turmoil had been temporarily pressed down. Yet she understood with painful clarity that if she wished to secure a foothold within this fraught and chaotic political landscape, relying solely on momentary wit and timely luck would never be enough.

She needed her own foundation, something that belonged to her alone, something that could not be taken away with a change of wind at court.

Therefore, she began to search.

She inquired after the legendary hairpin artisan renowned for peerless skill, the craftswoman whose name still drifted through the markets like a half-remembered refrain. This person had long vanished from the official artisan registers, her whereabouts difficult to trace.

Qin Nianyin asked from the southern city to the western market, following scraps of hearsay, paying for tea and rumours, hearing a dozen false leads for every one that sounded remotely true. At last, the trail led her into a remote, dilapidated neighbourhood of broken paving stones and collapsing eaves, where even the daylight seemed reluctant to linger.

A neighbour, leaning in a doorway with an indifferent expression, mentioned offhandedly, "You're looking for her? Why bother? That old woman stopped taking apprentices years ago. Drunk all day, a complete soak. If you have silver to spare, spend it elsewhere."

Qin Nianyin refused to give up. She waited at the doorstep for an entire day, standing through dust and idle stares, letting the hours pass without moving.

Finally, as twilight descended and the dying light of sunset stained the street entrance a deep crimson, a figure came swaying unsteadily into view. The person wore shabby, worn clothes, carried a half-full jug of wine, walked with a stumbling gait, and hummed a fragmented, intermittent tune as though the melody itself could not be bothered to remain whole.

Qin Nianyin was taken aback. Was this the legendary master artisan?

As the figure drew nearer, she could see it was an elderly woman, her face etched by wind and frost, her hair carelessly pinned, her gaze blurred at the edges by drink. Qin Nianyin had assumed it would be an old male master, a stern craftsman with a long beard and soot-blackened hands. Instead, this was a woman who looked like she had been worn down by years, not merely aged by them.

The woman's voice was hoarse, her tone carrying the weight of fatigue. "Little girl, what are you doing stationed here?"

Qin Nianyin stepped forward and bowed in a formal salute, earnestly stating her purpose.

The old woman narrowed her eyes, looking her up and down several times. Suddenly, she laughed, a sound full of scorn. "You? This craft is no pretty occupation. You deal with fire and stone daily, smoked and scorched by fumes until your lashes are damp, tears and sniffles streaming constantly. It is bitterly arduous. Someone of your delicate, pampered appearance likely wouldn't last a few days."

Qin Nianyin's expression remained unmoved, yet her voice was steady. "I am not afraid."

The old woman raised an eyebrow, tilted her head back for another swig of wine, and sat down unsteadily on the doorstep as if her bones were made of loose joints. "It's not that I refuse to teach you. But do you know I can only produce one full headdress set a year? You think I'm lazy? No. It's because kingfisher feathers are exceedingly rare. To gather enough for a complete set of hair ornaments often takes a full year of struggle. Without adequate materials, the finest skill is useless."

Qin Nianyin stared blankly for a moment, a pang of sorrow striking her heart. So that was the reason. No wonder this craft was famously never taught to outsiders. No wonder its finished works were so exceedingly few.

She said softly, "So that's how it is…"

But soon, she lifted her head, her gaze sharpening into resolve. "Even so, I still beg to acknowledge you as my master. I understand the rarity of kingfisher feathers and dare not make presumptuous demands for them. Yet if I can learn a true skill to rely upon, in the future I can strive to prevail through ingenuity. With novel and clever designs, they may still find favour. But without establishing a foundation in genuine craftsmanship, any amount of clever thought is ultimately hollow."

The old woman stared at her. The mockery in her eyes gradually faded, replaced by a glimmer of latent interest, as though something long dormant had been lightly tapped.

"Little girl…" she murmured, the corners of her mouth slowly twisting into a faint smile. "Heh. Such bold words. Very well. This old woman will see for herself just how long you can endure."

* * * * *

The old woman's eyes were half-lidded, as if the wine's influence had not yet lifted. Suddenly, she let out a low, gruff chuckle.

"Little girl, what did you say your name was again?"

Hearing this, Qin Nianyin smiled wryly. Between her previous life and the present one, she was likely the same age as this elderly woman before her. To be addressed as "little girl" now felt absurd in a way that was almost dryly amusing.

"My surname is Qin, given name Nianyin."

"Miss Qin." The old woman made a lazy motion with her wine jug, as though it were a sceptre. "This old woman's surname is Lin. You may call me Granny Lin. Since you possess this determination, you may stay. It so happens I am in need of someone to handle cleaning."

Qin Nianyin was momentarily taken aback, but quickly comprehended what was being tested. Her expression unchanged, she simply performed an earnest bow. "This disciple is willing."

Granny Lin shot her a glance and snorted. "Do not be so quick to call me 'Master.' This old woman has not agreed to accept you yet. If you truly wish to learn, you will start by sweeping floors, fetching water, chopping firewood, and tending the forge. On a day when my mood is favourable, I might deign to teach you a trick or two. If you cannot endure it, see yourself home."

With that, she hugged her wine pot and shuffled, unsteadily, into the house.

The courtyard settled into quietness, leaving behind a scene of disorder: scattered wood scraps, cloths stained with grease, and the sooty ashes of the forge piled where they had fallen. The air itself carried a faint bitterness, like old smoke lodged in timber.

Qin Nianyin lowered her head. Without the slightest hesitation, she hitched up her sleeves, secured her hair more firmly, and began by retrieving a broom.

Daylight faded into dusk. A neighbour peered in through the gateway, observing the scene, and could not resist whispering to another, "Is that girl simple-minded? She's truly intending to be that old drunkard's drudge?"

Qin Nianyin turned a deaf ear, but her sweeping became more diligent. Dust rose in faint clouds around her ankles, grey against the last scraps of light, yet her gaze remained unwavering. She was not here for transient ornaments or pretty decoration. She was here to acquire a genuine skill, one that would allow her to stand on her own feet. Even if it meant starting from the most humble chores, even if it meant being laughed at first, she was willing.

Inside the house, Granny Lin reclined against a table, the wine pot still in her hand. In dim, yellowish lamplight, she watched the small, busy figure in the courtyard through the partially open door. A faint, derisive smile tugged at the corner of her mouth, as if she did not quite believe what she was seeing.

"Foolish girl," she muttered. "She actually stayed."

* * * * *

Qin Nianyin returned from the city districts as dusk neared, the sky deepening toward darkness. Warm light spilled from the courtyard lanterns of the Su residence, yet a heaviness settled in her chest. She knew the words she was about to speak would likely cause Madam Qin distress, and she did not wish to wound her, yet she also knew she could not retreat simply because it was uncomfortable.

She knelt formally in the main hall and began, her tone earnest. "Madam Qin, I wish to learn the craft of jewellery-making. I have found a master and intend to stay by her side for a time, residing there temporarily."

Madam Qin, startled, immediately shook her head. "How could that be? It's dirty and arduous out there. How could it compare to the Su residence? The estate provides everything one could need. What could you possibly lack here? Why must you subject yourself to such hardship?"

Qin Nianyin replied softly, "Do not worry. It is not a permanent departure, merely a period of study. Once I have acquired the skill, I will naturally return."

Just as Madam Qin prepared to protest further, the hall door creaked open and Su Ze entered with measured steps. He glanced at Qin Nianyin, his gaze steady. There was no indulgent softness in his face, yet in his eyes lay the faintest hint of approval, restrained but unmistakable.

"Let her go," he said. "She is young. Going out to temper herself is no bad thing."

"Master." Madam Qin's voice rose at once, threaded with reproach and alarm. "How can you say that? Is our large, esteemed household incapable of supporting her? Why must she suffer this hardship outside?"

Su Ze shook his head, his tone calm. "Do not be upset. Have you not noticed? She does not find true ease of heart within these mansion walls. If we do not allow her to venture forth, her inner discomfort will only grow. This child is not seeking frivolous amusement. She genuinely wishes to accomplish something."

Madam Qin fell silent for a moment. Her heart was tugged in a hundred directions, reluctance and worry tightening her throat until she could not force out another argument.

Qin Nianyin kowtowed, her voice firm. "Thank you, Uncle, for your permission."

She rose and withdrew from the hall.

Only Madam Qin and Su Ze remained. Madam Qin's eyes reddened. "Really… how can we be so permissive? Although she was adopted, my brother and his wife cherished her since she was small. Now, for her to go and perform menial tasks, sweeping floors for others, hands blackened by soot… what face do I have to meet my brother and his wife? It pains my heart."

Su Ze gently patted her hand, soothing her in a measured voice. "Do not fret. Your brother and his wife undoubtedly treated her with immense kindness from childhood. But remember, she endured that great flood disaster. She may be stronger than you think. Perhaps, after tasting a few days of bitterness outside, she will return of her own accord."

Madam Qin bowed her head in silence. A long moment passed before she released a quiet sigh. "I suppose it must be so."

The lantern light flickered, illuminating the worry etched between her brows, a profound concern she could not conceal, no matter how she tried to steady her expression.

Chapter 69: Moving Out of the Su Residence

The night lay heavy. Wind slapped against the lattice windows, and the lamplight wavered, throwing restless shadows across the walls. Inside, the room was so quiet it felt unnatural.

Qin Nianyin sat at the dressing table, folding her garments one by one and laying them neatly into a wooden chest. Each scrape of cloth against wood, each soft rasp of the lid's rim, seemed to press directly onto her chest, dull and weighty, making it hard to breathe as though the air itself had thickened.

Mei hovered beside her, passing her folded cloth wraps and spare ribbons, her eyes tight with panic.

"Young Miss… are you truly going?" she whispered at last, forcing her voice low. "It's bitter out there, wind and rain without end. If that master is really as downcast as the neighbours say, I fear even the place you sleep will be uncomfortable. Let me go with you. At the very least, I can look after you."

Qin Nianyin's hands paused, but she did not lift her head. Her voice was even, steady to the point of severity.

"No. You remain in the Su residence. Looking after Madam Qin is the proper duty. This path, I must walk it myself."

Mei's eyes reddened instantly. She swallowed and tried to speak again, but at that moment the courtyard gate creaked open with a harsh sound, shoved hard from outside.

Cold air rushed in. The lamp flame jolted and bent.

Su Zhang strode in, his robe swept back by his own momentum, the hem still carrying the chill of the courtyard. His gaze locked onto her half-packed chest and the bundle of travel cloth laid out beside it. His face was set, hard as iron.

"You intend to move out?"

"Yes." Qin Nianyin did not soften it. Her answer was simple, final.

"Why?" His voice scraped hoarsely, the word forced out as if it had been held too long.

It sounded like anger, yet beneath it was something sharper and more vulnerable, like a question asked by someone already wounded.

Qin Nianyin's fingers stiffened. She looked up and met his eyes, her gaze cool and blank. She said nothing else. She turned back and resumed folding as though his presence had not altered the room's air at all.

Su Zhang stepped closer in two quick strides. He reached out and blocked her hands, his palm catching her wrist before she could tuck the next garment away. His voice dropped, urgent and pressed.

"Nianyin. I told you long ago, after that arrow, I will marry you. I will take responsibility. I will ensure that you will never lack food or clothing in this life, that you will live in comfort and finery. You… why must you force yourself to such extremes?"

He spoke too fast. His breath came uneven. The insistence in his words left no room for debate, as if this were a conclusion already decided.

Qin Nianyin wrenched her arm free and turned fully to face him.

The lamplight caught the hard edge in her eyes. Her voice struck the room with a clean, decisive force that made even Mei freeze.

"Minister Su. Cousin. I will say this only once, so listen carefully. I am not blessed with such fortune, and I have no desire to cling upward through marriage. I will never accept your promise of marriage. Not now. Not in this lifetime. I would rather become a nun than marry you."

Her words fell like a blade. One cut, clean and absolute, severing every possibility without leaving ragged threads.

Su Zhang stood rigid. Shock spread through his face, and his throat tightened as if he had swallowed something sharp.

"Why?" The question came out raw.

It was a question he had carried too long. In his own mind, he had every reason not to be refused: his talent, his reputation, his rising career, his bearing, his family. No matter which measure one chose, he should not have been turned away.

And yet she would not yield.

Qin Nianyin's chest rose and fell, but her tone remained cold, almost indifferent.

"There is no why. I am not worthy of you. You should be with someone like Shen Lingyan, a noble young lady of an eminent household. A well-matched pair, in status and in name. If you truly mean what you say, then do not waste more time. Do not waste more feeling on me."

Her gaze was sharp, unflinching. Once the sentence ended, she turned back to the table and continued packing as though closing a ledger.

Su Zhang's throat worked. His fists clenched so tightly the joints stood out.

"Not worthy?" His voice trembled. "You think so little of yourself?"

He took a step forward, close enough that the heat of his breath reached her. His hand lifted, almost as if to seize her shoulder, to stop her from turning away again.

"Nianyin, I have never despised your birth. In my heart, you have always been the most…"

"Enough." Qin Nianyin cut him off, cold and forceful.

The light in her eyes was hard, unyielding.

"The more you say such things, the more humiliated I feel. Do you understand what a true mismatch actually is? What you offer me is pity. It is charity. It is not the respect I want."

She did not even bother with softened address anymore. Each word landed heavily, as if she were striking something brittle inside him.

The room became terrifyingly silent. Even the faint crackle of the oil lamp sounded sharp and harsh.

Su Zhang's lips parted. They trembled slightly. No sound came.

The woman before him had once been gentle, once spoken to him with mild warmth, once even laughed in his presence. Now she looked at him the way one looked at a stranger in the street.

Something in his chest seemed to choke. He took a step back without meaning to. His fingertips trembled, betraying him.

"You say… not worthy…" he murmured, and the light in his eyes dimmed bit by bit, as though the lamp inside him were being starved of oil.

Mei stood frozen, staring between them, the atmosphere so heavy it felt like it pressed against the ribs.

Qin Nianyin did not look at him again. She lowered her head, folded the final garment, and placed it in the chest with meticulous care. Then she shut the lid.

Her movements were calm, almost gentle. Yet it was as if she were closing the lid on something else entirely, sealing it down and refusing to let it breathe.

Su Zhang's throat rolled. After a moment, he asked abruptly, voice low and strained.

"Then… the one you desire in your heart, is it Gu Xiao?"

The lamplight shook. Qin Nianyin snapped her eyes up. For a split second, a faint, scornful laugh flashed across her expression, quick as a knife's glint.

Her lips curved coldly.

"What, then? If it is not you, it must be another man? And it must be Young Master Gu?"

Su Zhang went still, as though struck.

Qin Nianyin's smile vanished. Her face settled into a sober, clear severity.

"It is not you. It is not Gu Xiao. There is no one in my heart right now. And in the future, there will not be, either."

For an instant, the only sound was her breathing.

Su Zhang's chest rose and fell sharply. His feelings twisted into something bitter and complex, relief and resentment entangled together. He was relieved it was not Gu Xiao, and yet the thought that there was no one at all only sharpened the truth that he still could not step into her heart.

After a long moment, he gave a low laugh. The sound held no warmth.

"Nianyin. If there is no one in your heart at this moment, then that means I still have a chance."

He stepped forward, not touching her, but pressing closer all the same. His gaze burned with stubborn determination.

"Remember this. I am not someone who speaks of giving up lightly."

Then he turned sharply and strode out. His sleeve lashed behind him like a snapped banner.

The door slammed. The lamplight shuddered.

Qin Nianyin stood alone before the chest. Her fingers were clenched so tightly her knuckles whitened. Pain flickered through her eyes for the briefest moment, and then she pressed it down until her face was smooth again.

Her heart felt cold to the bone.

In these following days, Qin Nianyin's life became a world entirely separate from the Su residence.

By day, she chopped firewood, hauled water, washed clothes until her fingers ached, and squatted in the kitchen for the better part of an hour simply to coax a pot of congee into being. The firewood refused to catch cleanly. Smoke rolled into her eyes until tears streamed down her cheeks, and her hands, unused to such labour, quickly turned red and swollen, roughened by fresh blisters and new calluses.

Granny Lin leaned against the threshold with her wine pot cradled in her arms, eyes half-lidded, watching without a word, as if silence itself were part of the lesson.

Yet on the second morning, Qin Nianyin woke to something that made her still.

A pile of firewood sat by the courtyard gate, split and stacked with unnatural neatness. The clothes in the basin had already been scrubbed clean, rinsed thoroughly, hung in proper order. On the stove, a pot of plain white congee was already simmering, the steam curling steadily as if someone had tended it with patient care.

Granny Lin took a sip of wine and glanced sideways, her mouth tilting into a crooked smile.

"Girl, you are fortunate. Someone is holding you in the palm of their hand."

Qin Nianyin stared for a beat, then lowered her eyes. She did not answer.

In the palm of their hand. That kind of tenderness was precisely what she wanted to flee.

That night, the sky pressed down dark and heavy. She dragged a small stool to the kitchen and kept watch by the weak lamplight, leaving only the faint crackle of embers to keep her company.

Near the third watch, a thin, almost imperceptible sound came from the corner of the wall. Qin Nianyin's fingers tightened. She struck a flint and the lamp flared up at once, light snapping into the room like a whip.

Two dark figures were already withdrawing, but her voice stopped them, crisp and cold.

"Stand still."

In the flickering light, both intruders were women. Their clothes were plain, suited for movement, the posture of trained fighters, their eyes alert and wary. They exchanged a glance, stiff with unease.

"Who are you?" Qin Nianyin demanded.

The two looked at each other. Neither spoke.

"Who sent you?" Her gaze sharpened, cutting straight at them. "Speak."

After a pause, the woman on the left said in a low voice, as if choking on the words, "Su… Su Zhang."

The woman on the right immediately blurted, too fast, as though terrified of being slower than the other.

"It was Young Master Gu. Gu Xiao is very concerned for you, Miss."

The air went rigid.

Qin Nianyin's eyes turned even colder, her voice measured, each word distinct.

"Su Zhang. Gu Xiao."

Both women nodded, uncomfortable and tense.

"What else did they instruct?"

They hesitated, stammering. At last they forced out, "Nothing. Only… to protect Miss Qin, to ensure you are attended properly."

Attended.

Watched, more like.

A cold smile touched Qin Nianyin's lips. Her voice rang out, clear and sharp.

"I do not need it. Leave. Both of you."

The two women glanced at each other, at a loss, and then withdrew stiffly into the night.

Outside, the wind howled. The moment they cleared the courtyard, their restraint snapped like a cord pulled too tight.

"Shameless!" the left one hissed angrily. "You are the one whose concealment was poor. The young lady discovered us and you dragged me into it."

"You have the cheek to speak?" the right one sneered. "If your technique were not so crude, would she have noticed at all? And now you blame me. Disgusting."

"Spare me your twisting tongue."

"Hmph. You learnt the art of shifting blame quickly enough."

Their voices rose. Their bodies shifted. In the next instant, they were trading blows, right there under the moonlight, fists cutting through air, sleeves whipping, the grass and shrubs shaking with each sharp movement.

"One more word and I will cripple your hand."

"Come, then. Let us see who falls first."

The sounds of impact carried through the night, harsh and grating.

Inside, Qin Nianyin heard everything through the half-closed door. She lowered her gaze. Her fingers curled under the lamplight, tightening slightly as a faint ache rose in her chest.

Two men's concern, so fierce it had reached this point. Another woman might have been moved.

She only felt cold.

She did not want to be held in anyone's palm. She did not want a life built on another person's protection, no matter how tenderly it was offered. She did not want to owe her steps to anyone's shadow.

After a long moment, she lifted her hand and covered the lamp flame. The light died with a soft puff.

In the darkness, only her quiet, determined breathing remained.

And a sudden, bitter absurdity rose in her mind: they fought with such blade-bared hostility, yet not one of them had ever asked what she truly wanted.

The road she wanted could only be walked by her alone.

Chapter 70: The Hearth Relit

The covert guard knelt on one knee, his voice low, carrying unmistakable embarrassment. "Young Master… Miss Qin discovered us."

Su Zhang had been reviewing memorials at his desk. At those words, his fingers paused for the briefest instant on the page. Then he lifted his gaze and looked at the man with measured calm.

"She discovered you?"

Fine sweat seeped from the guard's forehead. "Yes. And moreover… the Gu family's covert guards appeared at the same time. Miss Qin seemed to have been waiting in the small kitchen. The moment the lantern was lit, she intercepted both pairs of us. In the end… she ordered us all to withdraw."

Silence settled in the room, heavy and still, as though even the air dared not shift.

After a long moment, Su Zhang suddenly let out a soft laugh—quiet, almost amused—yet a sharp glint flashed deep in his eyes.

"As expected of a brother of many years," he said. "What I can conceive, Gu Xiao can also conceive."

The laughter held a thread of self-mockery, and also a chill.

"One person," he murmured, as if speaking to himself, "yet she compels both of us to station guards by her side at the same time…"

His gaze lowered slightly, and his voice softened into something quieter, more dangerous.

"A woman such as this… who could truly hold her in their grasp?"

The guard dared not answer. He kept his head bowed.

Su Zhang raised his hand and flicked his sleeve lightly. The composure on his face returned, smooth and controlled, as if nothing had occurred.

"Let it be. Henceforth, observe only from the shadows. Unless her life is in peril, do not intervene further."

His tone was calm and unruffled, yet it could not fully conceal the undercurrent that darkened his eyes for an instant—like ink spreading beneath clear water, quick and silent.

The afternoon courtyard held nothing but the shrill, ceaseless noise of cicadas.

Qin Nianyin crouched amid the wild grass, her hands still damp with soil. Her gaze was fixed intently on a circular stone furnace hidden beneath weeds and tangled roots. Cracks ran across its surface, faint traces of soot-black still clinging to the grooves. She traced the edge carefully with her fingertips, the grit rough against her skin.

"This was…" she murmured, voice low, as if afraid to startle the years asleep inside it. "Used for what?"

She remained crouched for a long time, studying it from different angles. In the fissures and scorched seams, there seemed to be the remnants of intense heat—evidence of a fire that had once burned fiercely here, only to be buried and forgotten.

As she was lost in thought, stumbling footsteps sounded outside the courtyard gate. The smell of liquor arrived on the breeze before the person did. Granny Lin shuffled in, clutching a half-empty wine pot, her other hand propped on a broom like a walking stick. She muttered curses under her breath, her voice rasping and uneven.

When she caught sight of Qin Nianyin crouched beside the derelict furnace, she stared for a heartbeat, blank and caught off guard.

Then she burst into loud laughter.

The sound was harsh, bitter, threaded with something that scraped like old wounds.

"Heh! You've got a sharp eye," she said, laughing as though the laugh itself hurt. "Digging out even this old thing!"

She walked over and slapped the furnace wall heavily. The stone gave a dull, dead thud beneath her palm.

"It's a kiln," she barked. "A firing kiln. I wasted the prime of my youth inside this very pit."

Her eyes narrowed, and her hoarse voice rose, as if the memory dragged her by the throat.

"And the result? Coloured glass jewellery, clever artistry—what nonsense. Not a single piece succeeded! Not one!"

Qin Nianyin stared at her. Confusion and doubt flickered across her eyes, not because she disbelieved, but because she could not reconcile the abandoned kiln with the craft Granny Lin was famed for. If this had been such a futile obsession, why had it been built at all? Why had it been kept, rather than smashed?

Granny Lin tilted her head back and took another swig of wine. The laugh that followed turned desolate, like wind whistling through a broken doorframe.

"You're still young. You've got a full life ahead of you," she said, voice suddenly hoarse in a different way. "Where there's comfort to be had, go and enjoy it. Don't end up like this old woman—burying your entire lifetime in a fiery pit!"

Before her words had fully faded, she suddenly swung the broom in her hand and swept it fiercely near Qin Nianyin's feet, sending dust and dry weeds scattering.

"Go!" she snapped, voice raw. "Don't waste your time here! Get out!"

Qin Nianyin was forced to retreat several steps, the broom's bristles nearly brushing her shoes. Yet she showed no panic. No anger, either. Only a deeper, more concentrated contemplation settled into her gaze— like someone staring straight into a wound and refusing to blink.

The ruined stone wall of the kiln and Granny Lin's weathered, vehement face overlapped under the setting sun, forming a stark, poignant picture: one of failure, and of a fire that had once been bright enough to ruin a lifetime.

The morning mist had not yet dispersed when Qin Nianyin walked alone into the backyard.

The confrontation from the previous afternoon—Granny Lin's laughter, her curses, the broom sweeping her away—Qin Nianyin held onto none of it. Not a single word lodged in her heart.

Instead, it was the abandoned kiln that refused to leave her mind.

She rolled up her sleeves and moved the scattered stones covering the kiln's mouth. Dust rose as she pried them loose. The smell of damp earth and old soot clung to her fingers. She began shovelling away the accumulated grime of many years, layer by layer. Where roots had wormed into the cracks, she tore them out with her bare hands, ignoring the sting as the rough fibers scraped her palms.

Her hands grew red and raw. Dirt embedded beneath her nails. Sweat slid down her temples. Still she did not stop.

By the time the sun stood high overhead, the kiln walls had been wiped clean by her hands. The fissures were still patchy and scarred, but the vessel's original shape had begun to emerge once more, like a forgotten backbone straightening after years bent beneath weeds.

She rummaged through corners and under broken boards. To her surprise, she unearthed several old tools: fire tongs, an iron ladle, and half of a mould streaked with rust. Some were warped, some cracked, as if they had been thrown aside in disgust. Yet in her hands, she placed them down carefully, one by one, arranging them as though setting bones back into order.

As if constructing a new world from what had been discarded.

In the afternoon, Granny Lin finally woke. Clutching her wine pot, she swayed unsteadily into the courtyard. The smell of alcohol still clung to her, her eyelids half-drooped, her mouth already set to hurl a few more insults.

But her movements halted abruptly.

She stared at the busy figure in front of the kiln.

Under the sunlight, Qin Nianyin's hair was slightly damp at the temples, loose wisps sticking to her cheeks. Her sleeves were rolled high, her forearms streaked with dust, and her fingers were scraped raw.

Yet her gaze was steady. Focused. Resolute.

In that instant, Granny Lin seemed to see a reflection of her own younger self—a time when she, too, had bent over this kiln, heedless of soot and heat, filled with nothing but the thought: Light it. Make it burn. Make it succeed.

She stood transfixed for a long moment. Then she raised her hand and drank, as if forcing the wine to drown the subtle sting rising in her chest.

"Do as you please."

Her voice was lazy, tinged with scorn, but her eyes betrayed something more complex—something that flashed and vanished too quickly to name.

Qin Nianyin did not turn around. She only pressed her lips into a faint smile and continued polishing the iron tongs in her hand, rubbing at the rust as if it were not merely decay, but a veil to be stripped away.

She knew.

She had taken the first step.

For several days consecutively, Qin Nianyin worked in the backyard without pause. The weeds were cleared entirely. The stone kiln stood revealed, scars and all. The scattered tools were wiped clean, one by one, and neatly arranged.

Granny Lin watched, outwardly indifferent, yet inwardly unsettled. On one evening, she returned with her wine pot, half-drunk and half-awake, but paused in the doorway.

The kiln fire had not yet been relit.

Yet Qin Nianyin's silhouette was brilliantly lit by the setting sun. She bent over, grinding away rust stains from the iron ladle, slow and meticulous, as though handling something precious enough to require reverence. There was no flourish to her movements, no attempt to look graceful—only stubborn, quiet persistence.

Granny Lin remained silent for a long time.

Finally, she let out a "Hmph," thumped the wine pot down on the table, and spoke in a deliberately lazy tone, as if doing so cost her nothing.

"Since you're so stubborn… If you want to learn, start by sorting through that quartz and sand. Not a single impurity is allowed to remain."

Qin Nianyin straightened. Her eyes brightened in an instant, like a lamp catching oil.

She said nothing. She only bowed deeply, formally—so solemn it made the gesture heavier than gratitude.

Granny Lin raised an eyebrow and sneered on purpose, as though to scold away the softness that might rise in her throat.

"Don't celebrate too soon. These are the stupidest, most arduous tasks. Working until your fingers bleed is nothing. I'm afraid you won't last three days."

Qin Nianyin answered with complete seriousness, without even a hint of hesitation.

"This disciple is not afraid."

Under the setting sun, her voice was clear and resolute, as if it had been forged from the very heat Granny Lin feared.

The old woman stared at her. For reasons she did not wish to admit, a faint ache stirred inside her—sharp and unexpected. She could only tilt her head back and drink again, forcing that tenderness down with the burn of wine.

The night was deep. Insects chirped in the courtyard in endless waves, rising and falling like a restless tide.

Qin Nianyin finished tidying the last basket of sand and gravel. Her arms were so sore she could barely lift them. Each time she flexed her fingers, pain pulsed along her knuckles as if the joints had been pried apart.

She dragged her feet back to the small hut and collapsed onto the simple bamboo bed.

The roof above was mottled and old. Through cracks in the wood, a few thin points of moonlight filtered down and fell across her face. With each breath, she could still smell the dust of sand and stone clinging stubbornly to her hands and hair, as if the kiln itself had marked her.

Her entire body ached—yet beneath that ache, something else seeped slowly into her bones: a strange, unfamiliar satisfaction, quiet and solid, like a foundation being laid.

She stared at the ceiling, and without meaning to, the corners of her lips curled upward.

This, she thought, is the life I truly desire.

Learning with my own hands. Working with my own hands. No matter how bitter, at the very least, it is a road I am walking myself.

Her thoughts shifted suddenly, uninvited. Somehow, she recalled a face from her past life—cold, detached, impossibly handsome, yet separated from her by countless mountains and rivers. That indifference had once pressed on her like frost, silent and suffocating, making her feel smaller and smaller until she could hardly breathe.

A tightness seized her chest.

She shook her head sharply, fiercely dispersing the shadow before it could root itself again.

"Useless thoughts should not be entertained," she murmured, voice soft in the dark.

She turned over, pulled the thin quilt up over her shoulders, and forced her eyes shut.

No matter how arduous, at least in this life, she was walking her own path.

Outside, the night breeze stirred gently. The bamboo bed creaked softly in response, a small, tired sound that blended into the insect chorus.

Soon, exhaustion swallowed everything. She sank into deep sleep, and between her brows, a faint trace of a smile lingered—subtle, stubborn, as if even in sleep she refused to retreat.

Chapter 71: Be Mindful of the Enemy

Dawn had only just broken and the mist in the courtyard had not yet dispersed. Qin Nianyin had already rolled up her sleeves, lifting basket after basket of sand and gravel cleared from the rear garden and emptying them outside.

Her back ached so sharply she could barely straighten and fine beads of sweat clung to her brow.

A sudden cough sounded from the top of the wall. She looked up and saw the two female shadow guards she had exposed the previous night now sitting openly and, indeed, rather brazenly along the ridge.

"Qin Nianyin, what are you doing?" asked the guard from the Gu household, her brows lifting with a hint of amusement. "Working yourself like a hired labourer. If you need something, we can fetch it for you."

"That is right," the guard from the Su residence chimed in, unable to resist. "The sky is barely light, yet here you are hauling stones and cleaning the stove. What exactly are you trying to accomplish?"

Qin Nianyin lifted her sleeve and wiped the sweat from her forehead. Her voice was calm, yet her tone carried unmistakable resolve. "This is my own path. I do not require your help."

The two exchanged a glance. A heartbeat later, they began bickering again as if unable to restrain themselves.

The Gu guard let out a cold snort. "Your Su master's mind twists in far too many directions. I would wager he is forcing her to suffer these hardships so he can reap the benefits afterward."

The Su guard shot back at once. "And your Gu household is any better? You claim you are here to protect her, yet every day you fight over who gets to chop wood and draw water for her. You dare accuse us?"

Qin Nianyin could not help a small, helpless laugh, though she did not bother to argue. She simply resumed cleaning the stove, methodically sweeping out the remaining sand.

Just as she tipped the final basket into place, the Gu shadow guard lowered her voice and said quietly, "Tomorrow, the army sets out."

The bamboo basket slipped from Qin Nianyin's fingers and struck the ground with a harsh clatter. sand scattered in all directions, the sharp sound cutting through the morning air.

She froze. Her fingertips trembled. Her gaze dulled for a heartbeat and the mist before her eyes seemed to billow and surge. Something tightened around her chest, invisible yet suffocating, as if her breath had been trapped mid-air.

She remembered.

That crucial piece ——the very one she had strained to recall for so long, yet could never grasp ——

had suddenly returned to her.

She drew in a sharp breath. In the next instant she turned abruptly, moving with a staggering urgency, her steps unsteady yet driven by a single desperate purpose. She ran straight toward the courtyard gate.

The two guards stared in shock before scrambling to their feet.

"Qin Nianyin!" they called after her.

But she was already gone and neither of them could stop her.

* * * * *

Warhorses cried out in long, echoing neighs while the banners overhead snapped sharply in the rising wind and the entire military camp moved in a restless tide of activity that swelled from one end of the encampment to the other.

Gu Xiao was still issuing detailed orders to his personal guards, his voice steady despite the noise around him, when the sound of hurried footsteps broke sharply through the tumult behind him, cutting across the clamour like a sudden blade through cloth.

He turned and what entered his sight was a figure he recognized even before her face became clear.

Qin Nianyin was running toward him from the dusty path that led into the camp, her steps uneven from the speed of her arrival and behind her followed Shadow Guard Seventeen ——the very guard he had assigned to watch over her.

It was obvious from the way the soldiers let them pass that Seventeen had used the token Gu Xiao had entrusted to him, a token that allowed her to move through every checkpoint without obstruction and reach the heart of the encampment with startling speed.

"Gu Xiao," Qin Nianyin called out as she reached him.

Her breath scattering apart in disordered bursts that made her voice tremble. She came to a halt only by instinct, her entire frame quivering as if her lungs were protesting every breath she forced through them and the sweat that slid from her temple traced an unsteady, gleaming line across her cheek before falling to the ground.

Gu Xiao was caught unprepared by the sight. He stepped forward out of reflex, both hands rising to steady her by the shoulders and although her body did not collide into him with much force, the faint trembling he felt beneath his palms rippled all the way into his chest, leaving a dull, lingering shock beneath his ribs.

"What happened?" he asked, his voice low yet taut, as if bracing for an answer he was not entirely prepared to hear.

Qin Nianyin struggled for several breaths before she could form any coherent sound. When she finally forced words past her lips, each one was strained, as though dragged out with effort.

"Remember this," she said, her voice unsteady. "Remain alert for an enemy who feints in one direction only to strike from another. And you must also watch the people closest to you, because danger may come from where you least expect it."

Gu Xiao instinctively wanted to laugh lightly and reassure her. He wanted to tell her she was being far too anxious and that she worried without reason.

"All the men in my unit are brothers who have survived life and death beside me, so how could they possibly ——"

Yet that sentence stopped abruptly.

Not because she interrupted him, but because her gaze fixed on him with a sharp, unwavering intensity.

Her eyes were trembling, yet beneath that tremor lay a clarity as cold and cutting as tempered steel, a clarity that forced the rest of his words back down his throat before they could emerge.

He remained silent for a brief moment, letting the weight of her warning settle. When he finally spoke, his tone was subdued but firm. "Very well. I will keep my guard up. Thank you for reminding me."

Qin Nianyin did not relax at all. She stepped closer instead, her expression drawn tight with fear she refused to acknowledge and she pressed out her words with deliberate clarity, as though carving them into his memory. "Come back alive."

* * * * *

That afternoon, the study within the Su residence was so quiet that it seemed to swallow even the faintest breath.

Outside the windows, cicadas chanted in long, rising waves and on the desk before Su Zhang lay stacks of bamboo slips arranged with meticulous order. He leaned forward over the table, his fingertip brushed with vermilion, yet the stroke he intended to make never descended, as though suspended in hesitation.

A female shadow guard glided into the room without stirring the air, her steps absence itself. She dropped to one knee, her voice low and steady as she delivered her report.

"Reporting to you, my lord. Early this morning, the moment Miss Qin Nianyin heard that General Gu's forces would depart at dawn, she ran from the marketplace straight to the military camp. She spoke to the general in front of the assembled troops and urged him to guard against an enemy who might feint in one direction only to strike in another. She also… she also told him that he must return alive."

The final word faded and the entire room fell into a silence so deep it seemed carved from stone.

Su Zhang lowered his gaze, appearing to listen with composed patience, yet he offered no immediate reply.

The vermilion brush twirled lightly between his fingers, but it never touched the paper again.

A fleeting shadow passed beneath his lashes ——an emotion too swift and too sharp for the eye to catch ——and he pressed it down, burying it within the calmness of his voice as he answered. "I understand."

The shadow guard bowed her head, a quiet ripple of apprehension tightening her shoulders. She dared not linger and withdrew in measured steps.

When the door shut behind her, only Su Zhang remained in the vast, quiet room.

He sat unmoving behind the desk, the faintest curve tugging at his lips ——a smile so slight it might have been mistaken for the trick of a wavering candle, yet it tasted of bitterness ground by sand and wind. His eyes remained as tranquil as ever, but his fingertips betrayed him. The vermilion brush snapped within his grasp with a muted crack, splintering between his fingers.

* * * * *

Night deepened around the imperial study and the silence inside grew so absolute it felt as though even a falling needle would resound.

The lamps flickered, their flames wavering like thin breaths of light, while Emperor Xuanwen turned page after page of the marriage registry.

His hands, steady in battles and court disputes, trembled faintly over the parchment.

"Three sons..." he murmured, the quiet breath bearing a weight too tangled to name.

The Crown Prince, Li Duan, was steady and restrained, his mind precise and deliberate. He was, without question, the most fitting heir. Yet if the emperor were to choose a bride from a powerful clan, it would be equivalent to placing an additional wing upon the crown prince's back.

The might of the aristocratic families was already difficult to contain and once bound to the next emperor by marriage, would he, as the reigning sovereign, still be able to hold the reins firmly?

However, should he choose a bride from a modest household or a rising family, the court would mock the prince's shallow foundation, forcing Li Duan to bear an undeserved slight.

Weighing the matter from every angle only revealed that neither path led to perfection.

The third son, Li Suo, had always appeared to be "useful precisely because he was useless."

He pretended to care little for worldly affairs, spending his days among poetry, wine and idle charm. Yet no matter how he feigned detachment, he remained a son of the imperial lineage.

A prince was a chess piece of the realm; he could not truly be set aside.

If he continued unmarried, the world would claim that the imperial house lacked propriety. When the ancestral temple asked for an account, how could the emperor answer?

As for the second son...

Emperor Xuanwen's expression darkened suddenly and a faint ache spread through his chest.

"This defeat..." he whispered, the words trembling in a way that startled even him. "If he had not been so impatient, so desperate to win, how would he have fallen to such a state?"

"The one who should have been able to stand toe-to-toe with the Crown Prince," he continued, closing his eyes as the veins on the back of his hand tightened, "now sits confined within the Imperial Clan Court."

He inhaled slowly, the breath strained. "Does he resent me? Naturally, he resents me. Yet in the imperial house… when has there ever been a day where brothers were truly allowed to devour one another?"

His voice halted and only after a long pause did a weary sigh escape him.

"Enough. The heart of a father and the duty of a sovereign are two roads that can never merge. Since he has already entered the Clan Court, he should stir no further waves. If I can at least arrange a marriage of decent standing for him, allowing him a stable life for the years that remain… then perhaps that is the only small reparation I can still offer."

He closed the registry with slow deliberation.

The candlelight flickered across his eyes and within that glow there was no warmth ——only a depth of cold that reached far beyond the shadows of the room.

Marriage, though it appeared to be a matter of the household, was in truth a battlefield of court politics.

Three sons meant three separate games of chess.

None of them were permitted to move beyond the emperor's hand.

None were allowed to take a step outside the board he had drawn.

* * * * *

Qin Nianyin was bent over in the courtyard, clearing fallen leaves and tangled weeds. A thin sheen of sweat gathered at her temples as she worked, her breath steady yet faintly strained.

All of a sudden, a soft crack sounded above her, something small striking the crown of her head with the weight of a careless tap. She frowned at once, lifted her hand to touch the spot and her fingers closed around a single roasted peanut.

"Who…" She lifted her head sharply and of course; a familiar indolent face lounged atop the courtyard wall.

Li Suo ——third son of Emperor Xuanwen ——wore a lake-blue robe embroidered with golden clouds, the silk catching sunlight with an arrogant gleam.

He held a folding fan between two fingers, half-open and half-shut and his smile was lazy in a way that made clear he rarely cared about consequences.

The sunlight glinted across his brows, granting him a roguish elegance that was, to her eyes, unbearably dazzling.

"It's you again? Why do you always throw peanuts at me?" Qin Nianyin snapped, irritation rising too swiftly for her to restrain. Her voice cooled instantly. "Is speaking properly beyond you?"

Li Suo flicked his fan open with a crisp snap, the motion practiced and almost theatrical. His lips curved and he lifted his chin slightly, as if issuing a decree rather than a suggestion. "Come. Walk with me."

Qin Nianyin felt a solid block rise in her chest, her grip on the broom tightening until the bamboo creaked faintly. Yet she could feel the weight of the neighbours' curious stares; the third prince, radiant in brocade, standing amid a heap of wilted weeds like a lantern dropped into mud, drew attention she could hardly counter.

She swallowed the sigh pressing in her throat, set the broom aside and pressed out a quiet, "Fine."

They walked side by side toward the nearby riverbank. The breeze brushed through the willow branches and the surface of the water shimmered with thin silver ripples.

Li Suo stood with an easy stance near the edge of the bank, tapping his fan lightly against his palm as he tilted his head toward her. "You could live a life of comfortand wealth," he said, his voice smooth yet edged with curiosity, "yet you choose to endure hardship in a place like this. What exactly are you seeking?"

Qin Nianyin lowered her gaze, brushing her fingers along a dangling willow leaf. Her reply was calm but sharp. "Your Highness has palaces of jade and gold, yet you wander down a country road like this. What exactly are you doing here?"

Li Suo burst into laughter ——bright, unrestrained and with an ease that did not quite match his reputation. But the sound faltered halfway and he folded his fan closed with a soft clap before letting the next words fall lightly from his tongue. "I came to propose."

"Propose?" She wondered if she had misheard something patently absurd.

"Yes."

"Here?" Her eyes widened, unable to process the notion.

"Yes." Li Suo's smile deepened, taking on a touch of wicked charm that had unsettled more than a few noble daughters.

She instinctively glanced around them, searching for any witnesses who might explain this strange turn, but aside from the two of them, the riverbank was empty.

A faint unease crawled up her spine. "With me?" she asked, a sinking feeling blooming in her chest.

"Yes." It was the third time he answered in that unhurried, maddeningly steady tone.

Qin Nianyin stopped walking entirely. She stared at him, stunned for a heartbeat, then lifted her gaze and glared with unmasked disbelief. "Stop repeating yes, yes, yes. Your Highness must not jest about matters like this."

The third prince of the empire, appearing in a countryside lane to make a proposal? How could such a thing be anything but a joke?

Yet Li Suo's expression shifted. Some of the idle frivolity drained from his brows, replaced by a trace of earnestness rarely seen upon his face. His next words came quieter, but weightier. "No jest. I truly came to propose to you."

Qin Nianyin froze, as though she had not understood a single word that had just fallen from his lips. "You… what nonsense are you talking about?"

"None at all." Li Suo's tone was light, as if he were merely stating the obvious. "I had intended to seek you at the Su residence. But then I heard you had abandoned the comfort of their grand estate and, for reasons unknown, chosen to remain in this humble little place. So I had no choice but to come personally."

"…" Qin Nianyin found herself speechless for a moment, unable to decide how much of what he said was truth and how much was nothing more than princely whim.

"My father intends to select proper consorts for the three of us." Li Suo spoke casually, yet each word carried the deliberate precision of someone weighing power.

"If I were to choose the daughter of a high-ranking official, Father might suspect me of harbouring ambition. If I were to choose the daughter of a minor official, it would seem as though she sought nothing more than a higher perch. After considering it over and over…"

His gaze drifted toward her, quiet and assessing. "You are fitting. You are Su Zhang's cousin, your reputation is clean and you are not like the others who claw upward with greedy eyes."

A tremor ran through Qin Nianyin's heart. She forced a cold laugh, masking the shift in her pulse. "And how does Your Highness know I have no such ambitions? If not for…" She paused, her gaze dimming with an almost imperceptible shadow. "Perhaps I once wished to rise as well."

Were it not for her previous life, she thought silently, she too would have been eager to grasp any branch within reach.

Li Suo's eyes flickered, but he merely tapped his folding fan and let out a low chuckle. "Then that is even better. This high branch of mine —— consider it specially reserved for you."

Hearing this, Qin Nianyin could not help giving him a sharp glare. Her voice was cold and clipped. "I have no such intentions. My thanks to Your Highness."

Li Suo looked at her as though he saw through every layer she attempted to hide behind. "If you truly wished to climb higher, you would not choose to toil here. Days like these ——what daughter who longs for elevation would endure them?"

Qin Nianyin's tone hardened. "Perhaps this is retreat in order to advance. Your Highness thinks far too simply."

Li Suo's lips curved in a smile that was neither mocking nor kind. He suddenly tapped her forehead lightly with his fan. "Do not pretend. As a prince, I possess at least a basic ability to discern people and gather information."

His gaze narrowed, with a gleam of teasing overlaying something sharper. "Do not think I am unaware that Gu Xiao and Su Zhang are already on the verge of turning against each other because of you."

A jolt went through Qin Nianyin's chest. Yet her face remained composed, her voice cool as frost. "Rumours. Baseless."

Li Suo laughed softly, not bothering to refute her. He merely closed his fan with a soft click, his eyes settling on her with an unreadable expression. "Consider it well."

A breeze stirred the willow branches overhead. The river murmured steadily at their feet. For an instant, the air itself seemed to still.

Chapter 72: Naming the Shadow Guards

Morning mist clung to the courtyard, leaving the air thick with dampness. Qin Nianyin had rolled her sleeves high and was bent over, sweeping away the ashes left from the previous night's fire. The coarse broom scraped against the stone pavement in a lonely, rasping rhythm, and fine grey dust rose in thin spirals before settling back onto her cuffs.

A soft cough sounded above the wall. She paused, lifted her head, and found the two female shadow guards she had exposed the previous night sitting openly atop the wall. One rested her chin on her palm, legs swinging idly; the other crossed her arms, posture rigid as if she were guarding a gate rather than loitering on it. Both looked entirely at ease, as though they had been there all along.

"Miss Qin, you are working far too hard," the one on the left said with a bright smile, her tone light and almost playful. "Up before dawn, hauling water and cleaning the hearth like a labourer. If you need anything done, just say the word. Our hands are quick. We will handle it for you."

"Hmph. Stop pretending to be kind," the one on the right cut in sharply, her voice edged. "You act as though you are the only one with hands. Whatever Miss Qin needs, I can do just as well."

The left guard answered immediately, scoffing. "You? With those clumsy hands? What could you possibly accomplish? Who was it last night who rushed to boil her water, burned her own hands red and still refused to let go?"

"You are lying!"

"I saw it clearly!"

Their bickering escalated at once. Sleeves fluttered, words clashed, and the two nearly toppled off the wall as they leaned at each other, furious and indignant. One reached out as if to shove; the other swatted her hand away, and both froze only when Qin Nianyin's gaze sharpened.

Qin Nianyin lifted her eyes with a helpless breath, her voice turning cool. "Enough."

Both guards stiffened and sat upright like chastened children. Even so, they still glared at each other, sparks flying silently between their eyes. Qin Nianyin returned to sweeping for two strokes, then stopped again, as if something else had finally surfaced in her mind.

After a brief pause, she spoke. "I have not asked, what are your names?"

The two exchanged a look. For a long moment neither answered. At last, the guard on the left murmured reluctantly, "This subordinate is Jia-number Seventeen."

The guard on the right bit her lip before replying, "This subordinate is Tian-number Eleven."

Qin Nianyin's brows drew together. She studied them quietly, from their plain clothing to the faint calluses along their knuckles, the kind earned by repeating the same movements for years. "So, you do not have names?"

The two looked at each other again, their movements oddly synchronized, as if the question had struck a place they never allowed themselves to touch.

Qin Nianyin asked softly, "Do you not remember your original names either?"

A faint tremor ran through both women. Their eyes flickered with a momentary vacancy, as though something deep in the hollows of their memories had been nudged. Then, without speaking, they shook their heads.

For once, the two who were always at each other's throats shared a rare, fragile expression of mutual understanding. Qin Nianyin felt something settle, heavy and slow, in the centre of her chest.

She thought of the floods she had lived through, of the muddy streets and broken roofs, of bodies shivering beneath makeshift awnings, of the countless displaced souls she had seen wandering with blank eyes and empty hands. Names were the first things lost when a life was torn apart.

Perhaps these two had also lost their families long ago, reduced to shadows who no longer bore names and no longer dared to want them back.

"You cannot recall?" she repeated, more quietly.

They shook their heads again, perfectly in unison.

A quiet ache rose in her heart. She wondered, if her adoptive parents had not taken her in, would she too have become a nameless shadow, drifting unclaimed between worlds, answering only to numbers and orders.

She had always regarded these two with wary irritation, believing them merely the eyes and ears that Gu Xiao and Su Zhang had placed around her. Yet now, seeing the uncertainty in their eyes, she suddenly felt that they too were little more than pieces sacrificed by others, forced to relinquish their identities before anyone ever bothered to ask what they truly wanted.

She let out a gentle sigh, her voice softening, her throat tightening ever so slightly. "Since you have no names, how should I address you from now on?"

"Eh?" Both blinked, startled, then turned to each other again, as if expecting the other to answer first.

Qin Nianyin's tone grew gentler. "In that case, from now on, I will call you Qiqi, and you Yiyi."

The names carried the mild, familiar rhythm of home, simple syllables that did not sound like orders. Both women froze for a heartbeat, then their eyes brightened in the same instant. Qiqi's smile bloomed like sudden sunlight; Yiyi's lips moved with a small, shy curve she could not quite conceal. They answered together with almost childlike delight. "Yes!"

Qin Nianyin's expression, however, cooled at once. Her voice turned firm. "But remember this. You may only help with simple cleaning. The firing of the kiln, the sorting of materials, the mixing of clay, these are tasks I must do myself. You are not to interfere."

Qiqi and Yiyi exchanged a look and for once there was no quarrel between them. They nodded at the same time, answering earnestly, "Understood!"

The courtyard quieted. Firewood crackled faintly in the hearth. The mist slowly lifted, pale strands thinning in the morning light. Qin Nianyin lowered her gaze and tightened her grip on the broom handle. Beneath the lingering chill in her chest, something small and steady began to take root. From this day onward, she would no longer face this place entirely alone, even if the road was still hers to walk.

* * * * *

The study was steeped in dim lamplight; only the inkstone breathed a faint trace of ink fragrance into the still air. A sealed letter rested between Su Zhang's fingers. The paper was thin and brittle, yet it weighed upon his hand as heavily as iron.

He unfolded it, his gaze drifting over the first few lines with composed ease. But the moment the words "Prince Li Suo" and "proposal of marriage" surfaced before him, his pupils tightened in a sudden, sharp contraction.

His grip tightened at once. The letter crumpled with a harsh rustle, and the sharp paper edge sliced across his palm, drawing a thin line of blood. A drop welled slowly at the cut and stained the pale paper. He did not seem to feel it at all. His eyes remained fixed on those few words while a cold gleam sank, inch by inch, into their depths.

After a long moment, he let out a quiet laugh. The sound was low and constrained, carrying the faintest shade of self-mockery. "Li Suo, a neat stroke. He strikes before the rest."

The curve of his lips lingered, yet frost had already settled across his brow. The plain letter, fragile as it was, was crushed ruthlessly in his hand until it became a twisted ball. His knuckles creaked with the force, and the fresh blood on his palm smeared into a darker red.

"In that case," he murmured, voice deep and hushed, steeped in restraint sharpened into something violent, "I can no longer afford to wait."

Under the lamp, his shadow stretched across the wall at an angle. Its outline was severe, and every line of his face was suffused with decisive, almost ruthless resolve. The board was not yet settled; he had intended to watch quietly from the side, to let others reveal their hands first. Yet with this sudden move falling into play, he could only act earlier than planned.

* * * * *

In the late afternoon, the courtyard had grown so quiet that only the faint sound of cicadas lingered in the air. Qiqi approached with a small cloth bundle in her hands, her expression threaded with faint tension. She offered the bundle with both palms and spoke in a low voice. "Miss Qin Nianyin, this was sent back to the capital together with the military dispatches. General Gu Xiao specifically instructed that it be delivered to you."

Qin Nianyin's brows narrowed slightly. She accepted the bundle and unfolded it. Inside lay a wooden horse, no larger than the span of her palm.

The wood was coarse, and the knife marks varied in depth. Its outline was upright and steady, yet it could hardly be called delicate. Some places were clumsy, as though the hand that carved it had fought the grain with stubborn force rather than coaxing it gently. A faint scent of resin and raw wood still clung to it, unmasked by lacquer or perfume.

Her fingertips brushed lightly across each carved stroke and her heart jolted. Such workmanship was not from a craftsman of the markets. It was the work of a man who wielded a blade for battle. She could almost picture him seated beneath a dim lamp inside the command tent, a military blade in his hand, shaping the wood stroke by stroke while the night deepened around him, while war reports piled at his elbow and soldiers' footsteps passed outside like distant waves.

"This was carved by General Gu Xiao himself," Qiqi added in a rush, her tone carrying a careful trace of defence, as if afraid Qin Nianyin might dismiss it too quickly. "He said you might dislike something so rough, but it was made by his own hands during his brief moments of rest. No matter the result, he wished for you to have it."

Qin Nianyin remained silent for a long time. Her brows tightened as if held by an unseen knot.

This was something she could neither accept nor return. To discard it outright would be trampling on the sentiment behind it. To send it back along with the military documents might unsettle the troops or stir needless whispers. Yet accepting it felt like allowing one more thread to wrap around her wrists, gentle and firm, until she could no longer claim she was walking entirely by herself.

Her fingers tightened around the cloth. At last, she breathed out softly, wrapped the wooden horse again, and said in a quiet but unyielding tone, "In that case, I will keep it for now." Yet in her thoughts she added, when he returns, I will return it to him myself.

Qiqi blinked in surprise. She seemed as if she wished to say more, but in the end she only bowed her head and answered in a subdued voice. "Yes."

The lamp's glow flickered. Qin Nianyin placed the cloth bundle at the bottom of a storage chest and lowered the lid. The faint scent of cedar rose as the wooden panels met, sealing the bundle away. A fleeting shadow crossed her gaze, a trace of emotion too faint and swift for anyone to discern.

It was a sentiment with no rightful place to rest, one that could only be locked away for the time being.

A breeze slipped past the window lattice, stirring a thin curl of dust. Qin Nianyin felt a sudden tightness in her chest, as though the curve of that little wooden horse had lodged itself somewhere deep in her memory, halted in place and unable to move again.

She prayed silently to the heavens that he had taken her warning to heart, that he would not throw himself into danger as if his life were an offering he could spend without regret.

Chapter 73: A Nation Gives What It Can

The bronze incense burner sent thin coils of smoke drifting upward, pale and wavering like threads of mist.

Within the Imperial Study, the quiet was so complete that even the soft rustling of pages seemed magnified, echoing against the carved beams above.

Emperor Xuanwen slowly closed the bamboo scroll in his hand.

His gaze fell past the dragon-carved desk, settling somewhere indistinct in the room's stillness as he spoke in a low, even voice:

"Gu Xiao and the Tiger Guard have already been on the march for fifteen days.

Once they pass Yongri Pass, they will enter the northern frontier directly.

If this campaign holds steady, the border will remain secure for five years.

But if even one thing goes amiss..."

He paused.

His fingertip tapped the surface of the desk twice ——slow, heavy taps that carried the weight of unspoken possibilities.

" ——military provisions will be our greatest threat.

The Ministry of Revenue has urged the release of grain, yet the distance is great and the carts heavy.

It may not arrive in time.

If necessary, we will need to divert supplies from the Western Commandery and send their stock ahead first, so as to prepare for unforeseen circumstances."

The Crown Prince, Li Duan, bowed his head as he answered.

His tone was steady, with the discipline of someone long accustomed to responsibility.

"Your son understands. I will assign men to supervise the matter closely and ensure no delay."

Emperor Xuanwen gave a faint nod, though he did not conclude the subject.

Instead, he exhaled slowly before speaking again ——his voice lower, more weighted:

"However,… there are already murmurs in court.

With provisions insufficient and the treasury depleted, there are those who have once again proposed the idea of a marriage alliance."

The words dropped like iron into the quiet chamber.

The air seemed to harden at once.

The Crown Prince lifted his eyes.

A sharpness flashed through them; his reply was cold, decisive, cutting cleanly through the stillness:

"Father, such a measure would undermine the dignity of our state. It must not be allowed."

The emperor did not appear surprised by his resistance.

He simply looked at him ——silent, measured ——waiting for what would follow.

The Crown Prince continued, his complexion composed but his voice ringing with clarity:

"Such a decision will first scatter the people's confidence and the consequences will ripple into years to come.

Since the founding of our Great Zhou, we have never sought survival through submission.

If we set such a precedent today, then each time conflict arises, shall we sacrifice another princess of the imperial clan in exchange for temporary peace?"

His words struck the quiet chamber with crisp resonance, echoing in the vaulted silence.

Emperor Xuanwen's brows pressed together.

His expression grew solemn, as though weighing considerations piled heavy in his mind.

The Crown Prince, sensing his father's contemplation, softened his tone ——but only slightly.

"Furthermore, among the imperial family… only the Second Princess remains unwed."

A quiet beat.

"Jing is a daughter of the imperial house," the emperor said at last. "She is raised by the realm. It is natural that she should bear the duties of a princess."

"Unless another noble lady of the clan is elevated to the rank of princess, she is the only candidate.

But… the Second Princess has long held affection for Su Zhang.

It is unlikely she would consent to such a marriage."

A shadow of thought crossed the emperor's expression.

His eyes darkened and after a long silence he spoke again ——each word deliberate and heavy:

"Su Zhang is young, yet capable.

If he were to wed a princess, he could no longer hold his central post.

That would be tantamount to you, as Crown Prince, losing an arm.

Such a matter must not happen."

After saying this, he leaned back abruptly into the dragon throne.

His gaze grew distant, sinking into some deep calculation.

His fingers curled once around the armrest before striking it with a firm knock.

"Still… calls for negotiation in court have not risen in merely a day or two.

Since you have just declared it impossible, then you must provide a way to make it impossible.

Words alone accomplish nothing.

If provisions run dry ——if soldiers hunger ——then tell me, who will bear that responsibility?"

The Crown Prince's brows tightened.

He lowered his head again and answered, voice deep with resolve:

"Father may rest assured.

Your son will work with the Ministry of Revenue and the Transport Commission to ensure the army's rations are delivered without fail.

Should corruption or obstruction surface, your son will see that it is investigated and punished at once."

Emperor Xuanwen held his gaze.

Little by little, the emperor's look grew colder, as though peeling away layers to examine the steel beneath the prince's calm exterior.

Not until some time had passed did he finally let out a short, chilly laugh.

"Very well.

Remember your words today.

If the northern frontier stands firm, the court will naturally align behind you.

But if the north falls… Crown Prince, you should already know what you will lose."

The Crown Prince's expression did not shift.

He bowed low, his voice steady as iron:

"Your son bears it in mind."

The candlelight trembled.

No other sound stirred within the vast Imperial Study ——only the faint, curling trails of incense smoke drifted upward, twining like unseen chains that bound father and son in their shared, unspoken burdens.

* * * * *

The bronze incense burner released slow coils of fragrant smoke that drifted upward like pale mist, veiling the rafters of the Golden Hall in a subdued haze. The ceremonial drums had already fallen silent, yet the court remained assembled in full array.

Civil officials stood to the left, military generals to the right, their robes arranged in precise order.

Upon the imperial throne, Emperor Xuanwen sat motionless, his gaze steady and faintly austere, offering neither approval nor rebuke.

From the ranks of the civil ministers, the Assistant Minister of Revenue stepped forward and bowed deeply. His voice was respectful yet carried a faint tremor beneath its formality.

"Your Majesty, the supply lines for the northern front grow perilously strained. What remains in the imperial treasury is scarcely sufficient. This humble servant believes that we should follow the precedent of former dynasties and send a princess to the northern tribes in marriage, thus securing fifteen years of peace."

476

His words fell into the hall like a stone into still water.

A murmur rippled through the officials.

From the left column, another minister stepped out in quick support. "The former dynasty concluded a marital treaty with the Bei Di (the Northern Di, a northern tribal confederation), which secured several years of peace and indeed secured several years of peace. The records attest to it clearly. Such a measure is neither without precedent nor without merit."

A few more voices rose in succession.

"When rations run short, soldiers cannot fight. Empty loyalty serves no purpose. Marriage diplomacy is a feasible path."

Before the wave of agreement could swell further, Crown Prince Li Duan advanced a single step. His expression was calm yet resolute and when he spoke, his voice carried across the hall like a blade drawn cleanly from its sheath. "Father, this son believes such a measure must not be taken."

The murmuring subsided at once. Every eye turned toward him.

Li Duan cupped his hands, his tone firm. "A marriage alliance may offer temporary reprieve, yet it would degrade the dignity of our Great Zhou. Should we seek safety through yielding, our prestige would fall before any treaty is even enacted. The border may not remain truly quiet, yet the people's hearts will already have grown cold. Once this precedent is set, every future conflict would invite the same proposal. Such appeasement is a grave mistake."

His words struck heavily, but the hall had never been short of dissent.

The Minister of Revenue stroked his beard and allowed a thin, pointed smile to appear. "His Highness speaks righteously, yet if not by such means, where shall provisions come from? Empty rhetoric does not fill granaries. Soldiers require sustenance. Should the court refuse a marriage alliance, the only remaining measure is to raise taxes."

Several ministers responded in eager support.

"Yes. Temporary taxation can ease the emergency."

"Though the people may suffer, it is preferable to letting the border fall."

The tide of voices swelled, forceful enough to threaten overpowering the prince's stance.

Li Duan's expression remained composed. He spoke again, his voice cool and unwavering. "This, too, cannot be done. The common people have endured two floods in recent years. Their strength is depleted. Should we impose further taxes, resentment will rise and greater calamity will follow."

A minister barked sharply, "Then what does His Highness propose? If marriage is forbidden and taxation forbidden, shall we conjure grain from the air?"

Dozens of gazes pressed toward him.

Emperor Xuanwen, seated upon the dragon throne, did not interrupt. His hands were folded behind his back. His eyes reflected both patience and scrutiny, as though he were weighing not merely the prince's words, but the heart behind them.

Li Duan took a slow breath. Then he bowed and declared clearly, "This son believes that the court may open a voluntary contribution."

The hall faltered into momentary confusion.

He continued, "When the nation faces peril, those who serve it must act first. This son is willing to contribute one thousand taels of gold to support the army."

A low gasp travelled through the officials.

Then silence.

Absolute, sudden, unnerving silence.

The sum he named was not trivial. It equalled half the yearly wealth of a mid-ranking noble household. More importantly, he had spoken these words in open court, under the gaze of the entire nation's governing body. The gesture stood like a pillar, casting its long shadow over every official present.

In the breathless stillness, a single soft chime sounded: jade striking jade.

Su Zhang stepped out from the ranks. His robe fluttered lightly as he bowed, his voice clear and steady. "The Su family is willing to contribute one thousand taels of silver."

The declaration was like a stone dropped into a still lake. Its ripples surged outward in widening circles.

With Li Duan and Su Zhang aligned so openly, who in the court could afford to remain unmoved?

The hall erupted.

"My household is humble, yet we are willing to contribute three hundred taels of silver."

"I offer my daughter's dowry jewels, worth five hundred taels in silver."

"This official… will contribute as well."

Voices rose one after another, spreading like a tide until the entire Golden Hall resounded with pledges and declarations. Officials exchanged hurried glances, each compelled to speak lest they be judged lacking in loyalty or courage.

Upon the imperial throne, Emperor Xuanwen watched the scene unfold. The sternness in his eyes softened only faintly, yet that faintness was enough to reveal a trace of satisfaction.

Another minister came forward. "Though my household has little, we are willing to contribute three hundred taels."

"Two hundred taels from mine."

"One hundred taels in platinum."

The shifting wave of contributions washed away the earlier discord. A new momentum filled the hall, firmer and more unified than the debate that preceded it.

At last, Emperor Xuanwen rose slightly. His voice was low, but it carried the weight of final judgment. "Good. Since all officials are willing to join in one accord, this is fortune for our realm."

He paused, his gaze sweeping over the assembled ministers with a solemn sharpness. "Pass down my decree. Beginning today, all officials shall contribute according to rank. The wealthy merchants of the empire shall follow thereafter. The military provisions must be gathered in full. As for the common people, their livelihood must not be disturbed even by a single grain."

A resounding reply rose in unison. "We obey."

The voices echoed against the gilded pillars of the Golden Hall, vibrating like distant thunder.

Above them, the smoke from the bronze incense burner spiralled upward, curling into shapes that seemed almost palpable. In the dim light, the drifting tendrils resembled chains, binding every heart in the hall to the fate of the northern front and to the decisions made on this day.

Chapter 74: Redirecting Donated Silver for Compensation

Several days later, within the Imperial Study.

The gilded bronze censer burned in quiet stillness, smoke curling and pooling in a soft haze. Crown Prince Li Duan, dressed in full court robes, lowered his head and reported:

"I submit to Father Emperor. The decree for voluntary contributions has already been issued, and officials of the various offices have been the first to respond. The Su residence gave generously—one thousand taels of silver at first, and then another thousand, for a total of two thousand taels. After the Ministry of Revenue completed its accounting, the tally stands at six thousand eight hundred taels of gold and more than ten thousand taels of silver. Merchants are continuing to deliver more, and the figures are still being compiled. This amount may not sustain us for long, but it can, for now, relieve the Northern Frontier's immediate crisis."

Emperor Xuanwen's gaze sank. His fingertips tapped lightly against the dragon desk. After a long while, he nodded slowly.

"Not bad. I had thought this measure might draw complaints, yet the results are such. It is better than issuing a tax increase with a single paper decree."

His eyes settled on the Crown Prince, and for once there was a faint, barely-there trace of approval.

"However—" Emperor Xuanwen's voice suddenly dropped. "These are life-saving funds. How they are delivered safely to the Northern Frontier is of the utmost importance. If even one coin is lost midway, it will not only unsettle military morale, it will also shake the court. Who should be sent to escort it?"

The Imperial Study fell into silence. The ministers held their breath, not daring to speak out of turn.

Emperor Xuanwen's gaze abruptly shifted to Li Suo at the side. The Third Prince wore splendid robes, idly rolling a jade fan between his fingers; his eyes flickered.

"Su." Emperor Xuanwen's voice was deep. "What is your view?"

Li Suo jolted. The fan snapped shut with a sharp clack. He forced a smile, yet panic seeped through it.

"Father Emperor, your son has never had experience in military affairs, and I am often deemed… idle and undisciplined. I fear I would be unable to shoulder such a great responsibility."

The air in the Imperial Study tightened at once. Emperor Xuanwen's brows knit sharply; a flash of exasperation—hatred that iron would not become steel—passed through his eyes.

In a low, stern voice he said, "Nonsense! You are of the imperial bloodline—my son. How can you forever use 'unfit' as your excuse?"

Li Suo only gave a light smile, wearing that same roguish, it-has-nothing-to-do-with-me look, and did not speak again.

After a long moment, the Crown Prince finally bowed and spoke with steady composure.

"Father Emperor, escorting and transporting the pay and silver funds must be handled with the utmost care. Your son believes… Su Zhang, Langzhong of the Civil Appointments Division in the Ministry of Personnel, is the most suitable. Though he serves as a Ministry of Personnel official, he is upright and trustworthy, and he is skilled in military and administrative coordination. He can adapt at once to any sudden change."

The moment those words fell, the entire room stirred.

Emperor Xuanwen lifted his brows slightly; the look in his eyes was unreadable.

"Su Zhang…" he repeated softly. His fingertips tapped the dragon desk once, as if weighing the matter. After a long pause, he finally issued the order.

"Appoint Su Zhang as the Transport Minister for this supply mission. He is to depart at once and proceed to the Northern Pass to support the army."

* * * * *

The following afternoon, Su Zhang left through the palace gates and returned to his residence. The sky was faintly overcast. A thin layer of dust had settled on the stone lions before the manor gate, and even the wind was so still it felt oppressively restrained.

When he reached the inner courtyard, the scene from morning court still circled in his mind—unexpected, and yet also expected. The Emperor's cold gaze, naming him in that deep voice, ordering Su Zhang to personally escort this "life-saving money." The weight on his shoulders was so heavy it made even breathing feel stuck.

As he passed a side corridor, he suddenly saw a slender figure standing ahead.

A plain blue robe and gauze skirt—not luxurious in the least, yet her focused brows and eyes made her look exceptionally steadfast.

It was Qin Nianyin.

Su Zhang's steps paused slightly. His heart jolted hard. Lately she had always been avoiding him, yet this time she had taken the initiative to wait for him here. Outwardly his expression did not change, but in the depths of his eyes a secret, restrained joy quietly surged.

"Nianyin—"

He stopped after a single word, forced himself steady, and asked in a calm voice, "You waited here specifically. Is there something you need?"

Qin Nianyin stepped forward. With both hands she produced a heavy gold ingot and placed it gently into his palm.

Su Zhang's mind shook. He lowered his gaze to that gleam of gold and asked hoarsely, "This is…?"

"It is the compensation silver the Third Prince gave before," Qin Nianyin said. Her tone was cool, yet her resolve was unmistakable. "Nianyin is a woman. Though I cannot go to the battlefield and kill the enemy, I still wish to do my part. Please, Cousin, take this gold and send it along with the rest."

Su Zhang frowned, lowering his voice. "If it is compensation the Third Prince gave you, then it was bestowed upon you. Why hand it to me again?"

Qin Nianyin's gaze flickered. She lowered her lashes and spoke softly. "Nianyin knows the whole capital is already in full flame, raising military funds. This is not much, but it is the only… sincerity I have."

A sour ache rose in Su Zhang's chest. He had meant to say "no need," yet seeing the stubborn insistence in her eyes, he swallowed the words back—hard. He accepted it slowly, though his palm trembled faintly.

For a moment, the ingot lay in his hand like a live ember. Its weight pressed into his skin, heavy enough that he could feel the ridge of gold biting against his palm, as if reminding him that this was not mere metal but a portion of someone's resolve.

He lowered his eyes and said nothing. The words he wanted to offer—refusal, reassurance, anything—rose to his throat and stuck there, swallowed back by the discipline he had worn for years. Outside the corridor, the overcast light bled thinly across the flagstones; even the air felt burdened, as though the capital itself was holding its breath for the Northern Frontier. In that single heartbeat, he understood: she was not handing him money.

She was placing a choice into his hands—her attempt to stand on her own, even while stepping toward a road that could bruise and break a person. His fingers tightened unconsciously, the tremor in his palm betraying him before his face ever could.

She turned as if to leave. His heart tightened in sudden urgency, and he blurted out, "Today, His Majesty has already issued the decree. I will personally escort the donated silver to the Northern Frontier."

Qin Nianyin halted.

She turned back. Her eyes were bright, yet carried a searching intent. "Then… is there anywhere else Nianyin can help?"

Su =Zhang looked at her, and warmth rose in him for no reason he could name. The corner of his lips could not help but lift into a faint curve.

"The court has called for voluntary contributions. Not only officials and merchants—many women in the capital have also gathered cloth and food. But…" His tone shifted; his expression sank slightly. "What the army lacks most now is not money. It is medicine and medical officers. The Northern Frontier is harsh and bitterly cold. Once war begins, the wounded will only increase. Yet if we requisition in haste, there are far, far too few physicians."

Qin Nianyin fell silent. Her fingers tightened slightly within her sleeve. She thought for a moment—only a moment—and then lifted her eyes again, her gaze as firm as before.

"If so—then, if Lord Su does not mind… Nianyin is willing to accompany you."

Su Zhang froze. His breathing turned faintly unsteady.

"Nianyin is not a physician," she continued, her voice not loud, yet each word fell with the weight of hammered iron, firm and unmistakable. "But I understand basic bleeding control and bandaging. I can also cook and tend to the wounded. If Lord Su does not find Nianyin foolish or slow, Nianyin is willing to go with the army to the Northern Frontier and offer whatever strength I can."

Su Zhang stared at her.

The curve of his lips finally spread, impossible to restrain.

Yet after Qin Nianyin delivered that last determined line, her chest tightened slightly.

In her mind, fragments she had once heard in her previous life rose up without warning.

Back then, in that Northern Frontier war, Gu Xiao fell on the road. For a time, the army's morale plunged into chaos. Though they ultimately relied on the Tiger Guard's desperate defence and the reinforcements that arrived just in time to win by a hair's breadth, they were still grievously wounded in strength.

Court and country sank into a period of gloom. Officials panicked, and even the Ministry of Revenue's storehouses were emptied by more than half.

And Su Zhang… in that life, he had been so busy he could scarcely be seen. Day and night he handled military funds, dispatched officials, soothed the court—yet his expression remained cold and severe, and he never exchanged so much as a single sentence with her. In that lifetime, his back had looked unbearably heavy. She had watched from afar and felt only that heaven and earth were cold, the weight on her chest so crushing she could hardly breathe.

Qin Nianyin snapped the shadow away. Her fingers clenched tight.

In this life, she would not be a powerless person who only stood aside and watched.

She spoke nothing aloud. Only in her heart did a silent vow form, her lips pressed tight.

Su Zhang merely looked at her quietly. At last, he gave another low laugh, husky yet gentle.

"If you are not afraid of the hardships of this journey, then come with me."

Qin Nianyin turned and walked away, her figure gradually swallowed by the deepening dusk. Su Zhang remained standing beneath the corridor, the heavy gold ingot in his hand seeming to take on a scorching warmth. A hundred flavours churned through his heart—an unspoken pride, and a bitterness he could not put into words.

Chapter 75: North With the Army

The twilight was thick as ink, pressing down heavily upon the courtyard. The firewood had burned to its end, leaving only a faint, dull red glow of embers in the furnace, flickering uncertainly in the deepening night.

Qin Nianyin gently placed the fire tongs, now smoothed by use, beside the kiln. She opened her palms, brushing away the grimy soot clinging to them. She stood still for a moment, then finally turned and walked with steady steps towards the interior of the house.

The old woman still slumped against the table, clutching the half-empty wine pot to her chest, her eyelids half-closed, appearing utterly lost to drunken stupor.

Qin Nianyin, however, knelt formally before her, her voice solemn and earnest. "Master, in the coming days, I must accompany His Excellency Su to escort military funds north. This journey is no childish game.

It is for the soldiers at the frontier and for a clear conscience within my own heart. It is not an abandonment of my path here. If I return safely, I will naturally come back to this place and continue my studies with you properly."

Qiqi started violently, blurting out, "What? To the Northern Frontier?"

Yiyi's eyes widened in shock, immediately following up with a question, her voice trembling, "You speak truly? The war is raging there. How can a woman like you go?"

Qin Nianyin lifted her gaze, her tone calm yet filled with resolve. "The army's medical corps needs reinforcement. If I can add even one more pair of hands, it is my duty to serve the state. I know well the limits of what I can do, but I cannot simply stand by and watch."

The two women listened, exchanging glances. Qiqi was the first to speak through gritted teeth. "If that is the case, then Qiqi wishes to accompany you, Miss!"

Yiyi immediately chimed in, her voice shaking yet unwavering. "Yes, I will go too! Since you are leaving, Miss, I will absolutely not stay behind."

Qin Nianyin was taken aback. Looking at the stubborn determination in their eyes, a pang of sorrow struck her heart, but she did not attempt to dissuade them further.

At this moment, the old woman slowly raised her eyelids. Usually lazy and often smirking, today her expression was uncharacteristically serious, her gaze seeming to pierce through to one's very core.

"The Northern Frontier is bitterly cold and harsh. You... truly have no fear?"

Qin Nianyin shook her head.

In her heart, she was not merely seventeen years old. Reckoning from her previous life to the present, her mind was that of one nearing half a century. She was no young girl and thus, naturally, she felt no fear.

"Girl..." the old woman rasped, her voice trembling slightly from the wine yet unusually clear, "You actually possess such courage... Then you should go."

She stared intently at Qin Nianyin, suddenly letting out a low, soft laugh, a complex emotion in her eyes. "If you return and this old woman isn't dead yet... based on this loyal heart of yours, I will teach you properly."

She understood then that what the old woman had given her was not permission, but a reckoning. Not encouragement, but a wager placed upon her life. To step onto the northern road was to stake her future, her return, even her breath itself. This was no longer merely about learning medicine, nor about youthful resolve. It was a vow that bound teacher and disciple across uncertainty and death alike.

In truth, fear had long since lost its hold on her. Though her body was young, her soul had already traversed a lifetime of endings. She had seen what it meant to arrive too late, to watch lives slip away while standing safely aside. If she remained behind now, sheltered and intact, that would be the true betrayal.

As the drums sounded and the procession moved, Qin Nianyin knew she herself had become part of the convoy's weight. Alongside the silver and medicine, her choice was being carried northward — fragile, resolute, and impossible to turn back.

These few, short words held the weight of a vow.

A sudden warmth surged in Qin Nianyin's chest, her eyes threatening to well up. She kowtowed deeply, her voice slightly tremulous. "Thank you, Master."

Outside the house, the night breeze stirred gently, With a chill that caused the lantern flame to shudder slightly.

* * * * *

The sky was gloomy and overcast, the beat of the drums deep and resonant. Su Zhang guided his horse alongside Qin Nianyin's. His gaze swept over her, noting her slender frame, yet her spine was ramrod straight, her expression resolute and unwavering.

He remained silent for a long moment before finally speaking his voice low. "This journey will mean sleeping in the wind and dew, enduring bitter cold and hardship. You will have to tend to the wounded with the army medics, carry water, brew medicines… It is an undeserved hardship for you."

Upon hearing this, Qin Nianyin shook her head. Her eyes were clear and held a steadfast determination. "It is no hardship at all. To be able to contribute in some small way for the common people, to contribute my humble efforts for the soldiers… I feel… profoundly honoured."

Su Zhang was slightly taken aback. As he prepared to speak again, she pressed her lips together briefly. Her voice was quiet, yet exceptionally distinct.

Her voice carried clearly in the morning air. "If I sought only comfort and ease, I would have remained within the Su residence. But I remember my adoptive parents."

During the great floods, they chose to sacrifice themselves to save others rather than compromise their integrity and spirit. If I only knew how to enjoy a life of luxury, I would be disgracing the profound intention in their hearts."

The wind whistled sharply around them, the morning mist thick and swirling. Having spoken, Qin Nianyin's gaze remained calm and steady, as if no amount of danger lying ahead could shake her even slightly.

Su Zhang turned his head to look intently at her. His heart suddenly constricted. He wanted to say something, but in the end, he pressed those deeply felt, tangled words of his heart back down into his throat, merely responding in a low voice, "...Alright."

Dawn had not yet broken; only a sliver of greyish-white touched the eastern horizon. Yet, on the official road leading out of the capital's outskirts, banners already snapped fiercely in the wind and warhorses neighed long and loud.

Rows of large carts stood in orderly lines. Each was loaded with sealed wooden chests containing tens of thousands of silver ingots, along with medicinal supplies, cloth and silk.

Though the supplies were heavy, for the sake of speed, everything was packed simply for efficient travel. The cart curtains were removed, covered only with coarse hemp cloth. The axles were reinforced with iron strips, giving them a sturdy, unyielding appearance.

At the very front of the procession was a contingent of cavalry clad entirely in black armour. Their plate armour was heavy, their face guards shut tight. Lances and banner-bearing swords were strapped to their backs.

With each fall of their horses' hooves, the ground trembled faintly. These were the Black Armor Guard, personally assigned by the Emperor, renowned as the "Iron Wall," specifically tasked with escorting vital shipments and preventing raids.

A drumbeat sounded ——boom ——low and weighty, seeming to strike deep into the very core of one's being.

Su Zhang, clad in blue-engraved battle armour, stood at the very front. His expression was stern and cold, his eyes burning like torches as they swept over the assembled troops.

His voice was clear, resonant and decisive. "This mission concerns the safety of the entire Northern Frontier! Not a single step can afford disorder! Relay my command ——"

"Move out!"

The cry echoed simultaneously and the procession began its march. Cart axles creaked and groaned; horses' hooves fell in unison. The Black Armor Guard flanked the front and rear, forming two sharp, formidable iron walls tightly encircling and protecting the silver-laden carts.

Qin Nianyin, along with Qiqi and Yiyi, was amidst the procession. She rode a horse with a dark mane, her posture erect. Shrouded in the morning mist, she gripped the reins tightly, yet her fingertips were slightly cold.

She understood clearly in her heart: this was no ordinary journey, but a high-stakes gamble where failure was not an option.

Looking into the distance, the procession gradually advanced further into the morning haze, resembling a heavy iron dragon winding its way towards the uncertain storms gathering at the frontier.

* * * * *

Deep within the Imperial Palace Gardens

Deep within the imperial palace gardens, green willows brushed the ground and the shadows of flowers layered delicately amidst the foliage.

Shen Lingyan had just accompanied her mother to pay respects to the Empress in the central palace.

While the elders conversed inside the hall, she had strolled alone into the gardens, her fingers gently tracing a cluster of peonies beaded with morning dew.

Suddenly, a light laugh sounded behind her. "Miss Shen, would you care to sit with this Prince for a while?"

She turned to see the Third Prince, Li Suo, leaning casually against a pine tree. He was dressed in robes the colour of a lake's blue, a folded fan swaying gently in his hand, his expression bearing its usual indolent and flirtatious air.

Shen Lingyan offered a slight bow, maintaining proper decorum and followed him into a small pavilion nestled within the garden.

Outside the pavilion, flowers bloomed in profusion, their fragrance hanging heavy in the air. Li Suo half-reclined against the stone table, his gaze resting on the vibrant, colourful blossoms in the garden.

He sighed softly. "Such peace and tranquillity here, the shifting patterns of light and shadow among the flowers… It must be a scene utterly different from the desolate, bitter cold of the Northern Frontier."

Shen Lingyan followed his gaze and offered a faint smile. "Indeed. All we women can do is join with a few sisters from other families to donate some jewellery and trinkets in a joint effort, merely to express our sentiment. It cannot compare to the young lady from the Su family… She actually went with the relief army to support the effort at the Northern Frontier."

Upon these words, a silence fell within the pavilion.

"Qin Nianyin?"

Shen Lingyan nodded gently. "Yes, Miss Qin. We are all not her equal."

Li Suo, who had been lounging, suddenly stilled. The folded fan in his fingers trembled slightly. He stared blankly for a long moment before slowly murmuring in a low voice, "...She went with them?"

Shen Lingyan, thinking nothing of it, continued, "I heard she accompanied His Excellency Su personally. Although she is a woman, she insisted on going to assist with the army's medical care and manage the medicines. I… truly rather admire her for it."

A gentle breeze swept through, causing the flower shadows in the pavilion to sway. A complex smile, tinged with both mockery and a hint of being genuinely stirred, curved Li Suo's lips. "So that's how it is… She actually went to the Northern Frontier with Su Zhang."

Shen Lingyan tilted her head to look at him. She saw the depth in his gaze, as if he were lost in thought, yet the true flavour of his reflections remained elusive.

Outside the pavilion, the wind rustled through the willow branches, scattering petals like falling snow. The scene reflected the subtle, unspoken thoughts colouring both their expressions.

Chapter 76: The Rush Toward the Cliff

After half a month of wind-beaten days and nights spent beneath open skies, the supply convoy escorted by the Ironclad Army finally reached the military camp of the Northern Frontier of Great Zhou.

The heavens above the borderlands were shrouded in a dim, oppressive gloom. The wind lashed at them with sand sharp enough to sting the skin, and beyond the camp gates, the banners snapped and cracked in the frigid air.

The moment a single horn sounded across the vast encampment, the entire garrison seemed to ignite into motion at once. Soldiers who had been drilling or standing guard surged forward in a single breath, their boots thundering across the ground like a flood released.

"They are back."

"The grain from the capital has arrived."

These rough, resonant shouts rose and fell without pause, one wave louder and more fervent than the one before it, as though their voices alone were enough to still the sweeping border winds.

Some men raised their long blades, others' eyes reddened and a few tore off their helmets and hurled them into the air, letting them trace bright arcs across the bleak sky.

The moment the carts crossed into camp, the soldiers rushed forward. They crowded around, hands reaching out to support and unload, yet their movements were careful to the point of reverence.

Crates, medicines and bolts of cloth were lifted down from the wagons and there were men whose eyes flushed red the instant they touched those precious supplies.

Their voices, usually coarse and unshaken, trembled with suppressed emotion. "Our thanks. Our deepest thanks to the capital."

One voice began the cry and ten more rose in fierce echo. Soon the shout rumbled across the entire encampment like a wave breaking upon cliffs.

"Our thanks. Our thanks."

The sound surged skyward, as though it meant to tear apart the clouds and sweep away every trace of gloom.

A deputy general, his face wind-scarred and travel-worn, strode toward them with quick steps.

His expression was blazing with relief, and he let out a laugh so bold it nearly broke with emotion. "Lord Su, for you to escort the supplies here yourself, the soldiers of the North owe you a debt they can never repay."

Su Zhang dismounted, the metal of his armour clattering against itself.

His expression was steady and composed, yet he offered a solemn bow. "This journey is nothing more than the fulfillment of duty. If it may offer even the slightest aid to all of you, then it is my honour."

The cheers continued to echo around them. Soldiers clenched their fists, their gazes blazing bright; some drew their blades and lifted them high, the steel catching the pale light, burning like a rising flame.

Yet amid that fervour, Qin Nianyin cast her gaze swiftly across the gathering troops. Her eyes searched with an urgency she could not suppress. In the next heartbeat, her pupils tightened. She did not see the tall, familiar figure she sought. Her heart clenched hard enough to hurt and without considering the eyes around her, she stepped forward abruptly. "Where is General Gu?"

Only then did Su Zhang realize Gu Xiao was nowhere in sight. He asked immediately, his voice pressed low. "Where is General Gu?"

The deputy general faltered. His earlier fervour dimmed, and a faint hesitation flickered between his brows. After a moment, he cupped his fists and answered in a subdued tone. "To report to Lord Su, General Gu and his adjutant took a small scouting party and departed to survey the routes ahead."

"His adjutant. What is his name?"

Qin Nianyin felt her heart lurch violently, as though something cold and poisonous had surged up without warning.

The deputy general, though confused, replied as protocol demanded. "The adjutant's surname is Liang. His personal name is Don."

"Liang Dong."

Around them, the soldiers were still cupping their fists in unison, voices crashing together in a single roar of gratitude—so loud the windborne sand seemed to hesitate midair. Yet for Qin Nianyin, all that fervour receded in an instant, as if someone had extinguished the fire inside her chest.

"The adjutant is Liang Zhong," the deputy general said, enunciating the name as though it were nothing more than a formality.

Zhong.

But what surged up in her mind was not Zhong.

It was Dong.

A single syllable—wrong, and yet dreadfully familiar—hooked into the shadows of her previous life and dragged them to the surface. Her breath caught. The world narrowed to the taste of iron at the back of her throat, to the memory of Gu Xiao not returning after this campaign, to the cold certainty that something must not be allowed to repeat.

"Liang… Dong?" she forced out, her voice turning knife-cold.

Qin Nianyin repeated the name, her voice dropping to a frigid edge. Her stance shifted as she stepped closer and her gaze cut as sharply as drawn steel.

The deputy general stiffened under that piercing stare. His foot slid half a step backward before he caught himself and forced a stiff nod.

In that instant, the colour drained from Qin Nianyin's face entirely. The fatigue of half a month fell away as swiftly as retreating tidewater. What remained in her eyes was a cold, hard clarity and a rise of unhesitating resolve. Her voice was tight when she demanded, "How long ago did they leave? and in which direction?"

"They set out roughly one hour ago." The deputy general hastily pointed toward the northwest. He had barely raised his hand before she spun and bolted forward, her figure already swallowed by the sweeping wind, her eyes filled with resolute purpose.

Qin Nianyin.

The soldiers had not yet reacted when she had already seized the reins of a tall warhorse. Her slender fingers tightened around the leather, her grip clearly unsteady and her entire body trembled with the effort.

Though she had learned to ride in childhood under her foster father's guidance, those skills had long fallen into disuse over the years. The horse pawed violently at the ground, snorting clouds of white mist, its immense strength nearly dragging her off balance.

She gritted her teeth, her knuckles whitening from force and whispered under her breath, "Do not be afraid. You must not be afraid."

With a final breath drawn through trembling lips, she gathered herself and vaulted upward. Her movement was imperfect, almost wavering, yet she managed to land upon the horse's back. The stallion reared with a piercing neigh, then sprang forward, breaking into a full gallop straight through the camp gates.

"Nianyin!" Su Zhang's eyes turned sharply cold, his voice cutting through the air in a deep command.

Qiqi and Yiyi were stunned for a heartbeat before they exchanged a quick look. In the next instant they mounted their horses and shot forward in pursuit.

But Qin Nianyin seemed utterly deaf to all the voices behind her. Her black hair was lifted by the rushing wind, her thin frame drawn taut with resolve and her figure disappeared into the sweeping haze of flying sand as though she were a shadow vanishing into storm.

Su Zhang's eyes narrowed, yet beneath that icy composure a thin fracture of pain spread across his chest.

Without sparing another word, he hauled on the reins and launched into the chase, the black armour on his body catching the sun with a harsh, cold gleam.

The wind howled around them and the pounding hooves roared like thunder rolling across barren plains.

Her silhouette was slipping farther and farther away, retreating step by step as though driven by an obsession no one could restrain.

A sudden realization struck Su Zhang with heavy force. Why was she so frantic? They had only just arrived. They had not even rested. How could the mere mention of the name Liang Dong hurl her into such a state of alarm, as though confronted with imminent peril?

Confusion and unease surged within his chest, yet there was no time to unravel them. Her figure was racing forward with unmistakable determination, as if she meant to disappear into danger itself.

His heart tightened. His brows drew together with cold severity. He jerked the reins sharply and spurred his horse onward.

The wind whipped past them. The earth beat beneath their hooves like drums of war. In Su Zhang's eyes, only one thought remained: regardless of what drove her to flee into the unknown, he could not allow her to face that darkness alone.

When Qin Nianyin had first thrown herself onto the horse, her foot had slipped. She nearly toppled sideways, her body pitching dangerously toward the ground.

Her palm clutched the reins in a desperate grip, though her fingers trembled uncontrollably. The horse beneath her gave a heavy, impatient snort. Her chest rose and fell in frantic motion, each breath burning through her lungs.

It had been far too long since she last rode. After leaving her foster parents' small courtyard, she had never again touched a saddle.

In her memory, her foster father had stood beside her, calmly holding the horse's bridle, guiding her little by little and steadying her shoulders with his warm, broad hands. But now, there was no one left to hold her upright.

The moment the hooves struck the earth, her entire body jolted violently. Every shock rattled through her bones, shaking her so hard her legs almost gave out beneath her, barely able to grip the horse's sides.

The wind lashed at her face with merciless sharpness and her eyes watered uncontrollably until tears were forced out, sliding down her cheeks mingled with sweat.

She was afraid. She was truly afraid ——afraid she would fall, afraid she would fail to stay upright, afraid that her strength would not last.

Yet the pressure crushing her chest was stronger than fear itself.

Liang Dong.

Gu Xiao.

The two names intertwined, pressing down upon her like the shadow of a past life she could never dispel.

She did not truly know what had happened back then; all she knew was that after this very campaign, Gu Xiao had never returned. That loss was a wound carved into the depths of her heart, one that time had never been able to erase.

It could not happen again. It must not.

She clenched her jaw, her fingers turning white as she tightened her grip. Her legs trembled uncontrollably, yet she forced them to press hard against the horse's sides. The stallion let out a sharp, pained neigh, then surged forward with renewed speed.

Mist and sand lashed her face as the wind roared past her ears. She felt as though she might be thrown from the saddle at any moment.

Her heart shook with every jolt, fear clawing at her chest. But she did not dare to stop. She could not stop.

Even if she fell and shattered upon the rocks below, she would still chase after them.

Before the cliff edge, the mountain winds howled, cold and sharp as blades.

Qin Nianyin's horse thundered across the ground, her vision stinging from the onslaught of wind, yet her gaze clung stubbornly to the path ahead.

The world streamed past her in blurred motion: patches of withered grass, jagged stones, looming cliff walls, all swept behind her in an instant. The bitter air sliced her breath apart inch by inch, burning through her chest, but she did not allow herself a single moment of hesitation.

In the distance, she finally caught sight of a solitary, upright silhouette

——

Gu Xiao stood before the cliff, hands clasped behind his back, his dark cloak billowing fiercely in the wind. His figure was tall, austere and solitary, like a blade forged in shadow.

Just then, something at the edge of her vision jolted violently ——

Not far behind him, a man knelt with one knee pressed to the ground, bow in hand, the bowstring drawn to its fullest. The arrow's cold gleam pointed straight at Gu Xiao's unprotected back.

"Gu Xiao ——!"

Her voice tore through the rushing wind, with a desperate tremor.

The archer's fingers twitched and the arrow flew.

A sharp hiss cut through the air. Qin Nianyin felt her heart seize, her blood turning cold in an instant.

Yet the next heartbeat brought a sudden reversal ——the arrow had been thrown off its original course by her cry.

A piercing whistle followed.

The arrow grazed Gu Xiao's shoulder, slicing through the air near his ear. In the instant he turned sharply around, the arrowhead brushed past the side of his sculpted face, carving a thin line of bright red across his skin.

His black hair lifted violently in the mountain wind, strands rising like a dark waterfall, the gleam of fresh blood cutting sharply across that motion.

A sliver of sunlight pierced through the clouds at that exact moment, falling upon his features ——clean, cold, unforgiving. His brows were sharp as blades, his gaze keen and unwavering, yet touched by a strange, fleeting sadness beneath that single stroke of crimson.

Qin Nianyin felt a violent tremor crash through her heart. The reins nearly slipped from her fingers and her entire being seemed frozen by the sight before her ——

In the instant he turned, it felt as though the world fell away.

There were only him and her.

The wind, the pounding hooves, the flash of blood ——all dissolved into the depths of his unfathomable eyes, becoming an eternal heartbeat suspended between them.

Her horse had not even fully stopped when she hurled herself downward, landing with staggering steps. Her feet barely found the ground before she stumbled forward, running straight toward Gu Xiao with unsteady, desperate urgency.

Somewhere behind her came Su Zhang's shout and the hurried footsteps of Qiqi and Yiyi closing in ——but all of it dissolved into nothing.

In her ears, there was only the pounding of her heart and the relentless cry of the wind.

She could hear nothing else at all.

Gu Xiao had only just recovered from the shock of the sudden arrow; as he turned sharply, he saw a familiar figure running toward him against the wind and sand ——skirts snapping wildly, hair dishevelled, her entire gaze fixed solely on him with a mixture of panic and fierce resolve.

He froze, his heart hollowing out in an instant before slamming violently against his ribs, each beat echoing like a war drum that drowned out the raging wind.

Was she ——

Was she running here for him?

The next moment, she was already upon him. His chest tightened and he reacted almost without thought, opening his arms and pulling her firmly into his embrace.

"Gu Xiao ——!"

Her breath was as chaotic as a storm tide, her voice trembling with tears even as she struggled against him. "Let go of me!"

But he held her even tighter, his chest burning, his voice low and unsteady. "Just… let me hold you for a moment."

Her tears would not stop. Her palms pushed uselessly against his armour, but he did not loosen his hold until she wrenched herself free with a desperate twist.

"I didn't come for this!" she cried, choking on each word, her voice shaking beyond control. "I came to save you!"

She stepped back, putting the length of an arm between them, her eyes urgently sweeping over him ——from shoulder to chest, from arms to waist ——searching for wounds that might be hidden beneath the armour.

Only after confirming that aside from the thin streak of blood on his cheek, he was unharmed, did her fingers loosen. The strength drained from her body and her knees buckled as she collapsed onto the ground.

"Thank heavens… thank heavens…"

The fear and remorse she had forced down finally broke loose. Her sobs spilled out uncontrollably, with the weight of two lifetimes of dread and grief, as though every sorrow lodged in her heart had found an escape all at once.

Gu Xiao looked down at her, a relentless tremor running through his chest. The arrow had grazed him moments ago, sharp enough to draw blood, yet the shock of that pain was nothing compared to the upheaval now rising because of her.

She had thrown everything aside ——fear, danger, reason ——simply to reach him.

In that instant, he understood clearly that the fierce longing he had buried in his heart could no longer be contained, no matter how he tried.

* * * * *

The wind howled, sand lashing harshly against his face.

Su Zhang urged his horse forward at full speed, stopping only when he reached the edge of the cliff. As he pulled hard on the reins, the iron-shod hooves skidded across loose gravel, striking sparks that scattered through the air.

All along the way he had chased after her shadow. She had ridden without hesitation, without the slightest regard for danger, as though she meant to break through the boundary between life and death itself.

That reckless determination sent a violent jolt through his chest —— shock, fury and a bleakness he could not even begin to name.

He had never known she possessed such skill on horseback.

She was ——

She was like a book he had never once opened, each page revealing something more startling, more unfathomable than the last.

But the person for whom she had risked everything, racing toward the cliff as if the world were ending ——was not him.

The sight before him struck like a blow.

Qin Nianyin was crying so hard she could barely breathe, collapsed in the swirling sand, while Gu Xiao knelt beside her, one arm wrapped tightly around her trembling shoulders.

The scene seemed to still the heavens themselves; even the mountain winds froze, suspended in the air.

Su Zhang's fingers clenched around the reins until the knuckles drained of all colour.

His lips curved ——not gently, but with a cold, cutting edge, a faint shape of a smile that was sharper than any blade buried in the desert wind.

The wind tore past his sleeves, swallowing every sound around him, leaving only the words that surged, heavy and unspoken, in the depths of his gaze ——

Absurd.

Chapter 77: First Come, First Claim

Qiqi and Yiyi had already moved with swift precision, forcing Liang Dong onto the ground and pinning him there. The snapped bowstring still quivered faintly in the harsh air, its vibration lingering beneath the rising dust.

Amid the drifting grit, Qin Nianyin had collapsed to her knees, tears falling as though a dam within her had burst.

Gu Xiao's chest rose and fell with violent breaths. Instinct urged him forward. He reached out, wanting to help her stand, wanting to steady the trembling line of her shoulders.

Before his hand could lower, another palm struck his aside with unhesitating force.

"Do not touch her."

The voice came from his left, cold and composed, with no hint of doubt.

Gu Xiao turned sharply. He met the dark, steady gaze of Su Zhang.

"What do you mean by that?"

Gu Xiao's voice was rough, threaded with anger that had not yet found its release.

Su Zhang held his stare without flinching. His eyes were clear, unyielding and sharp enough to cut.

"For so many years we have stood as brothers. Do you still not understand what lies in my heart?"

Gu Xiao paused for half a beat, the meaning striking him like a dull blow. His voice lowered.

"You… you have feelings for her."

"Yes."

Su Zhang's answer carried no hesitation. Each syllable was firm, deliberate and free of shame or denial.

Gu Xiao's breath caught. His gaze darkened.

"I was the one who cared for her first."

A faint, cold smile touched Su Zhang's lips.

"She has known me since childhood. The first person she met between you and me was me."

Gu Xiao clenched his teeth so tightly the sound felt like a tremor in the wind.

"That is not how affection is measured. It means nothing."

Su Zhang continued to watch him. His voice remained calm, but the quiet steel within it was unmistakable.

"You are right. It does not determine the outcome. But I once asked you plainly if you had affection for her. Tell me, Gu Xiao, what was your answer? You said there was nothing of the sort, that she merely amused you."

Gu Xiao stiffened. A storm moved through his eyes, deep and conflicted.

"You trapped me into saying that. You twisted the conversation so I would answer as you wished."

The final word had not fully left his lips before his fist struck forward.

A heavy impact landed against Su Zhang's cheek. His head snapped aside and blood gathered at the corner of his mouth.

The second punch followed with greater force. Su Zhang staggered half a step but remained upright. He lifted a hand and wiped away the blood with the back of his fingers, his expression steady. He did not retaliate.

Gu Xiao's fist trembled in the space between them.

"Fight back. Su Zhang. Fight back."

Su Zhang's gaze was firm, unmoving. His voice was deep and resolute.

"You may strike as you must."

The wind howled through the cliffs, wtih the echo of Gu Xiao's shout. Fury and pain tangled in his throat as his third punch fell, but it did not land on Su Zhang's face.

It struck the trunk of a nearby tree.

The sound was dense and heavy. Leaves shook loose and drifted down like muted fragments of the sky. Blood seeped through the cracks between Gu Xiao's fingers, falling onto the earth below.

The sting in his knuckles was sharp, but it could not compare to the turmoil inside his chest, which felt as though something vital had been torn open.

Between the two men, the wind hissed like drawn blades. Anger, hurt and unspoken truths clashed in the narrow space where neither would yield.

Behind them, Qin Nianyin's sobs slowly weakened. Her shoulders shuddered once and the strength drained from her limbs. Without a word, she collapsed, unconscious, onto the windswept earth.

Qiqi and Yiyi both gasped, their voices overlapping in panic.

"Miss!"

They surged forward at once, their hands lifting instinctively as if to catch Qin Nianyin before her body could fully collapse. The movement carried an urgency born not of duty alone, but of genuine fright ——her knees had given way so suddenly that even the wind seemed to flinch.

Yet Su Zhang lifted a hand. His voice cut through the wind with a chill that allowed no question.

"Stand back."

The two froze mid-step. They dared not disobey and could only withdraw quietly.

Su Zhang crouched beside her. His movements were unexpectedly gentle as he gathered her out of the dirt. Her brows were still drawn tight. Tear tracks stained her face, yet she had already slipped into unconsciousness, unaware of the world around her.

He lowered his gaze to her still features. His expression remained unreadable, but his fingertips tightened faintly against the strands of hair that brushed his palm.

So, in the end, the one who holds her is still me.

No matter whom she resists, no matter who else covets her, as long as she lies in my arms at this moment, I will not let go.

A shadow of cold satisfaction curled at the corner of his lips. It vanished in the next breath, leaving his eyes sharp as tempered steel.

Without another word, Su Zhang lifted her securely and swung himself onto his horse. He drew her carefully into his embrace, one arm shielding her, the other gripping the reins.

"Return to camp."

His voice was hard, yet beneath the firmness hid a tremor buried deep within his chest.

Gu Xiao watched the scene with a sensation like fire spreading beneath his ribs. Fury and regret churned together, consuming his breath. His gaze locked onto the two receding figures, unable to tear away from them.

"Bring Liang Dong."

He spun toward his guards, barked the order with a voice that struck like a blade.

Qiqi and Yiyi had already bound Liang Dong tightly, forcing him to his knees. Several tiger-guard soldiers strode forward, seized the prisoner and dragged him upright.

"Take him back to the main camp."

Gu Xiao's voice rolled across the cliffs, deep and unyielding. The soldiers answered in unison, their crisp reply echoing between the rocks.

A harsh wind swept over the precipice, with the remnants of blood and gunpowder. Gu Xiao's knuckles were split and bleeding, yet he paid them no mind. His gaze remained fixed ahead, following the shrinking silhouette of the man and woman riding away.

His breath came heavy. Anger, pain and something far more scalding churned within him.

* * * * *

Night settled over the military encampment. Firelight flickered unevenly, throwing shifting shadows across the tent walls. Smoke curled upward, clinging to the air with a cold, metallic bitterness.

Liang Dong hung bound to a wooden post. Numerous lash marks crossed his back and arms. Blood had dried in harsh streaks, yet fresh rivulets seeped from newly opened wounds. His breath was ragged. His chest rose and fell rapidly, but still he clenched his jaw and refused to speak a word.

Gu Xiao stood before him.

His armour remained on, the metal catching the dim firelight. His gaze locked onto the prisoner with a weight that could crush stone. His voice was hoarse, yet restrained fury pulsed through every syllable.

"Liang Dong, I will ask you one last time. Who ordered you?"

Liang Dong kept his eyes shut. His breath scraped through his throat, thin and broken.

"…General… your subordinate… dares not say."

"You dare not say."

Gu Xiao's eyes turned colder. With a sharp motion of his arm, he gave the command.

A whistle tore through the air.

The whip cracked down.

Blood splattered across the wooden post. Liang Dong's body jolted. A muffled groan escaped him as he pressed his forehead desperately against the wood. His fingers curled so tightly that the nails almost pierced his skin.

Gu Xiao stepped closer, the coldness in his gaze deepening. He seized Liang Dong's jaw in one hardened hand and forced his head upward. His stare pierced straight into the man's eyes, leaving no room for retreat.

Gu Xiao's breath was harsh and uneven. His voice dropped to a low, dangerous growl that trembled at the edge of a shout.

"Speak. Who sent you?"

Liang Dong's throat worked convulsively. His chest heaved with violent breaths. A flicker of madness crossed his eyes, a flash so sharp it looked as though he meant to bite through his own tongue.

"Hold him."

Gu Xiao's command lashed through the tent.

Two tiger-guard soldiers stepped forward at once. They forced Liang Dong's head down, crushing his attempt at self-destruction.

His eyes turned bloodshot, the whites veined with rage and despair. His lips trembled uncontrollably. At last, through a guttural rasp, he pushed out several shaking syllables.

"…It was… the Imperial Consort's husband."

The moment the words fell, the tent collapsed into silence.

Gu Xiao froze where he stood. His entire frame stiffened as if seized by cold iron.

His pupils contracted sharply. He had suspected many. The Crown Prince Li Duan, the Third Prince Li Suo, even Li Xuan.

But never, not once, had he imagined it would be that nearly-forgotten figure ——the consort prince, the quiet son-in-law of the throne, a man who lived far from politics and seemed content to drift like a shadow.

A man utterly without presence.

A man so silent he was nearly overlooked.

A man who had now revealed himself as the hidden venom behind the curtain.

The realization struck with the force of a falling mountain. His breath thickened, pressing hard against his ribs.

"The consort prince."

Gu Xiao repeated the title under his breath. His teeth nearly cut into his own lip.

"You followed me for years. I treated you as a brother. Yet you shot at my back. If that arrow had struck my heart, how would you have returned to answer for it?"

Liang Dong trembled uncontrollably. Struggle twisted in his gaze. His lips shook as though fighting some invisible chain, yet he kept them tightly closed. Sweat and blood trickled down his chin, drop by drop, seeping into the dirt.

His entire body shuddered again. His throat bobbed. At last, he forced out a laugh that sounded broken, a sound split between bitterness and despair.

"Brother? General… you are the heir of a great military clan. The moment you stepped into the northern army, you were a commander. And what am I? I spent ten years bleeding on the frontier, climbed out from piles of corpses, only to end up a deputy beneath you."

His voice shook, yet beneath the trembling lay resentment sharpened through years of silence.

"This world does not reward who fights hardest. It rewards whose name comes with lineage. You rise to the summit without effort. I, Liang Dong, no matter how fiercely I fight, am destined to remain beneath your heel."

Gu Xiao's body jolted. His brows knotted into a dark, severe line.

"So, you betray your brother and your nation?"

Liang Dong's eyes burned red. His hoarse voice ripped out from his throat.

"I did not want to betray anyone. But the consort prince promised… that if I succeeded, he would recommend me as the grand General of the

Northern Frontier. No longer your deputy. No longer the man forever in your shadow."

Silence spread through the tent like winter frost.

The firelight flickered, throwing jagged shadows across Gu Xiao's face. His eyes darkened until they resembled tempered iron.

Liang Dong's breath faltered. His voice dropped to a trembling murmur.

"I only wanted a life with dignity. I was tired of being treated as a shadow."

Blood slipped from the corner of his mouth. His words weakened, thinning like a dying flame. At last his head tilted to one side and he slid into unconsciousness.

The only sound left in the tent was the crackle of burning wood.

A vein bulged sharply at Gu Xiao's temple. He brought his fist down on the wooden table beside him.

The impact was so fierce that the corner of the table splintered apart.

His voice was low and cold, with the bite of a blade drawn in the dark.

"So, this is the consort prince."

Chapter 78: A Feint in the East

The lamps within the command tent glowed a muted amber, their light flickering against rising coils of medicinal fragrance.

Qin Nianyin lay on the pallet, her brow beaded with cold sweat. Her face tightened as though wrestling with unseen shadows.

At times her lips trembled with a broken sob; at others, a faint, hollow smile tugged at them. Disjointed murmurs escaped her throat, half-formed pleas and fragmented names, drifting like the delirium of someone caught between past and present.

Yiyi stood guard beside the bed, her nerves stretched taut. Panic flickered across her expression before she hurriedly pushed aside the curtain and stepped out. Her voice was low and unsettled when she addressed Su Zhang.

"Master Su… Miss Qin seems to have a slight fever. She is talking in her sleep, crying and laughing, as if trapped in a nightmare."

Su Zhang's face darkened at once.

"Fetch the military physician at once."

Before Yiyi could even move, heavy footsteps echoed outside. Gu Xiao strode in, his aura as cold as a storm rolling in from the steppes. The moment he crossed the threshold, his gaze locked onto the pale silhouette lying on the bedding.

"How is she?" His voice was low, pressed down so tightly it carried a near violent intensity.

Su Zhang looked up, his expression cool.

"Only a nightmare. Lower your voice. Do not disturb her."

"A nightmare?" Gu Xiao gave a short, humourless laugh. He stepped forward, fury simmering beneath the restraint in his tone. "Su Zhang, you had better not take advantage of her weakness."

"Gu Xiao." Su Zhang's reprimand cracked through the tent like a whip. He moved to stand before the bed, blocking Gu Xiao's advance. "She is not awake. If you truly care for her, you will not agitate her further."

The two men stood in a strained silence, the thick scent of herbs weighing down the air between them. At last, they stepped out of the tent, boots grinding against the cold earth. Under the snapping banners, they faced each other with barely veiled hostility.

Gu Xiao spoke first, his voice low and metallic.

"Liang Dong has confessed. The one behind him is the Great Prince Consort. I did not expect it… not him."

A brief shadow crossed Su Zhang's gaze, a rare flicker of solemnity.

"This must not be spread. The Great Prince Consort may sit quietly among the imperial kin, but once the border armies become entangled with him, the consequences will spiral beyond control."

Gu Xiao snorted coldly.

"You always calculate three steps ahead. But you, Su Zhang… your heart is deeper than any trench on this frontier. You plot with a calm face each time. Yet this time, you will not drag her into your schemes."

Su Zhang met his glare, his voice steady and sharpened like steel.

"She is not part of any scheme. My intentions are as clear as the sun and moon. I will not step back simply because you command it before any betrothal has been made. And if you presume you already possess her, without her consent, I will not accept that."

Gu Xiao's chest rose sharply, anger and restraint clashing within him. He leaned forward, a cold laugh escaping.

"You speak nobly enough. But you fear you cannot win against me. Otherwise, tell me… why was it me she ran toward at the cliff, without hesitation, ready to throw her life aside?"

Su Zhang's fingers curled slightly, though the faint, icy smile on his lips did not waver.

"A battle is upon us. If we quarrel now, we jeopardize tens of thousands of lives. If you are unwilling to let this go, wait until the war ends. Then we will settle this."

Gu Xiao's gaze sharpened, deadly cold, yet held back. After a tense breath, he turned away with a bitter sound in his throat.

Night wind surged, battering the banners until they cracked sharply against their poles. Even so, the violent currents of tension between the two men remained far more fierce than the raging wind outside.

* * * * *

The military physician set his fingers lightly upon her pulse. He listened in silence, his gaze steady, until at last he withdrew his hand.

"Miss Qin is merely exhausted from travel. Her vital energy is depleted and the sudden fright unsettled her spirit, causing a mild fever. Two doses of medicine and several days of rest should be sufficient. There is no grave concern."

Su Zhang rose and offered a restrained bow.

"Thank you."

The physician closed his medicine case and took his leave. The lanterns dimmed once more, leaving only the drifting scent of herbs suspended in the tent.

On the bed, Qin Nianyin's brows were tightly drawn. Beads of sweat slid down her temples, her lips pressed faintly together, breath uneven and hurried.

Su Zhang watched her for a long moment before finally leaning closer. He lifted a damp cloth and carefully wiped the cold sweat from her brow.

His movements were composed and exacting, his fingertips held in deliberate restraint. Yet the quiet certainty in each gesture left no room for anyone else to intervene. Her pale, unadorned face rested in the trembling candlelight and he did not look away, as though memorizing each fragile contour.

From her lips came broken sounds, wavering from soft whimpers to hoarse pleading.

"…no arrows… run… quickly…"

From her lips, the broken words did not sound like the ramblings of illness alone. They carried direction. Urgency. As though she were no longer trapped within the tent, but back at the cliff's edge, watching someone stand with his back exposed to death. It was not fear for herself that surfaced in her delirium, but a desperate insistence that another must live.

The same fragments struck both men —yet not in the same way. One felt them like a blade pressed against his ribs, sharp and immediate. The other bore them in silence, letting the weight sink inward, measured and restrained. Neither spoke. In that suspended breath, it became painfully clear: even in sleep, her heart was running toward danger ahead of her.

The words were slurred, but each syllable carried a sting.

Silence fell like a blade. Gu Xiao stiffened where he stood, his entire frame jolting. His eyes narrowed sharply and for a heartbeat he felt something heavy and breath-stealing crush against his chest.

Su Zhang's brows lowered in a sudden shadow and though his face remained composed, his fingers curled ever so slightly beside his knee.

Outside the tent, Qiqi could no longer hold herself still. Fury twisted across her features.

"Why should he be the only one allowed to stay with Miss?"

Before she finished, she moved to lift the curtain.

Yiyi caught her arm, her expression firm.

"No."

"Why not?" Qiqi's voice dropped, but her anger trembled just beneath the surface.

Yiyi only shook her head. Her tone was quiet, yet edged with a rare, steady certainty.

"My master will take care of her. If we charge in now, we will only disturb her."

Qiqi's chest rose and fell with agitation. She bit down hard on her lower lip, her knuckles whitening as her nails dug into her palm.

"No. I want to see her. I want to take care of her."

Yiyi held her back. Qiqi pushed forward. The two exchanged several quick moves, until Yiyi finally raised her voice in frustration.

"Can you truly not see who Miss holds in her heart?"

"Of course I can. It is General Gu. Miss has been nothing but cold toward Lord Su this whole journey, yet she ran herself breathless for General Gu's sake when danger struck…"

"Wrong." Yiyi's answer cut the air sharply. "She pushed him away."

Qiqi froze.

Lowering her voice, Yiyi forced the truth out with quiet gravity.

"If she truly felt nothing for Lord Su, she would not have gone to such lengths to appear indifferent. This is precisely the kind of distance born from concealment."

Qiqi fell silent.

Inside and outside the tent, two currents ——one motionless and one restless ——rose and churned in opposite directions. Yet both were suppressed, sinking heavy and unspoken into the stillness of the night.

* * * * *

The command tent blazed with light. Upon the sand table, the contours of mountains and plains stood stark beneath the glow, every ridge and valley marked by ranks of black and white flags thrust densely into the grit. Gu Xiao stood before it with his hands clasped behind his back, his brows drawn tight, his gaze honed to a blade's edge.

"Scouts have returned," the deputy general reported, pointing to a cluster of crimson markers. His voice carried the weight of a looming storm. "The enemy is massing its main force in the eastern plains. The terrain there is wide and open ——if they advance in full, we will be forced into a direct confrontation. As for the western border ——" He indicated a remote corner of the map. "There lies only a sheer ravine. Impassable. No army could possibly mount an assault from there."

The gathered officers nodded. A quiet, heavy pause followed.

Gu Xiao, however, did not speak. His gaze remained fixed upon the western edge of the sand table. In his mind flashed the image of Qin Nianyin racing toward the camp earlier that day ——her eyes fierce, her voice sharp:

"Remember. Guard against a feint."

His chest tightened. Then his expression shifted ——storm gathering beneath still water.

"…No."

The single word cut through the tent like a drawn sword. The officers stiffened.

Gu Xiao reached forward. With a swift, decisive motion, he plucked the crimson flag from the east and drove it into a narrow pass in the west. His voice rang out cold and unyielding, as implacable as iron:

"The enemy's true strength is not in the east. It lies here, in the west."

"General?" the deputy faltered. "But the western ravine is a natural barrier. Even scouts traverse it with difficulty ——how could an entire army cross it?"

"Precisely because it seems impossible," Gu Xiao replied, "it becomes the most perilous point. If they intend a surprise strike, they will choose the path no one believes can be taken. Their display in the east is nothing more than a diversion. The true blade lies in the shadows."

His knuckles tapped the sand table, each strike crisp, like the measure of an executioner's drum. His gaze swept the map with icy clarity, each word slicing through doubt:

"If the west falls, the entire northern frontier collapses. But if they truly dare approach through the ravine, then they step willingly into our net. Let them believe we guard the east and neglect the west. Once they enter the choke point, we crush them in a single blow."

The officers exchanged uneasy glances. One ventured a cautious objection.

"General… would this not be too great a risk? If we misjudge, then ——"

"'If'? " Gu Xiao's laugh was cold, sharp as steel striking stone. He surveyed the room, his voice lowering to a hard, unforgiving timbre.

"The battlefield favours no man who clings to imagined safety. A capable enemy never walks the road we expect. This is not recklessness. This is using their ambition to bury them."

"General… if we miscalculate, it could mean annihilation."

"Then tell me ——" His voice thundered with a restrained ferocity. "What commander fears defeat? No general under Heaven wins every battle. Send my orders! Fortify the west at once. In the east, maintain only the appearance of strength ——no more. Conceal our true intent. If the enemy dares descend that ravine, then let them enter and never return."

The officers straightened as one, their fists clasped.

"By your command!"

The air within the tent shifted ——sharpened, thickened. A killing aura surged like a rising tide. Outside, distant drums rumbled, as if heralding the bloodshed soon to come.

Gu Xiao's eyes returned to the sole crimson flag planted in the western pass. His chest tightened once more.

He did not know why he believed this so wholly. He only knew that the voice of the woman who had ridden to warn him ——her breathless certainty ——seemed to echo now within his own resolve.

He believed her.

Chapter 79: Whispered Dreams

The lamplight flickered against the canvas walls, casting wavering shapes that mingled with the faint scent of medicine and the sharper edge of cold sweat.

Upon the narrow cot, Qin Nianyin twisted restlessly, her brows drawn tight, her lips trembling with fragmented murmurs, as if wrestling with some unseen nightmare.

Su Zhang kept silent vigil at her side. His fingers tightened around the embroidered handkerchief he held, fine perspiration beading along his own temples. When her trembling worsened, he leaned forward at last, lifting the cloth to gently wipe the sweat gathering along her brow.

Just before the fabric touched her skin, her eyes snapped open.

Dark, deep and utterly lucid, they locked onto him with a chill that did not belong to this moment. For a heartbeat, Su Zhang froze, his hand suspended in mid-air.

"...Nianyin?" he whispered, the tentative note in his voice betraying his unease.

The woman on the bed slowly pushed herself upright. Then, with a curl of her lips, she smiled ——a thin, cold smile that cut like frost. Her voice was hoarse but clear, each word landing with the sharpness of steel.

"Lord Minister... what brings you back so early today?"

Su Zhang stiffened. His breath caught.

Lord Minister? He was but a ranking official of the Ministry of Personnel's selection bureau. How could he have leapt to the rank of Minister?

"What... what did you say?" His voice dipped low, yet tension coiled through his chest, winding tight.

Qin Nianyin's gaze flickered with scorn ——scorn laced with glistening tears. Her smile carried a quiet bitterness, the kind that cut deeply without raising its voice.

"There is no one else here. You need not pretend concern. We have been married for twenty years. I can care for myself. Go on with your duties."

"Married... twenty years?"

Su Zhang nearly choked on the words. A tremor rippled through his voice. His fingers clenched around the handkerchief until the knuckles blanched.

He leaned closer, throat tightening and asked urgently, "Then… who am I?"

Qin Nianyin's expression shifted into one of weary amusement, as though he had told a joke far beneath her notice. She gave a faint, humourless scoff.

"I am not yet so old as to forget names. Lord Minister Su, ranked third in the imperial examinations in the year of Gengzi, esteemed as Su Zhang, Minister of Personnel. Have you forgotten even yourself?"

All colour drained from his face. Cold sweat gathered along his spine. His heartbeat surged ——pounding, disordered, almost painful.

No… this is wrong…

The thought hammered violently inside him as he struggled to breathe.

He tried to steady himself, forcing control back into his shaking voice. "Tell me… what year is it now?"

Her eyes grew distant. Tears rolled down her cheeks, one after another, but she laughed softly ——a sound so brittle and aching it hollowed the air itself.

"How forgetful you have become. It is the fifteenth year of Taiwu. Eighteenth day of the sixth month."

Her voice faltered. A shadow crossed her gaze and her next words splintered with raw pain.

"You do not know, do you? Had our child lived… he would be twenty years old this year."

A hollow thunder seemed to crack through Su Zhang's skull.

His mind went blank.

His chest seized as if crushed by an invisible weight.

Breath deserted him.

He stood rooted to the ground, stunned, shattered by a life he had never lived.

"Child…?"

His voice trembled so faintly it was almost lost in the air.

The tears on Qin Nianyin's cheeks fell more rapidly, each drop like the splintered notes of a broken zither string, tugging mercilessly at the deepest part of his chest.

"I never told you… we once had a child. But when you entered the palace for ten days, you had no patience to hear me out before leaving and when you returned… the child was already gone."

Her voice wavered with anguish. She clutched the thin blanket tightly in both hands, her sobs suppressed yet piercing, as though years of unspoken pain had finally surged upward, unable to be contained any longer.

Su Zhang's entire frame shook. His hands lifted instinctively, then dropped again in helplessness. He stared at her, stunned, his throat clogged so tightly that not a single word could pass through.

"Impossible…" he whispered.

His knees weakened and he rose abruptly, the motion sharp and unsteady. As his sleeve swept outward, the small table beside the bed toppled with a harsh clatter and the porcelain bowl fell to the ground. The sound of shattering rang through the tent, sharp enough to sting the ears.

Qin Nianyin continued to cry without pause. Her tears soaked the pillow beneath her head, spreading into a darkened patch of sorrow. Little by little, the force of her sobs weakened.

Her voice sank to a faint murmur and at last, exhausted beyond resistance, her eyelids lowered and she slipped once more into a heavy sleep.

Silence fell inside the tent, broken only by the fragile rhythm of her breathing.

Su Zhang remained motionless where he stood. His face had drained of all color, turning as pale as the canvas walls. His hands hung stiffly at his sides, his fingertips icy to the touch.

His chest felt as though a massive weight had settled upon it, making each breath painfully difficult. Cold sweat gathered along his brow, dripping slowly, one drop after another.

He stepped backward without awareness, his footing unsteady, nearly stumbling. His gaze had lost its focus, drifting in the emptiness before him, as though he were still imprisoned within the echo of those words about twenty years of marriage and a child who never lived long enough to breathe.

"No..."

The whisper escaped him, hoarse to the point of breaking.

He could no longer remain inside the tent. With a sudden turn, he staggered outward, nearly tearing aside the tent flap. The night wind struck him full in the face, yet he felt even colder, his pallor rivalling the faint light of the moon.

He had never known fear like this.

* * * * *

At the same time, Su Zhang nearly fled the military tent. The night wind pressed against him, sharp and biting, but it did nothing to steady the turmoil inside his chest.

His breathing rose and fell unevenly, as though something heavy had lodged beneath his ribs, refusing to be dislodged. His steps faltered and he braced a trembling hand against a nearby wooden post to keep himself upright.

The encampment was unnaturally quiet. From the distance came only the muffled cadence of soldiers keeping time with the night watch. The moonlight cast an icy sheen across the ground, yet his face was even colder, drained of the last trace of warmth.

Beside him, a large water jar reflected his distorted figure. He leaned down and scooped up a handful of water. The chill of it bit into his palms and spread across his cheeks, helping him suppress the tide of breath he could not control.

Droplets trailed down his face and along his jaw, yet he remained unaware of the wetness. On the trembling surface of the water, his reflection quivered, lengthening and warping until it resembled a visage that was his and yet not his: a face etched with twenty years of weariness, aged by a life he had never lived.

The dreams she uttered, the fragments of another life, pierced him with relentless precision.

"Lord Minister..."

"Twenty years of marriage..."

Each phrase reverberated through his mind, leaving trails of cold dread in their wake.

"Taiwu, fifteenth year…"

"The child we lost…"

He drew in a slow breath, attempting to steady himself, yet the weight in his chest refused to loosen. No matter how he forced calm into his thoughts, the suffocating pressure only grew heavier, spreading through him like a rising tide.

He had never believed in spirits or fate, nor in any tale of w andering souls or divine premonition, yet at this moment, he trusted this dream far more than he would ever trust an omen carved upon stone.

Taiwu.

The reigning era was known as Xuanwen and no such reign title had ever been declared. If her words held truth, then it belonged to a future not yet written, named by an emperor who had yet to ascend.

What she spoke of came from a time beyond the present, a fragment of years he had not lived.

Lord Minister.

He was nothing more than a moderate role in the Personnel Directorate, still a long distance from the seat of a Minister. If he were to rise to that height, it would mean his path led straight into the very heart of the court, where only the most powerful of officials were permitted to stand.

Twenty years of marriage.

His heart throbbed with a violent jolt. She would marry him in that other life; they would share their days for two full decades, morning and night, in the same household and yet she would speak to him with such distant coldness.

What manner of marriage would that be, where two people lived side by side yet could not reach each other, not even across the span of twenty years?

A child.

The word cleaved through him with the force of a blade.

"We once had a child… but you left for the palace and when you returned, the child was gone…"

Her trembling voice in the dream had seared itself into his ears, burning with a pain he could not dispel.

His vision swayed and dimmed and for an instant he seemed to see an empty bundle of swaddling cloth, light as air in her arms, while she cried with a grief fierce enough to tear the sky apart, yet there was nothing ——nothing ——left for her to hold.

Su Zhang clenched his fist abruptly, the veins standing rigid across the back of his hand. His thoughts snarled into a tangled mass, each thread pulling against the next, filling him with a bewildering mixture of sorrow, fear and disorientation.

He lifted his gaze toward the moon, which hung suspended like polished silver in the night sky, looking down with an indifferent gleam, as though witnessing an ending long predestined.

If what she had seen truly belonged to the years ahead…

His voice wavered, the sound scarcely more than an unsteady whisper, fragile enough to crumble with a single breath.

"Then is that truly the end awaiting us?"

The night wind sharpened, cutting across his skin like a blade of frost. The ache in his chest tightened again, pressing so heavily that he could barely draw air.

Beneath the moonlight, his shadow curved upon the ground, unsteady, trembling, merging gradually with the aged and weary reflection he had glimpsed in the rippling water earlier.

If their past life had already ended in such desolation, and if she had returned now bearing every memory of it, then what chance did he possess?

The confidence he once held, the quiet pride that had followed him all his years, shattered completely within him, leaving only bare and trembling uncertainty.

It felt as though fate itself had reached out a cold hand.

Chapter 80: The Armies Begin Their March

The candle flame quivered in the draft, its shadows stretching and then drawing tight again across the table. Su Zhang sat at his desk, the tips of his fingers resting on a freshly copied list of military names.

The horn tore through heaven and earth.

Its long, guttural call rolled over the ridgelines and crashed down upon Wulan Ridge, where dust surged up like a waking tide and the ground itself seemed to shudder.

For a single breath, two armies stood locked in silence beneath the oppressive sky—iron scales, snapping standards and the harsh, animal cry of warhorses swelling until it felt as though the valley could no longer contain it. Then the drums answered, deep and relentless, and the air thickened into something that tasted of blood.

The banners of the Northern tribes snapped in the wind, the iron scales of their armour shimmered with a cold gleam and ten thousand horses shrieked in a chorus that shook the air.

Their war drums pounded in deep, thunderous rhythm, each beat echoing across the valley like distant mountains answering one another, filling the field with a suffocating force of violence.

The Great Zhou army formed its lines beneath the ridges. Standards rose in dense rows, armour glinted with sharp light and the faces of the soldiers were hard as iron. Spears lifted in unison until they resembled a forest of steel; shields locked tightly together and every breath they took deepened the pressure in the air.

Gu Xiao stood at the front of the formation. His expression was severe and the Tiger Guards behind him held their ranks like an immovable wall, waiting for the inevitable clash.

For a moment, the wind, drums and hooves collided in an overwhelming noise that made the heavens themselves seem to shake.

Suddenly, the Northern horn sounded again and dust erupted across the eastern flank. A tidal wave of iron cavalry burst forth, charging with the fury of a storm toward the Great Zhou lines.

The valley quivered to the roar of a single word.

"Kill."

The front ranks of the Great Zhou army met the impact at once. Blades collided, spears splintered and blood sprayed across white armour. The war drums beat with frantic urgency, yet the formation gradually shifted backward, step by measured step, fighting while retreating.

Young soldiers clenched their jaws until their teeth nearly cracked and even as their throats vibrated with hoarse growls, they refused to loosen their grip on their spears.

The Northern tribes sensed momentum and their cries surged skyward as they pressed toward the central encampment.

Just as the eastern line sank into a vicious stalemate, movement rippled across the western flank.

From the shadows of tangled forest and broken stones, countless dark figures erupted all at once. It was the second main force of the Northern tribes, the troops who had slipped into that treacherous terrain long before dawn.

They now revealed themselves in a sudden strike, intending to carve through the rear of the Great Zhou formation.

The leading general of the Northern tribes threw back his head in triumphant laughter.

"They have taken the bait. There is no way they could know a path exists here."

The narrow track lay hidden beneath overgrown weeds and scattered boulders, scarcely wide enough for a single horse. Only those born in the harsh borderlands would know that such a road existed at all. The Northern tribes had chosen it as their secret route and were brimming with confidence.

Yet just as they poured forth in full force, the ridges themselves answered.

Horns rose from every direction atop the cliffs.

The sound reverberated through the valley in a long, commanding call.

In the next moment, the Great Zhou ambush revealed itself. Shields lifted in tightly woven layers until they resembled a fortress of iron. Archers drew bowstrings in unison, their fingertips trembling but unwavering in resolve.

Gu Xiao stood upon the ridge, his eyes sharp as fire and with a single decisive sweep of his arm he gave the command.

"Loose."

Ten thousand arrows launched together. The sky darkened beneath the storm of steel. The arrowheads tore through the air with the sound of wind and thunder, plunging directly into the ranks of the advancing Northern cavalry.

Screams erupted across the valley as bodies fell from their horses. Blood sprayed across stone and mounts reared and bucked in terror. The Northern forces collapsed into chaos, crushed between their own momentum and the sudden rain of arrows.

Horses trampled footmen, armour collided in confusion and the formation twisted into a desperate struggle for space.

"This is impossible."

The Northern general's voice cracked as his eyes bulged with disbelief.

"It is impossible. How could the Great Zhou know this path existed."

Yet no explanation could change the outcome. Arrows continued to descend in relentless waves. The shield wall held its ground like a mountain. The roar of battle rolled like thunder.

The Northern army had meant to launch a brilliant surprise attack. Instead, they had charged straight into a trap. A sheer cliff blocked their escape on one side and on the other the unyielding shield wall prevented any advance.

To the left lay a storm of arrows and to the right swept the Tiger Guards who had already begun their flanking charge.

The cries of combat surged like rolling thunder. Blood and fire interwove in the narrow ridges. Horses screamed, fallen banners snapped under frantic hooves and the Northern general's figure vanished beneath the crush of panicked soldiers.

In the span of a heartbeat, the battlefield had turned completely.

The outcome had been decided.

* * * * *

The battlefield churned with blood-tinged smoke as the cries of slaughter rose to drown the sky. Gu Xiao rode to the highest rise at the front lines, his horse stamping at the blood-soaked earth below. From that vantage point he watched the western ambush erupt, watched the storm of arrows descend in seamless waves and watched the Northern army collapse in a single breath.

His chest tightened and a fierce, silent tremor spread beneath his ribs.

Remember. Guard against a feint in the east and a real strike in the west. And the people around you… you must be careful.

That day outside the encampment, she had spoken to him while barely able to breathe. Her voice had trembled, yet she had forced every word out with unwavering resolve. The memory of her warning cut through him now with the precision of a blade.

Had it not been for her… had she not repeated it again and again, he would certainly have made the same assumption as the other generals.

No one would have imagined that hidden beneath those weeds lay a narrow passage the Northern tribes could use. No ordinary strategist could have guessed it. Yet he had chosen to trust her, and he had staked the lives of the entire army on that trust.

Now the arrows had ceased, the enemy was in full retreat, and the battlefield shook with the sound of their collapse. However, no triumph rose within his heart. What filled him instead was a deep, indescribable shock.

How had she known?

Such foresight surpassed many who had weathered countless campaigns. Such clarity could not be learned from mere observation. It spoke of something deeper, something that unsettled him even as it compelled him.

Gu Xiao felt a violent pulse surge through his chest. From the moment she had ridden to the camp for him, reckless and fearless, until this instant when the tide of battle turned exactly as she had foreseen, he could no longer deceive himself.

Qin Nianyin was the miracle placed in his fate.

She was not a woman meant to hide behind anyone's sheltering hand. She was someone who could stand beside him on the battlefield, someone who could tip the balance of war, someone who could shift the heavens themselves.

His horse stepped through pools of blood and his heartbeat thundered against his ribs. A rough sound rose in his throat, half a roar and half a vow, yet he forced it back with effort.

If I live to return from this war, I will never let her go.

* * * * *

The fire inside the command tent wavered restlessly, casting a crimson glow across the enclosing walls. The lamps were dim, their flames trembling with each shift of the draft.

Su Zhang sat alone behind the low desk, his expression hidden in the shadow that pooled beneath the canopy.

Documents lay spread at his side, yet he had not turned a single page for a long while. The entire tent was wrapped in a silence so dense that only the faint crackle of burning oil could be heard.

Suddenly, the curtain was flung open.

Gu Xiao strode in with heavy steps. His armour was stained with fresh blood, his presence burdened with the metallic weight of the battlefield. He removed his helmet and threw it onto the desk with deliberate force.

His voice was low and thick with the remnants of battle, yet even the shadow of exhaustion could not conceal the exhilaration beneath it.

"We have won a great victory. The enemy has collapsed. Their casualties are countless, while our men have lost no more than a dozen."

Su Zhang lifted his gaze for a brief moment. His expression remained unchanged.

Gu Xiao, however, grew increasingly animated as he spoke. A fierce gleam rose in his eyes and the timbre of his voice sharpened with unrestrained pride.

"Do you know to whom this victory belongs?"

He did not wait for an answer. His lips curled slightly yet he spoke each word with intentional emphasis.

"Qin Nianyin."

The light in the tent seemed to pause, settling into stillness.

Gu Xiao approached slowly, as if savouring each step, his tone immersed in a heavy yet triumphant recollection.

"That day, when we set out from the capital, she came all the way to the outskirts of the camp. Her face was drenched with sweat, but her gaze cut like steel. Her voice trembled, yet she still forced out every word, telling me to beware of a false attack in the east and to guard against those near me."

He raised his hand slightly, as though tracing her desperate movement when she had reached for him. His voice dropped, rough and hushed.

"She was nearly in tears. Her hands were shaking, yet she held onto me with everything she had."

When he finished, he drew in a breath and let out a low laugh. Confidence shone across his face as if it were light itself.

"Would she have risked so much if she did not worry for me? If she did not ride here for my sake? Tell me, Zhang. Is she not the blessing Heaven granted me? She was there for me."

The last four words landed with the weight of iron.

Su Zhang's fingertips moved slowly over the surface of the wooden table, as though without intent. Yet the movement gradually tightened. The firelight caught the edge of his gaze, revealing a faint, razor-cold glint deep within.

He suddenly remembered the journey to Jiangnan—the instant she stepped into the path of the arrow, placing her body between him and death. The blow tore into her right shoulder; her clothes were soaked through with blood. Yet she had not hesitated, not even for a single breath, to place her own life aside.

Now she had done the same for Gu Xiao.

Why was it that she placed her life behind theirs, again and again, as if her existence were a thread tied between the two of them, pulling her toward danger without question?

The light shifted. Shadows washed across Su Zhang's face, obscuring half his features. He remained silent, seated with a stillness that seemed carved from stone, yet there was an invisible tension coiled tightly around him.

Gu Xiao, oblivious to the storm beneath that calm exterior, grew more impassioned. His voice rang louder with each sentence, every word striking the air like a hammer.

"Her face was covered in sweat and yet her gaze remained sharp as a blade. She warned me to guard against a feint in the east. She told me to beware of someone close."

"She was shaking, yet she grabbed my arm with all her strength. She was nearly in tears that moment."

Every phrase landed like a blow.

Su Zhang slowly lowered his gaze. His fingers curled beneath his sleeve, the knuckles paling as they tightened. A faint sheen of sweat gathered at his temples, yet his breathing remained perfectly controlled, not a trace of tremor allowed to surface.

Taking the silence for concession, Gu Xiao's pride swelled further. His voice rose, ringing with bold, triumphant certainty.

"Brother Su, you are always meticulous and cautious. But this time, you must admit it. She saved my life—and she saved Da Zhou."

The fire leapt suddenly, its light flaring across Su Zhang's eyes. For an instant, they shone—cold, unfathomable, sharp enough to cut.

In his mind, however, Gu Xiao's embellished recounting began to entwine itself with the strange fragments Su Zhang had personally experienced. One image after another surfaced, each slotting into place with unnerving precision.

The uncanny slip of paper he had found before leaving for Jiangnan, the one with its cryptic warning.

The moment during the assassination attempt when she threw herself before him, taking the arrow against her shoulder.

The fevered delirium in which she murmured unfamiliar words, as though recalling a time that did not belong to this world.

The instant Liang Dong betrayed them, she spurred her horse without hesitation to save Gu Xiao.

And most of all, the enemy ambush revealed in this battle—the very one she had warned of, her voice trembling with urgency.

These scattered pieces, each seemingly insignificant on its own, formed a single inescapable conclusion. Without knowing the future, how could any of it be explained?

Gu Xiao noticed Su Zhang's continued silence. He mistook it for subdued resignation, believing his own momentum had fully overwhelmed the other man.

Pride surged in his chest. He laughed—a loud, satisfied sound—seized his breastplate and turned toward the exit.

Just before stepping beyond the curtain, he paused and deliberately glanced back. His voice dropped, edged with a faint, taunting sharpness, each word pressed forward like a blade.

"Zhang, you should be grateful that such a woman stands at your side. Only…"

He lingered there, his gaze darkening, the curve of his lips touched with an unreadable gleam.

"With how fiercely she worries for me, even the coldest heart would be scorched open by her tears."

With that, he strode away. His laughter carried into the night, dissolving into the wind beyond the tent.

In the flickering firelight, Su Zhang's fingertips had already bitten into his own palm. A thin bead of crimson welled up and slid slowly across his skin.

His eyes darkened, the colour sinking deep, like ink left too long beneath winter frost. Within his chest, something violent and terrifying surged, hammering against his ribs.

His breathing grew heavier, his lungs rising and falling under strict restraint. Every emotion was forced down, crushed beneath the rigid line of his lips. Beneath his sleeve, his fingers curled hard, the knuckles aching as though he meant to grind this sudden fear into dust.

The military insight she possessed.

The incoherent words she spoke in fever.

Even the strange note.

It had likely all come from her hand. Otherwise—how could she have known events long before they ever occurred?

Everything that had transpired, every clue, every scattered fragment, all pointed toward one truth.

Qin Nianyin had truly lived another life.

* * * * *

The command tent returned to silence.

The lamplight flickered across the desk, casting shadows that stretched and shrank with each wavering flame.

Su Zhang remained seated. His fingers slowly uncurled, though his palm still bore the crescent marks he had carved into it moments ago.

Compared to Gu Xiao's glowing triumph, he felt only the crushing weight of a millstone on his chest. No surge of victory touched him.

He closed his eyes. Something dry and bitter kept rising in his throat.

Gu Xiao's words still reverberated in his ears, each syllable sharp as a needle, pricking through his composure.

Nianyin… truly the Savior of Great Zhou.

Had she not intervened, the battle would have turned to ruin. Of this he had no doubt.

And yet the notion of rebirth was so absurd it verged on heresy. If such a truth were exposed, others would never see her as a saviour, only as a monster—an ominous aberration. What would follow would not be recognition, but execution.

His throat constricted, as though seized by an unseen grip.

The words she murmured in fever. The moments of cold vigilance, the instinctive distance in her gaze.

If she truly had lived once before, then ——

In that former life, he had given her neither shelter nor warmth.

Worse ——he had likely been the very person who drove her heart to its breaking point.

A knife-like pain tore through his chest.

No wonder she kept her distance. No wonder her gaze never softened.

It was not indifference ——it was a wall built from wounds she still remembered.

He wanted to ask her.

Ask what she had seen of the past.

Ask what kind of marriage they once had, twenty long years.

Ask if, in this life… or even in the last… her heart had ever turned toward Gu Xiao.

But another voice whispered back at him, soft and merciless.

What would you do with her answers?

If every word she speaks is true, can you bear it?

If she speaks only of your failures, your cruelty, your inability to protect her ——will you survive it?

His fingers trembled. Cold sweat slid down his temples.

Every emotion surged inside him, but he forced them down until nothing remained on his face but rigid stillness. He lifted his eyes and stared at the wavering flame.

To ask… or to pretend he knew nothing?

His chest swelled painfully with the weight of it. No answer came.

Outside, the soldiers roared with laughter, celebrating a long-awaited victory.

But inside the tent, only the candle crackled softly, burning upon a face darkened like tempered steel.

Every cry of triumph from beyond the canvas struck him like a tolling bell ——heavy, hollow, pounding against his heart.

He could almost see it:

If he truly did confront her, how would she look at him?

A cold glance, telling him he had been a man without tenderness, without strength ——one who had broken her faith?

Or a quiet admission that her heart had already belonged to someone else?

Either possibility cut deeper than any blade and so, through the long night, he found no answer.

Chapter 81: The Sealing of the Princess Residence

Before the vesper bells had yet to sound, thunder suddenly rolled across the streets of Chang'an ——not from the heavens, but from iron-shod hooves striking stone.

The vanguard in black armour swept forward close to the ground, shadows streaking past deserted stalls.

From the ramparts, war drums boomed three times ——heavy, measured, resonant. One by one, the ward gates of the city dropped their iron bolts. Four major intersections were sealed in unison, the clatter of chains echoing like a verdict.

The Commander of the Imperial Guards rode at the front, a pale ash-coloured cloak whipping behind him. Under one arm he carried a lacquered yellow edict coffer; in his other hand he bore a military writ stamped in cinnabar. Behind him surged an uncountable tide of black-armoured soldiers.

They entered from the Gate of Heavenly Manifestation, drove straight into the offices of the Imperial City Division, then split into four prongs ——each heading for a single target: the residence of the grand Princess.

Residents were shouted back beneath the shelter of their eaves. They watched, wide-eyed, as waves of black armour surged into the narrow lanes, closing in like an iron ring. Spears rose like a forest; shields interlocked into a wall.

In front of the Princess Residence, the vermilion pillars and polished jade steps were swallowed in moments by heavy infantry. Crossbows were raised. Bowstrings tautened. Arrowheads glinted, dark as storm clouds.

The chief steward of the Princess Residence stumbled out, face drained of blood, limbs shaking like reeds in winter wind.

"Her Highness is still resting after her noon meal. My lords… w-what is the meaning of this?"

"By imperial command!"

The Commander flipped open the edict coffer. The golden-edged scroll unfurled; a blaze of yellow imperial script gleamed beneath the dusk light.

"Decree of Emperor Xuanwen: The Imperial Consort Prince, Zhao Ziqi, is charged with conspiring with foreign enemies and plotting the murder of a commanding general. Imperial Guards are to surround and search the premises at once, seize the accused and escort him into custody. The Princess Residence is to be sealed until further notice. Any who obstruct this order shall share his crimes."

Beside him, the Deputy Censor-in-Chief presented accompanying documents from the Censorate ——an emergency memorandum, the Tiger-Guards' military seal and original battle reports from the northern front. The vermilion wax was still soft; the parchment corners carried traces of windblown sand.

A collective hiss rippled through those gathered outside.

The steward, who had attempted to maintain courtesy, froze when he saw the envoys cast down the imperial writ of confiscation ——inked with the gold bell of authority. At last he could only whisper, trembling, "P-please… enter."

The Imperial Guards flooded into the residence like a steel tide. Their armour plates scraped against one another, the grinding sound rising and falling like the sea.

Serving maids in the front courtyard and the house stewards under the banner tent were all ordered to kneel facing the wall. Under the long eaves, wind bells shuddered violently, ringing in broken, frantic tones ——as if the building itself trembled.

"Your… Highness…"

A close attendant ran stumbling into the inner hall.

The grand Princess jolted awake. Her hairpins were still loose; a thin fur mantle lay folded across her knees, which she pulled hastily around her shoulders. Her voice cracked from sleep and indignation.

"The Imperial Guards have surrounded the residence? ——Absurd! There must be some mistake."

She descended from the dais barefoot, forcing calm into her posture.

"Summon the Consort Prince. I shall question him myself."

But the moment she stepped past the threshold, her breath caught.

Rows of bowed crossbows filled her vision.

The Deputy Censor-in-Chief stepped forward, offered a formal salute and spoke with a voice as cold and steady as steel that had been quenched a dozen times:

"Your Highness, there is no mistake. Reports from the northern border arrived first. Confessions and material evidence are complete. By imperial warrant, I am to read the charges."

He raised the scroll.

"One ——Zhao Ziqi, the Imperial Consort Prince, colluded with northern spies, transmitting military route maps through concealed threads woven inside sachets."

"Two ——he bribed Tiger-Guard Deputy Officer Liang Dong, placing him beneath General Gu Xiao's command to await an opportunity to assassinate."

"Three ——he forged western border markers, luring the enemy into a treacherous pass and placing the frontier army at risk of annihilation."

"Four ——he planned to plant oil along the grain route and ignite the supply wagons to sow panic among the troops."

"Five ——he secretly conspired with individuals in the capital, promoting peace negotiations to turn public sentiment and unsettle the court."

"Six ——..."

"Seven ——..."

With each charge read aloud, a piece of evidence was laid upon the table:

A heavy bow with a broken string.

An arrow whose feathers were still stained a dark, dried red.

From the hidden compartment in Liang Dong's armour, sealed letters were produced ——the fire-lacquer crest matching Zhao Ziqi's private seal.

A hollowed jade pendant containing a thin, folded map, marked with a blood-red dot at the western choke-point.

A pouch of northern coins, each edge engraved with the emblem of a nomadic clan.

The grand Princess ——Li Rong ——watched her complexion drain, shade by shade, as if blood abandoned her with every accusation. Her lips trembled so violently she could barely speak.

"Impossible... impossible... This is fabricated!"

She suddenly lifted her voice in anguish and fury.

"Where is Zhao Ziqi? Bring him out! I demand to see him!"

The curtains of the inner hall shifted.

Zhao Ziqi was dragged out by two captains, iron chains already clasped around his wrists. His blue robe had been yanked half off his shoulder, hanging crooked. Even so, he forced himself to lift his head, scraping together a faint smile.

"Do not fear, Your Highness ——"

But when his gaze swept across the courtyard ——across the cold weapons, the assembled evidence laid out upon the case table ——his voice broke abruptly.

The Deputy Censor-in-Chief spoke with an unyielding chill:

"Liang Dong has already confessed before the army. The military report bears the Tiger-Guards' seal. Zhao Ziqi ——have you any defense left to make?"

Zhao Ziqi lowered his lashes. His throat moved once, twice, as he swallowed. He remained silent for several breaths. Then, suddenly, he threw back his head and laughed ——a laugh that flared like an open flame touched by wine, wild and poisoned.

"Defend myself? Defend what?"

The grand Princess took a step and nearly threw herself toward him. She grasped his sleeve with trembling fingers.

"Say it! Say it now ——tell them this is all fabricated!"

He looked at her. The bloodshot veins in his eyes swelled slowly, one ring after another. When he finally spoke, each word seemed torn from between his teeth.

"Why? You ask me why?"

"Because I wanted revenge."

The wind in the courtyard stilled ——sudden and absolute.

He moved forward step by step, iron chains dragging behind him with a cold, rhythmic clang.

"You are the grand Princess ——placed on a pedestal, untouchable. And I? I am the dog you summoned into your household. You kept your lovers in the inner quarters, ordered me to share a table with your catamites, allowed handmaids to bark commands at me as if I were beneath them. Have you ever once treated me as even half a husband?"

534

Princess Li Rong's face drained to a paper-white pallor. She shook her head in desperation.

"…I acted in anger… I only…"

"You only wanted to grind me into the mud!"

Zhao Ziqi roared, the fury tearing at his voice.

"When I married a Princess, the entire capital mocked me as a man who married upward. Because of your arrogance ——your public humiliations ——they laughed, they whispered. At your banquet, you made me kneel until dawn as punishment before all your guests. My dignity ——bit by bit, you crushed it!"

He suddenly laughed, low and sharp, the sound cold as the spine of a blade.

"To make you truly kneel ——there is only one path. The fall of Great Zhou. The shattering of your divine pedestal. Without the title of 'Princess,' you are nothing. And when that day comes, I will make you crawl before the world as I did… beg as I did."

"Insanity!" the Censor barked. "Watch your tongue!"

But Zhao Ziqi did not flinch. His gaze grew more deranged, pupils burning with feverish triumph.

"I arranged everything flawlessly. You thought the western terrain impassable for cavalry? Perfect. Feign troops in the east, strike in the west. My men guide the way. Once Gu Xiao dies, the army collapses and the capital will clamour for peace. Then you ——"

He leaned forward, lips twisting.

" ——you will be used as a bargaining chip. Perhaps sent beyond the frontier, perhaps locked away for life. Have you ever imagined that fate?"

Princess Li Rong seemed to have her bones removed; she collapsed at the base of the jade steps, voice fraying into a thread.

"…You are mad… For my sake, you would sell out all of Great Zhou?"

"To drag you down from the heavens!"

He nearly howled the words.

"To crush you just once ——so you understand what my years have tasted like!"

A tremor rippled through the gathered officials and soldiers. The air itself felt colder.

The Commander of the Imperial Guards hesitated no longer. His order rang out like a blade striking stone:

"By imperial command ——seize him!"

Chains clamped over shoulders, waist stocks were locked, iron bars fitted around his arms. The Deputy Censor-in-Chief gathered the scrolls and sealed the written record on the spot.

"Treason, collusion with the enemy, conspiracy to murder a commanding general ——none of these crimes can be forgiven."

At that moment, an inner steward rushed into the courtyard with a freshly delivered vermilion edict. He knelt, lifted the scroll above his head and proclaimed in a trembling but loud voice:

"Imperial decree of Emperor Xuanwen: Zhao Ziqi's treason and collusion with the enemy are proven beyond doubt. He is to be executed at the Meridian Gate immediately to uphold the laws of the realm.

The grand Princess, for failing her duty of conduct, is to be confined to her residence and never permitted to depart.

The Princess Residence shall be sealed and held under the authority of the Imperial Household Department, pending further deliberation."

The grand Princess jerked her head up. Her fingers clawed at the edge of the bluestone steps, knuckles bleaching from the force.

"Father ——Father ——!"

Her cry shattered beneath the advancing footsteps of the Imperial Guards.

Zhao Ziqi, however, suddenly laughed ——laughed until tears welled in his eyes.

"Excellent... excellent. At last,... I don't have to pretend anymore."

* * * * *

Outside the Meridian Gate, the drum sounded three times.

The Registrar of the Ministry of Justice read aloud the scroll of crimes, each line struck with a clear, metallic finality:

"Criminal Zhao Ziqi ——who conspired with the enemy, bribed officers, leaked military secrets and nearly caused the annihilation of our border forces ——his crimes cannot be pardoned.

Execute by beheading!"

A flash of steel.

A burst of red spattering across the bluestone.

The crowd held its breath.

A gust of wind surged through the shadowed arch of the Meridian Gate, carrying with it a faint tang of dissipating blood.

* * * * *

The great doors of the Princess Residence were shut with a heavy thud, sealed by diagonal strips of white silk.

The grand Princess was escorted back into the inner courtyard by two female eunuchs. Each step she took wavered, as if her legs no longer remembered how to bear her weight.

She turned, casting one last look toward the direction of the Meridian Gate. Her lips were completely drained of colour; what escaped them was a whisper barely more than air:

"Surely… surely this is a mistake… it must be… a mistake…"

But the lock snapped shut with a crisp click, sealing her final illusion on the other side of the door.

In the depths of the palace, Emperor Xuanwen stood atop the imperial steps in silence.

The grand Academician bowed deeply before him.

From above, the Emperor spoke only four words ——each cold as hoarfrost:

"Purge the prisons. Purge the palace."

From that moment, the capital trembled. Court factions shifted like tides.

A treason born of love and hatred had pushed the grand chessboard of power into its next, irreversible move.

* * * * *

Night deepened over Yongning Palace; lantern light wavered softly across the lacquered screens.

Second Princess Li Jing burst into the hall as though waking from a nightmare. Her robe was in disarray, her shoulder sash slipping, hair loose as if she had torn through half the palace in a panic. The maids froze where they stood ——none dared step forward to restrain her.

"Third Brother!"

Her voice cracked, trembling with tears.

Inside the hall, Li Suo reclined against the couch, a bamboo scroll half-opened in his hand. The candlelight cast a calm glow over his features ——serene, unreadable, as though the storm outside belonged to an entirely different world.

"What happened to you?"

His tone was steady, not a single crease marring his brow.

Li Jing halted, but only for a heartbeat. Then the tears spilled over, unstoppable. Her voice shook as she forced the words out:

"Elder Sister… Elder Sister… and the Consort Prince… he ——he betrayed the realm!"

At the words betrayed the realm, her knees nearly buckled. She clutched her handkerchief so tightly it twisted between her fingers. Her breath hitched with each sob.

"Father has ordered… execution at the Meridian Gate… immediate execution!

Third Brother, what do we do?

Will… will we be implicated too?"

Her last question dissolved into a broken whisper, heavy with terror.

Her sobs tore through the night like the cry of a raven ——shrill, panicked, desolate.

Li Suo lowered his gaze slightly and closed the bamboo slip with deliberate gentleness. A flicker of cold light passed through his eyes beneath the wavering candle flame, yet his voice remained faint, composed:

"Treason is a crime that warrants the execution of nine clans."

He paused, then lifted his eyes toward Li Jing. His gaze was still and deep, as calm as a bottomless pool.

"But she is the grand Princess ——born of the imperial line. Father will not extend the purge lightly. If you doubt it, look to the Second Prince. He was implicated in the Jiangnan affair and yet he sits confined only within the Ancestral Court. His life is not in danger."

Li Jing froze where she stood. Tear beads still clung to her lashes, but her breath caught sharply in her chest. She bit her lip, voice trembling into a thin, wounded whisper.

"Third Brother… how can you speak of this so calmly? She is our sister ——our own blood!"

Li Suo turned his head. The candlelight carved a stark, cold angle along his profile. The corner of his mouth lifted ——barely, just a trace —— but his voice was a blade, honed and merciless:

"In the imperial family, there is only one way to survive."

"You may indulge in luxury. You may revel in pleasure. But there is one thing you must never ——ever ——allow."

"To give others a handle over you."

The words were few, but each fell like a heavy hammer, striking Li Jing's heart one blow after another.

She stared at Li Suo, stunned, tears sliding silently down her cheeks. The wild panic of moments before clogged her throat; now she could not force out even a single word.

For the first time, she felt it ——the dazzling palace of gold and jade was not a sanctuary.

It was a cage.

* * * * *

Night deepened.

After the maids withdrew, the bedchamber fell into a heavy quiet. Li Jing curled into the corner of her bed, her shoulder sash slipping down her arm without her noticing. Her tears had long since dried, yet her eyes still stung faintly.

Outside, the night drums sounded in slow, distant echoes ——

but in her ears, only two sentences repeated over and over:

"Treason warrants the execution of nine clans."

"The only thing you must never do is give others a handle."

She hugged her knees tighter, fingertips digging hard into her palms. A coldness pulsed through her chest again and again, like waves of icy water pushing against her ribs.

If the one dragged away today had not been my sister… but me?

The moment the thought surfaced, her entire body shuddered. Tears spilled again, uncontrollable. She suddenly thought of her elder sister ——her once overbearing, radiant elder sister ——dressed in brocade and jewels, dazzling as if born above all others...

Now reduced to a prisoner.

Her husband executed before the noon gate.

A Princess once seated upon a divine pedestal now stripped of all protection, incapable even of saving herself.

A fear she had never known before rose violently within her.

The dread of the rabbit watching another fall beneath the snare.

The knowledge that they were all the same ——birds in the same gilded cage.

Today it was her elder sister.

Tomorrow... could it be her?

Li Jing buried her face against her knees; lips drained of colour. For the first time in her life, the word future surfaced in her mind and it felt smaller, more fragile, than ever before.

Chapter 82: Bravado Gains Nothing

War drums rumbled in the distance, the smoke of the battlefield slowly thinned.

News of the crushing victory at Mount Wulan spread through the ranks like a sudden blaze. By dusk, the encampment in every direction was thick with the smell of roasting meat and spilled wine.

Rows of bonfires were lit, turning the night sky a deep, wavering red. Enemy captives had long been confined to the rear camp under heavy guard; their shackles caught the firelight with sharp, cold flashes.

Soldiers shed their heavy armour at last, their bodies still with the stench of blood and powder, but none cared. Some tore chunks of meat and skewered them over the flames ——the dripping fat sizzled, sending up a fragrant plume.

Others lifted bowls of strong liquor and gulped them down in long, reckless swallows, faces flushing hot.

"Glory to the General!"

"Victory to Great Zhou!"

Shouts shook the night, fierce and jubilant. The men crowded around Gu Xiao, pushing him toward the largest bonfire at the centre.

Gu Xiao's white armour, once drenched in blood, had been removed; he wore only a light robe now, though the killing aura of battle still lingered between his brows. He lifted a wine cup, gaze sweeping over the sea of rough, exhilarated faces. A booming laugh burst from his chest.

"This victory belongs not to Gu Xiao alone ——it belongs to every brother who fought beside me!"

"Good!"

"Well said, General!"

"Not a coward among Great Zhou's soldiers!"

Cheers erupted again and again. Wine cups clashed; flames roared; valor swelled with the heat, burning away the bloodshed and weight of the day, leaving only wild laughter and the relief of survival.

Gu Xiao tilted back his head and drained the cup. The burning liquor scorched its way down his throat, yet the heat in his chest was fiercer still. His laughter rang boldly, but when the crowd's attention finally scattered, it slowly faded from his lips.

The bonfire crackled fiercely; sparks spiralled upward like fireflies. But across the dark horizon, his gaze sank deep ——his thoughts drifting not toward the slaughtered battlefield, but toward a single familiar figure.

Qin Nianyin.

Sweat streaked her cheeks, but her eyes had been sharp as blades when she stood outside the military tents, voice trembling as she urged him to "feign east, strike west."

She had almost been crying. Her fingers had clutched his sleeve with desperate strength. In that fleeting instant, the shine of tears and iron determination in her eyes weighed more than a thousand cavalry.

Heat surged again in Gu Xiao's chest. He wiped the wine from his lips with the back of his hand ——the ache beneath his breastbone tightening, settling into a resolve forged between fire and strong drink.

Nianyin…

This time, he would return to the capital.

With this victory.

With the merit of thousands of soldiers.

With the stability of the northern frontier on his shoulders.

He would return to the capital, stand before the imperial hall and openly request a marriage decree ——letting the court and the world alike understand that Qin Nianyin belonged to him and that Su Zhang would have no further pretext, no argument to advance, no seam left to exploit.

"My things," Gu Xiao growled, "are not for anyone else to take."

The wine cup in his hand strained under his grip, giving a faint crack. His gaze burned ——scorching like a flame licking the darkness.

Around the bonfire, the soldiers still shouted and cheered, their laughter ringing through the night. But beneath all that revelry, Gu Xiao's resolve blazed hotter than the liquor, fiercer than the fire.

——When he returned to the capital, he would win not only honours of war.

He would win her.

* * * * *

Outside the command tents, the night pressed thick as ink. In one corner of the camp, firelight blazed bright; grease sizzled on iron racks, sending up a mist of roasted fat and wine fumes.

Soldiers clanged bull-horn cups together as they laughed, some stomping the rhythm of the war drums while others slapped blades in crude, triumphant chorus. The noise of victory beat against the flags and the night wind beyond the tents.

Yet inside the main command tent, an uncanny stillness ruled.

The candle flame quivered in the draft, stretching then shrinking the shadows cast across the sand table. Su Zhang sat at his desk, fingertips resting on a freshly copied column of military names.

He had not moved in some time. At the corner of his mouth, where a fist earlier had split the skin, a thin scab had begun to form.

He tilted his head slightly, as though listening from the medical tent came a faint cough, then quiet again.

Suddenly, the tent flap was swept aside in one brusque motion. Cold wind barged in, with smell of wine and the loud warmth of celebration.

Gu Xiao strode in with a fresh flask of strong liquor dangling from his fingers; cloak dusted with ash and the aroma of roasted meat. He crossed the threshold in one bold step; his voice, unrestrained and vibrant, shattered the last of the tent's quiet:

"Brother Su! The men outside are clamouring for you ——meat won't wait and wine waits even less!"

Su Zhang lifted his gaze. It passed over the golden fire outside, over silhouettes dancing in victory-drunk joy. His tone was steady as still water:

"Go enjoy it with them."

Gu Xiao dropped the wine onto the table with a heavy thud, the fragrance spilling instantly into the air. He leaned down, picked a clean cup, filled it to the brim —— and then paused.

His eyes drifted, almost against his will, to the corner of the tent.

There, a curtain hung low; from that direction drifted the faintest thread of medicinal scent carried on the air.

"How is she?"

The single word ——she ——fell softly, neither heavy nor light, yet impossible to ignore.

"The fever has eased a little," Su Zhang answered, tone cool, unhurried. "Qiqi and Yiyi take shifts watching over her. She is in no danger."

Gu Xiao let out a short hum ——half relief, half an attempt to hide it. His laugh came with a hint of bitterness:

"True enough. A grown man hovering at a sickbed does look somewhat improper."

He poured himself another full cup and drank it down in one burning swallow. His throat worked; his eyes glimmered hot, as if reflecting the bonfire itself.

"But speaking of that ——"

He spun the cup lightly between his fingers. His voice rose, sudden and full of force, like a war drum struck anew:

"When we return to the capital after this victory, I will request a marriage decree ——before the throne itself."

Su Zhang's fingers stilled on the table.

Gu Xiao's words flowed on, gaining momentum, laced with the confidence of a victor and the bluntness of a young general who had never learned to hide his heart.

"Our merit is for the realm. His Majesty will not withhold a marriage reward. And ——"

He leaned forward slightly, like a man laying down his final, decisive move on the board.

"This victory ——Miss Qin deserves half its credit. Without her reminder, we might have fallen at Xiling. When the time comes, I'll give her half the merit. She may even receive a county rank. Let her be remembered ——as she ought to be!"

(Xiling: West cliff).

The candle flame shuddered, as if pushed by an unseen gust of wind.

"No."

Su Zhang's voice was so faint it bordered on coldness, yet the sound cut through the air like an ice-honed blade striking iron.

Gu Xiao froze. The smile on his face snapped apart.

"What did you say?"

"This matter must not be done," Su Zhang replied. He lifted his gaze; the candlelight drew a thin, sharp line across his pupils. "Not now. Not in the future. Not ever."

A vein stood out sharply across the back of Gu Xiao's hand. He slammed the cup back onto the table, the spill seeping into the grain of the wood like a dark bruise.

"Why? What is it, Su Zhang ——are you afraid you cannot win against me?"

He stepped forward, voice lowered, heavy like muffled thunder in a storm.

"You and I both understand battlefields and officialdom. Love is no different. If I take the initiative and she nods her consent, is that a defeat you cannot stomach?"

Su Zhang met his stare. His lashes dipped just enough to cage whatever flickered beneath his calm.

"She is not someone who thrives under display. Push her into the center of the court, place her beneath every watching eye and she will recoil."

Gu Xiao gave a hostile, breath-like laugh.

"And you presume to speak for her?"

"I am speaking on your behalf."

Su Zhang did not take a single step back; his tone remained steady.

"You say you want to give her part of your military credit. But when others question it, what explanation will you offer? Will you claim that the entire strategy turned because of a warning she gave?

If you do, what happens to your reputation? You will become the general who won at Xiling not through judgment or command, but because he listened to the words of a young woman.

 and what will people say about the Tiger Guard? That their victory owed itself not to discipline or strength, but to a convenient piece of luck?"

He watched Gu Xiao directly, each word deliberates, each consequence brought down like the fall of an axe.

"How will the court censors twist it? How will foreign spies write of it? How will your rivals memorialize against you, accusing you of superstition, of altering military orders based on a woman's 'unfounded warnings'? If the storm turns on her, will you be able to shield her?"

A tightness seized Gu Xiao's chest. Something lodged in his throat. He did not step back, but his gaze slid away for the briefest instant.

Su Zhang did not press him. He simply delivered the final strike, quiet but merciless:

"And furthermore, if you claim her merit before the throne, someone will ask how she knew. Can you give an answer that does not endanger her and does not undermine your own command?"

The command tent fell into a heavy stillness.

Only the sound of wine dripping off the corner of the table broke the silence ——soft, rhythmic, like a cold accounting of costs.

The muscles across Gu Xiao's back contracted in a painful knot, a hard pull beneath the skin that made every breath feel tighter than the last.

He drew in air through his teeth, opened his mouth and almost hurled back the instinctive retorts already forming in his head, war thrives on deception, who fears rumours or I will bear the burden myself.

But the words did not rise.

They thickened, took on weight and settled heavily on his tongue as if turned to metal. No force of will push them out.

He stood there, jaw clenched, knowing in that unmoving silence that this was not Su Zhang grasping at pride, nor jealousy, nor petty rivalry.

The truth was written plainly in the other man's eyes ——cool, measured and stripped of all embellishment.

There was no resentment there, no desire to compete, only the stark calculation of risk and consequence. Each possibility had already been weighed; each cost had already been counted.

Gu Xiao understood then that what Su Zhang spoke was not a challenge, but the unsoftened truth. Every path he had imagined taking might lead not to honour or protection, but to consequences that would fall on her first.

and suddenly he understood: the fierce desire he carried, to win her a name and a rightful place ——once placed on the imperial court's scales, could instead become a proclamation that pushed her straight into the fire.

Gu Xiao said nothing. A thin layer of sweat appeared along his temples. The cloth bandage on his palm had already soaked through with faint red, an old wound split anew from his earlier grip.

He tipped his head back, forcing the trapped heat in his chest downward. The liquor burned his throat, but the laugh that escaped him was edged and bitter, like the flat of a knife scraped across bone.

"Su Zhang ——you with your eight hundred schemes and a mind that refuses to lose… all of this analysis, this endless reasoning ——because you fear you cannot best me."

"It is not about refusing defeat."

Su Zhang shifted slightly and moved the stack of military records away from the stain of spilled wine. His voice lowered, with a rougher honesty beneath the restraint.

"She should not be the one who loses. Least of all to either of us."

Gu Xiao's throat tightened. The heat in his eyes flared, then vanished.

He suddenly remembered the cliffside wind and the moment she, trembling and crying, still raised her sword to shield him.

A hand, unseen, seemed to twist the inside of his chest.

After a long moment, Gu Xiao exhaled a harsh, weighted breath. The tension in his shoulders finally dropped by a fraction. He dragged a hand over his face and said, hoarse and grudging, "...Fine. Not now."

Su Zhang lowered his eyes slightly and answered with a simple hum of acknowledgment.

Silence settled once more.

Outside, the cheers rose and fell in great waves, like the turning of a tide. Inside the tent, the candlelight stilled for a heartbeat, outlining each of their shadows ——one sharp-edged, the other restrained ——yet both held the same fatigue and the same fierce heat beneath the surface.

Gu Xiao grabbed the wine flask, splashed half a cup into his bowl, then halted mid-motion and drank straight from the mouth of the flask instead. He turned to leave. After taking one step, he stopped, glanced back at Su Zhang and lowered his voice.

"If she wakes… don't let me find out first."

Su Zhang met his eyes. His gaze was faint, unreadable.

"And I will not let her know what you said just now."

They held each other's stare for a brief instant. Neither of them smiled.

Gu Xiao finally swept the flap aside and stepped out. The night wind struck him with the scent of roasted meat and the thump of distant drums. He drew in a breath, but his steps did not immediately carry him toward the revelry.

When he lowered his gaze, he saw the bandage on his palm seeping a darker patch of blood. He laughed under his breath into the darkness.

This was a delay, not surrender. The marriage decree could wait. To pursue her and win her, he would have to take the steady path, the one she would not turn away from.

Inside the tent, Su Zhang eased back into his seat. His fingertips brushed the darkened mark left by the spilled wine and with a single quiet swipe, he wiped it clean.

He lifted his eyes toward the medical tent in the distance, where a single lantern gave off a dim, muted glow. His gaze deepened, inch by inch.

Bravado is useless; protection is the only path that matters. To keep her safe from the storm, the storm must be turned to blow where it should.

He closed the military records, rose and extinguished one of the two lamps at his desk, leaving only one burning. Its flame stood steady, silent, like a hidden blade or a heart being held down to prevent it from breaking free.

Outside, the celebration surged on, but in the quiet, he pressed a single thought deep into his chest.

If there is a contest to be had, it must be fought in a way she will not dislike.

Night deepened and the wind grew colder. The two men walked in opposite directions, yet each carried the same fire in his chest ——one determined to win in the open and the other determined to shield from the shadows.

Chapter 83: The Point of No Return

The tent was bathed in a dim, heavy glow of lamplight, the air thick with the lingering, bitter-sweet scent of medicinal herbs. The night was so profoundly still she could hear the wind whispering against the army banners outside.

On the bed, a faint stir. Then, the slightest tremble of fingers beneath the thin blanket.

"...Nianyin?"

Low, urgent voices rose almost in unison, one from each side of her bedside.

Her eyelids fluttered twice before slowly, heavily, parting. Two familiar faces swam into view, starkly contrasted: to one side, Gu Xiao, his features blazing with a fierce intensity, his very presence carrying the metallic reek of blood and the pungency of rice wine.

To the other, Su Zhang, his expression a mask of tranquil composure, yet his eyes shadowed by a layer of unconcealable weariness.

She stared blankly, her mind still a chaotic haze, but her throat burned with a raw, painful dryness. Her lips parted soundlessly.

"Water!" Gu Xiao was the first to react. His shoulder brusquely jostled Su Zhang aside, forcing him back a full half-step. The movement was so abrupt it nearly sent the cups and basin on the side table clattering to the ground.

He snatched up a cup, poured the lukewarm water himself, and brought it urgently to her lips.

"Here. Slowly now."

She took it, her hand trembling noticeably, and drank in small, careful sips. The coolness slid down her throat, soothing the fiery ache just a little.

"Nianyin!" Seeing her drink, a great weight seemed to lift from Gu Xiao's chest. Joy erupted on his face, and his words began tumbling from his lips in an unchecked torrent. "Do you know? It's all because I listened to you! This battle—we've won a decisive victory for Great Zhou!"

His speech was rapid, his voice vibrating with barely-leashed excitement. "The Northern Di are utterly routed, in disarray for over three hundred miles! The whole camp is celebrating. You are my lucky star, Gu Xiao's, and the lucky star of all Great Zhou!"

The woman on the bed remained pale as parchment, but the corners of her bloodless lips lifted into a faint, soft curve. She said nothing, only nodded quietly.

Yet in that moment, her heart was submerged in a wordless tide of solace and joy.

She had won.

This battle against fate was hers.

Great Zhou had triumphed.

Gu Xiao had survived.

And countless soldiers and officers of Great Zhou had lived to see this dawn.

Everything, everything was different from the previous life.

She tilted her head slightly, her gaze drifting instinctively toward the other side.

Su Zhang sat in silence, a still statue in stark contrast to Gu Xiao's vibrant fervour. He did not interject, only watched her. His gaze was like dark water at night—outwardly calm, yet heavy with untold, turbulent undercurrents.

His brows and eyes were as usual, even touched with a hint of fatigue, yet her heart gave a faint, inexplicable tremble. She couldn't articulate it, yet she sensed something in his bearing now that differed from his usual self.

"Nianyin, how do you feel? Is there anything you need?" Gu Xiao finally reined in his excitement, his voice softening into urgent concern.

She fell into a dazed silence, her fingers clutching tightly at the edge of the thin blanket.

Emotions churned in her chest, coalescing finally into a whisper so faint it seemed to dissolve into the night air: "...I want... to go home."

Gu Xiao was taken aback, then quickly offered a reassuring smile. "What's so difficult about that? The army is regrouping. We depart for the capital in three days. You'll be home then."

Yet the moment his words fell, silent tears began to trace gleaming paths down her cheeks. Her shoulders trembled slightly, each teardrop soaking dark into the pillow.

She shook her head and her voice choked and so faint it seemed about to scatter with the night wind. "...I can't go back... It's impossible now..."

What she meant was not the capital, nor Jiangnan, nor any physical place she could return to.

It was something far more distant, far more unreachable—a life that had already ended once before.

Gu Xiao stared, his face a mask of stunned confusion, utterly lost.

He grew frantic. "What do you mean, you can't go back? We're returning to the capital in glorious triumph! If we press the march, we can reach the outskirts in little over ten days!"

Gu Xiao heard only exhaustion and lingering fear.

To him, her tears were the aftershock of illness and battle, something that time and rest would surely mend.

He did not realize that what she mourned had nothing to do with distance—or recovery.

"I'm... so exhausted... so, so exhausted..." Her words were a breathless sigh, drained of all vitality.

They were spoken to a past that could never be revisited.

"What nonsense is this?" he insisted, worry etching his voice. "It's just a chill, a depletion of your energy. Once we're back, with proper rest and tonics, you'll be perfectly well!" He reached out, wanting to steady her.

But Qin Nianyin shrank from his touch, gently pushing his hand away. A few quiet, wrenching sobs escaped her before she lapsed back into murmuring, "...No... I can't go back..."

Her voice was a mere quiver, laced with a fragility that seemed ready to shatter into nothingness.

The candle flame in the tent flickered violently, once.

Gu Xiao stood frozen, as if struck a physical blow. His lips moved soundlessly.

"Nianyin," he whispered, the tone now raw, bordering on pleading, "Don't say such things. I'm here. Whatever you want, whatever you need, I will get it for you."

She lowered her gaze, her fingers whitening around the blanket's edge, and gave a weak, almost imperceptible shake of her head.

Her eyes, adrift and lost in the uncertain candlelight, finally lifted. And as if drawn by an invisible, taut thread, they met the gaze of the silent figure opposite.

In that single, suspended moment, her eyes locked with Su Zhang's.

The candlelight seemed to hold its breath, illuminating the silent space where their glances met and held.

For a fleeting instant, something raw and tumultuous swirled in the depths of his eyes—a tremor of understanding, a pang of heartache so profound it stole his breath—before it was violently suppressed, forced down into a silent, unfathomable abyss.

Her heart constricted painfully. Her breath hitched. But no more words would come.

—The night lay heavy and still, broken only by the tremble of the candle flame, casting its wavering light upon three souls, each adrift in their own raging, unvoiced sea of thought.

* * * * *

The night deepened into its coldest watch.

Outside the tent, the wind howled like a distant beast, and the army banners snapped with a sharp, lonely sound—a world away from the day's clamorous victory.

Su Zhang stood motionless just beyond the camp's periphery. The night cold pierced to the bone, yet he wore no cloak, letting the bitter wind and stray snowflakes whip through the folds of his robe, as if seeking physical penance.

Her voice echoed again and again in the chamber of his mind, a haunting refrain—"...I can't go back..."

His fingers clenched inside his sleeves, a subtle tremor in his palms—yet he refused to let that tremor betray him to the empty night.

After the fragments she had let slip in her fevered dreams, he understood with a chilling, absolute clarity—when she wept those words, she wasn't speaking of the capital, of Jiangnan's gentle shores, or even of the Su family mansion.

She was not speaking of the capital.

Not Jiangnan.

Not the Su residence.

What she was mourning was a life already sealed—a heart that could never return to what it had once been.

She was speaking of her previous life.

Her heart truly could never go back.

Gu Xiao had been all jubilant relief, believing her distress mere aftermath of illness and fear. But only Su Zhang knew—what she truly wept for was the chasm between two lifetimes, the fate she had rewritten yet remained trapped by.

He could scarcely believe it, resisted believing it, yet the evidence was undeniable: Nianyin... must have lived through a life before this one.

With near-divine foresight, she had predicted enemy manoeuvres, slipped that cryptic warning before the Jiangnan trip, orchestrated the rescue of Xu Wencai, unveiled Liang Dong's betrayal before it could blossom...

Su Zhang lifted his gaze to the heavens. The night was profound, the star river a cold, sharp tapestry—like a vast, indifferent net that had ensnared them both.

All his life, he had prided himself on his composure, his meticulous calculations. But in this moment, his chest was hollowed out by a powerlessness that left him reeling.

Should he continue to fight? To contend for her?

From her fragmented murmurs and guarded distance, he could already sense it—

the man she had loved in that former life had not been kind to her.

And that knowledge cut deeper than jealousy ever could.

From her fragmented murmurs, it seemed the "him" of that former life had been far from a worthy man. In this life, she had chosen Gu Xiao, then...

Or perhaps the Third Prince, Li Su?

One could offer her a love fierce and unguarded, a sun-blaze of passion; the other, a position supreme among women, a throne beside an emperor. Both were exceptional men, dragons among mortals, each capable of shielding her for a lifetime...

A corrosive bitterness seeped into his heart, but he dared not follow that thread of thought further.

The mere possibility was a blade twisting in his gut. Yet... if Gu Xiao could give her in this life the warmth, the uncomplicated devotion he himself seemed incapable of... should he let go? Should he, for once, step aside and enable their happiness?

But then... she had just said, her eyes holding his for that fleeting moment—I can't go back—

Did that mean, in the depths of her heart, in this present life he had been reborn into, he had nothing left to offer her?

Or worse—that she wanted nothing at all, not from him, not from anyone?

The cold wind lashed his face like a slap. Suddenly, a low, humourless laugh escaped him. The laughter was bitter, pressed so deep it seemed to seep into his bones and blood.

"Nianyin..."

He murmured her name into the devouring night, his voice so hoarse and faint the wind nearly stole it whole. "No, Nianyin... Forgive me. Even knowing all this... I find I cannot let you go."

In that moment, the stillness in his eyes resembled a solitary lamp burning in the deepest, most desolate hour of the night.

No one else could see it. No one else could know. But he knew—the last light in his heart had long since narrowed, focused, until it illuminated her alone.

In this life, he could afford to lose the world.

But to lose her? That was a defeat from which there could be no recovery.

Perhaps it was not that she had chosen another.

Perhaps she had chosen nothing at all.

Chapter 84: The Ceremony of the Triumphant Return

The horns of victory reverberated through the sky, ringing with a clarity that seemed to shake the very air.

Nearly half a month later, one hundred thousand soldiers marched southward from the northern frontier, their banners snapping sharply in the wind.

Rows upon rows of iron armour caught the light and gleamed like molten metal; long spears rose in dense lines; the thunder of hooves rolled continuously down the official road stretching from the borderlands to the capital, turning it into a river of silver that seemed to rush endlessly toward the horizon.

Gu Xiao rode at the front of the army in full armour. The wind lifted the strands of hair near his temples, sharpening the striking dignity of his features. His expression was bright with triumph and the pride between his brows signalled victory with unmistakable force.

Wherever he passed, the people lining the road knelt in greeting. Their voices rose and fell like waves, calling out, "Great Zhou, ever victorious!" and "General Gu, mighty and unmatched!"

Children waved colourful ribbons; elderly men leaned on their canes with tears in their eyes. Cheers surged from all directions and gathered like a rising tide around the silver-armoured figure at the head of the formation.

Gu Xiao rode with spirited confidence, the reins taut in his hand. His chest swelled with a sense of accomplishment he had never experienced before. This battle had proved that he was no longer merely a scion of a military clan, no longer just a young man known for brute bravery.

He had carved out his own feats and established his own authority, standing firmly with the empire itself.

Yet even amid this overwhelming brilliance and celebration, Qin Nianyin quietly noticed a contrasting presence.

Su Zhang.

Slender, austere and unyieldingly composed.

He also rode on horseback, yet he remained embedded within the ranks rather than at the forefront. In stark contrast to Gu Xiao's blazing visibility, Su Zhang wore a plain, ink-dark robe beneath a dark cloak and even his horse was the same sombre shade.

His lack of armour made him appear even more severe and the muted colour of his attire absorbed the sunlight instead of reflecting it. The restrained darkness created a solitary silhouette, a shadow moving with the army but never merging with its jubilant atmosphere.

Even in earlier years at court, he had been known for his unshakable calm. Now, however, there was something heavier beneath it. It was a quiet darkness that war smoke could not wholly explain, a heaviness that felt as if it came from someone having borne far too many things alone for far too long.

Qin Nianyin lifted her gaze instinctively and at that precise moment, Su Zhang turned his head. Their eyes met across the roar of thousands of voices.

For an instant, her chest tightened without warning.

His eyes were cold ——colder than the deep pools she had once compared them to. Yet this chill was not the distant indifference she was used to. It was the cold of ice that had existed for centuries, untouched by warmth, stripped of movement or life.

A faint tremor passed through her chest, and she unconsciously held her breath.

She did not understand. Why did he look at her like that?

She could not name the feeling, only that the look was too deep and too heavy, as if he had tried to pull her entire being into that silent darkness for a single heartbeat.

But the next moment, he had already turned away, withdrawing back into his usual reserved composure, as though the moment had been nothing more than her own imagining.

On this long journey home from the northern border, Gu Xiao had remained bold and warm, frequently speaking with her and calling out to others, energized by triumph.

Su Zhang, however, had remained composed and withdrawn, speaking little to her. Though she was relieved to see that he seemed to have finally set aside the sentiment he once held for her, she still could not dispel the faint unease resting in her heart.

Qin Nianyin lingered in thought for a moment. Something about him felt out of place, yet after thinking through every possibility and arriving at nothing, she finally lowered her gaze and pressed her lips together.

The army stopped near the outskirts of the capital, where only a selected number of officers would enter the city to report their victory. The imperial procession awaited not far ahead.

Before long, she stepped into the carriage prepared for her and the curtain fell, shutting out the wind and the distant tumult.

Yet the faint tremor in her chest would not subside, lingering stubbornly beneath her ribs.

At the far end of the long avenue, the tolling of bells and the beat of drums erupted without warning. The imperial city, layered with imposing towers and palace roofs, emerged gradually from the pale morning haze.

Gu Xiao drew his horse to a halt. When he looked upon the tiers of golden tiles rising toward the sky, a slow, swelling heat rose within his chest. The light in the capital was softer than that of the northern frontier, yet also colder.

He recalled the quiver in Qin Nianyin's voice when she had spoken to him and his fingers tightened unconsciously around the reins.

He could not suppress the impulse to publicly present her "contribution" before the Golden Throne, to let all under Heaven see how extraordinary she truly was. But Su Zhang's warning forced him to reconsider, to weigh the consequences again with a cooler head.

Even so, even if he spoke nothing of her "tactical insight" that had secured Great Zhou's victory, he had already reached a firm decision: he would use this triumph to petition for an imperial marriage decree.

The drums sounded again. The army advanced slowly. People knelt along both sides of the road and flower petals drifted through the wind like falling rain. The scent of crushed blossoms intermingled with the tang of iron in the air ——an aroma that felt like the meeting of victory and fate.

Inside the carriage, with only a thin curtain separating her from the clamouring cheers outside, Qin Nianyin felt her thoughts sinking.

She realized suddenly that this triumphant return was not an ending, but the beginning of something else entirely.

Gu Xiao's glory and Su Zhang's silence ——one bright, one dark —— pulled at her from opposite directions, neither willing to release their hold.

When the procession reached the Meridian Gate, she lifted her gaze toward the heavy palace walls.

Frost-coloured tiles glimmered faintly in the afternoon light. The weather was clear, yet the air felt cold enough to make one tremble. A quiet, inexplicable premonition rose within her.

The road leading into the imperial city would alter the fate of many.

* * * * *

The great road on the outskirts of the capital was packed with tens of thousands of people.

Officials in ceremonial headpieces had gathered, banners fluttered, gongs and drums resounded and citizens had streamed in since dawn just to witness the triumph of the returning army. When the vanguard banners appeared in the distance, the cheers surged forward like a rising tide.

At the centre of the road stood the imperial carriage, its canopy embroidered with a five-clawed golden dragon. The opulence of it commanded attention, radiating an authority no one could mistake.

Crown Prince Li Duan stood before his horse in formal dark-brocade court attire, his expression solemn. Yet there was a faint, unmistakable trace of a smile between his brows.

He was here under imperial command to greet the victorious forces, and to demonstrate to the world the demeanour and bearing of the heir apparent.

"The Crown Prince arrives ——!"

The high cry of the imperial attendant echoed outward, met by the thunderous response of tens of thousands.

Moments later, the army approached in full formation. Armor glinted like frost and spears rose in a dense forest of steel. At the front, two riders drew every eye.

One was clad in silver armour that gleamed like snow. Gu Xiao urged his steed forward with spirited vigour, wind lifting the strands of hair near his temples, his gaze sharp and filled with fire.

The other wore armour as dark as ink. His horse's mane was black as night. Su Zhang's expression was austere; his brows shadowed with restrained intensity. He rode slightly behind Gu Xiao's brilliance, yet his presence emanated a cold, cutting gravity that no one could dismiss.

All officials bowed deeply toward the approaching army, their voices overlapping in a grand wave of acclaim.

Li Duan stepped forward, his smile warm yet composed and addressed them in a clear, Nianyin voice.

"The soldiers of the realm have endured hardship and earned immense merit. With this victory at our borders, both I and the entire court take pride in your service."

Gu Xiao swung down from his horse and dropped to one knee with a heavy, resounding thud. His voice rang across the open field, clear and metallic, brimming with the fervour of a young general.

"Your servant has not failed the trust bestowed upon him. With this body, I shall continue to serve Great Zhou. May our dynasty endure for ten thousand years!"

The declaration carried a sharp, stirring force, igniting emotion among all who heard it. Even the most seasoned officials felt their hearts quake.

The Crown Prince Li Duan personally stepped forward to raise him up, his smile gentle, his tone warm.

"General Gu, brave and valiant in your youth ——truly, you are the blessing of our Great Zhou."

With those words, applause burst forth like rolling thunder, the gathered officials echoing their agreement in unison.

Just then, another voice drifted through the air ——smooth, leisurely, with a faint undercurrent of amusement.

"Elder Brother speaks true. General Gu's martial prowess is unmatched. Even I, your Third Brother, cannot help but admire him."

The crowd looked up.

There, approaching from the side path, was Third Prince Li Suo. Dressed in a robe of deep jade-green, he walked with measured poise, several guards following in orderly formation. His gaze swept the gathered soldiers before settling on Gu Xiao, holding both admiration and something harder to read, something edged, deliberate.

"Third Brother," the Crown Prince said lightly, though a hint of wariness flickered beneath his composed tone. "What brings you so late?"

Li Suo gave a bright, ringing laugh.

"Elder Brother is the Crown Prince. Naturally, the honour of greeting the army falls to you. As for me, merely joining in the festivities. A little tardiness hardly matters."

As he spoke, he turned his head. His eyes, sharp as a blade, fell upon Su Zhang. The corner of his lips lifted slightly.

"Especially Lord Su. Able to devise strategy with your pen and suppress the frontier with your mind. You organized the grain supplies, ensured their safe and timely arrival at the border, truly, the greatest unsung merit of this campaign lies with you."

A ripple passed through the assembled officials. The atmosphere shifted at once.

The Crown Prince's smile deepened almost imperceptibly as he looked toward Su Zhang. His tone was mild yet carried unmistakable praise.

"Lord Su's foresight and careful planning, such achievements stand no lesser than those of the warriors on the front lines. I am fully aware of his contribution."

Two brothers, speaking seemingly in admiration, yet beneath every word was a clash of intent.

Some sought to claim all credit for the Crown Prince.

The other insisted that Su Zhang's accomplishment was indispensable, and perhaps beyond the Crown Prince's control.

Gu Xiao's brows tightened. He could feel the subtle currents swirling around him, but he said nothing. His hand tightened around the hilt of his sword, his whole frame taut as a drawn bow.

There they stood ——three men before the Crown Prince and the victorious army.

One warrior, one court strategist, one imperial prince.

Their presences clashed even without steel drawn.

The Crown Prince smiled, yet his gaze was dark beneath its warmth.

The Third Prince spoke casually, yet every word hid a sharpened edge.

Gu Xiao radiated unrestrained momentum, impossible to overlook.

and Su Zhang… said nothing. His silence was an even deeper weight, his eyes calm yet with a faint, suppressed turbulence.

In that moment, the air itself seemed to tighten, full of unsheathed tension.

Only Qin Nianyin had been discreetly escorted back to the Su residence the moment the army reached the outskirts, spared from stepping into the heart of this swelling undercurrent.

 and yet, her name hung between these men like an invisible blade, poised above all of them, ready to slice open the grand façade of this triumphant ceremony at any moment.

Chapter 85: Three Men Seeking the Same Fate

The Su Residence.

Red walls stood in quiet composure. Beyond the gate, drums and cheers surged in rolling waves, pouring in from the streets outside, yet inside the estate a stillness held firm, forming a stark and almost cruel contrast.

Qin Nianyin was helped into a side chamber. Her outer robes had not yet been changed; dust from the road still clung to her temples and hairline. She sat upon the brocade couch, listening through the latticed window as the distant uproar swelled and receded.

The thunderous music and the shouts of the gathered crowds reached her ears, each call loud enough to shake the air, yet it all felt separated from her by a thick, heavy veil, as though a dense sheet of water stood between her and that blazing world.

"Great Zhou, ever victorious… General Gu, mighty and peerless…"

Voices merged into a single roaring mass, a mountain and sea of sound that made the window paper quiver. Yet her chest felt hollow, as though something vital had been scooped out. Her fingers tightened around her sleeve so hard the fabric wrinkled and creased in her grip. For a long while, not a single word left her lips.

The radiance of victory belonged to those hundred thousand iron riders.

It belonged to Gu Xiao.

It belonged to Great Zhou.

And yet at this moment, she had been brought back to the Su Residence by Su Zhang with no room for refusal, placed into this quiet courtyard, sealed away from all the heat and fervour outside. The celebration did not belong to her. The clamour did not reach her. It was as though the world had surged forward, and she had been set down behind a closed door to listen to it from afar.

"Miss," Mei's voice cut in softly, careful not to startle her. "Shall this servant bring you a cup of hot tea?"

Qin Nianyin blinked once, as if only then remembering she was not alone, and gave a faint nod. She lifted her gaze toward the window.

Night had deepened. In the direction of the capital's outskirts, the glow of fire still rose toward the sky, staining the darkness with a distant, restless light. All at once she felt as though she had been pushed away from the board, reduced to a spectator standing at the edge of a game she could not enter.

In her previous life, she had also been like this, smiling brilliantly before others, wearing a flawless mask, yet unable to lay a hand on any true matter. Even in this life, though she had fought with everything she had to change the course of fate, she had reached this point all the same. She could do nothing but watch, watch as those three names were driven by destiny to converge upon the same battlefield.

"Miss," Mei said again, voice trembling despite her efforts, "you finally returned. Mei missed you terribly."

As she spoke, her eyes reddened at once. Tears gathered at the corners before she could stop them.

Qin Nianyin's heart tightened abruptly, as if pinched by an unseen hand. Her voice dropped into a gentle murmur, low and steady, meant as much to calm Mei as to steady herself.

"Mei, don't cry. We are both safe. That is what matters most."

Great Zhou's triumph over the Northern Di meant Gu Xiao had escaped the fatal calamity of the previous life. It also meant that countless soldiers and officers had preserved their lives. That was what mattered most. That was the one fact she could hold onto without it breaking apart in her hands.

The tea arrived. Steam rose in soft spirals, drifting upward and dissolving into the lamplight. She reached out to take the cup, yet her fingertips trembled faintly as they met the warm porcelain.

In the distance, the drums continued to pound through the night. Each resounding beat struck against her chest like a hammer, heavy and deliberate, again and again.

* * * * *

Imperial Great Hall.

The palace hall was paved with cold gold bricks that gleamed beneath towering shadows. Below the vermilion steps, civil and military officials stood in orderly ranks.

News of the great victory at Wulan Ridge had already swept through the realm. Today's court assembly carried an unmistakable exhilaration, as if the entire hall had been lifted by a single tide of triumph.

Upon the high imperial throne, Emperor Xuanwen wore a bright yellow ceremonial robe. Even with his usual composure, a trace of pleasure still lingered between his brows.

"In this campaign, the border was secured and the state stabilized," the emperor declared. His voice was steady, resonant, echoing beneath the vast roof. "Gu Xiao led the army with valour and seized the foremost merit. Su Zhang, though stationed in the court, planned and coordinated, sending provisions north so the army lacked nothing. The achievements of you two, one in the field and one in the administration, complement each other well. One civil, one military, each fulfilling his role."

"His Majesty is wise!" the officials answered in unison.

Gu Xiao stood at the head of the assembled ministers. His posture was straight as a drawn spear; his expression carried the bright, unrestrained vigour of a man returned from victory. By all reason, he should have felt only joy.

Yet as the emperor's praise settled over the hall, heat surged violently through his chest. It rose too fast, too sharp, mingling pride, urgency, and something that could not be suppressed. He clenched his jaw hard, as if biting down on a storm.

In the next moment, he stepped forward, bowed, and dropped to his knees with a heavy thud that rang across the chamber.

A ripple of shock moved through the entire hall.

"Your Majesty," Gu Xiao said, voice ringing, firm, yet with a faint tremor pressed beneath it, "this subject, Gu Xiao, begs for imperial grace. As a commander of Great Zhou, to fight and guard the border is duty itself, and I do not dare claim merit. Yet in my heart there is one request I cannot set aside."

Officials exchanged glances. Palace attendants held their breath.

Emperor Xuanwen's gaze sharpened slightly, interest flickering at the arch of his brow. "Oh? General, speak freely."

Gu Xiao struck his forehead to the floor, the sound heavy, his voice booming like metal on stone.

"This subject wishes to request permission to marry…"

Before the sentence could finish, another impact echoed across the chamber, sharp and unmistakable.

"This subject, Su Zhang, also seeks an imperial decree."

Gu Xiao froze as though struck. He turned sharply.

Su Zhang was kneeling as well, robes perfectly arranged, posture restrained, expression calm. He mirrored Gu Xiao at the foot of the crimson steps as if the hall had suddenly split into two equal lines of will.

Their eyes collided in the air with force, like two blades crossing.

"Minister Su?" Emperor Xuanwen's brows lifted, the faintest amusement slipping into his tone. "You too?"

"Yes." Su Zhang raised his head. His expression was cool and composed, yet his gaze held a quiet firmness that did not bend. "Though this subject did not fight on the front lines, I oversaw the coordination of provisions and ensured every supply reached the border without delay, travelling day and night without pause. That may be considered a modest contribution. Today I dare to speak out, for the matter I seek is singular. Only this one."

He lifted his head higher. His clear, cold voice carried through every corner of the grand hall.

"These subject request an imperial marriage decree. I ask Your Majesty to bestow a union upon the daughter of the late Prefect of Jiangnan, Qin Shouyi, my cousin, Qin Nianyin."

The hall was struck as if by thunder.

Officials erupted in whispers. Even the empress seated above allowed a faint change to touch her expression.

Gu Xiao's face drained of colour in an instant. His pupils contracted sharply, as though a heavy blow had landed squarely against his chest.

"What…?" His voice cracked. His breath caught hard. Heat surged violently beneath his ribs; his fingers whitened as they curled into a tight fist.

He could scarcely trust his own hearing.

Trembling, he lunged forward and seized Su Zhang's collar, yanking him close. The strain in his expression was a mixture of pain and fury, raw enough to split him apart.

"Su Zhang, you… you told me… you told me before…"

Su Zhang's chest was pulled tight beneath the grip, yet his face did not change. His gaze remained cold, pressed down with an unshakable light.

"I'm sorry." Two words. Calm, decisive, like forged iron. "Only her, I will not yield."

Gu Xiao's breath slammed to a halt. Red fissured across his eyes like cracks spreading through glass. Rage surged up so fast it nearly blinded him. His arm jerked, his fist lifting, ready to strike.

"Enough!"

From the imperial throne, Emperor Xuanwen's voice fell heavy as rolling thunder.

"Xiao, do not be insolent!"

Silence stampeded through the hall, crushing every sound.

Gu Xiao's entire body jolted. His raised fist froze mid-air. Each knuckle trembled from the effort of restraint. His eyes were bloodshot; his chest rose and fell in violent waves. Yet under imperial authority, he slowly forced his fist down.

His breathing came ragged. His palm trembled uncontrollably. With a sharp motion, he flung Su Zhang aside, but the pain inside him only intensified, slicing through his chest as though a blade were carving him open stroke by stroke.

Su Zhang staggered back under the force, yet remained kneeling before the steps. His posture was perfectly straight, unshaken. Beneath his lowered lashes, his eyes were dark as midnight, yet lit with an obsession no one else could extinguish.

In that moment, the two men knelt side by side before the throne, but they were no longer brothers.

And the name Qin Nianyin burned in the centre of the hall like rising fire, illuminating every gaze, igniting every ambition, and marking the point from which none of them could turn back.

* * * * *

Imperial Study.

Candlelight wavered. The air felt so heavy it was almost solid.

Gu Xiao and Su Zhang knelt before the imperial desk. Their words differed, but both petitions pointed unmistakably to the same name. The ministers in attendance looked from one to another, stunned, wide-eyed, unable to conceal their shock.

Emperor Xuanwen's gaze drifted from one man to the other, deep and unreadable. Then the corner of his mouth lifted in an expression that hovered somewhere between amusement and something far colder.

"Gu Xiao. Su Zhang." His tone was unhurried, not loud, yet each syllable pressed down like iron. "The two of you would contend before Me, all for the sake of a single woman?"

Gu Xiao clasped his hands hard, voice ringing with unrestrained urgency, yet you could hear the shake beneath it, like a blade humming.

"Your Majesty. This subject's heart can stand witness before sun and moon. Miss Qin is an exceptional woman, righteous in mind and broad in spirit. I owe her a debt of gratitude, and I also hold her in deep affection. I beg Your Majesty to grant this union."

Then Su Zhang spoke, calm and measured, voice cool as still water. He did not raise it. He did not plead. Yet the steadiness in each word was its own kind of force.

"Your Majesty. Qin Nianyin is not only compassionate, but also discerning and courageous. During the Jiangnan affair, this subject personally witnessed her composure in danger and her ability to unravel treachery. This subject seeks marriage not solely for personal desire. If such a woman stands at my side, she can also assist in matters that serve the state. I ask that Your Majesty look kindly upon this petition."

The ministers exchanged uneasy glances. Their thoughts were the same. What manner of woman could inspire this?

Behind the imperial desk, Emperor Xuanwen listened without interruption. His fingers tapped lightly against the carved dragon surface, each soft tap tightening the atmosphere in the room.

After a long, deliberate pause, he let out a low chuckle. His gaze shifted slightly, the amusement edged with something that felt almost cruel.

"How intriguing… I find myself curious what sort of woman could cause both a tiger-born general and a scholar-official of the Hanlin to lose their composure so completely."

Gu Xiao's chest rose sharply, as if he wanted to argue again, to force the world back into sense. But the emperor's voice dropped, the undertone turning cool, playful at the surface and cold at the bone.

"Gu Xiao. Su Zhang. It seems neither of you are aware that only a few days ago, the Third Prince also submitted a memorial, requesting an imperial marriage decree."

His gaze hardened.

"And the woman he seeks to marry is also Qin Nianyin."

"What?!" The room erupted. Even seasoned ministers could not suppress their shock.

Gu Xiao stiffened violently, as if struck squarely in the chest. His eyes widened, voice cracking.

"The Third Prince… he also…?"

Su Zhang's fingers tightened imperceptibly within his sleeves. His gaze darkened, swallowing whatever surged in the depths.

Emperor Xuanwen regarded the two men with an expression almost amused, though the coldness beneath it was unmistakable.

"A single woman is enough to stir the heart of My son, My general, and My minister, driving all of you to contend before Me." His voice rolled across the chamber, forcing the officials into silence. "Tell Me. What, exactly, is Qin Nianyin?"

Moments later, he struck the imperial desk.

The sharp crack split the air like thunder.

"Attend Me. Announce My order."

The chief eunuch hurried forward, bowed, and rushed out.

Emperor Xuanwen's gaze turned cutting. His words came slow, distinct, sinking into bone.

"Summon Qin Nianyin. She is to enter the palace at once for questioning."

The doors of the imperial study swung open. Cold wind swept through the threshold. Candle flames fluttered violently. Shadows stretched long across the lacquered walls, tugged and torn by the gust.

Gu Xiao's breathing turned harsh, chest tightening as though something inside him were ready to burst. Su Zhang's face remained controlled and austere, yet the knuckles hidden within his sleeves were clenched to the point of bloodlessness.

The ministers felt their hearts tremble. All understood that what came next would be an imperial decision of rare weight.

Qin Nianyin, at this moment, had become the centre of the entire empire.

Chapter 86: Summoned to the Palace

The imperial guards moved with startling speed.

Qin Nianyin had barely surfaced from the feverish haze before she was already lifted upright, steadied by firm hands at her elbows, and a thin cloak was settled over her shoulders.

The cloth was light, almost too light for winter night air, yet it still carried the faint warmth of someone else's body. Outside, the wind cut like ice.

It slipped between the folds of her collar, crawled into her sleeves, and pressed against her skin with cold insistence. Yet none of it felt as sharp as the unease rising steadily within her chest.

The forbidden troops flanking her held halberds and remained wordlessly silent. Their formation, however, was tight as iron. Their steps were synchronized, their spacing exact, their presence unyielding. She was not being escorted so much as enclosed. Wherever she turned her head, she saw armour, dark silhouettes, and the hard gleam of weapon edges catching lantern light.

"Summoned to the palace for questioning."

Those four characters seemed to hover beside her ears. They fell over and over, like stones dropped one after another into a deep well, each one sinking, each one weighing down her breath. Her heartbeat stumbled into a frantic rhythm, her lungs refusing to fill properly, her mouth going dry as though she had been walking for hours.

The imperial palace.

She had been there in her previous life, too, entering its golden halls as the wife of a minister, attending banquets from the women's seats, smiling at the right moments, bowing when expected, trading polite words with titled ladies whose names carried more weight than truth.

Lanterns had glittered, dancers had twirled under carved beams, and music had floated across jade floors. Back then, she had witnessed power from a distance, wrapped in splendour. She had been close enough to see it, yet far enough to never touch it.

But tonight was different.

Tonight, she was not a minister's wife. Not anyone's spouse. Not even a proper lady of a household. She was merely the Su clan's nominal young cousin, a woman with no status to speak of no title to protect her, no position that could serve as armour. Why would the Emperor summon her? What did he intend to ask? What answer would satisfy him, and what answer would condemn her?

Stone tiles stretched before her, layer after layer. The palace gates rose in towering shadow, high as mountains. The closer she drew, the more the shadow seemed to swallow the sky. With every step, the pressure in her chest tightened, stacking higher and higher until her ribs felt as though they might splinter beneath it.

The wind seeped through her cloak. She scarcely noticed. Each step felt heavy, as though she were treading directly upon her own heart.

Whenever the distant echo of guards' boots crossed beneath a lantern, crisp and interlocking, she reflexively curled her fingers inward.

Her nails pressed into her palm. It was not pain she sought, but certainty, a small sharp point that could keep her from drifting. She feared that one moment of distraction, one brief haze, would be enough for this vast, cold palace city to swallow her whole.

Then, quite suddenly, memory surfaced.

The words the Third Prince had spoken that day returned with chilling clarity.

"I have already submitted a memorial to Imperial Father, requesting an imperial marriage decree."

At the time she had found his declaration absurd, almost laughable. She had dismissed it as distance, as arrogance, as something that belonged to princes and court games rather than her fragile, borrowed life. She had not truly carried it in her heart.

But now, now she was being summoned in the dead of night, escorted past gate after gate by forbidden troops. Was it related to that? Was this the consequence she had not taken seriously? Was she about to be questioned because a prince had spoken her name too boldly before the throne?

Her lips turned pale. Beneath her sleeve, her fingertips dug harder into her palm until the joints ached faintly.

Her thoughts spiralled in uneven waves, images from her previous life tangling with those of her present. Yet her feet had no choice but to keep pace with the guards leading her forward.

The wind whipped past the eaves, harsh and relentless. Deeper within the palace, rows of lanterns glowed with cold, disciplined order. Their light did not warm. It only revealed.

In that moment, she no longer felt like the quiet woman who had sat earlier in the Su residence side chamber. She felt herself shifting, becoming something else, becoming a single chess piece pushed, without warning, onto a board where every move was perilous, and where even standing still could be counted as a crime.

* * * * *

Still unsteady in mind and breath, Qin Nianyin was escorted toward a side hall adjoining an imperial garden. The area was hushed, the silence so complete that even the wind brushing through bamboo leaves seemed restrained, as if the palace itself demanded stillness.

A faint fragrance drifted from within, incense thick and lingering, the air heavy with it. Curtains hung low, their embroidery catching the light in dull glints. Upon the raised seat sat Emperor Xuanwen in formal attire. Beside him, in full regalia, sat the Empress, calm and luminous, the phoenix embroidery on her robes seeming almost alive under the candle glow.

Before she could think, before a single thought had fully formed, her body reacted on instinct.

She stepped forward and executed a complete formal court salute: kneeling, bowing, touching her forehead to the ground, rising, bowing again. Every gesture was flawless. The sequence flowed like water, steady and practiced, without any trace of hesitation or misstep.

The hall fell silent for a heartbeat.

For that single heartbeat, she realized what she had done too late. She had not adjusted for her present identity. She had not measured what was appropriate for a "nominal cousin" with no standing. She had simply followed the etiquette carved into her bones by an old life, and she had offered the highest form of palace greeting, the kind used at formal banquets before the main throne.

The Empress studied her, a flicker of surprise gliding across her eyes. Then her lips curved into a faint, controlled smile.

"You carry yourself with impeccable decorum. Such precision rivals that of the great clans' young ladies."

A tremor shot through Qin Nianyin's chest. Her pulse jumped. In that instant, memories from her previous life rose like branding marks pressed against her mind. During her years as a minister's wife, she had followed her husband into the palace again and again. She had watched ceremonies until the motions became instinct. She had bowed until the act of lowering herself felt as natural as breathing.

Emperor Xuanwen regarded her for several quiet moments, his gaze unreadable. Then he inclined his head with deliberate calm.

"You may rise."

Holding her breath, Qin Nianyin lifted herself slowly. She had barely found her balance when the Emperor's voice sounded once more, measured, firm, carrying the absolute authority of one accustomed to obedience.

"Do you understand why you were summoned tonight?"

Qin Nianyin lowered her gaze. "In reply to Your Majesty and Her Majesty the Empress, this humble woman does not know."

The Empress gave a soft laugh, light yet edged, as though amused by something she alone could see.

"Is that so? Then the situation grows even more curious. Three of the most promising young men of our dynasty have asked His Majesty for an imperial marriage decree, each wishing to wed you, and yet you claim you know nothing of it?"

Qin Nianyin's head snapped up. Astonishment froze on her face.

Only then did the Emperor's deeper voice follow, slow and heavy.

"In these past two days, Minister Su, General Gu, and even the Third Prince have all petitioned Us to grant them marriage with you. Are you aware of this matter?"

Her heart lurched violently. The strength she had only just regained slipped from her limbs, as if cut away. She dropped back to her knees at once. Her wide sleeves spread across the jade floor like pale wings. Her fingertips dug sharply into her palm, but her voice, though low, did not waver.

"Your Majesty, this humble woman begs forgiveness. This matter was unknown to this humble woman. Moreover, in this life I have no intention of marrying. If this is a fault, then I request punishment."

The air in the garden seemed to pause. Even the bamboo shadows outside the curtain looked suddenly still.

The Empress' expression changed openly for an instant, surprise written in her eyes. She turned slightly toward Emperor Xuanwen. The Emperor did not move, but the silence between them held a brief exchange, a moment of shared, quiet astonishment.

A woman with no title, no clan behind her, no name that carried weight, and yet three powerful men fought to stand before the throne for her. And at this critical moment, she had chosen to reject every path to glory laid at her feet.

What, exactly, was she thinking?

Emperor Xuanwen rested back upon the cushioned throne, hands behind his back. His gaze was fathomless, like deep water that never revealed what lay beneath.

"Among all the women under Heaven," he said evenly, "there are few whose dreams do not revolve around a marriage decree or a stroke of glory. Now, when General Gu, Minister Su, and the Third Prince all petition to wed you, you not only refuse them, but even request punishment."

His tone cooled further, and the hall tightened under it.

"Qin Nianyin. Is this so-called modesty, or is there something else you seek?"

Each word fell heavy, pressing down like stone.

Qin Nianyin bowed deeper. Her fingertips pressed into her palm until it blanched, yet her voice remained steady and rang clearly across the silent floor.

"Your Majesty, this humble woman is neither lofty nor scheming. My foster parents passed early, leaving me without kin. I have long relied upon the protection of the Su household for even the smallest foothold in this world. I know well my lowly station, and I do not possess the fortune needed to bear such weighty honour."

Her forehead lowered again, brushing the cold jade tiles.

"If marriage were forced upon me, it would bring calamity not only to myself, but to those entangled with me, and in time perhaps even to the court. Thus, rather than accept undeserved favour, I beg Your Majesty to punish me instead."

The Empress lifted her gaze, studying Qin Nianyin more carefully now. Not dazzling like the famed noble ladies of the capital, yet possessing a stark, clear-boned resolve. It was not softness. It was not calculation. It was something colder, something closer to refusal carved into the marrow.

Emperor Xuanwen tapped a knuckle lightly against the dragon table, once, twice. The sound was unhurried, deliberate, yet it tightened the air as surely as a drawn blade.

Then a faint curve touched his lips, almost mocking.

"Your words sound pleasant enough. But if you claim no interest in marriage, how is it that three men fight to stand before my throne on your behalf? Unless you have been enticing them."

The tension snapped taut.

A tremor passed through Qin Nianyin's spine. Yet she did not defend herself. She lifted her head only to strike it firmly against the floor. The crisp sound echoed under carved beams, sharp and clean.

"May Your Majesty judge clearly," she said. "This humble woman receives shelter from the Su family and is grateful beyond measure. General Gu protected me on the frontier. His Highness the Third Prince has shown occasional kindness. These are favours I dare not repay, let alone presume upon."

Her breath shook, but her words remained resolute.

"If any rumour or impropriety has arisen, the fault lies with me alone. Yet I swear upon my life, this humble woman harbours no ambition, seeks no glory, and has never desired a share of the world's power."

The Empress shifted slightly, her voice calm yet probing, the question precise as a needle.

"This palace has heard that the moment you arrived at the northern frontier, you rode off at once to seek General Gu. And some even say that at the cliff's edge, you rushed forward just as an assassin prepared to shoot an arrow at his back. Is that true?"

A cold tremor tightened Nianyin's fingers. She forced her breath to steady.

"In reply to Her Majesty," she said, "when I first reached the borderlands, I felt an inexplicable unease, an urgency I could not explain. I only wished to find General Gu quickly. By coincidence, it was at that moment I saw the assassin raise his bow. I acted before thinking."

The Empress observed her for a long moment before allowing a faint, unreadable smile.

"So, merely coincidence."

Qin Nianyin lowered her gaze again. Her posture remained impeccable.

"Indeed. My fortune is shallow. I would not dare speak of anything beyond that."

Emperor Xuanwen's voice cut through the air without warning.

"Then tell Me, do you harbour affection for General Gu?"

Qin Nianyin held her breath. Silence stretched. Then slowly, she raised her head.

"In reply to Your Majesty," she said, voice clear, "as with my cousin Su Zhang, I regard him as an elder brother. Nothing more."

The Empress exhaled softly, almost in disbelief.

"Such resolve truly does not sound like something one expects from a young girl."

Emperor Xuanwen's gaze deepened. He studied her for so long that the silence began to ring. At last, he spoke again, quieter, heavier.

"A fine 'desireless heart' you claim to have. Since you speak so firmly, then I shall remember it."

His tone sharpened suddenly.

"However, choosing none is not an option. Among the three, whom do you choose?"

Qin Nianyin remained kneeling, her forehead still brushing the floor.

"This humble woman knows her station is low. Any of them is far beyond my reach. And I wish only to learn my craft and establish myself by my own hands. I beg Your Majesties to grant me this freedom."

The hall held its breath.

Finally, Emperor Xuanwen waved a hand.

"Rise. Return to the Su residence for tonight. As for this matter, we shall discuss it another day."

The eunuchs echoed the command, drawing down the embroidered curtains. A cold wind slipped through the quiet garden outside, making the candle flames shudder.

Qin Nianyin rose slowly. Her heartbeat thudded like a drum beneath her ribs. She understood perfectly. She had not escaped. She had merely pressed this storm back, for now.

* * * * *

Behind the curtains of the imperial garden pavilion, Qin Nianyin had only just withdrawn when the eunuch leading her guided her along a narrow side path. Palace lanterns cast pale halos upon stone. Bamboo shadows trembled, then steadied, then trembled again.

"Miss Qin," he murmured, stopping, "please wait here for a moment. Someone wishes to see you."

The words had barely fallen when she noticed a dark silhouette standing quietly ahead, motionless, half-hidden among wavering shadows.

Su Zhang.

He wore plain ink-black robes. Under the lantern glow, the sharp restraint of his brows and eyes seemed carved even deeper, colder than the night itself. His posture was straight, too straight, as if he were holding himself in place by sheer will.

The eunuch retreated soundlessly, leaving only an expanse of hushed stillness.

A tremor ran through Qin Nianyin. She stepped back half a pace instinctively.

"Why is it you…"

The question had not finished before he moved toward her. His steps were controlled, but each one closed the distance with quiet inevitability.

Under the lantern light, his shadow stretched long across the flagstones. It was so long it felt as though the weight of the entire palace pressed upon his back. His gaze held a storm, turbulent and dark, yet forced down with ruthless discipline.

"I heard," he said.

His voice was low, hoarse at the edges, each word falling with contained force.

"You chose no one."

Qin Nianyin's breath faltered. Her fingers closed around her sleeve until the fabric creased beneath her grip. She did not look up. She could not afford to.

Su Zhang stared at her as if something inside his chest were being slowly, deliberately torn apart. At last, he forced out a single question.

"Why?"

There was a tremor in it, a thin crack he could not fully seal.

On the tip of his tongue hovered a deeper, more dangerous question, whether she had truly lived one life more than the rest of them. The words pressed up, urgent, burning. He swallowed them back at the final moment.

He wanted to ask.

He feared the answer.

Their gazes met, brief and sharp. The air seemed to freeze between them. Qin Nianyin's heartbeat scattered wildly. Her lips went pale. At last, she spoke, barely audible.

"Because I am unworthy."

She turned, meaning to leave.

In the next heartbeat, an arm wrapped around her from behind.

The hold was fierce, so tight it felt as though he meant to gather her into his bones. The suddenness struck the breath from her lungs. All she could hear was the thunder of her pulse, and the ragged, uneven sound of his breathing at her ear.

"Nianyin…"

His forehead pressed against her shoulder. His voice was hoarse, raw, close to breaking.

"Please, marry me. Will you?"

Qin Nianyin trembled. She stood frozen, unable to move.

Across two lifetimes, she had never seen Su Zhang like this, the man always composed, cold, self-possessed, now revealing cracks of fragility, and something painfully close to desperation.

Her throat tightened. A sting rose behind her eyes. Yet she still answered in a whisper.

"Cousin, it has been a long time since I last called you that. From now on, let me remain only your cousin. So, cousin, I beg you, forget me. Go and find your own happiness. I am truly unworthy of you."

The arms around her froze for a breath, then loosened, little by little.

Unworthy.

She kept saying she was unworthy, but for what reason?

Qin Nianyin lifted her hands and placed them over his, the hands still circling her waist. She pried his fingers away one joint at a time, patient, firm, as though dismantling a knot she could not afford to leave tied.

But Su Zhang drew her closer again, stubbornly, almost desperately, as if the act of letting go would undo him. The heat of his breath brushed the side of her neck, yet she felt a coldness spreading through her limbs in waves.

"Let me go, cousin."

"Your mind is set?"

"Yes, cousin."

The resolve in her voice struck him like a blade.

Su Zhang lowered his gaze. In the depths of his eyes burned a light that refused to be extinguished, quiet, fierce, unwavering.

He said nothing more.

At last, his arms loosened completely and he allowed her to step away, allowed her to follow the eunuch waiting at the far end of the path.

She walked further and further, her figure receding beneath the palace lanterns. The light swallowed her outline, then returned it, then swallowed it again, until at last she disappeared at the end of the corridor.

He remained where he stood.

His fingertips dug into his own palm so hard they nearly drew blood, yet he felt none of it.

His eyes stayed locked on the direction she had gone, sharp and unblinking, like a hunter fixed on the single prey he had marked.

It was a gaze filled with resolve.

It was a gaze filled with obsession.

Chapter 87: A Bitter Smile

Gu Xiao lifted a hand and gave his cloak a brisk shake. The silver plates of his armour caught the night light and glimmered with a frigid sheen, yet his brows were curved in an unmistakable smile.

"I've been waiting here," he said, standing at the path between the Imperial Garden and the palace gate, "for quite some time. Even if the night wind cut like ice, I intended to wait until you came out."

Qin Nianyin's heart stirred; a faint, soft smile brushed her lips.

"…There was no real delay."

But Gu Xiao's smile vanished. His expression tightened and he nearly ground out the words:

"Did Su Zhang see you first?"

Her lashes lowered. She said nothing.

and silence, in that moment, spoke more loudly than any answer.

A tightness struck Gu Xiao's chest. He muttered an oath under his breath:

"That sly old fox… He must have bribed the inner eunuchs long beforehand, lured you to some quiet corner of the palace, just so he could get ahead of me!"

His voice brimmed with frustration and fierce unwillingness, like a fiery-tempered youth whose victory had been stolen at the last moment.

Qin Nianyin only gave a light smile, her tone gentle and cool.

"You waited for me here. Was there something you wished to ask?"

Gu Xiao's expression changed instantly. His eyes lit with fierce vitality; lowering his voice, he asked:

"What did His Majesty and the Empress ask you?"

Qin Nianyin lowered her gaze. Her voice remained calm, almost airy.

"Nothing of importance. They merely asked after my well-being."

"Nianyin, do not hide the truth from me."

Gu Xiao stepped closer, his posture sharpening, his gaze burning straight into her.

"His Majesty and the Empress must have asked about your choice of husband.

Tell me ——did you choose me?"

Qin Nianyin looked at the spirited young general before her, so full of life and earnest passion. Her heart warmed with quiet affection.

Yet the smile that lifted at her lips was tinged with undeniable bitterness.

"The Emperor and Empress did ask," she replied softly, every word clear.

"But… knowing my own unworthiness, I refused all."

The colour drained from Gu Xiao's face.

"Why?"

His breath hitched; his chest rose and fell in uneven waves.

His mind flashed to the scene at the northern cliff, the moment she had rushed toward him despite danger, her slight figure shielding him from a hidden blade.

"If you felt nothing for me," he demanded hoarsely, "why would you risk your life for mine?"

Qin Nianyin shook her head gently. A shadow passed through her eyes.

"I truly have no wish to marry at all. As long as everyone I care for lives safely, as long as Great Zhou endures in peace… that alone is my greatest wish."

"Nonsense!"

Gu Xiao snapped, anger surging.

"You are neither an official nor a minister. Since when is it your place to worry about the nation's fate? You speak like ——like some weathered old matron who has survived half a lifetime of storms!"

The words struck her cleanly.

Her chest tightened. Her lashes lowered.

A weathered old matron?

He is not wrong… is he?

Two lifetimes added together, she was already over fifty.

"My heart is indeed old," she murmured, her voice soft yet resolute.

"I no longer have the strength to struggle."

She paused. Her fingertips trembled faintly. Then she looked up at him, truly looked at him, her gaze steady and luminous with finality.

"Do not press me further. Otherwise…"

She drew in a slow breath. The words that followed fell like a blade, severing the last fragile thread between them.

"Otherwise, I will go to Qin Mountain Temple and take vows."

The moment the words left her lips, it felt as though every sound in the world had been drained away.

Gu Xiao stared at her, as if struck clean through the chest by a blade.

For a long moment, he could only swallow hard, his throat moving with difficulty. When his voice finally emerged, it was hoarse and trembling.

"Nianyin… are you trying to frighten me?"

Qin Nianyin did not answer. She simply held his gaze.

Her eyes were calm, too calm. Yet within that stillness lay a bleak, unshakable resolve.

That look chilled more than the charge of ten thousand armoured soldiers.

A sudden harsh breath escaped Gu Xiao. Cold sweat seeped into his palms.

His mind flashed back to the northern cliff: her tear-filled eyes, her desperate sprint toward him, the way she had dragged him back from death with her bare hands.

He had been certain, absolutely certain, that her heart held him.

How could it not?

Otherwise, why risk her life?

But now she claimed her heart was old, claimed she would retreat to Qin Mountain Temple.

"Absurd!"

The word tore from Gu Xiao's throat. His jaw clenched so tightly that the lines of his face turned stark and pale.

He fixed his gaze on her, bloodshot veins spreading through his irises, his voice shaking with a fury he could no longer contain.

"Nianyin, you were willing to risk life and limb for me. How could you be without feeling? You may fool others, but you cannot fool me!"

Qin Nianyin's lips trembled faintly.

Yet in the end, she gave no answer. She only lowered her head.

A violent tide surged in Gu Xiao's chest, threatening to break free.

His hand lifted, instinctively reaching for her shoulders. At the last instant, his fingers froze in mid-air.

The palace gate was only steps away.

Around them, the shadows of guards and eunuchs hovered like silent witnesses. If he lost control here, if he touched her rashly, the consequences would fall not only on him, but on her.

So, he did not take that final step.

He clenched his hand into a fist, so tightly that his knuckles cracked aloud.

After a long, suffocating silence, a quiet laugh escaped him, bitter enough to taste of blood.

"Very well, Nianyin. You say your heart has grown old, that you will never marry again.

I believe you."

He stepped toward her, one step, then another.

His eyes burned with a fierce, unyielding blaze.

"But if you dare flee to Qin Mountain Temple, then you make yourself my enemy."

The wind howled through the courtyard.

Firelight flickered in his eyes, illuminating a wild, unwavering obstinacy, a devotion so fierce it bordered on madness.

Qin Nianyin's heart jolted. She pressed her lips together and offered no reply.

Gu Xiao's breaths came rough and fast. His chest rose and fell like a storm barely held at bay.

Then, without another word, he turned sharply. His cloak snapped behind him, slicing through the wind. His back was straight, sharp as a drawn blade.

Yet in the shadows, his eyes glowed red, burning with hurt, with anger, with a relentless vow.

For Gu Xiao had never, not once in his life, let go of what he wanted.

* * * * *

The room was deathly still, the air heavy with drifting threads of incense smoke. Princess Li Jing had just received the news: Gu Xiao had led the Tiger Guards to a triumphant return.

At that instant, her chest tightened violently.

It felt as though something had stripped her of all support, leaving her folding into the brocade-lined chair in silent collapse. Cold sweat rolled freely down her temples; the silk handkerchief in her grip had long been soaked through.

These past days, she had tossed and turned through every night. All her dreams were of the bitter northern plains, endless cold, choking smoke from beacon fires, and of herself being sent away for a political marriage.

If that future had unfolded, she would have been condemned to spend the rest of her life wandering the barren steppes, living the life of a nomad, never again seeing the warmth of the capital. Worse still was the memory of the elder princess and Zhao Ziqi's merciless rebuke. Their words still hammered at her eardrums like nails driven deep.

For Zhao Ziqi, the grand Consort's husband, to harbor such venomous resentment toward the princess that he had schemed with the enemy, sought to topple Great Zhou, and aimed to destroy the princess herself, the very thought sent another cold wave down Li Jing's spine.

It seemed laughable now, her naive belief that, with her noble birth, she could effortlessly choose her own beloved and secure a pleasing match. Looking back, it had all been nothing more than self-inflicted humiliation.

Now that the war had been won and the prospect of a diplomatic marriage dissolved, she should have felt relieved. Instead, her limbs had gone weak, utterly drained.

It was relief, but it was also the aftershock of standing at the very edge of an abyss.

Her lips trembled. She tried to force a smile yet found she could not lift the corners at all. Tears spilled silently down her cheeks.

"...Good… good… I don't have to go anymore…"

She whispered to herself, as though trying to convince her own trembling heart.

But then another piece of news reached her, whispers from today's imperial court. It was said that Su Zhang and Gu Xiao, along with the Third Prince, had all stood before Emperor Xuanwen, and each had asked for the same imperial marriage decree. Each had requested to marry the same woman.

Li Jing froze where she sat. A sharp pain twisted her heart, as though someone had seized it and pulled without mercy. A moment later, a fragile, sorrowed smile curved at her lips, one so faint it bordered on despair.

She was a princess of the imperial blood, born into privilege and prominence, yet she had been forced into a position where she had nearly agreed to marry beneath her, all in the desperate hope of avoiding a fate she could not bear.

And the one she had secretly admired, the man whose composed voice and steady demeanour had lodged themselves in her heart, that very man was now standing alongside others before the throne, openly contending for another woman's hand.

A woman with no noble status, no illustrious heritage. An ordinary girl, yet one who had somehow stirred the hearts of a prince, a general, and a powerful minister, all eager to fight for her sake.

"What a joke… what a cruel joke…"

She murmured, her voice dissolving into broken sobs, tears falling like beads of blood squeezed from the heart.

She was a princess, yet she lived lowlier, more fearfully, than any common woman. So humble that she was willing to accept whatever marriage could shield her, regardless of rank or dignity.

But the woman they sought had nothing, yet she was blessed with what Li Jing had never been granted.

Li Jing pressed a trembling palm to her chest. A suffocating heaviness swelled beneath her ribs. Half her face was wet with tears.

She knew, with painful clarity, that she had no time to hesitate. Whether it was the concubine-born son of a marquis' household or an impoverished yet respectable scholar, it no longer mattered.

What mattered was simple: as long as the man could shield her, her life, her safety, her fragile measure of freedom, then he would become the only path left to her, the single escape she could grasp.

And yet, deep in her heart, she understood the harshest truth.

What she truly yearned for, what she had always yearned for, was that cold, self-contained man whose every word struck like carved jade.

Su Zhang.

But in this world, there was no place left for someone like her in his story.

Chapter 88: The Capital in Uproar

The front hall of the Su residence blazed with lamplight, the shadows cast by the candles wavering across the carved pillars and lacquered screens. Su Wan's mother sat rigidly in the high-backed chair, the string of Buddha beads in her hand already damps with sweat.

Every bead clicked faintly under her tightened fingers, the sound heavy and rhythmic. Ever since the young servant returned with the report — —that Emperor Xuanwen had personally summoned Qin Nianyin into the palace.

Her heart had been suspended in her chest, weighed down as if a solid stone pressed against it, leaving her scarcely able to breathe.

"Why would His Majesty suddenly…" she murmured under her breath, the words trembling with anxiety and disbelief.

Su Wan had changed into a pale shawl and now sat quietly at her mother's side. When she noticed the coldness in her mother's palm, she reached out to cover it gently, her voice low and soothing.

"Mother, perhaps it was merely because of matters related to the returning army. It may even be that His Majesty intends to reward Cousin Nianyin. It does not necessarily mean anything ill. Please do not worry too much."

But Su Wan's mother shook her head, the fine wrinkles at the corners of her eyes trembling faintly. "You do not understand. The emperor personally calls for a young woman and he does so at such an hour… Tell me, how can a person not be troubled?"

Su Wan was silent for a moment. She still kept her tone calm and steady. "But Cousin has always been careful and composed. Her conduct and manners have never once fallen short of propriety.

She has never given anyone the slightest reason to find fault. Mother, let us wait for her return before letting fear take hold."

Yet Su Wan's mother remained restless. Her fingers slipped anxiously along the beads, the soft rasp of wood-on-wood betraying her unease.

Her voice quivered as she whispered, "Since ancient times, the palace gates have been as deep as the sea. She is only a young girl. At this moment she must be terrified. Those gates… once you enter them, they are not easily left behind. And she is still so young, with no powerful family standing behind her…"

Her words halted. A surge of painful emotion rose in her throat. She remembered how Qin Nianyin had appeared when she first entered their household ——cautious, restrained, careful with every gesture.

And she remembered how, in recent months, the child had been repeatedly drawn into matters of the military and the court. The more she thought on it, the more her unease grew.

"Where is Zhang? He should be in the palace now, should he not?" she asked quietly, as though afraid someone might overhear.

Su Wan lifted her gaze to the few strands of grey at her mother's temples. Her answer was gentle. "Do not think too far ahead, Mother. Cousin is not a foolish person. She keeps her dealings measured and always leaves room for retreat. If His Majesty summoned her, I do not believe he will make things difficult for her. And besides, Elder Brother will certainly look after her."

Hearing this, Su Wan's mother drew in a slow breath. Even so, she still murmured the Buddha's name under her breath, as though reciting it might press the swelling worry in her heart back down inch by inch.

She looked at her daughter again. Though the concern in her eyes had not faded, Su Wan's words had eased her anxiety by a small measure. She raised a hand to lightly pat Su Wan's shoulder and spoke in a muted tone. "Let us hope so. Let us hope…"

Seeing the tension still gathered between her mother's brows, Su Wan spoke again, her voice even gentler than before. "Mother, it is late. Too much worrying will only wear down your health. Cousin Nianyin is blessed. Heaven will protect her. She will surely return safely. Please rest your mind for now."

Su Wan's mother closed her eyes for a brief moment and the hand gripping the beads finally loosened. She breathed out a quiet "Amitabha," yet her gaze remained fixed on the doorway, watching the shifting lantern-light outside. She waited, longing to see a familiar silhouette appear in the wavering glow.

* * * * *

News that the imperial court had witnessed something unprecedented — —that Su Zhang, the newly appointed tan-hua; Gu Xiao, the famed young general; and Prince Li Suo had all requested imperial permission to marry the same woman ——spread across the capital with the speed of wildfire.

Within every household and every private women's quarters, astonishment erupted as though a storm had blown open the shutters.

In the inner courtyard of the Shen residence, Shen Lingyan had been checking newly acquired bolts of silk with her maid when a young servant hurried in.

Breathless and pale, she stammered out the report: Gu Xiao, Su Zhang and Prince Li Suo had all petitioned Emperor Xuanwen during morning court.

Each asking to marry a young woman of no known background, a simple commoner girl named Qin Nianyin.

In that instant, the light silk slipped from Shen Lingyan's hand. She stood rooted to the spot, unable to move. A dull roar filled her ears, drowning out every other sound.

"Gu… Gu Xiao?" she whispered, the name escaping her lips without thought, her voice barely audible.

She had always concealed her feelings well, wrapping them under layers of decorum and restraint. But at this moment, something in her heart was struck with a force she could not withstand.

She had grown up among the sons of noble families and had seen countless young men with talent and bearing, yet it was that one cold, steady figure ——one glimpse of his stern composure ——that had imprinted itself quietly in her heart.

She had never dared speak of it. She had not even dared to think deeply about it. But in dreams, or in the flicker of reflections on rippling water during spring gatherings, she had allowed herself to bury his name in the dimmest corners of her heart.

And now ——

A sharp ache rose beneath her breastbone. The corners of her eyes stung with heat. Her fingers clutched the edge of her sleeve so tightly the fabric twisted.

She had always assumed that he cared only for battle achievements and the path of military honour, that he would not easily form attachments.

She had never imagined he would stand in the golden hall alongside others and openly request a marriage decree ——for the sake of Qin Nianyin.

"So, it is… her," Shen Lingyan murmured, a fragile smile curving her lips, so faint it looked more like a cut than a smile.

She knew of Qin Nianyin ——Su Zhang's cousin, temporarily residing at the Su residence. A girl of gentle countenance, with skilful hands capable of crafting hair ornaments. But this knowledge brought her no comfort.

Instead, it tore open a hidden corner of her heart, leaving her exposed as though the night air itself carried a sting.

Seeing Shen Lingyan's pallor, her maid called softly, "My lady…" Her tone was cautious, afraid to touch whatever fragile thing lay beneath the calm surface.

Shen Lingyan merely shook her head, gathering up the fallen silk with steady hands, though her voice carried a slight tremor. "It is nothing. I am only… a little tired."

She turned and walked back into her inner room, leaving behind a single solitary lamp on the small desk, its glow outlining her quiet loneliness and the turmoil she could not voice.

In that moment, memories surfaced ——scattered yet sharp.

Years ago, Gu Xiao had been fifteen, already strikingly handsome, bright as the rising sun and fierce as a young hawk. She had heard him laughing beneath the carved eaves that year.

His brows had been direct, his voice clear. In the slanting light of dusk, his profile had looked almost sculpted, and her heartbeat had faltered without warning.

She had known he and her childhood friend Su Zhang were close as brothers. After that, she had sought excuses to visit the Su residence more often, pretending casualness even as her intentions remained carefully hidden.

Yet she understood the distance between them all too well. She was the daughter of a respectable household but not a daughter of the imperial clan. He was the empress's only nephew.

The thoughts of a young woman were easily misunderstood and even more easily scorned, so she had folded her feelings into poetry and pressed them into the strings of her zither, never allowing a single word to slip.

Now, hearing that he had sought marriage with another, the old longing she had silenced and chained away seemed torn open in an instant, leaving her with nowhere to hide.

She closed her eyes slowly, fighting the ache in her chest. Her voice was barely above a whisper. "There are thousands of beautiful sights in this world. None of them were meant for me."

Her fingertips passed over the smooth surface of the silk and in the quiet of the room, she could almost hear something delicate inside her quietly breaking.

* * * * *

By the next morning, every alley and street of the capital was speaking of the same name: Qin Nianyin.

Inside a bustling teahouse, the storyteller slapped his wooden clapper against the table, his voice loud and ringing as he addressed the packed audience.

"Have you all heard? After the great victory at Wulan Ridge, General Gu Xiao returned in triumph and ——in front of the entire court —— petitioned His Majesty for a marriage decree! But the astonishing thing is that kneeling beside him, asking for the very same woman, was none other than the newly appointed tanhua, Su Zhang!"

The main floor erupted instantly. Patrons leaned across tables, whispering, gesturing and repeating the news with incredulous faces.

In a nearby embroidery house, several young noble ladies gathered around a low table, their heads close together.

One girl, her eyes faintly reddened, spoke with a mixture of envy and bitterness. "She is merely a cousin taken in by the Su family ——a girl without a proper lineage ——yet she can make both General Gu and Su Dar ——Su Zhang ——fall for her at the same time?"

Another young lady, fanning herself lightly, let out a soft laugh tinged with mischief.

"You all truly haven't heard the rest? It's said that Prince Li Suo had already submitted a memorial requesting the same marriage. The three of them stood together in the hall before His Majesty. If this isn't a storm sweeping through the whole city, I don't know what is."

Gasps rippled through the group, sleeves lifted to cover mouths, eyes wide in shock.

At a small street stall, a man with a shoulder pole shouted as he arranged his goods. "For common folk like us, it's simple enough. If Miss Qin really enters the palace, that's rising to the heavens in one step!"

The candied-haw vendor beside him clicked his tongue repeatedly, shaking his head. "No, no, that won't do. A woman who draws the hearts of a general, a scholar and a prince all at once ——that sort of fate is as dangerous as it is enviable. Mark my words, blessings like that can turn to disaster. Heaven may very well envy the beautiful."

In the span of a single day, whether in the mansions of nobles or in the crowded markets, people spoke of nothing else.

The three characters of "Qin Nianyin" spread through the capital like a blaze, igniting curiosity, envy, admiration and fear in equal measure.

Chapter 89: The Woman in the Mirror

Night rain threaded softly through the darkness, dripping from the eaves in steady intervals.

In the Su residence's study, the lamplight hung low. The window paper, pressed by the wind, showed faint rippling patterns—like a thin imprint laid over it.

Su Zhang leaned against the armrest beside the desk, unusually still.

The weight that had pressed against his chest throughout the day had yet to fade. He rarely drank, but tonight he had broken the habit. Two sips of the warm wine had already brought a faint heat to his throat. By the third, he held the cup for a long time without lowering it, as though even that small descent required a decision.

His gaze lifted toward the desk.

The scattered pages had already been gathered. Only a pen-rest with a broken corner remained lying crosswise beside the inkstone—sharp and jarring like an old, unhealed splinter, a thorn that refused to blunt.

Wind and rain clashed outside the window, but inside he could hear only the thin thread of sandalwood drifting through the room—so light it was almost illusory, now near, now distant.

Stifling.

At last, he tipped back the cup and swallowed the third mouthful.

The warmth dropped heavily through his chest like a smooth, heated stone, pressing down the sharp edges that had been stirring inside him—subduing them for the moment, not erasing them.

His eyelids grew weighty. He closed the dossier, leaned back into the chair, and his fingers continued tapping unconsciously at the table—one tap after another, as if counting, or as if turning something over in his mind and refusing to let it go.

His breathing lengthened.

At the edge of his vision, the candleflame wavered like a flower brushed by a passing gust—brightening and dimming in turn. He meant to steady it with his hand, but his arm suddenly sank, as if the weight had been quietly reapportioned to his bones.

His consciousness felt as though someone had laid a gentle hand upon it, pressing it downward, letting it slide slowly into a pool of warm, rippling darkness.

The door… opened on its own—

He stood at the threshold.

Ink from the study still clung faintly to his fingertips, yet before him stretched a quiet, secluded bedchamber entirely different from the one he had left.

A gauze canopy hung low.

A small sandalwood table stood polished and clear.

On the dressing stand, a bronze mirror glimmered with the muted lustre of years.

The scent here was softer than in the study—like the first blossom of spring osmanthus, warm and gentle against the nose.

She was seated before the mirror.

Her long hair fell like a dark waterfall, cascading down the line of her back. Her movements were slow, careful—as though afraid to disturb something—guiding the comb's teeth through her hair inch by inch, strand by strand.

The candlelight flickered across her tresses, throwing a soft length of glow that sketched the quiet, clean curve of her cheek. The profile it drew was almost too still, too pure, as though even sound would startle it.

His heart shifted abruptly.

He reached out without thinking, wanting to touch the back of her hair— then immediately lowered his hand, as though he had caught himself in the act of trespassing.

Su Zhang rarely felt anything like this even in dreams:

A soundless tremor, like a smooth blade drawn lightly across the ribs— too gentle to wound, yet leaving behind a trace of heat that felt dangerously close to pain. It cut, and yet left no mark; it was almost worse for how quiet it was.

For an instant, he even felt a strange and perilous thought rise within him—

Go closer. Lean down. Gather that loose strand and tuck it behind her ear.

His fingertips moved half an inch.

Then, in the mirror, he met his own eyes.

No.

He denied it silently in his heart—light as breath, yet firm as a decree carved into stone, a rule he did not permit himself to bend.

A woman like her, with gentle brows and a soft voice and a smile that never rose beyond the faintest line—if she truly held him in her heart, why would every step be measured, every word proper, every expression so timed and controlled? If she revealed even the slightest hint of fondness now, would that not be precisely what she wished—to win what she sought?

What she wanted, he told himself again, was nothing more than his status and his position.

Fragments of memory rippled outward like rings on still water.

Her perfectly proper greetings. Her impeccable inquiries. Her modest restraint displayed just right before others—everything too calculated, too precise, too deliberate, as if polishing the title of "Madam" until it shone.

The comb paused.

As if sensing something, she turned her head slightly—not toward him, but toward her reflection. The corners of her eyes dipped faintly, as though from weariness… or from holding something back so it would not spill.

She reached into a small case and took out a white jade hairpin carved with a tiny orchid. Simple, warm, quietly polished—nothing like the dazzling gold and pearls of banquets, so ordinary it might be overlooked at a glance.

She slid it into her hair.

Her fingers lingered on the smooth surface for a heartbeat too long.

That pause was so brief it felt like an illusion—too quick to read, too quick to name, and yet unmistakably there.

Su Zhang's throat tightened.

He remembered that pin—something he had bought casually from a market stall simply because the carving was elegant. Not expensive. Not meant to impress.

She had accepted it with a small smile: no excessive delight, no polite refusal, everything neatly within "appropriate."

Appropriate. Proper. Measured.

A short, cold laugh almost formed in him. Yes—this was what he should never forget: her unerring grasp of "just right," never too much, never too little, so flawless that no fault could be found. How could such perfection not be calculation?

In the mirror, she suddenly lowered her head. Her lips moved the slightest bit—almost a smile, yet not one at all, more like swallowing back a sigh before it could become sound.

She pressed her fingertip lightly at the corner of her eye, the touch so gentle it seemed meant not to disturb anything—like she feared smudging her makeup, or feared letting something break its surface.

The bronze mirror did not gleam sharply, yet it still captured the faint flush beneath her touch with a clarity that felt too intimate.

His heart contracted.

Without realizing it, he stepped closer.

The fragrance around her became clearer; the embroidery threads along his robe seemed to drift like a silent tide, the entire room hushed as if it were waiting.

He saw her fingertips pause again atop the hairpin—another tiny hesitation, hidden in plain sight, a brief moment that did not fit within "proper measure."

He wanted to call her.

His tongue had already begun to move when another thought intruded coldly and without mercy:

If you call her, she will turn. She will bow her head softly and address you as "husband." You will remember her attentiveness, her gentleness, her finely measured deference behind closed doors. And afterward she will ask after your health, offer concern without fault, warmth without excess—everything perfect, everything "just right."

His knuckles tightened.

He forced the rising words back down his throat.

In the mirror, she noticed nothing.

She simply gathered that long dark hair again. The jade pin caught the light and flickered once, trembling faintly within the candleflame, as though even it were unsteady.

At last she lifted her gaze.

It passed through the reflection—not a direct look, not quite meeting him, and yet landing precisely at the space between his brows, as if she could see him without "seeing" him.

That glance was exceedingly brief.

Yet it landed like a needle, silent and exact.

His chest tightened.

Still, stubbornly, he told himself: pretence. All of it is pretence. If not for ambition, why should she be so flawlessly considerate?

She raised her hand and pushed a brocade box on the dressing table closer.

There were no jewels inside—only several sheets of thin paper, neatly stacked, aligned as carefully as everything else about her.

She unfolded the top one.

The bronze mirror reflected a line of elegant handwriting. Su Zhang could not see the words clearly—only sensed that the final strokes were drawn tight, as if holding something back, as if the sentence had been cut short by restraint.

She stared at the paper, eyes pausing for a brief moment.

Her fingertips smoothed its edge with an uncalled-for softness, as though afraid to wake something—or afraid to startle herself. The very next second, she smiled: a faint, pale curve that vanished almost as soon as it appeared, like tucking something quietly back into her heart.

A sound that was almost a scoff caught at his throat—barely audible.

Those words—who are they written for?

For him?

Or for the title of "Madam"?

The candle flame jumped suddenly. Light and shadow in the mirror stretched and warped.

Her profile seemed cut into two halves—one calm and obedient, brows and eyes smooth; the other tense, her lips pressed so tightly they had gone pale.

The comb slipped from her fingers and fell against the dressing table with a soft tap.

It was not loud.

Yet it struck his chest like a stone dropped into deep water.

At last, he reached out.

His fingertips brushed the ends of her hair—

And the entire scene shattered violently, as though someone had plunged a hand into water and stirred it apart. Mirror, hairpin, gauze canopy, her slender back—everything scattered into drifting fragments of light.

He snapped his eyes open.

The candle in the study was still burning. The rain outside had grown heavier, denser, more insistent.

Cold sweat dampened his forehead.

A sharp sting pulsed from his palm—only then did he realize his own nails had dug so deeply into his skin that they had left a ring of pale marks, biting into the web of his thumb as if he had been holding himself in place.

The heat in his chest had long dissipated. The wine had cleared from his head.

Yet that single moment—the instant in which he had almost called out to her—remained like a wavering flame lodged beneath his ribs, burning without showing itself: hot, and yet unwilling to declare its light.

Su Zhang did not move for a long time.

Only after quite a while did he slowly straighten his back, smooth his sleeve and allow his expression to cool, inch by inch, returning it to something controlled and unreadable.

Yet at the very end of that unspoken sentence, there remained a faint, unspeakable sting in his throat—

Like that small touch of red pressed at the corner of her eye in the mirror: light to the point of nearly invisible, and yet—impossibly hard to erase.

Chapter 90: A Measure of Balance

Night lay deep over the Imperial Garden. Bamboo shadows swayed in restless layers beneath the lowered curtains, while the lamps fluttered faintly in the wind.

Qin Nianyin bowed low and withdrew. Her eyes remained lowered as she retreated, following at a distance behind the eunuch who guided her until her slight figure disappeared into the far end of the palace path.

Within the hall, silence settled almost at once, leaving only the slow, hazy curl of incense smoke.

The Empress watched that fragile back recede into the darkness. Only when it was completely gone did she draw her gaze back, turning to Emperor Xuanwen with a softened voice.

"Your Majesty can see it as well. She truly bears no ambition for rank or power. If what she said is sincere—if her heart truly has no inclination toward marriage—then she is, at least, a clean-handed girl."

Emperor Xuanwen stood beneath the lamplight, hands clasped behind his back. His eyes, however, were cold, his expression carrying a restraint that was almost dismissive.

"Empress, you speak foolishly. What woman in this world is truly without desire? If she truly has no desire, then she is a calamity waiting to happen. Since ancient times, how many lessons have been written in blood by the so-called femme fatale? The fall of a realm often turns on a single thought."

The Empress parted her lips, wanting to argue, yet found that some of his words carried an undeniable weight. For a moment she could not find her footing. All that remained was a heavy, quiet sigh.

Emperor Xuanwen's voice deepened again, each syllable settling with deliberate force.

"This girl has already driven Gu Xiao and Su Zhang to compete before the throne. Now she is entangled with the Third as well. Such a woman—whether she herself intends it or not—once she has the power to bewilder, others will not let her go. And I will be the first not to let her go."

The Empress frowned, the crease between her brows tightening.

"Xiao... seems to have fallen for her truly and deeply. Yet she has no family standing, no background. How could she possibly bear the position of a principal lady? What are we to do..."

Emperor Xuanwen inclined his head slightly, his tone low and steady.

"If she is granted to Su or granted to Gu, the other side will be offended. They will not rest in peace, and neither will the court. Moreover, what is this girl's true capability? What has she done, that she can make the young talents of our dynasty—three men, each exceptional in his own right—stand together before the throne and petition for her? A woman like this is either a blessing... or the root of disaster."

His gaze turned colder, his reasoning sharpened to a point.

"If she is left among the common folk, who can guarantee she will not stir wind and waves in the future? If she becomes a spark, she will become a hidden threat."

The Empress nodded, suppressing the unease that rose in her chest.

"Then according to Your Majesty—what should be done?"

Emperor Xuanwen answered evenly, as though stating something entirely ordinary.

"To kill her would be the most stable solution."

"Your Majesty!" The Empress's eyes widened. The shock broke through her composure and her voice rose involuntarily. "Absolutely not!"

Emperor Xuanwen gave a faint, indifferent smile.

"Naturally not now. If she dies at this moment, the scale will collapse. It will harm the court and harm the state."

Only then did the Empress loosen the breath trapped in her throat.

"If Your Majesty were to make her die to atone... Xiao's heart would only drift farther and farther away from us."

Emperor Xuanwen nodded, his expression unreadable.

"Since she cannot be killed at present, the most proper course is to keep her directly under our eyes—place her within the palace sphere. Cut off her retreat, yet do not damage the wings of any of the three."

His voice remained calm, but the calculation within it was unmistakable.

"In that manner, Su, Gu, and the Third will have nothing they can openly object to. And my board remains whole."

The Empress's heart sank slightly.

"This matter can be delayed now, but in the end she must be given to one among them. If it is not Xiao, he will not accept it."

Emperor Xuanwen began to pace slowly, the lamplight shifting across his robe. His voice was low, cold, and controlled.

"In my view… then only one choice remains."

The Empress stilled. "Your Majesty means…"

"Suo."

The Empress's throat tightened. After a long pause she spoke, her voice lowered.

"Your Majesty's meaning is—to bestow Qin upon the Third Prince?"

Emperor Xuanwen nodded. His eyes were deep, like a pool under nightfall.

"In this arrangement, Gu dares not resent. Su dares not speak. Qin remains beneath my eyes—she can be soothed, and she can be watched."

Then his tone turned faintly sharper, almost amused—yet the amusement was cold.

"Most crucially: when two tigers contend, the fisherman profits."

His gaze did not waver.

"And that fisherman can only be me."

The Empress lowered her eyes. Her fingers trembled lightly against her lap. She knew that once such a decree descended, it would be iron netting drawing tight—no one would be able to escape.

Emperor Xuanwen let out a thin, chilly laugh and lifted his hand, signalling for the attendants.

"Prepare the decree. Summon—"

The lamp flame shuddered. The air in the Imperial Garden seemed to drop in temperature at once.

Yet at that instant, the Empress's fingertips quivered. She raised her hand and pressed against his sleeve, stopping the motion.

"Your Majesty—please wait."

Emperor Xuanwen turned, a crease forming between his brows. Suspicion flickered in his eyes.

"What does the Empress mean?"

The Empress lowered her gaze. The heaviness in her chest grew thicker, but her voice still carried a faint tremor.

"This concubine only… feels fear. Xiao… may not be able to endure it."

"Xiao?" Emperor Xuanwen's eyes narrowed.

The Empress pressed her lips together. At last she spoke softly, each word weighed down by helplessness.

"He is my nephew. He grew up beneath my care. How could I not know him? In his heart, he has already regarded Qin as the only one he will ever take as his own. Today, in the Great Hall, he knelt and begged in such a loss of control—he laid his feelings bare before the entire court."

Her voice paused. A flash of reluctance passed through her eyes.

"If Your Majesty bestows her upon the Third Prince at this moment… I fear Xiao's will may be damaged. I fear he may never recover the sharpness he once had."

Emperor Xuanwen's expression shifted, his voice turning stern.

"Absurd. A grown man—three feet tall—would lose his resolve over such petty affection between man and woman?"

"No—" The Empress's voice grew more urgent. "This Qin is different."

She swallowed, forcing herself to continue.

"This concubine has looked into it. Your Majesty also knows—Xiao once wandered through life as if it were play, indulging himself without restraint. Yet it was because of a few words from this Qin that he steadied himself and rose again. To Xiao, she is not a passing fancy. I fear… this may be calamity rather than blessing."

Emperor Xuanwen's gaze dropped, cold and assessing.

"Then the Empress means—Qin should be granted to Xiao?"

The Empress shook her head immediately, conflict tightening her voice.

"This concubine also knows: Qin may be clean in conduct, yet she has no family standing. If she were established as principal wife, she would not be an ideal choice. Xiao is crowned with military merit, but if he takes such a woman as the head of his household, how will others view the Gu family? What noble house would still be willing to send their daughter as secondary, if the principal seat is occupied by a woman without roots?"

Her voice lowered further.

"In time, within the household, resentment will gather, suspicion will grow. A husband and wife may end in discord. And discord will become disaster."

Emperor Xuanwen's eyes darkened.

"Then what is the Empress's plan?"

The Empress answered in a low voice, as though pushing her way through thorns.

"Perhaps… if Qin is placed as a secondary consort, it could soothe Xiao's heart without pressing down the title of the principal wife. Others may still be willing to marry into the Gu household with dignity."

Her voice fell even softer, until it was nearly a whisper.

"Only… after Xiao's conduct today in the Great Hall, if Qin is merely secondary, then what family would willingly send their daughter to be the principal wife? Everyone can see where his heart lies. If Qin and Xiao live in harmony, then the principal wife would be condemned from the very beginning—to a lifetime of being neglected by her husband."

At that point the Empress's voice stopped. She understood there was no clean answer—yet she still could not help grasping for a sliver of room to turn, for her nephew's sake.

The night wind in the garden turned colder. Emperor Xuanwen narrowed his eyes, watching her in silence. His gaze held scrutiny—and beneath it, a cold, faintly amused curve.

"In that case," he said at last, "I will think it over again. I will probe each of their hearts… and see what they truly dare to bear."

* * * * *

In the Golden Hall, behind the dragon-carved desk, Emperor Xuanwen sat with hands folded behind his back.

The uproar in the hall had not yet fully calmed. Su Zhang and Gu Xiao each remained in a deep bow, the name Qin Nianyin suspended over the minds of the officials like wildfire—burning without flame, yet scorching all the same.

The emperor sat steadily upon the dragon throne above the golden steps while the voices beneath could not settle.

A cold laugh flickered in his heart.

A woman with no power, no backing, no position—and yet able to tug three men at once.

Su Zhang: the Su clan's Tanhua, praised by the upright scholars, supported by the pure-stream faction.

Gu Xiao: the Gu clan's tiger general, whose military merit shook even the court.

And Suo—his third son. A prince known for frivolity and mockery of the world, and yet now he had also opened his mouth to request a marriage decree.

Ridiculous.

Love? True feeling?

In the emperor's eyes, they were merely the clumsiest excuse in the world.

If Qin truly held no intent, how could three men submit memorials at the same time?

If she held intent, then she could not be left outside even more.

Civil minister. Military commander. Imperial clan.

The three most difficult forces to hold in balance—now tangled together upon a single woman.

This was not fortune.

This was calamity.

His gaze deepened. His mind grew so calm it was almost frightening.

"You are all pillars of my realm," he said coolly, "yet you bring a dispute over a woman before the throne. If this is not severed early, it will become a hidden danger in the heart."

In an emperor's heart, love and hate were disposable.

What could not be broken was balance.

What could not be allowed was a crack in the greater game.

She was nothing more than a piece.

Yet since she could move the board, then she would be locked inside the emperor's own chessboard first.

Rather than let you fight over her, I will take her.

The emperor lifted his hand. At once the hall fell into dead silence.

"You are all pillars of my empire," he declared, voice flat as iron, "yet you contend over one woman before the throne. It is a loss of measure."

"To steady your hearts and preserve order: Qin of the Qin clan is hereby ordered to go to Qing Shan Temple and undertake consecrated cultivation for one year, with her hair unbound, praying for Great Zhou's fortune and prosperity. When the year is complete, an auspicious day will be chosen, and she shall be installed as a secondary consort of the Third Prince."

The hall became so still it seemed no one dared breathe.

Gu Xiao's chest surged like a war drum. Blood roared in his ears. For a heartbeat he nearly believed he had misheard.

"No… impossible…"

His eyes turned red. A hoarse sound forced its way out of his throat. His fingers dug into his palm so hard that a metallic trace of blood rose on his skin.

In that instant, he nearly lost control—nearly roared out in defiance—

But a blade of reason cut through him: if he lost control, he would not only ruin himself; he would fling her straight into an abyss from which there would be no return.

Su Zhang, however, was quiet to the point of unnaturalness.

His hand tightened slowly within his sleeve. The knuckles blanched white. In his palm, nail-marks broke the skin until a thin wetness rose.

His eyes were a dead stillness—and yet in that stillness, a suffocating dark fire burned.

So it is as I thought.

The fisherman profits.

He had calculated the court. He had weighed every route.

Yet he had still failed to account for this single stroke.

At this moment he did not move, did not speak, did not contend.

Only his lips drew into a straight, frozen line, and his gaze grew cold enough to crack stone.

Emperor Xuanwen's eyes swept the hall. Seeing the three men's faces, each different, the corner of his mouth lifted faintly.

His voice remained indifferent, iron-cold.

"This is the imperial decree. None of you may object."

"Court is dismissed."

The imperial bell thundered. The officials bowed as one, crying:

"Long live the Emperor, long live the Emperor, long live the Emperor…"

Chapter 91: The Shattering of His Resolve

Within the Su Residence study, the lamplight wavered in unsteady arcs across the walls.

Yefeng and Xiuyan stood opposite each other, both holding their breath, neither daring to speak. Since the court had adjourned that morning, their young master had locked himself inside the study, forbidding anyone to enter unless summoned.

A sudden crash came from within.

"Bang ——!"

Scrolls tumbled to the floor. A jade brush shattered. The gilt brush stand struck the blue bricks and broke apart, scattering sharp fragments across the ground with a sound that made their hearts clench.

The fragments skittered and rang as they struck the bricks, sharp, repeated, relentless, as though each crack were landing directly on their ribs. For a heartbeat, neither attendant could even tell whether the next sound was porcelain, wood, or the young master's restraint breaking apart.

"Master…" Yefeng called softly despite himself, but his voice was swallowed whole by the next violent crash.

The heavy desk was overturned with a single palm strike. Documents, inkstones and bamboo slips crashed down in a single wave. Ink spilled in a dark splash, spreading rapidly across the floor like a pool of night.

"How could it be ——!"

Inside the room, the man who had always kept his composure —— silent, restrained, unshakably calm ——now lifted eyes that burned red as if drenched in blood. The centre of his brow tightened in a pained knot, his expression edged with something close to madness. His fingers gripped the upended desk so hard the veins in his hands were raised and stark.

"It should have been mine."

His voice was low and hoarse, trembling with fury ——yet threaded through with an obsession so fierce it bordered on deranged.

He had never lost control like this. Not once.

Xiuyan and Yefeng exchanged a terrified look, cold sweat sliding down their backs. Since the first day they had memory, they had never witnessed Su Zhang in such a state.

The man who had always been steady as a mountain and clear as winter pine now resembled a lone wolf driven to the very edge, its eyes flickering with bloodlust and despair.

"Qin Nianyin…"

He murmured her name under his breath, but the sound was like a blade scraped across stone ——sharp, cold and lethal.

"This game… I will not lose. Even if I must exhaust everything I possess, regardless of the price, I, Su Zhang, will overturn this outcome ——and take her back."

Once the words left him, he kicked the fallen desk aside with a violent strike. The crash of splintering wood and the harsh echo of his outburst made the window frames of the study rattle in their grooves.

The attendants knelt outside the door, not daring to utter a single word. Everyone understood: the composure Su Zhang had suppressed for years ——restraint carved into his bones ——had finally ruptured.

It was not merely anger. It was something that had been forced down, day after day, year after year, until it had hardened into bone. And now that bone had snapped. The servants outside did not dare lift their heads, because one glance would make the truth undeniable: the master they relied on had been pushed past the point where calm could still be worn like a mask.

He had truly lost control.

A gust of night wind swept into the room, making the lamp flame shudder. Su Zhang stood amid the chaos, his gaze bloodshot, yet the corner of his lips curved upward in a thin, chilling arc.

"Third Prince… and Gu Xiao… neither of you have a chance. She can only be mine."

He spoke slowly, each syllable pressed down, colder and heavier than the last. The words did not sound like a vow meant to persuade anyone. They sounded like a sentence already written, already sealed, already waiting to be carried out.

His words fell one by one, each cold enough to freeze blood.

In his mind, the image rose again ——Qin Nianyin on the Jiangnan road, shielding him from an arrow with her own body. The memory struck him like a blade to the heart. She had risked her life to protect him. How could such a woman ——how could she possibly refuse to marry him?

"Impossible… Nianyin… why… why would you…"

The question broke in his throat, raw, pained and disbelieving ——yet no answer came, only the echo of his own shattering breath filling the ruined study.

* * * * *

The night was deep; outside the Su Residence, the long street was filled with a mingled scent of wine and cold wind.

"I refuse to accept this!"

The young general ——still in silver armour, his cloak dishevelled, a half-emptied jug of strong liquor clenched in his fist ——stumbled forward unsteadily.

Gu Xiao's eyes were bloodshot, and wine dripped from the corner of his mouth, burning his already hoarse throat.

He tilted his head back and roared into the pitch-black sky. The sound tore from him like something breaking open, loud enough to startle dogs into barking throughout the street.

"Why ——!"

"Why grant the marriage to the Third Prince?!"

"Nianyin… she was the one I protected!"

He staggered step by step until he reached the Su Residence gates and slammed his fist against the red-lacquered doors. His voice was cracked and raw, yet carried the stubborn force only a young general could wield.

"Su Zhang! Get out here!"

"Aren't you the one who calculates best?! What did you calculate this time?!"

Every word was steeped in wine, rage and a hatred that bordered on despair.

His breath reeked of spirits and iron-bitter grief. The street lamps threw broken light over his armour, and passersby shrank back as if afraid the violence in his voice might spill into their hands. Even the dogs that barked from the alleys sounded uncertain, as though the night itself had been grabbed by the throat.

Inside, Xiuyan and Yefeng exchanged alarmed looks. Behind them, Su Zhang sat motionless, silent in the shadows, a cold glint in his gaze as he rolled a single icy chess piece between his fingers.

Outside, the voice kept shouting again and again, as though it meant to split the night in two.

"I ——Gu Xiao ——have never feared ten thousand troops across a battlefield!"

"But this time… this time… I lost to the 'greater design'!"

"Nianyin…"

His voice dropped suddenly, weighted with choking grief. He pressed his forehead heavily against the cold wooden gate and whispered, each word sinking.

"Nianyin… how could you bear it…"

There was a long silence.

Then, from within the residence, a cold, emotionless command was spoken ——

"Drag him away."

The door opened a narrow crack and two guards rushed out. Before Gu Xiao could react, a heavy staff struck hard across his back, sending him stumbling to his knees.

"Stop! I can walk myself ——"

But another strike came down on the back of his head. His vision went black. His body collapsed without resistance.

The two guards, not daring to utter a word, seized the unconscious young general beneath his arms and dragged his limp weight down the steps, pulling him into the depths of the night.

Inside, the candlelight flickered.

Su Zhang stood within the shadows, listening quietly as the dragging sounds faded into the distance. His eyes were cold as forged iron.

After a long moment, he finally exhaled a low murmur.

"Xiao… forgive me. She can only be mine."

The chess piece in his hand snapped with a sharp crack. Powder sifted through his fingers and scattered onto the floor.

* * * * *

The embroidery room was deathly still.

Qin Nianyin sat collapsed on the small embroidery stool, her hands hanging weakly at her sides. Her fingertips still carried the faint tremor left from the imperial edict moments ago.

The candle flame flickered; her shadow wavered gently on the wall. Yet her chest felt as though a thousand-jin stone had been pressed atop it, making it difficult to breathe.

(A jin —— an ancient unit of weight.)

——She had never imagined Emperor Xuanwen would bestow such an edict before the entire court.

"…Bestowing marriage to the Third Prince, Li Suo, to wed the daughter of Qin Shouyi ——Qin Nianyin."

The eunuch's drawn-out announcement had struck her ears like thunder. She had frozen on the spot, almost forgetting to bow, until Mei tugged her sleeve with tear-brimming eyes. Only then had she knelt, stiff as a puppet, murmuring, "This humble woman… receives the decree."

Even now, when she replayed the moment, it still felt like a nightmare.

"Third Prince… Li Suo…"

She whispered the name, lips drained of colour. In her mind surfaced that night at the palace banquet, the words he had spoken with a smile that was not quite a smile ——

I have already memorialized Father, requesting marriage.

At the time she had taken it as a careless tease, a trivial provocation meant only to stoke Gu Xiao and Su Zhang's rivalry. Who could have foreseen, that he had meant every word.

A shiver ran through her. Cold spread across her back, beading into a sheen of sweat.

How had her previous life ended?

Was it not because she had entangled herself with power and in the end met betrayal on all sides, dying alone with no one to claim her corpse?

She had believed that in this life she had walked cautiously enough, avoiding every thread of that doomed path. Yet she was once again caught in the net of a royal marriage decree.

"I shouldn't have… I shouldn't have…"

Her hands clutched the fabric of her embroidered skirt so tightly that her knuckles turned stark white. The tension running through her arms would not ease, no matter how she tried to steady her breath.

The Third Prince ——whom the world viewed as nothing more than a frivolous, idle noble with no interest in state affairs ——had shown her, in one unguarded instant, something far different.

In his eyes she had glimpsed a hidden sharpness, restrained yet unmistakably real, a quiet blade waiting for the right moment to be drawn.

If he truly harboured intentions toward the throne, then this marriage was not the union of two people at all.

It was a tightening snare ——one that would bind her, Gu Xiao, Su Zhang and even the entire struggle for the position of crown prince into a single, inescapable web.

Her chest tightened violently; her breath broke into short, panicked gasps.

"No… I don't want this…"

Tears finally spilled, drumming onto the brocade surface of the embroidery stool.

Mei, frantic, rushed forward with water and cloth.

"Miss, please don't be like this…"

But Qin Nianyin only stared blankly at the candle flame and let out a soft, broken laugh ——one steeped in despair.

"Mei… tell me… has fate never intended to let me go?"

A faint night breeze brushed the paper window; beyond it, the distant murmur of the city's gossip could still be heard. Yet inside this quiet embroidery room, she felt as though she were trapped at the bottom of a deep well, unable to glimpse even a sliver of sky.

 This imperial marriage decree had once again turned her into a piece on the board of fate.

* * * * *

The wavering candlelight rendering Qin Nianyin's expression even paler.

She had still been lost in thought when a maid announced from outside, "Second Young Lady has arrived."

Moments later, Su Wan entered with an ornate, gilded carved box, a composed smile resting on her lips.

"Cousin," she said as she approached, "I had this box of jewels selected specially for you. Consider it a congratulatory gift."

Qin Nianyin slowly returned to herself. She lifted her gaze; under the lamp, the box gleamed brilliantly, yet none of it could outshine the oppressive weight pressing down on her chest.

She forced a faint smile. "Thank you, Sister Wan."

Su Wan studied her carefully. A subtle, complex glimmer passed through her eyes. "I never imagined you would have such fortune ——rising in one step to become a prince's secondary consort. From now on, when I see you… I will have to salute you."

Qin Nianyin blinked, then lowered her head with a bitter, fragile smile. "Wan, don't tease me. There isn't a trace of joy in my heart."

Her brows were tightly drawn; exhaustion and bewilderment clouded her gaze.

Su Wan saw it all and after a moment, let out a soft sigh. "Are you… not pleased?"

Qin Nianyin shook her head. Her voice was light, yet quivered faintly. "There is no surprise ——only shock. This imperial marriage decree came far too suddenly. I was completely unprepared."

Silence settled for a heartbeat. Su Wan's expression darkened slightly as she lowered her voice. "The world rarely grants us perfect choices. Especially for women like us… much of the time, all we can do is accept."

Her tone was gentle, but the weight beneath it pressed like a thousand catties. Qin Nianyin's heart trembled. She lifted her gaze slowly and only then noticed the hidden heaviness in Su Wan's eyes.

"Wan," she asked softly, "do you… also have someone in your heart?"

Su Wan's face flushed crimson. She quickly turned away, scolding in flustered embarrassment, "Nonsense! Don't speak such things!"

Qin Nianyin watched her quietly, then something stirred within her. She deliberately probed, "Could it be… His Highness the Crown Prince?"

The moment the words left her lips, Su Wan's complexion turned deathly pale. Her lips parted as though to speak, yet no sound came. She rose abruptly, panic flaring in her movements and turned to leave.

Qin Nianyin froze, a ripple spreading through her heart. Only now did she truly realize ——Su Wan had already placed her feelings upon the Crown Prince.

But the Crown Prince's principal wife had long been decided ——Shen Lingyan. Even if he might harbor some affection for Su Wan, the most she could ever receive… was the position of a secondary consort.

A knot tightened in Qin Nianyin's chest. She steadied herself against the embroidery stool, watching Su Wan's retreating figure. A faint ache rose in her heart.

——In this world, who is not struggling against the chains of fate?

She herself was so.

Gu Xiao was so.

Su Zhang was so.

and even Su Wan ——dignified, composed Su Wan ——was merely another woman with no real right to choose.

Wax tears slid down the candle. Night deepened outside. Qin Nianyin felt her thoughts tangle into an impossible knot, impossible to unravel.

Chapter 92: Tracing the Silver Veins

Rain had only just withdrawn from the night sky, leaving a damp breath lingering over the capital, clinging to eaves and stone alike.

Within the study of the Su residence, every lantern burned bright. Scrolls and dossiers lay strewn across the desk. Coils of sandalwood smoke drifted upward, delicate and pale ——yet unable to dispel the oppressive weight that pressed upon the room.

Yefeng stood to the side, scarcely daring to breathe. After a long hesitation, he finally lowered his voice.

"Master… you should rest. You have neither eaten nor drunk anything for an entire day."

"No. Stand down for now. I must look again. There has to be something I overlooked."

Yefeng exchanged a brief look with Xiuyan, then ventured, "Master… that man, Cao Ji, has already confessed. He named the Second Prince. At this point, should the case not… be considered concluded? You keep turning through these old files ——there may be nothing more to uncover for the moment. Please, rest first."

Su Zhang's fingers halted mid-page.

The candlelight trembled, tugging his shadow long across the wall —— yet his gaze was colder and sharper than that stretched silhouette.

"The case is concluded?" A quiet laugh slid from his throat, frigid and razor thin.

Yefeng tensed, bowing at once, no longer daring to utter another word.

Su Zhang closed the dossier. His palm tapped lightly against the surface of the desk ——each tap soft, yet one after another, they landed heavy as falling stones upon the heart.

——A man like Cao Ji, sly and calculating by nature. How could he suddenly 'confess everything'?

——His statement points directly to the Second Prince, but offers no further detail. This is no confession. It is deflection.

——The true trail lies in what he deliberately left unsaid.

He shut his eyes briefly. The accounts from Jiangnan flashed through his mind ——numbers, routes of silver, ledgers written by different hands.

The flow of money broke off at a small, obscure shop. Trace it upward from there and the trail snapped clean, like a kite whose string had been cut, vanishing into empty sky.

A fierce intuition gripped him ——the answer was hidden within this seemingly chaotic cluster of numbers.

"…No." His voice dropped, barely audible.

Yefeng started and looked up. His master's brows were drawn tight; his fingertips pressed hard into the corner of a dossier. His lips had thinned into a pale, severe line. It was the look of a man who had thrust his entire being into a single, labyrinthine game of strategy.

"Cao Ji is nothing more than a piece on the board," Su Zhang finally said, his voice cold and weighty. "What he has confessed is merely what His Majesty wished to hear. The true silver vein… remains hidden in the dark."

Yafen's heart gave a jolt. He was just about to speak when Su Zhang lifted a hand, cutting him off with a single, decisive gesture.

"No need to ask further."

Su Zhang rose and walked toward the window. Beyond the lattice frame, the night stretched deep and ink-dark.

Rain still clung to the roof tiles in the distance, dripping in slow, steady intervals ——each drop falling with a muted tick, as though hinting at something yet unspoken, something lurking beneath the surface.

His silhouette remained composed, but his voice was colder than the rain that had only just ceased.

"Go."

A single syllable, clipped and hard.

Yefeng froze for a brief breath, unable to muster any other response.

"M-Master, where are you planning to go?"

"Dayue." Su Zhang's tone was low, hoarse from long hours of silence, yet every word was etched with precision. "Prepare the horses. We shall pay Cao Ji another visit."

Yefeng startled but quickly bowed and withdrew to obey.

The study sank back into stillness.

Su Zhang stood alone by the window, turning a chess piece between his fingers. The cold jade pressed against his palm, but could not smother the heat rising in the depths of his chest.

——If someone truly used the gambling houses as a veil to launder silver, then this game runs deeper than imagined.

——Cao Ji cast out the Second Prince on purpose, a convenient smokescreen for his real master.

He let the chess piece fall. It struck the desk with a crisp, cutting sound ——pa ——sharp as a blade edge.

His gaze hardened to frost.

"This game…" he murmured, barely above a whisper, "I refuse to believe I cannot pierce through it."

Li Suo ——must fall.

A gust of night wind swept through the cracked window, lifting the curtain. The lamplight flickered wildly, shadows twisting against the walls. The air within the study felt crushed beneath an invisible weight of iron and stone ——so heavy it choked the breath from the room.

* * * * *

The dungeon was dim, its stone walls slick with moisture. Water seeped through the cracks and fell in slow, echoing droplets ——each one striking the ground like the beat of a dead man's drum.

Cao Ji was bound hand and foot, lashed tight in a five-flower knot. His face had turned an ashen blue; cold sweat streamed down his brow. A pool of blood spread beside his feet, its metallic stench saturating the confined space.

A pair of polished boots came to a halt in that blood.

Su Zhang bent down. His fingertips touched a drop of red and idly smeared it across his palm. Candlelight flickered over his face ——his gaze was cold, yet within that chill, something darker stirred, a glint foreign and unsettling.

"Cao Ji."

His voice was soft, but carried a pressure sharp enough to crush bone.

"You truly believe that shifting everything onto the Second Prince will allow you to walk out of this unharmed?"

Cao Ji trembled from head to foot. His jaw clenched tight. He forced a strained smile.

"Th-the lowly one… has already confessed all. I have hidden nothing…"

The words had barely left his mouth ——

Pa!

A sharp, cracking sound split the stale air.

The folding fan struck his cheek with such force that the stone wall behind him seemed to reverberate. Cao Ji's vision whited out; half his face swelled instantly, blood threading from the corner of his mouth.

"Confessed?"

Su Zhang let out a laugh ——low, cold, as if a blade were being honed against whetstone.

He raised his hand, took up a dagger and ——without a flicker of hesitation ——drew the blade cleanly across his own palm.

A wet shh broke the air.

Blood welled up at once, dripping onto the blue bricks with a soft tapping sound that sank straight into the ears.

The blade had sunk deep. The crimson spread swiftly.

Su Zhang did not so much as flinch.

The pain ——raw and tearing ——burst through the suffocating pressure locked in his chest. It felt as though the fire consuming his heart had been forced outward, dragged to the surface through the wound in his palm.

It hurt. But not nearly as much as the ache inside.

The faster the blood flowed, the clearer ——almost lighter ——he felt.

He lowered his gaze, watching the red bloom widen in his palm and a strange, deadly calm crept over his mind.

So, this is how it is.

Only the pain of the flesh can smother a madness capable of driving a man insane.

His lips curved slightly, the smile colder than grief itself.

"Look closely, Cao Ji. If I can push myself to this point… do you think I would spare you?"

Cao Ji's eyes bulged so far they nearly leapt from their sockets.

"L-Lord Su ——you… you're mad…"

But Su Zhang did not furrow a single brow. He simply watched the blood sliding from his hand, as though observing a painting that had nothing to do with him.

"Mad?"

His smile deepened, chilling to the bone.

"Good. If madness is required, then before I go mad, I will make sure you understand what despair truly is."

The moment the words fell, his fingers shot out and clamped around Cao Ji's throat.

The pressure tightened gradually.

Cao Ji's face flushed a dark, violent red. His breaths came in frantic rasps. In the next instant, he seemed ready to suffocate.

"Gh ——kh… khhh ——" His body convulsed. Eyes rolled upward. Veins burst across his neck; his tongue trembled soundlessly.

Su Zhang leaned in, gaze bleak and unblinking.

"According to the investigation, you have an illegitimate son. Do you?"

The single sentence sank into Cao Ji's chest like a knife.

His pupils contracted sharply. His entire body stiffened.

"If you refuse to speak the truth," Su Zhang continued, voice quiet as winter iron, "I will find him. And before your very eyes ——I will carve him apart. One slice at a time."

That was the moment Cao Ji shattered completely.

A rasping cry spilled from his raw throat, torn with terror.

"I ——I don't know! Truly don't! Only… only that the last of the silver… all of it… was sent to the Golden Fortune Gambling House in the capital!"

His voice shook so violently it dissolved into sobs.

Only then did Su Zhang release him. He cast him a single frigid glance, then turned to leave. His sleeves swept through the air, carrying the coppery tang of blood. His back, shadowed against the dim light, bore the austere solitude of a demon king walking away from carnage.

Cao Ji collapsed into the pool of blood, gasping in ragged heaves, trembling as though his bones had turned to water. Only now did he truly understand ——

This man, the gentle-faced top scholar the world praised as mild and refined ——

When he chose to corner someone, he was a hundred times more terrifying than any iron-blooded general.

* * * * *

Night pressed heavily upon the city. Rain lingered in the air and the stone roads of the capital still shone with a slick, treacherous sheen.

The Golden Fortune Gambling House blazed with lantern light. Silk and bamboo music trilled above the roar of voices; dice cups tumbled and clattered; shouts rose to the rafters. The air around the gambling tables reeked of wine, sweat and old copper ——blended into one choking scent, like a pot of oil boiling on the verge of eruption.

Then ——

the entrance darkened.

The rasp of iron armour approached from afar, sliding closer and closer, sharp as a cold blade dragging down the spine. In the blink of an eye, a mass of black-armoured soldiers surged forward and formed a curving formation, sealing all three doors of the gambling house.

Long spears rose like a forest; crossbow triggers were pulled taut; armour plates caught the lantern glow like scales of ice.

"Seal the grounds ——"

A low command rolled across the street, overturning the hall's merriment like a table struck from beneath.

The rider at the front dismounted, his cloak casting droplets of rain as it swept aside.

From the shadows of armoured men stepped Su Zhang ——robes of austere black, no official seal at his waist, only a narrow bandage wound around his sleeve.

Blood had seeped through it, staining a dark ring at the edge. His gaze was glacial, so cold it dimmed even the fire brazier beside the door.

The gambling-master was a round, oily man. Startled by the disturbance, he waddled forward quickly. His slick hair and fleshy cheeks gleamed in the lamplight, yet he kept a lazy composure, bowing from afar with a murky smile.

"Lord Su, this humble one is surnamed Li. Your distinguished visit at such an hour… why, it must be a prosperous omen for our business. Only, this house follows its own rules and behind us stands ——"

"Move."

Su Zhang uttered a single word, without lifting his eyes.

The gambling-master paused, but his smile did not fade. Instead, he jerked his chin upward, motioning for Su Zhang to notice the golden waist plaque hanging from the eaves.

The plaque bore the character "Treasure," sealed with crow-blue fire lacquer. The imprint was blurred, yet unmistakably unusual ——a silent boast of powerful patrons behind the establishment.

"Well?" he sneered. "Will you step aside ——or not? Lord Su, there is no need for such temper. You surely do not know the kind of backer this ——"

Clang ——

Cold steel left its sheath, the sound slicing the air like stone splitting.

A slanted flash of blade glimmered once.

Clean. Precise.

The sword swept past the man's shoulder and neck.

Blood beaded before pain even struck, scattering across the crimson carpet like blossoms of red plum blooming in the dark.

Pu ——

The gambling-master's eyes bulged; his throat managed only half a gasp before he collapsed with a heavy thud. Panic exploded instantly —— guests shrieked, cups shattered, chairs scraped across the floor with teeth-grinding shrills.

Su Zhang did not lift an eyelid.

With a flick of his wrist, he drew the blade back. A thin trail of blood rolled along the spine of the sword before he wiped it away with a white cloth. Then, with a light prod of his toe, he pushed the corpse into the shadows beneath a pillar.

"Impeded official duty," he said evenly. "A dead man with a name. Record it. Seal the body."

Yefeng answered at once. Two armoured soldiers stepped forward ——
one laying a sheet of white cloth over the corpse, the other opening the
registry to write down the name.

"Prepare to receive orders ——"

The clamour of the gambling house stilled under the iron weight of
command.

Su Zhang slid his sword back into its sheath. His voice was not loud, yet
every syllable carried with unnerving clarity ——

as though spoken directly beside each listener's ear.

"Search. External ledgers, internal ledgers, shadow ledgers ——every
book, sealed. One by one."

"Storerooms, money counters, hidden compartments, cellars ——comb
through them. Leave not an inch unchecked."

"Account-keepers, cashiers, token exchangers, floor enforcers ——
arrest them, name by name."

"Whoever resists ——kill on the spot."

"Yes, sir!"

Steel answered in unison, the sound reverberating through the rafters.

The hall immediately divided into three units:

one to seal the entrances and account for all present;

one to force open boxes and cabinets;

one to advance with torches into the deeper back quarters.

Locks on wooden chests shattered under hammer blows. Iron hinges
bent back; the contents spilled onto the floor in stacks of ledgers.

In the rear hall, the wooden floorboards were lifted, revealing fresh pine
planks beneath.

Decorative cases along the rafters were removed; their lids fell open
with crisp thuds, exposing booklet after booklet ——"shadow accounts"
mirroring the entries in the official ledgers.

Chaos, yet meticulously ordered.

Every object, once retrieved, was first covered with a sheet of white
paper for identification, stamped in the corner with the red seal of
"Imperial Censorate ——Sealed".

Then hemp cords bound each bundle into a cross-shape. A scribe recorded the contents on a seal slip ——item number, time of sealing, location found.

All movements were rapid. Silent. Precise.

The unit under Su Zhang moved like a cold, immaculate machine —— no wasted breath, no stray sound.

"Report ——!"

A shout rose from the rear courtyard.

"An underground shaft discovered ——connected to the outer alley!"

Su Zhang's gaze darkened.

"Seal the entrance. Block it from inside and out. Capture anyone slipping through."

"Understood!"

Two Eagle Guards vaulted away; blades flashed once before their figures vanished into the alley shadows.

At the centre of the hall, a thin account-keeper was forced to his knees. He still attempted to protest:

"M-my lord, these are but the daily turnovers of the gambling house, all of them ——"

Yafen's boot silenced him, cutting off the excuse.

He pushed a glossy-covered Daily Cash Ledger toward Su Zhang.

The pages were flipped to early August. The columns appeared neat, yet every few days there appeared an entry labelled "floating gold" —— sums suspiciously even, each listed under harmless-looking aliases:

"Spring Zhi," "Summer He," "Autumn Gui."

Only one season was missing.

Winter.

Su Zhang stepped toward the account-keeper ——his height casting a long shadow. He looked down at the man, voice glacial.

"Speak. Since there is Spring, Summer and Autumn ——

why is there no 'Winter' ledger?"

"The lowly one… truly does not know ——ah ——!"

His denial fractured into a scream as Yefeng stepped down hard, grinding the man's fingers against the floorboards.

Su Zhang did not spare the account-keeper a single glance.

Instead, he pressed lightly at the corner of the ledger page.

The hand wrapped in white bandage looked especially slender beneath the lamplight; the blood seeping through the cloth resembled a blossom that refused to close.

He suddenly touched his thumb to that faint red stain ——

Then pressed a single mark beside the characters "Autumn Gui."

The crimson spread outward, bleeding into the grain of the paper.

"Now… that matches," he said, his voice calm.

At another table, a scribe was busy assembling scraps of paper unearthed from beam joints, table legs and the underside of couches. Piece by piece, he aligned them by date and amount, forming a second set of accounts.

The texture of those scraps was different from the official ledger —— finer, nearly translucent. Held against the light, a faint watermark appeared: the shape of a half-moon.

Yafen's brows twitched at the sight of it.

"Matched!"

The scribe let out a sharp whisper, tapping rapidly between the two ledgers.

"August sixth, twelfth, seventeenth ——three entries of 'floating gold.' All marked under 'Winter Plum'… sealed with the same crow-blue fire lacquer!"

"Crow-blue…"

Yefeng murmured, his gaze drifting toward the plaque hanging beneath the eaves ——the one lacquered in that exact shade of dark, oily blue.

Crow-blue.

So "crow-blue" was where the silver trail truly ended.

Su Zhang lifted his eyes and gave the plaque a faint, humourless glance ——something between a smile and a threat.

"Do not test my patience. Whoever stands behind this ——no matter who they may be ——will be traced to the end."

Chapter 93: Crow-Blue Fire Lacquer

Su Zhang's expression was stone-cold. The candlelight sharpened the planes of his profile, rendering his face even more severe beneath its glow. He turned and stepped deeper inside.

The heavy back-room storeroom door had already been pried open. Inside, rows of pitch-black wooden chests sat stacked atop one another, each marked with a red character: "Chips."

One chest was lifted open ——

yet instead of gambling tokens, it was packed with silver ingots. Each bar had been coated with ink-black pigment, smothering their shine. At the tail end of every ingot, an almost invisible incision had been carved, as if someone had tested their authenticity one by one.

"Count the silver ——"

"Yes, sir!"

Two silver-counters stepped forward, one with a scale, the other with a testing knife. The scale hook trembled; clear metallic notes rang out. Every ingot weighed was recorded with a fresh stroke on a tally slip.

"Reporting, sir ——the total exceeds the registered accounts by more than thirty percent!"

"Where did the thirty percent go?"

Su Zhang's gaze cut like a blade.

The account-keeper was dragged before the chest of silver. His face turned the color of clay; he knocked his forehead against the floor again and again, shaking uncontrollably.

Su Zhang did not look at him.

Instead, he lifted his gaze toward the storeroom's beams.

"Dismantle the third side-beam on the left."

"My lord, that beam bears weight ——"

"Dismantle it."

The single word hit the ground like iron.

Two armoured soldiers immediately hoisted a long bench beneath the beam as support. Wood was pried loose; mortise joints cracked with sharp cracking sounds. The third side-beam fell to the floor, wood splinters scattering.

Inside the hollowed-out beam was a narrow, flat box.

Once retrieved, the box revealed a seal of crow-blue fire lacquer. The imprint was clear ——

a half-moon, flanked by three star-like dots. The engraving was so fine that without close attention, it would be impossible to discern.

"Open it."

Once the lacquer seal was split open, the box proved to contain neither silver nor gambling chips; instead, it held three slender stacks of yatie ledger slips arranged with deliberate care.

The headers of the slips bore phrases such as "New Jiangnan Levy" and "Transport of Southern Goods". Each ended with a single character —— "received." The strokes were thin and forceful, the brush-tip hidden deeply within the calligraphy.

Every recorded entry was a source of bribery.

Yefeng sucked in a sharp breath.

His mouth opened slightly, but he dared not make a sound.

Su Zhang distributed the three stacks to three different scribes:

"One ——copy out every port indicated in the yatie."

"Two ——trace the money transfer routes through the trade houses."

"Three ——match the final-character signatures to the corresponding clerks. Remember: write down the characters first, then the men."

He returned to the front hall.

The gamblers had already been driven to the walls, kneeling with their hands over their heads. The gambling-house thugs had been disarmed and now crouched against the pillars, ashen and silent.

Someone attempted to sneak a glance at Su Zhang, but the moment their eyes met, that icy stare forced his head back down immediately.

Suddenly, a steward clad in simple blue robes lurched out from the inner corridor, breathless and unsteady, lifting a command token high above his head as though it were the only thing keeping him upright.

In his hand, he raised a command token wrapped with a gold-thread binding, shouting frantically:

"This establishment is under ——"

He never finished.

The sword's cold gleam reappeared.

Pu!

The tip pierced his throat cleanly, cutting the words in half. He clutched at the gushing wound, collapsed backward and began to tremble violently, choking out half-formed pleas:

"M-mercy, my lord ——my lord, spare me ——!"

Su Zhang's voice was as frigid as carved ice. A few droplets of blood clung to the sharp angle of his jaw, sliding slowly down the blade-like line of his cheek. The sight made the entire crowd inhale sharply, their breath freezing in their chests.

"Who shelters this place?"

His sword slid back into the scabbard with a quiet, decisive motion.

"Speak clearly. If you do not, my blade does not care whose throat it cuts."

His tone was light, almost conversational ——

as though asking after the weather.

"Speak clearly and I will confiscate your accounts.

Fail to speak clearly ——and I will confiscate you as well."

Silence followed.

Nothing remained but the distant drip of rainwater falling from post-storm roof tiles.

Silence lingered—

heavy, watchful, broken by nothing but the measured fall of water from the eaves above.

Outside, hurried footsteps approached. Two Eagle Guards dragged back a pair of mud-covered spies who had tried to escape through the underground shaft. They were bound from shoulder to wrist, unable to lift their heads.

Su Zhang did not spare them a glance.

"Add them to the case."

Across the hall, a scribe suddenly lifted his head, unable to contain his excitement.

"Reporting to my lord! These ledgers match the half-moon watermark from the Jiangnan case entirely. The 'flying remittances' flow into three separate routes and all three terminate at money houses within the Inner City. Every tier of transfer ultimately ends with a single signature —— 'Crow-Blue.'"

"Three money houses?"

Su Zhang's gaze hardened.

"Record the names. Seal them."

"Yes, my lord! ——Qinyuan, Jingyun, de. All three."

Yefeng murmured under his breath, "All inside the Inner City… Without powerful backing, none of this could happen."

The moment the words left him, regret seized him. He lowered his head at once.

If Su Zhang heard, he showed no reaction.

He reached up and removed the crow-blue lacquered plaque hanging from the eaves. His thumb brushed lightly across its surface. The lacquer grew tacky beneath his touch, warmed by his skin, softening slightly at the edges.

A faint smile tugged at his lips ——so faint it resembled pity.

"You think that smearing them black will hide them?

You think three layers of money houses will keep your trail safe?"

He lifted his eyes. His gaze cut through the hall ——through fear, through chaos ——settling far into the deepest shadows.

"But silver that has been dirtied carries a scent.

Filth attracts vermin.

Bury it as deep as you like ——it will still be found."

He turned, speaking to Yefenga: "Send word to the Censorate. Have the Vice Censor prepare two public vaults for sealed storage. All ledgers will be held under my office's custody for now. And inform Commander Liu of the Left Garrison of the Capital Battalion ——those three Inner City money houses are to be sealed immediately. Not a single person or scrap of paper escapes."

"Yes, sir!"

Yefeng answered sharply, then sprinted off.

"And ——"

Su Zhang added, voice cool and unhurried,

"extract the entire 'Autumn Gui' column. Seal it separately. Copy it separately. Archive it separately. Press one drop of red on the corner."

The scribe nodded with crisp understanding.

He marked the column with a vivid red dot.

That touch of red ——small, stark ——looked like a bead of blood swelling between black and white lines.

The wind in the courtyard grew harsher. Torches flickered wildly, casting wavering shadows across beams, curtains and fearful faces. Golden Fortune Gambling House had fallen from clamorous heat to graveyard stillness in the span of half a tea's time.

The final hidden compartment was torn open.

The final shadow-ledger bound and sealed.

The final cry drowned beneath the grinding march of armour.

Su Zhang stood at the main entrance. He lowered his gaze and brushed the blood from his sleeve. The bandage around his arm had darkened again with fresh stain, but he seemed completely unaware.

His eyes travelled past the street, into the heavy darkness beyond.

——The half-moon watermark from the old Jiangnan accounts.

——The crow-blue lacquer sealing the gambling house.

——The unified signatures at the three money houses.

——The lines had connected.

He turned, his voice low and cold:

"Seal the establishment. Transport everything tonight. Before dawn —— enter the palace with me."

"Yes, my lord!"

Iron locks clanged shut. The great doors swung closed with a thundering weight.

On the street outside, those who had gathered felt a wave of cold wind sweep past. When they looked up again, the glittering row of lanterns that once hung before Golden Fortune Gambling House had vanished ——

leaving behind only two bare cords swaying in the night wind.

That night, the capital learned something it would not soon forget:

The top scholar, Su Zhang, was capable of killing.

When he did ——

he killed cleanly, decisively, without sound, without hesitation.

* * * * *

Night hung heavy; candle flames wavered in the still air.

Bang!

A weighty teacup crashed down mercilessly, striking the Third Prince Li Suo square on the forehead. White jade shattered. Tea splashed across the floor. Several droplets of fresh blood trailed down his temple.

Li Suo let out a muffled groan, yet he remained kneeling, head bowed, fingers digging tightly into the cold stone tiles.

"Such audacity!"

Emperor Xuanwen swept a sleeve, his voice sharp as a blade.

"I have not treated you poorly, yet you dare establish gambling houses in the capital ——using the Second Prince's name as a veil?!"

Behind the imperial desk, the emperor's expression was glacial, each word striking like thunder.

Li Suo lifted his head slowly. Blood slid down the side of his face, but it could not mask the dim, shadowed gleam in his eyes. His voice was low and hoarse, yet unnervingly calm.

"Father, your son did not act out of greed. The gambling houses… were merely tools to gather men and influence. Without anchoring the merchants of Jiangnan and the capital, your son… would have long been discarded from this struggle."

"Silence!"

Emperor Xuanwen's palm slammed against the dragon desk. The entire hall trembled.

"You think yourself clever? The stone-statue affair in Jiangnan —— evidence ironclad ——and the silver all funnelled into the capital by your hand! Had Su Zhang not delivered the ledgers, how long did you intend to deceive us?!"

Li Suo's pupils tightened. A shadow flickered behind his gaze.

He had not expected the one who broke the game to be that mild-mannered top scholar.

Yet he did not panic.

Instead, he smiled ——thin and cold.

"Father is perceptive. Your son sought only a line of retreat when the storm approaches. The Crown Prince's wings have long grown full. If your son does not plan for himself… then he will soon have no path to breathe, let alone survive."

"Impudent!"

A violent spark ignited in the emperor's eyes. His sleeve whipped across the desk; the inkstone toppled, ink splattering across the scrolls like spilled night.

The hall fell into a suffocating silence, only the drip of blood and the patter of ink disturbed the stillness.

Emperor Xuanwen's gaze darkened, voice dropping to a near growl.

"So, that is the truth. All these years of debauchery ——nightly revelry, endless indulgence ——were nothing but a façade? Cloaked in dissipation, you hid a meticulous heart, laying down the road to seize the throne?"

Li Suo lowered his head again. Blood and cold sweat slid from his jawline, yet the corner of his mouth curved upward ——slow, deliberate.

"Your son bears no desire to seize the throne…

But Father ——your heart already holds its decision. If your son does not carve out one measure of safety for himself… should he simply wait for death?"

Emperor Xuanwen's chest rose sharply. His eyes burned with fury —— and, for one fleeting breath, shock.

The son he had always regarded as disinterested in power ——

had concealed every intention beneath the mask of a wastrel.

"You… dared hide so much from me!"

Li Suo pressed his hands to the floor, kowtowing. His voice was ragged yet ice-cold in resolve.

"Your son dares not deceive his sovereign. I only beg Father, for the bond of blood, to allow your son one corner to stand upon."

Emperor Xuanwen stared at him. The veins on the back of his hand strained against the skin. At last, he swept his sleeve aside with a harsh snap.

"Leave my sight! If I hear one more word of these gambling houses ——do not expect mercy!"

Li Suo bowed deeply. Blood scattered onto the floor with each movement, yet his voice remained low and steady.

"Your son obeys."

As he backed away, blood still trailing from his brow, his figure weighed heavy against the wavering candlelight.

Just before he disappeared beyond the pillars, the corner of his lips curled —— a fleeting, razor-thin smile, gone as quickly as it appeared.

* * * * *

The night wind was sharp and cold. Beyond the palace gates came a flurry of rapid reports, each voice tense, each breath panting.

"His Third Highness… has been imprisoned."

That single sentence struck like a blade, driving straight into Princess Li Jing's chest.

The bronze ladle slipped from her fingers and clattered onto the floor. Broth splashed across her shoes, warm droplets scattering over the tiles ——she remained utterly unaware.

"How could… how could this be…"

She whispered, barely audible. Her fingertips trembled; all color drained from her face. The brother who had always cloaked himself in frivolity and indulgence ——now confined in the imperial prison for the crime of the gambling houses.

A chill raked down her spine.

If even he, the one who had always laughed beside her, the one who shielded and indulged her, had fallen to such a fate ——

What, then, awaited her?

The palace walls, vast and towering in the night, suddenly felt as though they were closing in ——each brick a weight pressing down upon her lungs, suffocating her with dread.

She gripped the sleeve at her wrist tightly.

A fear she had never known before crept through her chest, cold and merciless:

Inside this palace, the emperor's authority pressed over every corner like an immovable weight, the Crown Prince's influence was rooted so deeply it seemed impossible to shake.

The Second Prince watched from the shadows with his silent and unreadable intent and her Third Brother ——who had always seemed untouchable ——had now fallen with a speed so absolute it left the air colder than the night wind.

And she?

She was nothing more than a lone princess, unprotected, unanchored.

If even he… cannot safeguard himself, then what power do I have? What am I, truly?

The cold spread through her, layer by layer.

For the first time, she understood with unsettling clarity that being a princess was never a shield at all but a shackle that tightened whenever the imperial will shifted.

Her father's anger could sweep across the court like a storm; she was but a piece on his board, to be moved or struck down as he pleased.

Her eyes reddened at the corners, though she forced herself to breathe steadily. Her confusion shifted ——slowly, then all at once ——into a hard thread of resolve.

"No… I cannot remain like this."

Her teeth tightened as she forced herself to breathe; the panic flickering in her eyes slowly hardened into something steadier and far more dangerous, a resolve shaped not by impulse but by the suffocating reality closing in around her.

If remaining in the palace meant living with fear woven into every step, every room, every silence, then the only path toward survival ——let alone freedom ——was to carve out an escape of her own.

A clarity she had never experienced settled over her with a cold, almost surgical precision and she understood that she needed a person she could trust.

Someone competent and willing to act.

Someone capable of taking her out of this stifling, airless palace while she still had the chance.

Chapter 94: Will You Come With Me

The night rain receded into the distance, enveloping the capital in a shroud of damp chill.

The lamp oil was nearly spent. Su Zhang closed his eyes, his consciousness drawn into the depths by a sinister, creeping cold.

Thick fog materialized abruptly.

He advanced step by step, his boot soles crushing scattered gravel underfoot. Echoes of horse whinnies, human shouts and the clashing of metal reverberated in his ears, as if rising from a deep well of a past life.

"Nianyin ——!"

A cluster of cold stars suddenly shot upwards from within the mist, exploding into a quivering blossom of fire. That was her signal. The curtain of vapor was torn asunder by the flare's light ——

The cliff path twisted sharply. Wheel hubs spun madly. Black-clad figures rained down arrows from the woods on the slope. The terrified horses reared, their front hooves pawing the air. The carriage tilted, unbalanced.

The curtain was snatched away by the wind, her profile flashing once amidst the chaotic arrows and fire ——then, in the next instant, the carriage, along with splintered wood and torn silk, overturned completely. Dragging a long, fiery arc of sparks, it plummeted down towards the white fog below the cliff.

"No!"

He rushed to the cliff's edge, his fingertips brushing against a severed half-length of rein, his palm scorched and bleeding from the rough rope. His heart felt as if seized by a bare hand, wrenching him downwards.

He scrambled down the rocky slope, his arms, elbows and knees scraped raw, his robes torn by jagged stones. The scents of charred wood, the rankness of horse sweat and the raw metallic tang of blood flooded his lungs in the mist.

The valley floor was narrow. Shattered wheels were lodged amongst chaotic rocks, the carriage frame utterly demolished.

She lay on her back beside the ruptured canopy, her hair fanned out like spilled ink. Dried blood stained her face, a diagonal gash marring her temple. Her clothes were torn by wooden splinters, the seams caked with the marks of wind and dust.

He knelt, his hands trembling. "Nianyin…"

His fingertips brushed away the grime and blood from her face, seeking her breath ——none.

He pressed against her chest, searching for a pulse ——none.

The world contracted into a single, needle-sharp point of silence. Only from afar, a single, low strike of a temple bell drifted into the fog: " —— Hum ——"

He heard the sound tearing from his own throat, yet could not form a single word.

He gathered her into his arms, tucking her dishevelled hair behind her ear ——the white jade hairpin was broken in two, one piece stuck fast in the dried blood. He carefully picked up the broken pieces, but try as he might, he could not fit them back together.

"I came too late… I came too late…"

Just then, in the dream, her lips seemed to stir, ever so faintly, uttering a single name —— Zhang.

A second toll of the temple bell arrived, profound and distant, as if pointing the way from somewhere.

Yet he could not move a single step, his entire being swallowed by the dark mist. He bent his head, pressing his lips to her forehead. The taste of blood, salty and metallic, touched his lips. Deep within his chest, something fractured with a deafening finality.

He came too late.

* * * * *

"Whoever took her," Su Zhang said, his voice so low it seemed to seep from a fissure in stone, "none of them will live." His tone did not rise; its quietness made the threat sink deeper, like something pressed into bone.

The wind surged without warning. Forest leaves flattened as if forced down by an unseen weight and the fog rolled forward in a single, cohesive mass. It swept over the cliff base, over the bloodstains, the splintered wood and even the outline of his shadow, drawing everything into a thickening black.

The third toll of the distant temple bell drifted further away. Its fading resonance carried the faint suggestion of someone urging him to turn back.

He let out a quiet laugh, a sound drained of warmth. "There is no turning back."

The light in his eyes dimmed, the last traces of fire collapsing into the hardened shade of iron. In his chest, the thoughts he had fought to restrain twisted into sharp, bone-like spurs, pushing outward with a clarity that bordered on pain.

In that half-conscious haze, he held her cold body against him. Tears mixed with the blood on his cheek, yet the corners of his lips lifted into a slight, chilling smile.

He clutched her as though she were the final thread of clarity he could still grasp while he stepped deeper into the encroaching dark.

"If the world has betrayed me… then let all under heaven sink into ash."

A violent roar burst forth. The colours of heaven and earth shifted as if overturned. Within the dream, he plunged completely into demon hood.

Su Zhang jolted awake. His eyes snapped open, sweat running cold along his spine. His palm remained tightly clenched, as if still gripping the last wisp of her fading shadow.

He stared at the emptiness of his hand while his breath rose and fell in sharp, uneven bursts.

His voice, dry and hoarse, sounded unnaturally deep. "So… this was the end?"

The night lamp wavered. In his gaze lay both a flicker of horror and an obsession he could no longer suppress.

After a suspended moment, he pushed himself upright from the bed. The bedchamber was as cold as the bottom of a well. Sweat coated his palm, yet he continued to clench it with a force that blanched his knuckles.

His chest rose sharply with each breath and he tilted his head slightly, as though he could still hear the third toll of the temple bell fading behind layers of mist.

After some time, he pressed his palm against his eyes, his voice a ragged whisper. "So… I have lost you once before."

The lamplight flickered again. His gaze sharpened and gathered into something cold, unwavering. Within that hardened light lay a resolution ——and an obsession strong enough to drag a man into the abyss.

* * * * *

The palace city lay under a deep, cutting night wind. Outside the Dali Temple prison, the Imperial Guards stood in formation. Chains clattered as the Third Prince, Li Suo, was dragged out in irons. His expression was unnervingly calm; the corners of his lips even carried a faint, mocking curve.

Suddenly, flames burst into chaos at the far end of the street. Several dark figures leapt down from the rooftops, blades flashing. In one swift stroke, they severed the bronze lock of the prison cart. The ambush threw the Imperial Guards into stunned disarray and shouts erupted in every direction.

Li Suo moved with the speed of a striking hawk. He twisted, seized a fallen blade and slashed through the chains binding his wrists.

Blood splattered across the ground. The next instant, his gaze shifted sharply ——and locked onto Qin Nianyin, who was being escorted past by palace attendants not far away.

"Nianyin!"

His voice was hoarse, yet brimming with a wild, feverish joy. In a single leap, before anyone could react, he closed the distance. His hand clamped around her wrist and the long sword angled coldly against her pale throat.

Qin Nianyin's heart jolted. Around her, the palace maids shrieked in panic. The Imperial Guards raised their spears and blades, but none dared advance another step.

Li Suo laughed ——softly, yet with a coldness that bordered on madness. "Do you see it? These people… this entire world… all of them bow beneath the blade in my hand. Whoever dares take one more step —— I will cut her throat open immediately."

The light caught the steel and streaks of red reflected along the edge. Yet the eyes behind that blade were hollow, stripped of hope. Dragging Qin Nianyin with him, he backed into a side hall and slammed the heavy doors shut.

Outside, shouts and pounding fists reverberated through the stone.

Inside, the wavering candlelight cast long shadows across the floor. Forced to face him at such close distance, Qin Nianyin could see every fracture in his expression ——the mania, the desperation, the cornered loneliness that pressed directly against her chest.

"Your Highness," she said quietly, "why go this far? You still have a way back."

"A way back?" Li Suo let out a sharp, derisive breath. The blade pressed closer, its tip grazing her skin and leaving a thin line of blood.

"I lost every path long ago. Su Zhang exposed my schemes. Father is furious. The Crown Prince grows stronger by the day. Gu Xiao's influence in the army rises like the tide. Tell me ——where, in all of this, am I allowed to stand? Aside from you, Nianyin… aside from you, what else do I have left to hold on to?"

A tight ache spread through her chest. She remembered the previous lifetime ——Li Suo standing alone upon the imperial throne, victorious in the struggle for power, yet immeasurably isolated. Looking at him now, she felt as though she were staring at a beast driven to the edge of a cliff by fate itself.

She gave a faint, sorrowful smile, her eyes glimmering with unshed tears. "If killing me will bring you even a moment of peace… then do it."

Li Suo froze.

The sword trembled in his grip. His breath quickened and in his gaze, the madness cracked open by a thin, fragile line. "You… you're not afraid of death?"

Qin Nianyin shook her head. Her voice was soft, but absolute. "If it eases your heart, then go ahead."

She could not forget that in the past life, he had climbed to the highest seat in the empire ——yet in this life, because of her rebirth, the path before him had twisted into ruin. How could she not feel guilty?

Li Suo stared at her, dazed. Then, abruptly, he began to laugh. The laughter started low, then rose higher and higher, until it spilled out in a near-manic burst ——an echo filled with despair and something painfully close to grief.

"If I choose not to kill you… will you come with me?" he asked, his voice rough, but his eyes blazing with intensity. "I still have a small force loyal to me. As long as you go with me, I won't harm you. Just tell me ——will you come?"

Qin Nianyin merely shook her head, the movement faint but steady. "If you take me with you, you won't escape. Put down the sword and there will still be a path left open for you."

"Well said… Qin Nianyin. You truly ——" Li Suo's voice broke, twisted between laughter and anguish, " ——you truly mean to take my life."

"Don't hesitate," she replied softly. "If you intend to kill me, do it quickly. The soldiers are closing in by the moment."

His laughter stopped at once. A tremor ran through his voice, as though this were the final question he had held back for years. "From the first time I saw you, I knew you were unlike anyone else. I wasn't wrong… Tell me ——who is it you love? Is it Gu Xiao? Or Su Zhang?"

Qin Nianyin lowered her lashes. "That doesn't matter. What matters is that we both live… though it seems neither of us can escape what fate has already written."

Yet deep inside, a face surfaced clearly in her mind ——a face cold, severe, unforgettable. But no matter what happened in this life, she no longer dared to acknowledge it aloud.

"Nianyin…" Li Suo murmured, his voice shaking. "Are you… are you afraid?"

She lifted her gaze to him, meeting the bloodshot desperation burning in his eyes. "I was, once. But not now. If my death can ease your suffering, then kill me."

Li Suo's body jolted. The sword in his hand wavered and for a moment, a raw, undefinable sorrow rose within his eyes.

After a long, shuddering exhale, he suddenly drew the blade away. He seemed prepared to push her aside.

"Go," he said. A flicker of softness crossed his gaze ——only for a heartbeat ——before it hardened into something final. "If you will not leave with me, then don't ever appear before me again ——"

He never finished the sentence.

At that instant, the doors crashed open with a thunderous boom. The clash of metal armour filled the hall as a forest of spears surged forward, Imperial Guards pouring in and sealing every corner of the chamber.

Li Suo's blade still hovered at Qin Nianyin's throat. Candlelight caught the thin line of blood on her skin, turning it sharp and chilling. The madness churning in his eyes surged—then faltered, arrested by the unshaken calm on her face.

Beyond the ranks of guards, a figure in black strode into the hall with long, decisive steps. His robe swept sharply behind him. Su Zhang entered with a face carved from ice, a shadow pooled between his brows. His gaze—cold enough to cleave through darkness—fixed directly upon her.

In the candlelight, a red glint flickered in his eyes. It was the look of someone emerging from a nightmare, a gaze that could drag a soul back from the brink—or push another straight into the abyss.

Li Suo offered no further struggle. He threw his head back and laughed, a sound both deranged and demonic. Within it lay utter desolation and a sorrow so deep it bordered on madness. In this life, he had finally lost.

Su Zhang's voice cut through the hall, deep and sombre, as though rising from an abyss. "Li Suo. Release her."

He did not address him as 'Third Prince,' nor did he kneel in deference. He called him solely by his full name, his tone deceptively calm, yet seething like hidden, turbulent currents.

"Su Zhang. What is this?" Li Suo sneered, a trace of defiance lingering despite being pinned. "Have you finally shed your refined and courteous disguise and revealed yourself as a demon outright?"

"You should not have touched her," Su Zhang's voice was icy.

"So, it is for her? You would drag me down from my horse for her?" The light in Li Suo's eyes stalled, followed by a burst of manic laughter. "Hahaha… Just as I thought! So it's true! Even Su Zhang has…"

Amid his laughter, Li Suo abruptly yanked Qin Nianyin closer, pressing the long sword against her heart, a surge of bloodlust palpable. "You want her? You want her? A pity! She is my rightfully bestowed concubine! In life and in death, she belongs to me!"

Qin Nianyin, crushed against his chest, the sword tip pressing painfully, struggled to breathe. Yet she did not cry out. Only silent tears traced paths down her cheeks.

"Your Highness… you are mistaken," she murmured, her voice low. "I have never belonged to anyone."

Li Suo jolted, a flicker of confusion passing through his eyes.

Su Zhang's gaze was frigid. He advanced step by step, each footfall seeming to land directly on Li Suo's heart.

"Release her," his voice was low, with a murderous intent never before heard. "Or else ——I will make you regret ever being born into this world."

Li Suo threw his head back with a shrill, bitter laugh, his voice hoarse as if bleeding.

"Hahahaha! Regret? The only regret I, Li Suo, hold in this life is not having sent someone to run you through with a sword back in Jiangnan!"

Before the words fully faded, the sword edge suddenly shifted, narrowly slicing across Qin Nianyin's collarbone, sending droplets of blood flying.

"Nianyin!" Su Zhang's voice erupted in a low roar, bloody fury churning in his eyes.

In that instant, however, Qin Nianyin grew utterly still.

She looked at Li Suo, her voice very soft, yet each word fell like a blade. "Your Highness, let go. It is over."

Li Suo's entire body convulsed violently. The sword in his hand finally clattered to the ground. He tilted his head back with a long, loud laugh, filled with despair and madness.

"Go… then… go… Since you will not come with me… then go with him…"

The candle flames flickered precariously. The distant toll of a temple bell drifted in, each resonant note sounding like a final farewell.

Qin Nianyin stood rooted to the spot, the bloody mark on her chest cool, yet it paled in comparison to the rending pain in her heart.

"Enough talk. Take him away," Su Zhang commanded coldly, not a trace of his former scholarly elegance remaining.

Seemingly unwilling to yield completely, Li Suo laughed wildly, "Su Zhang, have you gone mad? Does she know? Has she ever seen you in such a demonic state? Haha…"

As the sword was finally knocked from Li Suo's grasp, he gasped for breath, his hand twisting in a final, desperate attempt to seize her.

Without a moment's hesitation, Su Zhang pulled Qin Nianyin into his embrace, shielding her tightly against his chest. Blood dripped from the unhealed wound on his palm, staining her garments with spreading blooms of dark crimson.

Li Suo turned his head to look at her, blood streaming from his forehead, yet a bitter smile still clung to his lips. In that moment, the madness vanished from his eyes, leaving behind only a trace of release.

"Nian Nianyin… So it seems… you were never… mine to begin with."

Soon, Li Suo was escorted out and placed into the prisoner's cart.

Qin Nianyin stood in a daze, witnessing everything that had transpired, watching the once-proud Li Suo being led away in disgrace by the black-armoured soldiers. She could scarcely believe what her eyes beheld… Su Zhang!

A Su Zhang she had never seen before bloodthirsty, frenzied, so chillingly composed it terrified her…

Chapter 95: The Mask Falls

"Nianyin, my wife!"

A deep, shadowed voice cracked through the air behind her like thunder contained beneath a mountain. Qin Nianyin's entire body jolted violently and she turned around in a rush. For that brief instant, even her breath froze.

In her past life, countless nightmares had begun exactly like this ——his voice calling out to her with that same mixture of calm restraint and suppressed madness, his gaze filled with an obsession that permitted no refusal.

"My wife…"

His voice was low and heavy, with a blood-deep resolve, as if the call had crossed two lifetimes to reach her.

Qin Nianyin stared at him blankly, a sharp pain bursting through her chest.

Could he have remembered their past life?

Impossible.

"My wife…Nianyin, it is time to go home."

Her heart clenched at once. That single sentence ——just meeting his eyes ——was enough. She understood at once.

This was not intuition, nor coincidence.

He had remembered everything.

In that moment, she realized the cruel symmetry of fate: in their previous life, she had exchanged her life for a marriage; in this life, he was exchanging his life for love. Yet no matter how fate twisted them together, they always missed each other by a step.

In their previous life, she had traded her life for a marriage.

In this one, he was trading his life for love.

Different bargains — the same ending.

Su Zhang advanced toward her one pace at a time. The cold reflection of the blade in his hand flickered across his eyes, yet he seemed blind to the blood on the floor around them. The world felt as if it had tilted off balance.

Fog rose thickly in his mind, heavy and dark as night.

The rumble of carriage wheels ——sharply severed.

Fire surging upward.

Her scream swallowed by chaos.

The images from their past life crashed violently over the present: her face smeared with blood, her body falling into the ravine, her chest already cold when he caught her. No matter how he called to her, no breath ever returned.

"Nianyin…"

That had been the moment he first lost control.

 and now, seeing her again with a sword pressed against her chest, blood seeping through her robe, his heart felt as though it had been carved open. His blood surged in reverse, his breath choking in his throat. If he failed to save her again, he would not survive it.

His knuckles whitened around the scabbard. The weapon trembled faintly in his grip. A low ringing filled his skull, drowning out all thought.

"Nianyin, my wife… my love…" He forced the word out, thick with blood and soul, as though tearing it from the depths of his chest.

Qin Nianyin froze at the sound.

She looked at him and for a brief moment, the world fell away. In his eyes she saw the same thing she had heard countless nights in her dreams ——the call filled with despair, pain and a devotion so consuming it left no room to escape.

Tears blurred her vision at once. The ache in her chest felt almost unbearable.

In Su Zhang's mind, the distant ringing of a temple bell rose faintly. The sound was soft yet relentless, pulling him out from the mire of blood and hatred, yet also reminding him clearly that the entanglement of two lifetimes had already become a destined calamity.

This time, I won't let you fall from that cliff again.

The unspoken vow settled like iron in his bones.

The sword in his hand let out a low, vibrating hum. His body trembled once, sharply. In that instant, every thread of reason, hatred and stubborn resolve within him condensed into the edge of a single blade and he turned it straight toward the Third Prince.

She suddenly understood ——he truly remembered everything.

"Nianyin, do not be afraid," he said softly. His voice shook, but the conviction in it held steady.

Her entire body went still in his embrace. Her chest was pressed against the rapid rise of his breath. His voice, the strength of his arms —— everything struck her with such sudden familiarity that she felt momentarily disoriented.

At that moment, the wind outside surged violently.

Armor clashed.

Footsteps pounded like thunder.

"Nianyin!"

Gu Xiao burst through the doorway, sword drawn, killing intent sharp and focused. But when his gaze landed on the scene in front of him, his steps faltered.

In the wavering firelight, Su Zhang held her tightly against his chest. His face was smeared with blood, distorted with a grim, unyielding desperation. Qin Nianyin's clothes were dishevelled, her breath uneven, her expression shaken.

The sight struck Gu Xiao like a blade driven straight into his heart.

His breath caught painfully. The tip of his sword trembled. A raw, almost absurd sense of rupture surged within him ——he had raced through the capital to reach her, had cut down danger after danger, only to arrive and see her held by another man.

"…Nianyin."

His throat tightened, his voice cracking and hoarse, his eyes burning with fury and pain.

Qin Nianyin jerked her head toward him, startled. The blood-red rims of his eyes made her lips part soundlessly.

Su Zhang only tightened his hold around her, drawing her completely into the protection of his body. His gaze locked onto Gu Xiao's —— cold, sharp and unyielding.

For a moment, their eyes clashed like blades.

Between the firelight and the scent of blood, a suffocating tension filled the chamber.

* * * * *

The stench of blood still clung heavily to the hall. The candles flickered weakly, as if crying. Dark stains and shattered chains remained scattered across the floor, the metallic scent so thick it suffocated the air.

Qin Nianyin had been placed in a corner of the chamber. Blood still marked her robes and the pallor of her face under the shifting firelight made her look even colder, even more fragile.

Her fingers curled tightly, her heart pounding wildly in her chest, yet she did not utter a single word.

At the centre of the hall, two figures faced each other across the trembling glow of the flames.

Gu Xiao had stabbed his sword into the crack between the stone tiles. His tiger-like eyes were bloodshot, his breath heavy and uneven. He stared at the man before him, feeling as though a thousand pieces of stones pressed against his chest.

That man was Su Zhang.

Su Zhang, who had always been calm and restrained, with features as refined as carved jade. The man everyone praised as a perfect gentleman, the last person in the capital one could imagine losing control.

But now ——

he was drenched in blood.

His white robes soaked through and stained.

His hands still smeared with dark, dried streaks.

His expression was cold and shadowed, yet the faint curl at the corner of his lips carried a hint of madness and bloodlust. It was the smile of something that had crawled up from the depths of the abyss.

A chill ran down Gu Xiao's spine.

"Su Zhang…" His voice was hoarse, scraped raw like gravel grinding against stone. "Why… why have you become like this…?"

Su Zhang lifted his gaze. His eyes, sharp as a blade, glided across Gu Xiao's face.

"Xiao," he said calmly, "you came one step too late."

The simple sentence cut like a sword, severing the last thread of brotherhood between them.

Gu Xiao stared at him, stunned, his mind blank for a brief second.

Was this still the brother he once knew?

When had the gentle, courteous Third Place Laureate turned into a cold, ruthless demon?

"I heard what you did," Gu Xiao said, his breath unsteady. "The evidence against the Third Prince ——you were the one who presented all of it?"

"Yes." Su Zhang replied without hesitation, every word ringing with iron.

Gu Xiao's chest rose and fell sharply. His eyes reddened.

"Executing the master of Jinbao Gambling House in the streets, torturing men through the night to force confessions… Su Zhang, are you still the elegant, scholarly brother I once knew?"

A thin, cold smile flickered across Su Zhang's lips, slicing through the air like a knife.

"Xiao, people change."

"No!" Gu Xiao roared, the veins on his hand bulging as he gripped the sword hilt. His eyes were filled with tearing pain. "You haven't changed ——you've simply finally taken off your mask!"

The candlelight wavered and a sharp glint flickered across Su Zhang's eyes.

"Perhaps," he said. His voice was cold. "The world forced me. If I want to save her, I have no other path."

Gu Xiao grit his teeth. "I can save her as well! I can stop her from being married to the Third Prince ——as long as I plead with Her Majesty ——"

"And what right do you have?"

Su Zhang's laugh was thin and icy, cutting straight into the bone.

"With your hot blood alone, how many times can you protect her? If I hadn't arrived in time tonight, she would already be a corpse on the floor."

Gu Xiao's breath caught, his chest rising sharply. He had no rebuttal.

Su Zhang stepped forward, his presence pressing down like a collapsing mountain. The red glint in his eyes grew sharper and more dangerous.

"You dare risk your life for her?" he asked, his voice low and cold enough to freeze air, each word as sharp as a blade. "I dare far more."

He laughed ——quiet at first, then edged with a chilling, near-mad intensity.

"You dare die with her? I dare make the entire world die for her."

For him, the world had already lost its right to survive without her.

A suffocating silence swept through the hall.

The words struck like thunder.

Gu Xiao's breath halted and the sword in his hand nearly slipped from his grip.

He had always been bold ——an untamed young general, sharp and unstoppable.

But in this moment, for the first time, he understood it plainly:

He had lost.

Lost completely.

The candle flames trembled.

Su Zhang's shadow stretched long across the bloodstained floor, as if he had stepped out from within the fire and carnage.

He closed the distance until only a single step separated them. His voice dropped, rough and almost broken.

"You want to win?" His blood-red gaze carved through the air. "You've already lost. Because you love her ——and still care about the world."

A faint, cold curve touched his lips, the expression sharp and merciless.

"But I love her ——and I dare to become the enemy of the world."

Gu Xiao's body shook violently.

The blade in his hand trembled; veins rose starkly along his wrist.

He could no longer keep hold of it.

Qin Nianyin stared at the scene, frozen where she stood.

Her chest tightened; her fingertips were icy cold.

In that instant, Su Zhang felt like a stranger ——frighteningly unfamiliar.

The noble young scholar she had once known was gone.

In his place stood someone blood-thirsty, unhinged ——a war demon stripped of restraint.

Gu Xiao finally let out a low, humourless laugh.

It was filled with bitterness and self-mockery.

"So that's it… I never had a chance from the beginning."

He swept his sleeve aside and turned away.

His back remained rigid with pride, but the faint tremor in his shoulders could not be concealed.

His footsteps were heavy, each one sounding like it landed directly on his heart.

The hall grew quiet again, leaving only Su Zhang standing amidst the blood, fire and the fading echo of the temple bell.

He lowered his head.

The red glint in his eyes mingled with the shifting firelight.

His fingers trembled once, then finally extended toward the slender figure in the corner.

"Nianyin…" His voice was low, threaded with madness and finality.

"You were always mine."

* * * * *

The hall still reeked of blood, the air heavy as iron. The last sparks of fire flickered weakly across the broken chains and dark stains on the floor.

Qin Nianyin was held against his chest. Her fingers were cold and stiff, her breath quick and shallow, unable to break free no matter how she struggled.

"Nianyin," Su Zhang said. His voice was hoarse, trembling beneath the surface, with a barely restrained edge of madness. It sounded like a blade dragged out of raw flesh.

"S-Su Zhang… what happened to you?" she whispered.

He stared at her without blinking, his eyes red as if fire itself was burning through them. "I remember everything," he said. "Everything from the last life ——every moment of that loneliness, that coldness. I remember it all."

Qin Nianyin's heart lurched violently, her breath tightening.

His hand clamped around her wrist, the pressure so harsh it felt as though her bones might snap. The blood-red glow in his eyes mixed with the quivering firelight, creating a terrifying, unhinged intensity.

"You can cry," he said, "you can hate me, you can resent me. But don't even think about leaving again. You died because of me in the last life. In this life, you will live because of me. Whether you love me or not, I will keep you at my side for the rest of your life."

Tears burst from her eyes, but she bit down hard, forcing herself to meet his gaze directly.

"Su Zhang," she said. Her voice trembled but remained steady, each word falling like a hammer. "You are wrong. In the last life, we were married ——yet we spent our entire life in coldness. You stood alone on the court like untouchable frost and I was nothing more than a caged bird in your household. We never warmed each other, not even once, not until the day we died. Do you really want to repeat that ending?"

Su Zhang froze for a heartbeat.

The tension in his shoulders loosened only slightly before a low laugh slipped out of him ——quiet at first, but turning colder with every breath.

His expression did not soften; if anything, it sharpened, as though her words had struck somewhere buried deep.

"Cold?" he echoed. "Yes. We were cold for an entire lifetime."

He spoke without hesitation, as if confronting a truth he had long avoided. "And that was my fault."

His gaze locked onto hers. The faint tremor in his voice vanished, replaced by a hardness that felt carved into bone ——unyielding, absolute.

"But this life is different. Heaven gave us another chance," he said, each word steady and certain, "And I will not waste it. I will change what was meant to be."

He stepped closer, his breath unsteadies but his resolve unwavering.

"If you won't give it," he murmured, "then I will take it."

His hand tightened around her wrist as though afraid she would vanish if he loosened his grip for even a moment. "If you try to run, I will chain you."

His voice dropped to a low, hoarse vow, the kind that came from a man who had broken once and would not break again.

"Nianyin," he said, "your fate can only be mine."

He pulled her even closer, his voice barely above a whisper yet bearing the weight of absolute resolve. "Nianyin… I'm sorry. I cannot let go. Not in this life. You will still be mine."

Qin Nianyin trembled. Her tears blurred her vision, her chest felt like it was being torn open. She dug her nails into her palm, forcing herself to speak clearly.

"In the last life, we wasted an entire lifetime," she said. "In this life… I will not waste another."

A tear slid down her cheek, but her voice was like a cold blade.

She looked at him then, truly looked at him, as if stripping away the layers of memory she had carried across two lifetimes.

What stood before her was no longer the distant, restrained man of the past, nor the silent husband who had once kept his heart sealed behind frost.

This man's gaze burned too fiercely, his grip held too tightly, as though fear itself had fused with devotion and hardened into something unyielding.

She suddenly understood that what bound him now was not tenderness reborn, but terror of loss, sharpened by regret and tempered into obsession.

He did not fear losing her love.

He feared losing her existence.

And that fear had already begun to eclipse reason.

"If loving you means reliving that same cold, empty life ——then I would rather not love you at all."

The hall fell deathly silent.

Su Zhang's breathing grew uneven. The corners of his lips lifted slightly, forming a cold, chilling smile. Standing amid the blood and fire, he looked almost like a demon born of madness.

"Not love…" he murmured. "You say you don't love…"

His eyes narrowed, the red in them deepening.

"Nianyin… then I'll wait. I'll wait until you finally do."

Qin Nianyin did not answer him.

She stood within his arms, yet felt as though she were standing far away, separated by something vast and irrevocable.

The warmth of his body, the tightness of his hold, the tremor beneath his breath — all of it was unmistakably real, and yet none of it could reach her heart.

For the first time, she understood with painful clarity that this life had not simply repeated the last.

In the previous one, she had loved him and lost herself.

In this one, he loved her — and was losing himself instead.

The symmetry was cruel, almost mocking.

And she knew then that no matter how fiercely he clung, no matter how long he claimed he would wait, the distance between them had already become something that could not be closed by devotion alone.

Chapter 96: Blood Over the Capital

Dawn had barely broken, yet the night's relentless rounds of pursuit, executions, and escorts had already swept through the capital like a cold, sinister storm, turning everything upside down.

From the Golden Treasure Gambling Hall to three major money houses, and even within the palace gates, there were marks everywhere of armoured boots grinding across stone.

The streets lay empty. Bloodstains from last night still clung to the flagstones, now layered over and over by the thin morning mist.

 Now and then a passerby would hurry by with their head down, not daring to speak, afraid even a lingering glance might draw calamity onto them. Even the morning drum and the cries of roosters, sounds that should have been familiar and lively, seemed strangely lonely.

An elderly woman pushing a cart of firewood passed by. The moment she caught sight of the blood on the ground, her face changed. She turned in panic and hurried into a side alley.

At a street corner, a young boy holding an empty basket peeked out to look around, only for his mother to seize him at once, drag him back, and scold him in a low voice. Yet panic could not be hidden in her eyes.

Wine shops and tea houses kept their doors tightly shut. Even the street vendors did not dare set up their stalls. The entire capital felt as though someone had clamped a fist around its throat overnight.

Outside the Censorate, stacks of sealed ledgers and locked crates were piled higher than a man. Red seals and smears of blood crossed over the wood, announcing last night's thorough investigation without a word. Inside and outside the palace gates, several advisers from the Third Prince's household were dragged past in iron shackles, their faces ashen. Not one dared to argue. Not one dared to lift their head.

"The Third Prince… has been thrown into prison."

That single sentence spread through the court and the city like a violent gale, stirring countless hushed discussions. Some could not believe it. Some felt cold sweat slide down their temples. Others were already calculating, their thoughts quietly shifting toward the Eastern Palace.

In one night, the capital seemed to have been washed in blood. Even the dawn light upon the city walls looked cold and pale, as though the sky itself had drawn a shadow over this upheaval.

And within this suffocating stillness, one emotion alone rang clearly: fear, suppressed and trembling beneath every breath. Everyone knew that after last night, Great Zhou would never return to what it once was.

On the other side of the capital, Qin Nianyin quietly packed her belongings.

She carried very little. Only a few plain garments and her embroidery tools, neatly placed into a cloth bundle. Supporting Madam Lin with her own hands, she walked step by step toward the mountain gate of Qing Shan Temple.

The morning mist had not yet dispersed. The mountain path was still and cool, broken only by the occasional call of a bird. Compared with the bloodshed and turbulence that had swallowed the capital, this place felt like another world entirely.

Madam Lin muttered the entire way. There was still a faint trace of wine on her breath. Half supported and half persuaded by Nianyin, she grumbled now and then under her breath, "This old woman has no wish to eat vegetables and chant sutras…"

Yet in the end, she still came.

The stone steps curved upward. Through the mist, the temple gate appeared, its red lacquer worn and faded, but its incense unbroken.

Qin Nianyin halted for a moment and looked back toward the distant capital below. A faint ache rose unexpectedly in her chest. The echoes of last night's slaughter still lingered in her ears, yet she had already decided she would never look back.

What belonged to her from this day on was neither contention nor struggle.

It was peace.

She drew a long breath, and with Madam Lin, slowly crossed the threshold of Qing Shan Temple.

Life at Qing Shan Temple proved even colder than she had imagined.

On windy nights, the distant mountain bell would be scattered and thinned by the gusts. When she bent over her desk to embroider, the lamplight flickered, and from far away came the slow, uneven chanting of monks, low and subdued, as though recounting dust-covered stories of lives long past.

She would lift her gaze toward the shadowed mountains outside the window and feel a brief emptiness open in her chest. The wrongs of her previous life, the burdens of this one, everything seemed to be stirred into the mist by the sound of sutras until it blurred into distance.

In that moment, she understood that true repentance was not spoken with a single "I regret."

It was found in sitting down day after day, in carrying water up the stairs day after day, in quiet labour that slowly ground the restless thoughts in one's heart into stillness.

She let out a low laugh and murmured, "So be it."

The smile was faint, yet it felt like closing a door gently behind herself.

Before dawn, the morning bell rang again. Its deep echoes rolled through the valley, as if reminding all beings that another day had begun.

Qin Nianyin often rose with the monks, wrapped herself in coarse robes, and went with Qiqi and Yiyi to fetch water behind the mountain. The stone stairs were damp, the spring water frigid. She lifted her sleeves. Her fingers trembled when they touched the icy stream, yet she still hoisted the full jar without complaint.

Madam Lin could not adapt to the temple's strict rules. She often hid a small flask of wine behind the kitchen courtyard, only to be caught by a young novice monk. Each time she would protest loudly, "This old woman is already half-buried in the earth. Why can't I drink a little?"

Then she would tug on Nianyin's sleeve, begging her to speak on her behalf.

Nianyin could only look at her helplessly. Laughter slipped out despite herself, and in the end she always managed to soften the punishment by a few degrees.

During quiet hours, Nianyin sat beneath the corridor, unfurling cloth and gold thread to practise the craft Madam Lin had once mastered.

Madam Lin's fingers were old, yet astonishingly steady. She lectured while working, her voice low: "This craft requires a still heart. If the mind wanders, the thread will never find its way back."

Nianyin listened. A faint ache rose in her chest, yet she too quieted, stitching her thoughts away, thread by thread.

Qiqi remained mischievous. She often ran outside to pick wildflowers and tuck them behind Nianyin's ear, giggling, "Miss, you look even prettier than the temple blossoms."

Yiyi was far more sensible, always trailing silently behind her, occasionally helping gather scattered threads.

Late at night, the mountain wind flowed gently. The lamplight cast Nianyin's shadow long across the wall. She would close her embroidery frame and sit quietly in her meditation room, listening to the distant tolling of the bell.

Its deep, lingering tone was almost identical to the one she had heard before her fall from the cliff in her past life, and her heart would tighten faintly.

Perhaps this was fate.

She had already lived through the loves and hatreds of the mortal world. In this life, in this moment, all she wished for was a place of quiet, and the strength to protect the few people she still could.

Life at Qing Shan Temple was austere, yet because of a few small creatures, it held a thread of warmth that softened its quiet days.

Between morning bells and vesper bells, Qin Nianyin often found a tiny sable curled beneath the eaves of her meditation room. Its tail flicked with lazy entitlement, bright eyes fixed on her hands as though it knew she always saved a few dried fruits for it.

The kitten was even more attached to her, forever stepping on her robes, climbing up her sleeves, or pawing at her ankles, mewling insistently until she lifted it into her arms, where it would immediately begin to purr.

Qiqi would laugh and say, "Miss looks just like the Bodhisattva. Both hands full, one holding a kitten, the other teasing the little sable."

Nianyin could not help but smile. She tapped Qiqi lightly on the forehead. "Nonsense. What kind of Bodhisattva behaves like this?"

Yiyi remained the quietest of them all.

She often helped settle the kitten once it tired itself out, tucking it into a reed basket to sleep. Or she humoured the sable by sewing a small cloth pouch filled with dried fruits and hanging it from the ceiling beam so it would not overturn the food box every night. Sometimes she even dusted off the sable's whiskers when it returned from rolling in the firewood shed, murmuring that it looked "far too pleased with itself."

Madam Lin was the least tolerant of animals. She complained that they disturbed her peace, yet still sneaked pieces of wine-soaked pork to them, stubbornly insisting, "Hmph, it's leftovers. If no one eats it, it'll go to waste."

The inevitable result was a drunken little sable rolling around the courtyard like a fallen chestnut, making the novice monks choke back their laughter until the elder emerged to scold the entire group.

Sometimes, while Nianyin worked beneath the corridor, her needle threading steadily through cloth, the kitten would curl up and doze on her lap, its soft breaths warming her knees. Meanwhile the sable climbed to her shoulder, peering curiously at the silver thread glinting between her fingers.

Occasionally it would reach out a paw to swipe at it, prompting her to murmur, "Don't make trouble," though her tone always betrayed a quiet fondness.

At night, when the wind moved through the forest and the temple bell hummed faintly from afar, Nianyin would lift her gaze from the wavering lamplight and notice the kitten nestled against her embroidery frame, and the little sable curled tightly on a meditation cushion beneath the Buddha statue, as if guarding the room.

A small warmth rose in her chest.

This once-quiet place, cold, distant, almost forbidding, now held the gentle murmur of ordinary life.

Days at Qing Shan Temple passed in steady, unchanging rhythm: morning bells and vesper bells, drawing water, gathering firewood, simple meals shared at long wooden tables. The quiet was so complete that at times it felt as though even time itself had been sealed within these mountains.

Chapter 97: Past-Life Misunderstandings

Every ten days or so, Mei would secretly make her way up the mountain.

The moment she saw Qin Nianyin, she would start complaining at once, her eyes already rimmed red. "Miss, you really don't want Mei anymore. You left me in the capital all by myself while you came here to suffer through this bitter life. Do you know how lively the capital has been lately? The Second Princess is hosting another flower-viewing banquet, and the newly selected scholars have been composing poems. It's spread through the whole city—everyone's talking about it!"

Qin Nianyin only smiled. She reached out and gently tucked away the strands of hair the wind had loosened around Mei's temples, her voice soft. "You silly girl… your fate is a good one. You're destined for wealth, blessings, and longevity. Why come here and endure hardship with me?"

Mei pouted, yet she still couldn't help lowering her voice, as if afraid the mountains themselves might overhear. She began to pour out every scrap of news she had gathered rumours shifting through the court, gossip rolling through the streets, even which young ladies in the capital had recently come into their beauty, and which households were suddenly being whispered about.

Each word carried the warmth and bustle of the mortal world, thinning the cold quiet of the temple like a hand warming ice.

Qin Nianyin listened in silence. Sometimes she laughed despite herself. Other times, a faint melancholy slipped across her eyes, so light it was almost hard to catch.

"Mei," she said suddenly. She reached out and gently cupped the girl's face, her palm warm against Mei's cheek. "Don't blame me for not bringing you here. This kind of life… it truly isn't one you should have to endure. When I complete my year of cultivation here, as ordered by His Majesty, I'll go back and arrange a proper marriage for you. I want you to live peacefully, safe and steady, for the rest of your life."

Mei's tears fell at once, yet she still mumbled her grievances through them, stubborn as ever. "Miss always says you want to take care of me, but you keep pushing me away… you even prefer Qiqi and Yiyi over me…"

Qin Nianyin couldn't help laughing softly. She pulled her into an embrace and whispered, "I only push you away because I can't bear to let you suffer."

Outside, the wind swept through the pine forest and the distant temple bell drifted in long, faint echoes.

Inside the small room, warmth lingered between the two of them—yet beneath that quiet tenderness, it brushed against the undercurrents stirring in the capital below. Loneliness and solace crossed like two threads in the same cloth, woven together so subtly one could hardly tell where one ended and the other began.

At noon in midsummer, the mountain wind swept through the pine forest and cicadas cried without pause.

Qin Nianyin was seated beneath the corridor sorting through silk threads when Qiqi suddenly rushed over, breathless. "Miss! The Second Young Lady of the Shen family came up the mountain with Madam Shen to offer incense. She wishes to see you. She's waiting outside the mountain gate."

Qin Nianyin paused, startled, then rose at once and followed Qiqi out of the front veranda.

Outside the mountain gate, the red lacquer on the doors had long since faded and chipped, worn thin by years of sun and rain. Incense smoke curled upward in pale strands.

Madam Shen was speaking with the abbot. Beside her stood Shen Lingyan, dressed plainly in a simple blue gown. Her features were delicate and serene, yet faintly touched with sorrow, as if something sleepless still lingered beneath her calm.

When she saw Qin Nianyin, she froze for a heartbeat, then offered a small smile. "Nianyin, have you been well?"

A young novice monk led them toward the tea pavilion in the rear courtyard. Madam Shen went to the main hall to burn incense, leaving Shen Lingyan and Qin Nianyin seated across from one another.

The tea fragrance was light. The mountain breeze carried distant echoes of Buddhist chants, slow and muted, as though the temple itself were breathing.

Qin Nianyin smiled first. "Qiqi said you came today to pray for a marriage match?"

A faint flicker crossed Shen Lingyan's eyes, and the corner of her lips curved into a quiet, self-mocking smile. "My mother's idea. Even if I prayed—what difference would it make?"

Seeing her lack of interest, Qin Nianyin asked gently, "The candidate… does he not suit your liking?"

Shen Lingyan let out a soft sigh. "If it's not the person in one's heart, then even praying ten thousand times is meaningless."

Something stirred in Qin Nianyin's chest. She hesitated, then asked carefully, "From the sound of it… you already have someone in your heart?"

Only then did Shen Lingyan seem to realize she had spoken too freely. Colour rushed to her face at once. "It's nothing. Forget I said anything."

But Qin Nianyin's curiosity only grew. "It's only the two of us here. Why not tell me? Perhaps your younger sister can help you think of a way."

Shen Lingyan fell silent for a long moment before finally releasing a quiet, weary breath. "If I said it aloud, it would only invite ridicule. It's impossible. It's nothing but my own foolish wish."

"So the person your mother favours… is not the person you favour?"

Shen Lingyan nodded.

"Father and Mother want me to marry the Grand General of Zhen."

A memory from Qin Nianyin's previous life flashed past like a shadow—Shen Lingyan had indeed married a general in the end, most likely that very Grand General. But because he spent so many years at war, Shen Lingyan's days had been long stretches of solitude.

Qin Nianyin studied her face and asked softly, "From your tone… it seems you are not fond of this Grand General?"

Shen Lingyan's expression trembled. She abruptly lifted her gaze, panic flickering through her eyes, and shook her head again and again. "What Grand General? Sister, don't speak nonsense!"

Qin Nianyin hesitated, yet still couldn't stop herself. "Then… what about Lord Su Zhang?"

Shen Lingyan froze. The tips of her ears turned red in an instant. "W-What Su Zhang… why would you think that?"

Her reaction did not seem feigned. Qin Nianyin was momentarily stunned.

So Shen Lingyan's sweetheart… was not Su Zhang?

Shen Lingyan lowered her gaze. Her fingers twisted tightly around the edge of her sleeve, as if she could wring out the pounding of her heart through the fabric. Her voice was so soft it was nearly a whisper.

"Fine… since it's just you and me today, I'll quietly bare my heart. The person I admire… is Gu Xiao."

The words fell like a pebble into the still centre of a lake, sending shock rippling through Qin Nianyin until she sat completely frozen.

In her previous life, she had believed that Su Zhang and Shen Lingyan were the ones fated for one another.

Only now did she realize that what Shen Lingyan had hidden in her heart was Gu Xiao.

Another memory surfaced—their first meeting in this lifetime, at Su Wan's Ningfang tea gathering. That day, Shen Lingyan had kept glancing around the garden, her gaze drifting again and again as if she were searching for someone. Qin Nianyin had even asked, half in passing, whether she was waiting for a particular guest, only for Shen Lingyan to shake her head and deny it.

At the time, Qin Nianyin had thought nothing of it.

But now, with today's confession laid bare, everything finally fell into place.

The person Shen Lingyan had been searching for that day—moving her eyes across the garden, lingering and restless—had never been Su Zhang. It had always been Gu Xiao.

Her feelings had already been there, quietly exposed in plain sight, and yet Qin Nianyin had failed to see them. Not until today.

A faint ache spread through Qin Nianyin's chest.

In her previous life, Gu Xiao had died on the northern frontier, his body soaked in blood, his bones never returned to their homeland. With no one left to cling to, Shen Lingyan had eventually accepted her parents' will and married that Grand General. And yet, only now did Qin Nianyin realise—so much of what she had believed, so much of what she had assumed about that fate, had been wrong.

Shen Lingyan pressed her lips together, her voice dropping even lower. "I have admired General Gu for many years. I never dared to say it aloud. Others believed I approached Su Zhang with ulterior motives, but..." She paused briefly, then continued softly, "...it was only because that way, I could see General Gu a few more times."

Qin Nianyin could only stare at her, her chest tightening with a quiet, helpless ache.

So that was the truth.

Only now did she realize how deeply she had been mistaken.

In her previous life, she had believed Shen Lingyan and Su Zhang shared a destined affection, and she had even thought herself the one who ruined their bond, carrying that guilt for years.

Yet the truth was that Shen Lingyan had always kept Gu Xiao in her heart from beginning to end.

In that lifetime, Gu Xiao died on the frontier and never came back. With no one left to rely on, Shen Lingyan finally accepted her parents' arrangement and married the Grand General.

Qin Nianyin had been wrong—not only about her own entanglement with Su Zhang, but also because she had failed to see through Shen Lingyan's heart, allowing fate to push her into a loveless path she never chose.

She realized now that Shen Lingyan's fate in the previous life had been just as tragic.

Shen Lingyan had watched, powerless, as the man she secretly loved for years died in battle. Then, in despair, she accepted a political marriage without affection.

A faint shimmer of tears gathered in Qin Nianyin's eyes, yet she tightened her grip around Shen Lingyan's hand, making a vow in silence.

This lifetime, she would not let that bond be lost again.

She clasped Shen Lingyan's hand more firmly, her tone steady. "In that case, why not try being brave? If you never speak, how will he ever know?"

Shen Lingyan's head snapped up, panic rising sharply in her eyes. "Sister, don't frighten me! What woman confesses first? If word spreads, how will a daughter of the Shen family show her face?"

Qin Nianyin let out a soft laugh. Her eyes were warm, and heat gathered faintly at her lashes. "How others think does not matter. If you miss it, you'll regret it for a lifetime. Lingyan, if you trust me, then don't let him slip away."

Shen Lingyan stared at her blankly. Only the distant toll of the temple bell filled her ears. The flush on her face deepened, and she whispered, "…I'm afraid."

Qin Nianyin gazed at her and silently thought: if she could change Shen Lingyan's fate from the previous life, then perhaps this was another bond she was meant to mend in this one.

Chapter 98: My Heart Has Grown Old

Six months later.

The mountain wind at Qing Shan Temple was still as cool and sharp as ever, and the days passed with the same unchanging calm.

Morning bell, vesper bell. Bamboo shadows scattered across stone. Qin Nianyin's figure gradually blended into the quiet of this place. Plain robes, pale sleeves. Even the brilliance that used to sit in her brows and eyes seemed to have thinned, as if the temple's austere air had slowly washed colour from her.

That day, the sound of hoofbeats rose at the temple gate.

When Mei ran in to report it, her eyes were full of surprise.

"Miss, it's General Gu… he's come again."

Qin Nianyin pressed her lips together with a small smile, as if she had already expected it. She walked out to greet him herself.

Gu Xiao approached without even removing his silver armour. Dust still clung to him from the road, and the faint scent of wind and travel sat on the edges of his cloak. He looked like a man who had not paused even to drink water before coming up the mountain.

"General," she greeted him gently, "you have taken another long trip."

Gu Xiao looked at her. The emotion in his eyes was impossible to hide, too direct, too hot to be concealed beneath courtesy. He stepped forward, but when he spoke, his tone carried a quiet bitterness, the kind that scraped against the throat.

"Look at this. Half a year has passed and the only one who still comes for you is me. Besides me, who else remembers you? And that man surnamed Su, has he come even once?"

Qin Nianyin's expression remained calm. Only the faintest shadow of a smile brushed the corner of her lips, thin as mist, neither warmth nor mockery.

"The temple is quiet. Whether anyone comes or not… it makes little difference."

"Little difference?" Gu Xiao let out a cold laugh, though his voice shook.

"Nianyin, is your heart truly made of stone? After all this time, can't you see? In this world, I am the only one who is sincere toward you."

His gaze burned, as if trying to pry open the door she kept shut in her chest, as if he could reach in and drag out the name she refused to say.

Qin Nianyin looked at him quietly, then finally parted her lips.

"Xiao, it isn't that I do not understand your sincerity. It is that… I cannot accept it."

"Why?" The word slipped out of him in a rush, fuelled by frustration and longing, almost raw.

She lowered her gaze and her voice, though gentle, carried a faint, almost teasing smile, so light it could have been mistaken for a sigh.

"Because I'm old."

"Old?" Gu Xiao stared at her, then let out an incredulous laugh, his eyes slowly reddening. He took a step closer, insisting stubbornly, as if he could force the answer to change by refusing it.

"Nonsense. How old are you? Not even twenty and you call yourself old. You're pushing me away, and you don't even bother to choose a convincing excuse."

Qin Nianyin raised her eyes to meet his. Her gaze held no coldness, no sharp rejection, yet there was a quiet, weathered clarity in it, something aged, something resolute, like stone that had been worn smooth by years of water and could no longer be reshaped.

"Xiao," she said softly, "my heart has already grown old."

Counting her previous life and this one, she had lived more than fifty years. How could her heart not feel ancient?

She had loved and hated, struggled and repented. She had already exhausted the kind of youth that could throw itself into fire without looking back. What remained was not innocence, but a tired sobriety, a calm that came from knowing the price of every desire.

Gu Xiao, who had no memory of their past life, was in truth only a little over twenty, a young general at the height of his early brilliance. His love was still sharp-edged, still believing it could cut through anything.

Su Zhang, after recovering the memories of his past life, had aged inwardly as she had. Whatever youth remained on the surface had long since been hollowed out by what he remembered.

But Gu Xiao… he was still too young to understand this kind of tiredness, too young to understand what it meant to feel one's heart grow old before the body ever did.

Qin Nianyin's simple words, my heart has grown old, were as light as the mountain wind, yet they cut cleanly through all of Gu Xiao's persistent longing.

He stood frozen where he was.

His chest felt as though struck by a heavy hammer. For a long moment, he could not speak.

The wind brushed through the pines.

A distant temple bell sounded, echoing through the mountains, sealing this moment of confrontation into the quiet scenery.

Night descended, still and deep.

The bell of Qing Shan Temple tolled again, slow and heavy, reverberating far into the distance.

In the courtyard, the lamplight trembled. Qin Nianyin was clearing away the teacups on the table when she heard slow, steady footsteps behind her. When she looked up, she saw Gu Xiao standing at the threshold, his features half-hidden in shadow, his expression restrained and cold, as if he had pressed every emotion down until it could only leak out in the hardness of his voice.

"In three more months, your year of seclusion at Qing Shan Temple will be complete," he said. "The Third Prince has already been sent to guard the imperial tombs. The Second Prince has been released. Fortunately, His Majesty never got the chance to issue the marriage decree that would have handed you to the Third Prince. So tell me, three months from now, will you consider becoming the wife of a general?"

Qin Nianyin smiled lightly.

"I heard from Mei that the Shen family has been quietly looking at potential matches for Lingyan. Shouldn't you go try your luck?"

Gu Xiao frowned and let out a long sigh.

"Even if you refuse me, you don't have to push me toward someone else. I'll have you know, I am in very high demand."

Qin Nianyin nodded, as if acknowledging a simple fact.

"Yes, the general is very impressive."

Gu Xiao returned a faint smile, and for a heartbeat it almost looked as though everything could end there, as if all the tangled grievances and emotions between them had quietly unravelled.

Then silence fell again.

He stared at her for a long moment, and when he spoke, his voice was hoarse, subdued, as though the words scraped against something raw in his chest.

"You've always loved him, haven't you?"

Qin Nianyin stiffened. The teacup nearly slipped from her hand. She forced her breath to steady and replied calmly.

"No."

Gu Xiao's eyes darkened. He stepped forward suddenly, his voice trembling with a mix of frustration and desperation, the stubbornness of someone who would rather be wounded than kept outside the truth.

"Don't deny it."

He stared at her, as if trying to peel away every layer she hid behind. His words came low, painfully earnest, almost like an accusation, almost like a plea.

"I can see it from the way you look at him. Even if you avoid it, even if you deny it, even if I hate admitting it myself… your eyes light up when you look at him."

Qin Nianyin's fingers trembled faintly before she lowered her lashes, refusing to meet his gaze.

Gu Xiao let out a dry, humourless laugh. He turned away, looking toward the distant mountains, as if the mountain darkness could swallow what he could no longer bear to say to her face.

"What's so good about Su Zhang anyway? After taking down the Third Prince, he's been acting like a madman in court for half a year. He bites at everyone he sees. Now people look at him like they're looking at a demon. I've even heard them calling him 'Mad Su' behind his back."

Hearing that, Qin Nianyin couldn't help laughing softly.

It was not mockery. It was something sharper and more complicated, like recognition. Yes. That was the Su Zhang she remembered from her past life, the man who eventually rose to the highest ranks, cold, ruthless, frighteningly brilliant. Once he decided to tear something apart, he would not stop until the bones were exposed.

When Gu Xiao saw her reaction, it felt as if someone had driven a heavy blow straight into his chest. Even his breath carried the strain of suppressed pain.

He let out a quiet laugh, bitter to the bone.

"So, that's how it is… I never had a chance from the beginning."

Qin Nianyin shook her head gently and sighed.

"You wouldn't understand even if I explained. But seeing you alive and well, still able to visit me like this… I'm already grateful."

In her past life, Gu Xiao never lived long enough to stand before her like this. His early death had been a knot she carried for years, a debt she could not repay, an ending she could not undo.

To see him safe and unbroken in this life, to hear his voice and watch him argue, stubborn and alive, this alone was one of her greatest comforts.

Gu Xiao watched her quiet, serene profile and he knew, with a sinking certainty, that she was never meant to belong to him.

"Fine," he said, his voice low. "I can't compete with that lunatic Su. And you love him. So I can only wish you happiness for the rest of your life."

"Mm."

Something suddenly came to her mind. She looked up and spoke softly.

"Wait here."

She turned and swiftly returned to her meditation chamber. From a small chest, she took out a little wooden horse.

Time had worn its edges smooth. The corners had been polished bright by years of handling. Yet the rough, childish knife marks were still visible, clumsy and earnest, as if the hands that carved it had poured all their stubborn youth into the blade.

She hurried after him by two steps and placed the wooden horse into his palm, her smile faint, her voice quiet, but carrying a weight that did not belong to this life alone.

"Good. I still have the chance to return it to you with my own hands… because you're alive."

Gu Xiao froze. His brows tightened slightly before he finally accepted it. He let out a short, scoffing laugh, trying to cover what flickered across his eyes.

"Such a childish thing. You actually kept it? I thought you would've thrown it away long ago."

Qin Nianyin only shook her head. Her voice was soft but unwavering, like someone stating a vow she had carried for years.

"How could I throw it away? I've been waiting to give it back to you… the you who lived."

"What lived or dead?" Gu Xiao muttered, forcing his usual swagger back into his tone. "I'm doing perfectly fine right now."

"Yes," Qin Nianyin said, and her smile lifted again, faint and clear, "General Gu, alive and vigorous."

There was a brief moment where they looked at each other and shared a quiet smile. In that moment, it felt as though everything that should have been said, and everything that could never be said, had both been placed gently down.

Gu Xiao thought to himself that his feelings, for all their depth, could only remain buried in his heart from now on, never to be spoken again.

The wind brushed across the paper windows. The lamplight trembled.

She stood there in silence, not arguing, not explaining, letting that silence cut the distance between them like a blade.

Gu Xiao's departing steps faltered. He had meant to leave with ease, to be the kind of man who could turn away cleanly. But he couldn't help wanting to turn back for one last look at her.

Several breaths passed.

In the end, he swallowed the impulse down and strode away from Qing Shan Temple without looking back.

Qin Nianyin remained where she was, watching Gu Xiao's figure disappear into the night until he finally vanished completely. The little courtyard returned to its quiet stillness.

She continued standing there, her fingertips still clenching the fabric of her sleeve, as though a weight pressed hard against her chest, leaving her breathless.

The lamp flickered. In the wavering light, she asked herself silently.

"Do I love him?"

The question pierced her heart like a sharp blade.

She closed her eyes. And in her mind, the face that rose was always the same, cold and noble, expression restrained, voice deep and controlled; sometimes cold enough to chill the bone, sometimes revealing a fleeting gentleness she could never forget.

Yes.

She loved him.

In her past life, she had loved him to madness, recklessly, desperately, so much that she forced marriage upon him through every means she had.

In this life, she still loved him.

But this love had long been worn thin and torn apart by the wounds of the past. It was no longer the kind of love that could bloom. It was the kind that bled.

She loved him, yet could no longer afford to love.

Because she understood now that such love did not only destroy her.

It destroyed him as well.

Tears finally slipped down her cheeks, falling silently onto her robe. She lifted a hand and pressed it lightly over her heart, and a trembling breath of a laugh escaped her throat, broken and quiet.

"Just like the last life… so it is in this one."

To love or not to love, either way, it was a calamity she could never escape.

* * * * *

The night was deep. The wind roared like a beast outside the walls.

Gu Xiao sank into sleep, yet his brows were tightly furrowed, as if some shadow in his heart was churning restlessly, rolling over and over without settling.

In his dream, he returned to the northern frontier.

The world was vast and bleak. Snow swept across the sky in a blinding storm. The roaring wind carried the stench of blood and fire. War drums thundered. Hooves pounded like rolling thunder. The shouts of slaughter pierced straight into the clouds, then were swallowed by the storm and flung back in broken echoes.

Gu Xiao wore silver armour. The plates over his chest were already stained dark with dried blood, cold and heavy. His long blade was steady in his hand. His gaze remained sharp, bright as a burning coal that refused to go out even in the snow.

He led the Tiger Guard at the front, charging first, striking first. He cut down enemies like breaking bamboo. Blood and snow blended into a hellish scene beneath his feet, splashing up onto his greaves, freezing, cracking, then staining again.

He could smell iron. He could taste smoke. He could hear men screaming his name and screaming for their mothers, all tangled together under the drums.

Suddenly, he felt something behind him.

Not footsteps.

Not the pressure of an enemy line.

A strange presence, silent, wrong. A cold and deadly intent that did not belong on the battlefield's front, because it was too close, too familiar, too patient. It slid toward him like a knife in darkness.

A sharp whistle tore through the air.

An arrow shot forward with ruthless precision and pierced straight through his back.

For one heartbeat, his body did not understand. Then pain detonated through his chest, crushing, violent, like a mountain collapsing inside him. The arrowhead burst out through the armour at his chest, and fresh blood sprayed across the snow in a bright, obscene red.

He choked.

"Kh…!"

Blood surged up his throat. His vision blurred. The sounds of battle and war drums seemed to recede, as if the world was being pulled away from him by the snowstorm.

His knees buckled, then forced themselves straight again. He fought to remain standing, fought to remain a general, even as his body betrayed him.

He forced himself to turn.

Through the swirling snow, he saw Liang Dong standing on a high ridge.

The bow in Liang Dong's hands had not yet lowered. The string still trembled, a thin vibration cutting through the storm. His eyes were chillingly emotionless, colder than the snow itself, and there was even a faint, cruel smile at the corner of his lips.

In that instant, the truth struck harder than the arrow.

So the arrow in his back had come from his own man.

Gu Xiao's pupils contracted sharply. Blood seeped from the corner of his mouth as he forced out a broken whisper, disbelief and fury twisting together until his throat burned.

"You… actually…"

Liang Dong remained indifferent. He said nothing. He stood firm in the snowstorm as though he had been waiting for this moment all along, as though he had rehearsed it in his mind a hundred times and now was simply finishing the last step.

Blood flooded from Gu Xiao's chest like a broken dam. His breath came in ragged jolts. His fingers loosened. His long blade slipped and fell with a metallic clang, biting into the ice.

His body tilted toward the edge of the cliff.

The snow beneath his boots cracked. Ice and stone shattered and skittered down into darkness.

"No…!"

He let out a strangled, blood-filled roar, reaching out to grab something, anything, a rock, a root, the edge of the world, but his fingertips touched only the cutting cold of the wind.

The next moment, the world overturned.

He plunged into the endless abyss.

The gale tore past him. Snow lashed across his face like blades. The only sound that remained was the frantic pounding of his own heart, wild, desperate, as if it could beat its way back into life.

The vast whiteness of the snowfield dissolved into darkness.

In the final instant before he lost all sense, he saw the snow below stained crimson with his blood, a scene carved into his soul like a nightmare from hell.

…

"Ah…!"

Gu Xiao jerked awake.

Cold sweat drenched his entire body. His chest heaved violently. His trembling fingers clutched at his heart as if he could hold it in place, as if it might burst open again.

But beneath his palm, there was only cold fabric.

No wound.

No blood.

His breathing was ragged in the darkness. Sweat trickled down his temples, drop by drop. The room was silent, yet his ears still seemed full of drums, full of screaming, full of that arrow's whistle.

The nightmare felt so real it was like dying a second time.

It wasn't a dream.

It was memory.

In that past life, he had died exactly like this on the northern cliff, an arrow through the heart, shot by the man he trusted most.

No grave.

No remains.

His lips trembled. A whisper slipped out, hoarse and broken, and the hatred in his eyes burned so red it almost looked wet.

Chapter 99: Fulfillment on Qing Shan Mountain

The afternoon wind drifted slowly across the mountain and bamboo shadows swayed back and forth over the stone steps.

Beside the water vat in the courtyard corner, Qiqi had her sleeves rolled up as she rinsed rice, while Yiyi crouched next to her picking through broken bean pods.

A small cat sprawled over the vat's rim, pawing at the water and the little sable nudged around with its nose, trying to steal pieces of dried radish.

Qiqi was the first to start grumbling, her voice lowered but full of fire.

"Hmph, I swear, Lord Su is really just a block of wood. Our lady has been at the monastery for a whole year, and he hasn't come even once. What is that supposed to mean? Our General Gu isn't like that at all ——he comes every now and then. You can at least see his shadow two or three times."

Yiyi didn't look up, calmly brushing bean shells into the basket.

"Stop running your mouth. Everyone has their reasons."

Qiqi pouted.

"What reason? It's obvious he doesn't care about our lady. If he really did, what mountain could stop him? If someone truly wants to come, there's no road they can't walk!"

Yiyi finally lifted her gaze. She flicked her finger and knocked it lightly but sharply against Qiqi's forehead, earning a loud "oof!"

"You know nothing. It's called 'fearing the nearness of home.'"

Qiqi hissed and covered her forehead, glaring at her.

"What kind of saying is that? Being too close means you don't dare to come? You think I'm a three-year-old you can fool?"

Yiyi wasn't annoyed. Her voice lowered, steady and certain.

"It is because he's too close that he doesn't dare. If Lord Su comes here and sees the lady, he might not be able to walk away again. Her year of cultivation isn't finished ——how dare he disturb her until then? He's someone whose thoughts run deep and his feelings run deeper. The more he loves, the less he dares to be reckless."

Qiqi clicked her tongue, half convinced, half unwilling to be.

"So he doesn't dare because he loves too much? …Don't make things up just to excuse him."

Yiyi shook out the last handful of bean shells, set the basket straight and said calmly,

"I'm not excusing anyone. I'm just telling you the truth. Some people love by stepping forward boldly. Others love by taking one step back waiting for the bell to finish ringing before they come. General Gu is fire; wherever he burns, the world brightens. But Lord Su is snow; he falls quietly, without a word, but he lays the road flat before letting someone walk upon it."

Qiqi froze for a moment, her eyes rolling as she mulled it over. Still, she muttered stubbornly,

"Hmph, sounds nice enough when you say it. But if he still doesn't come soon, I'm going to assume he truly isn't coming."

Yiyi gave her a look and suddenly smiled.

"What are you in such a rush for? Whether he has her in his heart or not ——when that day comes, you'll see it clearly."

Before her words finished, a wooden clapper echoed faintly from the mountain gate. A distant Buddhist chant drifted through the air and the wind carried incense into the little courtyard.

The cat sprang up with its ears pricked toward the entrance. The sable stopped stealing food and scrambled onto a beam to peek outside.

Qiqi was still muttering,

"What day?"

Yiyi smoothed her sleeves, her voice light and even.

"When the time is right, the one who ought to come will naturally arrive."

Qiqi snorted softly, but she still straightened her clothes a little and rubbed the red mark off her forehead. Under her breath, she added,

"Always talking like some wandering sage… Well, if he truly comes… fine. I'll just see what sort of entrance he plans to make."

* * * * *

In the June heat, the grove west of Qing Shan Temple lay beneath a shimmering canopy of phoenix trees, their shadows baked by the endless rasp of cicadas. Yet within the monastery, everything remained still as water. Each toll of the temple bell echoed along the covered walkways in slow, steady waves.

Qin Nianyin packed her belongings as simply as she could: two plain robes, a rolled embroidery screen and a small pouch of medicine.

Qiqi and Yiyi stood at the threshold holding the little sable, while she turned back again to warn Granny Lin to put away her wine jar before the young monks came to report her.

From the shaded pines behind the hall, the white-browed bhikkhuni approached with measured steps, holding in her palms a string of old sandalwood beads.

The beads were dark and warm, with a faint scent as though they had travelled a long road before settling again in her hands.

"Benefactor," the bhikkhuni said in her quiet, steady voice, "this rosary is bound to you by fate. In your past life and this one, it has always returned to your hands. Today, as we part, I entrust it to you once more."

The moment Qin Nianyin's fingertips touched the warm wood, something trembled in her chest. Wind and snow at the cliff's edge, the shape of blood spattered on stone ——these memories rose sharply, pulled back into focus by the weight of a single bead.

She faltered for a breath, heat gathering suddenly behind her eyes.

"Why cry?" the bhikkhuni murmured, lowering her sleeve to wipe away a thin trace of moisture from Nianyin's cheek. "The debts of your last life have been repaid. The road of this life is about to open. Fulfillment does not require a single ending. To let go ——this too is fulfillment."

Qin Nianyin bowed her head and answered softly, "Yes." She had not yet put the rosary away when a spill of sunlight entered the hall.

Someone stood at the threshold, outlined against the light. His robes were plain and still coated with travel dust, a rolled document held in his hand.

The harsh summer sun traced his profile clearly; his brows and eyes were cool, his expression calm and quiet.

Her heart gave a sudden, painful thump. Her fingers slipped and the sandalwood beads nearly fell from her hands.

He looked at her, his throat moving once before he spoke. His voice was low, steady and unmistakably clear. "Nianyin… I am here."

The temple bell rang with a deep, resonant strike. Qin Nianyin tightened her grip on the beads, but she could not suppress the warmth rising to her throat.

"You… what do you mean by that?" she asked, trying hard to steady her voice.

Su Zhang lowered the scroll and stepped lightly into the shadow of the hall. His gaze was steady and direct.

When he reached her, he held the scroll across his palms and offered it to her with formal reverence. "By imperial decree," he said, "Qin, having completed one full year of ritual cultivation, may leave the mountain and return home. These are the documents for release and reinstatement."

Qin Nianyin accepted the scroll; the paper felt cool against her fingertips. She lifted her eyes, about to speak, when he continued, "And the meaning is this ——I remember."

Her body jolted as though a temple bell had struck straight through her chest.

Su Zhang met her gaze. The coldness in his eyes had loosened, replaced by a quiet heaviness that still pressed downward.

"In our past life," he said, "you shielded me from that calamity. The carriage fell from the cliff with you inside it. I found you at the bottom ——bloodied, barely alive. I held you in my arms and in that moment, I had only one thought: if there is another life, I will never let go of you again."

He paused and swallowed, as though forcing down something bitter. "In this life, I nearly lost you once more."

Qin Nianyin's fingers tightened around the corner of the document. Her voice trembled. "How… how did you come to know all this?"

"In dreams." His lips curved slightly, though the smile was faint to the point of vanishing.

"Again and again, I watched you fall with that carriage ——cold, breathless, gone. I thought it was just a nightmare. Until every expression on your face matched those in my dream, I realized it wasn't a dream at all. It was the road we had already walked."

A breeze passed outside the hall, tilting the trail of incense smoke. Qin Nianyin's lashes quivered. "If it is truly our past life," she whispered, "then you know… the ending was not a good one."

"That is why," he said quietly, "in this life, it must change."

His voice was so low it seemed he feared even sound itself might disturb the fragile beads she held in her palm. "This year, I didn't come up the mountain because I was afraid of disrupting your practice… and afraid I might repeat my old mistakes. I ended what needed ending. I severed what needed severing. Only when I was completely clean did I dare to come."

Qin Nianyin lifted her gaze to him. His eyes were still cool and controlled ——yet no longer like the distant frost he once carried. Within that coldness was a trace of something burned, a scar of heat and resolve that had been tempered by fire.

She let out a bitter smile. "But I am already old."

Su Zhang was silent for a moment before lowering his gaze. "It isn't you who has grown old," he said quietly. "It is the wounds in your heart. Two lifetimes of running… all our youthful fire has been worn away. We are both weathered now."

He lifted his hand, his fingertips hovering near the corner of her eye, but he restrained himself and let it fall back to his side. "I am old as well. But if you are willing to trust me once more, I will spend this life repaying everything. I owed you before ——piece by piece. Not to force you to turn back, but to walk the rest of the way beside you."

Qin Nianyin's throat tightened until she could no longer speak. Tears were already sliding down her cheeks. The sandalwood beads in her palm knocked softly against one another, each touch like a knot being pulled loose from her heart.

Another bell sounded in the distance.

She finally drew a steady breath, held the scroll close to her chest, bowed deeply to the white-browed bhikkhuni and then turned toward him. In her eyes there was both clarities forged through hardship and a small, quiet yielding.

"Let's go," she said.

Su Zhang answered with a soft "Mm," then stepped aside to drape her outer robe over her shoulders. His palm was warm, yet his touch on her shoulder was light.

Together they stepped over the threshold of the hall. Sunlight poured down from the eaves, stretching their shadows over the stone path.

Ahead, Qiqi pulled Yiyi along the walkway, while the little marten climbed up Su Zhang's sleeve to perch on his shoulder, peering around as if scouting the road. Granny Lin stuffed her wine jar even deeper into her bundle, muttering, "Down the mountain now ——time for proper hot wine again."

The bell behind them released a long, resonant note that drifted down the slope. Qin Nianyin lowered her eyes to the sandalwood beads resting in her hand and felt, for the first time, that the path ahead was no longer narrow or suffocating.

She wound the beads around her wrist and walked beside him. The wind stirred the parasol trees, scattering their shadows like golden fragments and the broken light happened to fall upon their interlaced fingers.

By the time they reached the capital, it was already early autumn. A cool golden wind swept through the streets. Beyond the palace gates, the marketplaces remained lively, but after the storm of blood and upheaval the city had endured, even its bustle now carried a quieter undertone.

* * * * *

Li Jing vs Xu Wencai

The crack of ceremonial whips sounded as the wedding procession moved forward in steady rhythm. Princess Li Jing, dressed in her bridal robes, looked entirely different from the spoiled and impulsive girl she once was. Her expression now carried a quiet composure, soft and gentle.

She lifted her gaze toward her new husband ——Xu Wencai, a man of humble origins who had failed the examinations several times before finally earning his place on the imperial roster.

He was not a man of wealth or noble lineage, but he stood straight, his features clean and earnest and in his eyes was a sincerity that could not be faked.

Li Jing's heart settled.

She thought: Within the cold walls of the palace and beneath the shadow of imperial power, only someone like him would give me a lifetime of genuine devotion.

At the wedding ceremony, Xu Wencai had spoken only one sentence:

"Your Highness has chosen me. For the rest of my life, I will guard you with everything I have."

Li Jing's eyes grew warm and after a brief moment, she answered in a soft voice:

"One lifetime, one pair."

* * * * *

The Second Prince – Li Xuan

Long confined, was finally released.

His titles were stripped, his power taken, leaving him with nothing but a frail, sickly body.

He no longer harboured any desire to fight for the throne; all he wanted was to recuperate quietly in a secluded residence.

Some mocked him for his fall from grace, saying he was pitiful and broken.

He merely gave a cold, indifferent smile.

"Schemes and struggles… in the end, they amount to nothing. Now that I have nothing to fight for, I find that peace is the greatest blessing."

Only one person remained by his side, the woman who had weathered every storm for him in the shadows and who could finally stand beside him openly and without fear.

* * * * *

Gu Xiao vs Shen Lingyan

The Gu residence was filled with joy on the day of the wedding.

The bride, Shen Lingyan ——the legitimate daughter of the Shen family ——wore a phoenix coronet and scarlet wedding robes, dignified and quietly beautiful.

Guests all praised the match: the fierce young general of a military house paired with an elegant daughter of a noble lineage.

Only Gu Xiao, when he raised the nuptial cup and drank the ceremonial wine, showed a fleeting emptiness in his eyes.

Shen Lingyan lowered her gaze and smiled gently, choosing not to ask.

After the wedding, she treated him with great tenderness and Gu Xiao gradually let go of the longing he had once carried in his heart.

Yet on certain nights, when sleep pulled him back into old memories, he would dream of the cool, distant figure standing beneath the eaves of Qing Shan Temple.

and each time, a tightness would catch in his chest before the dream
faded.

* * * * *

Crown Prince Li Duan vs Su Wan

The Eastern Palace wedding was held with great splendours and the
entire court offered their congratulations.

The Crown Prince, Li Duan, was to marry Su Wan ——the younger
sister of Su Zhang. She entered the palace in her wedding robes, her
steps steady and calm, without the slightest trace of panic.

She had long understood that becoming the Crown Princess was the
Crown Prince's way of securing powerful alliances, not an act born of
affection.

Her own heart, however, did hold true admiration for him.

But she also knew that in this world, there were no choices that were
perfectly whole.

Since fate had arranged her path, she would walk it with resilience and
resolve, offering the Eastern Palace its most unshakable peace.

The Crown Prince never once spoke of love.

Yet on one quiet night after the wedding, he murmured a single line:

"Wan… thank you."

Hearing those words, Su Wan felt an unexpected sense of release settle
softly over her heart.

* * * * *

Mei's happy life

What comforted Qin Nianyin most was none other than Mei.

The little maid who had followed her for so many years ——always
quick to complain, yet loyal to the bone ——was finally married.

Her husband was a young steward from the Su household, steady in
temperament and pleasant in appearance.

Though still in his twenties, he already managed several shops; in time,
he would surely rise even higher.

On the day of the wedding, Mei clung to Qin Nianyin's hand and cried,
saying she couldn't bear to part with her.

Qin Nianyin only laughed gently and wiped her tears.

"Your silly girl," she said. "You deserve a home of your own and someone who will cherish you properly."

Mei's eyes were still red, but she finally broke into a smile ——one tinged with the shy sweetness of a young bride.

* * * * *

Epilogue

Outside Qing Shan Temple, the sun was sinking beyond the ridge.

Qin Nianyin stood at the temple gate, watching the distant lights of the capital flicker into the dusk.

She was no longer the young girl she once had been, yet her heart had never felt clearer.

Fate had pushed each of them into the storm and every person had found a different way to walk through it. Some faltered and never rose again; some endured long enough to see the clouds break.

Some finally reached the ending they had longed for, while others learned ——through years of regret ——how to loosen their grip and let go of what once held them fast.

Qin Nianyin slowly ran her thumb over the string of prayer beads in her hand. The wood had been warmed by time and touch; each bead carried a weight she could not quite name.

A quiet smile softened her features, not bright, but steady ——like someone who had finally made peace with herself.

She turned toward the temple gate and took a step back inside. The breeze lifted the hem of her robe as she walked, carrying with it the faint scent of incense that lingered beneath the eaves.

Behind her, the fireworks blooming over the capital cast brief colours across the horizon and the distant toll of the evening bell rolled down the mountainside.

The two sounds mingled in the fading light, forming a gentle farewell to everything that had belonged to the life she had already lived once before.

As she crossed the threshold, she understood ——quietly and without surprise ——that this was what true completion felt like. It was not a grand ending, nor a moment of triumph, but a simple, steady clarity that settled into the heart and stayed.

Extra Story 1: The Opening of Blossom Hall

Early summer in the capital marked the end of the blooming season, but also the busiest time for the markets. Stalls bustled, voices rose and fell and business thrived in every alleyway.

Qin Nianyin stood at the corner of the street, gazing at the two-story building across from her. Its walls were chipped, the beams beneath the eaves missing a patch of paint, yet its location was excellent ——close to both the lively market street and the government offices, with crowds constantly passing by.

"Miss!" Mei nearly bounced on her feet, her face bright with excitement. "Our Blossom Hall is really going to open!"

Qin Nianyin only curved her lips into a quiet smile. "Yes. And because of that, we'll need more hands. It's good that you're here to help. Once you're married… things do change."

Mei's cheeks flushed. "Miss, don't tease me. Wherever you are, I'll be there too. I'm never leaving you."

Old Madam Lin snorted by her side, leaning on her cane. "You're married and still clinging to your young lady. Fine, fine ——if you two have set your minds on this nonsense, this old woman will tag along and see it through."

Even as she grumbled, she had already pulled out her account book and begun calculating the cost of repairs.

Within a few days, the old building had a new owner. Fresh plaster brightened the walls, dark tiles were restored and a gold plaque reading Blossom Hall was hung above the entrance.

On the opening day, Qin Nianyin wore a simple light-green gown, her hair adorned with a single velvet blossom she had stitched herself.

Unlike other shops along the street ——whose entrances boomed with drums and loud calls ——Blossom Hall was quiet but refined. Delicate bead curtains hung beneath the eaves, catching and scattering the sunlight like drifting threads of light.

The first customers walked in with cautious curiosity. Behind the door, Mei clutched her handkerchief tightly, her palms moist with nerves.

Then Nianyin opened a lacquered box and lifted a phoenix-head hairpin onto her palm. It wasn't flamboyant, but its threads were fine and meticulous ——the layered feathers catching the light so vividly they seemed almost real.

"What a magnificent piece," a noblewoman breathed and she bought it on the spot.

Word spread quickly. Within days, Blossom Hall had become the talk of the capital's noble ladies.

Some claimed its hairpins surpassed even those crafted in the palace workshops; others whispered that since the stunning Miss Qin herself oversaw the designs, every blossom in the shop seemed to carry a touch of her grace.

One night, as lanterns were being lit, Qiqi whispered, unable to contain herself, "Miss, you really are remarkable. I still remember when you first started learning with Madam Lin ——your hands were always covered in needle pricks and you worked from dawn till night. And now look ——you've already secured a place on this grand street."

She smiled softly as she put away the finished hairpins. "When it's something you truly wish to do, the fatigue never feels like suffering. More often, you simply forget to rest."

Mei's eyes reddened at those words, though she only nodded hard in silence.

Madam Lin came in with a pot of freshly brewed wine and let out a hearty laugh. "That's my good apprentice! A woman who relies solely on a man's favour is grasping at smoke. Skill in her own hands —— that's what keeps her standing firm."

The lantern light danced across the hairpins, setting the room aglow.

From that day on, the name Blossom Hall gradually took root in the capital. Even the old street itself seemed brighter for its presence.

Standing at the upstairs window, Qin Nianyin watched the lights of the marketplace and thought quietly to herself. In her previous life, she had missed too much. In this one, she would rely on her own hands to carve out a new path ——for herself and for the people she cared for.

Extra Story 2: Li Jing and Xu Wencai

Late spring in the capital brought a drifting rain of apricot blossoms.

The palace examinations had just concluded. One hundred successful candidates stepped out of the palace gates in neat rows, their new spring robes crisp, their belts perfectly straight.

Each maintained rigid composure, afraid that the slightest misstep would tarnish their bearing. Palace maids were technically forbidden from whispering or laughing, yet several still hid behind the colonnade, stealing glances at this year's fresh-faced graduates.

Li Jing stood in the shade beneath the eaves, the crushed petal she had rolled between her fingers still faintly fragrant.

The past few months had been turbulent ——her elder sister, the Eldest Princess, had fallen from favour and her Third Royal Brother had soon followed. Inside the palace, everyone held their breath.

For someone as spoiled and high-spirited as Li Jing, this was the first time she had felt a hollow ache in her chest. On the urging of a few maids, she had come out simply to distract herself——nothing more.

Her gaze drifted across the line of scholars, faint and uninterested at first. Then, unexpectedly, a single figure caught her attention.

He stood neither at the front nor among the top ranks. He was positioned near the rear of the formation, yet his tall, slender frame made him quietly conspicuous. His robe was plain, his appearance modest, but he carried himself with a certain upright sincerity.

A breeze passed through the courtyard. The ceremonial flower pinned to his cap ——the symbol of a newly minted palace graduate —— quivered, then nearly slipped off.

The young man panicked for a moment and instinctively reached up to catch it. The movement was abrupt and completely out of place amid the solemn procession. A few palace maids behind the columns let out soft bursts of laughter they could not contain.

Li Jing had been wound tight with irritation for days, her mood trapped in a fog she could not dispel. Yet seeing that scholar's flustered but still stubbornly upright posture… something in her chest loosened.

She laughed.

Just a breath of laughter, light as a breeze ——yet even she was startled by it.

One of her maids leaned in and whispered cautiously, "Your Highness… that scholar looks handsome enough, though he seems a little foolish."

Li Jing lifted a hand to cover the small curve of her lips. The amusement lingering in her eyes surprised even herself. For the first time in months, she realized that the world was not built solely of court struggles and looming storms.

At least, in this moment of spring wind, there were still people who would lose composure over a falling ceremonial flower ——honest, human and real.

She did not remember his name then.

But that fleeting glimpse would remain with her for years ——a quiet, unexpected memory tucked between the cold walls of the palace.

* * * * *

Xu Wencai was preparing to withdraw when a clear, melodious voice called from above him.

"Were you the scholar who tried to catch his ceremonial flower just now?"

He stopped short and instinctively looked up.

Standing before him was a young lady in ornate robes. A golden hairpin trembled lightly at her temple. Her features were bright and striking, yet composed ——nothing like the distant, icy hauteur he expected from someone of high birth. Instead, she regarded him with a hint of curiosity, her expression edged with faint amusement.

That single glance seemed to knock the breath from his lungs.

Xu Wencai straightened abruptly and bowed, heart pounding.

"Forgive me, my lady. My behaviour just now was improper…"

"My lady?" she echoed.

Her lips lifted, not unkindly ——but with a subtle tilt that made him realize, belatedly and with a cold rush, that this was no ordinary noblewoman.

It was clear the young man still had no idea who she was.

Li Jing allowed herself a soft, bright laugh.

"Improper? Hardly. Compared to all those stiff faces in the line, you were the most genuine one."

Her tone was unhurried, with a natural confidence and an almost playful sharpness.

Xu Wencai felt heat surge straight up his neck. The palace maids whispered behind the pillars, but he could only hear the pounding of his heartbeat. Standing this close, he could even catch the faint trace of fragrance drifting from her sleeve.

"What is your name? and what rank did you receive?" Li Jing asked lightly, her eyes sweeping over him with open curiosity.

Being examined from head to toe by such a magnificently dressed young woman made Xu Wencai's ears burn red.

"I ——I am Xu Wencai. In this examination, I was placed twenty-sixth in the second tier."

Li Jing nodded, her expression brightening. She suddenly remembered why she had come out of the palace in the first place ——and as she studied the handsome but modest young scholar before her, an unexpected thought crossed her mind. Perhaps this man… might be the answer she had not dared consider.

She asked directly, "Are you married? Or betrothed?"

Xu Wencai blinked, taken aback, then hurriedly shook his head.

"My family is humble and both my parents have passed. I have no elders to arrange such matters, so I have not yet married."

The moment she heard this, Li Jing's satisfaction deepened. Her smile grew brighter, blooming like a peony in spring ——radiant, noble and dazzling enough to make his heart thump painfully.

A humble background was no flaw. In truth, she preferred someone unentangled with powerful clans. And no parents meant she would not be expected to bow and scrape to in-laws despite being a princess.

"Do you know who I am?" she asked.

From beginning to end, Xu Wencai felt as though he had been swept into a cloud. That a celestial-like young lady would stand here and speak to him ——this was nothing short of a dream. He could only shake his head dumbly.

"Then remember it well." Li Jing turned away gracefully, her steps steady, her skirt sweeping lightly across the stone steps.

"I am the Second Princess ——Li Jing."

Xu Wencai stood frozen, staring after her retreating figure. His lips were pressed tightly together, yet his chest surged with an unfamiliar, restless excitement.

Such a beautiful woman ——

had smiled at him.

Even knowing she was far beyond his reach, he still felt something inside him tremble, like the first pluck of a string.

Second Princess… Li Jing.

A name gentle and bright, like a verse from old poetry and in that moment, he thought ——

What a beautiful name indeed.

Extra Story 3: The Imperial Marriage Decree

Rain had hung over the capital for days, yet the palace was bright with lanterns and red silk. An imperial decree had been announced: the Emperor commanded that General Gu Xiao ——still unmarried —— was to wed Shen Lingyan, the daughter of grand Preceptor Shen.

Once the news spread, the court and noble families all exclaimed that it was a perfect match. A tiger of the battlefield paired with a noble daughter from a prestigious clan ——well-balanced in status and beneficial to both families. Teahouses throughout the city buzzed with envy and praise.

Only Gu Xiao himself felt an unshakable heaviness in his chest.

He knew he had no power to refuse an imperial marriage.

Yet he also understood that marriage should not be a tool to mend political fractures, nor a vessel for someone else's expectations.

* * * * *

That Evening

The night breeze moved through the bamboo, leaving shadows swaying along the corridor. Gu Xiao had just returned from camp, still in armour and was heading toward the main hall when he noticed a quiet figure standing beneath the eaves.

"Miss Shen?"

Shen Lingyan stepped from behind a pillar. She wore no jewels, only a single white jade hairpin that made her features seem even calmer. She bowed, her voice soft but unwavering.

"General Gu, forgive my impropriety. I came tonight because there is something I wish to say."

Gu Xiao frowned slightly but nodded.

"Please speak."

Lowering her gaze, Shen Lingyan's fingers curled tightly before she finally forced out the words:

"I know this marriage may not bring you joy. Even so, I want you to understand ——I will do everything I can to be a proper mistress of your household. And if there is someone else in your heart, I will not resent it. If one day you must take a concubine, I will not stand in the way."

Her tone remained steady, but beneath it was a quiet resolve.

Gu Xiao was taken aback. His eyes darkened for a moment before he spoke slowly.

"Why would you say such things? I always thought…the person in your heart was Su Zhang."

Shen Lingyan stiffened. For a brief moment her eyes trembled and then she let out a faint, sorrowful laugh.

"If not for that misunderstanding, how could I have found excuses to see you all those years?"

The realization struck him sharply.

At last, Shen Lingyan lifted her gaze. Her voice was quiet, but each word was clear.

"General Gu, you and I are both people who have lost things. I know who it is that you cherish. But the one in my heart…has never been Lord Su."

Her eyes held his ——steady, deep and carried with long-buried affection.

Tears rimmed her lashes even as she forced herself to smile.

"The Emperor and Empress have granted this marriage. I don't want to let the chance slip past again. Whatever the future holds, if I may stand beside you for even a single day, that one day will be enough. And if — —one day ——you are no longer here, then I will 守 your memory for the rest of my life."

Gu Xiao was silent for a long time. Shock, guilt and something unspoken churned beneath the armour he wore. The coldness in his eyes slowly eased beneath her unwavering sincerity.

"Miss Shen…" His voice was low, unsteady in a way it had never been.

"This marriage ——if anything ——I am the one indebted to you. The battlefield is unforgiving. Every step is danger. I cannot promise you a peaceful life. If I fall one day, what awaits you is loneliness and widowhood. That…is my burden on you."

Shen Lingyan's tears finally fell, but she shook her head.

"There is no debt. This is my own choice. If you die for our country, then that is an honour. I will carry no resentment."

Gu Xiao looked at her ——really looked at her ——and something inside him tightened. After a moment, he reached out, his fingertips cool from the night air, brushing the tears gently from her cheek.

"Silly girl…" he murmured. A rare softness surfaced in his gaze.

"I'll try to live a little longer, then. If I can stay by your side, I'll stay as long as I can."

Shen Lingyan stared at him, tears still clinging to her lashes, but a true smile finally appeared. What she had feared most was not hardship —— it was losing the chance to walk beside him at all.

The lanterns wavered softly in the night breeze. Their shadows stretched together on the ground beneath the corridor.

Clutching her sleeves, Shen Lingyan felt her heart tremble with a long-suppressed joy. After so many years, she had finally received a promise ——no matter how small ——that belonged to her alone.

Gu Xiao studied the quiet strength of her profile and let out a silent sigh. He had already lost too much in his past. He would not lose someone willing to share the weight of his life. If fate had brought her to him, he was finally willing to give her hope… and give himself a new beginning.

The faint scent of bamboo drifted across the courtyard.

Neither spoke again, but in their silence, they both let go of the burdens they had carried for so many years.

Some bonds did not need grand gestures.

To walk side by side ——that alone was rare enough.

Extra Story 4: Su Wan and the Crown Prince

Their First Encounter

Late spring in the capital brought the blooming of the crabapple trees in the Imperial Garden. The palace hosted a banquet and the ladies of the noble families were invited to attend.

Su Wan entered the palace with her mother that day. She had no intention of drawing attention and sat quietly at a side table, observing the festivities without joining in.

Midway through the banquet, a small commotion rippled through the hall.

The Crown Prince, Li Duan, had returned from the front of the palace and was passing along the veranda. Born of imperial blood, he carried himself with a natural elegance ——his posture straight, his robes perfectly fitted, his every movement calm and restrained.

Su Wan's gaze swept past him without much thought.

But in the moment, he paused, something tightened unexpectedly in her chest.

A fledgling sparrow had fallen from a nearby flowering branch, landing at the foot of the steps with frantic, trembling wings. The palace maids were thrown into momentary panic, yet none dared approach too hastily.

Li Duan simply bent down, lifting the tiny creature into his palm. His hand was steady, his expression composed and he placed the sparrow back onto the branch with quiet care.

The action lasted only a few seconds, yet it drew silence from everyone watching.

Sunlight filtered through the leaves, landing across his profile and outlining features that seemed almost carved.

Su Wan found herself staring, fingers unconsciously tightening against her sleeve.

For the first time, she understood that when the world spoke of imperial nobility, it was not only about power or rank.

In that moment, something within her truly stirred.

Even after the banquet ended, the image lingered with her all the way home.

The wheels of the carriage rolled over the blue stone road, yet in her mind she could still see him ——head lowered slightly, the trembling feathers of a sparrow in his palm catching the afternoon light.

* * * * *

The Imperial Decree

Rain had just cleared over the capital, leaving the bamboo in the Su estate cool and glistening.

Several days after the marriage decree was announced, the Crown Prince himself came to the Su residence to express thanks. The entire household was stunned. grand Preceptor Su personally welcomed him into the main hall. After the proper exchange of courtesies, the atmosphere grew warm ——until the Crown Prince suddenly rose and spoke with a faint, composed smile:

"Gr and Preceptor, affairs of the palace keep me occupied. I cannot stay long. There is a small gift I must present personally to your daughter."

The hall fell silent. grand Preceptor Su hesitated for a moment, then smiled and ordered his youngest daughter to come from the inner courtyard.

Su Wan wore a pale rose-coloured gown as she approached. Her steps were steady, but a faint tremor lingered at her fingertips. Pushing the door open, she saw the Crown Prince standing among the bamboo shadows ——robes pristine, posture straight, profile calm and striking.

She bowed gracefully.

"Your Highness."

Li Duan lowered his gaze to her. His expression remained cool, but never discourteous.

He handed her a small silk-covered box. His voice was low and even:

"These are congratulatory gifts prepared by the Empress. Since you will enter the Eastern Palace as my Primary Consort, palace rules may feel overwhelming at first. These ornaments are meant to offer you some reassurance."

Su Wan accepted the box. The moment her fingertips brushed the cold edge, a quiet tremor passed through her.

She lifted her eyes and met his gaze.

Her voice was soft, yet earnest.

"I understand Your Highness's intention."

Li Duan paused, a faint crease forming between his brows as if he intended to speak.

But Su Wan was the one who continued, her voice gentle yet unwavering.

"I understand," she said quietly. "Your Highness is marrying me for the strength of the Su family me for the strength of the Su family. It is a matter of political balance. In the future, if Your Highness takes other consorts, I will consider it natural."

Li Duan's pupils tightened. His voice deepened.

"Su Wan ——"

"There is no need to explain." She offered a calm smile, her eyes bright and clear. "I do not ask to be the only one in Your Highness's heart. I only wish that, before the eyes of the world, I may stand beside you with dignity."

Her voice was soft, but every word carried cleanly through the still air.

Li Duan watched her in silence. For a moment, something subtle shifted inside him.

He had believed this young woman from the Su family to be gentle, reserved and simply a chess piece and simply a chess piece complying with her clan's arrangements.

He had not expected her to speak with such clarity ——stating the harsh truths of their future without trembling and even accepting them with a steady smile.

For a brief instant, he felt a strange, unfamiliar stir of emotion.

Su Wan lowered her gaze, the faintest curve remaining at her lips.

"There was a time when I envied those who found true affection," she said softly. "But after witnessing what happened between my brother and Miss Qin, I finally understood ——some hearts cannot be won by effort or force.

To have even this moment is already a blessing."

Outside, bamboo shadows wavered gently. The breeze after the rain drifted through the corridor, with the scent of damp earth and fresh leaves.

Li Duan remained silent for a long while before he finally spoke, his voice low and steady.

"Wan… you will always be my Principal Wife."

A tremor ran through her heart, though she only answered with a composed murmur.

"Your Highness is gracious."

She turned to leave, her steps measured and elegant. In the corner of her vision, the Crown Prince's figure ——white-robed and composed —— etched itself clearly into her memory.

She did not know whether he would ever truly fall in love.

But she had already made her choice:

to follow him, as one follows a distant but unwavering light.

Extra Story 5: Perfect Ending

Late summer in the capital brought long, lingering light.

Before nightfall, a breeze drifted from the depths of the bamboo grove, with the cool freshness of recent rain. It swept across the stone path and brushed over the courtyard pond. The surface rippled with the colours of the fading sunset, soft waves spreading like overturned silk.

Qin Nianyin stood beneath the eaves with a thread-bound book in her arms. She had meant to read a few pages, yet the moment she lifted her gaze and saw the figure in the courtyard, her fingers stilled.

——Su Zhang.

He had set aside his court robes and changed into a pale moon-white gown. At his waist hung a simple jade ornament, free of embellishment. He was only standing there, quietly, yet the air around him seemed to shift. The evening wind and bamboo shadows felt as though they had been arranged solely to frame him.

He was reading through a set of documents on the table. His fingers were long, his movements slow and deliberate. From time to time, he paused to think, lowering his eyes slightly. The lamplight cast a gentle glow across his features, outlining a calm, refined silhouette.

Qin Nianyin watched him, momentarily unable to move.

In a night like this, with a figure like that before her, she felt as though she had stepped back into the past ——to a time before bloodshed and turmoil, when the young scholar who ranked as tanhua was elegant, warm and untouched by the chill of the world.

A faint ache stirred inside her.

At last, she took a small step forward.

Her footsteps were quiet. She didn't wish to disturb the stillness that wrapped around him, so she walked even more slowly. Her skirt brushed across the stone slabs in a barely audible whisper, blending into the night.

Only when she reached his side did he finally look up.

The candlelight swayed and his eyes softened in its glow. His lips curved into a subtle smile ——unhurried, steady, gentle as a pool of clear water.

"Why are you standing there?"

His voice was calm, with an ease that loosened the tightness in one's chest.

Qin Nianyin blinked, her heart tightening unexpectedly. She opened her mouth to speak, but no words came. Instead, she returned his smile, small and quiet.

Su Zhang reached out. His palm was warm as he wrapped his fingers around hers, guiding her to sit beside him. The gesture held no force, yet it carried a silent certainty ——as though he had long grown accustomed to keeping her within reach.

She sat down, still unsteady from the sudden shift in her emotions.

Then she felt it.

His hand settled over her lower abdomen.

Her breath caught.

For a heartbeat, she felt surrounded by something both weightless and overwhelming.

She turned to look at him.

Su Zhang was already gazing back. His eyes were clear, his smile faint. The coldness that once lived between his brows had disappeared, replaced by something softer ——something sure.

"Is the baby troubling you?" he asked.

She shook her head lightly. "The baby is very well."

He nodded. "Good. After everything… our child has finally returned to us."

Qin Nianyin's throat tightened and a warm sting rose suddenly behind her eyes. She lowered her head and placed her hand over the back of his, her fingertips trembling ever so slightly from the weight of emotion.

In the courtyard, bamboo shadows swayed gently; the wind moved like flowing water.

Su Zhang reached into his sleeve and took out a small object. It was wrapped in a tiny sandalwood box.

"I searched for a long time," he said quietly. "But I finally found this for you."

She accepted it with a small smile. "What is it?"

"Open it and you'll see."

She shot him a faint glare, though there was unmistakable laughter in her eyes.

"What sort of thing is this? Why are you being so mysterious?"

Even so, she lifted the lid with slender fingers.

Inside lay a single item ——silent, untouched, unmistakable.

Her eyes widened. For a moment, she couldn't speak.

It was the jade pendant she had pawned years ago to raise money for her hairpin workshop ——her mother's last keepsake.

He chuckled softly. "Too happy?"

Her eyes reddened at once. Tears slipped down before she could stop them.

"You… how did you know?"

He only smiled again, offering no answer.

He would never tell her that back then, he had known her every step, every burden, every quiet struggle.

"It's fine," he said, gently. "It's back now. Don't cry."

"Mm." She dabbed her tears with a handkerchief, her voice catching. "Thank you."

"No need for thanks. In this lifetime, you never have to say that word to me."

They sat side by side without another word.

Silence settled, warm rather than empty. Beneath it flowed countless unspoken things ——past mistakes, this life's reunion, former loneliness, the tenderness now replacing it.

Su Zhang never once looked away.

He reached out to smooth the stray strands of hair near her temple. His movements were slow, careful. The warmth in his eyes was soft but strong enough to melt every trace of hardship they had endured.

At last, Qin Nianyin leaned toward him, resting her face against his shoulder. She closed her eyes. There were no tremors of old memories left in her heart ——only a quiet, steady peace.

Candlelight flickered. Water shimmered in the pond.

The night held no grand vows, no upheaval of fate.

It was simply calm ——clear as spring water, gently filling the heart, certain never to run dry.

——Fulfillment, she realized, did not always come with thunderous passion.

Sometimes, it arrived in moments of quiet like this.